GEORGE PE

Three Great Novels

The Derek Strange Trilogy

Also by George Pelecanos

A Firing Offense
Nick's Trip
Shoedog
Down By the River Where the Dead Men Go
The Big Blowdown
King Suckerman
Shame the Devil
The Sweet Forever
Hard Revolution
Drama City

George Pelecanos

The Derek Strange Trilogy

Right as Rain
Hell to Pay
Soul Circus

ORION

This omnibus edition first published in Great Britain in 2005 by
Orion
An imprint of Orion Books Ltd
Orion House, 5 Upper St Martin's Lane,
London WC2H 9EA

A CIP catalogue record for this book is available from the British Library.

Typeset by Deltatype Ltd, Birkenhead, Merseyside
Printed and bound in Great Britain by
Clays Ltd, St Ives plc

www.orionbooks.co.uk

Contents

Right as Rain

For Emily

1

What Derek Strange was worried about, looking at Jimmy Simmons sitting there, spilling over a chair on the other side of his desk, was that Simmons was going to pick some of Strange's personal shit up off the desktop in front of him and start winging it across the room. Either that or get to bawling like a damn baby. Strange didn't know which thing he wanted to happen less. He had some items on that desk that meant a lot to him: gifts women had given him over the years, tokens of gratitude from clients, and a couple of Redskins souvenirs from back in the 1960s. But watching a man cry, that was one thing he could not take.

'Tell me again, Derek.' Simmons's lip was trembling, and pools of tears were threatening to break from the corners of his bloodshot eyes. 'Tell me again what that motherfucker looked like, man.'

'It's all in the report,' said Strange.

'I'm gonna kill him, see? And right after that, I'm gonna kill his ass again.'

'You're talkin' no sense, Jimmy.'

'Fifteen years of marriage and my woman's just now decided to go and start taking some other man's dick? You're gonna tell me now about sense? God *damn*!'

Jimmy Simmons struck his fist to the desktop, next to a plaster football player with a spring-mounted head. The player, a white dude originally whose face Janine's son, Lionel, had turned dark brown with paint, wore the old gold trousers and burgundy jersey from back in the day, and he carried a football cradled in one arm. The head jiggled, and the Redskins toy tilted on its base. Strange reached over, grabbed the player, and righted it before it could tip over.

'Take it easy. You break that, I can't even charge you for it, 'cause it's priceless, hear?'

'I'm sorry, Derek.' A tear sprang loose from Simmons's right eye and ran down one of his plump cheeks. 'Shit.'

'Here you go, man.' Strange ripped a Kleenex from the box atop his desk and handed it to Simmons, who dabbed tenderly at his cheek. It was a delicate gesture for a man whose last day under three hundred pounds was a faded memory.

'I need to know what the man looked like,' said Simmons. 'I need to know his name.'

'It's all in the report,' Strange repeated, pushing a manila envelope across the desk. 'But you don't want to be doing nothin' about it, hear?'

Simmons opened the envelope and inched out its contents slowly and warily, the way a child approaches an open casket for the first time. Strange watched Simmons's eyes as they moved across the photographs and the written report.

It hadn't taken Strange all that long to get the goods on Denice Simmons. It was a tail-and-surveillance job, straight up, the simplest, dullest, and most common type of work he did. He had followed Denice to her boyfriend's place over in Springfield, Virginia, on two occasions and waited on the street until she came out and drove back into D.C. The third time Strange had tailed her, on a Sunday night when Jimmy Simmons was up in Atlantic City at an electronics show, he had waited the same way, but Denice did not emerge from the man's apartment. The lights went out in the third-story window where the man lived, and this was all Strange needed. He filled out the paperwork in the morning, picked up the photographs he had taken to a one-hour shop, and called Jimmy Simmons to his office the same day.

'How long?' said Simmons, not looking up from the documents.

'Three months, I'd say.'

'How you know that?'

'Denice got no other kind of business being over in Virginia, does she?'

'She works in the District. She's got no friends over in Virginia—'

'Your own credit card bills, the ones you supplied? Denice has been charging gas at a station over there by the Franconia exit for three, three and a half months. The station's just a mile down the road from our boy's apartment.'

'You think she'd be smarter than that.' Simmons nearly grinned with affection. 'She never does like to pay for her own gas. Always puts it on the card so I'll have to pay, come bill time. She's tight with her money, see. Funny for a woman to be that way. And though she knows I'll be stroking the checks, she always has to stop for the cheapest gas, even if it means driving out of her way. I bet if you checked, you'd see they were selling gas at that station dirt cheap.'

'Dollar and a penny for low-lead,' said Strange.

Simmons rose from his chair, his belly and face quivering as if his flesh were being blown by a sudden gust of wind. 'Well, I'll see you, Derek. I'll take care of your services, soon as I see a bill.'

'Janine will get it out to you straightaway.'

'Right. And thanks for the good work.'

'Always hate it when it turns out like this, Jimmy.'

Simmons placed a big hat with a red feather in its band on his big head. 'You're just doing your job.'

Strange sat in his office, waiting to hear Simmons go out the door. It would take a few minutes, as long as it took Simmons to flirt with Janine and for Janine to get rid of him. Strange heard the door close. He got out from behind his desk and put himself into a midlength black leather jacket lined with quilt and a thin layer of down. He took a PayDay bar, which Janine had bought for him, off the desk and slipped it into a pocket of the jacket.

Out in the reception area of the office, Strange stopped at Janine Baker's desk. Behind her, a computer terminal showed one of the Internet's many sites that specialized in personal searches. Janine's brightly colored outfit was set off against her dark, rich skin. Her red lipstick picked up the red of the dress. She was a pretty middle-aged woman, liquid eyed, firm breasted, wide of hip, and lean legged.

'That was quick,' he said.

'He wasn't his usual playful self. He said I was looking lovely today—'

'You are.'

Janine blushed. 'But he didn't go beyond that. Didn't seem like his heart was all that in it.'

'I just gave him the bad news about his wife. She was getting a little somethin'-somethin' on the side with this young auto parts clerk, sells batteries over at the Pep Boys in northern Virginia.'

'How'd they meet? He see her stalled out on the side of the road or something?'

'Yeah, he's one of those good Samaritans you hear about.'

'Pulled over to give her a jump, huh.'

'Now, Janine.'

'This the same guy she was shackin' up with two years ago?'

'Different guy. Different still than the guy she was running with three years before that.'

'What's he gonna do?'

'He went through the motions with me, telling me what he was going to do to that guy. But all's he'll do is, he'll make Denice suffer a little bit. Not with his hands, nothin' like that. Jimmy wouldn't touch Denice in that way. No, they'll be doing some kind of I'm Sorry ceremony for the next few days, and then he'll forgive her, until the next one comes along.'

'Why's he stay with her?'

'He loves her. And I think she loves him, too. So I guess there's no chance for you and Big Jimmy. I don't think he'll be leaving her any time soon.'

'Oh, I can wait.'

Strange grinned. 'Give him a chance to fill out a little bit, huh?'

'He fills out any more, we'll have to put one of those garage doors on the front of this place just to let him in.'

'He fills out any more, Fat Albert, Roseanne, Liz Taylor, *and* Sinbad gonna get together and start telling Jimmy Simmons weight jokes.'

'He fills out any more—'

'Hold up, Janine. You know what we're doing right here?'

'What?'

'It's called "doing the dozens."'

'That so.'

'Uh-huh. White man on NPR yesterday, was talking about this book he wrote about African American culture? Said that doing the dozens was this thing we been doin' for generations. Called it the *precursor* of rap music.'

'They got a name for it, for real? And here I thought we were just cracking on Jimmy.'

'I'm not lying.' Strange buttoned his coat. 'Get that bill out to Simmons, will you?'

'I handed it to him as he was going out the door.'

'You're always on it. I don't know why I feel the need to remind you.' Strange nodded to one of two empty desks on either side of the room. 'Where's Ron at?'

'Trying to locate that debtor, the hustler took that woman off for two thousand dollars.'

'Old lady lives down off Princeton?'

'Uh-huh. Where you headed?'

'Off to see Chris Wilson's mom.'

Strange walked toward the front door, his broad, muscled shoulders moving beneath the black leather, gray salted into his hair and closely cropped beard.

He turned as his hand touched the doorknob. 'You want something else?' He had felt Janine's eyes on his back.

'No . . . why?'

'You need me, or if Ron needs me, I'll be wearin' my beeper.'

Strange stepped out onto 9th Street, a short commercial strip between Upshur and Kansas, one spit away from Georgia Avenue. He smiled, thinking of Janine. He had met her the first time at a club ten years earlier, and he had started hitting it then because both of them wanted him to, and because it was there for him to take.

Janine had a son, Lionel, from a previous marriage, and this scared him. Hell, everything about commitment scared him, but being a father to a young man in this world, it scared him more than anything else. Despite his fears, their time together had seemed good for both Strange and Janine, and he had stayed with it, knowing that when it's good it's rare, and unless there's a strong and immediate reason, you should never give it up. The affair went on steadily for several months.

When he lost his office manager, he naturally thought of Janine, as she was out of work, bright, and a born organizer. They agreed that they would break off the relationship when she started working for him, and soon thereafter she went and got serious with another man. This was fine with him, a relief, as it had let him out the back door quietly, the way he always liked to go. That man exited Janine's life shortly thereafter.

Strange and Janine had recently started things up once again. Their relationship wasn't exclusive, at least not for Strange. And the fact that he was her boss didn't bother either of them, in the ethical sense. Their lovemaking simply filled a need, and Strange had grown attached to the boy as well. Friends warned him about shitting on the dining room table, but he was genuinely fond of the woman, and she did make his nature rise after all the years. He liked to play with her, too, let her know that *he* knew that she was still interested. It kept things lively in the deadening routine of their day-to-day.

Strange stood out on the sidewalk for a moment and glanced up at the yellow sign over the door: 'Strange Investigations,' the letters in half of both words enlarged inside the magnifying glass illustration drawn across the lightbox. He loved that logo. It always made him feel something close to good when he looked up at that sign and saw his name.

He had built this business by himself and done something positive in the place where he'd come up. The kids in the neighborhood, they saw a black man turn the key on the front door every morning, and maybe it registered, put something in the back of their minds whether they realized it or not. He'd kept the business going for twenty-five years now, and the bumps in the road had been just that. The business was who he was. All of him, and all his.

Strange sat low behind the wheel of his white-over-black '89 Caprice, listening to a Blackbyrds tape coming from the box as he cruised south on Georgia Avenue. Next to him on the bench was a mini Maglite, a Rand McNally street atlas, and a Leatherman tool-in-one in a sheath that he often wore looped through his belt on the side of his hip. He wore a Buck knife the same way, all the time when he was on a job. A set of 10 × 50 binoculars, a cell phone, a voice-activated tape recorder, and extra batteries for his flashlights and camera were in the glove box, secured with a double lock. In the trunk of the car was a file carton containing data on his live cases. Also in the trunk was a steel Craftsman toolbox housing a heavy Maglite, a Canon AE-1 with a 500-millimeter lens, a pair of Russian-made NVD goggles, a 100-foot steel Craftsman tape measure, a roll of duct tape, and various Craftsman tools useful for engine and tire repair. When he could, Strange always bought Craftsman – the tools were guaranteed for life, and he tended to be hard on his equipment.

He drove through Petworth. In the Park View neighborhood he cut east on Irving, took Michigan Avenue past Children's Hospital and into Northeast, past Catholic U and down into Brookland.

Strange parked in front of Leona Wilson's modest brick home at 12th and Lawrence. He kept the motor running, waiting for the flute solo on 'Walking in Rhythm' to end, though he could listen to it anytime. He'd come here because he'd promised Leona Wilson that he would, but he wasn't in any hurry to make this call.

Strange saw the curtain move in the bay window of Leona's house. He cut the engine, got out of his car, locked it down, and walked up the concrete path to Leona's front door. The door was already opening as he approached.

'Mrs Wilson,' he said, extending his hand.

'Mr Strange.'

2

'Will you help me?'

They sat beside each other in the living room on a slipcovered sofa, a soft, crackling sound coming from the fireplace. Strange drank coffee from a mug; Leona Wilson sipped tea with honey and lemon.

She was younger than he was by a few years but looked older by ten. He remembered seeing her in church before the death of her son, and her appearance since had changed radically. She carried too little weight on her tall, large-boned frame, and a bag of light brown flesh hung pendulous beneath her chin. Leona wore a maroon shirt-and-slacks arrangement and scuffed, low-heeled pumps on her feet. The outfit's presentation was rushed and sloppy. Her shirt's top button had been lost, and a brooch held it together across a flat chest terraced with bones. Her hair had gone gray, and she wore it carelessly uncombed. Grief had stolen her vanity.

Strange placed his mug on the low glass table before him. 'I don't know that I can help you, ma'am. The police investigation was as thorough as they come. After all, this was a high-profile case.'

'Christopher was good.' Leona Wilson spoke slowly, deliberately. She pronounced her *r*s as *ah*-rahs. She had been an elementary teacher in the District public school system for thirty years. Strange knew that she had taught grammar and pronunciation the way she had learned it, the way he had learned it, too, growing up in D.C.

'I'm sure he was,' said Strange.

'The papers said he had a history of brutality. They implied that he was holding a gun on that white man for no good reason when the other police officers came upon them. But I don't believe it. Christopher was strong when he had to be, but he was never brutal.'

'I have an old friend in the department, Mrs Wilson. He tells me that Chris was a solid cop and a fine young man.'

'Do you know that memorial downtown, in Northwest? The National Law Enforcement Officers Memorial?'

'I know it, yes.'

'There are almost fifteen thousand names etched on that wall, the police officers in this country who have been killed in the line of duty since they've been keeping records. And do you know that the department has denied my request to have Chris's name put on that wall? Do you know that, Mr Strange?'

'I'm aware of it, yes.'

'The only thing I have now is my son's memory. I want other people to remember him for the way he was, too. The way he really was. Because I know my son. And Christopher was *good.*'

'I have no reason to doubt what you say.'

'So you'll help me.' She leaned forward. He could smell her breath, and it was foul.

'It's not what I do. I do background checks. I uncover insurance fraud. I confirm or disprove infidelity. I interview witnesses in civil cases for attorneys, and I get paid to be a witness in court. I locate debtors, and I have a younger operative who occasionally skip-traces. Once in a while I'll locate a missing child, or find the biological parent of an adopted child. What I don't do is solve murder cases or disprove cases that have already been made by the police. I'm not in that business. Except for the police, nobody's in that business, you want to know the plain truth.'

'The white policeman who killed my son. Did anyone think to bring up his record the way they brought up my son's record?'

'Well, if I recall . . . I mean, if you remember, there was quite a bit written about that police officer. How he hadn't qualified on the shooting range for over two years, despite the fact that they require those cops to qualify every six months. How he was brought onto the force during that hiring binge in the late eighties, with all those other unqualified applicants. How he had a brutality-complaint sheet of his own. No disrespect intended, but I think they left few stones unturned with regard to that young man's past.'

'In the end they blamed it on his gun.'

'They did talk about the negatives of that particular weapon, yes – the Glock has a light trigger pull and no external safety.'

'I want you to go deeper. Find out more about the policeman who shot my son. I'm convinced that he is the key.'

'Mrs Wilson—'

'Christopher was proud to be a police officer; he would have died without question . . . he did die, *without question,* in the line of duty. But the papers made it out to seem as if he was somehow at fault. That he was holding his gun on an innocent man, that he failed to identify himself as a police officer when that white policeman came up on him. They mentioned the alcohol in his blood . . . Christopher was *not* a drunk, Mr Strange.'

Nor an angel, thought Strange. He'd never known any cop, any man, in fact, to be as pure as she was making him out to be.

'Yes, ma'am,' said Strange.

He watched Leona Wilson's hand shake with the first stages of Parkinson's as she raised her teacup to her lips. He thought of his mother in the home, and he rose from the couch.

Strange walked to the fireplace, where a slowly strobing light shone behind plastic logs, the phony fire cracking rhythmically. An electric cord ran from beneath the logs to an outlet in the wall.

He looked at the photographs framed on the mantel. He saw Leona as a young woman and the boy Christopher standing under her touch, and another photograph of Leona and her husband, whom Strange knew to be deceased. There were a few more photographs of Christopher in a cap and gown, and in uniform, and kneeling on a football field with his teammates, the Gonzaga scoreboard in the background, Christopher's gaze hard, his eyes unsmiling and staring directly into the camera's lens. A high school boy already wearing the face of a cop.

There was one photo of a girl in her early teens, its color paled out from age. Strange knew that Chris Wilson had had a sister. He had seen her on the TV news, a pretty, bone-skinny, light-skinned girl with an unhealthy, splotched complexion. He remembered thinking it odd that she had made a show of wiping tears from dry eyes. Maybe, after days of grieving, it had become her habit to take her sleeve to her eyes. Maybe she had wanted to keep crying but by then was all cried out.

Strange thought it over, his back to Leona. It would be an easy job, reinterviewing the players, retracing steps. He had a business to maintain. He wasn't in any position to be turning down jobs.

'My rates,' said Strange.

'Sir?'

He turned to face her. 'You haven't asked me about my rates.'

'I'm sure they're reasonable.'

'I get thirty dollars an hour, plus expenses. Something like this will take time—'

'I have money. There was a settlement, as you know. And Christopher's insurance, his death benefits, I mean, and his pension. I'm certain he would have liked me to use the money for this.'

Strange went back to the couch. Leona Wilson stood and rubbed the palm of one hand over the bent fingers of the other. She was eye to eye with him, nearly his height.

'I'll need access to some of his things,' said Strange.

'You can have a look in his room.'

'He lived here?'

'Yes.'

'What about your daughter?'

'My daughter doesn't live here anymore.'

'How can I reach her?'

'I haven't seen Sondra or talked with her since the day I buried my son.'

Strange's beeper, clipped to his belt, sounded. He unfastened the device and checked the readout. 'Do you mind if I use your phone?'

'It's right over there.'

Strange made the call and replaced the receiver. He placed his business card beside the phone. 'I've got to run.'

Leona Wilson straightened her posture and brushed a strand of gray hair behind her ear. 'Will you be in church this Sunday?'

'I'm gonna try real hard.'

'I'll say a prayer for you, Mr Strange.'

'Thank you.' He picked his leather up off the back of a chair. 'I'd surely appreciate it if you would.'

Strange drove down South Dakota to Rhode Island Avenue and hooked a left. His up mood was gone, and he popped out the Blackbyrds tape and punched the tuner in to 1450 on the AM dial. Joe 'the Black Eagle' Madison was on all-talk WOL, taking calls. Strange's relationship with OL went back to the mid-sixties, when the station's format had first gone over to what the newspapers called 'rhythm and blues.' Back when they'd had those DJs Bobby 'the Mighty Burner' Bennett and 'Sunny Jim' Kelsey, called themselves the Soul Brothers. He'd been a WOL listener for, damn, what was it, thirty-five years now. He wondered, as he often did when thinking back, where those years had gone.

He made a left turn down 20th Street, Northeast.

Leona Wilson's posture had changed when he'd told her he'd take the job. It wasn't his imagination, either – the years had seemed to drop off her before his eyes. Like the idea of hope had given her a quick shot of youth.

'You all right, Derek,' he said, as if saying it aloud would make it so.

He'd been straight up with Leona Wilson back at her house, as much as anyone could be with a woman that determined. Her temporary hope was a fair trade-off for the permanent crash of disappointment that would surely follow later on. He told himself that this was true.

Anyway, he needed the money. The Chris Wilson case was a potential thousand-, two-thousand-dollar job.

Down along Langdon Park, Strange saw Ron Lattimer's Acura curbed and running, white exhaust coming from its pipes. Strange parked the Caprice behind it, grabbed his binoculars and his Leatherman, climbed out of his car, and got into the passenger side of the red coupe.

Lattimer was at the finish line of his twenties, tall and lean with an athlete's build. He wore a designer suit, a tailored shirt, and a hand-painted tie. He held a lidded cup of Starbucks in one hand, and his other hand tapped out a beat on the steering wheel. The heater fan was blowing full on, and jazzy hip-hop came from the custom stereo system in the dash.

'You warm enough, Ron?'

'I'm comfortable, yeah.'

'You doin' a surveillance in the winter, how many times I told you, you got to leave the motor shut down 'cause the *ex*haust smoke, it shows. Bad enough you're driving a red car, says, Look at me, everybody. Notice *me*.'

'Too cold to leave the heat off,' said Lattimer.

'Put that overcoat on you got there in the backseat, you wouldn't be so cold.'

'That's a *cashmere*, Derek; I'm not gonna wear it in my car. Get it all wrinkled up and shit, start looking like I picked it up at the Burlington Coat Factory, some bullshit like that.'

Strange took a breath and let it out slow. 'And what I tell you about drinking coffee? What you need to be doing, you keep a bottle of water in the car and you sip it, a little at a time, when you get good and thirsty. Coffee runs right through you, man, *you* know that. What's gonna happen when you got to pee so bad you can't stand it, you get out the car lookin' for some privacy, tryin' to find a tree to get behind, while the subject of your tail is sneaking out the back door of his house? Huh? What you gonna do then?'

'The day I lose a tail, Derek, because I been drinkin' an Americano—'

'Oh, it's an *Americano*, now. And here I was, old and out of touch like I am, thinking you were just having a cup of coffee.'

Lattimer had to chuckle. 'Always tryin' to school me.'

'That's right. You got the potential to be something in this profession. I get you away from focusing on your *lifestyle* and get you focused on the business at hand, you're gonna make it.' Strange nodded toward the faceplate of the stereo. 'Turn that shit off, man, I can't think.'

'Tribe Called Quest *represents.*'

'Turn it off anyway, and tell me what we got.'

Lattimer switched off the music. 'Leon's over there in that house, second from the last on the right, on Mills?'

Strange looked through the glasses. 'Okay. How'd you find him?'

'The address he gave the old lady, the one he took off? He hadn't lived there for a year or so. One of the neighbors I interviewed knew his family, though – both of them had come up in the same area. This neighbor told me that Leon's mother and father had both passed, years ago. Got the death certificate of his mother down at that records office on H, in Chinatown. From the date on that certificate, I found her obituary in the newspaper morgue, and the obit listed the heirs. Of the family, only the grandmother was still alive. Leon didn't have any brothers or sisters, which makes him the only heir to g-mom. I figured Leon, hustler that he is, is counting on the grandmother to leave him everything she's got, so Leon's got to be paying regular visits to stay in her grace.'

'That the grandmother's house we're looking at?'

'Uh-huh. I been staking it out all this week. Leon finally showed up today. That's his hooptie over there, that yellow Pontiac Astra with the rust marks, parked in front of the house. Ugly-ass car, too.'

'Sister to the Chevy Vega.'

'People paid extra for that thing 'cause it had the Pontiac name on it?'

'Some did. Nice work.'

'Thanks, boss. How you want to handle it?'

Strange gave it some thought. 'I think we need to brace him in front of his grandmother.'

'I was thinking the same way.'

'Come on.'

They got out of the Acura, Lattimer retrieving his overcoat first and shaking himself into it as they walked alongside Langdon Park toward Mills Avenue. A couple of young boys, school age, were sitting on a bench wearing oversize parkas, looking hard at Strange and Lattimer, not looking away as Strange glanced in their direction.

'Hold on for a second, Derek,' said Lattimer, putting a little skip in his walk and side-glancing Strange. 'I got to find me a tree. . .'

'Funny,' said Strange.

They were past the park and onto Mills. Lattimer said, 'You want me to take the alley?'

'Yeah, take it. I don't feel like running today if I don't have to. My knees and this cold aren't the best of friends.'

'I don't feel like running, either. You know how I perspire quick, soon as I start to buck, even in this weather.'

'I don't suspect he'll be going anywhere, but you never know. Speaking of which . . .'

Lattimer saw Strange pull the Leatherman tool from his pocket and flick open its knife as they neared Leon's yellow Astra. Still walking, Strange drew change from his pocket and dropped it on the street beside the door of the car. He got down on one knee to pick it up, and while he was down there, punctured the driver's-side tire with the knife. He retrieved his change, closing the tool and replacing it in his pocket as he rose.

'See you in a few,' said Strange.

He took the steps up to the porch of the row house as Lattimer cut into the alley. He waited half a minute for Lattimer to get behind the house, and then he knocked on the door.

Strange saw a miniature face peer around a lace curtain and heard a couple of locks being turned. The door opened, and a very small woman with prunish skin and a cotton-top of gray hair stood in the frame. The woman gave Strange a thorough examination with her eyes.

She looked back over her shoulder toward a nicely appointed living room that spread out off the foyer. Then she raised her voice: 'Leon! There's a police officer here to see you.'

'Thank you, ma'am,' said Strange. 'And tell him not to run, will you? My partner's out back in the alley, and he'll be awful mad if he gets to perspiring. The sweat, it stains his pretty clothes.'

Strange took Leon Jeffries out the kitchen door to a small screened-in porch. The porch gave to a view of a gnarled patch of backyard and the alley. After Strange got Leon out to the porch, he waved Lattimer in from there. Leon confessed to bilking the old woman from Petworth with a pyramid investment scheme shortly thereafter.

'What y'all gonna do to me now?' asked Leon. He was a small, feral, middle-aged man with pale yellow eyeballs. He wore a pinstriped suit jacket with unmatching black slacks and a lavender, open-collar shirt.

'You need to give our client back her money, Leon,' said Strange. 'Then everything'll be chilly.'

'I *planned* on gettin' her money back to her, with interest. Takes a little time, though. See, the way I worked it, I used the next person's investment to pay the, uh, previous person's investment, in installments. Sort of how some folks stay ahead of the game with multiple credit cards.'

'That's a *legal* kind of scam, Leon. What we're talking about here is, you were taking off old ladies that trusted you. How you think that's gonna look to a jury?'

'A jury trial for a small-claims thing?'

'You got a sheet, Leon?' asked Lattimer.

'I ain't never been incarcerated.'

'So you got a sheet,' said Lattimer. 'And this goes before a judge, forget about a jury, you get a judge on a bad day he ate the wrong brand of half-smokes for breakfast, some shit like that, they gonna put your thin ass *away*.'

'We need the money for our client now,' said Strange. 'That's all she wants. She's a good woman, which you probably saw as a weakness, but we're gonna forget about that, too, if you come up with the two thousand you took from her straightaway.'

'I'd have to get me a job,' said Leon. ''Cause currently, see, I don't have those kind of resources.'

'You gonna wear that outfit to the job interview?' said Lattimer.

Leon, wounded, looked up at Lattimer and touched the lapel of his lavender shirt. 'This right here is a designer shirt. An Yves Saint Laur*ent*.'

'From the Singapore factory, maybe. Man your age ought to be wearin' some cotton by now, too, instead of that sixty-forty blend you got on right there.'

Strange said, 'How we going to work this out with the money, Leon?'

'I ain't got no got-damn money, man; I told you!'

Some spittle flew from Leon's mouth and a bit of it landed on the chest area of Lattimer's overcoat. Lattimer grabbed Leon by the lapels of his jacket and pulled Leon toward him.

'You spit on my cashmere, man!'

'All right, Ron,' said Strange. Lattimer released Leon.

'Everything all right over there?' said an elderly man from the backyard of the house to the left. An evergreen tree grew beside the porch, blocking their view of the man behind the voice.

'Everything's fine,' said Strange, speaking loudly in the direction of the man. 'We're officers of the law.'

'*No*, they ain't!' yelled Leon.

'Go on inside now,' said Strange. 'We got this under control.'

Strange squared his body so that he was standing close to Leon. Leon backed up a step and scratched at the bridge of his dented nose.

'Well,' said Leon haughtily.

'Well *water*,' said Lattimer.

'Look here,' said Strange. 'What me and my partner are going to do now, we're going to go back inside and talk to your grandmother. Explain to her about this misunderstanding you got yourself into. I think your grandmother will see that she has to give us what we need. I'm sure this house is paid for, and from the looks of things around here, it won't be too great a burden for her to write the check. I know she doesn't want to see you go to jail. Shame she has to settle up the debt for your mistakes, but there it is.'

'Won't be the first time, I bet,' said Lattimer.

'What y'all are doin', it's a shakedown. It's not even legal!' Leon looked from Strange to Lattimer and drew his small frame straight. 'Not only that. First you go and insult my vines. And now you're fixin' to shame me to my granmoms!'

'Sooner or later,' said Strange, 'everybody's got to pay.'

Strange split up with Lattimer, drove down to the MLK Jr library on 9th Street, and went up to the Washingtoniana Room on the third floor. He retrieved a couple of microfiche spools from a steel drawer where the newspaper morgue material was chronologically arranged. He threaded the film and scanned newspaper articles on a lighted screen, occasionally dropping change into a slot to make photostatic copies when he found what he thought he might need. After an hour and a half he turned off the machine, as his eyes had begun to burn, and when he left the library the city had turned to night.

Outside MLK, Strange phoned Janine's voice mail and left a message: He needed a current address on a man. He gave her the subject's name.

'Hey, what's goin' on, Strange?' said a guy who was walking by the bank of phones.

'Hey, how you *doin'*?'

'Ain't seen you around much lately.'

'I been here,' said Strange.

Strange headed uptown and stopped at the Raven, a neighborhood bar on Mount Pleasant Street, for a beer. Afterward he walked up to Sportsman's Liquors on the same street and bought a six-pack, then drove to his Buchanan Street row house off Georgia.

He drank another beer and got his second wind. He phoned a woman he knew, but she wasn't home.

Strange went up to his office, a converted bedroom next to his own bedroom on the second floor, and read the newspaper material, a series in the *Washington Post* and a *Washington City Paper* story, that he had copied from the library. As he looked them over, his dog, a tan boxer named Greco, slept with his snout resting on the toe of Strange's boot.

When he was done, he logged on to his computer and checked his stock portfolio to see how he had done for the day. The case for *Ennio Morricone: A Fistful of Film Music* was sitting on his desk. He removed disc one from the case and loaded it into the CPU of his computer. The first few strains of '*Per Qualche Dollaro in Piu*' drifted through the room. He turned the volume up just a hair on his Yamaha speakers, sat back in his reclining chair with his hands folded across his middle, closed his eyes, and smiled.

Strange loved westerns. He'd loved them since he was a kid.

3

He locked the front door of the shop and checked it, then walked up Bonifant Street toward Georgia Avenue, turning up the collar of his black leather to shield his neck from the chill. He passed the gun shop, where black kids from over the District line and suburban white kids who wanted to be street hung out on Saturday afternoons, feeling the weight of the automatics in their hands and checking the action on guns they could buy on the black market later that night. Integras and Accords tricked out with aftermarket spoilers and alloy wheels were parked outside the gun shop during the day, but it was night now and the street had quieted and there were few cars of any kind parked along its curb. He passed an African and a Thai restaurant, and Vinyl Ink, the music store that still sold records, and a jewelry and watch-repair shop that catered to Spanish, and one each of many braid-and-nail and dry-cleaning storefronts that low-rised the downtown business district of Silver Spring.

He crossed the street before reaching the Quarry House, one of two or three neighborhood bars he frequented. About now he could taste his first beer, his mouth nearly salivating at the thought of it, and he wondered if this was what it felt like to have a problem with drink. He'd attended a seminar once when he had still worn the uniform, and there he'd learned that clock-watchers and drink counters were drunks or potential drunks, but he was comfortable with his own reasons for looking forward to that first one and he could not bring himself to become alarmed. He liked bars and the companionship to be found in them; it was no more complicated or sinister than that. And anyway, he'd never allow alcoholism to happen to him; he had far too many issues to contend with as it stood.

He cut through the bank parking lot, passing the new Irish bar on the second floor of the corner building at Thayer and Georgia, and he did not slow his pace. He neared a black man coming in the opposite direction, and though either one of them could have stepped aside, neither of them did, and they bumped each other's shoulder and kept walking without an apology or a threatening word.

On the east side of Georgia he passed Rosita's, where the young woman named Juana worked, and he was careful to hurry along and not look through the plate glass colored with Christmas lights and sexy neon signs advertising Tecate and other brands of beer, because he did not want to stop yet, he wanted to walk. Then he was passing a pawnshop and another Thai restaurant and a *pollo* house and the art supply store and the flower shop . . . then crossing Silver Spring Avenue, passing the firehouse and the World Building and the old Gifford's ice-cream parlor, now a day-care center, and across Sligo Avenue up to Selim, where the car repair garages and aikido studios fronted the railroad tracks.

He dropped thirty-five cents into the slot of a pay phone mounted between the Vietnamese *pho* house and the NAPA auto parts store. He dialed Rosita's, and his friend Raphael, who owned the restaurant, answered.

'Hey, amigo, it's—'

'I know who it is. Not too many gringos call this time of night, and you have that voice of yours that people recognize very easily. And I know who you want.'

'Is she working?'

'Yes.'

'Is there a *c* next to her name on the schedule?'

'Yes, she is closing tonight. So you have time. Are you outside? I can hear the cars.'

'I am. I'm taking a walk.'

'Go for your walk and I'll put one on ice for you, my friend.'

'I'll see you in a little bit.'

He hung the receiver in its cradle and crossed the street to the pedestrian bridge that spanned Georgia Avenue. He went to the middle of the bridge and looked down at the cars emerging northbound from the tunnel and the southbound cars disappearing into the same tunnel. He focused on the broken yellow lines painted on the street and the cars moving in rows between the lines. He looked north on Georgia at the street lamps haloed in the cold and watched his breath blow out into the night. He had grown up in this city, it was his, and to him it was beautiful.

Sometime later he crossed the remainder of the bridge and went to the chain-link fence that had been erected in the past year. The fence prevented pedestrians from walking into the area of the train station via the bridge. He glanced around idly and climbed the fence, dropping down over its other side. Then he was in near the small commuter train station, a squat brick structure with boarded windows housing bench seats and a ticket office, and he went down a dark set of stairs beside the station. He entered a fluorescently-lit foot tunnel that ran beneath the Metro and B & O railroad tracks. The tunnel smelled of nicotine, urine, and beer-puke, but there was no one in it now, and he went through to the other side, going up another set of concrete steps and finding himself on a walkway on the west side of the tracks.

He walked along the fence bordering the old Canada Dry bottling plant, turned, stood with his hands buried in his jeans, and watched as a Red Line train approached from the city. His long sight was beginning to go on him, and the lights along Georgia Avenue were blurred, white stars broken by the odd red and green.

He looked across the tracks at the ticket office as the passing train raised wind and dust. He closed his eyes.

He thought of his favorite western movie, *Once Upon a Time in the West.* Three gunmen are waiting on the platform of an empty train station as the opening credits roll. It's a long sequence, made more excruciating by the real-time approach of a train and a sound design nearly comic in its exaggeration. Eventually the train arrives. A character named Harmonica steps off of it and stands before the men who have come to kill him. Their shadows are elongated by the dropping sun. Harmonica and the men have a brief and pointed conversation. The ensuing violent act is swift and final.

Standing there at night, on the platform of the train station in Silver Spring, he often felt like he was waiting for that train. In many ways, he felt he'd been waiting all his life.

After a while he went back the way he came and headed for Rosita's. He was ready for a beer, and also to talk to Juana. He had been curious about her for some time.

Juana Burkett was standing at the service end of the bar, waiting on a marg-rocks-no-salt from Enrique the tender, when the white man in the black leather jacket came through the door. She watched him walk across the dining room, navigating the tables, a man of medium height with a flat stomach and wavy brown hair nearly touching his shoulders. His face was clean shaven with only a shadow of beard, and there was a natural swagger to his walk.

He seated himself at the short, straight bar and did not look at her at first, though she knew that she was the reason he was here. She had met him briefly at his place of employment, a used book and vinyl store on Bonifant, where she had been looking for a copy of *Home Is the Sailor*, and Raphael had told her that he had been asking for her since and that he would be stopping by. On the day that she'd met him she felt she'd seen him before, and the feeling passed through her again. Now he looked around the restaurant, trying to appear casually interested in the decor, and finally his eyes lit on her, where they had been headed all the time, and he lifted his chin and gave her an easy and pleasant smile.

Enrique placed the margarita on her drink tray, and she dressed it with a lime wheel and a swizzle stick and walked it to her four-top by the front window. She served the marg and the dark beers on her tray and took the food orders from the two couples seated at the table, glancing over toward the bar one time as she wrote. Raphael was standing beside the man in the black leather jacket and the two of them were shaking hands.

Juana went back to the area of the service bar and placed the ticket faceup on the ledge of a reach-through, where the hand of the kitchen's expeditor took the ticket and impaled it on a wheel. She heard Raphael call her name and she walked around the bar to where he stood and the man sat, his ringless hand touching a cold bottle of Dos Equis beer.

'You remember this guy?' said Raphael.

'Sure,' she said, and then Raphael moved away, just left her there like that, went to a deuce along the wall to greet its two occupants. She'd have to remind Raphael of his manners the next time she got him alone.

'So,' the man said in a slow, gravelly way. 'Did you find your Jorge Amado?'

'I did find it. Thank you, yes.'

'We got *Tereza Batista* in last week. It's in that paper series Avon put out a few years back—'

'I've read it,' she said, too abruptly. She was nervous, and showing it; it wasn't like her to react this way in front of a man. She looked over her shoulder. She had only the one table left for the evening, and her diners seemed satisfied, nursing their drinks. She cleared her throat and said, 'Listen—'

'It's okay,' he said, swiveling on his stool to face her. He had a wide mouth parenthesized by lines going down to a strong chin. His eyes were green and they were direct and damaged, and somehow needy, and the eyes completed it for her, and scared her a little bit, too.

'*What's* okay?' she said.

'You don't have to stand here if you don't want to. You can go back to work if you'd like.'

'No, that's all right. I mean, I'm fine. It's just that—'

'Juana, right?' He leaned forward and cocked his head.

He was moving very quickly, and it crossed her mind that what she had taken for confidence in his walk might have been conceit. 'I don't remember telling you my name the day we met.'

'Raphael told me.'

'And now you're going to tell me you like the way it sounds. That my name sings, right?'

'It *does* sing. But that's not what I was going to say.'

'What, then?'

'I was going to ask if you like oysters.'

'Yes. I like them.'

'Would you like to have some with me down at Crisfield's, after you get off?'

'Just like that? I don't even know—'

'Look here.' He put his right hand up, palm out. 'I've been thinking about you on and off since that day you walked into the bookstore. I've been thinking about you *all* day today. Now, I believe in being to the point, so let me ask you again: Would . . . you . . . like . . . to step *out* with me, after your shift, and have a bite to eat?'

'Juana!' said the expeditor, his head in the reach-through. 'Is up!'

'Excuse me,' she said.

She went to the ledge of the reach-through and retrieved a small bowl of chili *con queso,* filled a red plastic basket with chips, and served the four-top its appetizer. As she was placing the *queso* and chips on the table, she looked back at the bar, instantly sorry that she had. The man was smiling at her full on. She tossed her long hair off her shoulder self-consciously and was sorry she had done that, too. She walked quickly back to the bar.

'You're sure of yourself, eh?' she said when she reached him, surprised to feel her arms folded across her chest.

'I'm confident, if that's what you mean.'

'Overconfident, maybe.'

He shrugged. 'You like what you see, otherwise you wouldn't have stood here as long as you did. And you sure wouldn't have come back. I like what *I* see. That's what I'm *doing* here. And listen, Raphael can vouch for me. It's not like we're going to walk out of here and I'm gonna grow fangs. So why don't we try it out?'

'You must be drunk,' she said, nodding at the beer bottle in his hand.

'On wine and love.' He saw her perplexed face and said, 'It's a line from a western.'

'Okay.'

He shot a look at her crossed arms. 'You're gonna wrinkle your uniform, you keep hugging it like that.'

She unfolded her arms slowly and dropped them to her side. She began to smile, tried to stop it, and felt a twitch at the edge of her lip.

'It's not a uniform,' she said, her voice softening, losing its edge. 'It's just an old cotton shirt.'

They studied each other for a while, not speaking, as the recorded mariachi music danced through the dining room and bar.

'What I was trying to tell you,' she said, 'before you interrupted me . . . is that I don't even know your name.'

'It's Terry Quinn,' he said.

'Tuh-ree Quinn,' she said, trying it out.

'Irish Catholic,' he said, 'if you're keeping score.'

And Juana said, 'It sings.'

4

'Where's your car?' asked Juana.

'You better drive tonight,' said Quinn.

'I'm in the lot. We should cut through here.'

They went through the break in the buildings between Rosita's and the pawnshop. They neared Fred Folsom's sculpted bronze bust of Norman Lane, 'the Mayor of Silver Spring,' mounted in the center of the breezeway. Quinn patted the top of Lane's capped head without thought as they walked by.

'You always do that?' said Juana.

'Yeah,' said Quinn, 'for luck. Some of the guys in the garages back here, they sort of adopted him, looked out for him when he was still alive. See?' He pointed to a sign mounted over a bay door in the alley, a caricature drawing of Lane with the saying 'Don't Worry About It' written on a button pinned to his chest, as they entered an alley. 'They call this Mayor's Lane now.'

'You knew him?'

'I knew who he was. I bought him a drink once over at Captain White's. Another place that isn't around anymore. He was just a drunk. But I guess what they're trying to say with all this back here, with everything he was, he was still a man.'

'God, it's cold.' Juana held the lapels of her coat together and close to her chest and looked over at Quinn. 'I've seen you before, you know? And not at the bookstore, either. Before that, but I know we never met.'

'I was in the news last year. On the television and in the papers, too.'

'Maybe that's it.'

'It probably is.'

'There's my car.'

'That old Beetle?'

'What, it's not good enough for you?'

'No, I like it.'

'What do you drive?'

'I'm between cars right now.'

'Is that like being between jobs?'

'Just like it.'

'You asked me out and you don't have a car?'

'So it's your nickel for the gas.' Quinn zipped his jacket. 'I'll get the oysters and the beers.'

They were at the bar of Crisfield's, the old Crisfield's on the dip at Georgia, not the designer Crisfield's on Colesville, and they were eating oysters and sides of coleslaw and washing it all down with Heineken beer. Quinn had juiced the cocktail sauce with horseradish and he noticed that Juana had added Tabasco to the mix.

'Mmm,' said Juana, swallowing a mouthful, reaching into the cracker bowl for a chaser.

'A dozen raw and a plate of slaw,' said Quinn. 'Nothin' better. These are good, right?'

'They're good.'

All the stools at the horseshoe-shaped bar were occupied, and the dining room to the right was filled. The atmosphere was no atmosphere: white tile walls with photographs of local celebrities framed and mounted above the tiles, wood tables topped with paper place mats, grocery store-bought salad dressing displayed on a bracketed shelf . . . and still the place was packed nearly every night, despite the fact that management was giving nothing away. Crisfield's was a D.C. landmark, where generations of Washingtonians had met and shared food and conversation for years.

'Make any money tonight?' said Quinn.

'By the time I tipped out the bartender . . . not real money, no. I walked with forty-five.'

'You keep having forty-five-dollar nights, you're not going to be able to make it through school.'

'My student loans are putting me through school. I wait tables just to live. Raphael tell you I was going to law school?'

'He told me everything he knew about you. Don't worry, it wasn't much. Pass me that Tabasco, will you?'

He touched her hand as she handed him the bottle. Her hand was warm, and he liked the way her fingers were tapered, feminine and strong.

'Thanks.'

A couple of black guys seated on the opposite end of the horseshoe, early thirties, if Quinn had to guess, were staring freely at him and

Juana. Plenty of heads had turned when they'd entered the restaurant, some he figured just to get a look at Juana. Most of the people had only looked over briefly, but these two couldn't give it up. Well, fuck it, he thought. If this was going to keep working in any kind of way – and he was getting the feeling already that he wanted it to – then he'd just have to shake off those kinds of stares. Still, he didn't like it, how these two were so bold.

'That's not fair,' said Juana.

'*What* isn't?'

'You been asking about me and you know some things, and I don't know a damn thing about you.'

You *been*. He liked the way she said that.

'That accent of yours,' he said.

'What accent?'

'Your voice falls and rises, like music. What is that, Brooklyn?'

'The Bronx.' She shook an oyster off her fork and let it sit in the cocktail sauce. 'What's yours? The Carolinas, something like that?'

'Maryland. D.C.'

'You sound plenty Southern to me. With that drawl and everything.'

'This *is* the South. It's south of the Mason–Dixon Line, anyway.'

He turned to face her. Her hair was black, curly, and very long, and it broke on thin shoulders and rose again at the upcurve of her smallish breasts. She had a nice ass on her, too; he had checked it out back at the restaurant when she'd bent over to serve her drinks. It was round and high, the way he liked it, and the sight of it had taken his breath short, which had not happened to him in a long while. Her eyes were near black, many shades deeper than her brown skin, and her lips were full and painted in a dark color with an even darker outline. There was a mole on her cheek, above and to the right of her upper lip.

He was staring at her now and she was staring at him, and then her lips turned up on one side, a kind of half smile that she attempted to hold down. It was the same thing she had done back at Rosita's with her mouth, and Quinn chuckled under his breath.

'*What?*'

'Ah, nothin'. It's just, that thing you got going on, your *almost* smile. I just like it, is all.'

Juana retrieved her oyster from the cocktail sauce, chewed and swallowed it, and had a swig of cold beer.

'How do you know Raphael?' she said.

'He came in the shop one day, looking for Stanley Clarke's *School*

Days on vinyl. Raphael likes that jazz-funk sound, the semi-orchestral stuff from the seventies. Dexter Wansel, George Duke, like that. Lonnie Liston Smith. I knew zilch about it, and he was happy to give me an education. I call him when we buy those old records from time to time.'

'You always worked in a bookstore?'

'No, not always. What you want to know is, am I educated, and if so, why haven't I done anything with it. I went to the University of Maryland and got my criminology degree. Then I was a cop in D.C. for eight years or so. After I left the force, I thought I was ready for something quiet. I like books, a certain kind, anyway . . .'

'Westerns.'

'Yeah, and there's nothing quieter than a used book and record store. So here I am.'

She studied his face. 'I know where I've seen you now.'

'Right. I'm the cop that killed the other cop last year.'

'It's the hair that's changed.'

'Uh-huh. I grew it out.'

Quinn waited, but the usual follow-up questions didn't come. He watched Juana use her elbow to push the platter of oyster shells away from her. While he watched her, he drank off an inch of his beer.

'How about me?' asked Juana. 'Anything else you want to know?'

'Not really. What I know so far I like.'

'Not a thing, huh?'

'Can't think of anything off the top of my head right now.'

'Let me go ahead and get it out of the way, then, all right? My mother was Puerto Rican and my father was black. I'm comfortable in a few different worlds and sometimes I'm not comfortable in any of them.'

'I didn't ask you that.'

'You didn't ask me that *yet*.'

'What I mean is, I don't care.'

'You don't care tonight. Tonight there's only attraction and do we connect. But this world we got out here and the people in it, right now, they're not gonna let us *not care*. Like those two guys over there, been staring at us all night.'

'How about we deal with it as we go along?' Quinn signaled the barrel-chested man with the gray mustache behind the bar. 'Sir? You wanna shuck us a dozen more?'

'Thanks, Tuh-ree,' said Juana.

Tuh-ree. He liked the way she said that, too.

On their way out the door, Juana noticed Quinn glance over his shoulder at the two men who had been staring at them all night and give them both a short but meaningful look.

Out on the street Juana put her arm through his as they walked to her black Beetle, parked in the lot of a tire store. She was cold and it warmed her to be close to him, and it felt natural to touch him, like they had moved past something and were onto something else. He was easy to talk to and he listened, didn't seem to be the type of man who was always thinking of what he'd say next. He didn't boast, either, didn't talk about his big plans, hadn't tried too hard to impress her in any way, in fact, which had made an impression in itself.

'Where do you live?' she asked.

'I got a place down off Sligo Avenue. What about you?'

'I'm over on Tenth Street in Northeast. Near Catholic University?'

'You mind dropping me off before you head back?'

'What're you, kiddin'?'

''Cause I could walk.'

'Yeah, I heard you like to walk at night.'

'Raphael told you, huh?'

'And that you like westerns. He said you were reading one the first time he went into your shop, and every time since.'

'So what was all that "It's not fair, I don't know a damn thing about you" stuff?' Quinn laughed. 'You're a liar!'

'All right, I lied,' said Juana. 'But I promise you, I'll never lie to you again.'

She stopped the Volkswagen out front of his place, a small brick apartment building, and let it idle. A convenience store and beer market sat closed and dark across the street, and boys in parkas were standing around outside its locked front door. The apartment units were dark as well.

'Here we are,' he said.

'Thanks for everything. It was nice.'

'My pleasure. I'll see you around, okay?'

'Okay.'

He squeezed her hand and it felt like a kiss. Then he was out of the car and crossing the unlit street, his jacket black and flat against the night.

She drove home listening to a Cassandra Wilson tape, thinking of him all the way.

Quinn washed and got under the covers of his bed. He tried to read a Max Evans sitting on his nightstand but found it hard to concentrate on the plot. He turned off the light, thinking of Juana, trying not to expect too much, hoping it could work.

Just before dawn he dreamed that he had gotten into a violent argument with a black man in a club. Punches were thrown and a gun was drawn. Then there were screams, blood, and death.

When he woke he was neither startled nor disturbed. He'd been having dreams like this for some time.

5

Ray Boone's jaw was tight from the thick line of crank he'd done. He unglued his tongue from the roof of his mouth and licked his dry lips. Ray went behind the long mahogany bar he and his daddy had built themselves, looking to fix himself a drink.

'Daddy, where's that Jack at?' he hollered.

Ray couldn't hear his own voice above the old Randy Travis number that was coming from the Wurlitzer jukebox he'd bought at an auction of the furnishings from a bankrupt restaurant. Edna had turned up the volume, way high.

Earl Boone was sitting in front of a video screen playing electronic poker. He took a sip from a can of Busch beer and dragged on his cigarette.

He tapped ash off the cigarette into a tray without taking his eyes off the screen. 'Wherever the hell you left it, Critter, last time you took a drink.'

'I see it,' said Ray. The Jack was on a low shelf beside the steel sink, in front of a Colt automatic his daddy had hung on a couple of nails he'd driven into the wood behind the bar. Ray grabbed the black-labeled bottle and a tumbler, filled the glass with ice from a chest beside the sink, and free-poured sour mash whiskey halfway to the lip. He filled the rest of the glass with Coke and stirred the cocktail with a dirty finger.

'Ain't you gonna fix me one, baby?' asked Edna Loomis, sitting at a card table covered in green felt. Edna was speed wired, her usual condition this time of the afternoon. She was stacking and restacking a pile of white chips with one hand and playing with her feather-cut shag with the other.

'Don't want you gettin' wasted too early, now,' said Ray, talking to her as he would to a child.

'I won't. Just want a little somethin' to sip while I'm back at the house watching my shows.'

Ray mixed a weak one and walked it over to Edna, who stood to take it from his hand. She reached for the glass, running her long fingers over the backs of his, and clumsily licked her lips. He felt a stirring in his jeans.

'We got time?' she said, looking over his shoulder briefly at the old man.

'Uh-uh,' said Ray. 'Me and Daddy are about to make a run into D.C.'

'When you get back, then,' she said, tossing a head of damaged orange-blond hair off her shoulder, winking as she took a sip of her drink. She moved her hips awkwardly to the Travis tune as she drank, keeping her eyes on him over the glass, and sang as the chorus returned to the song, '"Forever and ever, ay-men."'

Ray looked her over. Boy, she thought she was so sexy. He wondered what she saw when she looked in the mirror. She was getting up around thirty, and it was showing in the lines around her mouth. Dimples had begun to pucker below her ass, too, and she'd never had young eyes. She did have a nice set, though, the kind that stood at attention, with sharp pink button-nips. She ever let those bad boys go to seed like the rest of her was doin', Ray'd have to think about trading her in for a new model.

'Huh?' she said. 'I asked you a question, *Critter*. We gonna make like bunny rabbits and do the deed when you get back, or what?'

Her mouth, that was the other thing. Proud titties or no, she didn't learn to shut her mouth some, he might trade her in sooner than she knew.

'Don't call me Critter,' said Ray. 'Only Daddy can call me that.'

'Well, are we?'

'Maybe,' he said. But she'd be sloppy as hell by the time he came back from the city, cooked on crank and drunk as a sailor on shore leave, too. He couldn't stand to fuck her when she got like that.

'Ray?'

'Huh?'

'You're gonna be gone a few hours, right?'

'Uh-huh.'

'Whyn't you leave me some of that ice?'

'You know you're likin' that stuff too much.'

'Please, baby?'

'A little bit, then. All right.' He looked past her and said, 'You about ready, Daddy?'

Earl Boone said, 'Yep,' and flicked ash into the tray.

Ray went to a large door at the back of the barn. The door was steel fortified and it was set in a fortified, fireproofed wall. He took the set of keys he hung from a loop of his jeans and opened the door, which he kept locked at all times. He went in, closed the door behind him, and threw the slide bolt.

On one side of the room sat a weight bench and barbells and plates, with mirrors angled toward the weight bench and hung on the walls. A workbench ran along the opposite wall, with shelves above it and a Peg Board with hooks holding tools. A couple of safes sat beneath the workbench, and in the safes were money, heroin, and guns. Beside the workbench stood a footlocker next to a stand-up case made of varnished oak and glass, in which four shotguns were racked.

On the third wall was a single-unit kitchenette with a two-burner electric stove, sink, and refrigerator stocked with bottled water and beer. Ray used the stove to make his private stash of methamphetamine, both the powder and the crystal, which he cooked on the stove in a small saucepan. On the steel countertop of the kitchenette were bottles of Sudafed and carburetor cleaner, and the other chemicals he used to make the crank.

Ray and his father had plumbed in some pipes and put a bathroom in the room, too. It was big and private, with a solid oak door. Ray could sit on the crapper and look at his stroke books back in there, and if he had a mind to, when he was done wiping himself clean, he could just turn around and pump a load off into the bowl and flush the whole dirty mess.

Beneath the carpet remnant that lay beside the weight bench was a trapdoor. Under that trapdoor was a tunnel that he and his father had dug out the summer before last. The tunnel was their means of escape, in the event that one was needed, and it went back about fifty, sixty yards or so, into the woods behind the barn and the house.

Ray Boone loved this room. Only he and his daddy were allowed back here, that was the rule. Nobody, none of Daddy's friends or his own friends or Edna, would think of coming back here, even if they had access to the key. Edna knew that the drugs she loved so much were in this room. Dumb as she was, though, and she was dumber than a goddamn rock, she was plenty smart enough to know not to try.

Ray picked up a set of barbells and stood before one of the mirrors. He did a set of twenty alternating curls. He dropped the barbells and checked himself out. His prison tats showed just below the sleeves of his white T-shirt. A dagger with blood dripping from it on one arm, a cobra wrapped around the staff of a Confederate flag on the other: standard-issue stuff. The good tattoos, a swastika between two lightning bolts and a colored guy swinging from a tree, he kept covered up on his shoulder and back.

Ray made a couple of serious faces in the mirror, raised his eyebrows, first one, then the other. He wasn't too good-looking so anyone would mistake him for a pretty boy, and he wasn't all that ugly, either. He had acne scars on his face, but they'd never scared any girls off, not that he'd noticed, anyway. And some women liked the way his eyes were set real deep under his hard, protruding brow. A couple of times when he was growing up, some boys called him cross-eyed, and he just had to go ahead and pop those boys hard, square in the face. If he was cross-eyed, he didn't see it himself. Edna said he looked like that guy on the *Profiler* TV series, always played a drug dealer in the movies. Ray liked that guy. There wasn't nothin' pretty about him.

When Ray was done admiring himself he grabbed a vial holding a couple of meth crystals and slipped it into a pocket of his jeans. He took off his sneakers and put on a pair of Dingo boots with four-inch custom heels, opened the safe, and removed a day pack holding plastic packets of heroin the size of bricks that he had scaled out earlier in the day. He found his nine-millimeter Beretta, checked the load, and holstered the automatic in the waistband of his jeans. From the footlocker he withdrew a heavy flannel shirt and jacket, and put them both on, the tail of the shirt worn out to cover the gun. He slung the day pack over his shoulder, left the room, and locked the door behind him.

Edna was waiting for him out in the bar. She gave him a wet kiss as he palmed the vial over to her, then left the barn with her drink in her hand.

'Ready, Daddy?'

'Sure thing.'

Earl hated the city. There was only one thing good about it, far as he was concerned. It was down in the warehouse they called the Junkyard. For him, it was worth the trip.

Earl Boone stabbed his cigarette out in the ashtray. He killed his beer and crushed the can in his hand, dropping the empty in a wastebasket beside the electronic poker game. He slipped a deck of Marlboro reds into his shirt pocket and watched his son take his own pack of 'Boros off the bar and do the same.

Earl stood as his son crossed the room. Earl was a weathered version of the boy, the plow lines on his cheeks somewhat masking the acne scars, and deep-set, flat eyes. He was taller than Ray by six inches and wider across the shoulders and back. Unlike the boy, he'd never lifted a weight when he wasn't paid to do so, and he didn't understand those who did. A hitch in the Marine Corps and hard work had given him his build.

'Let's do it,' said Ray.

Earl smiled a little, looking at those high-heeled boots on his boy's feet. Ray sure did have a thing about his lack of height.

'Somethin' funny?' said Ray.

'Nothin',' said Earl.

Earl picked up a cooler that held a six-pack and looked around the bar and gaming area before he shut down the lights. He was real proud of what they'd done here, him and his boy. The way they had it fixed up, it looked like one of those old-time saloons. The kind they used to have in those towns out west.

Edna Loomis filled the bowl of a bong with pot and dropped a crystal of methamphetamine on top of the load. She stood at the window of the bedroom where she and Ray slept in the house and watched Ray and Earl leave the barn and head for their car, a hopped-up Ford parked between an F-150 pickup and Ray's Shovelhead Harley.

Edna flicked the wheel of a Bic lighter and got fire. She held the flame over the bowl and drew in a hit of ice over grass. Holding in the high, she watched Ray dismantle the top of the car's bumper, then take the heroin out of the day pack and stuff the packets into the space between the bumper and the trunk of the car.

She coughed out the hit, a mushroom of smoke exploding against the glass of the bedroom window.

Ray put a strip of rubber or something over the heroin and replaced the top of the bumper, pounding it into place with the heel of his hand. Earl was facing the wide gravel path that led in from the state road, keeping an eye out for any visitors. The both of them, thought Edna, they were just paranoid as all hell. No one ever came down that road. There was a locked wooden gate at the head of it, anyhow.

Edna was still coughing, thinking of Ray and Earl and their business, and her head started to pound, and for a moment she got a little bit scared. But she knew the pounding was just the rush of the ice hitting her brain, and then she stopped coughing and felt good. Then she felt better than good, suddenly straightened out right. She lit a Virginia Slim from a pack she kept in a leather case, picked up her drink, and sipped at it, trying to make it last.

She went to the TV set on the bureau and turned up the volume. Some white chick with orange hair was up on a stage, sitting next to a big black dude. The white chick was fat and asshole ugly, not surprising, and now some bubble-assed black chick was walking out on the stage and, boy, did she look meaner than a motherfucker, too. Looked like she was about to put a hurtin' on the white chick for sleeping with her old man. And damn if she wasn't throwing a punch at the white chick now . . . Edna had seen this one, or it could have been that she was just imagining that she had.

She went back to the window and looked down at the yard. Earl and Ray were three-point turning, heading down the gravel and into the trees.

She checked the level of her drink. It was going down real good today. Nothing like a little Jack and some nicotine behind a hit of speed. Course, Ray wouldn't like it if he came home and found her drunk, but she didn't have to worry about that yet.

She had a sip from the glass and then, what the hell, drank it all down in one gulp. Maybe she'd go down to the barn and fix one more weak one, mostly Coke with just a little mash in it to change its color. Ray wouldn't be home for another few hours anyway, and besides, he'd be all stoked and occupied for the rest of the night. Ray liked to count the cash money he brought back after he made his runs.

Ray and Earl's property was set back off Route 28, between Dickerson and Comus, not too far south of Frederick, at the east-central edge of Montgomery County. There was still forest and open country out here, but not for long. Over the years the Boones had seen the development stretch farther and farther north from D.C., white-flighters, mostly, who claimed they wanted 'more land' and 'more house for the buck.' What they really wanted, Ray knew, was to get away from the niggers and the crime. None of them could stand the prospect of seeing their daughters walking down the street holding the hand of Willie Horton. That was the white man's biggest nightmare, and they ran from it like a herd of frightened animals, all the way out here. Ray could understand it, but still, he wished those builders would go and put their new houses someplace else.

Ray moved the car to the on-ramp of 270 and drove south.

'Here,' said Ray, handing his pistol butt-out to his father. Earl took the gun, opened the glove box, hit a button, and waited for a false back to drop. He placed the Beretta in the space behind the glove box wall.

Ray had bought this particular vehicle from a trap-car shop up in the Bronx. It was your basic Taurus, outfitted with more horses than was legal, more juice than Ford used to put in its high-horse street model, the SHO. The bumper was a false bumper, which meant it could withstand a medium-velocity impact and could also accommodate relatively large volumes of heroin between its outer shell and the trunk of the car. Hidden compartments behind the glove box, to the left of the steering column, and in other spots throughout the interior concealed Ray's guns and his personal stash of drugs.

Ray lit a cigarette off the dash lighter, passed the lighter to his daddy so he could light his.

'You'd know we was the bad guys,' said Ray, 'if this here was a movie.'

'Why's that?'

''Cause you and me smoke.'

'Huh,' said Earl.

'Down county, I hear they want to outlaw smoking in bars.'

'That so.'

'They can have mine,' said Ray, beaming at his cleverness, 'when they pry 'em from my cold, dead fingers. Right?'

Earl didn't answer. He didn't talk much to begin with, and he talked even less with his son. Ray had been absent the day God passed out brains, and when he did say something, it tended to be about how tough he was or how smart he was. Earl had twenty years on Ray, and Earl could take Ray on his weakest day. Ray knew it, too. Earl figured this was just another thing that had kept the chip on his boy's shoulder his entire life.

Earl popped the top on a can of Busch.

Ray dragged on his cigarette. It bothered him that his father barely gave him the time of day. It was him, Ray, who had set up this business they had going on right here. It was him, Ray, who had made all the right decisions. If he had left business matters up to his father, who had never even been able to hold a longtime job on his own, they'd have nothing now, nothing at all.

Course, it took a stretch in Hagerstown, where Ray had done a ten-year jolt on a manslaughter beef, for him to find the opportunity to connect to this gig he had here. Ray had been paid to kill some K-head who'd ripped off the stash of a dealer out in Frederick County. Ray had killed a couple of guys for money since high school, and he'd gotten a rep among certain types as the go-to man in that part of the state. He'd never intended to become a hired murderer – not that he ever lost any sleep over it or anything like that – but these were people who deserved to die, after all. After his first kill, who begged and didn't go quick, it had been easy.

This particular job, Ray's idea had been to do it in the bathroom of a bar where the K-head hung out, then climb out the window and make his escape. After he gutted the thief with a Ka-Bar knife, though, the bar's bouncer came in to take a leak and disarmed Ray, holding him until the pigs could get to the scene. Ray should've killed the bouncer, too, he had replayed it in his head many times, but the bouncer was one of those cro-mags, he broke Ray's wrist real quick, and then there wasn't all that much Ray could do.

What he did do, he claimed the dust bunny had attacked *him*, and lucky for Ray, a piece-of-shit .22 was found in the jacket pocket of the corpse. So the hard rap couldn't stick, and Ray drew manslaughter and Hagerstown.

Prison life was okay if you could avoid getting punked. The way to avoid it was some strong attitude, but mostly alliances and gangs. The whites hooked up with Christian Identity and the like. The blacks hung together and so did the Spanish, but the whites and Spanish hated the blacks more than they hated each other, so once in a while Ray made talk with a brown or two.

One of them was Roberto Mantilla. Roberto had a cousin in the Orlando area, Nestor Rodriguez, who worked for the Vargas cartel operating out of the Cauca Valley in northern Colombia. Nestor and his brother Lizardo made the East Coast run, selling powder to dealers in D.C., Baltimore, Wilmington, Philly, and New York. Purer heroin at a lower cost had expanded their market, crushed their foreign competition, and fueled the growth of their business. Roberto said that his cousins could no longer handle the logistics of the transactions themselves and would be willing to sell to a middleman who could make the back-and-forth into D.C. and satisfy the demands of the dealers more readily than they. For this, said Roberto, the middleman would receive a ten-thousand-dollar bounce per transaction.

Ray said, 'All right, soon as I get out, I'd like to give that a try.' A year later, after a parole board hearing at which he convinced the attendees that the good behavior he had exhibited during his term was not an aberration, he was out of Hagerstown. And two years after that, when he had completed his outside time and said good-bye to his PO, he was free to go to work.

Ray supposed he had Roberto Mantilla to thank for his success. But this was impossible, as Roberto had been raped and bludgeoned to death by a cock-diesel with a lead pipe shortly after Ray's release.

'This load we got, it's eighty-five-percent pure, Daddy,' said Ray, thinking of the heroin sealed in the bumper compartment at the rear of the car.

'Lizardo tell you that?' asked Earl, needling his son, knowing Ray hated the Rodriguez brother who never showed Ray an ounce of respect.

'*Nestor* told me. Down in Florida, they got brown heroin, it's ninety-five-percent pure when it hits the street.'

'So? What's that do?'

'For the Colombians, it kills the competition. I'm talkin' about the Asians, who were putting out seven-, ten-percent product, and the Mexicans, too. The Colombians upped the purity and lowered the price, and now they're gonna own most of the U.S. market. And what this pure shit does, it creates a whole new class of customers: college kids, the boy next door, like that. It's not just for coloreds anymore, Daddy. 'Cause you don't have to pop it, see, to get a rush. You can smoke it or snort it, you want to.'

'That's nice.'

'You're not interested in what we're doin'?'

'Not really, no. Get in, sell it, get out; that's all I'm interested in. Wasn't for the money, I'd just as soon never set eyes on that city again. Let them all kill themselves over this shit for all I care.'

'You wouldn't want that,' said Ray, smiling at his father across the bench. 'Wouldn't have no customers, they all up and died.'

'Critter?'

'What.'

'Someday, you and me, we're gonna wake up and figure out we got enough money. You ever think about that?'

'I'm startin' to,' said Ray, goosing the Ford into the passing lane.

Truth be told, Ray had been thinkin' on it for quite some time. Only piece missing was a way to get out. That's all he and his daddy needed: some kind of plan.

6

By the time Earl had killed another beer, Ray had gotten off the Beltway and was on New Hampshire Avenue, heading south into D.C. Later, on North Capitol, down near Florida Avenue, he made a call on his cell phone and told Cherokee Coleman's boys that he and his father were on their way in.

He turned left onto Florida when things were really starting to look rough, and went along a kind of complex of old warehouses and truck bays that had once been an industrial hub of sorts in a largely nonindustrial town but were now mainly abandoned. The entire area had been going steadily downhill since the riots of '68.

Ray passed by Cherokee Coleman's place of business, one of several small brick rowhouses in the complex, indistinguishable from the rest. Coleman's place was across the street from what folks in the area called the Junkyard, a crumbling warehouse where crack fiends, blow addicts, and heroin users had been squatting for the past year or so. They had come to be near Coleman's supply.

Ray drove slowly down the block. Coleman's army – steerers, pitchers, money handlers, lookouts, and managers – was spread out on the sidewalk and on several corners of the street. An M3 BMW, an Acura Legend, a spoilered Lexus, and a two-seater Mercedes with chromed-out wheel wells, along with several SUVs, were curbed along the block.

A cop car approached from the other direction. Ray did not look at its uniformed driver but rather at the large numbers printed on the side of the cruiser, a Crown Vic, as it passed.

'Ray,' said Earl.

'It's all right,' said Ray, matching the numbers on the car to the numbers he had memorized.

In the rearview, Ray saw the MPD cruiser make a right at the next corner, circling the block. Ray punched the gas and made it quickly to a bay door at a garage on the end of the block. He honked his horn, two shorts and a long. The bay door rose and Ray drove through, into a garage where several young men and a couple of very young men waited.

The door closed behind them. Ray got his gun out of the glove box trap and pushed his hips forward so that he could holster the nine beneath the waistband of his jeans. He knew his father had slipped his .38 into his jacket pocket back in the barn. He didn't care if the young men in the garage saw the guns. He *wanted* them to see. Ray and Earl got out of the car.

There was no greeting from Coleman's men, no nod of recognition. Ray knew from his prison days not to smile, or show any other gesture of humanity, because it would be seen as a weakness, an opening, a place to stick the knife. As for Earl, he saw hard black faces, one no different from the other. That was all he needed to know.

'Money, clothes, cars,' rapped a dead, even voice from a small stereo set up on a shelf. 'Clockin' Gs, gettin' skeezed . . .'

'It's behind the bumper,' said Ray to the oldest of the bunch, whom he'd seen on the last run.

'Then get it, chief,' said the young man, the manager, with a slow tilt of his head.

'You get it,' said Ray.

Now you're gonna look at each other for a while, thought Earl, like you can't decide whether to mix it up or fall in love.

That's what they did. Ray stared them down and they stared him down, and a couple of the older ones laughed, and Ray laughed some, and then there were more hard stares.

And then the manager said, 'Get it,' to one of the younger ones, who nodded to the guy next to him. Those two dismantled the bumper and got the heroin packs out of the space.

Coleman's employees scaled the heroin out quickly on an electronic unit that sat on a bench along a wall while Ray and Earl smoked cigarettes. They did not taste it or test it, not because they trusted these two but because Coleman had instructed them to leave it alone. Coleman knew that Ray and Earl would never try and take him off. What they had with him, it was just too tight.

'The weight's good,' said the manager.

'I know it's good. Call Cherokee and tell him I'm coming in. We'll be back for our car.'

The group began chuckling as the Boones walked from the garage, after one young man started singing banjo notes. Ray didn't care, all of them would be croaked or in the joint soon anyway. It felt good walking out of there, not even looking over his shoulder, like he didn't give a good fuck if they laughed themselves silly or took another breath. He felt strong and he felt tall. He was glad he'd worn his boots.

Ray and Earl stepped quickly down the block. The cold wind blew newspaper pages across the street. Ray met eyes with a young man talking on a cell, knowing that the young man was speaking to one of Cherokee Coleman's lieutenants. They kept walking toward Coleman's place, and when they neared it a door opened and they stepped inside.

They were in an outer office then, and four young men were waiting for them there. One of them frisked Ray and Earl and took the guns that he found. Ray allowed it because there was no danger here; if something was to have gone down it would have gone down back in the garage. Coleman didn't keep drugs, handle large amounts of money, or have people killed anywhere near his office. He had come up like everyone else, but he was smart and he was past that now.

The one who had frisked them nodded, and they went into Coleman's office.

Cherokee Coleman was seated in a leather recliner behind a desk. The desk held a blotter, a gold pen-and-pencil set, and one of those lamps with a green shade, the kind they used to have in banks. A cell phone lay neatly next to the lamp. Ray figured this kind of setup made Coleman feel smart, like a grown-up businessman, like he worked in a bank or something, too. Ray and his father often joked that the pen-and-pencil set had never been used.

Coleman wore a three-button black suit with a charcoal turtleneck beneath the jacket. His skin was smooth and reddish brown against the black of the suit, and his features were small and angular. He wasn't a big man, but the backs of his thick-wristed hands were heavily veined, indicating to Earl that Coleman had strength.

Behind Coleman, leaning against the frame of a small barred window, was a tall, fat, bald man wearing shades with gold stems. He was Coleman's top lieutenant, Angelo Lincoln, a man everyone down here called Big-Ass Angelo.

'Fellas,' said Coleman, lazily moving one of his manicured hands to indicate they take a seat before his desk.

Ray and Earl sat in chairs set lower than Coleman's.

'How's it goin', Ray? Earl?'

'How do,' said Earl.

'How do what?'

Angelo's shoulders jiggled, and a *sh-sh-sh* sound came from his mouth.

'Looks like everything checked out all right,' said Coleman.

'No doubt,' said Ray. 'The weight's there, and this load is honest-to-God high-test. Eight-five per.'

'I heard.'

Coleman didn't feel the need to tell Ray this purity-percentage stuff was straight-up bullshit. If the shit was eighty-five, ninety percent pure for real, you'd have junkies fallin' out dead all over the city, 'cause shit that pure was do-it-on-the-head-of-a-matchstick stuff only. Got so even the dealers were startin' to believe the press releases comin' out of the DEA.

'You hear it from the Rodriguez brothers?'

'Yeah. They called me to discuss some other business.'

'This business involve my father and me?'

'It could.' Coleman turned to his lieutenant. 'Looks like we got a killer batch on our hands, Angelo. What we gonna call it?'

Coleman liked to label the little wax packets of heroin he sold with brand names. Said it was free advertising, letting his 'clients' know that they were getting Cherokee's best, that there was something new and potent out on the street. He liked to think of the brand names as his signature, like the special dishes cooks came up with in those fancy restaurants.

Ray watched Angelo, staring down at the floor, his mouth open as he thought up names, a frown on his blubbery face. Angelo looked up, nodding his head, proud of what he'd come up with.

'Kill and Kill Again,' said Angelo with a wide grin.

'I don't like that. Sounds like one of those Chuck Norris movies, Angie, and you know what I think of him.'

'Death Wish Too?' said Angelo.

'Naw, black, we used that before.'

'How about Scalphunter, then?' Angelo knew that his boss liked those kinds of names. Coleman thought himself kin to the Indian nation.

Coleman pursed his lips. 'Scalphunter sound good.'

Earl shifted in his chair. The room was warm and smelled of oils or perfume, some shit like that. Colored guys with their paper evergreen trees hanging from the rearview mirrors and their scented crowns and their fancy fucking smells.

'About the Rodriguez brothers,' said Ray.

'Nestor,' said Coleman, 'now he's gone and added cocaine to that sales bag of his. Had to explain to him, I'm getting out of that business. Blow fiends and pipeheads, their money's green, too, don't get me wrong. But all the cash is in brown powder right now, and that's where I see the money of the future, too. And the cocaine I do buy, I buy from the Crips out of L.A. Thing I'm tryin' to say is, I don't want to be beholdin' to just one supplier. Gives 'em too much power with regards to the price structure and negotiations side of things, you know what I'm sayin'?'

Beholdin' to, with regards to, price structure and negotiations side of things . . . Christ, thought Earl, who the fuck does this nigger think he is?

'What'd Nestor say to that?' said Ray.

'He implied that it might imperil our business relationship, I don't buy all my inventory from him. And I don't like those kinds of words. Almost sounds like a threat, you understand what I'm talkin' about?'

'I'm hip,' said Ray. 'I'm with you.'

Oh, you hipper than a motherfucker, thought Coleman. And of course you're *with* me. Where the fuck else *would* you be, it wasn't for me? Out in the fields somewhere with a yoke around your neck, a piece of straw hangin' out your mouth, you Mr Green Jeans-lookin' motherfucker . . .

'We done?' said Earl.

'You in a hurry?' said Coleman with a smile. 'Got a lady waitin'?'

'What if I do?' said Earl.

Coleman's smile turned down. His voice was soft, almost tender. 'Now, you gonna flex on me, old man? That's what you fixin' to do?'

'C'mon, Cherokee,' said Ray. 'My daddy was only kiddin' around.'

Coleman didn't look at Ray. He kept his eyes on Earl. And then he smiled and clapped his hands together. 'Aw, shit, Earl, that little redbone don't mean nothin' to me anymore. I done had that pussy when it was fresh. You go on and sweet-talk your little junkie all you want, hear?'

'I guess that'll do 'er,' said Ray. He stood and looked at his father, who was still seated in the chair, one eyebrow cocked, his gaze on Coleman.

'Go ahead, Earl,' said Coleman. 'She's waitin' on you, man. Got that stall of hers all reserved. Guess she heard you was comin' into the big city today.'

Earl stood.

'Now, Ray,' said Coleman. 'Think about what I said about that Rodriguez thing. No disrespect to my brown brothers, but maybe you ought to talk to them next time they drop off the goods, tell them straight up the way I feel.'

'I hear you,' said Ray.

'Good. Your money will be waiting for you back in the garage. You can pick up your guns on the way out.'

'See you next time,' said Ray, and he turned for the door.

'Hey, Ray,' said Coleman, and when Ray looked back Coleman was standing, looking over the desk at Ray's feet. 'Lizardo Rodriguez, he asked me to check and see if you was wearing those fly boots of yours today.'

'Oh, yeah?'

'I see you are.'

Ray's expression was confusion. He said, 'Later,' and he and his father walked out of the room, closing the door behind them.

Coleman and Big-Ass Angelo laughed. They laughed so hard that Coleman had to brace himself atop the desk. He had tears in his eyes and he and Angelo gave each other skin.

'Oh, shit,' said Coleman. 'Ray Boone, walkin' tall. Just like Buford T. Pusser, man.'

'I am *hip*,' said Angelo, and Coleman doubled over, stomping his foot on the floor.

A little later, Coleman said, 'I got him to thinkin', though, anyway, about the Rodriguez boys, I mean.'

'We lose the Rodriguez boys—'

'We'll find someone else to buy it from, black. Got a price and purity war goin' on in the business right now. It's one of those buyer's markets you hear about.'

'That means we wouldn't be seein' Ray and Earl no more. Shame to lose all that entertainment. I mean, who we gonna laugh at then?'

'We'll find someone else for that, too.' Coleman looked up at his lieutenant. 'Angie?'

'What?'

'Crack that window, man. Smells like nicotine, beer, and 'Lectric Shave in this motherfucker.'

'I heard that.'

'Every time the Boones come in here, it reminds me: I just can't *stand* the way white boys smell.'

Ray and Earl picked up their guns in the outer office, lit smokes outside of Coleman's building, and walked across the street. They went through a rip in the chain-link fence that surrounded the old warehouse. Yellow police tape was threaded through the links, and a piece of it blew like a kite tail in the wind.

They stepped carefully through debris, mindful of needles, and over a pile of bricks that had been the foundation of a wall but was now an opening, and then they were on the main floor of the warehouse, puddled with water leaked from pipes and rainwater, fresh from a recent storm, which came freely through the walls. There were holes in all four walls, some the product of decay, others sledge-hammered out for easy access and escape. Pigeons flew through the space, and the cement floor was littered with their droppings.

A rat scurried into a dim side room, and Ray saw a withered black face recede into the darkness. The face belonged to a junkie named Tonio Morris. He was one of the many bottom-of-the-food-chain junkies, near death and too weak to cut out a space of their own on the second floor; later, when the packets were delivered to those with cash, they'd trade anything they had, anything they'd stolen that day, or any orifice in their bodies for some rock or powder.

Ray and Earl walked past a man, one of Coleman's, who held a pistol at his side, a beeper and cell attached to his waist. The man did not look at them, and they did not acknowledge him in any way. They went up an exposed set of stairs.

At the top of the stairs they walked onto the landing of the second floor, where another armed man, as unemotional as the first, stood. Arched windows, all broken out, ran along the walls of this floor. They went through a hall, passing candlelit rooms housing vague human shapes sprawled atop mattresses. Then they were in a kind of bathroom without walls that Ray guessed had once been men's and women's rest rooms but was now one large room of shit-stained urinals and stalls. Ray and Earl breathed through their mouths to avoid the stench of the excrement and vomit that overflowed the backed-up toilets and lay pooled on the floor.

In the doorless stalls were people smelling of perspiration and urine and wearing filthy, ill-fitting clothes. These people smiled at the Boones and greeted them, some caustically, some sarcastically, and some with genuine fondness and relief. Ray and Earl passed stalls where magazine photos of Jesus, Malcolm X, and Muhammad Ali, and Globe concert posters were taped up and smudged with blood and waste. They kept walking and at the last stall they stopped.

'Gimme some privacy, Critter,' said Earl. 'I'll meet you back at the stairs.'

Ray nodded and watched his father enter the stall. Ray turned and walked back the way he'd come.

'Hello, young lady,' said Earl, stepping into the stall and admiring the damaged, pretty thing before him.

'Hello, Earl.' She was a tall girl with splotched, light skin and straightened black hair that curled at its ends. Her eyes were tinted green, their lashes lined, the lids shadowed. She smiled at Earl; her teeth carried a grayish film. She wore a dirty white blouse, halfway opened to expose a lacy bra, frayed in several spots and loose across her bony chest.

Votive candles were lit in the stall, and a model's photograph, ripped from a *Vanity Fair* magazine, was taped above the commode. The bowl of the commode was filled with toilet paper, dissolved turds and matchsticks, and brown water reached its rim.

'Got somethin' for me, Earl?' Her voice was that of a talking doll, wound down.

Earl looked her over. Goddamn if she wasn't a beautiful piece, underneath all that grime. No thing like this one had ever showed him any kind of attention, not even when he was a strapping young man.

'You know I do, honey pie.' Earl produced a small wax packet of brown heroin that he had cut from the supply. She snatched the packet from his hand, making sure to smile playfully as she did.

'Thank you, lover,' she said, tearing at the top of the packet and dumping its contents onto a glass paperweight she kept balanced atop a rusted toilet-roll dispenser. She tracked it out with a razor blade and did a thick line at once. And almost at once her head dropped slightly and her lids fluttered and stayed halfway raised.

'Careful not to take too much, now,' said Earl. But she was already cutting another line.

When she was done, Earl gently pushed down on her shoulders, and she dropped to her knees on the wet tiles. He unzipped his fly because she was slow to do it and wrapped his fingers through the hair on the back of her head.

When he felt the wetness of her mouth and tongue, he put one hand on the steel of the stall and closed his eyes.

'Baby doll,' said Earl. And then he said, 'God.'

Ray checked his wristwatch. Fifteen minutes had passed and still his old man had not showed. Ray was ready to leave this place, the Junkyard and the city and the trash who lived in it. He flicked the ass end of a 'Boro against the cinderblock wall and watched embers flare and die.

It disgusted him, thinking of what his daddy was doing back there with that high-yellow girl. She did have white features, but she was mud like the rest of them, you could believe that. His father and him, they disagreed on a few things, but none more than this. What was Earl thinkin', anyway? Didn't he know how that girl got to keep that stall on the end of the row? Didn't he know what a prime piece of real estate that was, what you had to do to keep it? Ray knew. If you were a man you had to fight for it, and if you were a woman . . . girl was probably on her back or on her belly, or swallowing sword ten times a day just for the right to squat in that shit hole. Didn't his father think of that?

But Ray was tired of pressin' it. Once he had made the mistake of calling that girl common nigger trash, and his father had risen up, told him to call her by her name. Hell, he could barely *remember* her name. It was Sandy Williams, somethin' like that.

Ray Boone flipped open the top of his box and shook another smoke from the deck.

Sondra *Wilson*. That's what it was.

7

Terry Quinn was behind a display case, sitting beside the register reading a book, when he heard a car door slam. Quinn looked through the plate glass window of the store and out to the street. A middle-aged black guy was locking the door of his white Chevy. Then he was crossing Bonifant on foot and heading toward the shop.

The car looked exactly like a police vehicle, and the gray-haired, gray-bearded black guy looked like a plainclothes cop. He wore a black turtleneck under a black leather, with loose-fitting blue jeans and black oilskin work boots. It wasn't his clothes that yelled 'cop' but rather the way he walked: head up, shoulders squared, alert and aware of the activity on the street. The guy had called, said he was working in a private capacity for Chris Wilson's mother, asked if Quinn would mind giving him an hour or so of his time. Quinn had appreciated the direct way he had asked the question, and he'd liked the seasoning in the man's voice. Quinn said sure, come on by.

The chime sounded over the door as the guy entered the shop. Just under six foot, one ninety, guessed Quinn. Maybe one ninety-five. All that black he was wearing, it could take off a quick five pounds to the eye. If this was the guy who had phoned, his name was Derek Strange.

'Derek Strange.'

Quinn got out of his chair and took the man's outstretched hand.

'Terry Quinn.'

Strange was looking down slightly on the young white man with the longish brown hair. Five nine, five nine and a half, one hundred sixty-five pounds. Medium build, green eyes, a spray of pale freckles across the bridge of his thick nose.

'Thanks for agreeing to see me.' Strange drew his wallet, flipped it open, and showed Quinn his license.

'No problem.'

Quinn didn't glance at the license as a gesture of trust. Also, he wanted to let Strange know that he was calm and had nothing to hide. Strange replaced his wallet in the back right pocket of his jeans.

'How'd you find me here?'

'Your place of residence is listed in the phone book. From there I talked to your landlord. The credit check on your apartment application has your place of employment.'

'My landlord supposed to be giving that out?'

'Twenty-dollar bill involved, *supposed to* got nothin' to do with it.'

'You know,' said Quinn, 'you get your hands on the transcripts of my testimony, you'll be saving yourself a whole lot of time. And maybe a few twenties, too.'

'I'm gonna do that. And I've already read everything that's been written about the case in the press. But it never hurts to go over it again.'

'You said you were working for Chris Wilson's mother.'

'Right. Leona Wilson is retaining my services.'

'You think you're gonna find something the review board overlooked?'

'This isn't about finding you guilty of anything you've already been cleared on. I'm satisfied, reading over the material, that this was just one of those accidents, bound to happen. You got two men bearing firearms, mix it up with alcohol on one side, emotion and circumstance, preconceptions on the other—'

'Preconceptions?' You mean racism, thought Quinn. Why don't you just say what you mean?

'Yeah, you know, preconceptions. You mix all those things together, you got a recipe for disaster. Gonna happen from time to time.'

Quinn nodded slowly, his eyes narrowing slightly as he studied Strange.

Strange cleared his throat. 'So it's more about exonerating Wilson than anything else. Wiping out the shadow that got thrown across his name, what with everything got written and broadcast about the case.'

'I didn't have anything to do with that. I never talked to the press.'

'I know it.'

'Even his own mother should be able to see that.'

Quinn spoke quietly, in a slow, gravelly way, stretching his vowels all the way out. Out-of-towners would guess that Quinn was from somewhere south of Virginia; Washingtonians like Strange knew the accent to be all D.C.

'Have you spoken with his mother?' asked Strange.

'I tried.'

'She's single-minded. Probably didn't make it too easy on you.'

'No. But I can understand it.'

'Course you can.'

'Because I'm the guy who killed her son.'

'That's a fact. And she's having a little trouble getting beyond that.'

'The finer points don't matter to her. All those theories you read about, whether or not I was doing my job, or if I made a bad split-second decision, or if it was the lack of training, or the Glock . . . none of that matters to her, and I can understand it. She looks at me, the only thing she sees is the guy who killed her son.'

'Maybe we can just clear things up a little,' said Strange. 'Okay?'

'There's nothing I'd like more.'

Quinn put the paperback he had been reading down on the glass top of the display case. Strange glanced at its cover. Beneath it, in the case, locked and lying on a piece of red velvet, he saw several old paperbacks: a Harlan Ellison with juvenile-delinquent cover art, a Chester Himes, an *Ironside* novelization by Jim Thompson, and something called *The Burglar* by a cat named David Goodis.

Strange said, 'The owner of the shop, he into crime books?'

'*She's* into selling first editions. Paperback originals. It's not my thing. The collecting part, and also those types of books. Me, I like to read westerns.'

'I can see that.' Strange nodded to Quinn's book. 'That one any good?'

'*Valdez Is Coming*. I'd say it's just about the best.'

'I saw the movie, if I recall. It was a little disappointing. But it had Burt Lancaster in it, so I watched it through. That was a man, right there. Not known especially for his westerns, but he was in some good ones. *Vera Cruz, The Professionals*—'

'*Ulzana's Raid*.'

'Damn, you remember that one? Burt was a scout, riding with some wet-behind-the-ears cavalry officer, played by that boy was in that rat movie . . . yeah, *Ulzana's Raid*, that was a good one.'

'You like westerns, huh?'

'I don't read the books, if that's what you mean. But I like the movies, yeah. And the music. The music they put in those is real nice.' Strange shifted his weight. For a moment, he'd forgotten why he'd come. 'Anyway.'

'Yeah, anyway. Where do you want to talk?'

Strange looked over Quinn's shoulder. There were three narrow aisles of wooden, ceiling-high shelves that stretched to the back of the shop. In the far right aisle, a thin man in a textured white shirt stood on a step stool and placed books high on a shelf.

'He work here?'

'That's Lewis,' said Quinn.

'Lewis. I was thinking, you had the time, maybe *Lewis* could cover the shop and we could take a drive to the spot where it went down. It would help me to see it with you there.'

Quinn thought it over. He turned around and said, 'Hey, Lewis!'

Lewis stepped down off the stool and walked to the front of the store, pushing his black-framed glasses up on his nose. His eyes were hugely magnified behind the thick lenses of the glasses, and his hair was black, greasy, and knotted in several spots. There were yellow stains under the arms of his white shirt. Strange could smell the man's body odor as he arrived.

'Lewis,' said Quinn. 'Say hello to *Detective* Strange.'

Strange ignored Quinn's sarcastic tone and said, 'How you doin', Lewis?'

'Detective.' Lewis did not look at Strange. At least Strange didn't think he did; Lewis's eyes were as big as boccie balls, unfocused, all over the shop. Lewis fidgeted with his hands and pushed his glasses back up on his nose. It made Strange nervous to be around him, and the man smelled like dog shit, too.

'Lewis, you don't mind, me and Detective Strange are gonna go out and take a ride. Syreeta calls, you tell her I clocked out for a while. That okay by you?'

'Sure.'

'Nice meeting you, Lewis.'

'You, too, Detective.'

Quinn snagged his leather off a coat tree behind the counter. Strange and Quinn walked from the shop.

Crossing the street, Strange said, 'He blind?'

'Legally, he is. I know he can't drive a car. He says he ruined his eyes reading under the covers with a flashlight when he was a boy. Had a father who thought Lewis was unmanly or something 'cause he read books.'

'Imagine him thinking that.'

'Lewis is all right.'

'You're a friend to him, you *ought* to tell him about these new products they got on the market, called soap and shampoo. Got this new revolutionary thing called deodorant, too.'

'I've told him. So has Syreeta. But he's a good clerk. She doesn't like to work too many hours and neither do I. He's the kind of guy, *his* hours might as well be painted on the front door. Hard to find help like that today.'

'What, they got him in charge of the romance books or something? He looks like he might be an expert in that department.'

Quinn looked over at Strange. 'You'd be surprised.'

'For real?'

'I'm not saying he's a player or anything like that. He's one of those one-woman men. Matter of fact, he's been faithful to a girl named Fistina for the last twenty years.'

'They say that'll make you blind, too.'

'*I'm* not blind.'

'Neither am I. But you and me, we probably practice that kind of love in moderation. I bet Lewis in there, he just wears old Fistina out.'

They got into Strange's Caprice. Strange turned the ignition, and the engine came to life. He looked through the windshield at the gun shop across the street.

'Real nice how they're running that place a half mile over the District line. Makes it real convenient for those kids downtown, don't have to drive too far to buy a piece.'

'They don't buy them there. Too many restrictions, and who wants a registered handgun, anyway? They just kind of road-test the floor models.'

'Just as bad, you ask me.'

'You're thinking like a cop,' said Quinn.

'That so.'

'And you're driving a cop's cruiser. What's this, a ninety?'

'Eighty-nine. Three-fifty square block with a beefed-up suspension. Thicker sway bars and a heavy-duty alternator. Not as fast as those LTIs, you know, the ninety-six with the 'Vette engine. But it moves.'

'Don't your tails get burned, driving this thing?'

'Sometimes. When I'm doing a close tail I take out a rental.'

'I thought you *were* a cop when you pulled up out front of the place. Not just the car – the way you moved.'

'Yeah, I got made as one by this old lady yesterday down in Langdon Park. Once you put on the badge, I guess you never lose the look.'

'You tellin' me—'

'Yeah,' said Strange. 'I was a cop and then I wasn't. Just like you.'

'How long ago was that?'

'Been about thirty years since I wore the uniform. Nineteen sixty-eight.'

Strange pulled down on the tree and put the Chevy in gear.

They drove south on Georgia Avenue, music playing from the deck.

Just past Kansas Avenue, Strange pointed out his shop, set back off the main drag in the middle of a narrow strip.

'That's me right there,' said Strange. 'That's my office.'

'Nice logo.'

'Yeah, I like it.'

'You sell magnifying glasses, too?'

'Investigations, man. Little kid sees that symbol, he knows what it means. Hell, your boy Lewis sees it, he squints real good, *he* can tell—'

'I got you.' Quinn looked across the street at a bar called the Foxy Playground. 'What's that, your hangout over there?'

Strange didn't answer. He turned up the volume on the deck and sang under his breath. 'We both know that it's wrong, but it's much too strong, to let it go now . . .'

'I've heard this one,' said Quinn. 'Guy's hammering some married lady, right?'

'It's a little more subtle than that. Mr Billy Paul, he justified an entire career with this single right here. Glad I recorded it before I lost my album collection. Had to throw them all out after the pipes busted in my house, couple years back.'

'You can buy it on CD, I bet.'

'I have a player. But I like records. Was listening to this Blackbyrds tape yesterday, *Flying Start*? Thinking about the liner notes on the inner sleeve of the original record. I sure wish I had that record today.' Strange smiled a little, listening to the music. 'This is kind of beautiful, isn't it?'

'If you were there, I guess.'

'Don't you like music?'

'When it speaks to my world. How about you? You ever listen to anything current?'

'Not really. The slow jams got to be the end-all for me. Nothin' worth listening to, you get past seventy-six, seventy-seven.'

'I was eight years old in seventy-seven.'

'Explains why you don't have an appreciation for this song.' Strange looked across the bench. 'You're a D.C. boy, right?'

'Silver Spring.'

'I heard it in your voice.'

'Graduate of the old Blair High School. You?'

'Roosevelt High. Grew up in this neighborhood right here. Still live in it.'

Quinn looked at the blur of beer markets, liquor stores, dollar shops, barbers, dry cleaners, and chicken and Chinese grease pits as they drove south.

'My grandparents lived down this way,' said Quinn. 'We'd come to see them every Sunday after mass. Thirteenth and Crittenden.'

'That's around the block from where I live.'

'I used to play out in their alley. It always seemed, I don't know, *dark* down there.'

Because of all those dark *people*, thought Strange. He said, 'That's because you were off your turf.'

'Yeah. It made me a little bit afraid. Afraid and excited at the same time, you know what I mean?'

'Sure.'

'One day these kids came up on me while I was playing by myself.'

'Black kids, right?'

'Yeah. Why you ask that?'

'Just trying to get a picture in my mind.'

'So these kids came along, and the littlest one of them picked a fight with me. He was shorter than I was and lighter, too.'

'It's always the littlest one wants to fight, when he's in a group. Little dude got the most to prove. You fight him?'

'Yeah. I had walked away from a fight at my elementary school earlier that year, and I'd never forgiven myself for it. Matter of fact, I still can't bear to think of it today. Funny, huh?'

'Not really. This kid in the alley, you beat him?'

'I lost. I got in a punch or two, which surprised him. But he knew how to fight and I didn't, and he put me down. I got back inside the house, I was shaking but proud, too, 'cause I didn't back down. And I saw that kid a couple of years later, the day of my grandfather's wake. He was walking by their house and stopped to talk to me. Asked me if I wanted to play some football, down by the school playground.'

'And you learned?'

'What breeds respect. Not to walk away from a fight. Take a beating if you have to, but a beating's never as bad as the feeling of shame you get when you back off.'

'That's your youth talking right there,' said Strange. 'One day you're gonna learn, it's all right to walk away.'

8

Down past Howard University, at the Florida Avenue intersection, Georgia Avenue became 7th Street. They stayed on 7th and then they were in Chinatown, passing nightclubs, sports bars, and the MCI Center, which anchored the new downtown D.C. Farther along there were more nightclubs and restaurants and the short strip of the arts and gallery district, and at Quinn's direction Strange hung a left onto D Street, two blocks north of Pennsylvania Avenue. He parked the Chevy in a no-parking zone, along a yellow-painted curb, and killed the engine. Then he reached into the glove box, withdrew his voice-activated tape recorder, and placed the recorder on the seat between himself and Quinn.

'This is it,' said Strange. 'You were right about here?'

'Except that we parked it in the middle of the street. We came in just like this, from Seventh. My partner was driving the cruiser.'

'That would be Eugene Franklin.'

'Gene Franklin, right.'

'What made y'all pull over?'

'We were working. We had just come off a routine traffic stop, guy in a Maxima had blown a red up at Mt Vernon Square. Up around Seventh and N, you want the exact location.'

'So you were headed south on Seventh after that, and Franklin turned left onto D. He see something, or was that just some kind of pattern?'

'No, we hadn't seen anything yet until we made the turn. This stretch of D is unlit at night, and there's hardly any activity. Pedestrian traffic, none. Sun goes down, rats stroll across the street like they own the real estate.'

'What about that night? You pulled onto D, what did you see?'

Quinn squinted. 'We came up on a confrontation. A curbed red Jeep, a Wrangler, parked behind a shit box Toyota. Next to the Toyota, on the street, a guy with his knee on another guy's chest, pinning him to the asphalt. In the aggressor's hand, a pistol. An automatic, and he had the muzzle smashed up against the pinned guy's face.'

'Describe this aggressor.'

'Black, mid-to-late twenties, medium build, street clothes.'

'And the guy he had on the ground?'

'White . . .' Quinn looked over at Strange, then away. '. . . around thirty, street clothes, slight build.'

'So you and your partner, you happen on the scene of this *confrontation.* What happens then?'

Quinn breathed out slowly. 'Gene says, "Look!" But I'm ahead of him, I already got the mic in my hand. I've got it keyed and I'm calling for backup while Gene flips on the overheads and gives the horn a blast. The aggressor looks up at the whoop of the siren, and Gene stops the cruiser in the middle of the street. But our presence doesn't change the aggressor's mind.'

'You got a talent for reading minds?'

'I'll put it another way. The aggressor keeps the gun on the guy he's got pinned to the ground. He's made us as cops, but it hasn't changed his focus. From my perspective it hasn't changed his intent.'

'His intent being, the intent of this black aggressor I mean, to do harm to the white guy he's got pinned down on the street.'

'I saw a man holding a gun on another man in the street.'

'All right, Quinn. Keep going. Where are you now? You and your partner, I mean.'

'We're about twenty-five yards back from them, I'd say.'

'Okay,' said Strange.

Quinn rubbed his thumb over his lower lip. 'I'm out of the car right away, and I can hear Gene's door swing open as I draw my weapon. So I know he's behind the driver's-side door, and I know Gene's got his own weapon cleared from his holster as well.'

'You do what next?'

'I've got my gun on the aggressor. I yell for him to drop his weapon and lie facedown on the street. He yells something back. I can't really hear what he's saying, 'cause Eugene's yelling over him, telling him what I'm telling him: to drop his weapon. The lights . . . the red and blue lights from the overheads are strobing the scene, and I can hear the crackle of our radio coming from the open doors of our cruiser behind us.'

'Sounds like a lot of confusion.'

'Yes. Gene and I are both yelling now and there's the lights and the radio, and the aggressor, he's yelling back at us, not moving the gun from the guy's face.'

'What's Wilson – what's the *aggressor* yelling now?'

'His name,' said Quinn. 'His name and a number. It didn't register . . . it didn't register until later on that the number he was yelling, it was his badge number. But he never moved his gun away from the guy's face. Not until he looked at us, I mean.'

Strange stared through the windshield, trying to imagine the picture the young man was painting.

'What happened when he looked at you, Quinn?'

'It was only for a moment. He looked at me and then at Gene, and something bad crossed his face. I'll never forget it. He was angry at us, at me and Gene. He was more than angry; his face changed to the face of a killer. He swung his gun in our direction then—'

'He pointed his gun at you?'

'Not directly,' said Quinn, his voice growing soft. 'He was swinging it, like I say. The muzzle of it swept across me, and he had that look on his face . . . There wasn't any doubt in my mind . . . I knew . . . I *knew* he was going to pull the trigger. Eugene screamed my name, and I fired my weapon.'

'How many times?'

'I fired three rounds.'

'From where you stood?'

'They say I walked forward as I fired. That I don't remember.'

'According to the articles, the trajectory of the entrance wounds and the exit pattern of the shell casings for that particular weapon were consistent with your statement. But the three casings weren't found together in a group. Apparently you moved forward and fired the third round into him when he was down. The third casing was found about ten feet from the victim.'

'I don't remember moving forward,' said Quinn. 'I know what they said, and I know about the casings, but I don't remember. And I don't believe I shot him when he was down. He might have been *going* down, still pointing his gun—'

'Weren't you concerned with hitting the other guy?'

'At that point I was concerned primarily with the safety of myself and my partner. I've already admitted as much.' Quinn glared at Strange. 'Anything else?'

'Okay, Quinn. Take a deep breath and settle down.'

Strange's beeper sounded. He took it from his hip and checked the readout. He said, 'Excuse me, man,' reaching across Quinn to unlock the glove box and withdraw his cellular phone. He punched a number into the grid and spoke into the mouthpiece.

'What's up, Ron? . . . Uh-huh.' Strange frowned. 'Now, you gonna ask me to do this thing for you because you're down on K Street picking up a suit? . . . Yeah, I know you can't just pick it up, you got to try it on, too . . . Uh-huh . . . No, it's not 'cause I buy my shit off the rack that I don't understand . . . I do understand . . . Believe me, it's no thing. I got no problem with it, Ron. I sound like I do? Gimme the data, man.'

Strange took the information, using a pen on a cord, writing on a pad affixed to the dash. He cut the line without another word and dropped the phone in the glove box, shutting the door a little too hard.

'I got something I got to do. Man jumped bail on a B&E beef, and there's this snitch we use, been hangin' in a bar this man supposed to frequent. Turns out the bail jumper just walked into the bar.'

'Who was that on the phone?'

'My operative, young man by the name of Ron Lattimer, works for me.'

'You do skip-tracing, too?'

'Ron handles that. I don't like to chase people down. But Ron's busy, see, picking up a suit. So this one goes to me. Shouldn't be too serious. I've seen the sheet on this guy, and he's all of one twenty if he's a pound. It's out of my way, but you want, I'll drop you off.'

'I'll ride with you,' said Quinn. 'You can drop me when you're done.'

'Suit yourself.'

'Hold up a second.' Quinn put his hand on Strange's arm. 'Don't think I didn't notice what you were getting at with your questions there. All that black-aggressor, white-guy, black-this, white-that bullshit. What happened that night, you can try and paint it any way you want if it makes you feel any better. But it had nothing to do with race.'

'Don't tell me,' said Strange. 'Don't tell me, 'cause I'm a *black* man, twenty-five years your senior, and I *know*. I'm just trying to get at the truth, and if I hurt your feelings or hit a nerve somewhere along the line, so be it. I didn't drop by to see you today 'cause I was looking for a friend, Quinn. I got plenty of friends, and I don't need another. I'm just doing my job.'

Strange ignitioned the Caprice, engaged the trans, and swung a U in the middle of D.

'One more thing,' said Quinn. 'Knock off that "Quinn" shit from here on in. Call me by my given name. It's Terry, okay?'

Strange turned right on 7th and gave the Chevy gas. He reached for the sunglasses in his visor, chuckling under his breath.

'What's so funny?'

'You got a temper on you,' said Strange.

Quinn looked out the window, letting his jaw relax. 'People have told me that I do.'

'That story about fighting in the alley. How you were shaking, afraid and excited at the same time. You liked the action your whole life, didn't you?'

'I guess I did.'

'What you ended up becoming, that's not surprising. Guy like you, I bet you always wanted to be a cop.'

'That's right,' said Quinn. 'And I was a good one, too.'

9

The bar was on the end of a strip of bars off M Street in Southeast, surrounded by fenced parking lots, auto repair and body shops, and patches of dead grass. Strange parked and nodded toward the corner business, a brick, two-story, windowless structure. The sign over the door read, 'Toot Sweet: Live Girls.'

'Sign says they got live girls in there,' said Quinn.

'That's so the fellas who like dead ones don't get disappointed once they get inside,' said Strange. 'Should've known from the address Ron gave me it was gonna be a titty bar.'

'They got the bathhouses down here, too, I remember right.'

'They got everything down here for every kind. This particular place, guys come to look at women. Wait out here, you want to.'

'I like to look at women.'

'Suit yourself.' Strange replaced his sunglasses atop the visor. 'Let me do my job, though. And stay out of my way.'

Strange got some papers out of the trunk. As he turned, Quinn noticed the Leatherman, the Buck knife, and the beeper, all affixed in some way to Strange's waist.

'You got purple tights,' said Quinn, 'to go with that utility belt?'

'Funny,' said Strange.

At the door of the club, Strange paid the cover and asked for a receipt. The doorman, a black guy who looked to Quinn like he had some Hawaiian or maybe Samoan in him, said, 'We don't have receipts.'

'Go ahead and create one for me,' said Strange.

'Create one?'

'You know, use your imagination. We'll be over by the bar. When you get it done, drop it by.'

They walked through the crowd. At first Quinn pegged it as all black, but on closer inspection he saw that it was a mix of African

Americans and other nonwhites: dark-skinned Arabs and Pakis, taxi-driving types. His partner, Gene, used to call them Punjabis, and sometimes '*pooncabbies,*' when they rode together as cops.

The dancers, black and mixed race as well, were up on several stages around the club and stroking the steel floor-to-ceiling poles that were their props. They weren't beautiful, but they were nude above the waist, and that was enough. Men stood around the stages, beers in one hand, dollar bills in the other, and there were men drinking at tables, talking and tipping the waitresses who would soon be dancing up onstage themselves, and there were other men with their heads down, sleeping, dead drunk.

Strange and Quinn stepped up to the unkempt bar, damp and strewn with wet bev-naps and dirty ashtrays. Smoke rose off a live cherry in the ashtray before them, and Strange butted the dying cigarette out. The bar was unventilated and smelled of nicotine and spilled beer.

'Filthy,' said Strange, taking a napkin off a stack and wiping his hands. 'They got a kitchen in this joint, I expect, but damn if I'd ever eat the food.' He glanced over his shoulder. He was searching for one face, Quinn could tell.

Some of the black men down along the bar were looking at the two of them, not bothering to look away when Quinn eye-shot them back. Quinn knew it was unusual, and suspect, to see a black and a white together in a place like this. To the men at the bar, they were either cops or friends, maybe even faggots, the kind of friends who 'played for the other team.' Any way those men looked at it, the two of them together wasn't natural, or right.

The bartender was approaching, and Strange said to Quinn, 'You want a beer?'

'Too early for me,' said Quinn.

'Give me a ginger ale,' said Strange to the bartender, who sported a damp toothpick behind his ear. 'From a bottle.'

'I'll have a Coke the same way.'

Quinn turned and put his back against the bar. He found a dancer he could look at. He was studying her breasts, the color of them and their shape, and wondering if Juana's would look the same. He'd made out with black women but had never had one in bed, not all the way. He was going to see Juana tonight, over at her place. That would give him time to cool down; God help her if he was to run into her right now . . .

'Your soda's up,' said Strange. 'Gonna ruin your eyes like that, you stare too hard. Get like your boy Lewis, have to wear those glasses like he does. What kind of girl you gonna find to give you a second look then?'

Quinn turned back and faced the bar. He had a long swig from his glass. The sound system was pumping out a Prince tune from the eighties, and Quinn tapped his fingers on the glass.

'Remember this one?' said Quinn.

'Sure. Had that little Scottish freak in the video. That girl was delicious, man.'

'You like Prince? Just curious, seeing as how it's not your era and all that.'

'He's all right. But he's got a little too much bitch in him, you want to know the truth.'

'Hate to break it to you, but I think the little guy gets a whole lot of play.'

'Maybe so, but I listen to his music, I picture the way he's licking his fingers to smooth down his eyebrows, crawling across the floor, wearing that makeup and shit . . . can't get past it, I guess.'

'Racism's bad, but that kind of ism is all right.'

'Just being honest with you. You get to know me better, you'll see; I tell it straight, whether you're gonna like what I'm saying or not. All I'm saying is, your generation, y'all can deal with that homosexuality thing better than mine can.'

'It's black men in general who can't deal with that homosexuality thing, you ask me. If you were really honest, you'd admit it.'

'Now you're gonna tell me, *in general*, what black men can and cannot deal with.' Strange looked over his shoulder again, did a double take, and said, 'There's my boy. Be back in a few.'

Strange found his snitch back in the hall that led to the kitchen and bathrooms, and returned ten minutes later. He told Quinn that the subject of the skip, Sherman Coles, had gone upstairs an hour earlier.

'What's upstairs?'

'Private lap dances, shit like that.'

'I'll come with you. Don't worry, I'm not going to get in your way.'

'Look, I'm just checking out the situation. Might not be the right time and place to try and bring him in.'

'Understood.' Quinn picked a piece of paper up off the bar and handed it to Strange.

'What's that?'

'Your receipt.'

Strange inspected it: a playing card showing a photograph of a bare-breasted woman on its face. Across her breasts was written, 'In receipt of seven-dollar cover charge, for strip bar, Toot Sweet.'

'Funny boy,' said Strange.

'You told him to be creative.'

'My accountant's gonna like it, anyway.' Strange slipped the card into his jacket. 'Come April, all those hours he puts in, he needs a little something to pick up his day.'

They walked up a red-carpeted set of stairs. A guy was coming down, and he moved aside to let them pass, not looking them in the eye. There was an oval spot of wetness high on the front of the man's jeans, just below the crotch.

'You see that?' said Strange, as they hit the top of the stairs. 'Man must have spilled something on his self.'

'Yeah,' said Quinn. 'His seed.'

'Bible says you're not supposed to do that.'

'Probably on his way to confession right now.'

'I was him, I wouldn't be wearing those blue jeans into church.'

Up on the second floor, the lamps were conical and dimmed, and smoke hung in their light. Another bar ran along the wall, and there were tables spread around the bulk of the room, some in darkness, some barely lit. At the tables, a few guys were getting lap-danced by girls wearing G-strings, nothing else. The girls used their crotches, breasts, and backsides to rub one off for the customers, who were sitting low in chrome-armed chairs, languid smiles on their faces. The music up here was slow and funky, heavy on the wa-wa pedal, with a deep, silky male vocal in the mix.

Strange and Quinn had a seat at an empty deuce near the bar. Strange settled into his chair and patted the table in rhythm to the music.

'This here's more like it,' said Strange. '*Joy*, by Isaac Hayes. I had the vinyl on this one, too. You could hear the champagne bubbles rising when you listened to the record on a nice box. But on the CD the sound quality just doesn't make it.' He nodded to a light-skinned girl, on the thin side with a man's shirt worn open over panties, who was walking toward them with a drink tray balanced on her palm. 'Speaking of champagne, check this out. She's fixin' to sell us some now.'

'Can I get you gentlemen a drink?' asked the girl as she arrived.

'Waitin' on a third party to join us,' said Strange, who was squinting, not looking directly at the girl, looking around the room. He pulled the Coles photograph from his jacket pocket, along with the Coles papers he had taken from the file box in the trunk. He studied the photograph until the girl spoke again.

'How about a private dance?'

'Maybe later, baby.'

'We've got a special on champagne.'

'Later, hear?'

She gave him a look, then gave Quinn one for good measure, and walked away.

Strange said, 'They're selling some bullshit off-brand, two steps down from cold duck, for fifty dollars a bottle to these poor suckers in here. Guys making minimum wage, taking home one hundred and sixty a week, come in here on a Friday night and spend it all in an hour. Walk out of here after a hard week of work with nothin' to show for it but a headache and a big old stain on the front of their drawers.'

'You some kind of expert?'

Strange looked over Quinn's shoulder. 'Listen, you want to pay for a lady's time, I'll take you someplace you're gonna get your money's worth. This ain't nothing but a cheap hustle they got going on right here.' He stood abruptly from his chair. 'Excuse me for a minute while I do my job. Looks like I located Coles.'

'Need some company?'

'Been doin' this for a long time. I think I'll just go ahead and handle it myself.'

'Fine. I'll be back in the bathroom, taking a leak.'

Quinn watched Strange cross the room, moving around the tables, walking toward a four-top at the edge of the darkness, where a little man in a suit and open collar sat, a long cigarette in one hand, his other hand wrapped around a snifter of something brown.

The man wants to be left alone, thought Quinn, I'll leave him alone. He got up and moved toward a dark hall, where the head was always located in a place like this.

Strange was walking toward the table where Sherman Coles was sitting, and had gotten to within a few yards of it, when another man emerged from out of the shadows. He was a very big man, with wide shoulders and hard, chiseled features. The cut of his biceps showed beneath his shiny shirt.

Strange stopped walking just as the man flanked Coles. He could have averted his eyes, kept going past the table, but they had watched his approach all the way and would say something or stop him if he tried the dodge. He knew his shot at Coles was over for today. Any way he looked at it, he was burned. It made no sense for him to turn his back on them, though, or walk past them, anything else. He had to stop and let it play out. And he was curious to know what Coles had to say.

'You lookin' for someone, man?'

'I was,' said Strange, forcing a friendly smile. 'From across the room there, I thought you were this fella I knew, from back in the neighborhood where I came up.'

'Oh, yeah?' Coles's tone was high and theatrical. 'You got to have twenty years on me, though. So how could we have come up together? Huh?'

Strange shook his head. 'We *couldn't* have, you're right. Now that I'm up close . . . the thing of it is, I can't see too good in this low light. And don't even get me started about my failing eyes.'

Coles took a sip from the snifter before him and tapped ash off his cigarette. He glanced over his shoulder to the man behind him and said, 'You hear that, Richard?'

A crescent scar semicircled Richard's left eye. 'Man can't see too good in this light.'

'Or maybe he thinks *we* can't see too good,' said Coles. ''Cause we did see you, sittin' over there with your Caucasian partner, lookin' at whatever it is you put back in your pocket, tryin' to make me.'

'Trying to make you as what?' Strange chuckled and spread his hands. 'Brother, I told you, I just mistook you for someone else.'

'Oh, you *mistook* all right.' Coles smiled, then dragged on his cigarette.

'Whatever you're thinking,' said Strange, his voice steady, 'you are wrong.'

'Tell you what,' said Coles, looking past Strange. 'I'll just go ahead and ask the white boy. Here he comes now.'

Quinn had been turned away by a sign on the men's room door that told him it was closed for repair. He was coming back down the hall when he stopped briefly to look through the crack of a partially opened door. In the candlelit room, a young man in a chair was being fellated by the waitress who'd been talking to them minutes earlier. Her head was between the guy's legs, her knees sunk into orange shag carpet, and there was a bottle of bad champagne and two glasses on a small table beside them, the hustle just as Strange had described. A sculpture candle of a black couple standing up, intertwined and making love, burned on the table next to the glasses. Quinn walked on.

He came out of the hall and along the bar and saw Strange in a dark corner of the room, standing in front of the table where Coles sat. A big man stood behind the table, cracking the knuckles of one hand with the palm of the other. Quinn walked toward them.

Quinn knew Strange had warned him to stay off, and he considered this while he continued on, and then he was standing next to Strange, thinking, I'm here, I can't change that now. He spread his stance close to the table, looked down on Sherman Coles, and affected his cop posture. It was the way he used to dominate, standing outside the driver's-side window of a car he'd stopped out on the street.

'Here go your backup,' said Coles. 'What you think, Richard? This salt-and-pepper team we got here, they cops?'

'Look more like the Orkin army,' said Richard. 'What's with those jackets, huh? Those y'all's uniforms?'

Strange realized for the first time that he and Quinn were both wearing black leather. Another thing for these jokers to crack on, but he didn't care. Now that Quinn had made the mistake of joining him, he was focusing on how the two of them were going to walk away. And then he began to think about Quinn's short fuse. And Strange thought, Maybe we ought to stay.

'I don't think they're cops,' said Coles.

'White boy's too short to be a cop,' offered Richard.

No, I'm not, thought Quinn.

'Look more like bounty hunters to me,' said Richard. His voice was soft in a dangerous kind of way, and it was difficult to hear him over the wa-wa and bass pumping through the house system.

'Kind of what I was thinking, too, Richard.' Coles looked at Strange. 'That what you are, old man? A bounty hunter?'

'Like I said,' said Strange, keeping his voice on the amiable side. 'I thought you were someone else. I made a mistake.'

'Now, why you want to lie?' said Coles.

''Cause he scared?' said Richard. 'He does look a little scared. And *white* boy looks like he's about to dirty his drawers. How about it, white boy, that so?'

'How about what?' said Quinn.

'You gonna soil your laundry, or you gonna walk away right now before you do?'

'What'd you say?' said Quinn.

'Was I stutterin'?' said Richard, his eyes bright and hard.

'Let's go,' said Strange.

'Don't you know,' said Richard, smiling at Quinn, 'white man just *afraid* of the black man.'

'Not this white man,' said Quinn.

'Oh, ho-ho,' said Richard, 'now Little Man Tate gonna give us some of that fire-in-the-belly stuff. That's what you gonna do now, *bitch*?'

Strange tugged on Quinn's sleeve. Quinn held his ground and stared at Richard. Richard laughed.

'We're leaving now,' said Strange.

'What's a matter?' said Coles, holding his wrists out and together, as if he were waiting for cuffs. 'Ain't you gonna take me in?'

'Maybe next time,' said Strange, his tone jocular. 'See you fellas later, hear?'

Coles broke the imaginary chains on his wrists, raised the snifter in a mock toast. He drank and placed the glass back down on the table.

'When your bosses or whoever ask you why you came back empty handed,' said Coles, 'tell 'em you ran into Sherman Coles and his kid brother. Tell him it was us who punked you out.'

Strange nodded, the light draining from his eyes.

'We told you our names, white boy,' said Richard, his gaze on Quinn. 'Ain't you got one?'

Strange pulled harder on Quinn's jacket. 'Come on, man, let's go.'

This time Quinn complied. They walked toward the stairs, the Coles brothers' laughter on Quinn's back like the stab of a knife.

At the downstairs bar, Strange signaled the bartender for his unpaid tab and yelled out over the music for the tender to bring back a receipt. Strange turned to Quinn, who stood with his back against the bar, looking out into the crowd.

'Stupid, man. What'd I tell you about interfering with my shit?'

'I wasn't thinking,' said Quinn. It was the first thing he'd said since their conversation with the Coles brothers on the second floor. 'What do you do now? You ever gonna take him in?'

'Oh, I'll take him in. Didn't figure on Sammy Davis Jr. havin' a baby brother looked like Dexter Manley. Gonna be real calm about it, though, and wait for the moment. It's just work, got nothin' to do with emotion. I had the situation under control until you stepped in, tried to get all Joe Kidd on their asses. You got to learn to eat a little humble pie now and again.'

'Yeah,' said Quinn, watching Richard Coles come down the stairs and sidle-up next to a waitress. Richard was bending forward to whisper in the girl's ear. 'I've got to work on that, I guess.'

'Damn right you do,' said Strange, glancing back to see the subject of Quinn's attention.

Strange saw Quinn watch Richard Coles as he headed off down the hall past the end of the bar.

'Here you go, man,' said Strange, paying the bartender, taking his receipt.

'Appreciate it,' said the bartender, and Quinn turned and read the man's name, Dante, which was printed on a tag he wore pinned to his white shirt.

'You ready?' said Strange to Quinn.

'Gotta take a leak.'

'Another one? You just ran some water through it five minutes ago.'

'The upstairs head was out of order. I'll see you out at the car.'

Strange said, 'Right,' and walked from the bar. Quinn waited until he was gone and then headed down the hall.

On his way out, Strange told the doorman he'd be right back. He walked quickly to his car and pulled a set of handcuffs and a sap from the trunk, sliding the sap in to the breast pocket of his jacket, then went back into the club. He took the steps up to the second floor two at a time and moved through the table area to the four-top where Sherman Coles still sat.

Coles's eyes widened, watching Strange moving in his direction, purpose in his step. Coles's neck jerked, birdlike, as he looked around the bar, searching frantically for a familiar face.

'Right here, Sherman,' said Strange, and he kicked the table into Coles, sending him to the floor in a shower of drink and live ashes.

Strange got Coles up to his feet, turned him, and yanked his arms up, forcing Coles to his knees. Strange put his own knee to Coles's back while he cuffed him, and then he pulled Coles to his feet.

Strange drew his wallet, flipped it open, and showed his license to the room in general.

'Investigator!' shouted Strange. 'Don't no one interfere and everything's gonna be all right!'

He did this in situations like this one, and nearly every time it worked. It wasn't a lie and to most people, 'investigator' meant cop. The waitresses and patrons and the men who were being lap-danced all stopped what they were doing, but no one came near him and no one interfered.

Strange kept his wallet open, holding it out for all to see, as he pushed Coles along towards the stairs.

'Where my brother at, man?' said Coles.

'That white man I was with, he's talking to him, I expect.'

'Richard'll kill him.'

'Keep walkin', man.'

On the stairs, Coles lost his footing. Strange pulled him back upright with a jerk to his arms.

Coles looked over his shoulder and said, 'Bounty hunter, like I thought.'

'They call us bail agents now, Sherman.'

'Knew you'd be back,' mumbled Coles. 'You had that look in your eye.'

'Yeah,' said Strange. 'But you didn't know I'd be back so soon.'

Quinn walked down the hall, shakily singing along under his breath to another Prince tune that was playing now in the main portion of the club. There were small speakers hung in the hall, but their sound was trebly, not bass heavy like out near the stages, and this thin, shrill tone made his blood jump, as did the thought of what he was about to do.

'Gonna be a beautiful night, gonna be a beautiful night . . .'

Quinn went straight back to the end of the hall, pushed on a swinging door, and went through the frame into a fluorescent-lit, dirty kitchen. The light came up bright off the steel prep tables that were spread about the room.

'Amigo,' said Quinn to a small Salvadorian with a thin mustache, wearing a stained white apron, leaning against a prep table near the back of the kitchen and smoking a cigarette.

The man said nothing and his eyes said nothing. The kitchen radio blared in the room.

'Dante sent me back here,' said Quinn, shouting so the man could hear. Quinn scanned the kitchen quickly and went to where a steel tenderizing mallet lay atop an industrial microwave oven. He picked up the mallet, measured its weight in his hand, waved it stupidly, and said, 'Dante needs one of these out at the bar.'

The man shrugged and dragged on his cigarette, dropping the butt on the Formica at his feet and crushing it under a worn black shoe.

'I'll bring it right back,' said Quinn, but he knew the man didn't care. He was only talking now to hear his own voice and to keep the adrenalin going, and he was out of the kitchen just as quickly as he'd come in.

Now he was back in the hall and walking toward the men's room. Now he was pushing on the men's room door, walking through it and into the men's room, looking at Richard Coles taking a piss at one of the stand-up urinals against the wall.

Quinn kept moving. He said, 'Hey, Richard,' and when Richard Coles turned his head to the side, Quinn swung the mallet fast and hard and connected its ridged surface to the bridge of Richard's nose. Richard's nose shifted to the right, and blood sprayed off in the same direction. A stream of urine swung out and splashed at Quinn's feet.

Richard's legs gave out from under him, and Quinn kicked him in the groin as he hit the tiles. He kicked him in the cheekbone, and blood splattered onto the porcelain face of the urinal. Quinn heard his own grunt as he kicked Richard in the side and was about to kick him again when he saw Richard's eyes roll up into his head.

Quinn's hands were shaking. He waited for the rise and fall of Richard's chest. He said, 'Terry Quinn,' and he dropped the mallet to the floor.

Out in the bar there was a buzz, a sense that something had gone down. The dancers were moving on the various stages, but the patrons were turned away from them, talking among themselves.

Men moved out of Quinn's path as he walked through the club. He felt the power, and it was a familiar feeling, though he hadn't felt it for a while. It was like he was wearing the uniform again, and he knew now that this was what he had been missing for a long time. He felt *good.*

Quinn got into the passenger side of Strange's car and looked over the lip of the bench. Sherman Coles was stretched out and cuffed, lying on the backseat.

Strange nodded at the blood on Quinn's boots. 'You all right?'

'Yeah.'

'Where my brother at?' said Sherman from the backseat.

Neither Quinn nor Strange answered Coles.

'How'd you know I'd walk out of there?' said Quinn.

'I didn't know,' said Strange. 'What I did know, you'd give me enough time.'

'Where's my brother!' yelled Sherman.

Quinn said to Strange, 'You always go for the light work?'

'When I can.' Strange ignitioned the Chevy. 'I got to get little Sherman over to Fifth Street, process the paperwork. I know you don't want to stick around for that.'

'Drop me at the first Metro station you see,' said Quinn. 'I need to get home. I'm seein' a lady tonight.'

'Yeah,' said Strange, thinking of his mother. 'I'm seein' one, too.'

Strange pulled off the curb and drove toward M Street. He looked over at Quinn, still intense, sitting straight up in his seat, his knuckles rapping at the window.

'Gonna split the agent's fee with you on this one, Terry. How's that sound?'

'How's this sound: You and me work together on that other thing.'

'Together? You're the subject of my investigation, you forget about that?'

'I didn't forget.'

'Look, you got nothin' to worry about. The review committee said you were right as rain on that shooting. I got no reason to doubt it.'

'Right as rain. Yeah, I remember, that's exactly what they said.'

'And you couldn't get with me on this, anyway. You don't have the license to be doing the kind of work I do.'

'If you're going to stay on it, I want to be involved.'

Strange goosed the gas, coming out of the turn.

'Don't worry,' he said. 'You and me, we're not through.'

10

Derek Strange's mother, Alethea Strange, lived in the District Convalescent Home in Ward 3, the predominantly white and wealthy section of Northwest D.C. The home, a combination hospice and nursing facility, had been operating in the city since the nineteenth century.

Strange didn't like nursing homes, for the same simple reason he didn't care for hospitals or funeral parlors. After his mother had her stroke back in '96, he had brought her to his house and hired a round-the-clock nurse, but a clot sent her back to the hospital, where the surgeons took her right leg. She had gotten around before with a walker, but now she was permanently wheelchair-bound, paralyzed on her right side, and she had previously lost most of her speech and the ability to read and write. Alethea Strange managed to tell her only living child that she wanted to go somewhere else to live out her days, with people who were sick like her. He suspected she was only asking to go away so as not to be a burden on him. Still, he granted her wish and put her in the District Convalescent Home's long-term care facility, as they accepted patients on Medicaid and there was nothing else that he could see to do.

In the lobby of the home that night, they were having some sort of event, young folks with green shirts, a church group most likely, trying to lead the elderly residents in song. There was a dining facility and a library with an aquarium in it down here, too. Alethea Strange never attended these events or sat in these rooms, and she only came down to the first level when Derek brought her down. In the spring and early summer, she would allow her son to wheel her out to the nicely landscaped courtyard, where a black squirrel, a frequent visitor to the complex, drank water while standing on the lip of the fountain. She'd sit in a block of sun, and he'd sit on a stone bench beside her, rubbing her back and sometimes holding her hand. The sight of the squirrel seemed to bring something to her day.

Strange went to the edge of the hospice at the end of a long hall and took the elevator up to the third floor. He walked through another hall painted drab beige, and as he approached the long-term wing where his mother resided he smelled the mixture of bland food, sickness, and incontinence that he had come to dread.

His mother was in her wheelchair, seated at one of three round tables in a television room where the residents could also take their meals. Next to her was another stroke victim, an Armenian man whose name Strange could never remember, and next to him was a skeletal woman in a kind of reclining wheelchair who never spoke or smiled, just stared up at the ceiling with red-rimmed, hollowed-out eyes. At the table beside them a woman fed her bib-wearing husband, and next to them a man sat sleeping before an untouched tray of food, his chin down on his chest. No one seemed to be watching the basketball contest playing on the television set, or listening to the announcer who was loudly calling the game. Strange patted the Armenian's shoulder, pulled a chair from the other side of the room, and drew it to his mother's side.

'Momma,' said Strange, kissing her on the cheek and taking her hand, light and fragile as paper.

She smiled crookedly at him and slowly blinked her eyes. There was a bead of applesauce hanging on the edge of her lip, and he wiped it clean with the napkin that had fallen into her lap.

'You want a little of this tea right here?'

She pointed with a shaking hand to two sugar packets. Strange ripped the packets open and poured sugar into the plastic cup that held the tea. He stirred it and put the cup in her hand.

'Hot,' she said, the *t* soft as a whisper.

'Yes, ma'am. You want some more of that meat?'

He called it 'that meat' because he wasn't exactly sure if it was fowl or beef, smothered as it was in a grayish, congealed gravy.

His mother shook her head.

Strange noticed that the table beside them wobbled whenever the wife leaned on it to give her husband another forkful of food. He got up and went to a small utility room, where he knew they kept paper towels, and he folded some towels in a square and wedged the square under the foot of the table that was not touching the floor. The wife thanked Strange.

'I fixed the table,' said Strange to a big attendant as he passed her on the way back to his mother. She nodded and returned to her conversation with another employee.

He knew this attendant – he knew them all, immigrants of color, by sight. This one was on the mean side, though she was always polite in his presence. His mother had told him that this one raised her voice to her and teased her in an unkind way when she had his mother alone. Most of the staff members were competent and many were kind, but there were two or three attendants here who mistreated his mother, he knew. One of them had even stolen a present he had given her, a small bottle of perfume, off the nightstand in her room.

He knew who these attendants were and he hated them for it, but what could he do? He had made the decision long ago not to report them. He couldn't be here all that often, and there was no telling what a vindictive attendant would do in his absence. What he tried to do was, he let them know he was onto them with his eyes. And he prayed to God that the looks he gave them would give them pause the next time they had the notion to disrespect his mother in this most cowardly of ways.

'Momma,' said Strange, 'I had a little excitement on the job today.' He told her the story of Sherman Coles and his brother, and of the young ex–police officer who had come along. He made it sound funny and unthreatening because he knew his mother worried about him and what he did for a living. Or maybe she was done worrying, thought Strange. Maybe she didn't think of him out there, could no longer picture him, or her city and its inhabitants, at all.

When he was done his mother smiled in that crooked way she had of smiling now, her lips pulled over toothless gums. Strange smiled back, not looking at the splotchy flesh or the stick arms or the atrophied legs or the flattened breasts that ended near her waist, but looking at her eyes. Because the eyes had not changed. They were deep brown and loving and beautiful, as they had always been, as they had been when he was a child, when Alethea Strange had been young and vibrant and strong.

'Room,' said his mother.

'Okay, Momma.'

He wheeled her back to her room, which overlooked the parking lot of a post office. He found her comb in the nightstand and drew it through her sparse white hair. She was nearly bald, and he could see raised moles and other age marks on her scalp.

'You look nice,' he said, when he was done.

'Son.' Those eyes of hers looked up at him, and she chuckled, her sharp shoulders moving up and down in amusement.

Alethea Strange pointed to her bedroom window. Strange went to the window and looked out to its ledge. His mother loved birds; she'd always loved to watch them build their nests.

'Ain't no birds out there building nests yet, Momma,' said Strange. 'You're gonna have to wait for the spring.'

Walking from her room, Strange stopped beside the big attendant and gave her a carnivorous smile that felt like a grimace.

'You take good care of my mother now, hear?'

Strange went toward the elevators, unclenching his jaw and breathing out slow. He began to think, as he tended to do when he left this place, of who he might call tonight. Being here, it always made him want a woman. Old age, sickness, loss, and pain . . . all of the suffering that was inevitable, you could deny its existence, for a little while anyway, when you were making love. Yeah, when you were lying with a woman, coming deep inside that sucking warmth, you could even deny death.

'You want a little more?'

'Sure.'

Terry Quinn reached across the table and poured wine into Juana Burkett's glass. Juana sipped at the Spanish red and sat back in her chair.

'It's really good.'

'I got it at Morris Miller's. The label on the bottle said it was bold, earthy, and satisfying.'

'Good thing you protected it on your little journey.'

'I was cradling it like a baby on the Metro on the way over here.'

'You really ought to get a car, Tuh-ree.'

'Didn't need one, up until recently. My job is close to my house, and I can take the subway downtown, I need to. But I was thinking, maybe I should get one now.'

'Why now?'

'Your house is kind of a far walk from the Catholic U station.'

'You're pretty sure of yourself.' Juana's eyes lit with amusement. 'You think I'm gonna ask you back?'

'I don't know. You keep making dinners like this one, I'm not going to wait for an invitation. I'll be whining like a dog to come in, scratching on the door out on your front porch. 'Cause you are one good cook.'

'I got lucky. This was the first time I made this dish. Baby artichokes and shrimp over linguini, it just looked so good when I saw the recipe in the *Post*.'

'Well, it was.' Quinn pushed his empty plate aside. 'Next time I take you to dinner. A little Italian place called Vicino's on Sligo Avenue, they got a red peppers and anchovies dish to make you cry.'

'That's on your street.'

'We can walk to it,' said Quinn. 'Stay in the neighborhood, until I get my car.'

Juana went to get coffee and brandy from the kitchen. Quinn got up and walked to the fireplace, where a pressed-paper log burned, colored flames rolling in a perfect arc. He picked up a CD case from a stack of them sitting on top of an amp: Luscious Jackson. Chick music, like all the rock and soul with female vocals she had been playing that night.

Juana's group house was nicer than most. Her roommates were grad students, a young married couple named James and Linda. He had met them when he'd arrived, and they were good-looking and nice and, as they had disappeared upstairs almost immediately, considerate as hell. Juana told him that James and Linda had the entire top floor of the house, and she had the finished basement for a quarter of the rent. The furnishings were secondhand but clean. Postcard-sized print reproductions of Edward Hopper, Degas, Cézanne, and Picasso paintings were framed and hung throughout the house.

Juana came out of the kitchen carrying a tray balanced on one hand. She wore a white button-down shirt out over black bells, with black waffle-heeled stacks on her feet. Black eyeliner framed her night-black eyes. She placed the tray on a small table and went around the room closing the miniblinds that hung from the windows.

'Wanna sit on the couch?'

'Okay,' said Quinn.

Quinn pulled the couch close to the fire. They drank black coffee and sipped Napoleon brandy.

'I downloaded all the stories they did on you last year off the Internet,' said Juana.

'Yeah?'

'Uh-huh. I read everything today.' Juana looked into the fire. 'The police force, it sounds like it's a mess.'

'It's pretty bad.'

'All those charges of police brutality. And the cops, they discharge their weapons more times in this town, per capita, than in any city in the country.'

'We got more violent criminals, *per capita*, than in any city in the country, too.'

'And the lack of training. That large group of recruits from back in the late eighties, the papers said that many of those people were totally, just mentally unqualified to be police officers.'

'A lot of them *were* unqualified. But not all of them. I was in that group. And I had a degree in criminology. They shouldn't have hired so many so quick, but they panicked. The Feds wanted some kind of response to the crack epidemic, and putting more officers on the street was the easiest solution. Never mind that the recruits were unqualified, or that the training was deficient. Never mind that our former, pipehead mayor had virtually dismantled the police force and systematically cut its funding during his *distinguished* administration.'

'You don't want to go there, do you?'

'Not really.'

'But what about the guns they issued the cops?' said Juana. 'They say those automatics—'

'The weapons were fine. You can't put a five-shot thirty-eight into the hands of a cop these days and tell him to go up against citizens carrying mini TEC-nines and modified full-autos. The Glock Seventeen is a good weapon. I was comfortable with that gun, and I was a good shot. I hadn't been on the range the official number of times, but I'd take that gun regularly out to the country . . . Listen, believe me, I was fully qualified to use it. The weapon was fine.'

'I'm sorry.'

'It's okay.'

'You're thinking, She doesn't know what she's talking about. Now she's going to tell me about cops and what's going on out in the street.'

'I wasn't thinking that at all,' lied Quinn. 'Anyway, we've got a new chief. Things are going to get better on the cop side of things, wait and see. It's the criminal side that I've got my doubts about.'

Juana brushed her hand over Quinn's. 'I didn't mean to upset you.'

'You didn't upset me.'

'I've never been with someone who did what you did for a living. I guess I'm trying to, I don't know, tell myself it's all right to hang out with a guy like you. I guess I'm just trying to figure you out.'

'That makes two of us,' said Quinn.

She moved closer to him, her shoulder touching his chest. They didn't say anything for a little while.

And then Quinn said, 'I met this man today. Old guy, private investigator. Black guy, used to be a cop, long time ago. I can say that he's black, right?'

'Oh, please. You're not one of those people claims he doesn't see color, are you?'

'Well, I'm not blind.'

'Thank you. I was at a dinner party once, a white girl was describing someone, and her friend said, "You mean that black guy?" and the white girl said, "I don't know; I don't remember what color he was."

She was saying it for my benefit, see, trying to give me the message that she wasn't "like that". What she didn't realize was, black people laugh at people like her, and detest people like her, as much as they do flat-out racists. At least with a racist you know where you stand. I found out later, this girl, she lived in a place where you pay a nice premium just so you and your children don't have to see people of color walking down your street.'

'I hear you,' said Quinn. 'I used to live in the basement of this guy's house in this neighborhood, about a mile or two from where I live now.'

'You mean that nuclear-free bastion of liberal ideals?'

'That one.

'A lot of the people on the street I lived on, they had bumper stickers on their cars, "Teach Peace," "Celebrate Diversity," like that. I'd see their little girls walking around with black baby dolls in their toy strollers. But come birthday time, you didn't see any black *children* at those little white girls' parties. None of those children from "down at the apartments" nearby. These people really believed, you put a bumper sticker on your Volvo so your neighbors can see it and a black doll in your white kid's hands, that's all you have to do.'

'You're gonna work up a sweat, Tuh-ree.'

'Sorry.' Quinn rubbed at the edge of his lip. 'So anyway, I met this old *black* PI today.'

'Yeah? What'd he want?'

Quinn told her about his day. When he came to the Richard Coles part, he told her that he had kept Coles 'occupied' in the men's room while Strange, the old investigator, made his bust.

'You were smiling just then,' said Juana, 'you know it? When you were telling that story, I mean.'

'I was?'

'It made you feel right, didn't it, to be back in it.'

Quinn thought of the swing of the hammer, and the blood. 'I guess it did.'

'You like the action,' said Juana. 'So why'd you leave the force?'

Quinn nodded. 'You're right. I liked being a cop. And I wasn't wrong on that shooting. I'd give anything to have not shot Chris Wilson, to have not taken his life. But I was not wrong. They *cleared* me, Juana. Given all the publicity, though, and some of the internal racial stuff, the accusations, I mean, that came out of it . . . I felt like the only right thing to do at the time was to walk away.'

'Enough of that,' said Juana, watching the frown return to Quinn's face. 'I didn't mean to—'

'It's all right.'

Juana turned him and placed the flat of her hand on his chest. Quinn slipped his hand around her side.

'I guess this is it,' said Quinn.

Juana laughed, her eyes black and alive. 'You're shaking a little bit, you know it?'

'It's just because you're so fucking beautiful.'

'Thank you.' Juana brushed Quinn's hair back behind his ear.

'Well, what are you going to do now?'

'Keep working at the bookstore, I guess, until I figure things out.'

'I mean *right* now.'

'Kiss you on the mouth?'

'For an educated guy,' said Juana, 'you're a little slow to read the signs.'

'Thought it would be polite to ask,' said Quinn.

'Ask, hell,' said Juana, moving her mouth toward his. 'You nearly made me beg.'

11

Entering his row house, Derek Strange listened to a message from Janine, asking him over for a thrown-together dinner with her and her son, Lionel. She had made 'a little too much' chicken, she said, and she didn't want 'all that food to go to waste.'

Strange phoned a woman named Shirley whom he dated from time to time, but Shirley was either not at home or not taking calls. Strange fed Greco and walked him around the block.

When Strange returned he checked his portfolio on the Net while listening to a reissue of Elmer Bernstein's soundtrack to *Return of the Magnificent Seven.* He took a shower and changed into a sport jacket over an open-collared shirt. He phoned another woman and was relieved to find her line busy, as this was not a woman he was anxious to see. His stomach grumbled, and he phoned Janine.

'Baker residence.'

'Derek here.'

'Hello.'

'Got any of that chicken left?'

'I been keeping it warm for you, Derek.'

'Can I bring Greco?' asked Strange.

Janine said, 'I've got a little something for him, too.'

They kissed for a long time, and then Quinn removed his shirt and Juana removed hers. She began to unfasten her black brassiere.

'Can I get that?' said Quinn.

'Sure.'

He had some trouble with the clasp. 'Bear with me.'

She ran her fingers down his veined bicep. 'I thought you meant *may* I get that.'

'No, I can do it. Here we go, I got it, right here.' He removed her bra. She let him look at her and touch her. He kissed her shoulder blade and one of her dark nipples, and he kissed the soft flesh of her breast and tasted the salt on her skin.

'That's nice,' she said.

'Christ,' said Quinn.

He got out of his jeans, and when he turned back to her he saw that she was naked now, too, and they embraced atop the blanket she had thrown on the couch. He kissed her mouth and rubbed himself between her thighs, and she moaned beneath him and laughed softly and with pleasure as his fingers found her swollen spot. Her skin was a very deep brown against his pale, lightly freckled body, and he intertwined his white fingers with her brown fingers and kissed her hand.

'You know what we're doing now?' whispered Quinn.

'Celebrating diversity?'

'I like it so far.'

'We're all the same,' said Juana, 'deep down inside.'

Strange owned a '91 Cadillac Brougham V-8, full power, black over black leather with the nice chromed-up grille, that he used when he wasn't working, only for short trips around town. He drove up Georgia Avenue, listening to *World Is a Ghetto* coming from the deck. Greco sat on his right on a red pillow Strange kept for him there, his nose pressed up against the passenger-side glass.

Janine and Lionel Baker lived up on 7th and Quintana in a modest red-shingled house in Brightwood. Strange parked out front, got Greco out by his leash and choke chain, and walked him to the front door.

Janine, Lionel, and Strange had dinner together in a small dining room where a print of *The Last Supper* hung on one wall. Janine had given Greco the bone from a chuck roast she had cooked the week before, and the boxer had taken it down to the basement to gnaw alone.

'Pass me those mashed potatoes, young man,' said Strange.

Lionel was tall like his mother, and would be handsome soon but had not yet fully grown into his large features. He held the bowl out for Strange to take.

'Thank you,' said Strange, who spooned a mound onto his plate and reached for the gravy bowl.

'Where you goin' tonight, Lionel?' asked his mother.

'Got a date with this girl.'

'What's her name?'

'Girl I know named Sienna.'

'How you gonna take a girl out on a date when you got no car?'

'Could I get yours?'

'Lionel.'

'We're goin' out with Jimmy and his girl. Jimmy's got his uncle's Lex, gold style with some fresh rims.'

'Where Jimmy's uncle get the money for a Lexus?' asked Janine, her eyes finding Strange's across the table.

'I don't know,' said Lionel, 'but that joint is *tight.*' He gave Strange a sideways glance and said, 'Course, it ain't tight like no Caddy, nothin' like that.'

'You don't like my ride?' said Strange.

'I like it.' And Lionel smiled and sang, 'Best of all, it's a Cad-i-llac.'

Janine and Lionel laughed. Strange laughed a little, too.

'He's got a nice voice,' said Janine, 'doesn't he, Derek?'

'It's all right,' said Strange. 'Too bad no one sings anymore on the records, otherwise he might have a career.'

'I'm gonna be a big-time lawyer, anyway,' said Lionel, reaching toward the platter of fried chicken and snagging a thigh.

'Not if you don't get your grades up,' said Janine.

'You over at Coolidge, right?' said Strange.

'Uh-huh. Got another year to go.'

'So what movie you going to see tonight?' asked Janine.

'That new Chow Yun-Fat joint, up at the AMC in City Place.'

'Say you chewin' the fat?' said Strange.

'*That's* funny,' said Lionel.

Strange looked at the Tupac T-shirt Lionel was wearing, the one with the image of Shakur smoking a blunt. 'None of my business, but if I had a date with a young lady, I wouldn't be wearin' a shirt with a picture of another man on the front of it.'

'Oh, I'll be changing into somethin' else, Mr Derek. Bet it.' Lionel looked at the watch on his gangly wrist. 'Matter of fact, I gotta bounce. Jimmy'll be here any minute to pick me up.'

Lionel dropped the thigh bone and took his plate and glass and carried them off to the kitchen.

'See what I put up with?' said Janine.

'He's a good boy.'

'I do love him.'

'I know you do.'

Janine patted Strange's hand. 'Thank you for coming over tonight, Derek.'

'My pleasure,' said Strange.

Ten minutes later a horn sounded from outside, and they heard

Lionel's heavy footsteps coming down the stairs. Strange got up from the table. He walked into the foyer and met Lionel as he was heading for the front door.

'Later, Mr Derek.'

'Hold up a second, Lionel.'

Lionel looked himself over. He wore pressed jeans and a Hilfiger shirt with Timberland boots. 'What, you don't like my hookup?'

'You look fine.'

'Got me some brand-new Timbs.'

'Sears makes a better boot for half the price.'

'Ain't got that little tree on 'em, though.'

'Listen up, Lionel.' Strange took a breath. He wasn't all that good at this, but he knew he had to try. 'Don't be drivin' around smoking herb in a fancy ride, hear?'

'Herb?' Lionel said it in a mocking way, and Strange felt his face grow hot.

'All I'm telling you is, the police see a car with young black men inside it, 'specially a gold Lexus with fancy wheels, looks like a drug car, they don't think they need a reason to pull you over. They find blunt or cheeva or whatever you're calling it these days inside the car, you got a mark on your record you can't shake. You might as well go ahead, and forget about law school then. You understand what I'm saying?'

'I hear you, Mr Derek.'

'All right.' Strange reached into his back pocket and pulled a twenty from the billfold. 'Here you go. You don't want to be taking out a nice girl without a little extra money in your pocket. Take her over to that TGI Friday's they got up there after the show, buy her a sundae, something like that.'

'Thank you.' Lionel took the money and winked. 'Maybe after that sundae, she might even give me some of that trim.'

Strange frowned, put his face close to the boy's, and lowered his voice. 'I don't want to hear you talking like that, Lionel. You have a nice young woman, you treat her with respect. The same way you'd want a man to treat your mother, you understand me?'

'Yessir.'

Strange still had his wallet out, and he pulled a condom he kept for emergencies from underneath his business cards. He handed the condom to Lionel.

'In the event something *does* happen, though . . .'

'Thank you, Mr Derek,' said Lionel, smiling stupidly as he pocketed the rubber. The horn sounded again from out on the street. 'I'm ghost.'

'Have a nice time.'

Lionel left, and Strange locked the door behind him. Strange walked back to the living room wondering just how bad he'd fucked that up.

Janine was waiting for him there. She had put *Songs in the Key of Life* on the stereo and brought out a cold bottle of Heineken and two glasses and set them on the table before the couch. Janine was sitting on the couch with her stockinged feet up on the table. Strange joined her.

'You and Lionel have a little man-to-man?'

'Uh, yeah.'

'There's so much I can't give him alone.'

'I'm just a man, no smarter than any other.'

'But you are a man. He needs a strong male figure to guide him now and again.'

Strange smiled and flexed his bicep. 'You think I'm strong?'

'Go ahead, Derek.'

'I don't feel too strong tonight, I can tell you that.'

'That Sherman Coles pickup do you in?'

'Good thing I had that young man with me.'

Janine put a pillow behind Strange's head. 'Tell me about your day.' They talked about work. He told her the Coles story, and she told him how she'd taken care of some loose ends at the office. When they were done talking, and the beer bottle had been emptied, they went upstairs to Janine's room.

She had turned the sheets down, and he knew she had done it for him. Her clock radio, always set on HUR, had been turned on, and was softly emitting some Quiet Storm. The room was strong with the smell of her perfume, and as he undressed her, taking his time, the room grew strong with her female smell, too.

He got out of his outer clothes and stripped himself of his underwear. They were naked and they kissed standing. He got his hand on her behind and caressed her firm, ample flesh.

'*Damn,* Janine.'

'What?'

'You got some back on you, girl.'

'You don't like it?'

'You *know* I do.'

He pushed her large breasts together and kissed them, then kissed her mouth.

'Come on,' she said, short of breath.

'You in some kind of hurry?' Strange chuckled and sucked a little on her cool lips.

'Sit your ass down,' said Janine.

'Here?' asked Strange, pointing to the edge of the bed.

'You said you were tired,' said Janine. 'Let me do the work tonight.'

'Who's this right here?' said Quinn.

'Lauryn Hill,' said Juana. 'You like it?'

'Yeah, it's pretty nice. But you have any music with a guy singer?'

'I got the Black Album. You know, Prince. Does that count?'

'Oh, shit,' laughed Quinn.

'What's so funny?'

'I already had this conversation once today.'

Quinn adjusted himself. He felt his erection returning, and he moved his hips against hers. He gave her a couple of short strokes to let her know he was still alive.

'You tryin' to stay in or get out?'

'Just testing the water,' said Quinn.

'The water's warm.'

'Deep, too.'

'Cut it out.' Juana smiled. 'Some guys I know, they'd be tripping over themselves right about now, trying to get out the front door.'

'I'd be trippin' over somethin', I tried to leave right now.'

'Stop bragging.'

'Anyway, I want to stay right here.'

'You tellin' me you're not the type to hit it and split?'

'I've done it; I'm not gonna lie about that. But I don't want to do that with you.'

They were still on the couch. Quinn pulled an afghan up over them. The fire had weakened, and a chill had come in to the room. He looked at his white skin atop her brown.

'Think we can make this work?' asked Quinn.

'Do you want it to?'

'Yes.'

Strange was under the covers, lying beside Janine, when Greco walked into the room. He dropped the chuck bone at the foot of the bed, then moved it between his paws as he got himself down on the carpet.

'He's tellin' me it's time to go home.'

'I wish you didn't have to,' said Janine. 'It's nice and warm under this blanket.'

'It wouldn't be proper to have Lionel come home and know that I was here.'

'He already knows, Derek.'

'It wouldn't be right, just the same.'

Janine got up on one elbow and ran her fingers through the short hairs on Strange's chest.

'That lawyer I do business with from time to time,' said Strange. 'That Fifth Streeter with the cheap suit?'

'Markowitz?' said Janine.

'Him. He owes us money, doesn't he?'

'He's got an unpaid balance, I recall.'

'Give him a call tomorrow, see if he can't get us the transcripts of the review board hearings on the Quinn case.'

'You want to wipe out his debt?'

'See how much it is and settle it the way you see fit.'

'What's your feeling on this Quinn?'

Strange had been thinking of Terry Quinn all night. Quinn was violent, fearless, sensitive, and disturbed . . . all of those things at once. A cocktail of troubles, a guy who could come in handy in situations like they'd had today, but not the kind of guy who needed to be wearing a uniform, representing the law.

'I don't know enough about him yet,' said Strange. 'Next thing I'm going to do, I'm going to read those transcripts. Then I'm gonna go out and try and talk to the other players.'

'You think Quinn was wrong?'

'I think he's a white man who saw a black man holding a gun on another white man in the street. He reacted the way he's been programmed to react in this society, going back to birth.'

'You saying he's that way?'

'He's like most white people. Don't you know, most of 'em will tell you they don't have a racist bone in their bodies.'

'They're pure of mind and heart.'

'Quinn doesn't *think* he's that way,' said Strange. 'But he is.'

12

Nestor Rodriguez looked in the rearview mirror and spotted the green Ford, ten car lengths back. He punched a number into the cell phone cradled beside him, then snatched the phone up as it began to ring on the other end.

'Lizardo.'

'Brother.'

'We're almost there. I just now called Boone and told him to pick us up.'

'We have to do this every time for the midget?'

'The jerkoff doesn't want us to know where he and his father live. He insists.'

'Why can't we just make the trade in the parking lot?'

'Because the little one likes to scale out the *manteca* and test it at his house, in front of us. He's afraid of being ripped off.'

'Shit,' said Lizardo. It sounded like 'chit.'

The Rodriguez brothers did not have to worry about their conversation going out over the radio waves. Nestor had paid a young software engineer in Florida to alter his and his brother's electronic serial numbers and mobile identification numbers. Also, a Secure Cellular device called a Jammer Scrambler, attached to both of their phones, altered their voices.

Nestor was traveling north on 270 in a blue Ford Contour SVT. Lizardo Rodriguez followed in a green version of the same car. There were five kilograms of Colombian brown heroin in the trunk of Nestor's Ford and five in the trunk of Lizardo's.

The Contours looked liked family sedans, but at 200 horses were hardly that. The cars did 0 to 60 in 6.9 and could top out at over 140 miles per hour. The Fords' bland body styling was perfect for their runs, but the Rodriguez brothers preferred more flash driving on the streets of Orlando, their adopted city. Nestor in particular, who was the unmarried one of the two, was in love with pretty cars. He owned a new Mustang Cobra, also an SVT. His did 60 in 5.5. He was proud that he had not touched it cosmetically, as many Spanish were prone to do, but had left it stock. Well, not all the way stock. He had put two decals, silhouettes of naked girls with white-girl hair on the back of the car, with 'Ladies Invited' spelled out between the girls in neon letters. But that was the only extra thing he had done to the car.

'Who were you talking to a few minutes ago?' said Nestor.

'My woman,' said Lizardo. 'Her father doesn't want to change his crops. I tried to explain to him, the cartel will provide the fertilizer and the seeds, and a guarantee that what he reaps we will sell. The poppy will give him two crops a year, twice what he'll get from his single crop of coffee beans. And we'll pay his field-workers four times what they earn to harvest the crop.'

'What is the problem?'

'He is a peasant,' said Lizardo. 'That is the problem. He sees the American helicopters, the black Bells with the door gunners, and he is afraid. He sees me, his own son-in-law, and he is afraid. He sees his own shadow, brother, and he is afraid.'

'Farmers,' said Nestor with contempt.

'Yes. I'm only trying to help him, to get my woman off my back. So that maybe then she can get on *her* back, for a change.'

Nestor understood why Lizardo's woman did not care to sleep with him. Lizardo was often drunk, and when he was drunk he was not a gentleman in bed. When he was so drunk that he couldn't be a man, he hit her with his fists. Nestor believed that it was sometimes necessary to strike a woman, they expected it, even, but women lost their spirit if you struck them all the time.

'Bring him to stay with you in Florida,' said Nestor. 'You can afford it.'

'He doesn't want to come. And I don't want the filthy bastard in my house. He showers, but still he smells like the country.'

'Maybe your woman's brother can help, talk to your father-in-law for you.'

'The priest? Ah! He has trouble helping himself.'

'Is he struggling with his vow of celibacy?'

'He was never celibate. They have a saying in the old village: All the children call the priest father, except for his own children, who call him uncle!'

Nestor and Lizardo shared hearty laughter. Then Nestor hit his turn signal and got into the right lane, making sure his brother followed.

Nestor checked his face in the rearview. His black hair was combed back and set in place with gel, and he wore a neat Vandyke beard. He had shaved the hair that had been between his eyebrows his entire life, so that now he had two separate eyebrows. He wore two gold earrings, one small hoop in each ear. His clothing was neat but not flashy. Nestor studied the pictures in the *Esquire* and *GQ* magazines so that he could see the latest styles and the proper way to dress. Then he bought clothing that looked like it did in those pictures but without the fancy labels for which you paid extra. He shopped at the Men's Wearhouse and Today's Man.

A mile down the interstate stood a strip shopping center bordering a field where houses were being constructed. The parking lot was half filled. Nestor found a row of cars with two empty spaces. He pulled into a space and watched his brother pull into the other, situated at the very end of the row. Nestor reached beneath the seat and picked up his gun, a Sig Sauer .9 that held an eight-shot magazine. He slid the Sig into a leather holster inside his jacket.

'You talk to Coleman?' said Lizardo, still holding the phone.

'Not since the last time. I'll call him from Baltimore tonight.'

'Will he take the cocaine on the next run?'

'He said that he buys his cocaine from a supplier in Los Angeles and he doesn't want to change. But I told him, if he wants our *manteca,* he will have to take the cocaine. I told him that we can no longer sell one without the other. We are selling the *manteca* to the Boones for a very good price. Even with the bounce the Boones put on it, Coleman knows he cannot buy the heroin any cheaper.'

'What if he refuses?'

'We'll have the Boones sell the *manteca* to someone else.'

Lizardo reached across the seat, dropped the glove box door, and removed his Davis .32. It was a small gun, good at close range, and it fit neatly in the pocket of his pleated black slacks. He dropped it there and for a moment considered the situation. Nestor never asked for his business advice, but sometimes Lizardo came up with good ideas. He thought he had one now.

'Listen,' said Lizardo. 'We'll go back to selling Coleman direct. It'll be cheaper for him, right? Maybe that will convince him to take the coke as well.'

'You forget why we got the Boones involved to begin with?'

'We didn't. Our cousin Roberto did, when he and the little one were together in the joint.'

'*We* asked Roberto to find a mule for us, remember?'

'Oh, yeah.'

Nestor exhaled a long breath. He had to remember to be patient with his brother, whose brain worked very slowly.

'Lizardo. Do you want to go into that lousy city, deal with the niggers directly?'

'No.'

'Then we need the Boones. For now, anyway. So leave little Ray alone, understand? You are always trying to get him excited.'

'Fuck,' said Lizardo. It sounded like 'fawk.'

Edna Loomis had the Ford pickup bouncing on the gravel road, doing a real good number on the shocks but not really thinking on it, as she was in a big hurry to get on back to the house. Travis Tritt sang loudly in the cab. She had turned up the volume on the dash radio to keep herself pumped.

The night before, she had made an impression of Ray's key in some special putty she'd picked up at the hardware store, on the advice of a girlfriend of hers who loved to smoke crystal, too. This girlfriend, a big-hair girl named Johanna, got her convinced that Ray would never miss a little here and there if she was to take it, and besides, all the good stuff Edna was giving away to Ray for free, it was owed her to get some of that stash on a regular basis. Edna was Ray's woman, after all, almost a wife, and why should a wife have to ask every time she wanted to get high? After a couple of Courage and Cokes, Edna began to see Johanna's point.

So, the night before, after Ray had gone to sleep, Edna'd slipped the key off that ring of his with the chain attached to it. He woke up in the morning, the key was right where it had been when he'd hung his jeans over the bedroom chair, and Ray was none the wiser. She had taken the putty to this dude Johanna knew, and he'd fixed her up. She had a shiny new key in her pocket now.

Edna pulled the F-150 into the yard between the Taurus and Ray's Shovelhead. Ray's legs were hanging out the open door of the Taurus, his steel toolbox on the ground at his feet. He was always fooling with that car, that or the Harley. He got to his feet and stood, brushing himself off, as Edna came down out of the truck's cab.

'Thought I told you to go out to a movie or somethin',' said Ray. 'You know me and Daddy got business here today.'

'Forgot my tape box,' said Edna. 'Can't be drivin' around all day without my music.'

'Well, hurry up and get it, then get gone.'

'Where's Earl?'

'In the house, why you ask that?'

'No reason, just wonderin' where he was. Look, don't worry about me, you just finish up whatever it is you're doin'.'

Ray got back into the car and laid himself down between the bench seat and the gas and brake pedals, wondering why women talked so much about nothin'. He was putting the trapdoor by the steering column back together, having taken it apart and oiled the movable parts. The door had been dropping slow lately, and he couldn't have that. A little WD-40 to finish the job, then put everything back in place. After that, he and his father would be ready to meet the Rodriguez brothers, out by that mall.

Edna walked through the barn to the back of it real quick, running on adrenalin. She put her new key to the lock of the steel door and smiled as the key caught and turned. She went inside the drug room without even looking over her shoulder. Johanna had been right: If you had the guts, it was easy.

She didn't throw the slide bolt on the door because that would be worse, trying to explain to Ray why she was in here behind a locked door. The other way, he just walked in on her, she wouldn't look so guilty, and anyhow, she could always use that old excuse, female curiosity.

All right now, Edna, don't you go lingerin'.

She saw the stove where Ray cooked the meth straight away. Above it was shelf, and on the shelf were old prescription pill bottles, amber plastic with white plastic tops, and she opened one and found spansules, Ray's personal stash. This was not what she was looking for. She opened another and found it to be filled with rocks of ice. She dumped half the rocks out into her hand and dropped them in a film canister she carried in her pocket. What, was Ray going to count every piece of ice he had? Like Johanna liked to say, I don't *think* so.

Before she left the room she had a quick look around at Ray's tools and weights. Boys' toys. She'd never complain about his liftin' weights, though. Ray was on the short side, but he did make her damp down there when he took off his shirt at night. She liked that bulldog look.

Somewhere in here was the entrance to their little tunnel, too. She'd had a good laugh with Johanna over that one, after the two of them had had way too many drinks one time at this tavern, place that had the jukebox played Whitesnake and Warrant and those other groups Johanna liked, down near Poolesville. Ray liked to try and scare her, tell her about the snakes that lived down in the tunnel, but she didn't pay him much mind. She wasn't afraid of no snakes; snakes weren't nothin' but overgrown worms. And why would she want to go down in that dirty tunnel for, anyway?

She walked out of the room as confidently as she'd gone in. No one was in the saloon area of the bar that Ray and Earl had built and decorated themselves. No one had seen a thing.

She locked the door behind her, shaking hair off her shoulders. She'd done it, and she was proud of what she'd done.

Earl Boone sat on the edge of his bed, killing off a can of Busch beer. He crushed the can in his hand, dropped it in a wastebasket, where it clanged against other empties, and went to his bedroom window. He flipped open the lid on a box of Marlboros, shook out a smoke, and drew it from the box with his lips. He lit it with a Zippo that had a raised map of Vietnam on one side and the Marine Corps insignia on the other. Below the map were the words 'Paid to Kill.' Every time he looked at the lighter, he recalled with some bit of fondness that he was full of piss and vinegar when he was a kid.

Edna was coming out the barn like she was on fire, walking real fast and shaking that hair and ass of hers, heading for the truck. Girl was always going fast, 'cept in the morning, when she looked like somethin' that the cat wouldn't think of dragging indoors. Now she and Ray were talking or arguing over something, he couldn't never tell which. Earl didn't understand why Ray didn't just backhand the girl when she got to sass-talking like she was prone to do. Around other men, Ray had a temper he couldn't control, but put him near anything with a fur piece between its legs and he was tamer than a broke-dick dog.

Some men were like that, but not Earl. Back when Earl was married to Ray's mother, Margo, God have mercy on her soul, he'd shown her the back of his hand and even a fist once or twice, when she got real brave and disrespectful behind that gin she liked to drink. The gin took her liver eventually. At the end, when she was on those machines with the tubes running out her nose, waiting on a transplant, he'd almost apologized for those times he'd raised his hand to her, but it was not in his nature to do so, and the moment had passed. Hell, he knew she'd never get a liver from the start. It would go to some rich person, even if that person was below her on the list. That was the way the world worked. He'd known it from the time he'd fallen out his cradle and begun to walk on two feet.

Now Edna was driving the truck out of the yard and down the gravel road.

Earl got into his winter jacket. He put his smokes and lighter in one pocket and his .38 in the other. He picked up his six-pack cooler and turned out the lamp in his room. Looked like Ray was done tamperin' with the car, and right about now he'd be looking to move out, nervous and ready to roll. Nervous in that way he got, when somethin' was about to happen.

13

Nestor Rodriguez saw the Taurus enter the parking lot and snake up and down the rows of cars. Ray Boone always looked for cops and DEA types in unmarked vehicles when he pulled into the lot. Nestor had already checked and was satisfied that there was no problem, as these kinds of cars were very easy to spot. But Ray was the kind of person who needed to know this for himself.

Into the phone Nestor said, 'They're here,' and, still watching the Taurus in his rear- and sideview mirrors, added, 'Wait until I tell you, then lock your car down and walk on over to mine.'

Ray Boone parked the Taurus next to Nestor's Contour. Nestor's eyes went past the old man, unshaven and looking like a two-day drunk as usual, and on to Ray, who was seated behind the wheel. Nestor nodded to Ray as he spoke into the phone: 'All right, Lizardo, come on.'

'How do our friends look today?' said Lizardo.

'Don't be funny,' said Nestor, smiling slightly at Ray through the window as he spoke. 'The little jerkoff doesn't like your humor. We just want to do our business and get on our way. And no Spanish, Lizardo; he doesn't like that, either.'

'Okay,' said Lizardo. 'Here I come.'

Nestor cradled the phone. He didn't like the playful sound in his brother's voice. Going back to when the two of them were kids, Lizardo was always with the jokes.

Lizardo exited his car, locked it, checked the locks, and walked along the row of cars, dropping his keys in his pocket. He wore his hair in the same fashion as his brother's but did not shave between his eyebrows, leaving one long brow like a furry black caterpillar stretched out across the base of his forehead. He had a small mustache, but no hair on his chin, and dressed with less regard for style than his brother. He bought his clothing at Target and Montgomery Ward. He didn't like fabrics that wrinkled and wondered why fools paid extra for fabrics that did. At home, he often slept in his clothes when he'd had too much to drink.

Nestor got out of the Contour, locked it, and met Lizardo at the back of the car. He opened the trunk and flipped over the indoor/outdoor carpet piece that normally covered a well holding the spare but that now covered five identical gym bags with Adidas logos printed on their sides. He lifted two of the gym bags out, replaced the carpet, and locked the trunk. His movements were fluid, and both he and his brother were very calm.

Nestor and Lizardo split up, Nestor going to one side of the Taurus and Lizardo going to the other, and entered the backseat of the car.

'Hello, Ray,' said Nestor. 'Hello, Earl.'

'Ho-la, amigos,' said Ray.

'How do, Earl,' said Lizardo, clapping Earl on the shoulder.

'How do,' said Earl. He popped the ring on a can of Busch and took a long swig.

'Lie on down back there,' said Ray. 'It ain't far.'

They didn't protest. This small thing seemed to put Ray at ease. Nestor and Lizardo arranged themselves the way they had many times before. Nestor let his legs dangle off the bench and put his face down on the seat, and Lizardo did the same in the opposite direction. Nestor's face was inches away from Lizardo's ass.

'Here we go,' said Ray, backing out of his spot.

They had been on the interstate for a mile or so when Nestor heard a kind of sharp squeak. Then came an awful, wretched smell from the seat of Lizardo's pants.

'Lizardo,' said Nestor. 'Please.'

'I can't help it, Nestor. The *huevos rancheros* I had this morning, at the Denny's on the interstate . . .'

'You *can* help it! You're forcing it out; I can hear the sound!'

'I'm sorry,' said Lizardo.

But he wasn't sorry. And he couldn't help but giggle when he heard his brother gag.

Nestor felt the car slow down and then, after a sharp turn, the gravel beneath their tires as they drove onto the Boone property. The car kept going for a while, slowly, and finally came to a stop.

'Y'all can get up,' said Ray, as he killed the engine.

All of them got out of the car. The yard was cluttered with tires and oil drums, old brake pads, cinder blocks, upended logs, a rusted-out backhoe. A Prussian helmet was hung by its chin strap on the sissy bar of an old Harley, and a plastic buck's head was nailed over the barn door. The house beside the barn was badly in need of paint. A dead plant hung from the ceiling of the porch, and the porch listed to one side.

White trash, thought Nestor. You can give them money, but money will never buy them style.

'Let's go inside,' said Ray, 'warm up some while we work.'

They walked toward the barn. Ray checked out Nestor, holding the gym bags loosely at his side. Nestor with his shiny suit, big pads under the shoulders, and those pointed spick shoes he liked, weaved on the sides like a basket. Colder than the tits on an old sow today, and here goes Nestor, wearing shoes with holes in 'em. Ray knew Nestor liked the ladies, and he bet that this brown boy thought he looked pretty attractive, dressed the way he was. He once told Ray that the girls called him Nestor the Molester down in Florida, and he was proud of it, too. Well, maybe they went for that look down there, but up in Maryland, out here in the country? He looked pretty goddamned stupid, you asked Ray.

'Hey, Nestor,' said Ray, 'how much you drop on that suit, a buck?'

'Buck and a half,' said Nestor defensively.

'How about it, Daddy? Think I'd look good in a suit like that?'

'Huh,' grunted Earl.

It was warm inside the barn. They had a couple drinks, Ray insisting on pouring them shots of tequila, the gold kind he had sitting up on the top shelf behind the bar, to go with their beers. Earl sat with them at one of those tables with green felt on it, the type cardplayers used, while Ray went into that secret room of his to scale out the brown, make sure it weighed out to two full Ks. Ray claimed to have some chemical kind of test back there he ran it through, too, though Nestor had never actually seen the kit.

Earl didn't say much while Nestor and Lizardo sipped their tequilas and beers. He smoked a cigarette and then another, nodding when Nestor tried to include him in the conversation but not giving up more than the nod or a 'yep' or 'uh-huh' here and there.

'Take it easy with that,' said Nestor, pointing to the Cuervo bottle that Lizardo was lifting off the table and bringing to his glass.

'Just a taste,' said Lizardo, pouring three fingers and setting the bottle back down on the felt.

Nestor didn't like to be around Lizardo when he drank. Liquor made his brother more stupid, and much sillier, than he already was.

In the back room, Ray broke open a spansule of meth, poured the white speckled contents onto the crook of his thumb, and snorted it all into his nose at once. He paced around the room, hungry for a smoke, his heart beating rapidly. He did a set of preacher curls, then opened the door that led to the saloon area and stuck his head out into the room.

'Nestor, Lizardo! Come on back and get your money!'

Nestor looked at Lizardo and shrugged. They got up from the table and walked to the back room. Earl butted his smoke and followed. When all of them were in the room, Ray closed the door behind them.

Nestor had been curious about the back room. He had never been asked to come inside it, but now that he was here he felt somewhat disappointed. There was a tool bench, some shotguns in a case, a setup to cook drugs, a couple of safes, a weight bench, free weights strewn about, and a stack of porno magazines on a small table near the bathroom. It looked very much like the room Nestor kept in the basement of his house.

'Everything all right?' said Nestor.

'It all checked out fine,' said Ray.

'Then we'll just take our money and get on our way.'

'You got the rest of the run to make, right?'

'This is our first stop, Ray, same as always.'

'Must be worried about the rest of your load, settin' back there in the trunks of those cars.'

'If I'm worried,' said Nestor, smiling cheerfully, 'then it is *my* worry.'

Lizardo laughed a little. Nestor could see from the familiar glassy sheen to Lizardo's eyes that his brother was feeling the tequilas and beers.

'Somethin' funny?' said Ray.

'It's the boots, *menino,*' said Lizardo, his eyes traveling down to the custom Dingos on Ray's feet.

'What's that word, *me-nino*?' said Ray.

Nestor nearly winced. *Menino* meant 'little man.' It was something you would call a boy.

Nestor said, 'It's another word for amigo, Ray. It's like calling you a friend.'

'I *like* the boots,' said Lizardo. 'Honest, Ray. And the heels! Tell me, where could I get some like those?'

'What for?' asked Ray suspiciously.

Lizardo grinned. 'I'd like to bring a pair back for my woman.'

Ray took a step forward. Earl stifled a grin.

'He don't mean nothin', Critter,' said Earl. 'He's just havin' a little fun with you, is all. Go on and give these boys their money.'

Ray went to the tool bench, picked up the gym bags the Rodriguez brothers had brought with them, and handed them to Nestor. Nestor unzipped one bag and looked inside.

'Count it,' said Ray.

'I don't need to count it,' said Nestor. 'We are going to be in business together for a long time.'

'Hey, Ray,' said Lizardo, nodding to the weight bench. 'You really pick up all that yourself?'

'Damn straight,' said Ray. 'Two hundred and fifty pounds. I'll bench that motherfucker all day.'

'Let's go, brother,' said Nestor.

'What,' said Ray, 'you don't think I can?'

'I don't know,' said Lizardo, winking at Nestor. 'You look pretty strong, but . . .'

'I'll show you,' said Ray. 'And not just one, either. I'm gonna do a set of ten, how about that?'

Lizardo made a spreading motion with his hands. 'You want to show me, man, pfft, show me.'

'Jerkoffs,' said Nestor, stepping between Earl and the weight bench.

Ray stripped off his flannel, leaving on only his white T-shirt. He lay back on the bench, the pad of which had the word *Brutus* spelled across it. He got a grip on the bar, took a couple of deep breaths, and pushed the bar off the towers on which it rested. He bench-pressed the barbell once, twice, three times, counting aloud the reps, veins emerging on his forehead and neck. He benched it ten times and gently returned the bar to its place on the towers.

Ray sat up, checked his arms briefly, and smiled up at Lizardo. 'Now you.'

'You don't think I can?'

'Now you,' said Ray.

'*Vamonos,* Lizardo,' said Nestor.

'Y'all ain't gonna *vamonos* nowhere until he benches this bar,' said Ray. 'I did it; now he's gonna do it. C'mon, Li-zardo, can't you do it?'

'I can do it,' said Lizardo. 'But do I have to take off my shirt?' It sounded like 'chirt.'

Lizardo laughed shortly and lay down on the bench. He gripped, ungripped, and regripped the bar. He took a deep breath and held it in. Ray moved behind the towers and centered himself for the spot.

'One!' shouted Lizardo, as he raised the bar. Immediately he knew that he could only do but two or three. The weight was much heavier than he had imagined it would be.

'Two!' he said, his voice weak. He barely got the bar up to where his elbows locked. He brought it down slowly to his chest, breathed in, and pushed with everything he had.

He didn't count this time. It was difficult to get the bar up at all. His arms burned and shook, and he felt his face grow hot. The bar was only halfway up and it wouldn't, couldn't go any farther. He looked up pleadingly at Ray.

'I got it,' said Ray. He reached over the towers and gripped the bar, pulling it up toward him.

'You got it?' said Lizardo.

'I got it,' said Ray.

Lizardo let go of the bar and allowed his hands to fall to his sides. Ray drew the bar up to the height of the towers. He looked over at his father and smiled stupidly.

'Hey, Daddy,' said Ray, as he released the bar.

Lizardo screamed, watching the barbell fall. The bar crushed his Adam's apple and windpipe, and broke his neck. For a moment, but only for a moment, Lizardo saw the spray of blood that he coughed up into the room.

Nestor dropped the gym bags. His hands shook wildly as he fumbled inside his jacket for the .9.

Earl drew his .38 and shot Nestor in the back of the head. Nestor's black hair crested, a wave of crimson arcing out above it, and as he pitched forward Earl shot him between the shoulder blades. When Nestor hit the ground, his legs kicking, Earl put his palm out above the hammer of the .38 and shot Nestor once more behind his ear.

Ray laughed nervously, squinting at his father through the cordite. There was only Ray's laughter for a while, and a ringing sound in their ears.

Earl slipped the .38 back into his jacket. He checked his clothing for blowback and saw that he was clean. He was glad he'd put his palm out as a shield. He washed his hands in the sink.

'Got a smoke, Daddy?'

'Yep.'

Earl shook one out for himself and one for his son. He flipped open the Zippo, thumbed the wheel, and got flame.

Earl dragged and exhaled. 'You plan that?'

'Kind of came to me,' said Ray, 'while we were out in the saloon, havin' our drinks.'

'You were plannin' it, you shoulda told me.'

'Seemed like an opportunity. Coleman was havin' a problem with those boys—'

'He asked you to talk to 'em, is all.' Earl hit his smoke. 'Guess you better get you a shovel, Critter.'

'Ground's too hard for that. I got somethin' else in mind, least until this cold spell breaks. Meantime, I got to get over to that shopping center before it empties out. Clean those trunks out and get on back.'

Earl nodded and smoked.

Ray smiled. 'Well, Daddy, you said you wanted out.'

'Uh-huh.'

'Well, we are out now, aren't we? And we are going to be rich. Ain't nothin' we can't have.'

'I could use some company,' said Earl, thinking of that pretty little colored junkie, down in D.C.

'A woman, you mean?'

'You don't have someone to share it with,' said Earl, 'all this good fortune, it just don't mean a thing.'

14

Strange sat in his office, reading the transcripts of the Quinn hearings, Greco asleep at his feet. A red rubber ball with rubber spikes on it rested between Greco's paws.

Strange brought the boxer into work with him once or twice a week, when the dog begged. Earlier that morning, when Strange had headed for the front door with the car keys in his hand, Greco had looked up at him with those big browns of his and whined something fierce. Strange couldn't bear to think of the dog standing in the foyer all morning, pacing back and forth, barking at every car that slowed down or parked on the street.

He picked up his phone and hit Janine's extension.

'Yes, Derek.'

'Anything on Kane's address?'

'I've got it out here. He lives with his mother, apparently.'

'What about his phone number?'

'I've got that, too. But it cost us twenty dollars. I put it on your credit card.'

'Damn.'

'You can get anything off the Internet, for a price.'

'Ron out there?'

'Uh-huh.'

'What's he doin'?'

'Looks like he's reading the newspaper to me.'

'I pay him to read the paper?'

'You know I don't get into your business, Derek.'

'Print out a copy of that page where you gave them my Visa. I need to show it on my expense sheet.'

'I already did it.'

'Good. And call Lydell Blue over at the Fourth District, see if he ran a sheet for me yet on Ricky Kane.'

'I'll do it.'

'I'll be out in a few.'

Strange finished reading the transcripts. Much of the information had been duplicated in the newspaper and television reports. He carefully read Quinn's statement and the corroborating statement of his partner, Eugene Franklin. Then he read and reread the testimony of Ricky Kane.

On the night of the shooting, Kane, a restaurant and bar worker, was driving across town after his shift at the Purple Cactus, a trendy eatery on 14th and F, when he pulled over on D Street to urinate. Kane explained that he had downed 'a beer' after work, had begun to feel the effects of a weak bladder, and saw that D Street was deserted as he drove east. Standing beside the open door of his Toyota, 'I pulled out my penis and prepared to urinate,' when a Jeep, 'the military-looking kind,' came from around the corner, its brights tapped on, and stopped behind his Toyota.

The lights from the Jeep were in his eyes and blinding as Kane 'tucked myself back in' and zipped up his fly. A 'large black man' came through the glare of the lights and was upon him at once, yelling in an extremely agitated manner for Kane to produce a license and registration.

'What did I do?' Kane asked the black man.

'You were pissin' in the street,' said the black man. 'And don't even think of lyin' about it, 'cause I saw you holdin' your little pecker plain as day.'

The man was broad, 'like a weightlifter,' and taller than Kane by a head. Later, Kane would be told that the man's name was Chris Wilson and that he was an out-of-uniform cop.

Kane said here that he detected the strong smell of alcohol on Chris Wilson's breath.

When a man had been drinking, even one beer, thought Strange, it would be difficult to smell alcohol on another man's breath. Strange made a line through this statement with a yellow accent marker.

'Who are you?' asked Kane. 'Why do you need to see my license?'

'I'm a cop,' replied Wilson.

Kane was frightened, but 'I knew my rights.' He asked to see Wilson's badge or some other form of identification, and that's when Wilson 'became enraged,' grabbing Kane by the lapels of his shirt and throwing him up against the car. Kane suffered severe back pain immediately, he said.

'Aw, shit,' said Strange, under his breath. That was for the benefit of a future lawsuit, right there. Greco opened his eyes, lifted his head up, and looked up at Strange.

Kane claimed to have 'a moment or two' of blackout then. He next recalled lying on his back in the street, with Wilson crouched down upon him, one knee on his chest. There was a gun in Wilson's hand, 'an automatic, I think,' and he was holding it 'point-blank' in Kane's face.

Kane said that he had never known that kind of fear. Spittle had formed on the edges of Wilson's mouth, his face was 'all twisted up with anger,' and he was repeating, 'I'm gonna kill you, motherfucker,' over and over again. Kane had no doubt that Wilson would. He was 'embarrassed to say' that when Chris Wilson pressed the muzzle of the gun to his cheek and rolled it there, Kane 'involuntarily voided' his bowels.

Strange read the police report from the scene. Going by the statement of one officer who reported that he detected a strong fecal smell coming off him, Strange concluded that indeed, Ricky Kane had dirtied his drawers that night.

Kane said that at the point when Wilson had him pinned to the ground, a marked police cruiser pulled onto the scene. Two police officers, one black and one white, got out of the cruiser and ordered Wilson to drop his weapon. Kane's description of the events that followed were roughly in keeping with the statements made by officers Quinn and Franklin.

Strange opened his newspaper clipping file. He went to a section he had marked, an interview with Chris Wilson's girlfriend, who had been with him earlier that night. The girlfriend confirmed that Wilson had been drinking on the night of the shooting and that 'he seemed upset about something.' She didn't know what it was that was making him upset, and he 'didn't say.' He made a mental note of the girlfriend's name.

Strange dialed a number, got the person he was trying to reach on the other end. After some give and take, he managed to make an appointment for later that afternoon. He said, 'Thank you,' and hung the receiver in its cradle.

''Scuse me, old buddy,' said Strange, pulling his feet gently from beneath Greco's head. 'I gotta get to work.'

Strange got into his leather. The dog followed him out of the room.

In the outer office, Strange stopped to talk to Janine while Greco found a spot underneath her desk.

'You talk to Lydell Blue?'

Janine Baker handed him a pink message note, ripped off her pad. 'Lydell ran Kane's name through the local and national crime networks. Kane has no convictions, no arrests. Never got caught with a joint in his sock. Never got caught doing something besides what he was supposed to be doing in a public restroom. No FIs, even, from when he was a kid. No priors whatsoever.'

'Okay. Remind me to give Lydell a call, thank him.'

'He said he owed *you*. Somethin' about somethin' you did for him when the two of you were rookie cops. Good thing you still know a few guys on the force.'

'The ones who aren't dead or retired. I know a few.'

'Hey, boss,' said Ron Lattimer from across the room. Ron wore a spread-collar shirt today with a solid gold tie and deep gray slacks. His split-toe Kenneth Coles were up on his desk, and a newspaper was open in his hands.

'What?'

'Says here that leather of yours is out. The zipper kind, I mean. You need to be gettin' into one of those midlength blazers, man, with a belt, maybe, you want to be looking up-to-the-minute out there on the street.'

'You readin' that article about that book came out, on black men and style?'

'Uh-huh. Called *Men of Color,* somethin' like that.'

'I read the article this morning, too. That lady they got writing about fashion, she's got a funny way of putting things. Says that black men have developed a dynamic sense of style, their "tool against being invisible".'

'Uh-huh. Says here that we black men "use style like a sword and shield",' said Lattimer, reading aloud.

'*All* of us do?'

'See, now, there you go again, Derek.'

''Cause I was wonderin', that old man, practically lives out on Upshur, with the pee stains on the front of his trousers? The one gets his dinner out the Dumpster? Think he's using style as a tool against being invisible? I seen this young brother gettin' off the Metrobus yesterday out on Georgia, had on some orange warm-up suit with green stripes up the side; I wouldn't even use it to cover up Greco's droppings. And look at me, I went and forgot to shine my work boots this morning . . .'

'I get you, man.'

'I just don't like anybody, and I don't care who it is, tellin' me what black men do and don't do. 'Cause that kind of thinking is just as dangerous as that other kind of thinking, if you know what I mean. And you know some white person's gonna read that article and think,

Yeah, *they* spend a lot on clothes, and yeah, *they* spend a lot on cars, but do they save money for their retirement or their children's education, or do they do this or do they do that? You know what I'm sayin'?'

'I said I heard you.'

'It's just another stereotype, man. Positive as it might look on the surface, it's just another thing we've got to live with and live down.'

'Damn, Derek,' said Lattimer, tossing the paper on his desk. 'You just get all upset behind this shit, don't you? All the article's saying is we like to look good. Ain't nothin' more sinister behind it than that.'

'Derek?' said Janine.

'What is it, Janine?'

'Where are you off to now?'

'Workin' on this Chris Wilson thing. I'll be wearing my beeper, you need me.' Strange turned to Lattimer. 'You busy?'

'I'm working a couple of contempt skips. Child-support beefs, that kind of thing.'

'Right now?'

'I was planning on easing into my day, Derek.'

'Want to ride with me this morning?'

'That Chris Wilson case isn't going to pay our bills. I do a couple pick ups, it helps us all.'

'Like to get your thoughts on this, you have the time.'

'Okay. But I got to do some real work this afternoon.'

'Give Terry Quinn a call,' said Strange to Janine. 'The name of the shop he works in is Silver Spring Books, on Bonifant Street. Tell him I'll be by in an hour, he wants to make arrangements to take some time off.'

'You're gonna let the guy you're investigating ride with you?' said Lattimer.

'I'm getting to know him like that,' said Strange. 'Anyway, I told him I'd keep him in the loop.'

Lattimer stood, shook himself into his cashmere, and placed a fedora, dented just right, atop his head.

'Don't feed Greco again,' said Strange to Janine. 'I gave him a full can this morning.'

'Can I give him one of those rawhide bones I keep in my desk?'

'If you'd like.'

On the way out of the office, Strange looked into Janine's eyes and smiled with his. That was just another thing he liked about Janine: she was kind to his dog.

Out on Upshur, Strange nodded at the fedora on Lattimer's head.

'Nice hat,' he said.

'Thank you.'

'That function as a sword or a shield?'

'Keeps my head warm,' said Lattimer, 'you want the plain truth.'

15

Strange drove the Caprice into Southeast. He popped 3 + 3, in his opinion the finest record in the Isley Brothers catalog, into the deck. Ronald Isley was singing that pretty ballad 'Highway of My Life,' and Strange had the urge to sing along. But he knew Lattimer would make some kind of comment on it if he did.

'This is beautiful right here,' said Strange. 'Don't tell me otherwise, 'cause it's something you can't deny.'

'It is pretty nice. But I like somethin's got a little more flow.'

'Song has some positive lyrics to it, too. None of that boasting about beatin' up women, and none of that phony death romance.'

'You know I don't listen to that bullshit, Derek. The music I roll to is hip-hop but on the jazz tip. The Roots, Black Star, like that. That other stuff you're talkin' about, it doesn't speak to me. You ask me, it ain't nothin' but the white music industry exploiting our people all over again. I can see those white record executives now, encouraging those young rappers to put more violence into their music, more disrespect for our women, all because that's what's selling records. And you know I can't get with that.'

'The soul music of the sixties and seventies,' said Strange. 'Won't be anything to come along and replace it, you ask me.'

'Can't get with that, either, Derek. I wasn't even born till nineteen seventy.'

'You missed, young man. You missed.'

Strange turned down 8th Street and took it to M.

'Where we headed?' said Lattimer.

'Titty bar,' said Strange.

'Thank you, boss. This one of those perks you talked about when you hired me?'

'You're staying in the car. This is the place I picked up Sherman Coles for you while you were admiring yourself in a three-way mirror. I just got to ask the doorman a question or two.'

'About Quinn?'

'Uh-huh.'

'I heard Janine say that the man Wilson pulled that gun on, he was clean.'

'Maybe he was. One thing's certain, he made out. According to the papers, the department paid him eighty thousand dollars to make him happy. For the *emotional trauma* he went through and the back injury he sustained when Wilson threw him up against the car.'

'What did Wilson's mother get?'

'A hundred grand, from what I can tell.'

'Cost the police department a lot to make everyone go away on that one.'

'The money was never going to be enough to satisfy his mother, though.'

'You can dig it, right?'

Strange thought of his brother, now thirty years gone, and a woman he'd loved deep and for real back in the early seventies.

'When you lose a loved one to violence,' said Strange, 'ain't no amount of money in the world gonna set things right.'

'How about revenge? Does that do it, you think?'

'No,' said Strange, his mind still on his brother and that girl he'd loved. 'You can never trade a bad life for a good.'

Strange parked on the street, alongside one of the fenced-in lots fronting the strip-bar and bathhouse district. He said to Lattimer, 'Wait here.'

The doorman who'd been at Toot Sweet when Strange had picked up Coles was there again today. He'd gotten his hair cut in a kind of fade, and he wore a baggy sweatsuit, which didn't do a whole lot to hide his bulk. Boy looked like some cross of African and Asian, but Strange figured the majority of it was African, as he'd never seen any kind of Chinaman that big.

'How you doin',' said Strange.

'It's still seven dollars to get in. We ain't gone and changed the cover since the other day.'

'You remember me, huh?'

'You and your friend. White boy did some damage back in the bathroom.'

Strange palmed a folded ten-dollar bill into the doorman's hand. 'I'm not coming in today, so that's not for the cover. That's for you.'

The doorman casually looked over his shoulder, then slipped the ten in the pocket of his sweatpants. 'What you want to know?'

'I was wonderin' about what happened back there in the bathroom.'

'What happened? Your partner fucked that big boy *up*. Went into the kitchen and got a tenderizing mallet, then went into the bathroom and broke big boy's nose real quick. Kicked him a couple of times while he was down, too. I had to clean up the blood myself. There was plenty *of* it, too.'

'What you do with the big guy?'

'One of my coworkers drove him to D.C. General and dropped him off. They got a doctor over there, this Dr Sanders, we've seen him put together guys got torn apart in this place real nice. So we figure we put him in good hands.'

'Why didn't you phone the cops?'

'The big guy didn't want us to. Right away I'm thinkin' he's got warrants out on him, right? And the management, they don't want to see any cops within a mile of this place. Not to mention, you and your buddy, I know you're not cops, but whatever the fuck your game is, you probably know enough real policemen to make it rough on the owner to keep doing business here, know what I'm sayin'? I mean, we're not stupid.'

'I didn't think you were.'

'Next time you bring white boy around here, though—'

'I know. Put him on a leash.'

The doorman smiled and patted his pocket. 'You want another receipt?'

'It's tempting,' said Strange. 'But I'll pass.'

On the way back to the car, Strange thought, Maybe I'm giving this Terry Quinn too much credit. Sure, it could have gone down the way he said it did with Wilson. But maybe it was just that some switch got thrown, like all of a sudden the 'tilt' sign flashed on inside his head. A young man with that kind of violence in him, you couldn't tell.

Quinn was shaking the shoulder of a guy called himself Moonman, sleeping by the space heater in the room at the back of the shop. Moonman's clothes were courtesy of Shepherd's Table, and he showered and ate in the new Progress Place, a shelter off Georgia, behind the pool hall and pawnshops, back along the Metro tracks. Daytime he spent out on the street. Today was a cold one, and when it got bitter like this Quinn let Moonman sleep in the science fiction room in the back.

'Hey, Moon. Wake up, buddy, you gotta get going. Syreeta's coming in, and you know she doesn't like you sleeping back here.'

'All right.'

Moon got himself to his feet. He hadn't been using the showers at Progress Place all that often. That bad smell of street person that was body odor and cigarettes and alcohol and rot came off him, and Quinn backed up a step as Moon got his bearings. There were crumbs of some kind and egg yolk crusted in his beard. Quinn had given him the coat he was wearing, an old charcoal REI winter number with a blue lining. It was the warmest coat Quinn had ever owned.

'Take this,' said Quinn, handing him a dollar bill, enough for a cup of coffee, not enough for a drink.

'A ducat,' said Moon, examining the one. 'Do you know, the term refers to an actual gold coin, a type of currency formerly used in Europe? The word was appropriated as slang by twentieth-century African Americans. Over the years it's become a standard term in the Ebonic vocabulary . . .'

'That's nice,' said Quinn, gently steering Moonman out of the room toward the front door.

'I'll spend it well.'

As he walked behind him, Quinn saw the paperback wedged in a back pocket of Moonman's sorry trousers. 'And bring that book back when you're done.'

'*The Stars My Destination*, by Bester. It's not just a book, Terry. It is a mind-blowing journey, a literary achievement of Olympian proportions . . .'

'Bring it back when you're done.'

Quinn watched Moonman walk out the front door. People in the neighborhood liked to treat Moon as their pet intellectual, speculating on how such a 'mentally gifted guy' could slip through society's cracks, but Quinn didn't have any interest in listening to Moonman's ramblings. He let Moonman sleep in the back because it was cold outside, and he gave him his coat because he didn't care to see him die.

Quinn stopped by the arts and entertainment room and looked inside the open door. A middle-aged guy with dyed hair and liver lips studied a photography book called *Kids Around the World*. He faced the wall and held the book close to his chest. He had the same look as the wet-eyed fat guy who hung back in the hobbies and sports room, and the young white man with the very short haircut, his face pale and acned, who lingered in the military history room and stared half smiling at the photos in the Nazi-atrocity books shelved there. Quinn recognized them all: the ineffectual losers and the creeps and the pedophiles, all the friendless fucks who didn't really want to hurt anyone but who always did. Syreeta said to leave them alone, that the books were a healthy kind of outlet for their unhealthy desires, the alternative was that they would be out there on the street.

Quinn knew that they *were* out there on the street. Syreeta was all right, a good woman with good intentions, but Quinn had seen things for real and she had not. Sick motherfuckers, all of them. He'd like to get them all in one room and—

'Hey, Terry.' It was Lewis, standing before him, a box of hardbacks in his arms. Lewis's eyeglasses had slipped down to the tip of his nose. 'I finished racking the new vinyl. Now I've got to get these fictions shelved. You want to watch the register for me?'

'Yeah, sure.'

Quinn went up to the front of the shop. He phoned Juana to confirm their date for that evening. He'd had a long phone conversation with her the previous night. He'd gotten an erection just talking to her, listening to the sound of her voice. It was driving him crazy, thinking of her eyes, her hair, those dark nipples, that warm pussy, her fine hands. It had been that way with other girls who'd turned him on, but this was *different,* yeah, he wanted to hit it, but he wanted to just *be* with her, too. He left a message on her machine.

Quinn went behind the register counter and read some of *Desperadoes,* a western by Ron Hansen. It was one of his favorites, a classic, and he was reading it for the second time, but he found it hard to concentrate, and he set the book down. He stood and flipped through the used albums in the bins beside the register area. Another Natalie Cole had come in, along with a Brothers Johnson, a Spooky Tooth, and a Haircut 100. He picked up a record that had a bunch of seventies-looking black guys on its cover, three different pictures of them jumping around out on a landing strip. He read the title on the album and smiled.

The bell over the door chimed as Syreeta Janes walked into the shop. Syreeta was at the tail end of her forties, on the heavy side, with a nice brown freckled face, high cheekbones, and deep chestnut eyes. Half of her time was spent in the shop, the other half at book conventions or in her home office, working on her Web site, where she bought and sold rare paperbacks. She wore her usual, a vest and shirt arrangement worn out over a flowing long skirt and clogs, with a brightly colored kufi atop dreads. Lewis, in one of his less serious moments, had described her look as 'Harlem by way of Takoma Park.'

'Terry.'

'Syreeta.'

'Taking off?'

'Soon as my ride comes. I might be asking for more time off, too.'

'Long as Lewis covers, I don't mind.' Syreeta put her canvas bag down on the glass counter. 'Don't you need the money, though?'

'My pension's keeping me flush.'

Quinn looked out the window as a white Caprice pulled to the curb. He rang the register, put money in the drawer, and cradled the record he had found in the bin as he grabbed his leather off the tree.

'That your ride?'

'Yeah.'

'Looks like a cop car.'

'It is.'

'Terry?'

'Huh.'

'Smells funky in here.'

'Moonman. He borrowed a paperback, too. *The Stars My Destination,* you want to knock it off the inventory.'

'That's a good one.'

'Olympian,' said Quinn.

'You're gonna let him sleep here,' said Syreeta, 'spray a little Lysol through the place before I get in.'

Quinn didn't hear her. He was already out the door.

16

'After I went through all that trouble,' said Strange, 'now you're gonna tell me you can't go?'

'I apologize,' said Lattimer. 'I know you went and got the tickets and all that, but Cheri said she doesn't want to go to some dark auditorium and watch two men beat the fuck out of each other all night.'

'That girl of yours must be special, you gonna pass up tickets to a title bout. This is a Don King production, too, ain't no thing someone's puttin' on in their basement. You should have told me she was gonna act like that before I bought the tickets, man.'

'I didn't know.'

Strange watched Quinn cross the street, a record under his arm. 'There he is.'

'What's with white boys and flannel shirts?' said Lattimer. 'A chain saw come with that outfit when he bought it?'

'Everybody's got their own thing.'

'He don't look all that violent to me. And he doesn't look like a cop.'

'He is on the short side,' said Strange. 'But, trust me, he can rise up.'

Quinn opened the passenger-side door and got into the backseat.

'Terry. Meet Ron Lattimer, an investigator on my staff.'

'Ron, how you doin'?'

'I'm makin' out.'

Quinn reached his hand over the front bench, and Lattimer shook it.

'What you got there, Terry?' said Strange.

'It's for you.'

Quinn passed the Blackbyrds' *Flying Start* up to Strange. Strange smiled as he examined the cover. He opened it and studied the inner sleeve, a photo of the group in an airplane hanger.

'Damn, boy. On the Fantasy label, too. I never thought I'd see one of these again.'

'It just came in today.'

Strange scanned the liner notes. 'Just like I remember it. These boys were students at Howard when they cut this record. They were studying under Donald Byrd, see—'

'Derek,' said Lattimer, 'I got things to do this afternoon.'

'Yeah, okay, right.' Strange put the record on the seat beside him. 'Y'all hungry?'

'There's a Vietnamese around the corner,' said Quinn. 'The soup there rocks.'

'I'm into that,' said Strange.

Strange engaged the trans and pulled off the curb. He went up to Georgia, turned left at Quinn's direction, and drove south. At the stoplight he opened the record again, chuckled to himself as he checked out the period threads and oversized lids on the members of the group.

'That was real nice of you, Terry.'

'I know you're not looking for any friends,' said Quinn, catching Strange's eyes in the rearview. 'I just thought you'd like it, that's all.'

Strange, Lattimer, and Quinn got a window table at My-Le, a former beer garden, now a *pho* house on Selim. Their view gave to the traffic on Georgia Avenue and the railroad tracks beyond.

'They're doing something over there,' said Quinn, nodding to the station by the tracks. A blue tarp covered the roof, and plywood boards had replaced the windows.

'Looks like they're restoring it,' said Lattimer.

'Either that or tearing it down. They're always tearing down things here now.'

'Get rid of all these pawnshops—'

'Yeah, and the nail and braid parlors, and the barbershops, and the cobbler and the key maker, the speed shops and auto parts stores . . . the kinds of places working people use every day. So the yuppie homeowners can brag that they've got the music-and-book superstore, and the boutique grocery store, and the Starbucks, just like their counterparts across town.'

'I take it,' said Strange, 'you're not all the way into the revitalization of Silver Spring.'

'They're erasing all of my memories,' said Quinn. 'And to tell you the truth, I kind of like the decay.'

The lone waiter, a genial guy named Daniel who painted houses on the side, served them their soup and fresh lemonade.

Lattimer stared into his bowl and frowned. 'There's none of that bible tripe or tendon or nothin' like that in there, is it?'

'Number fifteen,' said Quinn. 'Nothing but eye round.'

The soup was a rich mixture of rice noodles, meat, and broth, with bean sprouts, hot green pepper, lime, and fresh mint served on the side. Strange and Quinn prepared theirs and added hot garlic sauce from a squeeze bottle. Lattimer slung his tie back over his shoulder, watched them, and followed suit.

'Were you a cop, too?' asked Quinn, the fragrant steam from the soup warming his face.

'Me?' said Lattimer. 'Nah.'

'He didn't like the way the uniforms were cut,' said Strange.

'Go ahead, Derek. I always wanted to do the kind of investigative work I'm doing right now. Never wanted to do anything else. Besides, you don't mind my sayin' so, all the problems they got on the force, I feel lucky I *didn't* join up.'

'There's a helluva lot more good cops on the force than there are mediocre ones,' said Quinn. 'And there's not many who are plain bad. The ones who weren't ready to be out on the street, that wasn't their fault. The situation you had back then, the fish stank from the head down.'

'That explain all those shootings?' said Strange.

'Firing on unarmed suspects, firing at moving vehicles . . .' said Lattimer, picking up the ball from Strange.

'Who's gonna decide whether they're armed or unarmed in the heat of the moment, when some guy's reaching into his jacket, huh?' said Quinn. 'In this climate we got now, out there on the street? With all the criminals having access to guns, the attitudes, the cold-blooded murder of cops . . . it's not much of a leap to make the assumption that, if you're wearing a uniform, you're in harm's way. Look, man, what I'm trying to tell you is, a lot of us out there, we were scared. Can you understand that?'

Lattimer didn't answer, but he held Quinn's gaze.

Strange broke apart his chopsticks and used them to find some eye round in the bottom of his bowl. 'Like I said, that doesn't explain everything.'

'It's complicated,' said Quinn. '*You* know that. You were out there, Derek. You *know.*'

'All right, then,' said Strange. 'You had a couple of brutality complaints in your file, right?' He swallowed meat and noodles and wiped a napkin across his mouth.

'That's right,' said Quinn. 'So did Chris Wilson. So do a lot of cops. Legitimate or no, once a complaint gets made, it stays in your file.'

'What were yours about?'

'Mine were about bullshit,' said Quinn. 'Guy hits his head on the lip of the cruiser's back door when you're putting him in, guy claims you slapped the cuffs on him too tight . . . like that. It never goes into the report what was said to you, how many times *you're* disrespected in the course of a night.'

Strange nodded. He remembered all of that very well. He remembered, too, how cops got hardened after a while, until what they saw in certain parts of town were not the citizens they had sworn to protect but potential criminals, men and women and children alike. A white cop looking at a black face, that was something further still.

'Listen,' said Quinn. 'You guys remember a few years back, this black cop pulled over a drunken white woman, coming out of Georgetown or somewhere like it, late one night?'

'That's the girl that cop handcuffed to a stop sign,' said Lattimer, 'made her sit her ass down in the cold street. Some photographer happened to be there, caught a picture of the whole thing.'

'Right,' said Quinn. 'Now, Derek, tell me what you thought about that incident, the first time you read it.'

'I know what you're gettin' at,' said Strange. 'That the police officer, he didn't just do that to that girl for no reason. That she must have said something to him—'

'Like what?'

'I don't know. How about, "Get your hands off me, you black bastard," somethin' like that.'

'Or maybe she even called him a nigger,' said Quinn.

Lattimer looked up from his bowl. He didn't like to hear that word coming from a white man's mouth, no matter the context.

'Maybe she did,' said Strange.

'The point is, whether it happened that way or not, those kinds of conversations go on in the street every night between cops and perps and straight civilians. And what's said, it never sees the light of day.'

'You goin' somewhere with this?' said Strange.

'Yeah,' said Lattimer, 'I was kind of wondering the same thing.'

'All right,' said Quinn, leaning forward, his forearms resting on the four-top. 'You want to know what happened that night? As far as my role in it, it's in the transcripts and the news reports. There's nothing been left out, no secret. A man pointed a gun at me, and as a police officer, I reacted in the manner I was trained to do. In retrospect, I made the wrong decision, and it cost an innocent man his life. But only in retrospect. I didn't know that Chris Wilson was a cop.'

'Go on,' said Strange.

'Why was Chris Wilson holding a gun on Ricky Kane? Why did Wilson have that look of naked anger that I saw that night on his face?'

'The official line was, it was a routine stop,' said Strange. 'Must have just degenerated into something else.'

'An off-duty cop takes the time to pull over and hassle a guy for pissin' in the street?'

'Doesn't make much sense,' said Strange. 'I'll give you that. But let's suppose Wilson did just pull over and decide to do his job, whether he was wearin' his uniform or not.'

'We don't know what happened between Wilson and Kane,' said Quinn. 'We don't know what was *said.*'

'We'll never know. Wilson's dead, and all we've got is Kane's version of the event. Kane's got a clean sheet. *Kane* didn't shoot Wilson, so there wasn't any reason for the inquiry to be directed toward him.'

'I'm not tellin' you guys how to do your jobs,' said Quinn. 'But if it was me got hired to make Wilson's memorial look better, I'd start by talking to Kane.'

'I plan to,' said Strange.

'But Kane's got no incentive to talk to anyone,' said Quinn.

'It's gonna be difficult, I know.'

'And he sure as hell's not gonna talk with me around,' said Quinn.'

'That's not why I picked you up today.'

'Yeah? Who we goin' to see?'

'Eugene Franklin,' said Strange. 'Your old partner. We're meetin' him in a bar in an hour or so.'

Quinn nodded, then placed his napkin on the table and went to the small bathroom next to the restaurant's karaoke machine.

Lattimer drank off the remaining broth from his bowl and sat back in his chair. 'You gonna drop me off at the office on the way to that bar?'

'Sure,' said Strange. 'What do you think?'

'The man is troubled,' said Lattimer. 'But what he's saying, it makes sense.'

They split the check and went to the car. Driving down Georgia Avenue, they passed the Fourth District Police Station, renamed the

Brian T. Gibson Building in honor of the officer who was slain in his cruiser outside the Ibex nightclub, shot three times by a sociopath with a gun. Officer Gibson left a wife and baby daughter behind.

17

Down on 2nd Street, blocks away from the District Courthouse and the FOP bar, was a saloon called Upstairs at Erika's, located on the second floor of a converted row house, across from the Department of Labor. The joint had become a hangout for cops, cop groupies, U.S. marshals and local and federal prosecutors. Next door was another bar and eatery that catered to rugby players, college kids, government workers, and defense attorneys, most of them white. There was business enough for both establishments to exist side by side, as the clientele at Upstairs at Erika's was almost entirely black.

Strange got a couple of beers from the bartender, a fine young woman favored by the low lights, tipped her, and asked for a receipt. When she returned with it he asked her to put some Frankie Beverly and Maze on the house box. He'd met a woman for drinks here one night, not too long ago, and he knew they had it behind the bar. Maze was a D.C. favorite; though recorded years ago, you still heard their music all over town, at clubs, weddings, and at family reunions and picnics in Rock Creek Park.

'Which one you want to hear?' asked the bartender.

'The one got "Southern Girl" on it.'

'You got it.'

He carried the two bottles of beer back toward a table set against a brick wall, where he had left Quinn. Quinn was standing and giving a hug to a black man around his age, the both of them patting each other on the back. Strange had to guess that this was Eugene Franklin.

'How you doin'?' said Strange, arriving at the table. 'Derek Strange.'

'Eugene Franklin.' Strange shook his hand, but Franklin's grip was deliberately weak, and the smile he had been sharing with Quinn began to fade.

Franklin was the size of Strange, freshly barbered and fit but with a face with features that did not quite seem to belong together. Strange thought it was the buck teeth, pronounced enough to be near comic, and Franklin's large, liquid eyes; they did not complete the hard shell he was trying to project.

'You want a beer, somethin'?'

'I don't drink,' said Franklin.

They sat down and spent an uncomfortable moment of silence. A couple of guys with the unmistakable look of cops, a combination of guard and bravado, walked by the table. One of them said hello to Franklin and then looked at Quinn.

'Terry, how you doin', man?'

'Doin' okay.'

'You look good, man. Long hair and everything.'

'I'm tryin'.'

'All right, then. Take it light, hear?'

Strange saw the other man give Quinn a hard once-over before he and his partner walked away. He figured that Quinn still had some friends and supporters on the force and that there were others who would no longer give him the time of day.

'You gonna be all right in here?' said Strange.

'I know most of these guys,' said Quinn. 'It's cool.'

Strange glanced around the bar. By now word had gotten around that Terry Quinn was in the place, and he noticed some curious looks and a few unfriendly stares. Maybe Strange's imagination was running wild on him. It wasn't any of his business, and he wasn't going to worry about it either way.

'You called,' said Franklin, 'and I'm here. Not to rush you, but I'm due for a shift and I don't have all that much time.'

'Right.' Strange pushed a business card across the table. As Franklin read the card, Strange said, 'I appreciate you hookin' up with us.'

'You said you were working for Chris Wilson's mom.'

'Uh-huh. She was concerned about her son's reputation. She thought it got tarnished in the wake of the shooting.'

'The newspapers and the TV,' said Franklin, with a bitter shrug. 'You know how they do.'

'I'm just trying to clear things up. If I can take away some of that shadow that got thrown on Wilson . . . that's all I'm trying to accomplish.'

'It's all in the transcripts. You're a private investigator' – Strange caught the kernel of contempt in Franklin's voice – 'you ought to have a way of getting your hands on the files.'

'I already have. And Terry here has given me his version of the event. You don't mind, I'd like for you to do the same.'

Franklin looked at Quinn. Quinn drank off some of his beer and gave Franklin a tight nod. Strange took his voice-activated recorder from his leather, turned on the power, and set the recorder on the table.

Franklin pointed a lazy finger at the unit. 'Uh-uh. Turn that bullshit off, or I walk away.'

Strange made a point of pressing down on the power button but did not press it hard enough to turn it off. He slipped the recorder back into his jacket.

'All right, man,' said Franklin. 'Where you want me to begin?'

Strange told him, then sat back in his chair.

Their beer bottles were empty by the time Franklin was done. Strange had to smile a little, watching Franklin watch *him*, waiting for some kind of reaction or reply. Because it was almost funny how identical Franklin's account was to Quinn's. And no two recollections of a single event could be that on-the-one, that tight.

'What?' said Franklin.

'Nothin', really,' said Strange. 'Not that it's significant or anything like that . . . What I was wondering is, if the danger was that imminent, that clear, why didn't you fire down on Wilson, too?'

'Because Terry fired first.'

'You would have shot Wilson if Terry hadn't?'

'I can't say what I *would* have done.'

'But you're sayin' he was right.'

'He was *all* the way right. I saw where Wilson's gun was headed. I saw in his eyes what he planned to do. There's no doubt in my mind, if Terry hadn't shot Wilson, Wilson would have shot me. You understand what I'm sayin'? No doubt at all.'

Strange ran his thumb along his jawline. 'You're so sure . . . and that's what's botherin' me, Eugene. See, I was at MLK, pulling up all the newspaper stories, the ones they did at the time and the follow-ups, too, and there was this one thing I read that I just can't reconcile.'

'Oh, yeah? What's that?'

'After your partner left the force, you joined that group of cops, called itself the Concerned Black Officers. Y'all had flyers put up tellin' the brothers in uniform to stage a protest. I believe you signed the petition your own self, too.'

Franklin's eyes flickered past Quinn's. 'I did.'

'If Quinn was so right—'

'Look here,' said Franklin. 'Terry *was* right, in that particular case. But since ninety-five, we've had three off-duty African American police officers shot by white cops. It's bad enough, the danger I put myself in every day, without having to be a target for the guys on my own team. So yeah, I was concerned. And anyway, Strange, that's internal police business, understand? It is not any business of yours. It's between me and my fellow cops, and my partner.'

'Your ex-partner, you mean.'

Something passed between Franklin and Quinn. Strange could see that their bond was strong. Maybe it even bordered on affection. But however strong it had been, it was tainted by the shooting, and what had been ruined was most likely beyond repair.

Franklin shook his head and looked down at the table. 'You're somethin', Strange.'

'Just doin' my job.'

'Punch out your time card, then. 'Cause I am done talkin' for today.'

'Yeah, I guess we covered it for now.' Strange stood from his chair. 'I'll leave the two of you alone for a few minutes. This beer goes through me quick.'

As Strange went along the bar toward the head, Franklin watched his walk, the hint of swagger in it, the straight shoulders and back.

'Man walks like a cop,' said Franklin.

'He was one,' said Quinn, 'a long time ago.'

'Wasn't till I saw him move,' said Franklin, 'that it showed.'

Strange stopped at the bar to talk to a cop he knew, now retired, named Al Smith. Smith had been partnered up for years with a guy named Larry Michaels. Smith had gone gray, and his paunch told Strange that this was where he spent his days.

'I buy you one?' said Smith.

'One's my limit in the daytime, Al, and I already had it.'

'Next time. And if I don't see you here, I'll *see* you, hear?'

Strange chuckled. Al Smith had been using the same cornball expressions for the past thirty years.

Strange nodded to a big man with a high forehead and a flat-bridged, upturned nose, sitting at the bar and smoking a thick cigar, who looked at him dead-eyed as he passed. The man didn't nod back. He moved his gaze into his beer mug, raised it, and took a deep drink. Strange noticed that the MPD T-shirt fit tightly on the man's broad chest, his bulked-up arms stretching the fabric of the sleeves.

In the bathroom, he took a leak into a stand-up urinal, singing along to 'Joy and Pain' as it came trebly through small wall-mounted speakers. He zipped up and turned around as the man in the MPD T-shirt entered, tall and looking like a bear on two feet, pushing the bathroom door so hard it hit the wall.

All right, you're drunk, thought Strange. Tell the world.

'Excuse me, brother,' said Strange, in a friendly way, because the man was blocking his path. 'Can I get by?'

But the man didn't move or react in any way. His expression was dull, and his face was shiny with sweat. Strange was going to ask him again but decided against it. He moved around the man, his back brushing the wall in the cramped space, and went out the door.

Strange had known plenty of uniforms like this one. Guy had a day off from all the bad shit out there, and instead of relaxing, he was in a bar, wearing his MPD shirt, getting meaner with every beer and looking to start a fight. One of those cops who was carrying serious insecurities, always trying to test himself. Well, if he was wantin' to try someone, he'd have to find someone else. Strange had left all that bullshit behind a long time ago.

'How you been makin' out?' said Franklin.

'I'm doin' okay,' said Quinn. 'Working in a used book store over the District line. It's real . . . *quiet*.'

'Gives you time to read those cowboys-and-Indians books you like.'

'I do have time.'

'Seein' anyone?'

'I have a girl. You'd like her. She's nice.'

'She fine, too?'

'Uh-huh.'

'Dog like you. Never known you to be with an ugly one.'

'No one could say the same about you.'

'Go ahead and crack on me. But it's one of the reasons I stopped drinkin'. Got tired of waking up next to those *fugly*-ass girls I was meetin' in the clubs.'

'Wonder how many of them stopped drinkin' when they got a look at you.'

'I guess I did send a few off to church.'

Franklin and Quinn shared a laugh. Franklin's odd looks had always bothered him, along with his inability to make time with attractive women. Quinn had been one of the few who could broach the subject, and joke about it, with Eugene.

Quinn looked around Erika's. He recognized Al Smith, sitting on his usual stool, and a patrolman named Effers he'd played cards with once, and an ugly, friendless cop he knew by sight only, Adonis Delgado, who was pushing away from the bar.

'You miss it,' said Franklin, 'don't you?'

'I do.'

'Listen, Terry . . .'

'What?'

'That thing Strange was talking about, the group I joined – Concerned Black Officers, I mean.'

'I knew about it already.'

'Didn't have anything to do with how I felt about you, or whether you were right or wrong on the Wilson thing. You understand that, don't you?'

'Sure.'

'We'd been asking for radios for off-duty officers for years, so that if you did get into a situation when you were in street clothes, you could call it in, let the dispatcher know that you were a cop and you were on the scene.'

'I know it.'

'If Chris Wilson had had that radio that night, and we had known who he was when we pulled up on him, he'd be alive today.'

'Y'all got your radios now. I read about it, that the issue finally went through.'

'It took that last shooting, and the threat of a protest, to get it done. And Chief Ramsey, he's toughened the firearms instruction requirements, instituted retraining. Got a whole lot of new initiatives drafted, with new hiring standards on the way, too.'

'You tryin' to tell me it was a good thing that Wilson died? Don't go blowin' smoke up my ass, man, 'cause I've known you too long.'

'I'm tellin' you that some good came *out* of it. Whatever I thought about what happened that night, it was on me to get involved, make sure that somethin' like that couldn't happen again.'

'I bet it was good for your conscience, too.'

'There was that.'

'Don't worry, Gene. I don't blame you for anything. I would have liked to hear from you once in a while, but I don't blame you for a thing.'

'I thought about calling you,' said Franklin. 'And then I thought, Outside of our shift, me and Terry never hung out, anyway. I don't recall us speaking on the phone more than once or twice when we were riding together, do you?'

'You're right. We never hung out.'

'We got different things. Different kinds of lives, interests, different friends. You and me used to talk about it, remember? Ain't no kind of crime for people to want to hang with their own kind.'

'It's a shame,' said Quinn. 'But it's no crime.'

'Anyway,' said Franklin, 'I gotta bounce.'

'Go ahead. Nice seeing you. Gene. Stay away from the fuglies, hear?'

Franklin blushed. 'I'm gonna try.'

They stood, hugged again, and broke apart awkwardly. Franklin did not meet Quinn's eyes before walking away. Franklin passed Strange on his way back from the head but did not acknowledge him at all.

'Friendly place they got here,' said Strange as he arrived at the table. 'Your boy Eugene is a card-carrying member of my fan club, and some Carl Eller-lookin' sucker back in the bathroom was wantin' to take my head off.'

'You know cops,' said Quinn. 'They like to stick to their own kind.'

'I've got a couple more stops today,' said Strange. 'I'd take you home, but it's not on my way.'

'Drop me at the Union Station Metro,' said Quinn. 'I'll catch the Red Line uptown.'

Strange pulled the Caprice away from the curb. '*Nevada Smith* is on TNT tonight. You know that one?'

'Uh-huh. That's a good one. McQueen was the real thing.'

'That's the one ends with that old guy from *Streets of San Francisco,* with the nose—'

'Karl Malden.'

'Yeah, him. McQueen shoots him a couple of times, but he doesn't kill him. Gets off of that revenge trip he's been on right there, finds his humanity, and leaves Malden in the river. McQueen's riding away on his horse, and Malden's yellin' at him to finish him off, screaming, over and over, "You're yella . . . you haven't got the guts!" I get the chills thinkin' about it, man.'

'You gonna watch it?'

'I'm takin' a woman to the fights.'

'Your girlfriend?'

'More like a friend kind of thing, the woman who runs my office, Janine Baker. I been knowin' her for a long time. Nothin' all that serious.'

'Friend kind of thing's the best kind, you ask me.'

'Yeah, I believe you're right. What about you?'

'I got a date myself. Girl named Juana I been seeing.'

Strange looked across the bench. 'Y'all got specific plans?'

'We were just going to go out, figure it out then.'

'Why don't the two of you come with me and Janine? I got extra tickets, man.'

'I wouldn't mind. But I have to see if Juana's into it.'

'Check it out with her and give me a call. My beeper number's on that card I gave you.'

'I will.'

Strange turned onto North Capitol. Quinn said, 'Here's good,' and opened the door as Strange slowed the car to a stop.

'Hey, Terry. Thanks again for the record, man.'

'My pleasure,' said Quinn.

They shook hands. Quinn walked toward Union Station. Strange drove north.

18

Strange stood in Chris Wilson's bedroom, examining the objects on his dresser. There was a cigar box holding cuff links, a crucifix on a chain, a Mason's ring with a black onyx stone, ticket stubs from the MCI Center and RFK, and a pickup stub from Safeway. There were shoehorns and pens in a ceramic police-union mug. A small color photograph of Wilson's sister, pretty and sharply dressed, had been slipped beneath the mug. A nail clipper, a long-lensed camera, a pearl-handled knife, a bottle of CK cologne, and a crystal bowl holding matches from various bars and restaurants sat atop the dresser, as did a well-used, autographed hardball, scuffed and stained by grass and mud.

Beside the dresser mirror, hung on the wall, was a framed photograph of Chris Wilson as a boy, standing under the arm of Larry Brown, with a message from Brown and his signature scrawled across the print. Team photographs of the Redskins going back fifteen years and posters, framed cheaply and mounted, of college and professional basketball players, local boxers, and other athletes and sporting events were hung on the walls as well. The room reflected an unsurprising blend of boy and man.

'I've left it exactly as it was,' said Leona Wilson, standing behind Strange. 'He was so proud of that picture we took with Larry Brown.'

'I've got a signed photo of Larry myself,' said Strange. 'Proud to have mine, too.'

'I remember one time I was straightening the picture, and Chris walked in and just got so upset, told me to leave it alone. Of course, he hardly ever raised his voice to me.'

'Some things special to a man might seem trivial to others. I got this Redskins figure on my desk, got a spring for a neck—'

'Chris grew up in this room. He never lived anywhere else. I suppose if he had moved out and gotten his own place, his new room wouldn't have looked like this. He kept it much the same way as he did when he was a boy.'

'Yes, ma'am.'

'I never asked him to stay, Mr Strange. After his father died, he took it upon himself to become the man of the house. He felt it was his role, to take care of me and his sister. I never asked him to do that. He took it upon himself.'

Strange looked around the room. 'Chris keep any kind of journals? He keep a diary, anything like that?'

'Not that I'm aware of.'

'You don't mind, I'd like to take these matchbooks from this bowl here. I'll return them, and anything else I take.'

Leona Wilson nodded and wrung her hands.

'Chris had a girlfriend at the time of his death, didn't he?' said Strange. 'I'm talking about the one gave the statement to the newspapers.'

'That's right.'

'Think it would be possible to talk to her?'

'She's been wonderful. She has dinner with me once or twice a month. She and her little girl, a lovely child she had before she met Chris. I'll call her if you'd like.'

'I would. Like to meet with her as soon as possible, matter of fact. And I'd like to speak to your daughter, too.'

Leona lowered her eyes.

'Mrs Wilson?'

'Yes.'

'Do you know how I can get ahold of your daughter?'

'I don't.' Leona shook her head. 'We lost her to drugs, Mr Strange.'

'What happened?'

'How can anyone know? She was in college out at Bowie State and working as a hostess in a restaurant downtown. She was a beautiful girl. She was doing so well.'

'She was living here then?'

'Sondra had gotten her own place, and that's when we began to lose touch. Chris and I saw her less and less frequently, and when we did see her . . . she had changed, physically, I mean, but also her attitude. I didn't recognize her, couldn't confide in her the way I always could before. It was Chris who finally sat me down and told me what was wrong. I didn't believe it at first. We were so watchful of her during her high school years, and she had gotten through them fine. After she got in trouble, it was as if she had forgotten everything she had learned, here at home and in church. I didn't understand. I still don't understand.

'The day of the funeral, she showed up at the cemetery. I hadn't seen her for a month or so. Her phone had been disconnected, and she had been fired from her job. She had dropped out of college, too.'

'If you hadn't seen her, then how did you know all of those events had taken place?'

'Chris knew.'

'He was in contact with her?'

'I don't know how he knew. He was close to her . . . He was very upset, Mr Strange. But in the end, even he had lost track of her. We didn't know if she had a roof over her head, if she was eating, where she lived, where she slept. We didn't know if she was living or dead.'

'So she was at the funeral.'

'She looked barely alive that day. Her eyes, even her steps were without life. I hadn't seen her for so long. I haven't seen her since.'

'I'm sorry.'

'If Chris were here, he'd find her.' Tears broke and ran down Leona's sunken cheeks. 'Excuse me, Mr Strange.'

She turned and walked quickly from the room.

Strange did not follow. After a while he heard her talking on the living room phone. He went to the dresser and emptied the crystal bowl of matchbooks, transferring them into the pockets of his leather. He slid the photograph of Sondra Wilson out from beneath the mug and placed it in his wallet. He paced the room. He sat on Chris Wilson's bed and looked out the window.

Strange could imagine Wilson as a boy, waking up in this room, hearing the songbirds, recognizing the bark of the same dogs every morning. Looking out that same window and dreaming about catching the winning pass, knocking one out of the ballpark with the bases full, a pretty girl he sat near in class. Smelling breakfast cooking, maybe hearing his mother humming a tune in the kitchen as she prepared it, waiting for her to poke her head through the door, tell him it was time to get up and off to school.

Strange heard Leona Wilson's sobs from out in the living room. Trying to stifle it, then crying full on.

'You all right, Derek,' said Strange under his breath, feeling useless and angry at himself for having given the Wilson woman false hope.

He walked out to the living room and stood beside her where she sat on the couch, clutching a cloth handkerchief. Strange put a hand on her bony shoulder.

'It's so hard,' she said, almost a whisper. 'So hard.'

'Yes, ma'am,' said Strange.

She wiped her face and looked up at him with red-rimmed eyes. 'Have you made any progress?'

'I'll have a report for you very soon.'

Leona handed Strange a slip of paper off the coffee table. 'Here's Renee's address. She's going to pick her daughter up at day care, but she'll be home soon. She'll see you if you'd like.'

'Thank you,' said Strange.

He patted her shoulder impotently again and walked away.

'Will I see you in church this Sunday, Mr Strange?'

'I hope to be there,' said Strange, keeping his pace.

He couldn't get through the door fast enough. Out on the sidewalk, he stood for a moment and breathed fresh air.

Renee Austin lived in a garden apartment complex set behind a shopping center in the Maryland suburbs, out Route 29 and off Cherry Hill Road. Strange waited in the parking lot, listening to an old Harold Melvin and the Blue Notes, as Renee had not yet returned from picking up her daughter. Strange was singing along to 'Pretty Flower,' closing his eyes and trying to mimic Teddy's growl, when Renee's red Civic pulled into the lot.

They sat at her kitchen table, drinking instant coffee. Renee's daughter, a darling little three year old named Kia, sat on the linoleum floor. Kia had a dark-skinned doll in one hand and a freckly faced, cartoonish-looking white baby in the other, and she was pressing their faces together, loudly going, 'Mmm, mmm, mmm.'

'Honey,' said Renee, 'hush, please. We are trying to talk, and it's hard to hear ourselves with those sounds you're makin'.'

'Rugrat kissing Groovy Girl, Momma!' said Kia.

'Yes, baby,' said Renee. 'I know.'

Renee was a good-looking, dark-skinned young woman with long painted nails and a sculpted, lean face. Her hair had been chemically relaxed, and she wore it in a shoulder-length, fashionable cut. She worked as an administrative assistant for an accounting firm on Connecticut and L, and she stayed there, she said, not for pay or opportunities but for the firm's flexible schedule, which allowed her more time with Kia.

She was a tired-looking twenty-one. Renee told Strange that she had planned to register for community college courses but that Kia's arrival and the father's subsequent departure had dimmed those plans. Strange noticed all the toys, televisions, and stereo equipment spread about the apartment, and Renee's Honda had looked brand-new. He wondered how far she was overextended, if she had dug a credit hole so deep that she couldn't even see the light from where she stood.

'Maybe when she gets into a full day of school,' said Strange, 'you can go after that college degree.'

'Maybe,' said Renee, her voice trailing off, both of them knowing that it would never happen that way.

Renee talked about Chris Wilson, how they had met, what kind of man he was. How he had been 'a better father' to Kia than Kia's own blood had been.

'How about when he drank?' said Strange. 'Was he good to her then?'

'Chris hardly drank more than one, maybe two beers at a time. When I first met him, he barely drank at all.'

'What about the night he was killed?'

Renee nodded, looking into her coffee mug. 'He had been drinking pretty heavy, here at the apartment, earlier that night. He had gone through, I don't know, maybe a six-pack over the course of the night.'

'Unusual for him, right?'

'Yes. But the last few weeks before he died, he was drinking more and more.'

'Any idea why?'

'He was upset.'

'And he was upset the night he was killed, wasn't he?'

'Yes.'

'Over what?'

'I don't know.'

Renee bent forward from her seat and handed Kia a Barbie doll she had dropped. Then Renee sat up straight and sipped at her coffee.

'Renee?'

'Huh.'

'What was Chris upset over? You told the newspeople you didn't know. But you *do* know, don't you?'

'What difference would it have made to talk about it? It didn't have nothin', *anything* to do with his death. It was family business, Mr Strange.'

'And here I am, only tryin' to help the family. Chris's mother hired me. Chris's mother sent me *over* here, Renee.'

Renee looked away. She looked up at the clock on the wall and down at her daughter and around the room.

'Was it about his sister, Sondra?' said Strange.

She nodded hesitantly.

'Had he been in contact with her?'

'I don't know.' Renee met his eyes. 'I'm not lyin'; I do not know.'

'Go on.'

'After Sondra lost her job and her place, Chris got more and more distant. He was trying to find her, and do his job as a policeman, and make time for his mother, and me and Kia . . . it got to be too much for him, I guess. And I learned not to ask too many questions about Sondra. It only upset him more when I did.'

'Where was Sondra working when things started to fall apart on her?'

'Place called Sea D.C., at Fourteenth and K. She had been a hostess there for a short while.'

'Her mother said she was basically a good girl, got in with the wrong crowd.'

'Wasn't like she was wearing a halo or nothin' like that. Sondra always did like to party, from what Chris told me. And I had some friends who worked in restaurants and clubs downtown, and I'd hung with these people a few times after the chairs got put up on the tables. So I knew what time it was. In those places, at closing time? Someone's always holding something. In that environment, it's easy to fall into that lifestyle, if you allow yourself to fall into it, Mr Strange.'

'Call me Derek.'

'Sondra got into that heroin thing. Chris said she was always afraid of needles, so he figured she started by snorting it. Probably thought it was okay, doin' it like that, like she couldn't get a jones behind it in that way. Another mistake future junkies make. I know because I had an uncle who was deep into it. It's a slower way to go down is all it is. How you end up, it's all the same.'

'The night Chris was killed. Describe what happened here before he went out.'

Renee moved her coffee mug around the table. Her voice was even and unemotional. 'He got a phone call on his cell. He took the call back in my bedroom. I didn't hear what was said and I didn't ask. But he was agitated when he came out of the bedroom, for real. He said he had to go out. He said he was going to a bar or something to grab a beer, that he needed to get out of the apartment and think. I didn't think it was a good idea, what with him already having been drinkin' and all, and I told him so. He told me not to worry. He kissed me and he kissed Kia on the top of the head, and then he left. Two hours later, I got a call from Chris's mother telling me he was dead.'

Strange sat back in his chair. 'Chris had some brutality complaints in his file. He ever talk about that?'

'Yes,' said Renee. 'He told me he had to get rough with suspects sometimes, but he said he never went off on someone didn't deserve it. And yes, he had been drinking heavily the night he was killed, just like they said. The newspapers and the TV and his own department, they can paint their pictures any way they want. None of that explains why he was murdered. Bottom line is, if that white cop hadn't come up on the scene, Chris would be alive today.'

'That white cop didn't know Chris was a policeman,' said Strange. 'He saw a man with a gun—'

'He saw a *black* man with a gun,' said Renee. 'And you and I both know that's why Chris is dead.'

Strange didn't reply. He wasn't certain that on some basic level she was wrong.

Strange leaned forward and touched Kia's cheek. 'That your baby, pretty little girl?'

'*My* baby,' said Kia.

'I hope I helped you,' said Renee.

'You did,' said Strange. 'Thank you for your time.'

Strange sat at the downstairs bar of the Purple Cactus, sipping a ginger ale, watching the crowd. It was mostly young white money in here, new money and livin'-off-the-interest kind of money as well. The waitresses and bar staff were pretty young women and pretty boys, working with a kind of rising intensity, serving the early, preshow dinner patrons who were just now beginning to flow through the doors. The dining room chairs were hard, and triangles and other geometric designs hung on the walls. Dim spot lamps brought an onstage focus to each table, so the patrons could be 'seen' while eating the overpriced cuisine.

Upon its opening, the Cactus had been touted in the *Post*'s dining guide and in *Washingtonian*, and had become 'the place' for that particular year. Strange had come here once when he was trying to impress a woman on a first date, always a mistake. He had dropped a hundred and twenty-five on three appetizers, portioned to leave a small dog hungry, and a couple of drinks. Then the waiter, another bright-eyed boy with bleached-blond hair, had the nerve to come out with a dessert tray, and try to get them to sample a 'decadent,' twelve-dollars-a-slice chocolate cake that was, he said with a practiced smile, 'architecturally brilliant.' It had ruined Strange's night to feel that used. And to make things worse, the woman he was with, she hadn't even given him any play.

A waiter wearing a thin line of beard came up to the service end of the bar and said to the bartender, 'Absolut and tonic with a lemon twist,' then added, 'Did you see that tourist with the *hair* at my four-top? Oh my God, what is she, on chemo or something?' The waitress standing next to him, also waiting on a drink and arranging her checks, said, 'Charlie, keep your voice down, the customers will hear you.'

'Oh, *fuck* the customers,' said Charlie, dressing his vodka tonic with a swizzle stick as it arrived.

Strange wondered how a place like this could stay in business. But he knew: people came here because they were told to come here, knowing full well that it was a rip-off, too. Same reason they read the books their friends read, and went to movies about convicts hijacking airplanes and asteroids headed for earth. Didn't matter that none of it was any good. No one wanted to be left out of the conversation at the next cocktail party. Everyone was desperate to be a part of what was new, to not be left behind.

'You okay here?' asked the bartender, a clear-eyed blonde with nice skin.

'Fine,' said Strange. 'I do have a question, though. You remember a guy used to work here, name of Ricky Kane? Trying to locate him for a friend.'

'I'm new,' said the bartender.

'*I* remember Ricky,' said Charlie the waiter, still standing by the service bar. Would be like old Charlie, thought Strange, to listen in on someone's conversation and make a comment about it when he wasn't being spoken to.

'He's not working here any longer, is he?' said Strange, forcing a friendly smile.

'He doesn't need to anymore,' said Charlie. 'Not after all that money he got from the settlement.' Charlie side-glanced the brunette waitress beside him. 'Course, he never did need to work here, did he?'

'Cause old Ricky had his income set up from dealin' drugs, it suddenly occurred to Strange.

'Charlie,' admonished the waitress.

Charlie chuckled and hurried off with his drink tray. The bartender served the brunette waitress her drinks and said, 'Here you go, Lenna.'

After Lenna thanked her, the bartender came back to stand in front of Strange. 'Another ginger ale?'

'Just the check,' said Strange, 'and a receipt.'

Strange walked around the corner and four blocks up Vermont Avenue, then took the steps down to Stan's, a basement bar he frequented now and again. It was smoky and crowded with locals, a racial mix of middle-class D.C. residents, most of them in their middle age. Going past some loud tables, he heard a man call his name.

'Derek, how you doin'!'

'Ernest,' said Strange. It was Ernest James from the neighborhood, wearing a suit and seated with a woman.

'Heard your business was doin' good, man.'

'I'm doin' all right.'

'You see anything of Donald Lindsay?' asked James.

'Heard Donald passed.'

'Uh-uh, man, he's still out there.'

'Well, I ain't seen him.' Strange nodded and smiled at Johnson's lady. 'Excuse me, y'all, let me get up on over to this bar and have myself a drink.'

'All right, then, Derek.'

'All right.'

Strange ordered a Johnnie Walker Red and soda at the bar. At Stan's, they served the liquor to the lip of the glass, with the miniature mixer on the side, the way they used to at the old Royal Warrant and the Round Table on the other side of town. When Strange felt like having one real drink, and being around regular people, he came here.

Sipping his scotch, he felt himself notch down. He talked to a man beside him about the new Redskins quarterback, who had come over from the Vikings, and what the 'Skins needed to do to win. The man was near Strange's age, and he recalled seeing Bobby Mitchell play, and the talk drifted to other players and the old Jurgensen-led squad.

'Fight for old D.C.,' said the man, with a wink.

'Fight for old *Dixie,* you mean.'

'You remember that?' said the man.

'That and a lot of other things. Shame some of these young folks out here, talkin' about nigga this and nigga that, don't remember those things, too.'

'Some of our people get all upset 'cause the word's in *Webster's* dictionary, but they hear it from the mouths of their own sons and daughters and grandkids, and they let it pass.'

'Uh-huh. How are white people gonna know not to use that word when our own young people don't know it their *own* got-damn selves?'

'I heard that.'

Strange's beeper sounded. He read the numbers, excused himself, went to the pay phones back by the bathrooms, and made a call. It was Quinn on the other end of the line.

'Lookin' forward to it,' said Strange, when Quinn was done talking.

'Us too,' said Quinn. 'Where should we meet?'

Strange told him, racked the phone, and checked his wristwatch. He paid his tab, bought the man at the bar another round, and left Stan's.

At his row house, Strange dumped all the matchbooks and the photograph of Sondra Wilson onto his office desk, went through his mail, and changed into sweats. He went down to his basement, where a heavy bag hung from the steel beams of the ceiling, and listened to the soundtrack of *Guns for San Sebastian* on his boom box while he worked the bag. He fed Greco, then stripped off his damp clothing and went to take a shower. If he hurried, he'd have time to visit his mother at the home before picking up Janine for the fights.

19

Ray and Earl Boone stopped at the red light on Michigan and North Capitol. Ray dragged on his cigarette and Earl sipped from a can of Busch beer. On the corner, a neon-colored poster was stapled to a telephone pole, announcing some kind of boxing event that was scheduled for that night.

'Feel like goin' to the fights tonight, Daddy?' said Ray, knowing full well that his father didn't even like to step outside the car in D.C. 'They got some good ones over at that convention center. Looks like Don King's gonna be there, too.'

'Don King?' said Earl. 'I'd sooner have a dog lick peanut butter out the crack of my ass.'

'That a no?'

'You got a green light, Critter. And stop bein' so silly, too.'

Ray made a call to Cherokee Coleman's office, told one of Coleman's people that he and his father were coming in. They drove into the old warehouse district off Florida Avenue.

Ray saw an MPD cruiser idling on the street near Coleman's office. He recognized the small numbers on the bumper of the Crown Vic and the same numbers, printed larger, on its side. Coasting past the driver's-side window, Ray caught a quick glance of the uniform behind the wheel, a big, ugly spade who was staring straight ahead. Coleman had once told him the name of their pocket cop, funny kind of name for a man, funnier still for such a big one, but Ray could not exactly remember what the name was. Sounded like Madonna, some bullshit like that.

They dropped the kilo off at the garage. The usual types were waiting, with a couple of new, young faces in the bunch, skullcap stockings worn over the tops of their heads, dead eyes, kill-you-while-I-laugh smiles. There was a north side–south side argument going on as Ray and Earl stepped out of the car, one kid playfully feinting and jabbing another as the rest moved their heads to some jungle-jump coming from a box. Ray could give a good fuck about any of them. And as he and his father smoked and watched them scale out the heroin, he could only think, Everything goes right, this'll be the last time I ever set foot in this shit hole of a city again.

Tonio Morris came out of the dark room on the first floor of the Junkyard, where he lived with the other last-stage junkies and the bugs and the rats, lying on a moldy mattress in his own filth. When he was not here he was out on the street, stealing or begging, or collecting cigarette butts gathered along the curbs, or rummaging through the garbage cans in the alleys behind the houses in Trinidad and LeDroit Park.

Here in the Junkyard, he experienced mainly boredom, relieved by the threat of drama, the occasional quick act of physical violence, or the odd joke that struck him funny and made him laugh deep in his wheezy chest. He slept fitfully and ate little, except for the small bites of chocolate he cadged from the others. Mostly his life was blocks of time between getting high, and mostly he waited, sometimes knowing but not caring that he was only waiting for death.

Tonio crossed the big room, his feet crunching pigeon droppings, puddles dampening his brown socks, water entering where the soles had split from the uppers of his shoes. He stood by the brick wall, in a place that had been hammered out, and watched the Ford Taurus pass, driving by the cop car that idled on the street. They were here, on schedule, and he turned and headed for the stairs.

He passed one of Coleman's and went up to the second floor, to the open-stalled bathroom area where those who were still strong and those who had something to trade had staked out their spots. The once-beautiful girl named Sondra was in the last stall, leaning against the steel wall, rubbing her arm with her hand as if she were trying to erase a stain.

Tonio went into the stall and stood very close to her so that he could make out her face. He was beginning to go blind, the final laughing insult of the plague.

'Hello, Tonio.'

'Hello, baby. Your boys are here.'

Sondra smiled and showed filmy teeth; zero nutrition had grayed them. Her lips were chapped and bleeding in spots, raw from the cold. She wore a heavy jacket over her usual outfit, the white shirt and black slacks. An old woman back near Gallaudet College had seen her on the street a week ago and handed the jacket to Sondra out the front door of her row house.

'You better get fresh for your man,' said Tonio.

'I got some water here,' she said. She had found an empty plastic Fruitopia container in a Dumpster and filled it with water from a neighborhood spigot.

'Use this to clean your face,' said Tonio. He handed her a filthy shop rag from his back pocket. 'Go on, girl.' She took it, examined it, and poured freezing water from the bottle onto the rag. She dabbed it on her cheeks. The oily dirt from the rag smudged her face.

'You're good to me,' said Sondra.

'And don't you forget to be good to Tonio, hear?'

'I won't forget you, T. I always get a little bit for you.'

He eyed her in a hungry but completely asexual way. He wanted things from her but not that. Tonio could no longer make it with a woman even if he wanted to. He no longer wanted to or thought of it at all.

'I better be goin' back down,' he said.

'See you later,' she said, watching him walk away, hitching his pants up where they had slipped down his behind.

Sondra was fond of Tonio. He never tried to do her like the others did. Tonio was her friend.

'What's wrong, Cherokee?' said Ray. 'Thought you'd be happy. Way you were talking last time, thought you wanted to get out from under the pressure the Rodriguez brothers were puttin' on you.'

'Didn't ask you to doom 'em, Ray,' said Coleman.

'They asked for it their own selves.'

'Committed suicide, huh?'

'Damn near like it. Anyway, I can't wake neither of them up now, so we're wasting time frettin' on it, right? Besides, I handled it, you can believe that.'

Cherokee Coleman sat behind his desk, his hands tented on the blotter, staring at Ray. His lieutenant, Big-Ass Angelo, stood behind him, his face a fleshy, impassive mask. Earl Boone got a kick out of Angelo's sunglasses, the Hollywood-looking kind with the thick gold stems. Dark as it was already in here, with that green banker's lamp the only light in the room, Earl wondered how fat boy could even see.

'You want to go ahead and tell us how you handled it?' said Cherokee.

'The day after their visit,' said Ray, 'I called Lizardo's wife, asked her where in the hell he and Nestor was. Said that they was due but hadn't showed up or called. 'Bout a New York minute later I get a call on my cell from one of the Vargas people down in Florida. I told him the same thing I told the wife. He mumbled somethin' in Spanish and hung up the phone. Next thing we did was, me and Daddy made two trips with those Contours they was drivin', drove those cars down to Virginia and dumped 'em near Richmond, off Ninety-five south. Dripped some of Nestor's and Lizardo's blood on the seats of those cars. Pulled some hairs from their heads and scattered them in the cars, too. When the cops break into those cars and trace the owners, gonna look like the brothers got killed down there on their way up north.'

'What about the bodies?'

'The bodies I got stashed on my property, until this weather turns. I'm gonna take care of that, too.'

'What happens,' said Cherokee, 'when I get the call from the Vargas family?'

'Hell, Cherokee, you're just gonna have to tell 'em the same. That you heard from me and that Nestor and Lizardo never showed.'

'Why would I do that?'

''Cause partners gotta stick together,' said Ray.

'We're partners now. You hear that, Angie?'

'Look here.' Ray leaned forward in his chair. 'I got nine keys of pure brown I'm sittin' on right now.'

'Got it with you?' said Coleman.

'Nah, man,' said Ray. 'I ain't stupid!'

Ray laughed. Coleman and Angelo laughed, and kept laughing long after Ray was done. Ray frowned, watching them. Were they fuckin' with him now? He couldn't tell.

Coleman drew a handkerchief from the breast pocket of his pretty suit and wiped his eyes.

'Anyhow,' said Ray. 'Me and Daddy, we been wantin' to get out of this business for a while now. What I was thinkin' is, we unload the rest of that brown to you directly, at a price you're really gonna like, and we are gone.'

'Oh, yeah? What kind of price is that?'

'You were payin' a hundred a key, right?'

'Including your bounce. It's *all* bounce now, so you don't have to add that back in, seein' as how there wasn't any, what do you call that, *cost of goods* involved.'

'That's right. So I was gonna say sixty a key you take the load. Nine keys time sixty—'

'Five hundred and forty grand.'

'Five forty, right. But, 'cause I like you, Cherokee—'

'You like me, Ray?'

'I do. And 'cause of that, I'm gonna sweeten the pie even more.'

'How you gonna sweeten it?'

'Say an even five hundred grand to you, Cherokee, for the whole shebang.'

'Generous of you, Ray.'

'I think so.'

'So when you gonna bring it in?'

Ray looked over at Earl, back at Coleman. 'We were kind of thinkin', Daddy and me, I mean, that we wouldn't have to come into the city again for this last deal.'

'Got somethin' against D.C.?'

'We prefer the country, you want the truth.'

'For real?'

Coleman and Angelo laughed again. Ray and Earl, expressionless as stones, waited until they were done.

'Tell you what,' said Coleman. 'We'll split the difference, hear? You bring in the first half of the load straight away, and for the last half, I'll send someone out your way to pick it up.'

'What's this half stuff?'

'You don't think I can get my hands on five hundred grand all at once, do you? Think I can walk on over to NationsBank and take out a loan?'

'No, but—'

'Got to turn that inventory first, man, get some cash flow goin' in this motherfucker. Only way we can do this deal, Ray.'

'I don't know,' said Ray.

'Fuck it,' said Earl, surprising Coleman with his voice. It was the first time Earl had spoken since he and his son had walked through the office door.

'You got somethin' on your mind, *Daddy*?' said Coleman.

'We'll bring the next load down,' said Earl, 'that's what you want. But I want somethin', too.'

'Let me guess,' said Coleman. 'This somethin' got light skin and green eyes?'

'That's right,' said Earl. 'I want to take that pretty girl home with me, the one you got livin' over there across the street. I'm gonna take her with me today.'

'Shit, Daddy.'

'Hold up, Critter. I'm talkin' now.'

'Aw, you're sweet on her,' said Coleman. 'That's real nice.'

'Got no problem with me takin' her, do ya?'

'No problem at all. I ain't got no kind of claim on it. Course, some of the fellas over at the Junkyard, they might want to up and flex on you, you try to take her away. 'Cause most of them been kickin' it, one behind the other, the last month or so.'

'Kickin' it?'

'Fallin' in love with her, Ray.'

Big-Ass Angelo went *'ssh, ssh, ssh,'* his shoulders jiggling hard.

Earl ignored him and said, 'That'll do it, then. We'll be on our way.'

Ray stood. 'I'll call you. We'll be back with that first load in a couple of days. Then you can come on out and get the rest.'

'Oh, I don't think I'll be makin' the trip personally, Ray. I'm gonna send out a po-lice escort, make it nice and official.'

'You're gonna send that guy Madonna?'

Coleman chuckled. 'Sure, Ray. I'll send Madonna.'

'All right, then. See you fellas later.'

'Ray,' said Coleman. 'Earl.'

Coleman and Angelo watched them go out the door.

Coleman said, 'Call all our dealers, Angie. Tell 'em we got a lot of good product comin' in. And don't forget to call that white boy, too. He can move it on the other side of town, and we need it moved out quick. Get that first load out on the street so we can do the same with the second. This a big opportunity we got right here. We gonna make some large bank on this motherfucker, Angie.'

'Yeah, but we got to go all the way the fuck on out to Hooterville to pick it up.'

'That's all right. Got to throw dirt on the Boones sooner or later, might as well do it while we're out there. Make a nice pile of bodies, them and the Rodriguez brothers. Get it lookin' like Jonestown out there and shit. Make it right for those Colombians. 'Cause you know I don't want to see the Vargas family in town, lookin' to start a war.'

'*I* ain't goin'.'

'Don't worry, big dawg. I'm gonna send Adonis and his shadow.'

Angelo grinned. 'You mean *Madonna,* don't you?'

'Ray Boone,' said Coleman. 'That's a real genius, right there.'

'I ain't *stupid*!' said Big-Ass Angelo.

Coleman cracked up and held out his palm. Angelo gave him skin.

Earl Boone walked along the doorless stalls, stopping at the very last one in the row. Sondra Wilson stood there, the flame from a single candle throwing light upon her face. Her white blouse was filthy, and dirt streaked her cheeks. She seemed unsteady on her feet.

'Hey, honey girl,' said Earl.

'Earl.'

He stepped in close and looked into her eyes. One was brown and one was green.

'What happened to your eyes, young lady?'

'I lost a contact, I guess.' She tried to curl her lip seductively. 'You got somethin' for me, Earl?'

'I got it. But not here. I'm takin' you out of this place.'

'Where we goin'?' she said.

'You're coming to live with me for a while. You're gonna have a shower and new clothes and clean sheets to sleep on every night.'

'What about the other thing?' she said, because that was all she cared about now.

'You're gonna have plenty of that, too.'

Sondra turned to the wall and untaped the magazine photo of the model. She folded it and picked up the paperweight off the toilet-paper dispenser and looked around for her other possessions. She picked up a wet, half-used book of matches from the tiles and realized that there was nothing else.

'Come on, baby doll. Ray's waiting on us out in the hall.'

'Can I get a little somethin' for my friend Tonio before we go?'

'Forget about him. We want to get out quiet and quick. I understand some of the other fellas in here might have fallen in love with you, and we wouldn't want them getting jealous.'

'Love?' said Sondra. She rubbed her nose and laughed.

They took her down the stairs and went through a large hole in the brick wall. From deep in the darkness of the side room, Tonio Morris watched Sondra leave with the old white man and his son. He wondered why Sondra would go without saying good-bye. He was sad for a moment, then felt a shudder of panic, realizing that maybe his source was gone for good.

In the street, the cop behind the wheel of the idling cruiser watched the Boones emerge from the Junkyard with the pretty junkie from the second floor. The three of them were headed for the garage where the others were holding their car. The cop snapped the cigar that he was holding between his fingers and tossed it to the floor.

20

'Sharmba Mitchell,' said Strange. 'That's a beautiful fighter right there.'

'Look at that left,' said Quinn.

'I had a left like that one, I'd never throw a right.'

Strange and Quinn sat in the bleachers of the Washington Convention Center, drinking a couple of four-dollar drafts. In the crowd of four thousand, Quinn was among a small number of whites, the others being the parents of a light heavyweight Texan, four frightened-looking fraternity boys, and several white women accompanied by black men. The convention center was a grim, outdated white elephant that had underserved the city from day one. But the sport almost lent itself to unattractive, spartan arenas; as boxing venues went, this wasn't a bad place to see a fight.

The white, light heavyweight Texan, who fought under the name of Joe Bill 'Rocky' Jakes, was walking along the edge of the stands, having changed into street clothes after his disastrous defeat. His face was marked and puffy, and one eye was swollen shut.

'Hey, Rocky!' shouted a guy from the stands.

'Yo, Adrian!' shouted another.

'You'll get 'em next time, Rock,' shouted a third, with a Burgess Meredith growl, to much laughter from the spectators in the surrounding seats.

'They're usin' the hell out of that guy,' said Quinn.

'You ever notice,' said Strange, 'how many white fighters call themselves Rocky?'

'I think there's been one or two.'

'There's that hook again,' said Strange, pointing to the ring.

Takoma Park's Sharmba Mitchell was defending his WBA super lightweight title against Pedro Saiz, out of Brooklyn. Saiz, a late replacement for a scratched William Joppy, had not been expected to show too much, but he was proving himself tonight. Mitchell wore trunks cut in strips of red, white, and blue. Saiz wore white.

The fourth round ended. As the fighters went to their corners, a blonde showing a whole lot of leg climbed into the ring and walked around the edge of the ropes, a round-card held up in her hands.

'You see the ladies?' said Strange.

'I liked Round Two, myself,' said Quinn.

'Shame about the face.'

'Hey, I bet she's got a big heart.'

'A big *inverted* heart, you mean.'

'Her ass *was* pretty big. But I thought you guys liked that.'

'You thought. Anyway, I'm not talkin' about the ring girls, Terry, I'm talkin' about *our* ladies. Our dates.'

'They went to get a couple of beers.'

'Fifteen minutes ago.'

'They're okay. Probably down there with their faces together, having a firefight. Talking about us.'

'I hope they are. It's when they stop talkin' about us, then we're in trouble.' Strange sipped his beer and looked at Quinn out of the corners of his eyes. 'You didn't tell me about Juana, man.'

'That she was fine?'

'That she was a sister.'

'She's half Puerto Rican.'

'Half nothin'. You got a drop of black in you, you are *black.*'

'Got a problem with it?' said Quinn.

'Uh-uh. I mean, I'm not gonna lie to you, it took me back at first, 'cause I didn't expect it.'

'It's the way we're programmed, is all it is.'

'Now you're gonna tell me what it is.'

'I was up in Wheaton Plaza a couple of weeks back, the mall? Half the young couples, some of 'em had babies in strollers, were interracial. Fifteen years ago, when I was hanging out up at the Plaza, you wouldn't have seen it. It's just natural for these kids now. And it made me think, the way my generation is, and especially the way your generation is, it's *our* hang-up, man. It's something *we've* got to get over, 'cause the world's changing whether we like it or not.'

'Case you didn't notice, you been getting a lot of looks here tonight. From people in all sorts of generations.'

'She's been drawing the looks, and I don't blame the guys who been lookin'.'

'You're gonna have to at least face this, Terry: there's a whole lot of people, black and white, they just don't believe in mixin', man. That doesn't make them racists or anything like that. It's just their opinion, straight up.'

'Long as they stay out of my business, they can have any kind of opinion they want.'

The fifth round began. A fight broke out by the men's room to their right, and security guards swarmed the guilty parties, carrying one man out as he kicked his legs and yelled obscenities over his shoulder. There had been a few fights in the crowd that night, and they had occurred with more frequency as more beer and liquor had been served.

'You been seein' Juana long?'

Quinn rolled his eyes. 'Shit, man, you still on that?'

'I got to admit, when we came up on the two of you, first thing I thought was, Terry got himself a one-time date with a black woman for my benefit. Trying to make an impression on old Strange, like, Here I am, Terry Quinn, lovin' all the people, can't you see I just want us *all* to get along?'

Quinn laughed. 'I'm through trying to impress you, Derek. You ought to know that by now. I've told you everything I know. I mean, can we just hang out and not deal with it for one night?'

'So how long you been seein' her?'

'Not too long, I guess. I'm crazy about her, too, you want to know the truth.'

'I got eyes.'

'How about you and Janine?'

'Shoot. We been seein' each other now, I don't know, about ten years. Not exclusive, nothin' like that.'

'She's in love with you.'

'Go ahead, man.'

'Look, I got eyes, too.'

'My mother always tells me that old parable about the guy, went all around the world lookin' for diamonds, when all the time he never did think to look in his own backyard.'

'Diamonds in your backyard. I've heard that one plenty of times.'

'Yeah, she didn't make it up. But when it's your mom tellin' you, you tend to listen. Anyhow, I guess me and Janine, we're good for each other in a lot of ways.'

Strange knew it was deeper than that between him and Janine. But he was a private man, and that was all he could bring himself to say.

Saiz issued a flagrant low blow to Mitchell, sending him to his knees. The increasingly raucous crowed booed loudly as the ref directed Saiz to his corner and deducted a point. At Mitchell's nod, the ref restarted the fight. Mitchell came out with fury, throwing a flurry of punches in a blur of speed and power.

'You're gonna see somethin' now,' said Quinn.

'Yeah,' said Strange. 'Sharmba's gonna fuck him up.'

Mitchell decisioned Saiz unanimously. Janine and Juana walked up the stands carrying two beers each. An elderly couple on the end got up to let them pass.

'Damn, where y'all been?' said Strange, as they took their seats. He sounded mildly cross, but it was plain from the relieved look on his face that he had been worried about Janine.

'Juana wanted to see Sugar Ray,' said Janine. 'He's down at ringside.'

'You see him?'

'Mm-huh,' said Juana, and she and Janine laughed.

'Saw Don King, too,' said Janine.

'Must have made you hungry for some cotton candy,' said Strange.

'Wondered why my stomach was growling,' said Janine, 'looking at that hair of his.'

'How you doin'?' said Quinn, touching Juana's hand.

'Janine's really nice,' she whispered.

'Havin' fun?'

'Uh-huh.'

He kissed her lips.

A tuxedoed man came into the ring, pulled down the hanging microphone, and began to describe, with flourish, the participants in the main event.

'Who's that guy?' said Quinn.

'Discombobulating Jones,' said Strange, with affection. 'Best ring announcer in D.C.'

'Here we go,' said Quinn. 'Bernard Hopkins.'

'Hopkins took out Simon Brown,' said Strange. 'You know that?'

The main event had Hopkins in a rematch with Robert Allen for the IBF middleweight crown. Their first pairing, in Vegas, had been marred by Allen's shoves and holds, and ended as a no contest when Hopkins fell through the ropes and sprained an ankle.

'Allen's doin' it again,' said Strange, well into the first round. 'He's headlockin' him, man; he doesn't want to fight.'

Allen seemed to fake an injury, claiming himself the victim of a low blow. The spectators became angry, calling Allen a punk and a bitch. As they grew more boisterous, they moved en masse toward the ring. The fight continued, with round after round the same. The crowd's taunts became louder and more threatening.

'These people want blood,' said Strange.

'Let's get out of here,' said Quinn. 'This fight stinks anyway, and you know Hopkins is gonna win.'

The four of them moved through the dense crowd. The young women in the crowd were mostly attractive, with shoulder-length, relaxed hairstyles that Juana called Brandy cuts. The oversized look was out for the young men. Many wore baseball jackets with leather sleeves and colorful sayings embroidered on the back. Someone bumped Quinn and he kept on, not knowing and trying not to care if it was intentional or not. But he felt his face flush as he walked away.

Out in the auditorium, as they walked down the carpeted lobby, a young man in a group of three made a comment directed at Juana, saying how he'd like to 'kick that shit deep.' Quinn felt his face grow hot and the tug of Juana's hand on his leather. He kept walking, and the movement calmed him.

Once outside, they walked down 10th. Strange and Quinn followed Janine and Juana, who were stepping quickly, talking to one another up ahead. A young black man was standing on the median, yelling at passing cars. 'I hate cracker motherfuckers!' he screamed. 'I swear to God, I'm gonna kill the next white motherfucker I see!'

'Sounds like the man's got some kind of *hang-up*,' said Strange, a playful light in his eyes. 'Doesn't he know, Terry, that the world is *changing*?'

'Think I ought to go tell him?' said Quinn.

'Go ahead,' said Strange, with a small grin. 'I'll make sure your lady gets home safe.'

Juana and Quinn followed Strange and Janine over to Stan's, where they had a round, and then another, before last call. By now they were all a little bit drunk, and Juana and Janine didn't seem to want the evening to end, so they agreed to meet up at Strange's row house for 'one more.'

Strange bought a twelve-pack at a market and drove up Georgia. Janine sat beside him on the bench, her thigh touching his, while Strange messed with the stereo, popping in *War Live* and fast-forwarding the tape to a song he liked.

'What you lookin' for?' asked Janine.

' "Get Down." Here it is.' Strange turned the bass dial and put more bottom into the mix. 'What's Ron doin' on Monday, you know?'

'He's workin' a couple of jumpers, I think.'

'I could use his help.'

'We need the money he's gonna bring into the business, Derek.

Don't tell me this Wilson thing is going to result in a big payday, 'cause I know you're not gonna end up charging his mother enough. Let Ron do his thing and go on and do yours.'

'Yeah, you're right.' Strange turned up the volume and sang, ' "The po-lice . . . We're talkin' 'bout the po-lice." '

Janine laughed. 'You're in rare form tonight, honey.'

'Havin' a good time, I guess.'

'Me, too. I like Juana. That's a together young lady right there. Going to law school down at GW, you know that? Might have her talk to Lionel about it, let him know in a backdoor kind of way that anybody can do anything, they set their mind to it. You know she didn't come from any kind of privilege or nothin' like that.'

'What about Terry? You think he's good for her?'

'They stay together, they're gonna have problems they don't even know about yet. Not to mention, all you've got to do is look in his eyes and see, that's an intense young man. He's got a lot of things to work out his own self before he can take on the responsibilities of a real relationship. But I do like him.'

Strange nodded, looking in the rearview mirror at the black VW following his car. 'So do I.'

In the Bug, Quinn shifted the stick while Juana worked the clutch and steered with her left hand. Her right hand was going through a box of tapes that sat in her lap.

'How about Lucinda Williams?' said Juana.

'The chick on *Laverne and Shirley*?'

'You're thinkin' of *Cindy* Williams.'

'I'm fuckin' with you, girl.'

'Here, put this in, you'll like it.'

Quinn slipped the tape into the deck. 'Metal Firecracker' came through the system, filling the interior of the car.

'This rocks,' said Quinn.

'Yeah, Lucinda is bad.'

Quinn chuckled, looking through the windshield. 'Derek's got that Caddy all waxed up. I bet he really loves that car.'

'What's wrong with that?'

'Nothin'. I'm sayin' he's proud of it, is all. His age group, the symbol of success is a Cadillac. *You* know what I mean.'

'I guess I do.'

When Juana was a kid, she heard a white boy in her elementary school class call a Cadillac a 'nigger boat.' She had told herself from the start that Terry wasn't 'like that' in any kind of way. But how could you know what was really in a person's heart? He had downed more than a few beers tonight, and maybe this was him for real, loose and talking truly for the first time. Maybe what he believed was out of his control, that everything he had learned had been taught to him, and had been ingrained in him irreversibly, long ago. And maybe she was just being too sensitive. Once you started going in that direction, you could drive yourself crazy over something that was probably nothing at all.

'What's wrong?' said Quinn, looking at her face.

'Nothing, Tuh-ree,' said Juana, finding his hand and giving it a gentle squeeze. 'I was just thinking of you, that's all.'

21

Strange was doing something he called 'the chicken leg,' Janine dancing beside him, as 'Night Train' blared through his living room stereo. Quinn was nearby, shouting out encouragement between hits from a can of beer. Juana sat on the couch, twisting up a number from some herb and papers she had found in her purse. Greco lay on the floor with his head between his paws, his tail slowly thumping the carpet.

'Sonny Liston used to train to that one,' said Strange, as the song ended.

'Like you were doin' right there?' asked Quinn.

'Naw, man, that was a dance we used to do. Check this out.' Strange held up a CD with a photograph of a sixties-looking white girl on its cover. 'Mr Otis Redding. *Otis Blue.*'

'You already played that Solomon Burke. What, are we working our way up to modern times here?'

'This is the man right here,' Strange said, as Steve Cropper's bluesy guitar kicked it off on 'Ole Man Trouble,' the horns and then Otis's vocal coming behind it.

'Got any Motown?'

'Shoot, Terry, Motown ain't nothin' but soul music for white people, man.'

'How do I know? I wasn't even alive when this shit was playin' on the radio.'

'And I was still gettin' press-and-curls,' added Janine. 'Barely a child.'

'*I* was there,' said Strange. 'And it was right.'

Juana walked over with a joint in her hand. 'You guys want some of this?'

'I do,' said Quinn.

'Been a while for me,' said Strange.

'Come on,' said Juana.

'You all aren't gonna start acting funny now, are you?' asked Janine.

'What's this "you all" stuff?' said Strange.

The four of them stood in the middle of the living room floor and smoked the joint. Strange took Quinn's shotgun, but Juana refused it. Janine just waved her hand and laughed. By the time the joint was a roach, they were all alternately giggling and arguing over the next piece of music to be played.

Strange put *Motor Booty Affair* on the CD player and turned up the volume. 'The power of Parliament. Now we're gonna roll with it, y'all.'

The four of them danced, tentatively at first, to the complex, dense songs. The bass line was snaky and insistent, and the melodies bubbled up in the mix, and as the rhythms insinuated themselves into their bodies they let go and found the groove. They had broken a sweat by the fifth cut.

Strange dimmed the lights and put on Al Green's *The Belle Album.*

'Reminds me of those blue-light parties we used to have,' said Strange.

'That was before my time, too,' said Janine, kissing him on the mouth.

They slow-dragged to the title tune. Janine had her cheek resting on Strange's chest, moving in her stocking feet. Quinn and Juana made out like high-schoolers as they danced. As the cut ended, Janine checked her watch and told Strange that it was time to go.

'Lionel ought to be getting back to my house by now,' she said. 'I want to be there for him when he arrives.'

'Yeah, we need to clear out of here,' said Strange.

'Where's the head?' asked Quinn.

'Up the stairs,' said Strange.

Quinn went up to the second floor. He saw the bathroom, an open door that led to a bedroom and sleeper porch, and two more bedrooms, one of which had been set up as an office. Quinn looked over his shoulder at the empty flight of stairs and walked into the office.

The office appeared to be well used. Strange's desk was a countertop set on two columns of file cabinets. Atop the desk was a monitor, speakers, a keyboard, and a mouse pad, and scattered papers and general clutter. Quinn went around the desk.

Beside the desk, Strange had mounted a wooden CD rack to the wall. In the rack were western movie sound tracks: the Leone *Dollars* trilogy, *Once Upon a Time in the West, The Magnificent Seven, Return of the Magnificent Seven, My Name Is Nobody, Navajo Joe, The War Wagon, Two Mules for Sister Sara, The Professionals, Duel at Diablo,*

The Big Country, The Big Gundown, and others. There was no evidence in this room of the funk and soul music from the sixties and seventies that Strange loved so much. Quinn wondered if Strange was hiding this collection here, if he was embarrassed to have his taste for western sound tracks on display for his friends.

Quinn looked at the papers on the desk. Stock related documents, mostly, along with report forms with the Strange Investigations logo printed across the top. A heap of matchbooks and a faded photograph of a pretty young woman. He picked the photograph up, recognizing the image as that of Chris Wilson's striking sister. Quinn remembered her from the newspaper stories and television reports that had been broadcast the day of the funeral.

'You see a toilet in here?' said Strange from the doorway.

Quinn looked up. 'Sorry, man. I'm naturally nosy, I guess.'

Strange's eyes were pink and lazy. He folded his arms and leaned on the door frame.

'Why have a photo of Wilson's sister?' said Quinn.

'For the simple reason that I'm beginning to think Sondra Wilson's the key to this whole thing.'

'You talk to her?'

Strange shook his head. 'Gonna have to find her first. Her own mother doesn't know where she is. Sondra's a junkie, man, got a deep heroin jones. Been away from the house a long while now. Wilson was looking to hook up with her, maybe bring her back home, is what I think. And another thing I think is, on the night he was killed, Chris got a phone call had something to do with Sondra.'

Quinn dropped the photograph to the desktop. 'You think Ricky Kane had something to do with that?'

'I like your instincts, Terry.'

'Well, do you?'

'It crossed my mind.'

'You need to talk to Kane.'

'If he's involved, it won't do any good to talk to him. It would shut him up for real, and I got no kind of leverage. It might even hurt my chances of finding Sondra.'

'That's what you're looking to do now?'

'Yeah,' said Strange. 'Finish what Chris Wilson started. Bring her home.'

'Because you know you got nothing else for Leona Wilson, right? You know there was nothing deeper than what got put on the record about my involvement in the death of her son.'

'You tellin' me?'

'I'm *asking* you, Derek.'

'Look here, man.' Strange rubbed his cheeks and exhaled slowly. 'God *damn*, I am fucked up. Haven't smoked herb in years, you want the truth. Don't know why I did tonight. But I got to blame it on something, I guess.'

'Blame what?'

'The crazy thing I'm gettin' ready to ask you to do. See, my associate, Ron, he's gonna be busy next week. And I could use your help.'

'Name it.'

'A tail and surveillance on Ricky Kane, for starters. I was thinkin' Monday morning.'

'Tell me what time.'

'You don't even have a car.'

'I plan to go out tomorrow and buy one.'

'Just like that.'

'Gettin' tired of Juana chauffeuring me around.'

'Okay, then. I'll call you in the evening, let you know where we can meet.'

'Derek?'

'What?'

'This mean I'm off the hook?'

'Aw, shit,' said Strange, chuckling from deep in his gut. 'You're somethin', man.'

'I'm serious, Derek.'

'Okay.' Strange unfolded his arms. 'That hook you're talkin' about, you put yourself on it. You got to admit to yourself the reality of the situation. You got to free your *own* self, man.'

'You just said—'

'I said that I suspect there was something with Chris Wilson and his sister. That her lifestyle is what drove him to D Street that night. But you yourself admitted that Wilson was tryin' to tell you and your partner that he was a cop. He was screaming his badge number out to you, man, but you wouldn't listen.'

'Look—'

'You wouldn't *listen.* You saw a black man with a gun and you saw a criminal, and *you made up your mind.* Yeah, there was noise and confusion and lights, I know about all that. But would you have listened to him if he had been white? Would you have pulled that trigger if Wilson had been white? I don't think so, Terry. Cut through all the extra bullshit, and you're gonna have to just go ahead and admit it, man: you killed a man because he was black.'

Quinn stared into Strange's eyes. Quinn wanted to say more in his defense, but the words wouldn't come. He was certain that any words he could choose would be insufficient. How could a white man ever tell a black man that he wasn't that way without sounding self-serving or duplicitous?

They heard Janine's voice, calling them from the bottom of the stairs. Strange lowered his gaze to the floor.

'C'mon, Terry,' he said, his voice nearly a whisper. 'We better go.'

Quinn and Juana drove east to her row house on 10th. They went straight to her bedroom, where he stripped naked and undressed Juana from behind. He ran both hands up her inner thighs and slipped two fingers inside her. She arched her back and moaned as he pinched her swollen nipples. Then, very quickly, they were fucking on the bed, Juana on the edge of it with her calves resting on his shoulders, and Quinn thrusting with his feet still on the floor. It was fast and nearly violent; Juana came with a groaning howl. Quinn was right behind her, veins standing out on his forehead and neck. The bed had slid across the room, stopping when it hit the wall.

Quinn pulled out and slid Juana up to the center of the bed, putting a pillow under her head. They got beneath the blankets, holding a tight embrace, and what was left from them wet each other and the sheets. She stared up at him, not saying a word, her eyes saying everything. Soon she was breathing evenly. Her eyes fluttered, then closed completely, and she fell asleep.

Lionel Baker came home at one forty-five in the morning, nearly two hours past his curfew. Janine had been waiting in the living room, parting the curtains of the front window every few minutes to check for her son, as Strange sat patiently beside her. A Lexus finally pulled up on Quintana in front of her house, and when she saw her son emerge from the car, Janine said, 'Thank the Lord.'

Strange knew Lionel had been smoking herb, or doing something other than just drinking, as soon as he walked through the front door. Lionel's pupils were dilated, his movements awkward and slow. He didn't look his mother in the eye as he greeted them with a 'Hey' and tried to get past them and up the stairs without another word.

'Hold on a minute, Lionel,' said Janine.

'What is it?' he said, looking at her directly for the first time. He glanced at Strange, then back at his mother, and an impudent smile threatened to break on his face.

'Where you been, son?'

'Out with Ricky, just rollin', listenin' to music. . . Can't you just let me go up to my room for a change? You always be *stressin'* and shit.'

Janine rose up from her seat. 'Don't you be takin' a tone with me, young man. Me and Mr Derek been sitting up, worried that you were in some kind of trouble, or worse. And now you come walking in here late, lookin' all red-eyed—'

'How about y'all?'

'*What?*'

'Forget it, Mama,' said Lionel, with a wave of his hand. He turned and went up the stairs.

Janine froze for moment, then moved to follow her son. Strange took hold of her arm.

'Hold up, baby. I'll talk to him, all right?'

On the second floor of the house, Strange knocked on Lionel's closed door. Lionel did not respond. Strange turned the knob and walked inside the bedroom. Lionel was standing, looking through his window, which gave to a view of the street. Strange crossed the room and stood beside him. Lionel turned to face him.

'Lionel?'

'What?'

'You know your mother loves you, right?'

'Sure.'

'When she asks you where you been all night, it's just her way of lettin' off a little steam. She's been sittin' down in that living room, worried sick about you, for the last two hours, and you come through that door, she's got to give you a taste of what you been puttin' *her* through all night.'

'I know it. It's just . . . I'm nearly a man, Mr Derek. I don't need all these questions all the time, see what I'm sayin'?'

'While you're livin' under her roof, and she's payin' for that roof, it's something you're just gonna have to deal with.'

'And there goes Mama, tellin' *me* my eyes are lookin' red, when y'all look like you been smokin' cheeva your own selves.'

'We drank a few bottles of beer, tonight, that's all,' lied Strange. 'I don't know, maybe we had one too many, but we did have fun. I'm not gonna go and apologize for that, 'cause your mama deserves it, hard as she works. But I never did claim I was perfect, even when I was trying to warn you about all the ways you can mess your life up before you even get out of the gate. Now, I told you what I thought about you drivin' around in that fancy car, gettin' high. I still think you're setting yourself up for something that could affect you your whole life. And your life ain't even started, son.'

'You're not my father,' said Lionel softly, and at once his eyes filled with tears. 'Don't call me son.'

Strange put his hand on Lionel's shoulder. 'You're right. I never did have the kind of courage it takes to be a father to a boy for real. But there's sometimes when I look at you, when you're making one of your jokes at the dining room table, or when I see you dressed up, lookin' all handsome and ready to go out and meet a girl, and I get a sense of pride . . . There's sometimes when I *look* at you, Lionel, and I get the kind of feeling that I know a father must have for his own.'

Strange pulled Lionel to him. He felt Lionel's heart beating hard against his chest. He held Lionel for a little while and let him break away.

'Mr Derek?'

'Yes?'

'The way it is with you and my mother . . . What I'm tryin' to say is, I know what time it is, see? I know you're tryin' to not disrespect her by staying in her room while I'm here, but I was thinkin' . . . I was thinkin', see, that you disrespect her even more in some way by not waking up in her bed.'

'Huh?'

'What I'm sayin' is, I'd like it if you just went ahead and stayed the night.'

'I'll, uh, talk to your mother,' stammered Strange. 'See if that's all right.'

Strange went down the hall to Janine's room. Inside, Janine was sitting on her bed, the toes of her stocking feet touching the floor. Ronald Isley was singing 'Voyage to Atlantis' from the clock radio set on her nightstand, and she had turned the light down low.

'Everything okay?' she said.

'Fine,' said Strange. 'He wants me to spend the night.'

'Do you want to?'

'Yes.'

'You feed Greco?'

'I opened a can of Alpo for him before we left my house.'

'Come here,' said Janine. She smiled and patted the empty space beside her on the bed.

Quinn got out of bed, covering Juana to the neck with her own blanket and sheets. He had been watching the numbers change on the LED display on Juana's clock for the last two hours, and he knew that he would not fall asleep.

He was sober now. He stretched and walked naked to her window, turning the rod of the miniblinds to open an angle of sight. He looked out the window to the sidewalk on 10th, illuminated by street lamps. A young black man was walking down the sidewalk in an oversize, hooded jacket, glancing in the windows of the parked cars he passed.

Quinn made some immediate presumptions about the young man, all of them negative. Then he tried to think of other explanations for why the kid would be out at this hour on the street. Maybe the young man had been unable to sleep, like Quinn, and was simply taking a walk. Maybe he was just leaving his girlfriend's place, was feeling bold and proud, and was checking out his reflection in the windows of the cars. These were logical scenarios, but they were not the *first* scenarios he had thought of when he had seen the young black man.

Quinn thought of the first time he had seen Juana, when she had walked into the bookstore on Bonifant.

Strange had been right about something, whether Quinn had been fully conscious of it at first or not: he had approached Juana initially to make some kind of point, to himself and the world around him.

'God damn you, Terry,' whispered Quinn. He closed his eyes tightly and pinched the bridge of his nose.

22

On Sunday morning, Strange ate breakfast with Janine and Lionel at the Three Star Diner, on Kennedy Street in Northwest. The Three Star was owned and operated by Billy Georgelakos, the son of the original owner, Mike Georgelakos. Strange's father, Darius Strange, had worked for Mike as a grill man at the diner for twenty-five years.

Billy Georgelakos and Strange were roughly the same age. On Saturdays, when Mike and Darius both had of their sons with them, Billy and Strange had played together on these streets while their fathers worked. Strange had taught Billy how to box and make a tackle, and Billy had introduced young Derek to comic books and cap pistols. Billy was Strange's weekend playmate, and his first white friend.

When Mike Georgelakos died of a heart attack in the late sixties, Billy had dropped out of junior college and stepped in to take over the business, as there was no insurance or safety net of any kind for the family. He had not intended to stay, but he did. The neighborhood had gone through some changes, and the menu had moved closer to soul food, but Billy ran the place the same way his old man had, breakfast and lunch only, open seven days a week.

Strange knew that Mike Georgelakos had bought the property long ago – the Greeks from that generation were typically smart enough to secure the real estate – and consequently the nut at the Three Star was very low. The diner had sent Billy's two sons to college and had managed to support his mother as well. The other thing Billy did like his old man was to cut the register tape off two hours before closing time. With a cash business like this, you could hide a whole lot of money from the IRS.

'Pass me that hot sauce, Lionel,' said Strange.

Lionel slid the bottle of Texas Pete down the counter, past his mother to Strange. Strange shook some out onto his feta cheese-and-onion omelet, and a little onto the half-smoke that lay beside it.

'Good breakfast, right?' said Strange.

'Mm-huh,' said Janine.

'The breakfast is tight,' said Lionel, 'but they could play some better music in this place.'

'The music is fine,' said Strange. Billy played gospel in the diner on Sunday mornings, as many of the patrons were coming straight from church. His father had done that, too.

'Why you name your dog Greco?' said Lionel. ''Cause of this Greek joint right here?'

'Nah. I knew this other Greek kid back when I was a boy, kid named Logan Deoudes. His father had a place like this, John's Lunch, over on Georgia, near Fort Stevens. Anyway, Logan had this dog, a boxer mix, called him Greco. Bad-ass dog, too – *excuse* me, Janine – and I always liked the name. Decided back then, when I got a dog of my own, I was gonna name him Greco myself.'

Billy Georgelakos walked down the rubber mat behind the counter, carrying a pot of coffee he had drawn from the urn. He wore a white shirt rolled up to the elbows and had a Bic pen wedged behind his right ear. Billy was big boned, with large facial features, most prominently his great eagle nose. With the exception of two patches of gray on either side of his dome, he had lost most of his hair.

'Want me to warm that up for you, Janine?' said Billy, chin-gesturing in the direction of Janine's coffee cup.

'A little bit more, thanks,' said Janine. Billy poured her some coffee and filled Strange's cup to the lip without asking.

'How's your mom doin', Derek?'

Strange made a so-so, flip-flop movement of his hand. *'Etsi-ke-etsi,'* he said.

'Yeah,' said Billy, 'mine, too. Tough old women, though, right?'

He walked down to the grill area to talk with his longtime employee Ella Lockheart, who had come up in the neighborhood as well.

'You speak Greek, Mr Derek?'

'Little bit,' said Strange mysteriously. Billy had taught him one or two useful expressions and a whole lot of curse words.

'Dag,' said Lionel.

'You got somethin' planned today?' said Strange to Janine.

'What'd you have in mind?'

'Want to stretch my legs. I'll be gettin' real busy tomorrow, and I might stay that way. It's cold, but with all this sunshine I was thinkin' I'd take Greco for a walk down in Rock Creek. Maybe go by the home and visit my mother after that.'

'I'm up for it,' said Janine.

'Lionel?'

'I got plans,' said Lionel. 'That Wilderness Family trip sounds good and all that. But if you don't mind, I'd just as soon spend my day lookin' at the women up at the mall.'

Billy rang them up at the register. On the way out, Strange stopped, as he always did, at the wall by the front door, where several faded photographs were framed and hung. In one, Strange's father stood tall, with his chef's hat cocked rakishly, a spatula in one hand, a smile on his chiseled, handsome face. Mike Georgelakos, short and rotund, stood beside him.

'That's him right there,' said Strange, and neither Lionel nor Janine said a thing, because they knew that Strange was just having a moment to himself.

'*Yasou,* Derek,' said Billy Georgelakos from behind the counter.

'*Yasou, Vasili,*' said Strange, turning to wave at his friend. Strange winked at Lionel, who was obviously impressed, as they headed for the door.

Quinn walked south on Georgia Avenue, through Silver Spring and down over the District line, sometime after noon on Sunday. He passed tattoo parlors and car washes, auto detailers, African American-owned barber shops and clothing stores, beer markets and fried-chicken shacks, and stores selling cell phones and pagers. He walked for an hour without stopping. The day was cold, but the sun and his movement kept him warm.

He stopped at a small used-car lot on the west side of Georgia. Multicolored plastic propellers had been strung around the perimeter, and they spun in the wind. There was a trailer on the edge of the lot where salesmen went for the close, and above the trailer door a large sign had been mounted and encircled with marquee-style lights. The sign read, 'Eddie Rider's, Where Everyone Rides!' Quinn walked onto the lot.

Quinn wasn't a car freak, but his stint as a police officer had put him in the habit of mentally recording models and model years. The trouble he'd had the last few years of his job, and the trouble he was having now, standing in the lot and looking at the rows of cars, was distinguishing one manufacturer from another. Most of the cars from the early nineties on looked the same. The Japanese had built the rounded prototypes, and the Americans and the Koreans and even some of the Germans had followed suit. So the back end of a late-model Hyundai was, at a glance, indistinguishable from that of a Lexus or a Mercedes. A fifteen-thousand-dollar Ford looked identical to a forty-thousand-dollar Infiniti. And all the Toyotas – especially the ultra-vanilla Camry, the nineties equivalent of the eighties Honda Accord – were as exciting as the prospect of a house in the suburbs and an early death. Quinn had done without a car for so long because nothing he saw turned him on.

'How ya doing today, sir?' said a startlingly nasal voice behind Quinn.

Quinn turned to find a short, thin, middle-aged black man standing before him. The man wore thick glasses with black frames and a knockoff designer sport jacket over a white shirt and balloon-print tie. He gave Quinn a toothy, capped grin.

'Doin' fine,' said Quinn.

'The name's Tony Tibbs. They call me *Mr* Tibbs. Ha-ha! Just kiddin', man. Actually, they call me Tony the Pony round here, '*cause I give good ride*, y'know what I'm sayin'? I didn't catch your name, did I?'

'It's Terry Quinn.'

'Irish, right?'

'Uh-huh.'

'I never miss. Pride myself on that, too. Hey, you hear about the two Irish gay guys?' Tibbs frowned with theatrical concern. 'You're not gay, are you?'

'Listen—'

'I'm playin' with you, buddy; I can see you're all man. So let me ask you again: you hear about the two Irish gay guys?'

'No.'

'Patrick Fitzgerald and Gerald Fitzpatrick. Ha-ha!' Tibbs cocked his hip. 'You lookin' for somethin' special today, Terry?'

'I need to buy a car.'

'I don't think I can help you, man. Just kiddin'! Ha-ha!'

Quinn looked Tony Tibbs over: pathetic and heroic, both at once. The privileged, who had never had to work, really work, to pay their bills, could ridicule guys like Tibbs all they wanted. Quinn liked him, and he even liked his lousy jokes. But in the interest of time, he thought he needed to set him straight.

'Listen, Tony,' said Quinn. 'Here's the program. I see something I like here and the price seems fair, I'm not gonna haggle with you over it, I'm just gonna pull out my checkbook and write you out a check, today, for the full amount. I don't want to finance anything, hear, I just want to pay you cash money and drive the car off the lot.'

Tibbs looked a little hurt and somewhat confused. Places like this were selling financing, not cars, and they were selling it at a rate of over 20 percent. The no-haggle bit seemed to knock Tibbs down a notch, too.

'I understand,' said Tibbs.

'Also, we go in that trailer there, I don't want to buy a service contract. You even mention it, I'm gonna walk away.'

'Okay.'

'Good,' said Quinn. 'Now sell me a car.'

Nothing stoked Quinn as they walked around the lot. Then they came to a small row of cars beside the trailer, where three old Chevys sat waxed and gleaming in the sunlight.

'What are these?' said Quinn.

'Eddie Rider's pets,' said Tibbs. 'He loves Chevelles, man.'

'They for sale?'

'Sure. He turns them over all the time.' Tibbs saw something in Quinn's eyes. He smelled blood and straightened his posture. 'That's a high-performance sixty-seven right there. Three-fifty twelve bolt.'

Tibbs pointed to a red model with black stripes. 'There goes a seventy-two. Got a cowl induction hood and Hooker headers, man.'

'What about that one?' said Quinn, chin-nodding to the last car in the row, a blue-over-black fastback beauty with Cregar mags.

'That's a pretty SS right there. Three ninety-six, three hundred and fifty horses. Four-on-the-floor Hurst shifter, got those Flowmaster mufflers on it, too.'

'What year is that?'

'Nineteen sixty-nine.'

'The year I was born.'

'You ain't nothin' but a baby, then.'

'Pop the hood on it, will you?'

Quinn got under the hood. The hoses were new, and the belts were tight. You could pour a holsterful of french fries out onto the block and eat off the engine. He pulled the dipstick and smelled its tip.

'Clean, right?' said Tibbs. 'You don't smell nothin' burnt on there, do you?'

'It's clean. Can I take it for a ride?'

'I got the keys inside.'

'How much, by the way?'

'I'm gonna go right to the bottom,' said Tibbs, 'seein' as how you don't like to *haggle*.'

'How much?'

'Sixty-five hundred. That's grand theft auto right there. Boss finds out I sold it for that, I might have to just go ahead and clean out my desk.'

'Sixty-five hundred is right for this car?'

'Sixty-five?' said Tibbs, pursing his lips and bugging his eyes. 'It's right as rain.'

Quinn chuckled.

'What's so funny?'

'Nothin',' said Quinn. 'This car rides as good as it looks, you got yourself a deal.'

23

Quinn met Strange for breakfast on Monday morning at Sweet Daddy's All Souls Paradise House of Prayer, occupying much of M Street between 6th and 7th in Northwest. The church was a modern, well-funded facility serving the community through religious and outreach programs, with a staff of motivated individuals who kept an eye on the grounds in what was a marginal neighborhood at best. Quinn parked his Chevelle in the church-owned, protected lot, and went to the cafeteria on the ground level of the complex.

Uniformed and plainclothes police, community activists, businessmen, parishioners, and local residents ate here every morning. The portions were generous and the prices dirt cheap. The staff's cheer and pleasant manner were fueled by religion.

Quinn built a tray of scrambled eggs, bacon, toast, and grits, and had a seat across from Strange at a long table where several other chairs were occupied by people of various colors and economic backgrounds. Strange was working on a plate of scrapple, eggs, and grits.

A white guy with a friendly smile named Chris O'Shea came over to the table and had a brief conversation with Strange.

'You take it easy now, Derek,' said O'Shea.

'All right then, Chris,' said Strange. 'You do the same.'

Quinn noticed that everywhere they went in D.C., people knew Strange.

'You ready to go to work?' said Strange, pushing his empty tray aside.

'What've you got lined up?'

'We'll hang out near Ricky Kane's house this morning. He lives with his mother out in Wheaton. If he leaves, we'll follow him, see how he fills up his day. Here.' Strange slipped a cell phone out of his jacket along with a slip of paper. 'Use this, it's Ron's. My number is on there and so is yours.'

'No two-way radios?'

'This is easier, man. And unlike a two-way, no one double-takes you these days if you're walking down the street talking on a phone.'

'Like all the other dickheads, you mean.'

'Uh-huh. You got yourself a car, right?'

Quinn nodded. 'Think you're gonna like it, too.'

Out in the lot, Strange laughed when he saw the Super Sport Chevelle with the racing wheels.

'Somethin' wrong?' said Quinn.

'It is pretty.'

'What, then?'

'You youngbloods, always got to be drivin' something says, Look at me. Ron Lattimer's the same way.'

'That Caprice you got looks exactly like a police vehicle. We got less chance of gettin' burned in mine than in yours.'

'Maybe you're right. Anyway, we'll take both of 'em, see how things shake out.'

Ricky Kane's mother owned a small house, brick based with siding, off Viers Mill Road on a street of houses just like it. The builder who'd done the community in the 1960s had showed little ambition and less imagination. From the activity he'd observed in the last hour or so, Strange could see that the residents here were what was left of the original middle-class whites and America's new working-class immigrants: Spanish, Ethiopian, Pakistani, and Korean.

Strange phoned Quinn, who was parked down the street at the next corner.

'You still awake?'

'I got coffee in a thermos,' said Quinn.

'Bet you gotta pee, too.'

'Now that you mention it.'

'You see our boy when he came out?'

'I saw him.'

'Another little punk with a big dog.'

Kane had walked his tan pit bull halfway down the block an hour earlier while Strange took photographs with his long-lensed AE-1. Kane, medium height, blond, and thin, was wearing a thermal vest under a parka, a knit watch cap, and oversized jeans worn low on his hips. He had a hint of a modified goatee on his bony face.

'Tryin' to be an honorary black man,' said Strange.

'He looks like every other white kid I see in the suburbs these days.'

'Yeah, till they figure out what it means to be a black man in America for real.'

'But this guy's got to be close to my age.'

'Uh-huh. He sure doesn't look like the same guy was on the TV interviews, does he?'

'Check out that car of his, too. Kane got rid of that shit-wagon Toyota.' There was a new red Prelude with shiny rims and a high spoiler sitting in the driveway of Kane's house.

'I see it. He did get a settlement.'

'Yeah. That could be it.'

Quinn took a sip of coffee from the thermos. 'I tell you how much we enjoyed meeting Janine the other night?'

'She's cool. Hell of an office manager, too. You got yourself a fine young lady there as well.'

'I know it,' said Quinn.

'All right, here comes our boy.'

Kane was coming out of the house with a gym bag in his hand. He opened the trunk of the Prelude and dropped the gym bag in, closing the lid and locking it.

'Goin' to work out,' said Quinn. 'You think?'

'Maybe.'

'I'll go first,' said Quinn.

'Yeah,' said Strange. 'Wouldn't want him to burn me or nothin' like that.'

Strange and Quinn circled the block while Kane went into a 7-Eleven for coffee and smokes, then picked him up again as he headed south into D.C. They hung back several car lengths, as Kane's red car was easy to track. He took 13th Street all the way downtown, cutting over to 14th and pulling into a Carr Park garage down past F.

'Should I follow him into the garage?' asked Quinn.

'Park on the street,' said Strange into the phone. 'Park illegal if you have to; I'll pay the ticket.'

Quinn curbed the Chevelle. Strange did the same to the Caprice, a half block south.

'What now?' said Quinn.

'Elevators in that garage go up into that building to the left of it. Unless he's got business in that building – and I don't think he does – he'll be coming out those double glass doors right there in about three or four minutes.'

'Why don't you think he's going up into the building?'

''Cause he's goin' to that restaurant, the Purple Cactus, across the street.'

'Want me to follow him?'

'He knows what you look like, but not since you grew that lion's head of hair you got. So go ahead. You got shades?'

'Sure.'

'Wear 'em. Only kind of disguise you'll ever need without overdoin' it. And when you're following a man, use the city, Terry.'

'Explain.'

'Keep the subject's image in your mind all the time, but indirectly. Watch where he's goin' in the reflection of the plate glass windows, in the car windows, in the metal of the cars themselves. Lose yourself in the crowd.'

'There he is.'

'Go on.'

Quinn got out of the car and loitered near the building. Kane emerged from the building's glass doors. Strange watched Quinn follow, staying back in the moderate, late-morning throng moving along the sidewalk. With his shades and the hair, Quinn looked more like a rocker with shoulders than he did a cop. Kane crossed the street and entered the Purple Cactus.

Strange phoned Quinn. 'Go on in. They'll be settin' up for lunch; just tell 'em you're thinking of bringing a date there or somethin' and you're checking the place out. Try and see what he's doin' in there.'

'Don't let Kane recognize me, right?'

'Funny.'

Quinn came out of the Purple Cactus five minutes later and crossed the street. He got into the Chevelle and phoned Strange.

'He was talking to a couple of the waiters and a bartender downstairs. Old home week, I guess. He's coming out now.'

When Kane pulled the Prelude out of the garage and onto 14th Street, Strange said, 'Let's roll.'

Kane parked four blocks north in another garage. Strange followed him on foot this time, making a bet to himself that he knew where Kane was headed.

Kane walked into Sea D.C., the fancy seafood dining room and bar at the corner of 14th and K. The restaurant was fronted in glass, so Strange didn't need to risk going inside. Kane was talking to a man behind the bar, which was elevated on a kind of platform above the rest of the dining room.

Back in the car, Strange said into the phone, 'He's making the rounds.'

'What is he, a food broker?'

'He sellin' *something*; that's a bet. Usually, you see a guy hangin' around with restaurant employees like that, it means he's making book.'

'Or taking orders for something else.'

'I heard *that*. Here he comes, man. Get ready to move.' Strange pushed the 'end' button on the cell phone. He didn't tell Quinn that Sea D.C. was the last place Sondra Wilson had worked before she disappeared.

Kane drove to a velvet-rope, exclusive club over at 18th and Jefferson, where people were often refused entry for having the wrong haircut or the wrong label on their trousers. He next hit a Eurodisco on 9th, across from the old 9:30, a notorious nightspot for beret wearers and Middle Eastern trust-fund kids with coke habits. He drove to U Street and parked in front of a buppie nightclub. The pattern was the same: five minutes, in and out.

Kane drove east on Florida Avenue. Quinn and Strange followed.

Cherokee Coleman took a gold pen off his desk and tapped it on the blotter before him. 'You lookin' large, Adonis.'

Adonis Delgado, seated in front of the desk, glanced down at his crossed arms, defined beneath the blue of his uniform. He flexed a little, and the folds and wrinkles in his sleeves disappeared. 'I been workin' on it.'

'Looks like you have been. Think he looks bigger, Angie?'

Big-Ass Angelo stood behind Coleman, who was in his leather chair. Angelo shrugged, his face impassive behind his designer shades.

'You ain't been using them steroids, have you?' asked Coleman with mock concern.

'You know I don't use that shit,' said Adonis. He had shot himself up that very morning, after a two-hour session at the gym.

''Cause you know those drugs fuck up your privates. Make you tiny as a Chinaman and shit.'

'My privates are fine,' said Adonis with a scary smile, his mouth a riot of widely spaced, crooked teeth.

Adonis Delgado was an ugly, light-skinned man. His forehead was high and very wide, and he had a stoved-in nose with nostrils that flared upward in a porcine manner. His eyes were dead black and Asian in shape. Big-Ass Angelo said that Delgado looked like one of those mongoloid retards, like the one on that television show he used to watch on Sunday nights when he wasn't much more than a kid. Angelo called Delgado 'Corky,' but never when he was in the room.

'So what do we owe this honor to today, Adonis?' said Coleman. 'Ain't many times you like to face-to-face it with us. Mostly you just drive around the perimeter, makin' the streets safe for our citizens. Me and Angie, we were gettin' the idea you didn't like associatin' with us types anymore.'

'I came in to make sure we're clear on that Boone thing. Time comes, I want to make the last run out there myself.'

'You and Bucky, you mean.'

'Sure.'

'He gonna be down with it?'

'He does what I tell him to do.'

'Okay.' Coleman cocked an eyebrow. 'You seem kind of tense. You're not mad at me, are you, Adonis? Wouldn't be because I let Earl Boone take away your girlfriend, is it?'

'Shit. You talkin' about that skeeze over in the Yard?'

'So you're not *mad*.'

Coleman and Delgado stared each other down for a moment.

Delgado sniffed and rubbed his nose. 'Like I said, she's just a fiend attached to a set of lips. I let her suck my dick once or twice is all it was. I'm through with Ray and Earl, I'll just go ahead and add her to the pile.'

'You want my advice, you're gonna kick it with her one last time, I'd wear two or three safes, man.'

'I always double up,' said Delgado. 'Four-X Magnums, too.'

'No doubt,' said Coleman.

The cell phone rang on Coleman's desk. Coleman answered it, said, 'Okay,' and killed the connection.

'What is it, Cherokee?' said Angelo.

'Our little Caucasian brother is on his way in.'

'I'll wait right here,' said Adonis, 'you don't mind.'

'You got personal business with him?'

'He owes me money.'

'Hittin' him up, too. Nice to see you expandin' your client base, *Officer* Delgado.'

'I did plenty for that white boy. And I don't do a got-damn thing for free.' Delgado pulled a cigar from his blue jacket hung on the back of his chair.

'Prefer you didn't smoke that in here,' said Coleman. 'Me and Angie, we can't take the smell.'

Quinn and Strange followed Kane to a side street just east of Florida and North Capitol. As Strange saw the drug setup and the boys on the street, he said into the phone, 'Hold up, Terry; I'm gonna take off and go up ahead. Tail me until I pull over and pick me up.'

'Right.'

Kane pulled up to an open garage door and drove through it into a bay. Strange watched him, then made a right turn. Quinn followed. Strange got back on Florida and went east to the Korean food market complex, parking his car in the lot. He grabbed his AE-1, jumped out of his car, and got into Quinn's Chevelle.

'Punch it,' said Strange.

Quinn drove quickly back to the street off Florida where all of the drug activity was in plain sight. He parked far away, three blocks back from the action, and let the engine idle. Up ahead, young men stood lazy as cats against brick walls, on corners, and around a decaying warehouselike structure encircled with broken yellow police tape. Along with Japanese and German sedans, and several SUVs, an MPD cruiser was curbed on the street in front of a short strip of row houses, many of their windows boarded.

'You see that Crown Vic?' said Quinn.

'I see it,' said Strange, his voice little more than a whisper.

'You need me to get closer?'

Strange leaned out his open window and snapped off several photographs. 'I'm all right. Five-hundred-millimeter lens, it's like having a nice set of binos.'

'There's our boy.'

They watched Ricky Kane come out of the garage and cross the street like he owned it. He met a couple of the young men on the corner of the strip of houses and was escorted into the row house nearest the cop car parked beside the curb.

'What the *fuck* we got goin' on here?' said Strange.

'You tell me,' said Quinn.

'Ever hear of Cherokee Coleman?'

'Yeah, I've heard of him. Like every cop and most of the citizens in D.C. What do you know about him?'

'Coleman played guard for the Green Wave over at Spingarn. He came out in eighty-nine. He could go to the hole, but he didn't have the height and his game wasn't complete, so college wasn't in the picture. Rose up in the ranks down here real quick after committing a couple of brazen murders they couldn't manage to pin on him. So the high school that gave the world Elgin Baylor and Dave Bing also gave us one of the most murderous drug dealers this town's ever seen.'

'I read this interview the *Post* did with some of the kids over in LeDroit Park. They talk about Coleman like he's some kind of hero.'

'He employs more of their older brothers and cousins than McDonald's does in this city, man.'

'Cherokee,' said Quinn, side-glancing Strange. 'Why do so many light-skinned black guys claim they got Indian blood in 'em, Derek? I always wondered that.'

''Cause they don't want to admit they're carrying white blood, I expect.' Strange lowered the camera. 'Coleman works out of this area right here.'

'Everybody knows it, and it keeps goin' on.'

'Because he's smart. Drugs don't ever touch his hands, so how they gonna bust him, man? You see those boys out there on that street? All of 'em got a separate function. You got the steerers leading the customers to the pitchers, making the hand-to-hand transactions. And then there's the lookouts, and the moneymen who handle the cash. The ones just gettin' into the business, always the youngest, they're the ones who touch the heroin and the rock and the cocaine. And even they don't carry it on 'em. You look real close, you see they're always nearby a place where you can hide a crack vial or a dime in a magnetic key case or in a space cut in a wall. And they're always close to an escape route where they can get out quick on foot: an alley or a hole in a fence.

'Once in a while the MPD will come through here and run a big bust. And it doesn't do a *god*damn thing. You can bust these kids, see, and you can bust the users, but so what? The kids serve no time on the first couple of arrests, especially if there's no quantity to speak of. The users get a night in jail, if that much, and do community service. And the kingpins go untouched.'

'You sayin' that Coleman'll never do hard time?'

'He'll do it. The Feds'll get him on tax evasion, the way they get most of 'em in the end. Or one of his own will turn him for an old murder beef on a plea. Either way, eventually he'll go down. But not until he's fucked up a whole lot of lives.'

Quinn nodded toward the warehouse, where addicts were walking slowly in and out of large holes hammered out of brick walls. A rat scurried over a hill of dirt, unafraid of the daylight or the humans shuffling by.

'There's where they go to slam it,' said Quinn.

'Uh-huh. I bet a whole lot of junkies be livin' in there, too.'

Quinn said, 'What about Kane?'

'Yeah, what about our boy Ricky Kane, huh? You ask me right now,

I'd say he's makin' a pickup. I'd say he was takin' orders back there from the staffs of those restaurants and bars. What do you think?'

'I was thinkin' the same way.'

Kane came out of the row house. He crossed the street quickly and headed in the direction of the warehouse structure.

'Fuck's he doin' now?' said Strange, looking through the lens of the camera and snapping off two more shots.

'Derek,' said Quinn.

Kane ducked inside one of the large holes that had been opened in the warehouse walls.

'We can't be hangin' out here too long, Derek. We can't wait for Kane to come back out.'

'I know it. One of Coleman's boys is gonna burn us soon for sure, and that cop, wherever he is, he's gotta be getting back to his car.'

'Let's take off. We've got enough for today.'

'Get me to within a block of that cruiser, man, then book right.'

Quinn pushed the Hurst shifter into first gear, worked the clutch, and caught rubber coming off the curb. He slammed the shifter into second. A couple of the boys on the corner turned their heads, and one of them began to yell in the direction of the car. Strange got himself halfway out the window and sat on the lip, his elbows on the roof of the car. He took several photographs of the police cruiser, shooting over the roof, and got back into the car just as Quinn cut a sharp right at the next side street. In the rearview, Quinn saw one of the boys chasing them on foot.

'God damn, Terry. I tell you to make all that noise? You must have left an inch of tread on the asphalt.'

'I'm not used to the car yet.'

'Yeah, well, we can't bring it down here again.'

'Why, we comin' back?'

'*I* am,' said Strange, sitting back in the seat and letting the cold wind blow against his face. 'There's more to learn, back there on that street.'

24

Quinn woke up on Tuesday morning in the bedroom of his apartment and sat up on the edge of his mattress, which lay directly on the floor. There was a footlocker in his room and a nightstand he had bought at a consignment shop, with a lamp and an alarm clock on the nightstand and four or five paperback westerns stacked beside the clock. There were no pictures or posters of any kind on the bedroom walls.

Quinn rubbed his temples. He had downed a couple of beers at the Quarry House the night before, then walked by Rosita's, but Juana was not on shift. He went down to his apartment on Sligo Avenue, phoned her and left a message on her machine, and waited a while for her to call him back. But she did not call him back, and he left the apartment and walked down the street to the Tradesmen's Tavern, where he shot a game of pool and drank two more bottles of Budweiser, then returned to his place. Juana had not phoned.

Quinn made coffee and toast in his narrow kitchen, then changed into sweats and went down to the basement of the apartment building, where he had set up a weight bench and a mirror and mats, and had hung a jump rope on a nail driven into the cinder-block wall. The resident manager had allowed him this space if he agreed to share the exercise equipment with the other tenants. A handful of black kids and a Spanish or two from nearby apartment buildings found out about the basement and occasionally worked out with Quinn. He often helped them, if they were not the kind of boys with smart mouths and attitudes, and sometimes he even learned their names. Mostly, though, he worked out down here alone.

After his shower, Quinn went to the bottom drawer of his dresser and retrieved the nine-millimeter Glock he had purchased several months earlier after a conversation with a man at the bar of a local tavern off Georgia. He took the gun apart and used his Alsa kit to clean it, then reassembled the weapon. He had no logical reason to own the Glock, he knew. But he had felt naked and incomplete since he'd turned in his service weapon when he left the force. Cops got used to having guns, and he felt good knowing there was one within reach now. He replaced the Glock in its case, which sat alongside a gun belt he had purchased at a supply house in Springfield, over the river.

He watched a little television but quickly turned it off. Quinn phoned Strange at the office and got Janine.

'He's out, Terry.'

'Can you beep him?'

'Sure, I'll try. But he might be into something, you know, where he can't get back to me right away.'

Quinn heard something false and a bit of regret in Janine's voice.

'Let him know I'm looking for him, Janine. Thanks a lot.'

Quinn got off the phone. Juana had been avoiding him since Saturday night. Now it seemed like Strange was ducking him, too.

Strange stood before Janine's desk.

'Ron call in?' he said.

'He's out there working a couple of skips. They should bring some money into the till this week.'

'Good. You go to the bank for me?'

'Here,' said Janine, handing Strange a small envelope. 'Two hundred in twenties, like you asked.'

'Thanks. I'm gonna be out all day. It's an emergency, you know how to get ahold of me. Otherwise, just take messages here, and I'll check in from time to time.'

'You're puttin' all your focus into this Wilson case.'

'I'm almost there. Pick up those photographs I put in yesterday, will you? And phone Lydell Blue for me, tell him I might be callin' him for another favor.'

'You keeping track of your hours, Derek? Your expenses?'

'Yeah, I'm doin' all that.'

Janine crossed her arms, sat back in her chair. 'I didn't like lying to Terry like that.'

'You're just doin' what I told you to do. The next couple of days, I got to work this thing by myself. It's too tricky for two. Time comes, I'll bring him back in.'

Strange went for the door.

'Derek?'

Strange turned. 'Yeah.'

'This weekend was nice. It was nice waking up next to you, I mean.

Good for Lionel, too. The three of us going out for breakfast on Sunday morning, it was like a family—'

'All right, Janine. I'll see you later, hear?'

Out on 9th, Strange buttoned his leather against the chill and walked toward his Caprice, passing Hawk's barber shop, and Marshall's funeral parlor, and the lunch counter that had the 'Meat' sign out front. He thought of Janine and what she'd said. She was right, the weekend had been pretty nice. Knowing she was right scared him some, too.

Strange decided that he ought to call that woman named Helen, the one he'd met in a club over Christmas, see if she wanted to hook up for a drink. He'd been meaning to get up with her, but lately, busy as he was, the girl had just slipped his mind.

Strange parked the Caprice on North Capitol, near the Florida Avenue intersection, and walked east. He walked for a while, and as he approached Coleman's street he picked up a handful of dirt and rubbed it on his face, then bent over and rubbed some on his oilskin workboots. He had upcombed his hair back in the car. He wore an old corduroy jacket he kept folded in the trunk.

On the street he began to pass some of Coleman's young men. He put a kind of shuffle in his step, and he didn't look at them, he looked straight ahead. He passed a crackhead who asked him for money, and he kept walking, toward the warehouse surrounded by the broken yellow tape. Today, the cop cruiser was not on the street. He walked over a large mound of dirt, stumbling deliberately as he came down off the other side, and he headed for a hole in the warehouse wall. He stepped through the hole.

The room was large, its space broken by I beams, bird shit, and puddled water on the concrete floor. Pigeons nested on the tops of the I beams, and some flew overhead. Strange liked birds, but not when they were flying around indoors. He kept the dead look in his eyes, staring ahead, as he heard the flap of their wings.

From the shadows of his room, Tonio Morris watched the broad-shouldered brother come into the main room of the first floor, mumbling what Tonio recognized as an early rap off a Gil Scott-Heron LP he'd owned once and sold. The man, square in his middle age, was moving slow and had a zero kind of look on his face like he had the sickness, and he was dirty and wearin' fucked up clothes, but he wasn't who he was tryin' to appear to be. Tonio had lived it and lived around it for too long. He *knew.*

Tonio watched the brother cross the room, mumbling to himself, sloshing through the deep puddles without bothering to pick up his feet, heading for the stairs. He wasn't no cop. No cop would come in this motherfucker right here alone. The man wanted somethin', thought Tonio. Had to want it bad to come into a place like this, too.

'Kent State,' said Strange, 'Jackson State . . .'

Strange neared a young man at the bottom of the stairs who was holding an automatic pistol at his side. The young man looked him over as he passed, and Strange slowly went up the exposed steps. He mumbled the spoken verse to 'H2Ogate Blues' under his breath; he knew the entire piece by heart, and reciting it allowed him to ramble on without having to think about what he would say, and it calmed his nerves.

'The chaining and gagging of Bobby Seale,' said Strange. 'Someone tell these Maryland governors to be for real!'

He was upstairs in a hall and followed the sounds of muted chatter and activity to a bathroom facility with open stalls. A man yelled something in his direction, and he kept walking, taking measured breaths through his mouth, steeling himself against the stench. Candles illuminated the stalls. The floor was slick with excrement and vomit. He came to the last stall, which was occupied by a man in a sweater, the cuffs of which completely covered his hands. The man, a skeleton covered in skin, was smiling at Strange, and Strange turned around and headed back the way he'd come. There was nothing here, no one to talk to or see, nothing at all.

The brother was back in the main room, heading toward the hole he'd come through, pigeons fluttering above his head. Walking slow but not as slow as before, Tonio Morris thinking, he didn't find nothin', and now he's fixin' to get out quick.

'Psst,' said Tonio, his face half out of the shadows of his room. 'Got what you're lookin' for, brother.'

The man slowed his pace but he didn't stop or turn his head.

'Got information for you, man.' Tonio wiggled his index finger, keeping his voice low. 'Come on over here and get it, brother. Ain't gonna hurt you none to find out. Come on.'

Strange turned and regarded a sick little man standing in the open doorway of a black room. The man wore a filthy gray sweatshirt, and his trousers were held up loosely with a length of rope. His shoes were split completely, separated from the uppers at the soles.

Strange walked toward the man, stopping beside a large puddle by an I beam six feet from the doorway. The I beam blocked the sight line of the young man standing by the stairs. Strange stared at the skinny man's face; his eyes were milky and glaucomic. Over the years he'd seen this death mask many times on the faces of those who were ready to pass, when he visited his mother at the home.

'What do you want?' said Strange, keeping his voice low.

'What I want? To get high. Higher than a motherfucker, man, but I need money for that. You got any money?'

Strange didn't answer.

'Suck your dick for ten dollars,' said Morris. 'Shit, I'll suck that motherfucker good for five.'

Strange turned his head and looked back toward the hole in the wall.

'Hold up, man,' said Morris. 'The name is Tonio.'

'I ask you your name?'

'You lookin' for somethin', right? Something or someone, ain't that *right.* Any fool can see you ain't one of us. You tryin', but you ain't. You can dirty yourself all you want, but you still got your body and you still got your eyes. So what you lookin' for, brother. Huh?'

Strange shifted his posture. Water dripped from an opening in the ceiling and dimpled the puddle pooled beside his right foot.

'White boy come in here yesterday afternoon,' said Strange. 'Don't imagine you get too many of those.'

'Not too many.'

'Skinny white boy with a knit cap, tryin' to be down.'

'I know him. I seen him, man; I see *every*thing. You got money for Tonio, man?'

'This white boy, what's he doin' in here? Is he slammin' it upstairs?'

'The white boy ain't no fiend.'

'What, then? What kind of business he got with Coleman?'

'Do I look crazy to you? I ain't know a *mother*fuckin' thing about no Coleman, and if I did, I still don't know a thing.'

Strange pulled folded twenties from his wallet. He peeled one off, crumpled it in a ball, and tossed it to the floor at Morris's feet. Morris picked the bill up quickly and jammed it in the pocket of his trousers.

'What was the white boy doin' in here?' said Strange.

'Lookin' for a girl,' said Morris. 'A friend of mine. Old friend to him, too.'

Strange's blood ticked. 'A girl?'

'Girl named Sondra,' said Morris.

'This girl got a last name?' said Strange, his voice hoarse and odd to his own ears.

'She got one. I don't know it.'

'This her right here?'

Strange pulled the photograph of Sondra Wilson from his corduroy jacket, held it up for Morris to see. Morris nodded, his mouth twitching involuntarily. Strange slipped the picture back into his pocket.

'He find her?' asked Strange.

'Huh?'

'Is she *here*?'

Morris licked his dry lips and pointed his chin at the bankroll in Strange's hand. Strange crumpled another twenty and dropped it on the floor.

Morris smiled. His teeth were black stubs, raisins stuck loosely in rotted gums. 'What'sa matter, brother? You don't want to touch my hands?'

'Where is she?'

'Sondra *gone*, man.'

'Where is she?' repeated Strange.

'Two white men took her out of here, not too long ago. Little cross-eyed motherfucker and an old man. I don't know 'em. I don't know their names. And I don't know where they went.'

Strange didn't speak. He balled and unballed one fist.

'They're comin' back,' said Morris playfully.

'How you know that?'

'Word gets out in here . . . The ones across the street, that one by the stairs . . . they know when we be gettin' too hungry. They tell us when we're about to be fed. And we are about to be fed. Those white men are bringin' it in.'

'When?'

'Tomorrow. Leastways, that's what I hear.'

Strange reached into his breast pocket and withdrew one more folded twenty. Morris held his hand out, but Strange did not fill it.

'What do you know about the girl?'

'The white boy, he used to bring her with him when he made his visits. He'd take her with him to that place across the street. One day he left her in there. She was across the street for a few weeks, comin' and goin' in those pretty-ass cars. A month, maybe, like that. Then she made her way over here. She kept her own stall up there on the second floor. But she never did make it back across the street.'

'You know what time those two white men are coming back tomorrow?'

'No,' said Morris, looking sadly at the twenty, still in Strange's possession.

Strange placed the bill in Morris's outstretched hand. 'You see me around here again, you don't know me, 'less I tell you that you know me. Understand?'

'Know who?'

Strange nodded. Most likely he'd just given that junkie more money than he'd seen at one time in the last few years.

Strange turned and shuffled off toward the hole from which he'd entered. There was a racing in his veins, and he could feel the beat of his own heart. It was difficult for him to move so slowly. But he managed, and soon he was out in the light.

25

Strange woke from a nap in the early evening. His bedroom was dark, and he flicked on a light. Greco, lying on a throw-rug at the foot of the bed, lifted his head from his paws and slowly wagged his tail.

'Hungry, buddy?' said Strange. 'All right, then. Let this old man get on up out of this bed.'

After Strange fed Greco, he listened to the soundtrack of *A Pistol for Ringo* as he sat at his desk and went through the matchbooks spilled across it: Sea D.C., the Purple Cactus, the Jefferson Street Lounge, the Bank Vault on 9th, the Shaw Lounge on U, Kinnison's on Pennsylvania Avenue, Robert Farrelly's in Georgetown, and many others. These were Chris Wilson's matchbooks; Wilson *knew.*

Strange reached for the phone on the desk and called the Purple Cactus. He got the information he needed and racked the receiver. Strange rubbed his face and then his eyes.

He stripped himself out of his clothes. He took a shower and changed into a black turtleneck and slacks, then phoned the woman named Helen. Helen was busy that night and on the upcoming weekend. He called another woman he knew, but this woman did not pick up her phone.

Strange got into his black leather, slipped a few items into its pockets, patted Greco on the head, and left his house. He drove his Cadillac downtown, listening to *Live It Up* all the way, repeating 'Hello It's Me,' because he really liked the Isleys' arrangement of that song. He parked on 14th at H, walked to the K Street intersection, and entered Sea D.C.

The dining room and the dining balcony were full, and the patrons were three deep at the elevated bar. Many were smoking cigarettes and cigars. A narrow-shouldered manager with a tiny mustache was trying to get a group of men, all of them smoking, to step closer in toward the bar. His emotional, exasperated, high-pitched voice was making the men laugh. A television mounted above the call racks was set on the stock market report, and some of the fellows at the bar were staring up at the ticker symbols and figures traveling right to left across the screen as they sipped their drinks.

Strange politely muscled his way into a position at the end of the stick. White people, in a setting like this one, generally let a black man do whatever he wanted to do.

Strange waited for a while and finally caught the bartender's eye. The bartender was trim, clean shaven, and of medium height. He had a false smile, and he flashed it at Strange as he leaned on the bar and placed one hand palm down on the mahogany.

'What can I get ya, friend?' said the bartender.

'Ricky Kane,' said Strange, giving the bartender the same kind of smile.

'What, is that a drink?'

Strange placed his hand over the back of the bartender's hand. He ground his thumb into the nerve located in the fleshy triangle between the bartender's thumb and forefinger. The color drained from the bartender's face.

'Saw you talkin' to Ricky Kane yesterday,' said Strange, still smiling, keeping his voice even and light. 'I'm an investigator, *friend.* You want me to, I'll pull my ID and show it to you right here. Show it to your manager, too.'

The bartender's Adam's apple bobbed, and he issued a short shake of his head.

'I don't want you,' said Strange, 'but I don't give a *fuck* about you, understand? What I want to know is, was Ricky Kane hooked up with Sondra Wilson?'

'Sondra?'

'Sondra Wilson. She worked here, case you've forgotten.'

'I don't know . . . maybe he was. He picked her up once at closing time when she was working here, but she didn't work here all that long. She lasted, like, a week.'

'She get fired?'

'She had attendance problems,' said the bartender, his eyes going down to the stick. 'My hand.'

'Barkeep!' yelled a guy wearing suspenders, from the other end of the bar.

Strange said, 'Kane and Sondra Wilson.'

'He met her over at Kinnison's, that seafood restaurant over near George Washington. She was working at Kinnison's before she came here. He was a waiter over there before he took the gig at the Cactus.'

'Bartender!'

Strange leaned forward. 'You tell Kane or anyone else I came by, I'm gonna send my people in here and shut this motherfucker down. Put you in the D.C. Jail in one of those orange jumpsuits they got, in a cell with some real men. You understand what I'm tellin' you, friend?'

The bartender nodded. Strange released him. He bumped a woman as he turned and he said, 'Excuse me.' He unglued the smile that was on his face, shifting his shoulders under his leather jacket as he went out the door.

Strange went over to Stan's on Vermont Avenue and ordered a Johnnie Walker Red with a side of soda. The tender was playing Johnnie Taylor's 'Disco Lady' on the house system, the one that had Bootsy Collins on session bass. Strange liked the flow of that song. A man took a seat next to him at the bar.

'Strange, how you doin'?'

'Doin' good, Junie, how *you* been?'

'All right. You look a little worn down, man, you don't mind my sayin' so. You all right?'

Strange looked at his reflection in the bar mirror. He took a cocktail napkin from a stack and wiped sweat from his face.

'I'm fine,' said Strange. 'Little hot in this joint, is all it is.'

Strange sat at the downstairs bar of the Purple Cactus. There were several empty tables in the dining area of the restaurant, and Strange was alone at the bar. The smiles and relaxation on the faces of the waitstaff told him that the evening rush had ended.

Strange ordered a bottle of beer and drank it slowly. The brunette named Lenna, the sensible girl with the intelligent eyes he'd seen on his earlier visit, was working tonight. He knew she'd be here; he'd phoned earlier to confirm it. Strange caught her eye as she dressed a cocktail with fruit and a swizzle stick down at the service end of the bar. The woman smiled at him before placing the drink on a round tray with several others. Strange smiled back.

The next time she passed behind him he swiveled on his stool and said, 'Pardon me.'

She stopped and said, 'Yes?'

'Your name is Lenna, right?'

She brushed a strand of hair off her face. 'That's right.'

Strange handed her a cocktail napkin with the words 'one hundred dollars' printed in ink across it.

'I don't understand,' she said.

'It's yours for real if you give me fifteen minutes of your time.'

'Now wait a minute,' she said, making the 'stop' sign with her palm, but he could see from her crooked smile that she was more curious than annoyed.

'I'm an investigator,' said Strange, and he flipped open his wallet to show her his license. 'Private, not police.'

'What's this about?'

'Ricky Kane.'

'Forget it.'

'I'm not lookin' to get you or anyone you work with in any trouble. This isn't about him or what he does here. You've got my word.'

Lenna crossed her arms and looked around the room.

'Meet me at the upstairs bar,' said Strange. 'I'm gonna double your take tonight for fifteen minutes of conversation. And I'll buy the drinks.'

'I've got to close out my last table,' said Lenna, not meeting his eyes.

'Half hour,' said Strange.

Strange watched her drift. Prostitutes and junkies were the best informants on the street. Waitresses, bartenders, UPS drivers, and laborers were pretty good, too. They cost a little more, but whatever the cost, Strange had learned that most people, the ones who knew the value of a dollar, had a price.

'How long did Ricky work here?' said Strange.

'Not too long,' said Lenna. 'The incident with the police officer happened about a month after he came. The settlement came pretty quickly after that, and then he was gone.'

Strange hit his beer, and Lenna took a sip of hers. Her eyes were a pale shade of brown, her lips thick and lush. She had changed into her street clothes and combed out her shoulder-length, shiny brown hair. Strange noticed she had sprayed some kind of perfume on as well.

'What'd you think when it went down? Given that you knew Kane was dealing drugs, did you have any doubts about what you read in the papers? Did you think that maybe there was something else going on that night that they had missed?'

'Sure, it crossed my mind.' Lenna looked around her. The nearest couple was seated four stools down the bar, and the tender was working under a dim light by the register. 'A few of us talked about it between ourselves. Look, I put myself through undergrad waiting tables, and this place has financed half of my grad school tuition so far. Over the years I've worked at some of the most popular restaurants in this city. You got any kind of late-night bar business, you're gonna have someone on the payroll, whether you're aware of it or not, who's a drug source for the staff and the customers. A restaurant has a natural client base, and a bar's about the safest place you can cop. I mean, it's not unusual or anything like that, given the environment.

'And then there's the perception most of the people in this city have of the police. What I'm saying is, you're talking about two different issues here. Ricky Kane was a dealer, but nobody really believed he had been stopped that night for selling drugs. He probably got stopped and hassled for urinating in the street, just like they said. The feeling was, it could have been any of us out there. At one time or another, we've all had some kind of negative experience with the police.'

'All right. How you feel about him now, then?'

'What do you mean?'

'Old Ricky is still comin' in here, doin' business. He was in here yesterday, taking orders, right?'

'I told you I wasn't going to talk about my co-workers and friends. They want to get involved with Ricky, it's their business, not mine.'

'You must have an opinion about what he's doing, though, right?'

Lenna nodded, looking at the glass of beer in her hand. 'I don't like Ricky. I don't like what he does. I'm no user now, but I walked through that door when I was younger. For me it was coke. Now it's heroin for the younger ones and the after-hours crowd. That's the low ride down. The ones who are using it don't know it or won't admit it, but there it is. Anyway, like I say, it's none of my business. Anything else?'

'One more thing.' Strange slipped the photograph of Sondra Wilson from his leather. 'You recognize this woman? Ever see her with Kane?'

'No,' said Lenna, after examining it closely. 'Not exactly.'

'What's that mean, not *exactly*?'

Lenna shrugged. 'Ricky liked light-skinned black women, exclusively. She fits the bill. None of them had grass growing under their feet, I can tell you that. I don't recall ever seeing him with the same one twice.'

Strange took a long pull off his beer. He set the bottle on the bar and slipped five folded twenties into Lenna's palm. 'I guess that's it. Sorry if I insulted you earlier. I didn't mean to imply that I was offering you money for something else.'

Lenna shook hair off her shoulder and smiled, the light from the bar candle reflecting in her eyes. 'You're a handsome man. I noticed you when you were in the other night, as a matter of fact. I was kind of hoping it *was* something else.'

'I'm flattered,' said Strange. 'To be honest with you, though, I'm spoken for.'

'I understand.' Lenna got off her stool and drained her beer standing. 'Nice to meet you.'

'And you.'

He watched her leave the restaurant and walk north on 14th. Strange finished his beer, realizing that he was hungry, and maybe a little drunk. Lenna was a good-looking young woman, and he was feeling the need. And it always was nice to get hit on by a woman twenty-five years his junior. These days, it happened less and less. But this Lenna girl didn't interest him. The truth of it was, white women had never been to his taste.

26

Terry Quinn sat at the bar at Rosita's, on Georgia Avenue in downtown Silver Spring, waiting for Juana Burkett to finish her shift. While he waited, Quinn read a British paperback edition of *Woe to Live On* and drank from a bottle of Heineken beer. Juana had smiled at him when he came through the door, but he had lived long enough to know that it was a smile with something sad behind it, and that maybe things between them were coming to an end.

As the last of the diners left the restaurant, Juana came out of the women's room, still dressed in her wait outfit but washed and combed, with a fresh coat of lipstick on her mouth.

'I tipped the busboy out extra to finish my side work. You ready?'

'Yeah,' said Quinn, slipping the paperback into the back pocket of his jeans. 'Let's go.'

Raphael, sitting at a deuce and putting dinner tickets in numerical order, waved them good-bye as they were going out the door.

'Got something in today you'd like,' said Quinn. 'An old George Duke – from the Dukey Stick days.'

' "Talk to me quick," ' said Raphael. 'Hold it for me, will you? I'll be in to pick it up.'

Quinn walked with Juana down Georgia to where the Chevelle sat parked under a street lamp. It shone beautifully in the light.

'This is me,' said Quinn. 'What do you think?'

'For real?'

'C'mon. Let's go for a ride.'

Quinn headed into Rock Creek Park, driving south on the winding road that was Beach Drive, Springsteen coming from the deck. The night was not so cold, and Quinn rolled his window down a quarter turn. Juana did the same. The wind fanned her hair off her shoulders and bit pleasantly at her face.

'Now I know what you like to listen to,' said Juana.

'It speaks to the world I came up in,' said Quinn. 'Anyway, you buy a new ride, you got to christen it with *Darkness on the Edge of Town*. There is no better car tape than that.'

'I like this car,' said Juana.

Juana's hands were in her lap, and she was rubbing one thumb against the knuckle of the other. Quinn reached over and separated her hands. He took hold of one and laced his fingers through hers.

'I'm gonna make this easy on you,' said Quinn.

'Thanks.'

'I got all this baggage, Juana. I'm aware of it, but I don't know what to do about it. If I didn't care about you I'd say, I'm gonna stick around and *let her* work it out. Because I'd stay with you as long as you let me, you know?'

Juana nodded. 'I thought when we met that it could work. But then, out in the world, when other guys were staring at us, making comments when we were walking down the street, I could see that you couldn't handle it. And it's not like it was going to go away. In this wonderful society we got here, no one is ever going to let us forget. There were times, I swear to God, it seemed like you wanted the conflict. Like the promise of that was what got you interested in me in the first place. I never wanted to be your black girlfriend, Tuh-ree. I only wanted to be your girlfriend. In the end, I wasn't sure what was really in your heart.'

'I'll tell you,' said Quinn. 'Maybe, in the beginning, you were some kind of symbol to me, a way to tell everyone that, inside, I was right. But I forgot about that, like, ten minutes after we were together. After that, in my heart, there was only you.'

'It's too intense with you,' said Juana. 'It's too intense *all the time*. Even sometimes when we're making love. The other night—'

'I know.'

'I'm young, Tuh-ree. I got my whole life to deal with the kinds of relationship problems that everyone has to face eventually. Money problems, infidelity, the death of love . . . but I don't want to deal with those things yet. I'm not ready, understand?'

'I know it,' said Quinn, squeezing her hand. 'It's all right.'

Quinn turned left on Sherril Drive and headed up the steep, serpentine hill toward 16th. He downshifted and gave the Chevy gas.

'Nice night,' said Quinn. 'Right?'

Quinn drove back into Silver Spring and parked on Selim. He said to Juana, 'You up for a little walk?'

They crossed the pedestrian bridge over Georgia and came to the chain-link fence.

'I'll give you a leg up,' said Quinn.

'You said a walk, not a climb.'

'C'mon, it's easy.'

On the other side of the fence, they walked by the train station and along the tracks. A Metro train approached from the south. Quinn stopped and embraced Juana, holding her tight to his chest. He looked over to the traffic lights, street lamps, and neon of Georgia Avenue.

'It's beautiful, isn't it?'

Her fingers touched his face.

'Don't forget me,' said Quinn.

He kissed her on the mouth as the train went by, and held the kiss in the storm of dust and wind.

Strange was starving, and he decided he could handle another beer. He left the Purple Cactus and drove over to Chinatown. He parked in an alley, behind a strip on I Street, between 5th and 6th. There was a hustler in the alley, and Strange gave him five dollars to watch his car, promising another five when he returned.

Strange entered the back door of an establishment that fronted I. He went by a kitchen and down a hall, passing several closed doors, and on through a beaded curtain into a small dining room that was sparsely decorated and held a half dozen tables. Several young Chinese women and an older one were working the room. A single white guy sat at a four-top, looking about as much like a tourist as a man could look, drinking a glass of beer.

'Gonna have some dinner, mama,' said Strange to the older woman. She rattled off something to one of the young ones, who led him to a table.

'You like drink?' said the girl.

'Tsingtao,' said Strange.

She brought him a beer and a menu while the other young women tried to catch his eye. There was a slim one with a little bit of back on her that he had already picked out; he had noticed her when he'd walked in.

One of the girls was talking to the tourist sitting at the table, who had set one of those booklet maps next to his beer.

'Whassa matter,' said the young woman to the tourist. 'You neeby be ray?' The other girls laughed.

Strange ate a dish of sesame chicken and white rice, with crispy wontons and a cup of hot-and-sour soup. He drank another beer, listening to the relaxing string music they were playing in the place. When he was done he broke open a fortune cookie and read the message: 'Stop searching forever, happiness is right next to you.'

Strange dropped the message on his plate. He signaled the older woman and told her what he wanted and who he wanted it from.

'Whassa matter,' said the young woman to the tourist, who now looked somewhere between confused and frightened. 'You neeby be ray?'

Strange left money on the table and got up from his chair. The tourist said, 'Excuse me,' and Strange went over to his table.

'Yeah?'

'Do you know what they're trying to ask me?' said the tourist.

'I think she's sayin', ain't you never been *laid*.' Strange went through the beaded curtain, muttering 'stupid' under his breath. He opened one of the closed doors in the hall and entered a series of rooms.

Strange undressed and took a hot shower in a tiled stall. Then he went to a clean white room, dropped the towel he had wrapped around his waist, and lay down nude on a padded table. The young woman he had chosen came into the room and began to give him a full massage. He felt her bare breasts brush his back as she straddled his hips, and he became aroused. She asked him to turn over. It was a relief to lie on his back, as he had a full erection now.

The young woman pumped her fist a couple of times and smiled. Strange said, 'Yes, baby,' and squeezed one of her nipples between his thumb and forefinger. She rubbed lotion on her hands and jacked him off. Afterward, she cleaned him with a warm wet towel.

Strange dressed and dropped forty dollars into a porcelain bowl set by the door. The young woman gave him a look of disappointment, and made a clucking sound with her tongue. But Strange was unmoved; he knew that forty was the price.

Out in the alley, he handed the hustler another five on the way to his car.

'All right,' said the hustler.

Strange said, 'All *right*.'

Strange drove north and parked his Caddy on 9th, directly in front of his business. He turned the key in the front door, went inside, and flicked on the lights. He walked toward his office, glancing at the neatness of Janine's desk. The woman just didn't go home until she had taken care of all the details of her day. He kept on walking to the back room.

In his office, he had a seat at his desk. Janine had picked up the packet of photographs he'd taken down off Florida Avenue. He went through the pictures: Ricky Kane had come out clearly, as had the numbers on the bumper and side of the police cruiser parked out on the street.

Strange reached for the phone. He called his old friend Lydell Blue and left a message on his machine. He didn't want to leave the cruiser's identifying number on Lydell's tape. He phoned Quinn, got his machine, told him they had work to do the next day, told him where and when he'd pick him up.

It was going to be an early day. I shouldn't have drunk so much tonight, thought Strange. I shouldn't have . . .

'Ah, shit.'

Strange saw a PayDay bar sitting on a piece of paper on the corner of his blotter. He lifted the bar and looked at the paper. Janine had drawn a little red heart on the paper, nothing else. Strange looked away and saw the Redskins figure, the one Lionel had painted for him, staring at him from the back of the desk.

'You all right, Derek,' said Strange. But his voice was unconvincing, and the words sounded like a goddamn lie.

27

Edna Loomis was straddling Ray Boone atop their bed, sliding up and down on his thick, short cock, moving her hips in awkward rhythm to the Alan Jackson tune that was blasting in the room. Her head was bent forward as she whipped her orange-blond, feather-cut hair across his pale chest, shaking her head in time to the music.

'She's gone country,' sang Edna. 'Look at them boots!'

Ray chuckled and grabbed one of her tits real good and hard. Edna kind of grunted. He couldn't tell if it was from pleasure or pain.

Ray shot off inside her, and right after that she faked like she was coming, too. He almost laughed, watching her shiver and howl, making a sound like a dog did when you went and stepped down on its paw. She must have seen some actress do that on one of her TV shows. Ray didn't know why she felt the need to fake it; he didn't care if she came or not.

Edna got off him and walked across the room. She turned the music down, then lit a Virginia Slims cigarette from that leather pouch of hers. The hand holding the lighter shook some from the speed that was still racing through her body.

'Turn that music off all the way,' said Ray. 'I'm tired of listenin' to it.'

Edna clicked off the compact stereo. Ray watched her, and when she caught him looking at her she sucked in her stomach. Aside from those dimples she had all over the tops of her legs, the girl was gettin' a belly on her, too.

'Me and Daddy gotta get goin',' said Ray, sitting up on the edge of the bed. He squeezed the rest of his jiz out and wiped it off on the sheets.

'You gonna leave me a little somethin', so I'll have somethin' to do while you're gone?'

'You just smoked up a mess of that crystal before we fucked, girl.'

'Bet your daddy's gonna leave *his* girlfriend a little somethin'.'

'Aw, shut up about that,' said Ray.

Edna stuck her tongue out playfully at Ray, then dragged hard on her cigarette. She wasn't going to make a fuss over it or nothin' like that. She still had that key to the room where he kept his stash, out there in the barn.

Earl Boone zipped up his trousers and looked at the girl stretched out there on his bed. She drew the sheets up to her birdlike shoulders and gazed at him with those funny, sexy, different-colored eyes. He didn't have no, what did you call that, *delusions* about her or anything like that. Sure, once he had got her out here in the country and cleaned her up, and kept her showered and smelling nice, she almost looked like any other good-looking young lady you'd see out there on the street. She was just a junkie, he knew, and if she kept up that pace of hers, she wasn't gonna live too much longer. But damn if she wasn't the prettiest junkie he'd ever seen.

'You gonna be all right, honey girl? 'Cause me and my boy, we got to make a trip into the city.'

'You'll leave me somethin', Earl?'

'Course I will. You know I wouldn't let you have any pain.'

Ray finished dressing. He heard that godawful music Edna was playing in Ray's bedroom down the hall. He hated that new stuff sung by those pretty boys with the department store-bought hats and the tight jeans, wondered why anyone would want to listen to that shit when they could be listenin' to Cash, Jones, Haggard, or Hank. Just when he thought he couldn't stand to listen to it any longer, the music ended. He figured his boy was getting himself ready for their last run.

Ray took a small wax packet of brown heroin from his coat pocket and dropped it on the dresser.

'Be back in a few hours,' he said.

Sondra Wilson watched him leave, closing the bedroom door behind him. She tried not to look at the packet on the dresser. She didn't want to do it up now; she wanted it to last. But then she began to shake a little, thinking of it sitting up there all alone. She thought of her mother and her brother, and began to cry. She wasn't sure why she was so sad. Everything she wanted was here, ten feet away from where she was lying now.

She wiped the tears off her face and got out of the bed. She walked naked across the room.

From the bedroom window, Edna Loomis watched Ray and Earl out in the yard, arguing over something, Earl pointing to a row of stumps at the edge of the woods, where Ray had set up empty beer cans. Ray had his gun in his hand, and Edna figured he was getting ready to shoot the cans off the stumps. Ray liked to do that before their runs, said it got him 'mentally prepared' to deal with those coloreds down in D.C. Earl didn't like Ray shooting off that pistol; he didn't care for all that noise.

He must have talked Ray out of it, because Ray left, then came out of the barn with his gym bag and loaded the heroin into the space behind the bumper of the car. Edna drained her third Jack and Coke of the afternoon, watching him complete his task.

She felt kind of funny, clammylike, and her heart was racing really fast.

You can always be higher, though. Ain't no question about that.

She rattled ice in the glass and sucked out the last few drips of mash as Ray and Earl got in the Taurus and drove away.

Edna got dressed, slipped the barn key into her jeans, and went down the hall, knocking on the door to Earl's room, where that half-colored junkie, Sondra, spent all her time. She opened the door and went through it when the girl didn't respond.

Sondra was naked, sitting on the edge of the bed, using a razor blade to cut out lines of heroin on a glass paperweight. Edna didn't think she'd ever seen a girl that skinny, not even those New York models she'd seen on TV. She didn't know what Earl saw in her, but it wasn't any of her business, and anyway she didn't care.

'I'm goin' for a walk,' said Edna.

'Okay,' said Sondra, not even raising her head.

'I feel like takin' a long one in the woods.'

'Okay.'

'Fine.'

Edna didn't know why she bothered covering her tracks with this one. She left the room.

Sondra bent forward and snorted up a thick line of heroin. She snorted the one beside it at once.

The warmth came almost immediately to the back of her neck. It spread behind her eyes and to the top of her skull. Then it was in her legs and buttocks and traveling like hot, beautiful liquid up her spine and racing through her veins. The edges of the room bled off, and Sondra lay back on the warm bed.

Sondra remembered that she had been crying moments earlier, but she couldn't remember why.

Edna patted her pockets as she walked into the barn and strode briskly through the saloon area toward the back room. She had her little brass pipe in one front pocket, the key in the other. She had wedged her leather pouch holding her pack of Slims and Bic lighter in the ass pocket of her jeans.

Edna used her key in the lock of the steel-fortified door, opened the door, and flicked on the lights. She closed the door behind her. She went quickly to the shelf mounted over Ray's homemade lab. She snatched a vial off the shelf and opened its lid. The vial was filled to the top with crystal rocks.

Edna shoved the entire vial into the pocket of her jeans. Ray wouldn't be back for some time. She was going to mix a tall drink and take a walk out in those woods for real. Smoke up those rocks and have a party her *own* self. She deserved a little treat, the way Ray always left her hangin' like that, when she was doing her best to service him good.

Edna heard a door open from the front of the barn. She turned her head and stumbled back, her own reflection in the weight-lifting mirror giving her an awful startle. Looking down at the floor, she saw the carpet remnant beside the weight bench, not completely covering the trapdoor.

Edna heard boot steps clomping on the barroom floor. She had always been a quick thinker, her friend Johanna told her that all the time. She thought fast and decided. There wasn't but one thing to do.

Ray and Earl had only gotten a mile down the interstate when Ray told Earl they had to turn around and go back to the property.

'I forgot somethin',' said Ray.

'What, that speckled powder?' said Earl.

'It gives me an edge when I'm dealin' with those rugheads.'

'Go on back if you need it,' said Earl, lifting a Busch from the six-pack cooler at his feet. 'Me, everything I need, it comes from a bottle or a can.'

Ray U-turned the Taurus and headed back for the property.

Earl cracked his window, then rolled it down halfway. 'Weather turned yesterday.'

'It'll get cold again.'

'It stays like this, them greasers are gonna get ripe. You best put 'em deep, first chance you get.'

'Ground's still too hard, Daddy.'

'You better get to it, Critter.'

'I'll take *care* of it, Daddy.'

Ray took a deep breath, wondering if his father would ever stop tellin' him what to do.

Ray walked hard across the saloon floor, his fists balled tight. He needed to calm down, but how could he, havin' to take care of all these people, and his business, and on top of it all having to take a boatload of shit from his old man. He pulled his keys off his belt loop and fitted one to the lock on the back door.

The lock had already been turned. He reached for the knob. God damn, the door was already open.

'Edna,' said Ray, shaking his head, because he knew it had to be her had been back here; somehow she'd gotten hold of his key. There wasn't anyone else stupid enough to test him like that.

Ray went to the shelf and took down the spansules of crystal meth. He shoved the vial into a pocket of his jeans. He scanned the shelf: that other vial, the one held the ice, was gone. Edna was probably out in the woods, smokin' it all up at once, greedy bitch that she was. He knew she hadn't driven anywhere, as the F-150 was still parked in the yard.

Ray turned at the sound of the car horn. That would be his daddy, just landin' on it, tellin' him it was time to go.

Ray looked around the room. Somethin' wasn't right . . . Damn, there it was, too, the carpet remnant had been moved off the trapdoor. Must have been moved with all that activity they'd had back here with the Colombians, what with them all floppin' around and shit. Even so, thought Ray, as he moved the carpet aside and lifted the trapdoor, holding his breath against a familiar smell, it doesn't hurt to check.

He looked down the wooden ladder that led into the tunnel. The lights were on down there, but that didn't mean nothin', they worked off the master switch.

Earl landed on that horn again.

'All right!' yelled Ray, though he knew his daddy couldn't hear him.

Ray closed the trapdoor, placed the carpet remnant over it, and dragged the weight bench over a few feet. Now the weight bench sat atop the trapdoor.

Ray shut down the lights before he locked the door from the outside. He took no pleasure in hurting Edna. But he sure was gonna give her some when he came back home.

Edna wasn't scared, not really. Even when Ray had shut the lights down, because she never had been frightened of the dark. She sat on the cold dirt patiently, waiting to make sure Ray had gone away for good, and when she was satisfied, she kind of crawled around some until she found the ladder, and climbed up it to the trapdoor.

The door wouldn't budge. Ray had put somethin' over it. She wasn't surprised. She went back down the ladder and sat, gave herself some time to think.

She'd seen enough of the tunnel, when the lights had been on, to know that it went straight back fifty yards or so, then went off hard to the right. It was a narrow open shaft, and she'd have to go through it like a dog, on her hands and knees, but there wasn't nothin' tricky about it; *it went back and cut right.*

Edna had no doubt that Ray and Earl had rigged some kind of opening at the end of the tunnel, a way for them to escape into the woods from all those imaginary FBI and ATF boys they were always goin' on about. Even Ray, he wasn't dumb enough to go through all that trouble of diggin' a tunnel without providing for a back door.

There was the smell of expired animal down here. Ray said there was snakes in this tunnel, but she wasn't afraid of no snakes, either. She'd lost count of all the black snakes she'd killed with a hoe, growin' up out this way. Maybe there was rats. But rats weren't nothin' but overgrown mice. *Somethin'* had cacked down here, that was for certain, maybe one of those barn cats that were always hanging around. She knew that smell.

Anyway, if she lost her bearings or something, crawling around down here, she could use the disposable lighter she had in her pocket. She was glad she had brought it with her. And the drugs.

Edna had an awful headache. It seemed to be getting worse. She found the vial of ice and the lighter and the pipe, and she hit the lighter so that she could fill the pipe. A little pickup would motor her out of this place quick and just right.

She smoked the rocks, coughing furiously on the last hit, and let the flame go out. The buzz started to build. It was a pleasant buzz at first. Then it was violent and it left her shaking. She realized that maybe she had smoked too much. The space felt very close, and for the first time she was frightened, though she wasn't sure of what. She wanted to get out.

Edna put everything but the lighter back in her pockets. Her hands were trembling, and she couldn't do it fast enough. She thumbed the wheel of the lighter, looked ahead, and began to crawl.

She could hear her own breath as she crawled. She started to hum, thinking it would calm her, but it only scared her, and she stopped and crawled on. Her head pounded and it hurt something fierce. She crawled with sudden velocity and found good purchase on the hard earth.

'Shit!' she said, as her head hit a wall of dirt.

I am at the end of the straight shot now, she thought, and she scrabbled, turning right and finding more space. The smell had grown awful, and she gagged, but she crawled on. She was dizzy and she panicked at the thought that she might be running out of air.

She gagged again at the lousy stench, heard a kind of crunching sound, struggled to draw in breath as she kept on and touched something soft, and crawled over another thing that was cold and hard.

Edna raised the lighter in front of her and got flame. Two corpses covered in writhing maggots lay before her.

'Aaah!' screamed Edna. 'Oh, God, Ray, God, Ray, *God*!'

She turned, the lighter flipping out of her hand.

Edna fell forward onto her belly. She clawed at the cold earth. But she was too dizzy to move, and it seemed as if a hatchet had cleaved her skull. She vomited into the darkness of the tunnel and lowered her head to the ground, feeling the warmth of her own puke on her face. Her eyes were fixed and glassy, and her tongue slid from her open mouth.

28

'They're comin' out,' said Strange looking through the 500 millimeter lens of his AE-1.

'They weren't in there long,' said Quinn.

'Droppin' off the goods, I expect. Now they're goin' to get their money. Couple of *Mayberry R.F.D.*-lookin' motherfuckers, too.'

'The short one's got high heels on. You see that?'

'Like I told you, it's the little ones got somethin' to prove. Those the ones you got to keep your eye on.'

Strange and Quinn sat in a rented Chevy Lumina two blocks west of the Junkyard. They had been there for several hours, and Strange had filled Quinn in on everything he'd learned the day before.

They watched Ray and Earl Boone leave the garage, cross the street, and head toward the row house where Cherokee Coleman kept his office. Ray and Earl spoke briefly to a couple of unsmiling young men, who led them up the stoop and through a door.

'Gettin' the royal escort,' said Quinn. 'Wonder how many guns we got out here on this street.'

'They ain't nothin' but kids.'

'Just as deadly as anyone else. Anyone can pull the trigger of a gun.'

'They don't have to be out here, though. They think they do, but they don't. They watch television, they see what everyone else has, what they're supposed to have, they want some, too. But how they gonna get it, Terry?'

'Work for it?'

'C'mon, man, you're smarter than that. 'Cause of some accident of birth these kids came into the world in a certain kind of place. Where they were born, and learnin' from the older kids around them – the only examples they got, most of the time – a lot of these kids, their fate was decided a long time ago.'

'I'll give you that. But what would you do about it now?'

'Two things I would do,' said Strange. 'First thing, I'd legalize drugs.

Take away what they're all fightin' over, 'cause in itself it's got no meaning anyway. It's like those MacGuffins they're always talkin' about in those Alfred Hitchcock movies – just somethin' to move the drama along. Legalization, it works in some of those European countries, right? You don't see this kind of crime over there. The repeal of prohibition, it stopped a lot of this same kind of thing we got goin' on right here, didn't it?'

'Okay. What's the other thing?'

'Make handguns illegal, nationwide. After a moratorium and a grace period, mandatory sentences for anyone caught in possession of a handgun. A pistol ain't good for nothin' but killing other human beings, man.'

'You're not the first person who's thought of those things. So why isn't anyone talking about it for real?'

''Cause you put all those politicians down on the Hill in one room and you can't find one set of nuts swingin' between the legs of any of 'em. Even the ones who know what's got to be done, they realize that comin' out in favor of drug legalization and handgun illegalization will kill their careers. And the rest of them are in the pockets of the gun lobby. Meantime, nearly half the black men in this city have either been incarcerated or are in jail now.'

'You tellin' me it's a black thing?'

'I'm tellin' you it's a *money* thing. We got two separate societies in this country, and the gap between the haves and the have-nots is gettin' wider every day. And the really frustrating thing is—'

'No one cares,' said Quinn.

'Not exactly. You got mentors, community activists, church groups out here, they're tryin', man, believe me. But it's not enough. More to the point, some people care, but most people care about the wrong things.

'Look, why does a dumb-ass, racist disc jockey make the front page and the leadoff on the TV news for weeks, when the murder of teenage black *children* gets buried in the back of the Metro section every day? Why do my own people write columns year after year in the *Washington Post,* complainin' that black actors don't get nominated for any Academy Awards, when they should be writin' every goddamn day about the fucked-up schools in this city, got no supplies, leaking roofs, and fifteen-year-old textbooks. You got kids walkin' to school in this city afraid for their lives, and once they get there they got one security guard lookin' after five hundred children. How many bodyguards you think the mayor's got, huh?'

'I don't know, Derek. You askin' me?'

'I'm makin' a point.'

'You gotta relax,' said Quinn. 'Guy your age, you could stroke out . . .'

'Aw, *fuck* you, man.'

A block ahead, a Crown Vic cruiser rounded the corner and headed east, driving slowly by the Junkyard.

'That our friend?'

'I'd bet it,' said Strange, narrowing his eyes. 'Ain't nothin' I hate worse than a sold-out cop.'

'What did you find out?'

'Just got the pictures back last night.' Strange thought of the packet of photographs Janine had left on his desk and something stirred in his head.

'You gonna run the number?'

'Got a friend working on it now.'

'We better get out of here,' said Quinn. 'He'll be turning around, I expect.'

'I was thinkin' the same thing. Those rednecks, when they leave, most likely they'll be drivin' out of here the same way they came.'

'I'd go back over to North Capitol and park it there.'

Strange ignitioned the Chevy and said, 'Right.'

Quinn sipped coffee from the cup of a thermos and stared out the windshield. Strange uncapped a bottle of spring water and drank deeply from the neck.

'Me and Juana,' said Quinn. 'We broke up.'

'What's that?' said Strange. He had been thinking of Janine and Lionel.

'I said, me and Juana are through.'

'That's too bad, man.'

'She told me I was too intense.'

'Imagine her thinkin' that.' Strange shifted his position behind the wheel. 'That's a wrong move, lettin' a together young lady like that get away from you. It have anything to do with your color difference?'

'It did.' Quinn tried to smile. 'Anyway, like my old man used to say, women are like streetcars; you miss one and another comes along sooner or later. Right?'

'It sounds good. You're puttin' on a good face, but you don't see too many streetcars rollin' down the street lookin' like Juana. And you don't find too many with her heart, either.'

'I know it.' Quinn looked across the bench at Strange. 'Since you're givin' me the benefit of a lifetime of wisdom—'

'Go ahead.'

'When are you gonna marry Janine?'

'Marry her? Shit, Terry, I'm long past thinkin' about marrying anybody.' Strange capped his bottle and looked down at his lap. 'Anyway, she deserves better than me. But thanks for the advice, hear?'

'Just tryin' to help.'

'So you got a father. You know, that's one of the first personal things you've told me in the time I've known you. He alive?'

'My parents are both dead,' said Quinn. 'I got a brother out in the Bay Area who I almost never hear from. What about you?'

'It's just my mom now.'

'No brothers or sisters?'

'I had a brother. He's been gone thirty-one years.'

'That was about the time you left the force, right?'

'That's right,' said Strange, and he didn't say anything after that.

'Here they come,' said Quinn, as the Ford Taurus approached from the east.

'Pa and Son of Pa Kettle.'

'You got a full tank?'

'Yeah.'

'They don't exactly look like they're from around here,' said Quinn. 'I got a feeling we're in for a long ride.'

They drove out of the city to the Beltway, then hit 270 north. The Taurus, a nondescript vehicle to begin with, had the same basic body style as half the other cars on the road. The driver of the Taurus did the speed limit, and Strange stayed ten car lengths back, unconcerned that they would be burned. The heavy traffic was their cover.

'Don't you have one of those homing devices in this thing?' said Quinn.

'Yeah,' said Strange. 'Let me just go ahead and bring up their vehicle on the Batscreen.'

'I figured, you know, that you got everything else. All those things you hang on your belt line, and those night-vision goggles you got in that bag back there. You get those out of a cereal box or somethin'?'

'Don't go makin' fun of my NVDs, man.'

'What're we gonna do when we get there?'

'Wherever they're goin', that's where we're gonna find Chris Wilson's sister.'

'Because some junkie snitch told you?'

'You go with what you got.'

The traffic lessened as cars got off the highway at the exurban exits of Gaithersburg, Germantown, and Darnestown, the innermost fringes of the new megalopolis that was Washington, D.C. Strange eased off the gas and kept the Lumina farther back than it had been. Ten miles later, he saw the right-turn signal flare on the Ford up ahead. Strange took the off-ramp, keeping the Taurus in sight.

'We lose 'em?' said Quinn.

'I don't think so,' said Strange. They were on a long curve that ran along open country and then dense forest. When they came out of the curve and hit a straightaway, the Taurus was up ahead. The driver had parked it at a gate of some kind on a gravel path cutting a break in the woods.

'Drive past 'em,' said Quinn. 'Don't even slow down.'

'I look like Danny Glover to you? Do I look like white America's pet African American sidekick, man? I'm in *charge* of this investigation, Terry, case you've forgotten.'

'Drive past 'em,' said Quinn. 'Punch it, man.'

'What the fuck did you think I was *gonna* do?'

They blew past the Taurus. The short one, standing at the wooden gate and putting a key to a padlock, glanced up as they passed, giving them a brief and unfocused hard look.

'Boy is cross-eyed,' said Quinn. 'You see that?'

'Uh-huh. Noticed when I was looking at 'em through the lens. The older one has the same look, too. Got to be his daddy, right?'

They went into another long curve running beside more woods. Strange pulled over on the shoulder, cut the engine, and grabbed his day pack off the backseat.

'Let's go,' he said.

They walked into the woods, dense with oak and pine, past a No Trespassing sign affixed to a tree and peppered with buckshot.

Quinn said, 'This way,' and pointed northeast. There seemed to be a trail of sorts, and they followed it.

'Looks like there's a break in the woods up ahead,' said Strange.

'I see it. But we can't get too close to 'em, if that's where they are. This time of year there's no foliage on these trees. We got no cover.'

'Right.'

'And watch where you walk. Don't go snapping too many branches, 'cause the sound travels in the open country. This isn't the city, Danny. I mean, *Derek*.'

'Funny,' said Strange.

Quinn looked over his shoulder and made a halting sign with his palm. Both of them stopped walking. Quinn looked around and motioned with his chin to a deer blind that had been built in the low branches of an oak. He pointed to the blind, and Strange nodded his head.

Quinn went up first, using the ladder of wooden blocks that had been nailed to the trunk of the tree. Strange tossed his bag up to Quinn and followed. The platform was narrow and shifted a little under their weight.

'This gonna hold us?' said Strange, keeping his voice low.

'I guess we'll find out.'

They looked through the trees to a clearing, about one hundred and fifty yards away. They could see the father and son getting out of the Ford, parked between a pickup and a motorcycle in a cluttered yard. Past the vehicles was a large barn with a ramshackle house beside it. Strange looked through the lens of the AE-1, snapping photographs of the son as he took a gym bag from out of the trunk.

'I can't see anything,' said Quinn. 'My eyes are going on me, man.'

'Got a set of ten-by-fifty binos in the bag. Help yourself.'

Quinn dug the binoculars out and adjusted them for his nose and eyes.

The two men headed for the house, the son carrying the gym bag, looking back once into the woods before both of them stepped onto the leaning porch and went through the front door.

Strange squinted. 'She's in there, I expect.'

They waited, listening to the call of crows, twigs snapping, the wind moving the tops of the tall trees. Squirrels chased each other in the high branches of the oaks. They waited some more and neither of them spoke. A doe crashed through brush and went by them, disappearing down a rise that dropped west of the blind.

'Here they come,' said Strange.

The two men came out of the house. Sondra Wilson was beside the father.

'That's her,' said Strange.

The father took her arm as they descended the porch steps. Even at this distance, Strange could see that she was near death. Beneath the coat she wore, her shoulders were like garden shears, and her eyes were hollowed out above sunken cheeks.

Now they were all standing in the yard, and the son was gesturing wildly toward the woods, the anger in his voice carrying through the trees, reaching Quinn and Strange. The older man was talking to his son in a quiet way, trying to calm him down. Then the son grabbed hold of Sondra Wilson's arm and shook her violently. Her head kind of flopped around on her shoulders, and that was when the father took three steps forward and shoved the son in the chest, sending him down to the gravel and dirt.

The son got up slowly, not saying a word, not looking at his father anymore or at Sondra. The father took hold of Sondra gently and walked her back into the house.

The son waited until they were inside. He pulled a gun from beneath his jacket and began firing in the direction of the tree line. His face was twisted into something between a grimace and a smile. Strange blinked with each shot, the rounds ricocheting metallically into the woods.

'What the fuck did we just see?' said Quinn.

Strange was thinking about the photograph packet on his desk, once again. He pictured himself in Chris Wilson's room, the items on his dresser and in his cigar box. He saw himself talking to Wilson's mother, the pictures hung on his wall, *one picture . . .*

'Derek?'

'Sorry, man. Was thinkin' of something.'

'What?'

'Wilson had a stub from a grocery store, a Safeway, I think, in the cigar box on his dresser. There was a camera on that dresser, too.'

'So there are some pictures he never got around to pickin' up.'

'Uh-huh. Also, if he was trying to find his sister . . . if we been covering the same tracks he was makin', I mean, then he probably has some kind of documentation related to what he was doin'. I'm thinkin' that maybe I know where that is.'

'What are we waitin' on, then?'

'It's just that I hate to leave her,' said Strange. 'You got a look at her, man, she doesn't have much time.'

'We can't do anything today. Not unless you want to pull that Buck knife off your hip and wave it at that guy with the automatic.'

'You're right,' said Strange. 'But I'm coming back.'

29

Strange lifted the framed photograph of Larry Brown and a young Chris Wilson, and placed the photograph on Wilson's bed. As Strange had suspected, the frame covered a hole of sorts in the wall. A tablet-sized notebook was wedged inside the hole among chips of particle-board, covered with a thick coat of dust. The hole was just large enough to accommodate the notebook; it looked as if Wilson himself had punched it through.

Leona Wilson had said that Chris had become visibly upset when she'd gone to straighten the picture. From everything Strange knew, Chris Wilson seemed to be the type of young man who would need an awful good reason to rise up at his own mom. Whatever Wilson had found – and Strange was certain that what he'd found was reflected in the notebook – he had kept it from his mother, his girlfriend, and the department as well.

Strange stashed the notebook in his day pack, along with the ticket stub from Safeway. The stub was redeemable at the Piney Branch Road location in Takoma, D.C., near his church.

In the living room, Leona Wilson peered out from behind her parted curtains at the Lumina parked on the street. She released the curtain and turned as Strange walked into the room.

'Did you find what you were looking for?'

'I did.'

'Then you're making progress.'

'Yes, I am.' Strange slung the day pack over his shoulder. 'Mrs Wilson?'

'Yes.'

'I believe I've located your daughter.'

Leona Wilson's lip trembled up into a smile. 'Thank you. Thank the good Lord.' She rubbed her hands together in front of her waist. 'Is she . . . what is her health?'

'She's gonna need help, Mrs Wilson. Professional help to get her off the kind of trouble she's found. You best . . . you *need* to start lookin' into it right away. There's programs and clinics; you can get a list through the church. You need to set that up *now*, understand? Do it today.'

'Why?'

''Cause I plan on bringin' Sondra home.'

Strange headed for the door.

Leona Wilson said, 'Who is that white man in the car out front? I'm afraid I can't make anything out but his color without my glasses.'

'An independent I been using.'

'Is he helping you with this?'

'Uh-huh.' Strange opened the door.

'Mr Strange—'

'I know. Just doin' what you're paying me for, Mrs Wilson. Don't forget, you *will* be gettin' a bill.'

'I'll say a prayer for you this Sunday, Mr Strange.'

'Yes, ma'am.'

He stepped outside and stood for a moment on the concrete porch. He'd gone and promised this woman something, and now he'd have to see it through.

'I saw the Wilson woman looking at me through the curtains,' said Quinn. 'She recognize me?'

'She wouldn't recognize her own face in the mirror without her glasses on,' said Strange. He blew a late yellow on Georgia, catching the red halfway through the intersection.

'I went to Chris Wilson's funeral. I tell you that?'

'No.'

'Word must have gotten around with the relatives that I was there. There weren't many white faces to begin with, except for a few cops. Anyway, Mrs Wilson found my eyes through the crowd – she was wearing her glasses *that* day – and I nodded to her. She gave me the coldest look—'

'What'd you expect?'

'It wasn't that I was expecting anything, exactly. I was hoping for something, that's all. I guess I was wrong to even hope for that.'

Strange didn't feel the need to respond. He passed Buchanan and continued north.

'Hey,' said Quinn, 'you missed your house.'

'I'm droppin' you off at your place, Terry. When I get close like this I need to think everything out my own self.'

'You're not gonna cut me out of this now, are you?'

Strange said, 'I'll phone you later tonight.'

After he dropped off Quinn, Strange stopped at the Safeway on Piney Branch. When the woman behind the glass handed him the packet of photographs, she said, 'These been in here a long time, Mr Wilson,' and Strange said, 'Thanks for keepin' 'em safe.'

He drove back to the car rental on Georgia, dropped off the Lumina, and picked up his Caprice, which he had left on the lot. Back at his row house, he fed Greco, showered, changed into sweats, went into his office, and had a seat at his desk. There was a message from Lydell Blue on his machine: the numbers on the cruiser matched up with a Crown Vic driven by a street cop named Adonis Delgado. Strange wrote down Delgado's name.

Strange angled his desk lamp down and studied the photographs he had picked up at Safeway. Halfway through them, his blood jumped. He said, 'I'll be goddamned,' and said it again as he went through the rest. He opened the notebook and read the ten log-style pages of text, detailing by date, time, and location the progress of Chris Wilson's own investigation. Strange reached for the phone, lifted the receiver, then replaced the receiver in its cradle. In an envelope in his file cabinet, he found the taped conversations he had recorded. He listened to them through. He rewound the tape to the sections that interested him and listened to those sections two more times.

Strange sat back in his chair. He reached down and patted Greco's head. He folded his arms and stared at the ceiling. He ran his finger through the dust that had settled on his desk. He exhaled slowly, sat forward, and pulled the telephone toward him. He dialed a number, and on the third ring a voice came on the other end of the line.

'Hello.'

'Derek here. You remember which house is mine?'

'Sure.'

'Better get on over here, man.'

'I'll be right there,' said Quinn.

Cherokee Coleman pressed 'end' on his cell and laid the phone on the green blotter of his desk. 'They're here.'

Big-Ass Angelo adjusted his shades so that they sat low on his nose. 'We ready for them to finish this thing?'

'Tomorrow night. We been sellin' this shit faster than I thought we would. We'll send our boys out there to Shitkickersville and let them bring back the last load. Bring back our money, too. Doom all those motherfuckers out there, so I can tell my Colombian brothers I went and avenged the deaths of their own. Stay in their good graces so we can keep on makin' that bank. Like to see those cracker cops out in Fredneck County when they find all those bodies, scratchin' their fat heads and shit, tryin' to figure out who and what and how come.'

'Let God sort 'em out.'

Coleman looked up. 'That's a good name for this next batch, Angie.'

'We used it, man.'

'Fucked in D.C.?'

'That ain't bad, right there.'

Coleman got up from his chair and walked to the office window. Two men got out of a black Maxima and were met by several younger men.

'Delgado got himself a brand new short,' said Coleman. 'Got some nice rims on it, too.'

'He just wants what we got,' said Angelo.

'Let him keep wantin' it. The want is what makes this world go round, black.'

'How his partner look?'

'Boy has *got* some teeth.'

'Wil-bur,' said Angelo, whinnying like a horse and using his foot, dragging it front to back on the floor, to count to three.

Coleman and Angelo were still laughing as the two men entered the office.

'Somethin' funny?' said Delgado.

'Angelo here was just tellin' me a joke,' said Coleman.

'How you doin', Bucky?' said Big-Ass Angelo to the second man.

'I told you not to call me that,' said the man. 'The name's Eugene Franklin, understand?'

30

Quinn sat on a hard-back chair in Strange's living room, the tablet-sized notebook and an empty bottle of beer on the floor at his feet, the package of photographs clenched in his hand. There were two photographs of Eugene Franklin and Adonis Delgado in the bunch, wearing street clothes and walking from Eugene's civilian car to the row house of Cherokee Coleman. Quinn had yet to read the contents of the notebook, but Strange had filled him in on the pertinent details.

'You want another beer, man?' said Strange, who sat on a slightly worn living room sofa.

'No,' said Quinn. 'I better not.'

Quinn's eyes were blown out in his pale face, and jaw muscles bunched beneath his tight skin.

'Play me the tape again. The part where Eugene was talking in Erika's.'

Strange played the tape. Eugene's voice filled the silence of the room: '*I saw where Wilson's gun was headed. I saw in his eyes what he planned to do. There's no doubt in my mind, if Terry hadn't shot Wilson, Wilson would have shot me.*'

Strange hit the stop button on the micro recorder.

'Wilson would have shot *me*,' said Strange. 'Franklin slipped right there.'

Quinn nodded obtusely at the recorder. 'Play the tape of me. The first conversation we had, down at the scene, on D Street.'

'We already did this once.'

'Play it,' said Quinn.

Strange popped in another tape. He cued up the spot that he knew Quinn wanted to hear.

Strange: '*You do what next?*'

Quinn: '*I've got my gun on the aggressor. I yell for him to drop his weapon and lie facedown on the street. He yells something back. I can't really hear what he's saying, 'cause Eugene's yelling over him—*'

Strange stopped the tape. 'Your partner was *yelling over him* 'cause he didn't want you to hear what Wilson was sayin'. He was adding to the confusion, and he didn't want you to know that Wilson was a cop.'

'Play the other part,' said Quinn.

Strange: '*What happened when he looked at you, Quinn?*'

Quinn: '*It was only for a moment. He looked at me and then at Gene, and something bad crossed his face. I'll never forget it. He was angry at us, at me and Gene. He was more than angry; his face changed to the face of a killer. He swung his gun in our direction then—*'

Strange: '*He pointed his gun at you?*'

Quinn: '*Not directly. He was swinging it, like I say. The muzzle of it swept across me and he had that look on his face . . . There wasn't any doubt in my mind . . . I* knew *he was going to pull the trigger. Eugene screamed my name, and I fired my weapon.*'

'That's enough,' said Quinn.

Strange stopped the recorder.

'Here's the way I see it,' said Strange, speaking softly. 'Your partner was driving the cruiser that night. Y'all comin' up on Chris Wilson like that, it wasn't an accident. Franklin turned down D Street because it was a setup. He knew Kane was going to lure Chris Wilson there. He knew it wouldn't take much for Kane to get Wilson to draw his gun.'

'Or for me to fire mine,' said Quinn.

'Maybe. The fact remains, your partner was involved. We got the photographs and Chris Wilson's notebook. That young man did some really fine police work, putting it all together. The tapes I got corroborate—'

'I just don't want to believe it, Derek.'

'Believe your own words,' said Strange. ' "He looked at me *and then at Gene*, and something bad crossed his face." "His face changed to the face of a killer" when he saw Eugene. Your own words were, "The muzzle of the gun swept *across* me." Chris Wilson wasn't lookin' to hurt *you*, Terry. He was pointing his gun at a sold-out cop. A dirty cop who was in the pocket of the drug dealer who had put his sister in a junkhouse. You understand what I'm tellin' you, man?'

'Yes,' said Quinn, staring at the floor.

'All right, then. Now, who's Adonis Delgado?'

'Big, bad-ass cop. He was sitting at the bar of Erika's the day we spoke to Eugene.'

'Muscle-bound and ugly, with a stoved-in nose?'

'Yeah.'

'That's the one tried to step to me in the bathroom. Wanted to send me some kind of message, I guess.'

'Eugene,' muttered Quinn.

'You're goddamn right, *Eugene*.'

Quinn stood out of his chair. He lifted his leather off the back where he'd hung it and put it on.

'Where *you* goin'?'

'To get the rest of it.'

'You need my help?'

'This one's me,' said Quinn. He turned as he reached the front door. 'Don't go to sleep.'

'I'm gonna see you again tonight?'

'Yeah. Gonna bring somethin' back for you, too.'

Eugene Franklin had a one-bedroom apartment in a high-rise across the road from the Maine Avenue waterfront in Southwest. Franklin, like many single cops, considered his apartment little more than a place to eat, sleep, and watch TV. The living area was sparsely decorated and furnished, with a couch and chair facing a television, a coffee table, and a telephone set on a bare end table beside the couch. Franklin answered the ringing phone.

'Yeah.'

'Gene, it's Terry, man. I'm at the front door in the lobby.'

'Terry—'

'Buzz me in, buddy. I got somethin' I need to talk to you about.'

Franklin pressed a button on the phone. He stood from the couch and ran his finger slowly over his protruding upper lip. It was a habit of his to do this when he was troubled or confused.

Franklin went to the door of his apartment, opened it, and stood in the frame. Quinn was walking toward him, down the long, orange-carpeted hall.

'Hey,' said Quinn, a smile on his face.

Quinn's long hair bounced as he walked. He was moving very quickly down the hall, his head pushed forward. Franklin was thinking, He's like one of those cartoon characters, determined, walking with purpose . . . and now he could see that Quinn's smile was not really a smile but more of a grimace, a forced smile that had pain in it and something worse than pain.

'Hey, Eugene,' said Quinn as he reached him, not slowing down, and Franklin saw the automatic come up from beneath the waistband of Quinn's jeans.

Franklin stepped back from the doorway as Quinn swung the barrel of the gun viciously, its shape a blur cutting through the fluorescent glare of the hall. The gun connected at Franklin's temple, and the room spun instantly as he stumbled back.

Franklin's feet were gone beneath him. He began to fall, and as he fell through the dimming light the gun streaked toward him, and this time he barely felt the blow. At the end, he saw his partner's face, ugly and angry and afraid, and Franklin loved him then. Falling into a soft bed of night, Franklin felt only relief.

Quinn stood in the center of Eugene Franklin's living room, the automatic held loosely in his hand.

Franklin sat on the couch, his head tilted back, holding a damp towel tight to his temple. The towel was pink where the blood of a deep gash had seeped through. Quinn had placed a yellow legal pad on the coffee table before him and set a pen on top of the pad.

'How'd you turn, Gene?'

'How?' repeated Franklin.

'Delgado drew you in.'

'Yeah. Used to see him down at Erika's all the time. In there every night, drinkin', talkin' mad shit, then goin' home alone. Delgado, he was like me. Neither one of us had many friends or was gettin' any play. So we got to talkin,' Adonis and me. I knew he was all bad; everyone knew. But I talked to him anyway.'

'What'd you talk about?'

'This and that, you know. Went from one thing to the other, until it came to this other thing. Delgado was tellin' me how a man with some money in his pocket didn't have to worry about finding women, they'd find *him*. How you could kick it with anyone out there if the woman had the idea you were holdin' bank. I knew his mouth was overloadin' his asshole, man, but with the alcohol runnin' through me and shit—'

'How'd it go to the next level?'

'He started talkin' about Cherokee Coleman's operation, down off Florida. How Cherokee wasn't never gonna see no time, how no one could touch his ass 'cause he was too smart. That the operation would keep goin' on as long as there was a market for drugs, and fuck all those junkies, anyway, they weren't nothin' but the low end of Darwin's theory. And then he told me how he was making a little extra on the side, how he figured out that if Cherokee was gonna be all that and no one was gonna do a goddamn thing about it, why didn't he, Adonis, deserve to get some, too.

'It wasn't no big deal, he said. A load came in twice a month to Coleman's, and twice a month Delgado cruised the perimeter of the area during drop-off day and made sure there wasn't anything goin' on out there in the way of interference, local or federal law. Never even got out of his car. He said it wasn't any more complicated than that.'

'Why tell you? Why did he need to cut you in?'

''Cause he couldn't always be there. And because they had a problem that Delgado couldn't or didn't want to handle on his own. Course, I didn't know what that problem was when I got in.'

'Chris Wilson.'

Franklin's eyes moved to the floor. 'That's right. His sister had got hooked up with Ricky Kane. He followed Kane's trail the same way y'all did, and it took him to Coleman's. On one of those trips, Kane went into the office with Sondra Wilson, and when he came out, he was alone. Sondra was Coleman's woman, just like that, and it pushed Wilson way over the edge.'

'You were in at this point?'

'Right about then, yeah. It was easy, just like Delgado said; wasn't nothin' but drivin' around the block a couple of times, twice a month. I didn't see anything all that wrong with it at the time.'

'Bullshit.'

'Just trying to explain it to you, how it was.'

'Bullshit,' said Quinn, a catch in his voice. 'What happened next?'

'Wilson was surveilling now in his street clothes, by the Junkyard and on the corners. I guess that's when he got those pictures of me. He knew he couldn't go up against Coleman's army himself, and he didn't know who to trust anymore inside the department. But by now he was all fucked up over his sister, and he was gettin' out of control. He threatened Delgado outside of Erika's one night. He threatened me.'

'You and Delgado went to Coleman.'

'Delgado did. They decided to get rid of Chris Wilson. For Delgado, it was easy. By then I'd found out he'd killed before for Coleman. It didn't matter what I knew at that point; I was damn near one of them. They wanted me all the way in, locked in for real.'

'They wanted you to kill Wilson.'

'That's right.' Franklin dropped the towel at his feet. A drop of blood burst from his cut and trickled down his cheek.

'They had Kane call Wilson out?'

Franklin nodded. 'Kane told Wilson he'd gotten his sister back. To meet him on D Street at a certain time. They knew Wilson would lose it when he got there and found Kane alone. I drove us up on the scene. You know what happened next.'

'You tell me, Eugene. You tell me what happened next.'

'I never shot a man. Never even shot *at* one, Terry. I had my gun out and I had it pointed at him, but—'

'Why *didn't* you shoot him, Eugene?'

'Because you shot him first.'

Quinn looked down at the gun in his hand. 'You knew I would.'

'No, I didn't know. But I knew you were more capable of it than I was. And I knew . . .'

'What?'

'I knew *you*. I knew what you'd see when you saw Chris Wilson holding a gun on Ricky Kane.'

Quinn raised the gun to his hip, pointing it at Franklin on the couch. Franklin's lip trembled, and his eyes filled with tears.

'You won't do it, Terry. There's a part of me that wishes you would. But you won't.'

'You're right,' said Quinn, and he moved the muzzle of the Glock, pointing it at the pad on the table. 'Write it out. All of it, Gene. Go ahead. I'm going to disgrace you to your family, and your fellow cops, and to all the folks you came up with over in Northeast. They're all gonna know what a lowlife you are. And I'm gonna make good and goddamn sure your fellow inmates know you used to wear the uniform when they haul your ass to jail.'

'I'm sorry, man.'

'Fuck you, Eugene. Fuck your apologies, too. Write it down.'

Franklin wrote a full confession out on the yellow pad, signed and dated the bottom of the last page, and dropped the pen when he was done.

'I'd like to talk to my father before this makes the news,' said Franklin. 'When are you going to turn this in?'

'After we get the girl home.'

'She's not in D.C.'

'I know it,' said Quinn. 'Me and Strange, we were out there today. We followed those rednecks out to their property, where they're keeping her.'

Franklin dabbed at the cut on his temple. The bleeding had stopped, and he lowered the towel. 'I'm going to be there with Delgado tomorrow night.'

'Why?'

'We're dropping off money and bringing back a load of drugs.'

'Thought you never had to do anything but drive around the block.'

'We met with Coleman earlier,' said Franklin. 'Those rednecks you followed, the Boones: the short one's named Ray, and his father's name is Earl. They killed a couple of Colombian mules, out at that property. Coleman wants us to kill the Boones, to make himself right with the Colombians.'

'What about the girl?'

'They didn't mention the girl, maybe because they knew I wouldn't like what they had to say. Delgado used to hit it himself, and he still has her on his mind. He starts killin', though, I don't see him stopping until everyone's put to sleep.'

'And you'll do what?'

'I can't shoot anybody, Terry. I already told you—'

'This is going down tomorrow night?'

'I'm meeting Delgado at eight . . . That would put us out there near nine o'clock. They're going to pick us up somewhere else, then drive us back to the place.'

'There's a barn and a house there.'

'Yeah. Coleman says the Boones like to do business in the barn. They got a full bar in there; it's set up like one of those old-time casinos or some shit like that.'

'Sondra stays in the house?'

'Far as I know.'

Quinn holstered the Glock in the waistband of his jeans. 'Tomorrow night, you keep them all in the barn, hear? Give me and Strange the chance to get Sondra Wilson out of that house.'

'What am I gonna do when Delgado starts all that killin'?'

'I don't care what you do. It makes no difference to me.' Quinn picked up the legal pad off the coffee table and slipped his pen into the breast pocket of his shirt. 'Whatever you decide to do tomorrow night, I want you to know it won't change what I'm going to do with this.'

'I didn't think it would.'

'So long, Gene.'

Quinn walked away. The door clicked closed behind him.

Strange was sleeping on the couch when the doorbell buzzed. Greco's barking woke him up. Strange opened the front door after checking the peephole. Quinn stood on the porch, his breath visible in the night.

'I got it,' said Quinn, holding up Franklin's confession for Strange to see.

'Fill me in on what I don't know,' said Strange.

Quinn told him everything, standing there.

When Quinn was done, Strange said, 'Tomorrow night, then.'

And Quinn said, 'Right.'

31

Strange hit the intercom-system buzzer on his desk and spoke into its mic: 'Janine?'

'Yes, Derek,' came the crackly reply.

'Come on in here a minute, will you?'

Strange leaned over, picked up a package, a padded, legal-sized envelope, off the floor, and placed it on his desk. In the package, addressed to Lydell Blue at the Fourth District Station, was the full evidence file Strange had collected on the Wilson case.

Strange had come in early that morning, made Xerox copies of the evidence, and dropped the duplicate package in the mail, addressed to himself. Next he'd called his attorney and confirmed that his will was up to date. He had filled his attorney in on the whereabouts of his modest life insurance policy, for which he had named Janine and Lionel joint beneficiaries.

Janine Baker came into the room.

'Hi,' said Strange.

'Hi.'

'I'm gonna be gone for the rest of the day, maybe a little bit into tomorrow.'

'Okay,' said Janine.

'You need me, you can get me on my beeper.'

'Just like always. Nothing unusual about that.'

'That's right. Nothin' unusual at all.' Strange rubbed an itch on his nose. 'How's Lionel doin'?'

'He's doing well.'

'Listenin' to you, gettin' all his homework done, all that?'

'He's got his moments. But he's fine.'

'All right then.' Strange leaned forward and tapped the padded envelope on his desk. 'You don't hear any different from me, say by noon tomorrow, I want you to take this package here and drop it in the mailbox, understand?'

'Sure.'

'Keep it in the safe until then. There's another package like it, will be coming *here*, in the mail, a couple days from now. When it arrives, I want you to put *that* one in the safe.'

'Okay.'

'You got the billing done for Leona Wilson?'

'Soon as you tell me you've concluded the case, it'll be done.'

'It's done. Bill her for eight more hours, and don't forget to add in all those receipts I collected in the way of expenses, too.'

'I'll do it.'

'Good. I guess we're all set.' Strange got up from his chair, took his leather off the coat tree, and shook himself into the jacket. He walked up close to Janine and glanced at the open office door. 'Ron out there?'

'He's off on an insurance fraud thing.'

Strange slipped his arms around Janine's waist and pulled her to him. He kissed her on the lips, and held the kiss. She looked up into his eyes.

'First time you ever did that in here, Derek.'

'I'm not all that good at putting things I got in my head into words,' said Strange. 'Listen, I'm tryin' to say—'

'You did say it, Derek.'

Still in his arms, Janine wiped her thumb across his mouth, clearing the lipstick she had left there.

'I need to be gettin' out of here.'

'It's early yet.'

'I know it. But I wanted to spend the day with my mom.'

Janine watched him walk away, through the outer office and out the front door. She picked up the package off his desk and headed for the safe.

Quinn put in an early shift at the bookstore, then came back to his apartment, worked out in the basement, showered, and dressed in thermal underwear, a flannel shirt, Levi's jeans, and hiking boots. He microwaved a frozen dinner, ate it, made a pot of coffee, and drank the first of three cups. He put *London Calling* on the stereo. He listened to 'Death or Glory' while he sat on the edge of his bed. He put on *Born to Run* and turned 'Backstreets' up loud. He paced his bedroom and found his gun and belt in the bottom drawer of his dresser.

Quinn stood in front of his full-length mirror. He wrapped his gun belt around his waist and buckled it in front, the holster riding low and tight on the right side of his hip. He had taken the Mace holder, bullet dump, pen holder, and key chain off the belt, leaving only his set of handcuffs, in their case and positioned at the small of his back. He holstered the Glock, cleared it from its holster, holstered it and cleared it again.

Quinn released the magazine and checked the load. He picked up the Glock, closed one eye, sighted down the barrel to the white dot on the blade, and dry-fired at the wall. The black polymer grip was secure in his palm. He slapped the magazine back into the butt of the gun and slid the Glock down into its holster.

The phone rang, and Quinn picked it up.

'Hello.' Quinn could hear symphonic music on the other end of the line.

'Derek here. I'm ready to go.'

'I'm ready, too,' said Quinn. 'Come on by.'

Strange hung up the phone. He was sitting at his desk at home, the Morricone soundtrack to *Once Upon a Time in the West* filling the room. The main title theme was playing, and Strange briefly closed his eyes. This was the most beautiful piece of music he owned, and he wanted nothing more than to sit here and listen to it, into the night. But the sky had darkened outside his rain-streaked window, and Strange knew that it was time to go.

Adonis Delgado's black Maxima cruised north on 270, its segmented wipers clearing the windshield of the rain that had lightly begun to fall. The rush hour traffic had thinned out an hour earlier, and the road ahead was clear.

'They like to do their business in the barn,' said Delgado, sitting low under the wheel. Delgado wore a black nylon jogging suit, his arms filling the sleeves, with a gold rope chain around his horse-thick neck.

'I know it,' said Eugene Franklin, beside him in the passenger bucket.

'Back when the Colombians were still breathin', they used to laugh about it with Coleman, tell 'em how it went down. We call 'em after we get off Two-seventy, and they meet us in the parking lot of a strip mall. They drive us back—'

'I know all this.'

'They drive us back, *Eugene*. They like to pour a few cocktails out in the barn before the business gets transacted.'

'I don't drink.'

'Have one or two to be polite, but don't go gettin' drunk. What I'm gonna do is, I'm gonna excuse myself, pay a visit to that little junkie. I'll take care of her, then come back to the barn.'

'You think that's a good idea?'

'Fuck you mean by *that*?'

'Maybe you better take care of the girl after. I mean, the sound of a gunshot in that house is gonna travel back to the barn.'

'I'll take care of the sound.'

'You got a suppressor or somethin'?'

'You got a suppressor or somethin'?' said Delgado, imitating Franklin's shaky voice and issuing a short laugh. 'Shit, Eugene, I don't know who in the fuck was ever stupid enough to give you a badge. I don't need no god-damn suppressor, man. I'll put a pillow over her face and shoot her through that.'

Delgado kicked up the wiper speed. The intensity of the rain had increased.

'Now,' said Delgado. 'When I come back in the barn, and I mean as soon as I come back in, I'm gonna walk straight up to Ray and do him quick. You do his father the same way, hear? I don't want to have to worry about you backin' me up.'

'You don't have to worry,' said Franklin.

'There's our exit,' said Delgado, pushing up on the turn signal bar. 'Grab my cell phone out the glove box, man. Call that little cross-eyed white boy, tell him we're on our way in.'

Ray Boone broke open a spansule of meth and dumped its contents onto a Budweiser mirror he had pulled off the wall. He used a razor blade to cut out two lines and snorted up the blue-speckled, coarse powder. He threw his head back and felt the familiar numbness back in his throat. He swigged from a can of beer until it was empty and tossed the can into the trash, wiping blood off his lip that had dripped down from his nose.

'Phone's ringin', Daddy.'

'I hear it,' said Earl. He had a cigarette in one hand and was playing electronic poker with the other.

'That's them.'

'Then answer it, Critter.'

Ray lifted his cell phone off the green felt table where he sat. He spoke to one of Coleman's men briefly, then pushed the 'end' button on the phone.

'They're down the road,' said Ray.

Earl nodded but did not reply.

Ray had everything he needed on his person. His Beretta 92F was loaded and holstered on his back, in the waistband of his jeans. He had a vial of crystal meth spansules in one of his coat pockets and a hardpack of Marlboro Reds in the other. As for the heroin, he had brought the rest of it out earlier and placed the bags behind the bar.

Ray had brought the heroin out because he didn't want to go back in that room more than one time tonight; it was beginning to smell somethin' awful back there. His daddy had been right, and knowing that made Ray even more disturbed than he already had been since Edna up and left him. The weather had warmed unexpectedly, and those dead greasers down in the tunnel were gettin' ripe.

Earl picked up his six-pack cooler full of Busch, patting his coat pockets to check that he had brought his cigarettes and his .38. He and Ray left the barn. Out in the yard, Earl flicked his cigarette toward the woods and said, 'I'll be back. Need to check on the girl.'

Ray knew that his father was going in the house to give that colored junkie a bag of love, but he couldn't bring himself to care. He wasn't even mad at his father for pushing him down the day before. He had problems of his own that were weighing on his mind.

Ray went to the edge of the woods and looked into its darkness, letting the rain hit his face. Where the fuck was Edna? All right, so she'd gone into his stash and smoked it up, and now she was scared. But a day had passed, and he'd heard not one thing from her. He'd called that big-haired, smart-as-a-stump girlfriend of hers, Jo-hanna, and she claimed to not know where Edna was either. Lyin'-ass bitch, she *had* to know where Edna was, the two of them was asshole buddies goin' way back to grade school. That Jo-hanna, she'd even acted suspicious when he called, like he'd done somethin' to Edna his own self. Shit, he'd never hurt Edna. Course, he'd have to slap her around a little when she did come back, but that was something else.

'You're gettin' wet, Critter,' said Earl, standing behind Ray. 'Gonna mess up the leather on them boots of yours, standing out in this rain.'

'Just thinkin' on something, Daddy,' said Ray.

'I know what you're thinkin' on. We get through tonight, you can buy a whole bunch of heifers, you want to, take your mind off that girl.'

'I guess you're right. C'mon, let's go pick up those boys.'

They walked to the car. Earl said, 'Startin' to smell back in the barn.'

'I'll bury 'em tomorrow,' said Ray.

'Told you that warm weather was comin' in.'

What with Edna, and his daddy always tellin' him what to do, and the speed rushing through his blood, Ray had a mind to bite clear through his own tongue.

*

'You all set?' said Strange, standing in Quinn's bedroom, nodding at the day pack in Quinn's hand.

'Yeah,' said Quinn. 'How about you?'

'Spent the day with my mother. Doctors say she's shuttin' herself down. She's just kinda layin' in her bed, looking out her window. Wanted to be with her, just the same.'

'I worked at the bookstore myself. Kept me busy, so I didn't have to think about things too much.'

'How's Lewis doin'? He keepin' his hand away from it?'

Strange and Quinn chuckled, then stared at each other without speaking. Strange handed Quinn a pair of thin black gloves.

'Wear these when we get out there. They'll warm you some, and they're thin enough, you can pick up a dime with 'em on.'

'Thanks.' Quinn dropped the gloves into his pack.

Strange looked toward Quinn's bedroom window. 'Rainin' like a motherfucker out there. Gonna be messy, but the rain'll cover a lot of noise.'

'And the clouds will cover our sight lines, goin' through those woods.'

'My NVDs will get us through those woods.'

'You and your gadgets,' said Quinn. He looked at Strange's belt line, where his beeper, the Leatherman, the Buck knife, and the case holding his cell were hung.

'Speaking of which,' said Strange, 'put this on.' He took his beeper off his hip and handed it to Quinn. 'We'll take two cars in case we don't leave at the same time.'

Quinn nodded. 'Otherwise I'll meet you at that No Trespassing sign on the second curve.'

'Okay, but if we get separated or somethin'—'

'I'll see you,' said Quinn, 'back in D.C.'

32

Ray Boone went behind the bar and found the bottle of Jack where he'd left it, by the stainless steel sink next to the ice chest. His Daddy's Colt was where it always was, hung on two nails, the barrel resting on one and the trigger guard on the other, driven into the wood over the sink. Ray put the bottle of Jack on the bar, took a glass down from the rack behind him, and filled the glass near to its lip.

'You boys want a taste?' he said, shouting over the George Jones coming from the Wurlitzer.

Ray watched the funny-lookin' coon with the buck teeth, sitting glumly with a beer can in his hand at the felt-covered card table, shake his head. The other rughead, the big ugly one with the fancy running suit, didn't even acknowledge the question. He was standing in the middle of the room, rolling his head on his stack of shoulders like he was trying to work something out of his fat neck. A cigar was clenched between his teeth.

'How about you, Daddy?' said Ray.

'I'll have a little,' said Earl. He was at the jukebox, punching in numbers and drinking from a can of Busch beer.

Ray poured one for his father. He almost laughed, thinking of him and his daddy and their guests, all of them still wearing their coats in the heated barn. Ray knew, and each and every one of them knew, that they all were carrying guns. It was part of the game. Ray and Earl wanted out, and with all this money they were makin', they really didn't need to be doing this anymore. But when Ray thought about it, he had to admit he would miss this part, the drinking with the customers, the tension, the guns . . . the game.

Coleman's pocket cops had put the bag of money up on the bar, near the end. Ray had put the bags of heroin right next to it. Neither of them had made a move to weigh or even have a look at the drugs. Ray had said it would be rude for them not to have a drink first, and they had complied.

Ray broke open a spansule of meth and poured it out onto the bar. He didn't bother to track it out with his blade. He leaned over the bar and snorted it all up his nose. Fuck it, he didn't care what his daddy or the rughead cops thought, he was gonna celebrate the end of this thing tonight.

'Whoo!' said Ray. He lit up a smoke.

'Tonight, the bottle let me down,' came the vocal from the juke.

Country-ass, cracker trash, thought Adonis Delgado, killing the rest of the cheap, piss-tastin' beer they'd given him. First they make him lie down in the backseat of that Ford with his head in Eugene Franklin's ass, making his neck all stiff, and now he had to listen to this backwoods bullshit on the record machine. Delgado had a throw-down automatic, a Browning .9, in his clip-on holster. He was gonna enjoy pulling it, the time came.

Eugene Franklin watched Earl Boone walk by him and take a seat on a stool set in front of a video game that had playing cards on its screen. Franklin reached into his coat pocket and touched the Glock 17, his service weapon, sitting loosely there. He checked his wristwatch, thinking of Quinn and Strange.

'Got someplace you need to be?' said Ray, coming around the bar with a glass of whiskey in his hand, a cigarette dangling from his lips. 'Huh, Eugene? It's Eugene, ain't that right?'

'I'm comfortable,' said Franklin, not looking into the fucked-up eyes of Ray Boone. 'I'm fine.'

'*I'm* not fine,' said Delgado. 'I need to use the bathroom.'

'Piss outside,' said Ray, 'like we been doin' all night.'

'I gotta take a shit,' said Delgado. 'Ain't you got a toilet in this place?'

'Got one in the back, but it's broke,' said Earl.

'Use the one in the house,' said Ray. 'It's open.'

Delgado saw the father turn his head and give the son a look.

'Don't worry, I won't touch nothin',' said Delgado. 'Where's it at?'

'Top of the stairs,' said Ray.

'Be right back,' said Delgado to Franklin. Delgado snapped his cigar in half and tossed it in the card table ashtray.

Franklin watched Delgado leave by the barn door. He raised the beer can to his mouth and was thankful for the loud music and the sound of the rain hitting the roof. He could feel his teeth chattering lightly against the can.

Quinn and Strange hiked through the woods. Strange had his goggles on, and Quinn stayed close behind him. The wind and water whipped against their faces. They wore layers of clothing under their coats and the thin black gloves on their hands, but it wasn't enough. Strange slipped once on a muddy rise, and Quinn grabbed his elbow, keeping him on his feet.

They made it to the area at the edge of the woods and dropped their day packs on wet brown needles in a dense stand of pine. A spot lamp mounted above the barn door illuminated the yard, and the heavy rain slashed through its wide triangle of light. In the house, a dim light shone beyond the darkness of a bedroom window.

Strange dropped his goggles in his bag and withdrew a short crow bar. Quinn reached into his bag and pulled the gun belt. He stood and buckled it, unsnapping its holster.

'Look at you,' said Strange. 'Gettin' all Lee Van Cleef.'

'Somebody's got to.'

'Yeah, I know. I always take the light work, when I can.'

Strange looked up at the second floor of the house. He looked back at Quinn, dripping wet, his long hair slick and stuck to the sides of his face. 'I guess she's in there. And I guess the rest of them are in the barn.'

'Lotta guessin'.'

'Anyway, we're gonna find out.' Strange took a couple of deep, even breaths. 'Put that beeper on that gun belt, man.'

Quinn clipped it to his left hip. 'Okay, it's on.'

'If I get back out here and I don't see you, I'm gonna keep right on goin' with Sondra, you understand? I don't like leavin' you, man, but we accomplish one thing here tonight, it's to get that girl back to her mother, Terry—'

'I hear you.'

'So I'm not gonna stop and wait for you, man. I get Sondra back to my vehicle, I'm gonna phone you from my cell. That beeper goes off, it's your signal that I got her out safe, hear? You get out then, but only then. Till you hear from me, you hold them in that barn.'

'I'll hold 'em till hell freezes over or you say different.'

'God damn, you are somethin', man.'

'Get goin', Derek.'

'Listen, Terry . . .'

'Go on,' said Quinn. 'I'll see you out front of Leona Wilson's house, hear?'

Strange went into the yard, zigzagging combat style through the light. He got up onto the leaning porch of the house, ready to use the crowbar in the jamb of the door. But the knob turned in his hand, and Strange opened the door and walked inside.

Quinn removed his coat. He dropped it on his day pack, lying on the pine needles at his feet.

Adonis Delgado stripped off his shirt and pants, and left them in a heap on the floor. He got out of his briefs and dropped them atop the rest of his clothing, walking naked across the bedroom to where the girl sat, backed up against the headboard atop the sheets. He thought he heard a creak on the stairs outside the closed door but then became distracted as he caught a glimpse of himself in the dresser mirror; he looked good, hard in the stomach and pumped in the arms, shoulders, and chest. His erection was fully engorged as he reached the foot of the bed.

'C'mere, girl,' he said to the Wilson junkie, depleted to bones and drawn skin, a mile away from the way she'd looked when he'd had her the first time, over in the Junkyard. That was all right. Her irises were pinpoints. He knew she'd just gotten high, and that was all right, too.

'Please,' said Sondra Wilson, her voice little more than an exhaled whimper.

Delgado grabbed hold of one of her thin wrists. 'Trick-ass bitch.'

Outside the bedroom, past the landing, Strange ascended the stairs.

'Where's your shadow?' said Ray. 'He's been gone twenty minutes.'

'He'll be back,' said Franklin.

'I'll *get* him back,' said Earl, standing from the seat in front of the electronic poker game.

'I will, Daddy,' said Ray. 'I gotta drain my lily, anyhow.'

Earl watched his son go out the barn door. He went behind the bar to mix himself a drink, keeping an eye on the one with the horse teeth. The bottle of Jack was sitting on the sink. While his hands were down there, Earl took the Colt off the nails and racked the slide, placing the gun on its side on the stainless steel.

Earl had his .38 in his coat pocket, but he thought he'd keep another weapon live and within reach. You never could have too many guns around when you were dealing with common trash.

'This is a good one right here,' said Earl, motioning with his chin to the jukebox. 'Orange Blossom Special.' But the colored cop sitting at the card table didn't respond. 'Whatsa matter, fella? Don't you like Johnny Cash?'

Quinn rolled out into the yard as he saw the barn door begin to open. He got up on his haunches and pinned himself against the Ford pickup that was parked beside the Taurus. He drew his Glock and jacked a round into the chamber, keeping the barrel pointed up beside his face. He rose slowly, watching the son, the one named Ray, go by and head for the house.

For a moment, Quinn studied the rhythm in Ray's stride. Quinn silently counted to three and stepped out into the yard, walking behind Ray, closing in quickly on Ray, and then shouting, 'Hold it right there!' as Ray put one foot up on the porch steps.

Ray stopped walking. Quinn said, 'Put your arms up and lace your fingers behind your head. Do it and spread your legs!'

Ray put his arms up, turning his head slightly. He was slow to spread his legs, and Quinn moved in and kicked one of Ray's legs out at the calf.

'Who the *fuck* are you?' said Ray.

'Shut up,' said Quinn, pressing the barrel of the Glock to the soft spot behind Ray's right ear. Quinn frisked Ray quickly, found an automatic holstered at the small of his back, pulled it, nimbly released the magazine, let it drop to the muddy earth, and tossed the body of the gun far aside. Quinn nearly grinned; he hadn't lost a step or forgotten a goddamn thing.

'Walk back into the barn,' said Quinn.

'Easy,' said Ray.

'I said walk.'

Ray turned, and Quinn turned with him. They moved together, the gun still at Ray's ear, and made it to the barn door. Then they were through the barn door, Quinn blinking water from his eyes. Then they were inside.

Quinn speed-scanned the scene: the father was behind the bar, his eyes lazy and unfazed, his hands not visible. Eugene was sitting at some kind of card table, drinking a beer. Delgado was not in sight.

'Get your hands up, both of you!' shouted Quinn. 'Don't come up with anything, or I swear to God I'll blow his shit out across the room.'

'Take it easy, fella,' said Earl, as he slowly raised his hands.

Quinn could barely hear him. The music coming from the jukebox echoed loudly in the big room.

'You at the table,' said Quinn. 'Lay your hands out flat in front of you!'

Franklin did as he was told.

'Move over to that bar,' said Quinn, giving Ray a shove. 'Put your back up against it, hear?'

Ray walked to the bar, stopping about six feet down from where his father stood on the other side. He turned and leaned his back against the bar and placed the heel of one Dingo boot over the brass rail. His forearms rested on the mahogany, and his hands dangled limply in the air. Blood trickled from one nostril and ran down his lip.

Quinn moved the gun from father to son. He moved it to Franklin and then quickly back to the Boones.

'You,' he said, his eyes darting in the direction of Franklin. 'Get up and pull the plug on that jukebox. Do it and get back in your seat.'

Eugene Franklin got out of his chair, walked to the jukebox, got down on one knee, and yanked the plug out of the receptacle. The music died instantly. Franklin walked back to his chair, sat down, and placed his hands flat on the green felt of the table.

Now there was only the sound of the rain. It beat against the wood of the barn and clicked steadily on the tin roof.

'What're you?' said Ray. 'FBI? DEA?'

'Whatever he is,' said Earl, 'he's all alone.'

'Must be one of those agents likes to do it solo,' said Ray. 'A cowboy. That what you are?'

That's what I am, thought Quinn.

They heard the muffled scream of a woman. Then the rain alone, then the woman's steady, muffled scream.

'You hear that, Critter?'

'I hear it.'

'Just shut your mouths,' said Quinn.

Delgado wrapped a meaty hand through Sondra Wilson's hair and dragged her toward him across the sheets.

The door burst open. Delgado turned, naked. A man was rushing toward him with a crowbar raised in his hands. Delgado took the blow on his forearm and used his fist to clip the man on the ear as the man body-slammed him into the dresser. Delgado threw the man off of him, the crowbar flipping from his grasp. The man stumbled, gained his footing, and took a stance, his feet planted firmly, the fingers of his hands spread wide.

'Strange,' said Delgado, and he laughed.

Strange saw Delgado glance at his clothing heaped on the floor. Strange kicked the clothing to the side. Delgado balled his fists, touched one thumb and then the other to his chin, and came in, Strange backpedaling to the wall.

Delgado was on him then. He led with a left jab that stung Strange's ribs, then hooked a right. Strange tucked his elbows in tight, his left bicep absorbing the blow down to the bone. Strange grunted, exploded with an uppercut, connected to Delgado's jaw. It moved

Delgado back a step and brought rage to his eyes. He crossed the room in two strides. The right came furiously. The right was a blur, and it caught Strange on his cheek and knocked him off his feet.

Strange rolled, came up standing, and shook the dizziness from his head. His hand found the sheath on his hip. He unsnapped it and freed the Buck knife. He pulled the blade from the handle and hefted the knife in his hand. Delgado smiled from across the room. His gums were red with blood.

'I am gonna take that motherfucker *from* you, old man.'

'Take it,' said Strange.

Delgado bobbed, moved in, feigned a left and threw a right, putting everything into the right and aiming three feet behind Strange's head. Strange slipped the punch. The momentum carried Delgado through, and he stumbled, slipping so that he was on one knee before Strange and looking up at him, his eyes wide and white. Strange came down violently with the knife, burying the blade to the handle in Delgado's thick neck. The blade severed his carotid artery and pierced his windpipe. A crimson fountain erupted into the room. Sondra screamed.

Delgado pawed weakly for the handle as he crashed to the floor. He coughed out a mist of red and fought for air. Delgado's brain died, and he kicked like an animal as his head dropped into a spreading pool of blood.

Strange put the sole of his boot to the side of Delgado's face and withdrew the knife. He wiped the blade off on his jeans, pushed down on the brass safety, and folded the blade back into its handle. Sheathing it, he turned to the girl. She had balled herself up against the headboard, and her screams were shrill in the room. Strange picked up the crowbar and slipped it into the back pocket of his jeans.

Strange crossed the room and slapped Sondra hard across the face. He slapped her again. She stopped screaming and began to sob and shake. She was afraid of him, and that was good. He ripped the wool blanket off the bed and wrapped it around her shoulders.

Strange picked Sondra up and carried her from the room, out onto the landing, and down the stairs. He managed the front door and walked out to the porch, down the steps, and out into the rain. He didn't look at the barn. He stopped at the stand of pine, laid Sondra down, slung his day pack over his shoulder, and picked her up again. He saw Quinn's pack and coat and left them there. He moved quickly into the dark shelter of the trees and did not look back.

'Screamin' stopped,' said Ray.

'I know it,' said Earl, looking over at Franklin.

'I told you to shut your mouths,' said Quinn, side-glancing Franklin, seeing Eugene's right hand slip off the green of the table.

'I'm just gonna go ahead and keep talkin',' said Ray, 'it's all the same to you.'

'Keep talkin', Critter.'

'Makes me feel better. Don't it make you feel better, Daddy, to talk all this out?'

'Yep,' said Earl, who scratched his nose.

'Keep your hands on the bar,' said Quinn.

'Yessir,' said Earl, and Ray laughed.

'What is it you want, exactly?' said Ray. 'Money? Drugs? Hell, boy, it's right up there on top of the bar. Get it and get gone, that's what you're here for.'

Quinn said nothing.

'Your gun arm must be gettin' tired,' said Earl.

The rain sheeted the walls of the barn.

'You gonna stand there like that all night?' said Ray. 'Shit, boy, you gotta do *somethin'*. I mean, shoot us or rob us or walk away. What's it gonna be?'

The beeper sounded on Quinn's hip. No one said anything, listening to it. Then the beeping ended.

Quinn began to walk backward, still covering the men with his gun. Ray laughed, and Quinn felt the blood rise to his face.

'Look at that, Daddy. He's gonna back on out of here now.'

'I see him,' said Earl, the lines of his cheeks deepening from his thick smile.

'That what you gonna do, pussy-boy? Just walk away?'

Quinn stopped. He stood straight and holstered his weapon. He glanced at Eugene Franklin, turned, and gave them his back. Quinn headed for the barn door.

Earl picked up the Colt and slid it down the bar to his son. Ray's boot heel caught momentarily on the brass rail as he swiveled his hips. He lost a second of time, reached out for the Colt's grip, got his hand around it, and swung the muzzle toward Quinn as Earl found the .38 and drew it from his coat pocket.

'Hey, Terry,' said Franklin in a quiet, even way.

Quinn cleared his Glock from his holster. He crouched and spun and fired from the hip. The bar splintered around Ray. Quinn fired again, and the slug tore open Ray's shirt in the center of his chest. Ray dropped his gun and fell to the slatted wood floor.

A gunshot exploded into the room. Earl's pistol jumped, and Quinn felt air and fire burn at the side of his scalp.

Franklin kicked the card table over as he stood. He squeezed the trigger on his Glock four times, the gun jumping in his hand. Earl was thrown back into the bar mirror. The bottles on the call rack exploded around him in a shower of glass and blood. Earl spun, dropped, and disappeared.

A bell tone rang steadily in Quinn's ears. He heard someone moan. Then a short cough and only the ringing sound and the rain.

Quinn walked through the roiling gun smoke. He kicked the .38 away from Ray's corpse. He went around the bar with his gun arm locked and looked down at the father. Quinn holstered his gun.

'The girl,' said Franklin.

'Strange got her,' said Quinn.

'Delgado?'

'If Strange got the girl, he got Delgado, too. Let's go.'

Quinn picked up his coat and pack in the stand of pine. He and Franklin entered the woods and headed for the row of lights on the interstate, glowing faintly up ahead.

An hour later, Quinn parked the Chevelle in the lot of Franklin's apartment house and let the motor run.

Franklin said, 'What now, Terry?'

'You've got a little bit of time,' said Quinn. 'Strange sent a package off today to someone he trusts in the department. Chris Wilson's notebook and the photographs.'

'What about my confession?'

'Strange made a copy of that.' Quinn reached across Franklin and opened the glove box door. 'I've got the original right here.'

Franklin took the yellow piece of paper from Quinn's hand. Quinn nodded, and Franklin slipped the paper into the pocket of his coat. 'Thank you, Terry.'

Quinn stared through the windshield and pushed hair behind his ear, careful not to touch the tender spot where Earl Boone's bullet had grazed his scalp.

'You're not off the hook. The evidence Strange mailed in is enough to convict you. However you want to plead your defense, that's up to you. As far as what happened tonight, and the girl—'

'Ain't no one ever gonna know about what happened tonight, or about the girl. Not from me.' Franklin swallowed. 'Terry—'

'Go on.'

Franklin offered his hand. Quinn kept his grip tight on the steering wheel.

'All right, then,' said Franklin. He stepped out of the car and crossed the parking lot, his head lowered against the rain.

Later, and for the rest of his life, Quinn would not forget Eugene Franklin's sad, odd face, or the hang of his outstretched hand.

Near dawn, Derek Strange exited the house of Leona Wilson, closing the front door softly behind him. The rain had ended. He stood on the concrete stoop and breathed the cold morning air, turning his collar up against the chill.

Down on the street, parked behind his Caprice, was a pretty blue Chevelle. A long-haired young white man sat behind the wheel.

'Thank you, Lord,' said Strange.

He locked eyes with Quinn and smiled.

33

That evening, the suicide of Eugene Franklin made the six o'clock news.

A resident in the apartment next door had heard a gunshot around noon and phoned the police. They found Franklin upright on the couch. His eyes were bugged from the gas jolt, and his nose was blackened and scorched. Blood and bone and brain matter had been sprayed on the walls and the fabric of the couch. His service weapon lay in his lap. A letter written in longhand had been neatly placed on the coffee table before him.

On the eleven o'clock news, Franklin's suicide was eclipsed by the discovery of a mass homicide on a wooded property at the east-central edge of Montgomery County. Six bodies had been found in various stages of decomposition. The police had been alerted by a friend of one of the victims, a woman named Edna Loomis. The friend, Johanna Dodgson, had not heard from Loomis for days and had called the local cops when her concern became great. After two bodies were discovered in the barn, and another in the house, police found three additional bodies, including the corpse of Edna Loomis, in a tunnel underneath the property. Johanna Dodgson had mentioned the existence of the tunnel in her initial call to the police.

The Out-County Massacre, as it was immediately dubbed by the press, dominated the news for the next three days. A rumor surfaced that one of the victims was a D.C. cop, and then the rumor was publicly confirmed. Drugs and large amounts of money were said to have been found at the scene. Another rumor surfaced, alleging that the suicide of Officer Eugene Franklin was somehow related to the Out-County Massacre, but this rumor remained unconfirmed. Police spokesmen promised a speedy resolution to the case, claiming that an announcement regarding the findings was 'imminent.'

Strange went to work daily and kept to his general routine. He followed the news reports closely but did not discuss them, except with Ron and Janine, and only then in passing. He phoned Quinn and spoke to him twice, and on both occasions he found him to be uncommunicative, remote, and possibly in the grip of depression. He visited Leona and Sondra Wilson briefly and was pleased with what he found.

It was a tentative time for Strange, and though he picked up a couple of easy jobs, mostly he waited. By the end of the next week, he welcomed the phone call that he knew with certainty would come. The call came on Saturday morning, when he was returning from a long walk with Greco, as he stepped into the foyer of his Buchanan Street row house.

'Hello,' said Strange, picking up the phone.

'Lydell here. You ready to talk, Derek?'

'Name the place,' said Strange.

Oregon Avenue, south of Military Road, led into a section of Rock Creek Park that contained a nature center, horse stables, and miles of hilly trails. A huge parking lot sat to the right of the entrance, where people met to train and run their dogs on the adjacent field. The parking lot was a popular rendezvous spot for adulterous couples as well.

Strange and Lydell Blue sat in Strange's Caprice, parked beside Blue's Park Avenue in the lot and facing the field. Blue's hair had thinned and it was all gray, as was his thick mustache, which he had worn for thirty years on his wide, strong-featured face. His belly sagged over the waistband of his slacks. He held a sixteen-ounce paper cup of coffee in his hand, steam rising from a hole he had torn in its lid.

Over a dozen large-breed dogs ran and played in the field, all of their owners white, well-off, and dressed in casual, expensive clothes. At the far end of the lot, near the tree line, a middle-aged man and a younger woman necked in the front seat of a late-model Pontiac.

'You shoulda brought Greco,' said Blue, looking through the windshield at an Irish wolfhound and a white Samoyed sitting side by side on a rise, a woman in a Banana Republic jacket telling them to hold from fifteen feet away.

'Greco's not a dog lover,' said Strange. 'Right about now, he'd be barin' his teeth at those two.'

'Wouldn't want to bust on all these folks' perfect day.'

Strange looked over at Blue. 'Tell me what you got, Lydell.'

'You gonna be up front with me if I do?'

'How long we been knowin' each other, man?'

'Okay, then. Okay.' Blue ran his thumb along his mustache. 'The cops who found Eugene Franklin found a suicide note at the scene. More like a confession, really.'

'You see the note?'

'Got a copy of it from a friend over in Homicide. Written with an ink pen on a plain white sheet of paper. Handwriting was clean and precise, like he was under no kind of duress when he wrote it. Signature on it matched the signature of Franklin we had on file.'

'What'd the note say?'

'Franklin admitted that he and Adonis Delgado were on the payroll of that drug lord, Cherokee Coleman. He detailed his role in the Chris Wilson shooting. How Wilson had gotten onto him and Delgado, and how Coleman had ordered a hit on Wilson. They used Ricky Kane, who was a drug dealer to the restaurant trade, not the clean-cut suburban boy the papers had made him out to be, to get Wilson out there in street clothes and make him look wrong. Franklin was supposed to shoot Wilson. But his partner, Quinn, who Franklin claimed was clean, shot Wilson first.'

Strange digested what Blue had told him. 'The news-people been talkin' about these rumors, that Franklin is somehow connected to the Out-County thing. If he was hooked up with Delgado—'

'Franklin put it all in the note. Him and Delgado were sent by Coleman out to that property to make a drug transaction, and also to kill the two wholesalers, Earl and Ray Boone. Somethin' about makin' it right for Coleman over two Colombians the Boones had murdered out there. That part checks out; two men were found in a tunnel on the property, their death date much earlier than the date of death on the Boones. They've ID'd the corpses as two Colombian brothers, Nestor and Lizardo Rodriguez, who were recently reported missing down around Richmond.'

'What about the Boones and Delgado? Who killed them?'

'Franklin claimed that he did. Claimed he had a crisis of conscience and had to end the whole thing the only way he saw fit. He and Delgado fought over it in the house, they went at it, and he killed Delgado. Then Franklin went down to the barn and shot the father and son. He left the drugs and the money sitting in the barn and drove back to D.C. Ate his own gun the next day.'

'There was a girl found in that tunnel, too.'

'Edna Loomis. Died of natural causes. That is, if you call a woman having a stroke at thirty years old "natural." Methamphetamine will do that to you, you ingest enough.'

'Hell of a story,' said Strange.

'Yeah. Trouble is, it doesn't check out.'

'What's wrong with it?'

'Plenty of things. Start with the crime scene, out at the barn and the house. Okay, so Franklin says he had a change of heart, and he and Delgado got down to it. Why was Delgado naked, then? And Delgado was stabbed. Why wouldn't Franklin just go ahead and shoot him like he did the others?'

'I don't know.'

'They found a boot print tracking out of Delgado's blood, too. Size twelve, I believe it was. Franklin wore a ten.'

'What else?' said Strange.

'The Boones were killed by the same type of gun, a Glock seventeen. But it was two *different* Glock seventeens that killed 'em. The markings on the slug found in the body of the son and another bullet found in the wood of the bar were inconsistent with the markings of those found in the father and those found around the father. The trajectory angles were inconsistent, too. There were two shooters that night, Derek. *Had* to be.'

'No fingerprints, nothin' like that?'

'No prints other than those of the deceased, Franklin, and another, unidentified woman.'

'A woman, huh?'

'They found vaginal fluid and pubic hairs in the same bedroom where they found Delgado.'

'The Loomis girl?'

'Didn't match. But if there was some kind of phantom woman there, it explains why Delgado died in his birthday suit.'

'Sounds like y'all got a genuine head-scratcher.'

'Uh-huh.'

Blue turned his head and stared at Strange.

'Why'd you call me here, Lydell?'

'Well, Derek, I'll tell you. I got an anonymous package in the mail, no return address, mailing label out of a printer just like any thousand printers in this city. Had Chris Wilson's investigation detailed in a notebook, and photographs of Franklin and Delgado headin' into Coleman's compound.' Blue took a sip of coffee. 'That was you sent me that, right?'

'It was,' said Strange.

'Didn't take a genius to figure it. You had called me and asked me to run the numbers of Delgado's cruiser, remember?'

'I do.'

'So tell me how you came to get all that information.'

Strange shrugged. 'I was hired by Leona Wilson to try and clear her son's reputation. Among other things, she wanted his name etched onto that police memorial they got downtown. I started by interviewing Quinn, and then Franklin, and the natural progression was to follow Ricky Kane and see what he was all about.'

'Okay. What'd you find?'

'Same thing Wilson did. Kane led me to Coleman, and that was when I noticed the same Crown Vic cruiser patroling the perimeter of the operation on two separate days. I called you and got Delgado's name. I found Wilson's notebook and the photographs and mailed them off to you. See, I saw that this thing was bigger than me, Lydell. I thought if y'all could connect the dots, Wilson's story would naturally get told. I didn't give a goddamn about no conspiracy thing, man, I was only trying to do what Leona Wilson had hired me to do.'

'A couple of cops came forward, said they saw you and Quinn talking to Franklin down at Erika's.'

'That's right.'

'They're gonna bring you in for questioning, man. They're gonna bring Quinn in, too.'

'You tell them I mailed you the information?'

Blue drank the rest of the coffee in one long gulp. He dropped the empty cup at his feet.

'They don't even know I got it,' said Blue. 'The notebook and photographs, they're in the trunk of my Buick, man. Gonna give it all back to you before you leave.'

'You can't use it?'

'How could I explain the fact that it was sent to *me* in the first place?'

'You couldn't, I guess.'

'Either I'd have to lie or I'd have to implicate you. And those are two things I'm not gonna do. Anyway, the department doesn't need the notebook or the photographs to make the case. Kane's been picked up. What I hear, he's already rolled over, and he's confirmed the background information that was in Franklin's note. They're gonna get him to turn Cherokee Coleman in exchange for some kind of country club jolt. Whether it sticks to Coleman or not, we'll see. Nothin' has so far.'

'Kane say how he got Wilson out in the street that night?'

'Kane said he heard that Wilson had a sister was hooked on junk. He told Wilson he'd found her and to meet him on D.'

Kane *heard* that Wilson had a sister . . . Lyin' motherfucker, thought Strange, tryin' to make himself look good.

'You knew about the sister?' said Blue.

'She lives with her mother,' said Strange, with a casual nod. 'Everything that family's been through, I'd hate to see that junkie sister rumor get thrown out to the press.'

'We know what that family's been through. How Kane got Wilson out to the street that night is immaterial. Far as anybody's ever gonna know, the sister's clean.'

'And Chris? What about him?'

'Yeah, Chris Wilson. It's delicate, how the department's gonna handle that. For obvious reasons, they don't want too much play on this bad-cop thing, and they don't want the public to think that what Wilson did – being some kind of rogue enforcer out there – is something they condone, exactly. In the end, I don't know how this will be spun for the general public. But I do know what they're saying about Wilson down at headquarters. He's gonna get some kind of posthumous, low-key commendation from Chief Ramsey.'

'Good,' said Strange. 'That's real good.'

'You stirred the pot, Derek.'

'I guess I did.'

'Funny about that other cop. Quinn, I mean.'

'Yeah. He's not gonna come out of this smellin' any better than he did to begin with.'

'You think he should?' said Blue.

'He made a mistake,' said Strange. 'I've gotten to know Quinn a little, and I can tell you, he's still payin' for what he did. I think he's always gonna pay.'

'Ending a fine young man's life the way he did, that's not just a mistake. And you can't tell me that if Chris Wilson had been white—'

'I know it, Lydell. You don't have to tell me, 'cause I know.'

Strange cracked his window. The afternoon sun had warmed the interior of the car.

'All the good people in this city,' said Blue. 'And all you ever hear about is the bad in D.C. Now you're gonna hear about bad cops, too, when most of 'em are good. And most of the people I come across every day, they come from good families. I'm talkin' about the people in the church, people who go to work every day to take care of their own, good teachers, good, hard workers . . . and here we are, all these years we been out here, fuckin' with the bad ones. Why'd we choose this, Derek?'

'I don't know. I guess it chose us.'

'If we'd only known, when we were young men.' Blue chuckled, looking over at his friend. 'Lord, I been knowin' you now for nearly fifty years. I even remember the way you used to run when you were a little boy, with your fists balled up near your chest, back in grade school. And I can remember the way you looked in your uniform, as a young man, back in sixty-eight.'

'Sixty-eight,' said Strange. 'That was some kind of year, Lydell, wasn't it?'

'Yes it was.'

A look passed between Strange and Blue.

'Thank you, Lydell.'

'*You* know how we do.'

Strange shook Blue's hand. 'So the department's gonna be callin' me in.'

'Any day,' said Blue. 'The way you just explained it—'

'What, somethin' about it you didn't like?'

'It was just a little rough, is all. I'd work on it a little, I was you.'

Strange returned to his row house and phoned Terry Quinn. He relayed the conversation he'd had with Lydell Blue.

'I hated to lie to my friend,' said Strange. 'But I didn't know what else to do.'

'I guess Eugene destroyed the original confession,' said Quinn.

'Looks like he did. The one the police found was written on plain white paper. I'm fixin' to destroy some things, too. Gonna lose the clothing I wore that night, my boots, my knife . . . you need to do the same. Get rid of your day pack and that Glock.'

'It's already done.'

'I don't like the way you sound, Terry,' said Strange. 'Don't do anything stupid, hear?'

'Don't worry,' said Quinn. 'I'm not as brave as Eugene.'

The phone clicked dead in Strange's ear.

34

On a Sunday morning in early April, when the cherry blossoms along the tidal basin were full and brilliant, and magnolias and dogwoods had erupted pink and white on lawns across the city, Strange, Janine, and Lionel met at church.

Strange had not been to services for some time. He decided to go this day, the weekend after Easter, to pray for his mother, and though he did pray in the privacy of his home from time to time, he thought it might be wise to be in the Lord's home for this, considering his mother's dire condition. He knew that attending church for personal favors was wrong and, on some level he didn't fully understand, hypocritical, but he went just the same.

The pews inside the New Bethel Church of God in Christ, on Georgia and Piney Branch Road, were nearly full. Strange paid some attention to the sermon, prayed intently for his mother while Janine rested her hand atop his, and enjoyed the gospel singing from the choir, his favorite part of the service.

Outside, as the congregation exited, Strange recognized many. In the faces of some of the children he saw their parents, whom he'd known since they were kids themselves. And he saw several former clients, whom he greeted and who greeted him with firm handshakes and claps on the arm. Though he had often given these people less-than-happy news, he was glad he'd never padded his hours with them or done a second-rate job. They knew who he was and what he was about, and he was proud that they knew.

'We goin' to that Greek joint for breakfast?' said Lionel.

'Billy's closed today,' said Strange. 'It's his Easter Sunday.'

'I was gonna make a nice turkey,' said Janine. 'Will you come over for dinner?'

'Was thinkin' I'd take Greco for a long walk down in Rock Creek,' said Strange. 'But yeah, I'd love to come over for dinner, long as it's early. Need to spend the evening with my mom.'

'We'll have it early, then,' said Janine. 'See you around five?'

'Lookin' forward to it, Janine.'

He kissed her there, in a cluster of azalea bushes planted beside the church.

'Look at y'all,' said Lionel. 'In front of God, too.'

Strange walked to his Caddy, parked on Tuckerman. Along the curb, on the other side of the street, sat a gray Plymouth K-car. Leona Wilson had opened the passenger door for her daughter, Sondra, who was ducking her head to get inside. Strange caught a quick look at Sondra, still thin and shapeless in her dress, her hair salon done and shoulder length, her eyes bright and a bit unfocused. Not there, but *getting* there, Strange could see.

As Strange crossed the street to greet Leona Wilson, Terry Quinn's face flashed in his mind. He hadn't seen Quinn or spoken to him for quite some time.

Leona Wilson walked around the K-car to the driver's-side door, stopping as she saw Strange approach. For a moment she didn't seem to recognize him, dressed as he was, but then she smiled at the broad-shouldered, handsome man in the pinstriped suit. She reached out with a white-gloved hand and cocked her head.

'Mrs Wilson,' said Strange.

'Mr Strange.'

Strange sat behind the wheel of his Cadillac Brougham, parked on Bonifant Street in Silver Spring. Greco was snoring, lying on his red pillow on the backseat. Strange and the dog both had a bellyful of Janine's cooking inside them, and Greco had taken the opportunity to nap.

Across the street, Terry Quinn locked the front door of the bookstore, checked it, and turned to go up the sidewalk.

Strange leaned his head out the window. 'Hey, Terry!'

Quinn found the source of the voice and smiled. He crossed the street and walked toward the car. Strange thought that Quinn had lost weight but realized that it was the hair that had given him that mistaken impression; Quinn had cut it short.

'Get in for a minute, man,' said Strange.

Quinn went around the Caddy and dropped into the passenger seat. Greco woke, sat up, and smelled the back of Quinn's neck as Quinn and Strange shook hands.

'Derek.'

'Terry.'

'What brings you out this way?'

'Was thinking of you, is all,' said Strange. 'And look at you, all cleancut.'

'Yeah. Went down to this barbershop on Georgia, Elegant and Proud?'

'I know that joint.'

'They didn't look too happy to see me in there. But all I wanted was a close cut, and they gave it to me. Anyway, it feels good to get rid of all that hair.'

'You look like a cop again.'

'I know.' Quinn thumbed his lip. 'You said you were thinkin' of me. Why?'

'Well, we're friends, for one.'

'We're friends now, huh?'

'Sure.'

'What else?'

'I saw Leona and Sondra Wilson today, at church.'

Quinn nodded. 'How's the girl doin'?'

'You know what that road's like. Once you're in, you're in forever. Always gonna be a struggle. But her mother got her into one of the city's best programs. She'll make it, I expect.'

'You did good.'

'So did you.' Strange looked over at Quinn. 'Chris Wilson got a commendation. They did a quiet kind of ceremony, but he got it. And they put his name up on that wall.'

'I heard about it,' said Quinn. 'The department didn't get the press involved in it, but word reached me from inside.'

'Yeah, the department's played the press pretty good on this whole thing. But what else they gonna do? They don't have all the answers their *own* selves. They've got Franklin's confession, and the conflicting forensic evidence from the scene, and Kane's self-serving testimony. They know there's more, but they can't seem to get to it.'

'They didn't get anything out of you and me.'

'No.' Strange studied Quinn. 'You're lookin' better.'

'I'm doin' all right.'

'You out of that funk you were in?'

'I guess I am,' said Quinn. 'You said that someday I'd learn to walk away from a fight. Maybe I'm getting to that place.'

'I guess, workin' in that bookstore over there, with Lewis and all them, you have plenty of time for meditation.'

'Yeah, Derek, I've got nothin' but time.'

'I was thinkin', you know, there are special instances when I could use another operative. You did some pretty good work with me, man.

I was wonderin', would you ever consider taking on a case for me, now and again?'

'While you do the light work?'

'Funny.'

'What about Ron Lattimer?'

'This time of year, Ron's busy pickin' out his spring wardrobe and shit. Haven't seen him much the last week or so.'

'I don't have an investigator's license.'

'Easy enough to get one.'

'I'll think about it, okay?'

'Sure, do *that*. With all that time you got . . . to think.'

Greco licked Quinn's neck. Quinn turned in his seat and scratched the boxer behind his ears.

'You seein' a woman?' said Strange.

'Nobody special. How's Janine?'

'She's good. Just left her and Lionel.'

'Spending a lot of time with her, huh?'

Strange nodded. 'Finally woke up. Was always lookin' for someone else . . . chasing after women who didn't care nothin' for me, even goin' after that anonymous kind of sex—'

'Hookers, you mean.'

'Yeah. Always lookin' for somethin' else, when the best thing was right next to me, staring me right in the face. Just like my mother always said. Not that I'm thinkin' of getting married or anything like that. But I do plan to be there, for her and the boy.'

'Tell her I said hey.'

'I will.'

Quinn looked at his watch. 'I better be goin'.'

'Me too. Where's your car at?'

'I didn't bring it.'

'You need a lift back to your place?'

'No, thanks. I think I'll walk.'

Quinn reached for the door handle. Strange put a hand on Quinn's arm.

'Terry.'

'What?'

'I just want you to know, in light of how all this ended up, I mean . . . I wanted you to know that I was wrong about you, man.'

Quinn smiled sadly. 'You were wrong about some things, Derek. But not everything.'

Quinn stepped out of the car. Strange watched him cross the street in the gathering darkness.

*

Terry Quinn walked up Bonifant and cut left on Georgia Avenue. The street lamps and window lights glowed faintly in the cool dusk. As Quinn went down Georgia, a group of four young black men in baggy clothing approached on the sidewalk from the opposite direction. They split apart, seeing that Quinn was not going to step aside. One of the young men bumped him lightly on the arm, and Quinn gave him an elbow as he went by.

I lied to Strange, thought Quinn. I'm lying to myself. I am never going to change. I am never going to walk away.

Quinn heard laughter from the group and he kept walking, past Rosita's without looking through its window, then left into the breezeway, where he patted the head of the bronze Norman Lane bust as he went on into the alley. He took the alley south.

Quinn crossed Silver Spring Avenue and continued through the alley to Sligo Avenue, then across to Selim and along the Napa auto parts shop and the My-Le *pho* house and foreign-car garages that faced the railroad and Metro tracks. Then he was on the pedestrian bridge spanning Georgia Avenue, and on the other side of it he jumped the chain-link fence and went past the commuter station and down the steps into the lighted foot tunnel beneath the tracks.

Quinn walked the wooden platform beside the fence that bordered the Canada Dry bottling plant. He turned, his hands dug in the pockets of his jeans, and watched the close approach of a northbound train.

This place had always been his. But now he shared it with a woman he'd kissed here on a clear and biting winter night.

Quinn closed his eyes and listened to the sounds of the train, felt the rush of the cars raising wind and dust.

He didn't come here for answers. There were no answers. There was only sensation.

No answers, and there would be no closure. Chris Wilson had been exonerated, but for Quinn nothing had changed. Because Strange had been right all along: Quinn had killed a man because of the color of his skin.

Strange walked down the drab, third-floor hall of the District Convalescent Home, passing a couple of female attendants who were laughing loudly at something one of them had said, ignoring a man in a nearby wheelchair who was repeating the word 'nurse' over and over again. A television played at full volume from one of the rooms. The hall was warm and smelled of pureed food and, beneath the mask of disinfectant, urine and excrement.

Strange entered his mother's room. She was lying on her side, under the sheets of her bed, awake and staring out the window. He walked around to the side of the bed.

'Momma,' said Strange, kissing her clammy forehead. 'Here I am.'

His mother made a small wave of her hand and smiled weakly, showing him the gray of her gums. Her body was tiny as a child's beneath the sheets.

Strange found a comb in the nightstand and ran it through her sparse white hair, pushing what was left of it back on her moley scalp. When he was finished, she pointed past Strange's shoulder. He went to the window and looked to the corner of the ledge.

A house wren had built a nest there and was sitting on her eggs. The small bird flew away at the sight of Strange.

Strange knew what his mother wanted. He tore off several paper towels from the bathroom roll, found some Scotch tape on a supply cart out in the hall, and taped the squares of paper to the window. His mother had done this every spring in the kitchen window of the house in which he'd been raised. She had explained to him that a mother bird was like any mother, that she deserved to tend to her children privately and in peace.

From her bed, Alethea Strange blinked her eyes with approval at her son, examining the job he'd done.

Strange brought a cushioned chair over to the side of her bed and had a seat. He sat there for a while, telling her about his day.

'Janine,' she said, very softly.

'She's good, Momma. She sends her love.'

'Diamonds . . .'

'. . . In my backyard. Yes, ma'am.'

Sitting in the chair, Strange fell asleep. He woke in the middle of the night. His mother was still awake, her beautiful brown eyes staring into his.

Strange began to talk about his childhood in D.C. He talked about his father, and the mention of her husband brought a smile to Alethea's lips. He talked about his brother, the trouble he'd had, and how even with the trouble his brother's heart had been good.

'I love you, Momma,' said Strange. 'I'm so proud to be your son.'

As he talked, he held her hand and looked into her eyes. He was still holding her hand at dawn, and the birds were singing outside her bedroom window as she passed.

Hell to Pay

To Dennis K. Ashton Jr, seven years old,
shot to death on June 27, 1997,
by a criminal with a handgun in Washington, D.C.

'Don't Look down
On a man . . .
Unless you gonna
Pick him up.'

Written on a mural outside Taylor's Funeral Home, on the corner of Randolph Place and North Capitol Street, NW, Washington, D.C.

1

Garfield Potter sat low behind the wheel of an idling Caprice, his thumb stroking the rubber grip of the Colt revolver loosely fitted between his legs. On the bench beside him, leaning against the passenger window, sat Carlton Little. Little filled an empty White Owl wrapper with marijuana and tamped the herb with his thumb. Potter and Little were waiting on Charles White, who was in the backyard of his grandmother's place, getting his dog out of a cage.

'It don't look like much, does it?' said Potter, looking down at his own lap.

Little grinned lazily. 'That's what the girls must say when you pull that thing out.'

'Like Brianna, you mean? *Your* girl? She ain't *had* no chance to look at it, 'cause I was waxin' her from behind. She *felt* it, though. Made her forget all about you, too. I mean, when I was done hittin' it she couldn't even remember your name.'

'She couldn't remember hers either, drunk as she had to be to fuck a sad motherfucker like you.' Little laughed some as he struck a match and held it to the end of the cigar.

'I'm talkin' about this gun, fool.' Potter held up the Colt so Little, firing up the blunt, could see it.

'Yeah, okay. Where'd you get it at, man?'

'Traded it to this boy for half an OZ. Was one of those project guns, hadn't even been fired but once or twice. Short barrel, only two inches long, you'd think it couldn't do shit. But this here is a three fifty-seven. They call it a carry revolver, 'cause you can carry this shit without no one knowin' you strapped. I don't need no long barrel, anyway. I like to work close in.'

'I'll stick with my nine. You don't even know if that shits works.'

'It works. Yours jams, don't be askin' me for mines.'

Potter was tall, light skinned, flat of stomach and chest, with thin, ropy forearms and biceps. He kept his hair shaved close to the scalp, with a small slash mark by way of a part. His irises were dark brown and filled his eyes; his nose was a white boy's nose, thin and aquiline. He was quick to smile. It was a smile that could be engaging when he wanted it to be, but more often than not it inspired fear.

Little was not so tall. He was bulked in the shoulders and arms, but twiggish in the legs. A set of weights had given him the show muscles upstairs, but his legs, which he never worked on, betrayed the skinny, malnourished boy he used to be. He wore his hair braided in cornrows and kept a careless, weedy thatch of hair on his chin.

Both wore carpenter jeans and button-down, short-sleeve plaid Nautica shirts over wife-beater Ts. Potter's shoes were whatever was newest in the window of the Foot Locker up at City Place; he had a pair of blue-and-black Air Maxes on now. On Little's feet were wheat-colored Timberland work boots, loosely laced and untied.

Little held a long draw in his lungs and looked ahead, exhaling a cloud of smoke that crashed at the windshield. 'Here comes Coon. Lookit how he's all chest out and shit. Proud about that dog.'

Charles White was walking his pit bull, Trooper, past a dying oak tree, its leaves nearly stripped bare. A tire hung on a chain from one of the branches. When he was a puppy, Trooper had swung on the tire for hours, holding it fast, strengthening his jaws.

'That ain't no game dog,' said Potter. 'Coon ain't no dog man, neither.'

White had Trooper, brown with a white mask and golden-pink eyes, on a short leash attached to a heavy-ringed, wide leather collar. Trooper's ears were game-cropped at the skull. White, of average size and dressed similarly to his friends, moved toward the car, opened the back door, and let the dog in before getting inside himself.

'S'up, fellas,' said White.

'Coon,' said Little, looking over the bench at his friend. Others thought White's street name had something to do with his color, dark as he was. But Little knew where the name had come from. He'd been knowing Coon since they were both kids in the Section Eights, back in the early nineties, when White used to wear a coonskin hat, trying to look like that fool rapper from Digital Underground, that group that was popular then. There was the other thing, too: White had a nose on him, big and long like some cartoon animal. And he walked kind of pitched forward, with his bony fingers spread kind of like claws, the way a critter in the woods would do.

'Gimme some of that hydro, Dirty.'

Dirty was Little's street name, so given because of his fondness for discussing women's privates. Men's, too. Also, he loved to eat all that greasy fast food. Little passed the blunt back to White. White hit it deep.

'Your champion ready?' said Potter.

'What?' said White.

It was hard to hear in the car. Potter had the music, the new DMX joint on PGC, turned up loud.

'I said, is that dumb animal gonna win us some *money* today?' said Potter, raising his voice.

White didn't answer right away. He held the smoke down in his lungs and let it out slow.

'He gonna win us *mad* money, D,' said White. He reached over and massaged the dense muscles bunched around Trooper's jaw. Trooper's mouth opened in pleasure and his eyes shifted over to his master's. 'Right, boy?'

'Sure he's strong enough?'

'Shoot, he was strong enough to drag a log down the block yesterday mornin'.'

'I ain't ask you can he do circus tricks. Can he hold his shit in a fight?'

'He will.'

'Well, he ain't showed me nothin' yet.'

'What about that snatch we did with that boy's dog over on Crittenden?'

Potter looked in the rearview at White. 'That dog at Crittenden wasn't nothin' but a cur. Trooper a cur, too.'

'The hell he is. You're gonna see today.'

'We *better* see. 'Cause I ain't wastin' my time or my green paper on no pussy-ass animal.' Potter slid the Colt under the waistband of his jeans.

'I said, you're gonna see.'

'C'mon, D,' said Little. 'Let's get a roll on, man.'

Garfield Potter's street name was Death. He didn't care for it much since this girl he wanted to fuck told him it scared her some. Never did get that girl's drawers down, either. So he felt the name was bad luck, worse still to go and change it. His friends now called him D.

Potter turned the key in the ignition. It made an awful grinding sound. Little clapped his hands together and doubled over with laughter.

'Ho, shit!' said Little, clapping his hands one more time. 'Car's already started, man, you don't need to be startin' it *again*! Maybe if you turned that music down some you'd know.'

'Noisy as this whip is, too,' said White.

'Fuck you, Coon,' said Potter, 'talkin' mad shit about this car, when you're cruisin' around town in that piece-of-shit Toyota, lookin' like a Spanish Cadillac and shit.'

'All this money we got,' said Little, 'and we're drivin' around in a hooptie.'

'We'll be gettin' rid of it soon,' said Potter. 'And anyway, it ain't all that funny as y'all are makin' it out to be.'

'Yeah, you right. It just hit me funny, is all.' Little took the blunt that White handed to him over the front seat and stared at it stupidly. 'I ain't lyin', boy, this chronic right here just laid my ass out.'

The dogfights were held in a large garage backing to an alley behind a house on Ogelthorpe, in Manor Park in Northwest. The fights went down once a week for several hours during the day, when most of the neighbors were off at work. Those neighbors who were at home were afraid of the young men who came to the fights, and did not complain to the police.

Potter parked the Chevy in the alley. He and the others got out of the car, White heeling Trooper to his side.

They went down the alley, nodding but not smiling at some young men they knew to be members of the Delafield Mob. Others were standing around, holding their animals, getting high, and drinking from the lips of bottles peeking through the tops of brown paper bags. Little and White followed Potter into the garage.

Ten to twenty young men were scattered about the perimeter of the garage. A group was shooting craps in the corner. Others were passing around joints. Someone had put on *Dr Dre 2001*, with Snoop, Eminem, and all them, and it was coming loud from a box.

In the middle of the garage was a fighting area of industrial carpet, penned off from the rest of the interior by a low chain-link fence, gated in two corners. Inside one corner of the pen, a man held a link leash taut on a black pit bull spotted brown over its belly and chest. The dog's name was Diesel. Its ears were gnarled and its neck showed raised scars like pink worms.

Potter studied a man, old for this group, maybe thirty or so, who stood alone in a corner, putting fire to a cigarette.

'I'll be back in a few,' said Potter to Little.

''Bout ready to show the dogs,' said Little.

'Got a mind to put money on that black dog. But go ahead and bet Trooper, hear?'

'Three hunrid?'

'Three's good.'

Potter made his way over to the cigarette smoker, short and dumpy, a raggedy-ass dude on the way down, and stood before him.

'*I* know you.'

The smoker looked up with lazy eyes, trying to hold on to his shit. 'Yeah?'

'You run with Lorenze Wilder, right?'

'I seen him around. Don't mean we run together or nothin' like that.' But now the smoker recognized Potter and he lost his will to keep his pride. His eyes dropped to the concrete floor.

'Outside,' said Potter.

The older man followed Potter into the daylight, not too fast but without protest. Potter led him around the garage's outer wall, which faced the neighboring yards to the west.

'What's your name?'

'Edward Diggs.'

'Call you Digger Dog, right?'

'Some do.'

'Lorenze called you that when we sold him that hydro a few weeks back. You were standing right next to him. Remember me now?'

Diggs said nothing, and Potter moved forward so that he was looking down on Diggs and just a few inches from his face. Diggs's back touched the garage wall.

'So where your boy Lorenze at?'

'I don't know. He stays in his mother's old house—'

'Over off North Dakota. I know where that is, and he ain't been there awhile. Leastways, I ain't caught him in. He got a woman he cribs with on the side?'

Diggs avoided Potter's stare. 'Not that I know.'

'What about other kin?'

Diggs took a long final drag off his cigarette and dropped it to the ground, crushing it beneath his sneaker. He looked to his right, out in the alley, but there was no one there. Everyone had gone inside the garage. Potter spread one tail on his shirt and draped it back behind the butt of the Colt, so that Diggs could see.

Diggs shifted his eyes again and lowered his voice. He had to give this boy something, just so he'd go away. 'Lorenze got a sister. She be livin' down in Park Morton with her little boy.'

'Maybe I'll drop by. What's her name?'

'I wouldn't . . . What I'm sayin' is, you want my advice—'

Potter open-handed Diggs across the face. He used his left hand to bunch Diggs's shirt at the collar, then yanked Diggs forward and slapped him again.

Diggs said nothing, his body limp. Potter held him fast.

'What's the sister's name?'

Diggs's eyes had teared up. He hated himself for that. All he meant to do was advise this boy, tell him, don't fuck with Lorenze's sister or her kid. But it was too late for all that now.

'I don't know her name,' said Diggs. 'And anyway, Lorenze, he don't never go by the way or nothin'. He don't talk to his sister much, way I understand it. Sometimes he watches her kid play football; boy's on this tackle team. But that's as close as he gets to her.'

'Where the kid play at?'

'Lorenze said the kid practices in the evenings at some high school.'

'Which school?'

'He live in Park Morton, so it must be Roosevelt. It ain't but a few blocks up the street there—'

'I ain't asked you for directions, did I? I live up on Warder Street my own self, so you don't need to be drawin' me a map.'

'It ain't too far from there, is all I was sayin'.'

Potter's eyes softened. He smiled and released his grip on Diggs. 'I didn't hurt you none, did I? 'Cause, look, I didn't *mean* nothin', hear?'

Diggs straightened his collar. 'I'm all right.'

'Let me get one of those cigarettes from you, black.'

Diggs reached into his breast pocket and retrieved his pack of Kools. A cigarette slid out into his palm. He handed the cigarette to Potter.

Potter snapped the cigarette in half and bounced the halves off Diggs's chest. Potter's laugh was like a bark. He turned and walked away.

Diggs straightened his shirt and stepped quickly down the alley. He looked over his shoulder and saw that Potter had turned the corner. Diggs reached into his pocket and shook another cigarette out from a hole he had torn in the bottom of the pack.

Diggs's boy Lorenze was staying with this girl he knew over in Northeast. Lorenze had kind of laughed it off, said he'd crib with that girl until Potter forgot about the debt. Didn't look to Diggs that Potter was the type to forget. But he was proud he hadn't given Lorenze up. Most folks he knew didn't credit him for being so strong.

Diggs struck a match. He noticed that his hand was shaking some as he fired up his cigarette.

Back in the garage, Potter sidled up next to Little. The owner of the garage, also the house bookie, stood nearby, holding the cash and taking late bets.

In one corner of the pen, Charles White finished sponging Trooper down with warm, soapy water. Diesel's owner, in the opposite corner, did the same. Many dogs were treated with chemicals that could disorient the opponent. The rule in this arena was that both dogs had to be washed prior to a fight.

White scratched the top of Trooper's head, bent in, and uttered random words into his ear with a soothing tone. The referee, an obese young man, stepped into the ring after a nod from the owner of the garage.

'Both corners ready?' said the referee. 'Cornermen out of the pit.'

White moved behind his dog into the space of the open gate, still holding Trooper back.

'Face your dogs,' said the referee. They did this, and quickly the referee said, 'Let go!'

The dogs shot into the center of the pit. Both of them got up on their hind legs, attacking the head of the other with their jaws. They snapped at each other's ears and sought purchase in the area of the neck. In the fury of their battle, the dogs did not make a sound. The garage echoed with the shouts and laughter of the spectators crowding the ring.

For a moment the dogs seemed to reach a stalemate. Suddenly their motions accelerated. Their bodies meshed in a blur of brown and black, and the bright pink of exposed gums. Droplets of blood arced up in the center of the ring.

Diesel got a neck-hold and Trooper was taken down. Trooper, adrenalized, his eyes bright and wild, scrambled up and out of the hold. One of his ears had been partially torn away, and blood had leaked onto the dog's white mask. Diesel went in, back to the neck. And now Trooper was down again, in the jaws of Diesel, squirming beneath the black dog.

'Stop it!' shouted White.

Potter nudged Little, who nodded by way of reply.

'That's it,' said the referee, waving his arms.

White went into the ring and grabbed Trooper's hind legs, pulling back. Diesel's owner did the same. Diesel relaxed his jaws, releasing Trooper to his man. The spectators moved away from the pen, laughing, giving one another skin, already trying out stories on one another that exaggerated the details of the fight.

'You were right,' said Little. 'That dog was a cur.'

'What I tell you?' said Potter. 'Dog's personality only as strong as the man who owns it.'

White arrived with Trooper, back on his leash. 'I need to fix him up some,' said White, not looking into his friends' eyes.

'We'll do it now,' said Potter. 'Let's go.'

A couple of blocks away, near Fort Slocum Park, Potter pulled the Chevy into an alley where there seemed to be no activity. He cut the engine and looked over the backseat at White; Trooper sat panting, his hip resting against his owner's.

'Dog needs to pee,' said Potter.

'He went,' said White. 'Let's just take him to the vet place.'

'He already bleedin' all over the backseat. He pees back there, too, I ain't gonna be too happy. Gimme the leash, man, I'll walk him.'

'*I'll* walk him,' said White. His lip quivered when he spoke.

'Let D walk him if he wants to, Coon,' said Little. 'Dog needs to pee, don't make no difference who be holdin' the leash.'

Potter got out of the car and went around to White's side. He opened the door and took hold of the leash. The dog looked over at White and then jumped his lap and was out of the car.

Potter walked Trooper down the alley until they were behind a high wooden privacy fence. Potter looked around briefly, saw no one in the neighboring yards or in the windows of the houses, and commanded the dog to sit.

When Trooper sat, Potter pulled the .357 Colt from his waistband, pointed it close to the dog's right eye, and squeezed the trigger. Trooper's muzzle and most of his face exploded out into the alley in a haze of bone and blood. The dog toppled over onto its side and its legs straightened in a shudder. Potter stepped back and shot the dog in the ribcage one more time. Trooper's carcass lifted an inch or two off the ground and came to rest.

Potter went back to the car and got behind the wheel. Little was holding a match to the half of the White Owl blunt he had not yet smoked.

'Gun works,' said Potter.

Little nodded. 'Loud, too.'

Potter put the trans in gear, draped his arm over the bench seat, and turned his head to look out the rear window as he reversed the car out of the alley. White was staring out the window, his face dirty from tears he had tried to wipe away.

'Go on and get it out you,' said Potter. 'Someone you know see you cryin' over some dumb animal, they gonna mistake you for a bitch. And I ain't ridin' with none of that.'

Potter, Little, and White bought a kilo of marijuana from their dealer in Columbia Heights, dimed out half of it back at their place, and delivered the dimes to their runners so they could get started on the evening rush. Then the three of them drove north up Georgia Avenue and over to Roosevelt High. They went into the parking lot at Iowa Avenue and parked the Chevy beside a black Cadillac Brougham. There were several other cars in the lot.

Potter looked in the rearview at White, staring ahead. 'We straight, Coon?'

'Just a dumb animal, like you said. Don't mean nothin' to me.'

Potter didn't like the tone in White's voice. But White was just showing a little pride. That was good, but he'd never act on his anger for real. Like his weak-ass dog, he wasn't game.

'I'll check it out,' said Potter to Little.

He walked across the parking lot and stood at the fence that bordered the stadium down below. After a while he came back to the car.

'You see him?' said Little as Potter got back behind the wheel.

'Nah,' said Potter. 'Just some kids playin' football. Some old-time motherfuckers, coaches and shit.'

'We can come back.'

'We will. I'm gonna smoke that motherfucker when I see him, too.'

'Wilder don't owe you but a hundred dollars, D.'

'Thinks he can ignore his debt. Tryin' to take me for bad; you *know* I can't just let that go.'

'Ain't like you need the money today or nothin' like that.'

'It ain't the money,' said Potter. 'And I can wait.'

2

Derek Strange was coming out of a massage parlor when he felt his beeper vibrate against his hip. He checked the number printed out across the horizontal screen and walked through China town over to the MLK library on 9th, where a bank of pay phones was set outside the facility. Strange owned a cell, but he still used street phones whenever he could.

'Janine,' said Strange.

'Derek.'

'You rang?'

'Those women been calling you again. The two investigators from out in Montgomery County?'

'I called them back, didn't I?'

'You mean *I* did. They been trying to get an appointment with you for a week now.'

'So they're still trying.'

'They're being a little bit more aggressive than that. They're heading into town right now, want to meet you for lunch. Said they'd pick up the tab.'

Strange tugged his jeans away from his crotch where they had stuck.

'It's a money job, Derek.'

'Hold up, Janine.' Strange put the receiver against his chest as a man who was passing by stopped to shake his hand.

'Tommy, how you been?'

'Doin' real good, Derek,' said Tommy. 'Say, you got any spare love you can lay on me till I see you next time?'

Strange looked at the black baggage beneath Tommy's eyes, the way his pants rode low on his bony hips. Strange had come up with Tommy's older brother, Scott, who was gone ten years now from the cancer that took his shell. Scott wouldn't want Strange to give his baby brother any money, not for what Tommy had in mind.

'Not today,' said Strange.

'All right, then,' said Tommy, shamed, but not enough. He slowly walked away.

Strange spoke into the receiver. 'Janine, where they want to meet?'

'Frosso's.'

'Call 'em up and tell 'em I'll be there. 'Bout twenty minutes.'

'Am I going to see you tonight?'

'Maybe after practice.'

'I marinated a chuck roast, gonna grill it on the Weber. Lionel will be at practice, won't he? You're going to drop him off at our house anyway, aren't you?'

'Yeah.'

'We can talk about it when you come back by the office. You got a two o'clock with George Hastings.'

'I remember. Okay, we'll talk about it then.'

'I love you, Derek.'

Strange lowered his voice. 'I love you, too, baby.'

Strange hung up the phone. He did love her. And her voice, more than her words, had brought him some guilt for what he'd just done. But there was love and sex on one side and just sex on the other. To Strange, the two were entirely different things.

Strange drove east in his white-over-black '89 Caprice, singing along softly to 'Wake Up Everybody' coming from the deck. That first verse, where Teddy's purring those call-to-arms words against the Gamble and Huff production, telling the listener to open his eyes, look around, get involved and into the uplift side of things, there wasn't a whole lot of American music more beautiful than that.

His Rand McNally street atlas lay on the seat beside him. He had a Leatherman tool-in-one looped through his belt, touching a Buck knife, sheathed and attached the same way on his right hip. His beeper he wore on his left. The rest of his equipment was in a double-locked glove box and in the trunk. It was true that most modern investigative work was done in an office and on the Internet. Strange thought of himself as having two offices, though, his base office in Petworth and the one in his car, right here. His preference was to work the street.

It was early September. The city was still hot during the day, though the nights had cooled some. It would be that way in the District for another month or so.

'"The world won't get no better,"' sang Strange, '"if we just let it be . . ."'

Soon the colors would change in Rock Creek Park. And then would come those weeks near Thanksgiving when the weather turned for real and the leaves were still coming down off the trees. Strange had his own name for it: deep fall. It was his favorite time of year in D.C.

Frosso's, a stand-alone structure with a green thatched roof, sat on a west-side corner of 13th and L, Northwest, like a pimple on the ass of a beautiful girl. The Mediterranean who owned the business owned the real estate and had refused to sell, even as the offers came in, even as new office buildings went in around him. Frosso's was a burger-and-lunch counter, also a happy-hour bar and hangout for those remaining workers who still drank and smoked or didn't mind the smell of smoke on their clothes. Beer gardens in this part of downtown were few and far between.

Strange made his way through a noisy dining area to a four-top back by the pay phone and head, where two women sat. He recognized the investigators, a salt-and-pepper team, from an article he'd read on them in *City Paper* a few months back. They worked cases retrieving young runaways gone to hooking. The two of them were aligned with some do-goodnik, pro-prosti organization that operated on grants inside D.C.

'Derek Strange,' he said, shaking the black woman's hand and then the white woman's before he took a seat.

'I'm Karen Bagley. This is Sue Tracy.'

Strange slid his business card across the table. Bagley gave him one in turn, Strange scanning it for the name of their business: Bagley and Tracy Investigative Services, and below the name, in smaller letters, 'Specializing in Locating and Retrieving Minors.' A plain card, without any artwork, Strange thinking, They could use a logo, give their card a signature, something to make the customers remember them by.

Bagley was medium-skinned and wide of nose. Her eyes were large and deep brown, the lashes accentuated by makeup. Freckles like coarse pepper buckshotted her face. Sue Tracy was a shag-cut blonde, green-eyed, still tanned from the last of summer, with smaller shoulders than Bagley's. They were serious-faced, handsome, youngish women, hard boned and, Strange guessed – he couldn't see the business end of their bodies, seated at the table – strong of thigh. They looked like the ex-cops that the newspaper article had described them to be. Better looking, in fact, than most of the female officers Strange had known.

Tracy pointed a finger at the mug in front of her. Bagley's hand was wrapped around a mug as well. 'You want a beer?'

'Too early for me. I'll get a burger, though. Medium, with some blue cheese crumbled on top. And a ginger ale from the bottle, not the gun.'

Tracy called the waitress over, addressed her by name, got a burger working for Strange. The waitress said, 'Got it, Sue,' tearing the top sheet off a green-lined pad before turning back toward the lunch counter.

'You're a hard man to get ahold of,' said Bagley.

'I been busy out here,' said Strange.

'A big caseload, huh?'

'Always somethin'.' A glass was placed before Strange. He examined a smudge on its lip. 'This place clean?'

'Like a dog's tongue,' said Tracy.

'Some say that about a dog's hindparts, too,' said Strange. 'But I wouldn't put my mouth to one.'

'Maybe they ought to put that on the sign out front,' said Tracy, without a trace of a smile. 'Good food, and clean, too, like the asshole on a dog.'

'Might bring in some new customers,' said Strange. 'You never know.'

'They don't need any new customers,' said Bagley. 'The regulars float this place.'

'I take it you two are numbered with the regulars.'

'We used to come here plenty for information,' said Tracy. 'Here and the all-night CVS below Logan Circle.'

'Information,' said Strange. 'From prostitutes, you mean.'

Bagley nodded. 'The girls would be in the CVS at all hours, buying stockings, tampons, you name it.'

'Them and the heroin lovers,' said Strange. 'They do crave their chocolate in the middle of the night. I remember seein' them in there, grabbing the Hershey bars off the racks with their eyelids lowered to half-mast.'

'You hung out there, too?' said Bagley.

'Back when it was People's Drug, which must be over ten years back now, huh? Used to stop in for my own essentials when everything else was closed. I was a bit of a night bird then myself.'

'The demographics have shifted some the last couple of years,' said Tracy. 'A lot of the action's moved east, into the hotel cluster of the new downtown.'

'But this here tavern was a known hangout for prostis, wasn't it?'

'More like a safe haven,' said Bagley. 'Nobody bothered them in here. It was a place to have a beer and a smoke. A moment of quiet.'

'No more, huh?'

Bagley shrugged. 'There's been an initiative to get the girls out of public establishments.'

Tracy moved her mug in a small circle on the table. 'The powers that be would rather have them shivering in some doorway in December than warm in a place like this.'

'I guess y'all think they ought to just go ahead and legalize prostitution, right? Since it's one of those victimless crimes, I mean.'

'Wrong,' said Tracy. 'In fact, it's the only crime I know of where the perp *is* the victim.'

Strange didn't know what to say to that one, so he let it ride.

'What about you?' asked Bagley. 'What do you think about it?'

Strange's eyes darted from Bagley's and went to nowhere past her shoulder. 'I haven't thought on it all that much, tell you the truth.'

Bagley and Tracy stared at Strange. Strange turned his head, looked toward the grill area. Where was that burger? All right, thought Strange, I'll have my lunch, listen to these Earnest Ernestines say their piece, and get on out of here.

'You come recommended,' said Bagley, forcing Strange to return his attention to them. 'A couple of the lawyers we've worked with down at Superior Court say they've used you and they've been pleased.'

'Most likely they used my operative, Ron Lattimer. He's been doing casework for the CJA attorneys. Ron's a smart young man, but let's just say he doesn't like to break too much of a sweat. So he likes those jobs, 'cause when you're working with the courts you automatically got that federal power of subpoena. You can subpoena the phone company, the housing authority, anything. It makes your job a whole lot easier.'

'You've done some of that,' said Bagley.

'Sure, but I prefer working in the fresh air to working behind a computer, understand what I'm saying? I just like to be out there. And my business is a neighborhood business. Over twenty-five years now in the same spot. So it's good for me to have a presence out there, the way—'

'Cops do,' said Tracy.

'Yeah. I'm an ex-cop, like you two. Been thirty-some-odd years since I wore the uniform, though.'

'No such thing as an ex-cop,' said Bagley.

'Like there's no such thing as a former alcoholic,' said Tracy, 'or an ex-Marine.'

'You got that right,' said Strange. He liked these two women a touch more now than when he'd walked in.

Strange turned the glass of ginger ale so that the smudge was away from him and took a sip. He replaced the glass on the table and leaned forward. 'All right, then, now we had our first kiss and got that over with. What do you young ladies have on your minds?'

Bagley glanced briefly over at Tracy, who was in the process of putting fire to a cigarette.

'We've been working with a group called APIP,' said Bagley. 'Do you know it?'

'I read about it in that article they did on you two. Something about helping out prostitutes, right?'

'Aiding Prostitutes in Peril,' said Tracy, blowing a jet of smoke across the table at Strange.

'Some punk-rock kids started it, right?'

'The people behind it were a part of the local punk movement twenty years ago,' said Tracy, 'as I was. They're not kids anymore. They're older than me and Karen.'

'What do they do, exactly?'

'A number of things, from simply providing condoms to reporting violent johns. Also, they serve as an information clearinghouse. They have an eight-hundred number and a Web site that takes in e-mails from parents and prostitutes alike.'

'That's where you two come in. You find runaways who're hookin'. Right?'

'That's a part of what we do,' said Bagley. 'And we're getting too busy to handle all the work ourselves. The county business alone keeps us up to our ears in it. We could use a little help in the District.'

'You need me to find a girl.'

'Not exactly,' said Bagley. 'We thought we'd test the waters with you on something simpler, see if you're interested.'

'Keep talking.'

'There's a girl who works the street between L and Mass, on 7th,' said Tracy.

'Down there by the site for the new convention center,' said Strange.

'Right,' said Tracy. 'The last two weeks or so a guy's been hassling her. Pulling up in his car, trying to get her to date him.'

'Ain't that the object of the game?'

'Sure,' said Bagley. 'But there's something off about this guy. He's been asking her, Do you like it rough? Telling her she's gonna dig it, he can *tell* she's gonna dig it, right?'

Strange shifted in his seat. 'So? Girl doesn't have to be a working girl to come up against that kind of creep. She can hear it in a bar.'

'These working women get a sense for this kind of thing,' said Bagley. 'She says there's something not right, we got to believe her.

And he doesn't want to pay. Says he doesn't have to pay, understand? She's scared. Can't go to the cops, right? And her pimp would beat her ass blue if he knew she was turning down a trick.'

'Even a no-money trick?'

Strange stared hard at Tracy. Her eyes did not move away from his.

Tracy said, 'This is the information we have. Either you're interested or you're not.'

'I hear you,' said Strange, 'but I'm not sure what you want me to do. You're lookin' for me to shake some cat down, you got the wrong guy.'

'You own a camera, right?' said Tracy.

'Still and video alike,' said Strange.

'Get some shots for us,' said Bagley, 'or a tape. We'll run the plates and contact this gentleman ourselves. Trust me, we can be pretty convincing. This guy's probably got a wife. Even better, he has kids. We'll make sure he never hassles this girl again.'

'Damn,' said Strange with a low chuckle, 'you ladies are *serious*.'

The waitress came to the table and set Strange's burger down before him. He thanked her, cut into it, and inspected the center. He took a large bite and closed his eyes as he chewed.

'They cooked it the way I asked,' said Strange, after he had swallowed. 'I'll say that for them.'

'The burgers here are tight,' said Bagley, smiling just a little for the first time.

Strange wiped some juice off his lips. 'I get thirty-five an hour, by the way.'

Tracy dragged on her smoke, this time blowing the exhale away from Strange. 'According to our attorney friend, he remembers paying you thirty.'

'He remembers, huh?' said Strange. 'Well, I can remember when movies were fifty cents, too.'

'You can?' said Tracy.

'I'm old,' said Strange with a shrug.

'Not too old,' said Bagley.

'Thank you,' said Strange.

'You'll do it, then,' said Tracy.

'I assume she works nights.'

'Every night this week,' said Tracy.

'I coach a kids' football team early in the evenings.'

'She'll be out there, like, ten to twelve,' said Tracy. 'Black, mid-twenties, with a face on the worn side. She'll be wearing a red leather skirt tonight.'

'She say what kind of car this guy drives?'

'Black sedan,' said Bagley. 'Late-model Chevy.'

'Caprice, somethin' like that?'

'Late-model Chevy is what she said.' Tracy stubbed out her cigarette. 'Here's something else for you to look at.' She reached into the leather case on the floor at her feet and pulled out a yellow-gold sheet of paper. She pushed it across the table to Strange.

The headline across the top of the flyer read, IN PERIL. Below the head was a photo of a young white girl, unclear from generations of copying. The girl's arms were skinny and her hands were folded in front of her, a yearbook-style photo. She was smiling, showing braces on her teeth. He read her name and her statistics, printed below the photograph, noticing from the DOB that she was fourteen years old.

'We'll talk about that some other time,' said Bagley, 'you want to. Just wanted you to get an idea of what we do.'

Strange nodded, folded the flyer neatly, and put it in the back pocket of his jeans. Then he focused on finishing his lunch. Bagley and Tracy drank their beers and let him do it.

When he was done, he signaled the waitress. 'I see on the specials board you got a steak today.'

'You're still hungry?'

'Uh-uh, baby, I'm satisfied. But I was wondering, you guys got any bones back there in the kitchen?'

'I suppose we do.'

'Wrap up a few for me, will you?'

'I'll see what I can do.'

The waitress drifted. Strange said to the women, 'I got a dog at home, a boxer, goes by the name of Greco. Got to take care of him, too.'

Later, Bagley and Tracy watched Strange exit the dining room, his paper bag of steak bones in hand. Bagley studied his squared-up walk, the way his muscled shoulders filled out the back of his shirt, the gray salted nicely into his close-cropped hair.

'How old you figure he is?' said Bagley.

'Early fifties,' said Tracy. 'I liked him.'

'I liked him, too.'

'I noticed,' said Tracy.

'Like to see a man who enjoys his food, is all it is,' said Bagley. 'Think we should've told him more?'

'He knew there was more. He wanted to find out what it was for himself.'

'The curious type.'

'Exactly,' said Tracy, draining her beer and placing the mug flat on the table. 'I got a feeling he's gonna work out fine.'

3

Strange turned down 9th, between Kansas and Upshur, one short hop east of Georgia. He saw a spot outside Marshall's funeral home, steered the car into the spot, and locked the Chevy down. He walked past a combination lunch counter and butcher shop, the place just said 'Meat' in the window, and nodded to a cutter named Rodel, who was leaning in the doorway of Hawk's Barbers, dragging hard on a Newport.

'What's goin on, big man?'

'It's all good,' said Strange. 'How about you?'

'Same old soup, just reheated.'

'Bennett workin' today?'

'I don't know about workin'. But he's in there.'

'Tell him I'll be by in forty-five or so. Need a touch-up.'

'I'll let him know.'

Strange looked up at the yellow sign mounted above the door to his agency. The sign read 'Strange Investigations,' half the letters bigger than the rest on account of the picture of the magnifying glass laid over the words. Strange really liked that logo; he'd made it up himself. He made a mental note that there were smudges on the light box of the sign.

Strange stood outside the windowed door of his offices and rapped on the glass. Janine buzzed him in, a bell over the door chiming as he entered. George 'Trip Three' Hastings, his hands resting in his lap, sat in a waiting area to the right of the door.

'George.'

'Derek.'

'I'll be with you in a minute, soon as I get settled.'

Hastings nodded. Strange turned to Ron Lattimer, seated behind his desk. Lattimer wore an off-the-rack designer suit with a hand-painted tie draped over the shirt, had one of those Peter Pan–looking collars, the kind Pat Riley favored. A little too pretty for Strange's taste, though he had to admit the young man kept himself cleaner than the White House lawn. And he made the office his home as well; Lattimer sat in an orthopedically correct chair and had one of those Bose compact units, always playing some kind of jazz-inflected hip-hop, set back behind his desk.

'What're you workin' on, Ron?'

'Faxing a subpoena right now,' said Lattimer.

'You still on that Thirty-five Hundred Crew thing?'

'Many billable hours, boss.'

'Shame, clean as you look, can't nobody see you in here. I mean, you go to all that trouble to be so perfect, how's anybody gonna know?'

'*I* know.'

'Let me ask you somethin'. You ever walk by a mirror you forgot to look into?'

'SUVs are pretty good, too,' said Lattimer, his eyes on the screen of his Mac. 'The windows they got in those things, they're just the right height.'

Strange passed a desk topped with loose papers and gum wrappers and stood in front of Janine Baker. He picked up the three or four pink message slips she had pushed to her desk's edge and looked them over.

'How was lunch?' said Janine.

'Nice women,' said Strange. 'C'mon in the back for a second, okay?'

She followed him back to his office. Lamar Williams, a gangly neighborhood boy of seventeen, was emptying Strange's wastebasket into a large garbage bag. Lamar took classes at Roosevelt High in the mornings and worked for Strange most afternoons.

'Lamar,' said Strange, 'need some privacy for a few. Why don't you get yourself the ladder and Windex the sign out front, okay?'

'Aiight.'

'You comin' to practice tonight?'

'Can't tonight.'

'You got somethin' more important?'

'Watchin' my baby sister for my moms.'

'All right, then. Close the door behind you on your way out.'

The door closed, leaving Strange and Janine alone. She came into his arms and he kissed her on the lips.

'Good day?'

'Now it is,' said Strange.

'How about dinner tonight?'

'If we can eat right after practice. I got a job from those women and I'm gonna try and knock it out late.'

'Sounds good to me.'

Strange kissed her again and went behind his desk. He had a seat and noticed the PayDay bar set beside his phone.

'That's you,' said Janine, her liquid eyes looking him over. 'Thought you'd like to cleanse your palate after that lunch.'

'Thank you, baby. Go on and send George in.'

He watched her walk to the door in her brightly colored outfit. She was the best office manager he'd ever had. Hell, she ran the damn place, he wasn't afraid to admit it. And, praise God, the woman had an ass on her, too. It moved like a wave beneath the fabric of her skirt. All these years, and it still stirred Strange to look at her. The way she was put together, some people who knew something about it might say it was poetry. He'd never been into poems himself. The best way he could describe it, looking at Janine, it reminded him of peace.

George Hastings and Strange had known each other since the early sixties, when both had played football for Roosevelt in the Interhigh. In those days he ran with George and Virgil Aaron, now deceased, and Lydell Blue, also a football player, a back who was the most talented of the four. Strange and Blue had gone into law enforcement, and Hastings had taken a government job with the Bureau of Engraving.

'Thanks for seeing me, Derek,' said Hastings.

'Ain't no thing, George. *You* know that.'

Strange still called Hastings George, though most around town now called him Trip or Trip Three. Back in the early seventies, Hastings had played the unlikely combination of 3-3-3 and hit it for thirty-five grand. It was a fortune for that time, and it was especially significant from where they'd come from, but, with the exception of the new Deuce and a Quarter he'd purchased, Hastings had been smart and invested the money wisely. He'd bought stock in AT&T and IBM, and he had let it ride. By neighborhood standards, Strange knew, Hastings had become a wealthy man.

He also knew that Hastings liked to hear Strange call him by his given name. George was a name out of fashion with the younger generation of blacks. It had been a generic name used by plantation owners to refer to their male slaves, for one. And in the modern world it had become a slang name to refer to a boyfriend, as in, 'Hey, baby, you got yourself a George?' So young black people didn't care much for the name and they rarely considered it as a name for their own babies. But George Hastings's mother, a good old girl whom Strange had regarded with nearly as much affection as his own, had thought it was just fine, and that made it all good for Hastings and for Strange.

Hastings leaned over and flicked the spring-mounted head of the plaster Redskins figure that sat on Strange's desk. The head swayed from side to side.

'The old uniform. That goes back, what, thirty-some-odd years?'

'Forty,' said Strange.

'Who painted his face brown like that? I know they weren't sellin' 'em like that back then.'

'Janine's son, Lionel.'

'How's he doin'?'

'Finishing up at Coolidge. Just applied to Maryland. He's a good boy. A knucklehead sometimes, like all boys tend to be. But he's doing all right.'

'You see Westbrook the other night?'

'Boy made some catches.'

'Uh-huh. Still makin' that first-down sign when they move the sticks. That drives the defenders crazy. He is cocky.'

'He's got a right to be,' said Strange. 'Some call it cocky; I call it confidence. Westbrook's ready to have the season of his career, George. Gonna bust loose like Chuck Brown and all the Soul Searchers put together.'

'He ain't no Bobby Mitchell,' said Hastings. 'And he sure ain't no Charley Taylor.'

Strange smiled a little. 'No one is to you, George.'

'Anyway,' said Hastings. He reached inside his lightweight sport jacket. Strange figured from the material that the jacket went for five, six hundred. Quiet, with a subtle pattern in there. Good quality, and understated, like all George's possessions. Like the high-line, two-year-old Volvo he drove, and his Tudor-style house up in Shepherd Park.

Hastings dropped a folded sheet of paper on Strange's desk. Strange picked it up, unfolded it, and looked it over.

'I got what you asked for,' said Hastings.

Strange read the full name of the subject: Calhoun Tucker. Hastings had provided the tag number for the Audi S4 that Tucker owned or leased. Mimeographed onto the sheet of paper was a credit card receipt from a nightspot that Strange recognized. It was located on U Street, east of 14th. Hastings had scribbled a paragraph of other incidental character details: where Tucker said he'd lived last, where he'd last worked, like that.

'How'd you get the credit card receipt?' said Strange.

'Looked through my little girl's purse. They went to dinner, he must have said, Hold on to this for me, will you? Didn't like going through her personal belongings, but I did. Alisha's getting ready to step off a cliff. I mean, young people, they decide to get married, they never do know what it means, for real.'

'I heard that.'

'My Linda, God love her, she'd be doing the same thing, she was still with us. She was harder on Alisha's boyfriends than I ever was, matter of fact. And here this boy just rolls into town six months ago – he's not even a Washington boy, Derek – and I'm supposed to just sit on my hands while everybody's world gets rocked? I mean, I don't even know one thing about his family.'

Strange dropped the paper on the desk. 'George, you don't have to justify this to me. I do this kind of background check all the time. It's no reflection on your daughter, and as of yet it's no reflection on this young man. And it damn sure is no reflection on you. You're her father, man, you're *supposed* to be concerned.'

'I'd do this even if I thought the boy was right.'

'But you don't think he's right.'

Hastings ran a finger down his cheek. 'Somethin' off about this Tucker boy.'

'You sure the off thing's not just that some young man's getting ready to take away your little girl?'

'Sure, that's a part of it; I can't lie to you, man. But it's somethin' else, too. Don't ask me what exactly. You live long enough, you get so you know.'

'Forget about exactly, then.'

'Well, he's drivin' a luxury German automobile, for one. Always dressed clean, too, real sharp, with the gadgets that go with it: cells, pagers, all that. And I can't figure out what he does to get it.'

'That might have meant somethin' once. Used to be, you had to be rich or a drug dealer to have those things. But look, any fool who can sign his name to a lease can be drivin' a Benz these days. Twelve-year-old *kid* can get his own credit card.'

'Okay, but ain't no twelve-year-old kid gonna march my baby girl down to the altar. This here is a twenty-nine-year-old man, and he's got no visible means of support. Says he's some kind of talent agent, a manager. Puts on shows at the clubs around town. He's got this business card, says "Calhoun Enterprises." Anytime I see "Enterprises" on a business card, way I look at it, might as well print the word "Unfocused" next to it, or "Doesn't Want No Real Job," or just plain "Bullshit," you know what I'm sayin'?'

Strange chuckled. 'Okay, George. Anything else?'

'I just don't like him, Derek. I plain do not like the man. That's somethin', isn't it?'

Strange nodded. 'Let me ask you a question. You think he's into somethin' on the criminal side?'

'Can't say that. All I know is—'

'You don't like him. Okay, George. Let me handle it from here.'

Hastings shifted in his seat. 'You still gettin' thirty an hour?'

'Thirty-five,' said Strange.

'You went up.'

'Gas did, too. Been to a bar lately? Bottle of beer cost you five dollars.'

'That include the two dollars you be stuffin' in their G-strings?'

'Funny.'

'How long you think this is gonna take?'

'Don't worry, this won't take more than a few hours of my time. Most of it we do from right here, on computers. I'll have you happy and stroking checks for that wedding in a couple of days.'

'That's another thing. This reception is gonna cost me a fortune.'

'If you can't spend it on Alisha, what you gonna do with it? You got yourself a beautiful girl there, George. Lovely on the outside, and in her heart, too. So let's you and me make sure she's making the right decision.'

Hastings exhaled slowly as he sat back in his chair. 'Thank you, Derek.'

'Strictly routine,' said Strange.

4

Strange dropped the paper Hastings had given him on Janine's desk.

'You get time, run this information through Westlaw and see what kind of preliminary information you can come up with.'

'Background check on a . . . ' Janine's eyes scanned the page. ' . . . Calhoun Tucker.'

'Right. George's future son-in-law. I'll pick up Lionel and swing him back with me after practice.'

'Okay.'

'And, oh yeah. Call Terry; he's workin' up at the bookstore today. Remind him he's coaching tonight.'

'I will.'

Lattimer looked up as Strange passed by his desk. 'Half day today, boss?'

'Need a haircut.'

'Next door? You ever wonder why they got the butcher and the barber so close together on this block?'

'Never made that connection. One thing I don't need is to be spending forty dollars on a haircut like you.'

'Well, you better get on over there. 'Cause you're startin' to look like Tito Jackson.'

Strange turned and looked into a cracked mirror hanging from a nail driven into a column in the middle of the office. 'Damn, boy, you're right.' He patted the side of his head. 'I need to get my shit correct.'

Strange dropped a couple of the kids off at their homes after practice. Then he and Lionel drove up Georgia toward Brightwood in Strange's '91 black-over-black Cadillac Brougham, a V-8 with a chromed-up grille. This was his second car. Strange had an old tape, *Al Green Gets Next to You*, in the deck, and he was trying hard not to sing along.

'Sounds like gospel music,' said Lionel. 'But he's singing it to some girl, isn't he?'

'"God Is Standing By,"' said Strange. 'An old Johnny Taylor tune, and you're right. This here was back when Al was struggling between the secular and the spiritual, if you know what I'm sayin'.'

'You mean, like, he loves Jesus but he loves to hit the pussy, too.'

'I wasn't quite gonna put it like that, young man.'

'Whateva.'

Strange looked across the bench. 'You got studies tonight, right?'

'I guess so.'

'Don't want you to let up now, just 'cause you already applied to college. You need to keep on those books.'

'You want me to stay in my room tonight, just say it.'

'I didn't mean that.'

Lionel just smiled in that way that drove Strange around the bend.

Janine Baker's residence was on Quintana Place, between 7th and 9th, just east of the Fourth District police station. Quintana was a short, narrow street of old colonials fronted with porches. The houses were covered in siding and painted in an array of earth tones and bright colors, including turquoise and neon green. The Baker residence was a pale lavender affair down near the 7th Street end of the block.

In the dining room they ate a grilled chuck roast, black on the outside and pink in the center, along with mashed potatoes and gravy and some spiced greens, washed down with ice-cold Heinekens for Strange and Janine. Lionel went upstairs to his bedroom as soon as he finished his meal. Strange had a quick cup of coffee and wiped his mouth when he was done.

'That was beautiful, baby.'

'Glad you enjoyed it.'

'You want me to come back after I'm done working?'

'I'd like that. And I've foil-wrapped the bone from the chuck for Greco, so bring him back, too.'

'Between you and me we're gonna spoil that dog to death.' Strange came around the table, bent down, and kissed Janine on the cheek. 'I'll be back before midnight, hear?'

Strange returned to his row house on Buchanan Street and hit the heavy bag in his basement for a while, trying to work off some of the fat he'd taken in from his meat consumption that day. He broke a sweat that smelled like alcohol when he was done, then showered and changed clothes up on the second floor, which held his bedroom and home office. In the office, Greco played with a spiked rubber ball while Strange checked his stock port folio and read a stock-related message board, listening to Ennio Morricone's 'The Return of Ringo' from the Yamaha speakers of his computer.

Strange checked his wristwatch, a Swiss Army model with a black leather band, and looked at his dog.

'Gotta go to work, old buddy. I'll be back to pick you up in a little bit.'

Greco's nub of tail made a double twitch. He looked up at Strange and showed him the whites of his eyes.

Strange drove down Georgia in his Chevy, through Petworth and into Park View. The street was up, Friday night, kids mostly, some hanging out, some doing business as well. Down around Morton a line had formed outside the Capitol City Pavilion, called the Black Hole by locals and law enforcement types alike. D.C. veteran go-go band Back Yard had their name on the marquee, as they did most weekends. In a few hours, Fourth District squad cars would be blocking Georgia, rerouting traffic. Beefs born inside the club often came to their inevitable, violent resolution at closing time, when the patrons spilled out onto the street.

Strange saw Lamar Williams, wearing pressed khakis and wheat-colored Timbies, standing in the line outside the club. Strange drove on. Between Kenyon and Harvard, kids sold marijuana in an open-air market set up on the street.

Georgia became 7th. Soon Strange was nearing the convention center site, a huge hole that took up several of D.C.'s letter blocks, on his right. On his left ran a commercial strip. His hooker, wearing a red leather skirt, was standing in the doorway of a closed restaurant, her hard, masculine face illuminated by the embers of her cigarette as she gave it a deep draw. Strange did not slow the car. He went west for a couple of blocks, then north, then east again, circling back to a spot on the east side of the future center, where he parked the Chevy on 9th, alongside a construction fence. He slipped a notepad into his breast pocket and clipped a pen there before exiting the car.

Strange opened the trunk of his Chevy. He pushed aside his live-case file, his football file, and his toolbox, and found his video camera, which was fitted in a separate box alongside his 500mm-lens Canon AE-1. He checked the tape and replaced it in its slot. Strange liked this camera, his latest acquisition. It was an 8mm Sony with the NightShot feature and the 360X digital zoom. Perfect for what he needed, perfect for this job right here. He'd gotten the camera in a trade for a debt owed him by a client; the camera was hotter than Jennifer Lopez in July.

Strange went over to a place by the fence at 7th and L, just north of the hooker's position, where there was an open driveway entrance breaking the continuity of the construction fence. He situated himself behind the fence in a position that would render him unseen by the passengers or drivers of any southbound cars. He stood there for a while, setting up the camera the way he wanted it and shooting some tape for a test. He watched the hooker talk to a potential john who had pulled up his Honda Accord beside her, and he watched the john drive off. The hooker smoked another cigarette. Strange's stomach rumbled, as he thought about AV, his favorite sit-down Italian restaurant, just around the corner on Mass. Hungry as usual, and having just eaten, too.

A black late-model Chevy rolled down 7th, slowed, and came to a stop near where the hooker stood. Strange leaned against the corner of the fence, brought the zoom in so the car was framed and clear, and shot some tape. Cigarette smoke came out of the driver's side of the car as the john rolled his window down. The hooker rested her forearms on the lip of the open window. She shook her head, and Strange could hear male laughter before the car drove off. The car wore D.C. plates. It was an Impala, the new body style that Strange didn't care for.

He waited. The Impala came out of the north once again, having circled the block. The driver stopped the vehicle in the same spot he had minutes earlier. The hooker hesitated, looked around, walked over to the driver's side but this time did not lean into the car. She seemed to be listening for a while, her face going from passivity to agitation and then to something like fear. Strange heard the laughter again. Then the driver laid some rubber on the street and took off. The hooker flipped him off, but only after the car had turned the corner and was gone from sight.

Strange wrote down the Impala's license plate number on the notepad he had placed in the breast pocket of his shirt. He didn't need to record it, not really; he had memorized the number at first sight, a talent that he had always possessed and that had served him well when he had worn the uniform on the street.

Anyway, the two letters that preceded the numbers on the plate had told him everything he needed to know. Bagley and Tracy must have known it, too. They had put him onto this, he reasoned, as some kind of test. He wasn't angry. It was just a job.

The letters on the plate read GT. Plainclothes, undercover, whatever you wanted to call it. The abusive john was a cop.

5

Hold on a second, Derek,' said Karen Bagley. 'I'm going to conference you in with Sue.'

Strange held the phone away from his ear and sat back in the chair behind his desk. He watched Lamar Williams climb a stepladder to feather-dust Strange's blinds.

'You coming with me to practice tonight, Lamar?'

'You want me to, I will.'

'I was just wonderin' on if you could make it. If you had to sit your baby sister again, I mean.'

'Nah, uh-uh.'

''Cause I saw you outside the Black Hole Friday night.'

Lamar lowered the duster. 'Yeah, I was there. After I did what I told you I had to do.'

'Kind of a rough place, isn't it?'

'It's a place in the neighborhood I can listen to some go-go, maybe talk to a girl. I don't eye-contact no one I shouldn't; I ain't lookin' to step *to* nobody or beef nobody. Just lookin' to have a little fun. That's okay with you, isn't it, boss?'

'Just tellin' you I saw you, is all.'

Strange heard voices on the phone. He put the receiver back to his ear.

'Okay,' said Strange.

'We all here?' said Bagley.

'I can hear you,' said Tracy. 'Derek?'

'I got what you needed,' said Strange. 'It's all on videotape.'

'That was quick,' said Bagley.

'Did it Friday night. I thought I'd let the weekend pass, didn't want to disturb your-all's beauty sleeps.'

'What'd you get?' said Tracy.

'Your bad john is a cop. Unmarked. But you two knew that, I expect. The flag went up for me when you said he was talkin' about 'I don't have to pay.' Question is, why didn't you just tell me what you suspected?'

'We wanted to find out if we could trust you,' said Tracy.

Direct, thought Strange. That was cool.

'I'm going to give the tape and the information to a lieutenant friend of mine in the MPD. I been knowin' him my whole life. He'll turn it over to Internal and they'll take care of it.'

'You've got a videotape of his car,' said Bagley, 'right? Did you get his face?'

'No, not really. But it's his car and it's a clear solicitation. He might say he was gathering information or some bullshit like that, but it's enough to throw a shadow over him. The IAD people will talk to him, and I suspect it'll scare him. He won't be botherin' that girl again. That's what you wanted, isn't it?'

'Yes,' said Bagley. 'Good work.'

'Good? It was half good, I'd say. You two ever see that movie *The Magnificent Seven*?'

Bagley and Tracy took a moment before uttering a 'yes' and an 'uh-huh.' Strange figured they were wondering where he was going with this.

'One of my favorites,' said Strange. 'There's that scene where Coburn, he plays the knife-carryin' Texican, pistol-shoots this cat off a horse from, like, I don't know, a couple hundred yards away. And this hero-worship kid, German actor or something, but they got him playin' a Mexican, he says something like, "That was the greatest shot I ever saw." And Coburn says, "It was the worst. I was aiming for his horse." '

'And your point is what?' said Bagley.

'I wish I could've delivered more to you. More evidence, I mean. But what I did get, it might just be enough. Anyway, hopefully y'all will *trust* me now.'

'Like I said,' said Tracy, 'there's no such thing as an ex-cop. Cops are usually hesitant to turn in one of their own.'

'There's two professions,' said Strange, 'teaching and policing, that do the most good for the least pay and recognition. But you want to be a teacher or a cop, you accept that goin' in. Most cops and most teachers are better than good. But there's always gonna be the teacher likes to play with a kid's privates, and there's always gonna be a cop out there, uses his power and position in the wrong way. In both cases, to me, it's the worst kind of betrayal. So I got no problem with turnin' a cat like that in. Only . . .'

'What?' said Tracy.

'Don't keep nothin' from me again, hear? Okay, you did it once, but you don't get to do it again. It happens, it'll be the last time we work together.'

'We were wrong,' said Bagley. 'Can you forget it?'

'Forget what?'

'What about the other thing?' said Tracy. 'The flyer we gave you.'

'I've got a guy I use named Terry Quinn. Former D.C. cop. He's a licensed investigator in the District now. I'm gonna give it to him.'

'Why not you?' said Bagley.

'Too busy.'

'How can we reach him?' said Tracy.

'He's not in the office much. He works part-time in a used-book store in downtown Silver Spring. He can take calls there, and he's got a cell. I'm gonna see him this evening; I'll make sure he gets the flyer.'

Strange gave them both numbers.

'Thank you, Derek.'

'You'll get my bill straightaway.' Strange hung up the phone and looked over at Lamar. 'You ready, boy?

'Sure.'

'Let's roll.'

Strange retrieved the videotape of the cop and the hooker, wedged in the football file box, and shut the trunk's lid.

'This here is you,' said Strange, handing the tape over to Lydell Blue.

'The thing you called me about?'

'Yeah. I wrote up a little background on it, what I was told by the investigators who put me on it, what I heard at the scene, like that. I signed my name to it, Internal wants to get in touch with me.'

Blue stroked his thick gray mustache. 'I'll take care of it.'

They walked across the parking lot toward the fence that surrounded the stadium, passing Quinn's hopped-up blue Chevelle and Dennis Arrington's black Infiniti I30 along the way.

Strange knew Roosevelt's football coach – he had done a simple background check for him once and he had not charged him a dime – and they had worked it out so that Strange's team could practice on Roosevelt's field when the high school team wasn't using it. In return, Strange turned the coach on to some up-and-coming players and tried to keep those kids who were headed for Roosevelt in a straight line as well.

'You and Dennis want the Midgets tonight?'

'Tonight? Yeah, okay.'

'Me and Terry'll work with the Pee Wees, then.'

'Derek, that's the way you got it set up damn near every night.'

'I like the young kids, is what it is,' said Strange. 'Me and Terry will just stick with them, you don't mind.'

'Fine.'

Midgets in this league – a loosely connected set of neighborhood teams throughout the area – went ten to twelve years old and between eighty-five and one hundred and five pounds. Pee Wees were ages eight to eleven, with a minimum of sixty pounds and a max of eighty-five. There was also an intermediate and junior division in the league, but the Petworth club could not attract enough boys in those age groups, the early-to-mid-teen years, to form a squad. Many of these boys had by then become too distracted by other interests, like girls, or necessities, like part-time jobs. Others had already been lost to the streets.

Strange followed Blue through a break in the fence and down to the field. About fifty boys were down there in uniforms and full pads, tackling one another, cracking wise, kicking footballs, and horsing around. Lamar Williams was with them, giving them some tips, also acting the clown. A few mothers were down there, and a couple of fathers, too, talking among themselves.

The field was surrounded by a lined track painted a nice sky blue. A set of aluminum bleachers on concrete steps faced the field. Weed trees grew up through the concrete.

Dennis Arrington, a computer programmer and deacon, was throwing the ball back and forth with the Midgets' quarterback in one of the end zones. Nearby, Terry Quinn showed Joe Wilder, a Pee Wee, the ideal place on the body to make a hit. Quinn had to get down low to do it. Wilder was the runt of the litter, short but with defined muscles and a six-pack of abs, though he had only just turned eight years old. At sixty-two pounds, Wilder was also the lightest member of the squad.

Strange blew a whistle that hung on a cord around his neck. 'Everybody line up over there.' He motioned to a line that had been painted across the track. They knew where it was.

'Hustle,' said Blue.

'Four times around,' said Strange, 'and don't be complaining, either; that ain't nothin' but a mile.' He blew the whistle again over the boys' inevitable moans and protests.

'Any one of you walks,' yelled Arrington, as they jogged off the line, 'and you *all* are gonna do four more.'

The men stood together in the end zone and watched the sea of faded green uniforms move slowly around the track.

'Got a call from Jerome Moore's mother today,' said Blue. 'Jerome got suspended from Clark today for pulling a knife on a teacher.'

'Clark *Elementary*?' said Quinn.

'Uh-huh. His mother said we won't be seein' him at practice for the next week or so.'

'Call her back,' said Strange, 'and tell her he's not welcome back. He's off the team. Didn't like him around the rest of the kids anyway. Doggin' it, trash-talking, always starting fights.'

'Moore's nine years old,' said Quinn. 'I thought those were the kind of at-risk kids we were trying to help.'

'They're *all* at risk down here, Terry. I'll let go of one to keep the rest of the well from getting poisoned. It'll school them on something, too. That we're tryin' to teach them somethin' more than football here. Also, that we're not gonna put up with that kind of behavior.'

'Way I see it,' said Quinn, 'it's the giving up on these kids that makes them go wrong.'

'I'm not giving up on him or anyone else. He straightens himself out, he can play for us next season. But for this season here, uh-uh. He blew it his own self. You agree with me, Dennis?'

Dennis Arrington looked down at the football that he spun in his thick hands. He was Quinn's height, not so tall, built like a fullback. 'Absolutely, Derek.'

Arrington gave Quinn a short look. Quinn knew that Arrington wouldn't agree with him on this or anything else. Arrington was quick with a smile, a handshake, and a back pat for most any black man who came down to this field. And Quinn did like him as a man. But he felt that Arrington didn't like *him*, or show him respect. And he felt that this was because he, Quinn, was white. Quinn had gotten that from some of the kids when he'd first started here as well. The kids, most of them, anyway, had gotten past it.

Strange turned to Quinn. Quinn's hair was cropped short. He had a wide mouth, a pronounced jaw, and green eyes. Among friends his eyes were gentle, but around strangers, or when he was simply in thought, his eyes tended to be flat and hard. In full winter dress he looked like a man of average height, maybe less, with a flat stomach and an ordinary build, but out here in sweatpants and a white T-shirt, his veins standing on his forearms and snaking up his biceps, his physical strength was evident.

'Before I forget it, some women might be callin' you, Terry. I gave them your number—'

'They already called me. Got me on my cell while I was driving over here.'

'Yeah, they do work quick. I brought you the information, if you're interested.'

'Do you want me to take it?'

'It's a money job for both of us.'

'It would mean more jack for you if you just took it yourself.'

'I'm busy,' said Strange.

The boys came back in, sweating and short of breath.

'Form a circle,' said Blue. He called out the names of the two captains who would lead the calisthenics.

The captains stood in the middle of the large circle. They commanded their teammates to run in place.

'How ya'll feel?' shouted the captains.

'Fired up!' responded the team.

'*How y'all feel?*'

'*Fired up!*'

'*Breakdown.*'

'*Whoo!*'

'*Breakdown.*'

'*Whoo!*'

'*Breakdown.*'

'*Whoo!*'

With each command the boys went into their breakdown stance and shouted, '*Whoo!*' This running in place and vocal psych-out lasted for a few more minutes. Then they moved into other calisthenics: stretches, knuckle push-ups, and six inches, where they were instructed to lie on their backs, lift their legs a half foot off the ground, keep their legs straight, and hold the position, playing their bellies like a tom-tom until they were told they could relax. When they were done, their jerseys were dark with sweat and their faces were beaded with it.

'Now you're gonna run some steps,' said Strange.

'Aw!' said Rico, the Pee Wee starting halfback. Rico was a quick, low-to-the-ground runner who could jook. He had the most natural talent of any of the players. He was also the first to complain.

'Move, Reek,' said Dante Morris, the tall, skinny quarterback who rarely spoke, only when he was asked to or to motivate his teammates. 'Let's get it done.'

'C'mon Panthers!' shouted Joe Wilder, sweeping his arm in the direction of the bleachers.

'Little man gonna lead the charge,' said Blue.

'They're *following* him, too,' said Strange.

A few more mothers had arrived and stood on the sidelines. Joe

Wilder's uncle had shown up, too. He was leaning against the fence that ran between the track and the bleachers, his hand dipped into a white paper bag stained with grease.

'Humid tonight,' said Blue.

'Don't make 'em run those steps too long,' said Strange. 'Look, I gotta run back up to my car for a second. Wanted to give you the Midget roster, since you'll be takin' them permanent. Be right back.'

Strange crossed the field, passing Wilder's uncle, not looking his way. But the uncle said, 'Coach,' and Strange had to stop.

'How's it goin?' said Strange.

'It's all right. Name's Lorenze. Most call me Lo. I'm Joe Wilder's uncle.'

'Derek Strange. I've seen you around.'

Now Strange had to shake his hand. Lorenze rubbed his right hand, greasy from the french fries in the bag, off on his jeans before he reached out and tried to give Strange the standard soul shake: thumb lock, finger lock, break. Strange executed it without enthusiasm.

'Y'all nearly through?'

'We'll be quittin' near dark.'

'I just got up *in* this motherfucker, so I didn't know how long you been out here.'

Lorenze smiled. Strange shifted his feet impatiently. Lorenze, a man over thirty years old, wore a T-shirt with a photograph of a dreadlocked dude smoking a fat spliff, and a pair of Jordans, laces untied, on his feet. Strange didn't know one thing for certain about this man. But he knew this man's type.

Blue called the boys off the bleachers. Exhausted, they began to walk back toward the center of the field.

'I'll be takin' Joe with me after practice,' said Lorenze. 'I ain't got my car tonight, but I can walk him back to his place.'

'I told his mother I'd drop him at home. Same as always.'

'We just gonna walk around some. Boy needs to get to know his uncle.'

'I'm responsible for him,' said Strange, keeping his tone light. 'If his mother had told me you'd be comin', that would be one thing . . . '

'You don't have to worry. I'm *kin*, brother.'

'I'm taking him home,' said Strange, and now he forced himself to smile. 'Like I say, I told his mother, right? You got to understand this.'

'I ain't *got*ta do nothin' but be black and die,' said Lorenze, grinning at his clever reply.

Strange didn't comment. He'd been hearing young and not-so-young black men use that expression around town for years now. It never did settle right on his ears.

They both heard a human whistle and looked up past the bleachers to the fence that bordered the parking lot. A tall young man was leaning against the fence, smiling and staring down at them. Then he turned, walked away, and was out of sight.

'Look,' said Strange, 'I gotta get something from my car. I'll see you around, hear?'

Lorenze nodded absently.

Strange walked up to the parking lot. The young man who had stood at the fence was now sitting behind the wheel of an idling car with D.C. plates. The car was a beige Caprice, about ten years old, with a brown vinyl roof and chrome-reverse wheels, parked nose out about four spaces down from Strange's own Chevy. Rust had begun to cancer the rear quarter panel on the driver's side. The pipe coughed white exhaust, which hovered in the lot. The exhaust mingled with the marijuana smoke that was coming from the open windows of the car.

Another young man sat in the shotgun seat and a third sat in the back. Strange saw tightly braided hair on the front-seat passenger, little else.

Strange had slowed his steps and was studying the car. He was letting them see him study it. His face was impassive and his body language unthreatening as he moved along.

Now Strange walked to his own car and popped the trunk. He heard them laughing as he opened his toolbox and looked inside of it for . . . for *what*? Strange didn't own a gun. If they were strapped and they were going to use a gun on him, he couldn't do a damn thing about it anyway. But he was letting his imagination get ahead of him now. These were just some hard-looking kids, sitting in a parking lot, getting high.

Strange found a pencil in his toolbox and wrote something down on the outside of the Pee Wees' manila file. Then he found the Midget file that he had come to get for Blue. He closed the trunk's lid.

He walked back across the lot. The driver poked his head out the window of the Caprice and said, 'Yo, Fred Sanford! Fred!'

That drew more laughter, and he heard one of them say, 'Where Lamont at and shit?'

Now they were laughing and saying other things, and Strange heard the words 'old-time' and felt his face grew hot, but he kept walking. He just wanted them gone, off the school grounds, away from his kids. And as he heard the squeal of their tires he relaxed, knowing that this was so.

He looked down toward the field and noticed that Lorenze, Joe Wilder's uncle, had gone.

Strange was glad Terry Quinn hadn't been with him just now, because Quinn would have started some shit. When someone stepped to him, Quinn only knew how to respond one way. You couldn't answer each slight, or return each hard look with an equally hard look, because moments like this went down out here every day. It would just be too tiring. You'd end up in a constant battle, with no time to breathe, just live.

Strange told himself this, trying to let his anger subside, as he walked back onto the field.

6

The Pee Wee offense said 'Break' in the huddle and went to the line. Strange saw that several of the players had lined up too far apart.

'Do your splits,' said Strange, and the offensive linemen moved closer together, placing their hands on one another's shoulder pads. Now they were properly spaced.

'Down!' said Dante Morris, his hands between the center's legs. The offense hit their thigh pads in unison.

'Set!' The offense clapped their hands one time and got down in a three-point stance.

'Go! Go!'

On two, Rico took the handoff from Dante Morris, bobbling it a little, not really having possession of the ball as he hesitated and was cut down by two defenders behind the line.

'Hold up,' said Quinn.

'What was that, Rico?' said Strange. 'What was the play?'

'Thirty-one on two,' said Rico, picking some turf off his helmet.

'And Thirty-one is?'

'Halfback run to the one-hole,' said Joe Wilder.

'Joe, I know *you* know,' said Strange. 'I was askin' Rico.'

'Like Joe said,' said Rico.

'But you weren't headed for the one-hole, were you, son?'

'I got messed up in my head.'

'Think,' said Strange, tapping his own temple.

'You had your hands wrong, too,' said Quinn. 'When you're taking a handoff and you're going to the left, where's your right hand supposed to be?'

'On top. Left hand down at your belly.'

'Right. The opposite if you're going right.' Quinn looked to the linemen who had made the tackle. 'Nice hit there. Way to wrap him up. Let's try that again.'

In the huddle, Dante called a Thirty-five. The first number, three, was always a halfback run. The second number was the hole to be hit. Odd numbers were the left holes, one, three, and five. Evens were the two-, four-, and six-holes. A number larger than six was a pitch.

They executed the play. This time Rico took the ball smoothly and found the hole, running low off a clean Joe Wilder block, and he was gone.

'All right, good.' Quinn tapped Joe's helmet as he ran back to the huddle. 'Good block, Joe, way to *be*.'

Joe Wilder nodded, a swagger in his step, his wide smile visible behind the cage of his helmet.

Close to dark, Strange blew a long whistle, signaling the boys into the center of the field.

'All right,' said Blue, 'take a knee.'

The boys got down on one knee, close together, looking up at their coaches.

'I got a call today,' said Dennis Arrington, 'at work. One of you was asking me how to make his mouth guard from the kit we gave you. Course, he just should have asked me before he did it, or better yet, listened when I explained it the first time. 'Cause he went and boiled it for three minutes and it came out like a hunk of plastic.'

'Tenderized it,' said Blue, and some of the boys laughed.

'You put it in that boiling water for twenty seconds,' said Arrington. 'And before you put it in your mouths to form it, you dip it in some cold water. You don't do that, you're gonna burn yourselves fierce.'

'You only make that mistake one time,' said Strange.

'Any questions?' said Blue.

There were none.

'Want to talk about somethin' tonight,' said Strange. 'Heard you all discussing it between yourselves some and thought I ought to bring it up. One of your teammates got himself in big trouble at school today, something to do with a knife. Now I know you already got the details, what you heard, anyway, so I won't go into it, and besides, it's not right to be talkin' about this boy's business when he's not here. But I do want to tell you that he is off the team. And the reason he is off is, he broke the deal he made with his coaches, and with you, his teammates, to act in a certain way. The way you got to conduct yourselves if you are going to be a Panther. And I don't mean just here on the field. I'm talking about how you act at home, and in school. Because we are out here devoting our time to you for no kind of pay, and you and your teammates are working hard, sweating, to make this the best team we can be. And we will not tolerate that kind of disrespect, to us or to you. Do you understand?'

There was a low mumble of yesses. The Pee Wee center, a quiet African kid named Prince, raised his hand, and Strange acknowledged him.

'Do you need to thee our report cards?' said Prince. The boy beside him grinned but did not laugh at Prince's lisp.

'Yes, we will need to see your first report card when you get it. We're especially gonna be looking at behavior. Now, we got a game this Saturday, y'all know that, right?' The boys' faces brightened. 'Anybody hasn't paid the registration fee yet, you need to get up with your parents or the people you stay with, 'cause if you do not pay, you will not play. I'm gonna need all your health checkups, too.'

'We gettin' new uniforms?' said a kid from back in the group.

'Not this season,' said Strange. 'I must answer this question every practice. Some of you just do not listen.' There were a couple of 'Dags,' but mostly silence.

'Practice is six o'clock, Wednesday,' said Blue.

'What time?' said Dennis Arrington.

The boys shouted in unison, '*Six o'clock, on the dot, be there, don't miss it!*'

'Put it in,' said Quinn.

The boys formed a tight circle and tried to touch one another's hands in the center. '*Petworth Panthers!*'

'All right,' said Strange. 'We're done. You that got your bikes or live close, get on home now before the dark falls all the way. Anyone else needs a ride, meet the coaches up in the lot.'

There were about ten parents and other types of relatives and guardians, dedicated, enthusiastic, loving, mostly women and a couple of men, who came to every practice and every game. Always the same faces. The parents who did not show were too busy trying to make ends meet, or hanging with their boyfriends or girlfriends, or they just didn't care. Many of these kids lived with their grandparents or their aunts. Many had absent fathers, and some had never known their fathers at all.

So the parents who were involved helped whenever they could. They and the coaches watched out for those kids who needed rides home from practice and to and from the games. Running a team like this, keeping the kids away from the bad, it was a community effort. The responsibility fell on a committed few.

Strange drove south on Georgia Avenue. Lamar and Joe Wilder

were in the backseat, Wilder showing Lamar his wrestling figures. Joe usually brought them with him to practice. Lamar was asking him questions, patiently listening as Joe explained the relationships among all these people, whom Strange thought of as freaks.

'You gonna watch Monday Nitro tonight?' asked Joe.

'Yeah, I'll watch it,' said Lamar.

'Can you come over and watch it?'

'Can't, Joe. Got my sister to look after; my moms is goin' out.' Lamar punched Joe lightly on the shoulder. 'Maybe we can watch it together next week.'

Strange brought Lamar along to practice to keep him out of trouble, but he was also a help to him and the other coaches. Both Lamar and Lionel were good with the kids.

Next to Strange sat Prince, the Pee Wees' center. Prince was one of three Africans on the team. Like the others, Prince was well behaved, even tempered, and polite. His father drove a cab. Prince was tall for ten, and his voice had already begun to deepen. Some of the less sensitive boys on the team tended to imitate his slight lisp. But he was generally well liked and respected for his toughness.

'There's my office,' said Strange, pointing to his sign on 9th. Whenever he could, Strange reminded his kids that he had grown up in the neighborhood, just like them, and that he owned his own business.

'Why you got a picture up there of a magnifying glath?' said Prince. He was holding his helmet in his hands, rubbing his fingers along the panther decal affixed to the side.

'It means I find things. Like I look at 'em closer so other people can see better. That make sense?'

'I guess.' Prince cocked his head. 'My father gave me a magnifying glath.'

'Yeah?'

'Uh-huh. One day it was thunny, and me and my little brother put the glath over some roach bugs that was outside on the alley porch, by the trash? The thun made those bugs smoke. We burned up those bugs till they died.'

Strange knew that here he should say that burning bugs to death wasn't cool. But he said, 'I used to do the same thing.'

Prince lived on Princeton Place, in a row house in Park View that was better kept than those around it. The porch light had been left on in anticipation of his arrival. Strange said goodnight to Prince and watched him go up the concrete steps to his house.

Some boys hanging on the corner, a couple years older than Prince, made some comments about his uniform, and then one of them said, 'Pwinth, why you steppin' so fast, Pwinth?'

They were laughing at him, but he kept walking without turning around, and he kept his shoulders erect until he made it to the front door and went through.

That's right, thought Strange. *Head up, and keep your posture straight.*

The light on the porch went off.

Strange returned to Georgia Avenue, drove south, and passed a small marijuana enterprise run by a half dozen kids. Part of the income made here funneled up to one of the two prominent gangs that controlled the action in the neighborhood. South of the Fourth District, below Harvard Street, was a smaller, independent operation that did not encroach on the turf of the gang business up the road.

At Park Road, Strange cut east and then turned into the Section Eight government-assisted housing complex called Park Morton. Kids sat on a brick wall at the entrance to the complex, their eyes hard on Strange as he drove by.

The complex was dark, lit only by dim bulbs set in cinder-block stairwells. In one of them a group of young men, and a few who were not so young, were engaged in a game of craps. Some held dollars in their fists, others held brown paper bags covering bottles of juice halved with gin, or forties of malt liquor and beer.

'That your unit, Joe?' said Strange, who always had to ask. There was a dull sameness to these dwellings back here, broken by the odd heroic gesture: a picture of Jesus taped to a window, or a string of Christmas lights, or a dying potted plant.

'Next one up,' said Lamar.

Strange rolled forward, put the car in park, and let it idle.

'Walk him up, Lamar.'

'Coach,' said Joe, 'you gonna call Forty-four Belly for me in the game?'

'We'll see. We'll practice it on Wednesday, okay?'

'Six o'clock, on the dot,' said Joe.

Strange brushed some bits of lint off of Joe's nappy hair. His scalp was warm and still damp with sweat. 'Go on, son. Mind your mother, now, hear?'

'I will.'

Strange watched Lamar and Joe disappear into the stairwell leading to Joe's apartment. Ahead, rusted playground equipment stood silhouetted in a dirt courtyard dotted with Styrofoam containers, fast-food wrappers, and other bits of trash. The courtyard was lit residually by the lamps inside the apartments. A faint veil of smoke roiled in the light.

It was a while before Lamar returned. He rested his forearms on the lip of the open passenger window of Strange's car.

'What took you so long?'

'Wasn't no one home. Had to get a key from Joe's neighbor.'

'Where his mom at?'

'I expect she went to the market for some cigarettes, sumshit like that.'

'Watch your mouth, boy.'

'Yeah, all right.' Lamar looked over his shoulder and then back at Strange. 'He'll be okay. He's got my phone number he needs somethin'.'

'Get in, I'll ride you the rest of the way.'

'That's me, just across the court,' said Lamar. 'I'll walk it. See you tomorrow, boss.'

Strange said, 'Right.'

He watched Lamar move slowly through the courtyard, not too fast like he was scared, chin level, squared up. Strange thinking, You learned early, Lamar, and well. To know how to walk in a place like this was key, a basic tool for survival. Your body language showed fear, you weren't nothin' but prey.

Driving home, Strange rolled up the windows of the Brougham and turned the AC on low. He popped a War tape, *Why Can't We Be Friends*, into the deck, and he found that beautiful ballad of theirs, 'So.' He got down low in the bench, his wrist resting on the stop of the wheel, and he began to sing along. For a while, anyway, sealed in his car, listening to his music, he found some kind of peace.

7

Sue Tracy sat in a window deuce, watching the foot traffic on Bonifant Street in downtown Silver Spring, as Terry Quinn arrived at the table carrying two coffees. They were in the Ethiopian place close to the Quarry House, the local basement bar where Quinn sometimes drank.

'That good?' said Quinn, watching her take her first sip. She had asked for one sugar to take the edge off.

'Yeah, it's great. I guess I didn't need the sugar.'

'They don't let the coffee sit out too long in this place. These people here, they take pride in their business.'

'That bookstore you work in, it's on this street, isn't it?'

'Down the block,' said Quinn.

'Near the gun shop.'

'Yeah, and the apartments, the Thai and African restaurants, the tattoo parlor. Except for the gun place, it's a nice strip. There aren't any chain stores on this block, it's still small businesses. Most of which have been wrecking-balled or moved, tucked under the rug to make way for the New Downtown Silver Spring. But this street here, they haven't managed to mess with it too much yet.'

'You got something against progress?'

'Progress? You mean the privilege of paying five bucks for a tomato at our new designer supermarket, just like all those suckers on the other side of town? Is that the kind of progress you're talking about?'

'You can always stick to Safeway.'

'Look, I grew up here. I know a lot of these shop owners; they've made a life here and they won't be able to afford it when the landlords up the square-foot price. And where are all these working people who live in the apartments going to go when their rents skyrocket?'

'I guess it's great if you own real estate.'

'I don't own a house, so I couldn't really give a rat's ass if the property values go up. I walk through this city and every week something changes, you know? So maybe you can understand how I don't feel all warm and fuzzy about it, man. I mean, they're killing my past, one day at a time.'

'You sound like my father.'

'What about him?'

'He thinks that way, too, is all.' Tracy looked Quinn over, held it just a second too long, so that he could see her doing it, and then reached down to get something from the leather case at her feet.

He was still looking at her when she came back up, holding some papers in her hands. She wore a scoop-neck white pullover with no accoutrements, tucked into a pair of gray blue slacks that looked like work pants but were probably expensive, meant to look utilitarian. Her breasts rode high in her shirt, its whiteness set off by her tanned arms. Black Skechers, oxfords with white stitching, were on her feet. Her blond hair was pulled back, held in place by a blue gray Scunci, with a stray rope of blond falling forward over one cheek. He wondered if she had planned it to fall out that way.

Quinn wore a plain white T-shirt tucked into Levi's jeans.

'What?' said Tracy.

'Nothing.'

'You were staring at me.'

'Sorry.'

'I don't know why I mentioned my father.'

'I don't either. Let's get to work, okay?'

Tracy handed Quinn a stack of flyers exactly like the one Strange had given him the night before. 'You might need more of these. We've got 'em posted around town, but they get ripped down pretty quick.'

Quinn picked up the Paper Mate sitting atop the notepad he had brought along with him. 'What else can you tell me about her?'

Tracy pushed another sheet of paper across the table at Quinn. 'Jennifer ran away from her home in Germantown several months ago.'

Quinn scanned the page. 'This doesn't say why.'

'She hit her teens and the hormones kicked in. Add to that, the kids she was hanging with were using drugs. It's the usual story, not so different from most that we hear. From interviews we did with her friends out in the county, it sounds like she started hooking before she split.'

'In the outer suburbs?'

'What, you think that part of the world is immune to it? It starts out, girl will take a ride with an older guy and fellate him so she can buy a night of getting high for her and her friends. Or maybe she lets herself get penetrated, vaginally or even anally, for a little more cash.

She doesn't get beat up or ripped up those first couple of times – she doesn't *learn* something, I mean – it accelerates pretty quickly after that. It gets easy.'

'She's only fourteen.'

'I'm hip.'

'Okay, so she leaves Germantown. What makes you think she's in the District?'

'Her friends again. She told them where she was going. But they haven't heard from her since.'

'You said she was using drugs. What kind?'

'Ecstasy was her favorite, what we heard. But she'd use anything that was put in front of her, if you know what I mean.'

'Anything else?'

'We haven't done a thing except interview her parents and a few of her friends. Like we told Derek, we're up to our ears in county business right now. That's why we were looking to hook up with you guys for the D.C. side of things. My partner wanted to meet you, but she's out rounding up a girl she found as we speak.'

'Rounding up?'

'Basically, we yank 'em right off the street when we find them. We've got this van, no windows—'

'This legal, what you do?'

'As long as they're minors, yeah. They have no domain over themselves, and if the parents sign a permission form for us to go after them it's all straight. If there are any repercussions, we deal with it later. We work with some lawyers, pro bono. Basically, we're out to save these kids.'

'That's nice. But this work here, Derek didn't say anything about it being pro bono. And on top of our hourly rate, I'm gonna need expense money.'

'Keep detailed records and you got it.'

'It could get rich.'

'We're covered by the APIP people.'

'They must have some deep pockets.'

'Grant money.'

'Because I got a feeling I'm going to have to pay some people to talk.'

'Okay. But I'm still going to need those details.'

Tracy's hand kept going into a large leather bag set on the table. She had been fondling something inside of it, then removing her hand, then putting it back in again.

'What've you got in there?'

'My cigarettes.'

'Well, you might as well stop romancing that pack. You can't light up in here.'

'You can't light up anywhere,' she said, adding by way of explanation, 'It's the coffee.'

'Gives you that urge, huh?' Quinn reached into a pocket and dropped a pack of sugarless gum between them. 'Try this.'

'No, thanks.'

'We'll be done in a minute, you can step outside.' Quinn tapped his pen on the notepad. 'The one thing I'm wondering is, a girl runs away from home, there's got to be good reason. It can't just be galloping hormones and drugged-out friends.'

'Sometimes there's an abusive parent involved in the equation, if that's what you're getting at. Emotional or physical or sexual abuse, or a combination of the three. Part of what me and Karen do is, we spend considerable time in the home, trying to figure out if that's the best place for the kid to go back to. And sometimes the home's not the best environment. But you're wrong about one thing: it often is just hormones and peers, and accelerating events, that make a kid run away. With Jennifer, we're convinced that's the case.'

'Where do you suggest I start?'

'Start with stakeouts, like we do. The Wheaton mall, it's near D.C. and it's been good for us before. The overground rave clubs, trance, jungle, whatever they're calling it this week. The ones play a mix of live and prerecorded stuff. What's that place, in Southeast, on Half Street?'

'Nation.'

'That one. Platinum is good, too, over on Ninth and F.'

'I don't like stakeouts. I'd rather get out there and start talking to people.'

'No one likes stakeouts. But suit yourself, whatever works for you.'

'Anything else?'

'Just in general terms. White-girl runaways tend to start out in far Northwest, where they're around a familiar environment.'

'Other white kids.'

'Right. Places like Georgetown. They get hooked into drugs in a bigger way, they get taken in by a pimp—'

'They move east.'

Tracy nodded. 'It's gradual, and inevitable. Last stop is those New York Avenue flophouses in Northeast. You don't even want to know what goes on in those places.'

'I already know. I was a patrol cop in the District, remember?'

Tracy turned her coffee cup slowly on the table. 'Not just any cop.'

'That's right. I was famous.'

'It's not news to me. We ran your name through a search engine, and there were plenty of hits.'

'Some people can't get past it, I guess.'

'Maybe so. But as far as you and me are concerned, this is day one.'

'Thanks.'

'Anyway, first impression, you seem like an okay guy to me.'

'You seem like an okay guy to me, too.'

'I bought a tomato at Fresh Fields once.'

'You probably spent too much for that shirt you're wearing, too.'

'It's a blouse. I paid about forty bucks for it, I think.'

Quinn touched his own T-shirt. 'This Hanes I got on? Three for twelve dollars at Target, out on Twenty-nine.'

'I better get out there before they run out.'

Quinn tapped the stack of flyers on the table. 'I'll phone you, keep you caught up.'

'You ready for this?'

'Been a while,' said Quinn. 'But yeah, I'm stoked.'

She watched him step out of the coffee shop, studying the way he filled out the seat of his Levi's and that cocky thing he did with his walk. Talking about her father, giving up something of herself to this guy who was, after all, a stranger, it was not what she would normally do. Add to that, Christ, she should have known better, he was a cop. But there was a connection between them already, sexual and probably emotional; it happened right away like that with her if it happened at all. She had known it two minutes after they had sat down together, and, she had seen it in his damaged green eyes; he had known it, too.

Strange looked over the file on Calhoun Tucker that Janine had dropped on his desk.

'Nice work.'

'Thanks,' said Janine. She was sitting in the client chair in Strange's office. 'I ran his license plate through Westlaw; everything came up easy after that. People Finder gave me the previous addresses.'

Strange studied the data. Tucker's license plate number had given them his Social Security number, his date of birth, his assets, any criminal record, and any lawsuits. Janine had printed out his credit history, with past and present employment, as well. Credit drove the database of information; it was the foundation of computerized modern detective services. It was useless for getting histories on indigents and criminals who had never had a credit card or made time-payment purchases. But for someone like Tucker, who was part of the system, it worked just fine.

Janine had fed Tucker's SS number into People Finder, a subprogram of Westlaw. From this she had gotten a list of his current neighbors and the neighbors of his previous addresses.

'He looks pretty straight, first glance.'

'No criminal record,' said Janine. 'Apart from a default on a car loan, he's barely stumbled.'

Strange read the top sheet. 'Graduate of Virginia Tech. Spends a few years in Portsmouth after college, working as an on-site representative for a company called Strong Services, whatever that's about.'

'I'll find out.'

'Looks like he owned a house in Portsmouth. Check on that, too, will you? Whose name was on it, any cosigners, like that.'

'I will.'

'Then he moved over to Virginia Beach.'

'Most likely that's where he got into entertainment,' said Janine. 'Got involved in promotions in clubs, hookups with fraternities, like that. Looks like that's what he's doing up here now, with the Howard kids along U Street and the upscale club circuit over around Ninth and on Twelfth.'

'That Audi he's driving—'

'Leased. Maybe he's beyond his means, but hey, he's in a business where image is half of what you are.'

'I heard that.' Strange dropped the file onto his desk. 'Well, let me get on out of here, see what I can dig up. Can't tell much until you face-time.'

'Tucker looks pretty clean to me.'

'I hope you're right,' said Strange. 'There's nothin' I'd like better than to give George Hastings a good report.'

Strange got up from his chair and walked around the desk. His office door was closed. He touched Janine on the cheek, then cupped his hand behind her neck, bent down, and kissed her on the mouth.

'You taste good.'

'Strawberry,' said Janine.

Strange clipped his beeper onto his belt and picked up the file.

'Terry phoned in,' said Janine. 'He was in Georgetown when he called. Asked Ron to run some girl's name, see if she has an arrest record in the District.'

'He's workin' a job those county women farmed out to us. Did you bill them for that one I did the other night?'

'It went out yesterday.'

'All right, then.' Strange headed for the door. 'See you later, baby.'

'Tonight?' said Janine to his back.

Strange kept walking. 'I'll let you know.'

8

Quinn parked his Chevelle on R Street along Montrose Park, between Dunbarton Oaks and Oak Hill Cemetery in north Georgetown. He walked over to Wisconsin Avenue with a stack of flyers, a small staple gun, and a roll of industrial adhesive tape that he carried in a JanSport knapsack he wore on his back.

Foot traffic was moderate in the business district, with area workers breaking for lunch, along with college kids and the last of summer's visitors window-shopping the knockoff clothiers and chain stores. There wasn't anything here that couldn't be had elsewhere and at a better price. To Quinn, and to most of D.C.'s longtime residents, Georgetown during the day was a charmless tourist trap and a parking nightmare to be avoided at any cost.

Quinn went along Wisconsin and west to the residential side streets, stapling the flyers to telephone poles and taping them to city trash cans. He knew the flyers would largely be gone, ripped down by residents and foot cops, by nightfall, maybe sooner. It was a long shot, but it was a start.

South of the P Street intersection he stopped to talk to a skinny man, all arms and legs, built like a spider, who was leaning in the doorway of Mean Feets, D.C.'s longtime trendsetting shoe boutique, dragging on a Newport. Inside the shop, Quinn saw a handsome older man smoothly fitting a shoe onto the foot of a young woman as a D'Angelo tune came from the open front door.

As a former cop, Quinn knew that urban shoe salesmen spent a good portion of their day standing outside their shops, talking to women walking down the sidewalk, trying to get them inside, into their web. As it was an occupational necessity, they tended to remember not just shoe sizes but faces and names as well. They also serviced many of the city's hookers and their pimps.

Quinn greeted the skinny man, then opened a leather holder, flashing his badge and license. To the public, it looked like a cop's badge. Beside a picture of the D.C. flag, it actually read, 'Metropolitan Police Department,' over the words 'Private Investigator.' It was Quinn's habit, suggested to him by Strange, to show the license and badge long enough for the flag and MPD moniker to register, then put it away just as fast.

'Investigator, D.C.,' said Quinn. Strange had taught him this, too. It wasn't against the law. It wasn't even a lie.

'What can I do for you, officer?'

'Name's Terry Quinn. You?'

'Antoine.'

Quinn unfolded a flyer he had kept in his back pocket and handed it to Antoine. Antoine squinted through the smoke curling up from the cigarette dangling from his mouth.

'Any chance you've seen this girl?'

'Don't look familiar.'

'You sell shoes to prostitutes from time to time, don't you?'

'Sure, I got my regular ladies, come in for their evening shoes. But I don't recognize this one. Been doin' this a long time in the District, too. She hookin'?'

'Could be.'

'I don't recall ever seeing one this young in my shop. Not that I knew of, anyway.'

'Do me a favor. Put this up in the back room, by the toilet, whatever.' Quinn handed Antoine his card. 'You or your coworkers, they see her, even if she's walking down the street, you give me a call.'

Antoine dropped the cigarette, ground it out. He reached for his wallet, slipped Quinn's card inside, and retrieved a card of his own, handing it to Quinn.

'Now you do *me* a favor, officer. You need a pair of boots or somethin', get you out of those New Balances you got on, somethin' a little more stylin', you give *me* a call, hear? Antoine. You walk in here, don't be *askin'* for anyone else.'

'I got a wide foot.'

'Oh, I'll fit you, now. Antoine can stretch some shoes.'

'All right,' said Quinn. 'I'll see you around.'

'The name is Antoine.'

Quinn walked north to a strip club up the hill on Wisconsin, stopping at an ATM along the way. He entered without paying a cover and was seated by a bouncer at a table in the middle of a series of tables set tightly in a row throughout the depth of the narrow club, facing one of several stages. Three men wearing ties, their shirtsleeves rolled back off their wrists, occupied the table. The men did not acknowledge Quinn. A nice-looking young woman in a sleeveless dress quickly arrived and took his order. She cupped her ear to hear him over the Limp Bizkit, their cover of 'Faith,' booming through the speakers.

Quinn checked out the dancers, working the poles on their stages, into the music, smiling politely at the audience but with their eyes someplace else. Thin, young, toned, and generally pleasant to look at. One of them was straight-up attractive, with a cheerleader's bright face and ruby red nipples. Connoisseurs claimed this place had the finest, cleanest-looking dancers in town. It was all perception and taste; Quinn knew men who swore by that joint near Connecticut and Florida Avenues. Quinn had been there once and judged it to be a skank-house.

The woman returned with a bottle of Bud, for which he paid dearly. He showed her the flyer. She barely looked at it and shook her head. Quinn paid her, tipped her, and asked for a receipt.

There were several bouncers working the room, all wearing radio headsets. The customers could go to the stages and tip the dancers, but they couldn't linger in the aisle, and if they did, one of the bouncers told them to get back to their seats. Patrons judged to be nursing their beers were encouraged to drink up and reorder or leave. This was the New World Order of strip clubs. To Quinn, it was all too bloodless and it didn't seem to be much fun.

Quinn recognized one of the bouncers, a black Asian-featured guy now standing by the front door, as a moonlighting cop. He didn't know the cop personally and didn't know his name. Quinn waited for his receipt, left his beer untouched, and walked over to the bouncer. He introduced himself, shook the guy's hand, and showed him the flyer.

'I don't know her,' said the cop. He looked closely at Quinn. 'Where'd you say you were at?'

'In the end, I rode Three-D.'

The cop got that look of recognition then, the clouding over of the eyes, that Quinn had seen many times.

'Keep the flyer,' said Quinn, handing the cop his business card as well. 'You see her, do me a favor and give me a call.'

Quinn walked out, Kid Rock screaming at his back. He knew the bouncer would throw the flyer and his card in the trash. He was one of those guys, once he figured out who Quinn was, he didn't want to have anything to do with him. He'd never get past the fact that Quinn had killed a fellow cop.

Quinn returned to his car and drove east, over the P Street Bridge and onto the edge of Dupont Circle. He found a spot on 23rd Street, walked past a gay nightclub that had been there since disco's first wave, and stopped at a coffeehouse at the next intersection. It was near P Street Beach, a stretch of Rock Creek Park that in years past had been known for sunbathing, cruising, and open-air sexual activity. Quinn remembered from his patrol days that this was also an area where ecstasy could be easily scored, as the 18th Street clubs were in the vicinity. It was a perimeter that young hustlers worked as well.

He bought a cup of regular and took it out to where tables were set on the sidewalk. He found a seat and checked out the crowd. Teenagers were interspersed in the mostly adult customer base of coffee drinkers and smokers. Some of the teenagers sat with friends; others, both boys and girls, sat with older men. Quinn guessed that some of these kids were cutting school, just slumming, and some were runaways who crashed wherever they could around town. That left the few who had gone professional and were working the crowd.

Quinn had the feeling, from the eye contact he was getting, that a couple of the kids had marked him as a cop. Strange claimed you never lost the look. Quinn was way too old to be one of them, too young to be a john, and, he told himself, too attractive to look like the type who would pay for it. He was mulling over all of this, sitting there trying to decide how to approach one of these kids.

Fuck it, he thought, getting up and crossing the sidewalk patio to a table where two teenage girls sat, empty cups in front of them, ashing the pavement with their cigarettes.

'Hey,' said Quinn, 'how you ladies doing?'

Both of the girls looked up, but only one of them kept her eyes on him.

'We're fine, thanks.' The girl, who had the look of hard money, someone who had been taught never to thank the waitress, said, 'Something we can help you with?'

Quinn had obviously made a mistake. 'I was wondering, can I snag a cigarette from you?'

She rolled her eyes and gave him one from her handbag without looking at him further. He thanked her and returned to his table, noticing a boy and his female friend laughing at him, feeling a flush of anger and trying to stifle it as he adjusted himself in his seat. Holding a cigarette and without even a match to complete the ruse.

He retrieved his cell from his pack and phoned the office. Janine switched him over to Ron Lattimer.

'Any luck?' said Ron.

'Nothing yet. Our girl got a sheet?'

'Jennifer Marshall. Got it right here.'

'Solicitation?'

'Man wins the Kewpie doll.'

'What about an address?'

'Listed as five seventeen J Street, Northwest. You might have a little trouble finding it, unless someone went and built a J Street in the last week or so—'

'There is no J Street in D.C.'

'No *shit*.'

'She's got a sense of humor, anyway.'

'Or the one who told her to write it like that does.'

'Thanks, Ron. I'll look over the rest of it when I come in. Derek around?'

'Uh-uh, he's out doing a background check.'

'Tell him I was looking for him, hear?'

'Call him on his cell.'

'He doesn't keep it on most of the time.'

'You can leave a message on it, man.'

'True.'

'I see him, I'll tell him.'

Quinn was replacing his cell in his bag when he noticed a girl standing before him. She wore boot-cut jeans and a spaghetti-string pink shirt with a cartoon illustration of a Japanese girl holding a guitar slung low, à la Keith. Her shoulder bag was white, oval, and plastic. Her dirty-blond hair fell to her shoulders. Her hips were narrow, her breasts small, mostly nipple and visible through the shirt. She was pale, with bland brown eyes and a tan birthmark, shaped like a strawberry, on her neck. She wore wire-rim prescription eyeglasses, granny style. She was barely cute, and not even close to pretty. Quinn put her in her midteens, maybe knocking on the door of seventeen, if that.

'You gonna smoke that?'

Quinn looked at the cigarette in his hand as if he were noticing it for the first time. 'I don't think so.'

'Can I get it from you, then?'

'Sure.'

She sat down without invitation. He handed her the cigarette.

'You got a light?'

'Sorry.'

'You need a new rap,' she said, rooting through her shoulder bag for a match. Finding a book, she struck a flame and put fire to the cigarette. 'The one you got is lame.'

'You think so?'

'You be hittin' those girls up for a smoke, you don't ask 'em for a light, you don't even have a match your own self?'

Quinn took in the girl's words, the rhythms, the dropping of the g's, the slang. Like that of most white girls selling it on the street, her speech was an affectation, a strange in-and-out blend of Southern cracker and city black girl.

'Pretty stupid, huh?'

'And if you was lookin' to score some ass, you went and picked the only two girls out here ain't even had their boots knocked yet. Couple of Sidwell Friends girls, trying out the street for a day before they go back to their daddy's Mercedes, got it parked around the block.' She grinned. 'You prob'ly don't even smoke.'

'I tried it once and it made me sick.'

'But you want something,' she said, no inflection at all in her voice, just dead. It made Quinn sad.

'I'm looking for a girl.'

'You a cop?'

'No.'

'You have to tell me if you are. It's entrapment otherwise.'

'I'm not a cop. I'm just looking for a girl.'

'I can *get* you some pussy, now.' She lowered his eyes, magnified behind the lenses, suggestively. 'Shit, you can have this pussy right here, that's all you want.'

Quinn found a flyer in his knapsack and slid it across the table. 'I'm looking for her.'

He watched her examine the face and data on the flyer. If she recognized Jennifer Marshall, her eyes did not give it up.

'I don't know her,' said the girl. 'But maybe I can hook you up with someone who does.'

'You work the middle,' said Quinn.

'When I can. It's rough out here, you know; I'm talkin' about the competition. My looks are, like, an acquired taste. Guys don't make passes at girls who wear glasses, and all that. My mother, when she was dolin' out one of her famous pearls of wisdom, used to remind me all the time. But contacts hurt my eyes. So here I am, lookin' like a magnet-school geek tryin' to peddle her ass. And my tits are too little, too. White johns like that black pussy, and with this kiddie pelvis I got, the brothers just tear my shit up. So maybe I'm not cut out for the life. You think I am?'

Quinn gave the girl a chin nod. 'What's your name?'

'Stella. Yours?'

'Terry Quinn. You were gonna hook me up, Stella.'

'It's gonna cost you fifty.'

'For a name?'

'It's a good name.'

'How do I know?'

''Cause I ga-ran-tee it, dude. Now how about that fifty?'

Quinn paid her discreetly. She finished her cigarette and dropped it to the concrete.

'There's a girl dances over at Rick's, on New York Avenue, on the way out of town, past North Capitol?'

'I know the place.'

'Black girl, goes by Eve. They call her All-Ass Eve; you see her, you'll know why. She knows this girl.'

'How do you know that she knows her?'

For the first time, Stella's confidence was visibly shaken. She recovered quickly, though, smiling crookedly like a child caught in a lie. And Quinn saw the little girl then, just for a moment, that someone had rocked to sleep, bought presents for, loved. Maybe not always – maybe the mother or the father had fucked up somewhere along the way. But he had to believe that this girl had been loved at one time.

'Okay, I don't know for sure that Eve knows this girl right here, but listen to me: this is the *kind* of girl Eve gets to know. She cruises through this intersection, and in bus stations and malls, lookin' for new talent so she can steer it to her pimp. Everyone workin' this area knows who she is. The ones been around know to stay away from her and stick to this side of the creek. But the girl in this picture right here? She is fresh meat. I mean, she looks like she don't know jack. It's the dumb ones, the desperate ones that go with Eve. I'm just connecting things, is all. Anyway, Eve don't work out for you, you come back, we'll start again.'

'For more money.'

Stella shrugged. 'I'm strugglin', dude.'

'How do I reach you?'

Stella gave Quinn her cell number. He used his to phone her right there at the table. Her cell rang in her shoulder bag. She fished it out and answered.

'Hellooo? Officer Quinn?'

'Okay.' He killed the call on his cell and gave her one of his cards. 'You want to talk, you call me, hear?'

'Talkin' don't pay my bills.' She looked him over. 'I'll suck your dick for another fifty, though.'

'This pans out, there's another fifty in it for you just for giving me the lead.'

'I'll take it. But don't use my name when you're talking to Eve.'

'You don't need to tell me that. Eight years on the force, I never once lost a snitch.'

'Knew you were a cop.'

'In another life,' said Quinn, getting up and stepping back from the table. 'Let's stay in touch, all right?'

9

Calhoun Tucker was tall and lean and visibly muscled beneath a crisp beige shirt tucked into tailored black slacks. He had a thin Billy D mustache and some kind of pomade worked into his close black hair that gave it shine. He wore expensive-looking shades and a small, new-tech cell clipped to his waistband. All of this Strange could see through his 10x50 binoculars as he sat in his Chevy, surveilling Tucker across the street from his residence, a rental town house near a medical park between Wheaton and Silver Spring.

Tucker went down the sidewalk toward his car, a cherry red S4, Audi's hopped-up model in the 4-series line, their version of the BMW M3. Tucker's complexion was a deep brown, not so dark as to hide his features, not so light as to suggest white blood. He walked with confidence, chin up, like the handsome young man he undoubtedly knew he was. He had the package women liked; the confidence thing, they liked that, too. Strange could see right away why Alisha Hastings had been attracted, surface-wise, to Tucker.

Tucker fired up the Audi and pulled out of his space. Strange followed him south, making sure there were plenty of cars between them all the way. Just over the District line, Tucker shot right on Alaska, then another right up 13th, into the cluster of 'flower-and-tree' streets, where he cut a left onto Iris. He was heading for George Hastings's house. Strange went around the block, counter to the route Tucker had taken, and parked in the alley behind Juniper. He got out of his car and left the alley on foot, his binos in his hand.

By the time Strange made it to the intersection of Iris and 13th, Alisha Hastings had come out of her father's house and was leaning into the driver's-side window of Tucker's ride, idling out front behind George's Volvo. Alisha had on some kind of casual, wear-around-the-house hookup that looked spontaneous but had probably been planned. Tucker had probably called her from his cell and told her he would be stopping by on his way into town. Strange didn't blame

Tucker for wanting to get a look at her before he started his day; Alisha was radiant and poised, with deep dimples framing her lovely smile. Tucker had his hand on her forearm and he was lightly stroking it, talking to her, making her laugh, making her so happy she had to look away. Seeing the two of them there, it reminded Strange of a girl he had loved hard back in the early seventies. He watched them kiss. A twinge of guilt snapped in his chest, and he went back to get his car.

He followed Tucker down into Shaw. Tucker parked on U Street, and Strange put his Chevy in a spot along a construction fence on 10th. He jogged up to the corner and saw Tucker walking west, carrying a briefcase of some kind. He followed Tucker until he went up the steps and into a nightclub that was a quiet bar and lunch joint during the day. Tucker came out ten minutes later and walked farther west to a similar club. He entered, and Strange stood back and leaned against a parking-meter pole stripped of its head. Back from where he'd come, he could see the lunch crowd going in and out of Ben's. His felt his mouth water and a rumble in his stomach, and he looked the other way.

It took Tucker a while to come out of the club. Strange knew the place. He used to drink there occasionally when it was a neighborhood bar, just a few short years ago. In the summer the management had strung speakers outside, and on some nights, driving slowly down U Street, Strange could hear James Brown doing 'Payback,' or a Slave tune, or Otis and Carla singing 'Tramp,' and that was enough to cause him to pull over and stop in for a beer. All types were in the bar then, even a few whites; you could wear what you wanted to, it was cool. But then they changed things over, instituting a dress code, and a race code, it seemed, as one night Strange had seen some fancy brothers punk out this one young white dude who was sitting at the bar quietly drinking a beer. The white dude, he wasn't bothering anyone, but he wasn't the right color and he wasn't wearing the right clothes, and they hard-eyed him enough to make him feel like he wasn't wanted, and soon he was gone. Strange hadn't gone back since. The truth was, he was too old for the crowd himself, and he preferred a working-class atmosphere when he sat down to have his drinks. Mostly, he didn't dig that kind of intolerance, no matter who was on the giving or the receiving end. He'd seen too much in his life to excuse that kind of behavior from anyone, even his own people. If this was the New U, then it wasn't for him.

Strange retrieved his car and kept it running on the street, waiting for Tucker to come out of the bar. Soon Tucker walked down the steps of the club, slipping his shades on, and went to his car. He pulled out onto U, and Strange followed.

Tucker went east, over to Barry Place, parking his Audi between Sherman and 9th, not far from Howard University. Strange kept going and circled the block.

He parked on the Sherman/Barry corner and got his AE-1, outfitted with a 500mm lens, out of his trunk, keeping his eye on Tucker, who was now walking down the street, talking on his cell. Strange returned to the driver's seat of his Chevy, where he had a clear view of Tucker, and snapped several photographs of him walking up the steps of a row house and waiting at its door. He got a last shot of Tucker going though the open door, and of the woman who let him in. He used the long lens to read the address off one of the brick pillars fronting the porch of the house. He used his cell to phone in the address to Janine. Janine had a reverse-directory program on her computer that would give them a phone number and name for the residence.

Strange sat there for an hour or so, sipping water from a bottle, listening to Joe Madison's talk show on WOL, while he thought of what was going on in the house. Maybe that was a business appointment in there, or it was a friend and the two of them were having lunch. More likely, right about now Tucker was knocking the back end out of that woman Strange had seen in the open door. Strange was disappointed but not surprised. Thinking about that young man and woman in there, it stirred something in him, too. He'd done enough today. He was hungry and he had to pee.

Strange ignitioned the Chevy and drove over to Chinatown, where he parked in an alley behind I Street. A man whom Strange recognized, a heroin addict who worked the alley, appeared like a phantom, and Strange handed him a five to look after his car. Then he went in a back door next to a Dumpster, down a hall where he passed a kitchen and several closed doors, and through a beaded entranceway into a small dining area where dulcimer music played softly. He took a deuce and ordered some hot-and-sour soup and Singapore-style noodles from an older woman who called him by his name. He washed the lunch down with a Tsingtao.

'Everything okay?' said the hostess.

'Yes, mama, it was good. Bring me my check.'

'You want?' she said, her eyes moving to the beaded curtain leading to the hall. 'Your friend here.'

Strange nodded.

He paid cash and went down the hall to a door opposite the kitchen. He went through the door and closed it behind him. He was in a white-walled room lit by scented votive candles. The music from the dining area played in the room. A padded table was in the center of the room, with a small cart set beside it holding lotions, towels, and a washbasin.

Strange went through another door, turned on a light, and undressed in a room containing a toilet, sink, and tiled shower stall. He hung his clothing on a coat tree and took a hot shower, wrapping a towel around himself when he was done. Then he returned to the candlelit room and lay facedown on the padded table. Soon he heard a door open and saw light spear into the room. The light slipped away as the door was closed.

'Hello, Stwange.'

'Hello, baby.'

Strange heard the squirt of an applicator and next felt the woman's warm, slick hands. She kneaded the lotion, some sweet-smelling stuff, into his shoulder muscles and his lats. He felt her rough nipples graze his back as she bent in to whisper in his ear.

'You have good day today?'

'Uh-huh.'

She hummed to the music as she massaged his back. The sound of her voice and the sensation of her touch made him hard. He turned over, the towel falling open. She massaged his chest, his calves, his upper thighs, working her way up to his balls. The lotion was warm there; Strange swallowed.

'You like?'

'Yeah, that's good right there.'

She applied more lotion to her hands and fisted his cock. Her movement was slow. As her hand went up his shaft, she feathered the head with her fingers. Strange opened his eyes.

The woman was in her twenties, with carelessly applied lipstick and eyes like black olive pits. She wore red lace panties and nothing else. She was short and had the hips of a larger woman. Her breasts were small and firm. He brushed his fingers across one nipple until it was pebble hard, and when the fire rose up in his loins he pinched her there until she moaned. He didn't care if it was all fake.

'Go now,' he said, and she pumped him faster.

His orgasm was eye-popping, his own jism splattering his stomach and chest.

'You need,' said the woman, chuckling under her breath.

As she wet-toweled him, Strange said, 'Yes.'

Dressed again, he left forty-five dollars in a bowl by the door.

Out in the alley, his beeper sounded. It was the office number. He debated whether or not to return the call. He got into his car and used his cell to dial the number. Quinn's voice came through from the other end.

'I stopped by the office to pick up Jennifer Marshall's sheet from Ron,' said Quinn. 'Where you at?'

'Chinatown,' said Strange.

'Uh-huh.'

'Had some lunch.'

'Okay.'

Strange had spilled his guts to Quinn one night when both of them had put away too many beers. Giving up too much of himself to Quinn had come back to him in a bad way. It was always a mistake.

'I'm headed down to Rick's, on New York Avenue,' said Quinn, then explained the reason. 'You wanna join me?'

'Yeah, okay.'

'C'mon over to the office. We can drive down together.'

'I'll meet you at Rick's,' said Strange. 'Say, half hour?'

'Fine,' said Quinn. 'Bring some dollar bills.'

Strange cut the line. He didn't want to go back to the office and have to small-talk Janine. He was relieved it hadn't been her on the phone when he'd called in.

On his way east, he drove by the row house on Barry Place, the site of Calhoun Tucker's afternoon tryst. Tucker's Audi was gone.

10

Rick's was a stand-alone A-frame establishment located a few miles east of North Capitol on New York Avenue, a bombed-out-looking stretch of road that was the jewel-in-the-crown introduction to Washington, D.C. for many first-time visitors who traveled into the city by car.

The building now holding Rick's had originally been built as a Roy Rogers burger house. It had mutated into its current incarnation, a combination sports bar and strip joint for working stiffs, when the Roy's chain went the way of corded telephones.

The conversion had been simple. The new owners had gutted the fast-food interior, keeping only a portion of the kitchen and the bathroom plumbing, and hung some Redskins, Wizards, and Orioles memorabilia on the walls. The omission of Washington Capitals pennants was intentional, as hockey was generally not a sport that interested blacks. The final touch was to brick up the windows that had once wrapped around three sides of the structure. Bricked windows generally meant one of three things: arson victim, gay bar, or strip joint. Once the word got around on which kind of place Rick's was, the owners didn't even bother to hang a sign out front.

Rick's had its own parking lot, an inheritance from the Roy's lease. A couple of locals had been shot in this parking lot in the past year, but pre-sundown and in the early evening hours, before the liquor turned peaceful men brave, then violent, the place was generally safe.

Strange pulled his Caprice alongside Quinn's blue Chevelle, parked in an empty corner of the lot. Quinn got out of his car as Strange stepped out of his. They met and shook hands. Quinn made a show of sniffing the air.

'Damn, Derek. You smell kinda, I don't know, *sweet.* Is that perfume?'

'I don't know what you're talkin' about, man.'

It was the lotion that girl had rubbed on him back in Chinatown. Strange knew that Quinn was remarking on it, in his own stupid way.

They walked toward Rick's.

Strange nodded at the JanSport hanging off Quinn's shoulder. 'What, we goin' mountain climbing now? Thought we were just gonna have a beer or two.'

'My briefcase.'

'You been waitin' on me long?'

'Not too long,' said Quinn.

'You coulda gone inside,' said Strange, giving Quinn a long look. 'I bet I would have spotted you right quick.'

'I'd be the one on the bottom of the pile.'

'With the red opening in his neck, stretchin' from one ear to the other.'

'Not too many white guys in this place, huh?'

'Seeing a white guy at Rick's be like spottin' a brother at a Springsteen concert.'

'I figured I'd just wait for you to escort me in.'

'No need to tempt fate. It's what I been telling you the past two years. You're learning, man.'

'I'm trying,' said Quinn.

They went into Rick's. Smoke hovered in the dim lights. The place was half filled, just easing into happy hour. A bar ran along one wall where the order counter for Roy's had been, and beyond it was a series of doors. Guys sat at the stick, watching the nostalgia sports channel, Packers uniforms dancing in a flurry of snow, 'Spill the Wine' playing on the stereo throughout the house. In two corners, women danced in thongs, nothing else, for groups of men seated at tables. Waitresses wearing short shorts and lacy tops were servicing the tables. Big men with big shoulders and no headsets were stationed around the room.

Floor patrons fish-eyed Strange and Quinn as they stepped up to the bar. Those seated at the bar barely noticed their presence, as their eyes were glued to the television set mounted on the wall.

Strange nodded up at the set. 'You want to get a man's attention, put on any Green Bay game where it got played in the snow. Guy'll sit there like a glassy-eyed old dog, watchin' it.'

'It's like when they run *The Good, the Bad and the Ugly* on TNT.'

'You mean, like, every week?'

'Tell me the truth; if you're scanning the channels with the remote and you see Eastwood, or Eli Wallach as Tuco—'

' "Otherwise known as the Rat." '

'Right,' said Quinn. 'So, when you recognize that movie, have you ever been able to scan past it? I mean, you always sit there and watch the rest of the film, don't you?'

'*The Wild Bunch* is like that, too,' said Strange. 'How many times you figure you've seen that one?'

Quinn pumped out two short strokes with his fist. 'With my pants on, or with them around my ankles?'

Strange chuckled as the bartender, a young guy with a hard face, arrived before them. 'What can I get y'all?'

'I'll take a Double R Bar burger and a saddle fulla fries,' said Quinn, but the bartender didn't smile.

'Heineken for me,' said Strange.

'Bud,' said Quinn.

'In bottles,' said Strange. 'And we're gonna need a receipt.'

The tender returned with their beers. Quinn paid him and dropped a heavy tip on the bar, placing his hand over the cash. 'Which one of the girls is Eve?'

'That's her right there,' said the bartender, chinning in the direction of a big-boned dancer working one of the corners of the room.

'When does she stop?'

'They work half hours.'

'Any idea how long she's been at it?'

''Bout ten years, from the looks of her.'

'I meant tonight.'

'Ain't like I been clockin' her.'

'Right,' said Quinn. He took his hand off the money, and the bartender snatched it without a word. He had never once looked Quinn in the eye.

Strange saw two men get up from their table near Eve's corner. He folded the bar receipt, put it in his breast pocket, and said to Quinn, 'There we go, that's us right there.'

They crossed the floor, one of the stack-shouldered bouncers staring hard at Quinn as they passed. 'Sweet Sticky Thing' came forward from the house system. Quinn and Strange had a seat at the deuce. Strange leaned forward and tapped his beer bottle against Quinn's.

'Relax,' said Strange.

'I get tired of it, is all.'

'You expect all the brothers to show you love, huh?'

'Just respect,' said Quinn.

They drank off some of their beers and watched the work of the woman the bartender had identified as Eve. She was squatting, her back to a group of men, her palms resting atop her thighs, working the muscles in her lower back. Her huge ass jiggled rapidly, seemingly disconnected from the rest of her. It moved wildly before the men.

'Someone ought to give that a name,' said Strange.

'She does have a nickname: All-Ass Eve.'

'Bet it didn't take long to come up with it.'

'You like it like that?'

'Is seven up?'

'She doesn't hold a candle to Janine.'

'That's what I know. You don't have to tell me, man.' Strange smiled and pointed to one of the speakers suspended from the ceiling by wires. 'Listen to this right here. The third verse is comin' up.'

'So?'

'The horn charts behind this verse are beautiful, man. The Ohio Players never did get much credit for the complexity in their shit.'

'That's nice,' said Quinn. 'You know, Janine was askin' where you were when I was back in the office.'

'You tell her I was in Chinatown?'

'I don't like lying to her.' Quinn's eyes cut off Strange's stare. 'No, I didn't say where you were.'

Strange had a sip of beer. 'You met with Sue Tracy, right?'

'Yeah.'

'What'd you think?'

'She's a pro. She's nice.'

'Bet you didn't find her all that hard to look at, either.'

'Knock it off.'

'Just wanted to make sure you still had some red blood runnin' through your veins. While you're sittin' over there judgin' me with your eyes.'

Quinn didn't respond. Strange said, 'Ron give you the sheet on the Marshall girl?'

'I got it.'

'What did it tell you?'

'She got popped for solicitation. It's a no-paper, so we won't be finding her in court.'

'She put an address on the form?' said Strange.

'A phony. But the spot where she wrote down her contact was interesting. A guy named Worldwide Wilson.'

'Worldwide.'

'Yeah, looks like she gave up the name of her pimp.'

'She give out his phone number, too?'

'She did write one down. But it's got one of those number symbols after it.'

'Must be his pager.'

'Genius.'

'Just tryin' to help you out, rookie.'

'Anyway, I'll find out tonight.'

They watched the rest of Eve's performance. The music programmer stuck with the Ohio Players and moved into 'Far East Mississippi' and 'Skin Tight.' Strange and Quinn ordered two more beers. Eve finished her shift and walked off through one of the doors behind the bar, accompanied by the stack-necked bouncer who had hard-eyed Quinn. A woman arrived, built similarly to Eve, and she began to dance in the same way Eve had danced, this time to a tune by the Gap Band. The woman's behind rippled as if it were in a wind tunnel.

'This here must be strictly an ass joint,' said Quinn.

'And they asked me when I took you on, Will he make a good detective.'

'It's like their signature dish.'

'Ledo's Pizza got pizza. The Prime Rib's got prime rib. Rick's got ass.'

'You black guys do love the onion.'

'Was wonderin' when you were gonna get to that.'

Soon Eve came out of the back room wearing a sheer top with no bra and matching shorts showing the lines of her thong. She was going around to the tables, shaking hands with the men, some of whom were slipping her money in appreciation of her performance. The stack-necked bouncer was never far from Eve. He had braided hair and a gold tooth. Quinn thought he looked like Warren Sapp, that football player. He was big as one.

'She'll be here in a second, Terry. I'll ask the questions, you don't mind.'

'My case. Let me handle it, all right?'

Eve was a large woman, in proportion with her backside. Her nose was thick and wide, and her lips, painted a bright red, were prominent; her hands and feet were the size of a man's. She had sprayed herself with some kind of sweet perfume, and it was strong on Strange and Quinn as she arrived at their table.

'Did you gentlemen like my performance?' she said, giving them a shy smile, her hand out.

'I did,' said Strange.

Quinn extended his hand, a twenty-dollar bill folded in it so that she could see the denomination. He pulled it back as she reached out for it.

'C'mon back when you have a minute,' said Quinn. 'My friend and I want to talk to you.'

Eve kept her smile, but it twitched at one corner. Strange noticed her bad teeth, a common trait among hos.

'Management says I can't sit down with the customers,' said Eve, ''less they buy me a cocktail.'

'Bet you like those fruity ones,' said Strange, 'loaded up with all kinds of rums.'

'Mmmm,' said Eve, licking her lips clumsily.

'We'll see you in a few,' said Quinn.

The bouncer gave him one long, meaningful look before he and Eve went off to the next table full of suckers.

'That drink's gonna cost you, like, another seven,' said Strange.

'I know it.'

'Won't even have no liquor in it.'

'Thanks, Dad.'

'Make sure you get a receipt. We'll charge it to your girl Sue.'

Eve returned after a while and pulled a chair over from another table, sliding it in between Strange and Quinn. She carried a collins glass filled with pinkish liquid and held it up by way of salute to her new friends before taking a sip. The bouncer had a seat on a stool positioned a table away and stared at Quinn. Kool and the Gang's 'Soul Vibration' played loud on the sound system. Strange watched the dancers bring it down a notch to catch the groove of the song.

'Thanks for the drink,' said Eve. She wiped her mouth and placed the drink on the table. Her lipstick had made a kiss mark on the glass. 'You two wouldn't be police officers, would you?'

'We're not with the police,' said Quinn, pushing the yellow flyer he had taken from his pack across the table. He dropped the twenty on top of the flyer, careful not to cover the photograph of Jennifer Marshall. 'You recognize this girl?'

Eve's eyes held their neutral vacancy. 'No.'

'You sure?'

'I said no. Was I talkin' too soft for you?'

'I can hear you fine. I don't believe you is what it is.'

Eve's smile, like a death rictus, remained upon her face. 'You're cuttin' me deep, white boy.'

Strange looked over at the bouncer, then around the room. He recognized one guy, an older cat with a cool-fish handshake he'd seen at church now and again. Anything went down, this cat would be no help at all.

Quinn leaned forward. 'You never seen her, like at a bus station, nothin' like that? How about over by P Street Beach?'

Eve's smile faded, and with it any façade of love.

'Ever hear of a guy named Worldwide Wilson?' said Quinn.

Eve's eyes were dead now, still on Quinn. She shook her head slowly.

'You steer girls over to Wilson, Eve. Isn't that right?'

Eve reached for the twenty on the table. Quinn put a hand over her wrist and pushed his thumb in at her pressure point. He pressed just enough for her to feel it. But if she felt it, it didn't show. In fact, the smile returned to her face.

'All right, Terry,' said Strange. 'Let her go.'

The bouncer was still staring at Quinn but hadn't moved an inch. Eve slowly pulled her hand free. Quinn let her do it.

'You know why you still conscious?' said Eve, her voice so soft it was barely audible above the sounds in the club. ''Cause you don't mean a *mother*fuckin' thing to nobody up in here.'

'I'm lookin' for this girl,' said Quinn just as softly, tapping his finger on the flyer.

'Then look to the one who gave you my name.'

'Say it again?'

'Do I look like I hang on P Street to you?' Eve took the twenty off the table and slipped it into the waistband of her shorts. 'White boy, you got played.'

Eve stood out of her chair, letting her eyes drift over Strange, then walked away.

'You done?' said Strange. 'Or you want another beer?'

'I'm done,' said Quinn, looking past Strange into the room.

'We could buy the house a round. Sing some drinking songs with all your new friends, like they do in those Irish bars—'

'Let's go.'

As they moved toward the bar, Quinn's and the bouncer's eyes met.

'Check you later, slim,' said the bouncer, and Quinn slowed his step. It was something you said to a girl.

Strange tugged on Quinn's T-shirt. At the stick, Strange settled the tab while Quinn kept his back at the bar, watching the patrons in the house, many of them now staring at him. Some were grinning. He felt the warmth of blood that had gone to his face. He wanted to fight someone. Maybe he wanted them all.

'We're gone,' said Strange, handing the receipt to Quinn.

Vapor lights cast a bleached yellow on the lot outside the club. They walked the asphalt to their cars.

'That was good,' said Strange. 'Subtle, like.'

Quinn kept looking back to the door of the club.

'Wanna go back in, huh?'

'Drop it.'

'Terry, one thing you got to learn to do is, don't take all this bullshit too personal.'

'Guess I ought to be more detached, like you.'

'You need to manage some of that anger you got inside you, man.'

'Tomorrow's Wednesday. We got practice in the evening, right Derek?'

'Six o'clock on the dot,' said Strange.

'I'll see you then.'

Quinn drove his Chevelle out of the lot while Strange killed some time, fumbling with his car radio and such. When Quinn was out of sight, Strange locked up his car and walked back into Rick's.

11

'Girl,' said Strange, 'you gonna bleed me dry.'

'House rules,' said Eve with a shrug. 'You want me to sit down with you, you gotta buy me one of these drinks.'

'Tell the truth, though. There's no liquor in that glass, right?'

'You *know* it ain't nothin' but sugar and juice.'

'Figured it was some kinda hustle,' said Strange.

They were seated at the far end of the bar, away from the sports junkies, near the service station. Eve's bouncer was nearby, talking to one of the dancers, keeping one eye on the house, one on Eve.

'That your man?' said Strange.

'Yeah. You got to have one, and he's as good as any I've had. Never has raised a hand to me once.'

Eve slid a cigarette from a pack the bartender had placed before her as she took her seat. Strange struck a match and gave her a light.

'Thank you, sugar.'

'Ain't no thing.'

'Say your name again?'

'Derek Strange.'

She dragged on the smoke, then hit it again. Strange took a ten from his wallet and placed it on the bar between him and Eve. Eve's head was moving to the 'Tower of Power' coming from the house system as she slipped the ten into her shorts.

'Clever Girl,' said Strange.

'I ain't all that. Would I be here if I was?'

'I'm sayin', that's the name of this song. Lenny Williams up front. Ain't no question, he was the best vocalist this group had, and they had a few.'

'Little before my time.'

'I know, darling.' Strange leaned in close to Eve. 'Let me just go ahead and ask you straight up, you don't mind. Do you know the girl in the flyer?'

Eve shook her head. 'No.'

'I didn't think you did.'

'I *told* your boy.'

'But you do know this cat Worldwide.'

'He was my pimp at one time.'

'Was?'

'I stopped trickin' last year. I can make a better living doing this right here. Plus, I got this thing at Lord and Taylor's, up in Chevy Chase? Givin' out perfume samples, like that.'

'Always wondered where they found those pretty girls in places like that.'

'Thank you,' said Eve, lowering her eyes for a moment and then fixing them again on Strange.

'Sounds like you're doin' all right.'

'I'm makin' it.'

'You just walked away from trickin', huh?'

'Worldwide specializes in those young girls. It wasn't like I went off to another pimp. That's something he wouldn't let happen, understand what I'm sayin'? What it was, he couldn't use me no more. I got old, Strange. So I clean-breaked and came on over here.'

'You're like, what, thirty? That ain't old.'

Eve tapped ash off her smoke. 'I'm twenty-nine. That's old for World.'

'What about the one who gave Quinn your name? You know her?'

'Oh, yeah. Had to be this little white bitch, name of Stella.'

'She told him you steered girls over to Wilson.'

'I ain't never done that. It's what *she* does. Can't sell her own ass; ain't nobody even wants that pussy for free. Trick-ass bitch hustled your boy out of his money, bringin' him my way. I knew straight off, he mentioned P Street, it was her. 'Cause that's her corner, right? She gets next to those young white-girl runaways and puts them up with World. She was doin' that shit when *I* was with him, and she still is, I guess. Thought she could make some quick change, givin' up my name. That's her, all the way.'

'Where's Worldwide base his self?'

'Uh-uh.' Eve took a final drag off her cigarette and crushed it dead in the ashtray. 'Look, I talked too much already. And I got to get myself back to work.'

'I need you, I can get up with you here, right?'

'Door's open, long as you just wanna watch me dance. Far as this goes, though, we are done. You do come back, don't be bringin' your Caucasian friend with you, hear?'

'Boy's got some anger management problems is what it is.'

'Needs to learn some manners, too.' Eve stood and straightened her outfit. 'Listen, you do run into World—'

'I don't know you no way. I never met you, and I don't even know your name.'

Eve's eyes softened. She looked younger then, and when she moved in and rested her hand on Strange's shoulder, it felt good.

'Somethin' else, too,' she said. 'Don't you even have a dream of fuckin' with that man. This is *not* somethin' you want to do.'

'I hear you, baby.'

Eve kissed him lightly on the cheek. 'You smell kinda sweet for a man, y'know it?'

Strange said, 'Take care of yourself, all right?'

She moved away and went through one of the doors behind the bar. Strange settled his tab and got his receipt. On his way out he stopped by the bouncer with the braided hair. He stood before him, looked him up and down, and smiled.

'Damn, boy,' said Strange, 'you got some size on you, don't you?'

'I go about two forty,' said the bouncer.

'Looks like most of it's muscle, too. Can you move?'

'I'm quick for my size.'

'You a D.C. boy, right?'

'Uh-huh.'

'Played for who?'

'Came out of Ballou in ninety-two.'

'The Knights. No college?'

The bouncer spread his hands. 'I ain't had the grades.'

'Well, all that natural talent you got, you ought to be doin' somethin' 'stead of standing in this bar, breathing in all this smoke.'

'I heard that. But this here is what I got.'

'Listen,' said Strange, 'thank you for handling that situation the way you did.'

'I don't reach out for trouble. But I only give out one get-out-of-jail card per customer, see what I'm sayin'? You need to tell your boy, he comes back in here again, I will kick his motherfucking ass.'

Strange put a business card into the bouncer's left hand, shook his right. 'You ever need anything, the name's Strange.'

Strange walked out, thinking on one of those golden rules his mother used to repeat, that one about the honey always gettin' the flies. His mother, she was full of those corny old sayings. Him and his brother, when he was alive, used to joke about it with her all the time. She'd been gone awhile now, and more than anything, he missed hearing her voice. The longer he lived the more he realized, damn near everything she'd taught him, seemed like it was right.

Quinn showered at his apartment on Sligo Avenue, then walked up to town, passing the bookstore on Bonifant, stopping to check the lock on the front door before he went on his way. He drank two bottles of Bud at the Quarry House, seated next to a dwarfish regular who read paperback novels, spoke rarely, but was friendly when addressed. Quinn had gotten a taste at Rick's and knew his evening would not be done without a couple more. These days, he almost always walked into bars by himself. He hadn't had a girlfriend since things between him and Juana, a law student and waitress up at Rosita's on Georgia Avenue, had fallen apart over a year ago. But he still frequented the local watering holes. He liked the atmosphere of bars, and he didn't like to drink alone.

After his beers, Quinn walked up to Selim Avenue, trying but failing to not look in the window of Rosita's, then crossed the pedestrian bridge spanning Georgia that led to the B&O train station alongside the Metro tracks. At this time of night the gate leading to the tunnel that ran beneath the tracks was locked, so he stayed on the east side. As he often did, he stood there on the platform, admiring the colored lights of the businesses and the pale yellow haloing the street lamps of downtown Silver Spring. A freight train approached, raising dust as it passed, and he closed his eyes to feel the stir of the wind. When the sound of the train faded he opened his eyes and went back in the direction of his place.

He came up here to the tracks nearly every night. The platform reminded him of a western set, and he liked the solitude, and the view. A construction crew had been working on the station, probably converting it into a museum or something, a thing to be looked at but not used, another change in the name of redevelopment and gentrification. Of course, he didn't know for sure what they were doing to the station, but recent history convinced him that it was something he would not like. In the last year Quinn's breakfast house, the Tastee Diner, had been moved to a location off Georgia, and he rarely ate there anymore as it was out of his foot range. Also, with its new faux-deco sign out front, it now looked liked the Disney version of a diner. He wondered when the small pleasure of his nightly walk would be taken from him, too.

Back at his apartment, Quinn checked his messages and returned a call from Strange, who had phoned from Janine's place. Strange told him what he had learned from Eve.

'Sounds like you ought to go back to that girl Stella,' said Strange.

'I will,' said Quinn. 'Thanks.'

Quinn was a little jealous that Strange had been able to get what he could not, but he was cognizant of his own limitations, and grateful that Strange had made the extra effort on his behalf.

After hanging up with Strange, he sat on his couch, rubbing his hands together, looking around at the spartan decor of his apartment, which was no decor at all. He was high from the beers and a little reckless from the high, and he felt as if his night was not done. He dragged his knapsack over to the couch, found Stella's phone number, and then saw Worldwide Wilson's number on Jennifer Marshall's sheet. He reached for his phone and dialed the number Jennifer had scribbled down.

It was a pager number, as he knew it would be. Quinn left his home phone number, waited for the tone that told him the number had been received, and cut the line.

He stared at the phone in his hand, looked around the room, stared at the phone some more, then dialed Stella's cell. She answered on the third ring.

'Hellooo. Officer Quinn?'

'You psychic or something?'

'Caller ID, duh.'

'I ought to get one of those 'number unknown' things.'

'Bet you're too cheap to pay for the service, Quinn.'

'It always comes back to money for you.'

'Well, yeah.'

'Why'd you do it, Stella?'

'You musta talked to Eve.'

'I had the pleasure.'

'She bugged on you, huh?'

'I guess I ought to ask you another way. Why'd you send me to her? You could've put me onto somebody who didn't know anything at all.'

'That's true. But I wanted you to come back to me. I wanted to see how bad you wanted Jennifer, baby doll. And I can see that you do. I mean, you didn't come looking to kick my ass or nothin' like that. You're callin' me like a gentleman and you don't sound angry. Are you angry at me, Quinn?'

'No,' he said, but it was a lie. 'Can you deliver Jennifer?'

'I'd deliver my mother for a price. Shit, I'd give you my mother for free, everything she done to me.'

'What's the price?'

'Five hundred will get you your girl.'

'How you gonna do that, Stella?'

'I got somethin' of hers. Somethin' I know she wants.'

'You stole from her?'

'Oh, *my* bad.'

'You're a piece of work.'

'Always good to have a little somethin' someone wants, information or merchandise, you know what I'm sayin'? Like I told you, it's rough out here.'

'What about Worldwide?'

Quinn heard the snap of a match and the burn of a cigarette.

'What about him?' said Stella.

'You're working for him. I don't think he'd take too kindly to you setting up one of his girls to get taken off the street.'

'Course not. Worldwide is a bad motherfucker, for real. But he ain't never gonna know, green eyes, 'less you thinkin' on tellin' him. You don't have to worry about me, 'cause I have done this before. Made some large money on it, too. Parents pay more than ex-cops, but I take whatever's there.'

'Always playing the middle.'

'When I can.'

'I won't worry about you, Stella. But I do want this girl. So I'll get you the money, with one condition. That you'll be right there with me when I make the snatch. Because I don't trust you, understand? I won't get burned by you again.'

'Fair enough.'

'When can we set it up?'

'Soon as you want, lover.'

'I need to get my hands on the money and a van. How's tomorrow night sound?'

'Sounds good.'

'I'll call you tomorrow, hear?'

Quinn hit 'end.' He phoned Sue Tracy and got her on her cell.

'Sue, it's Terry.' He cleared his throat. 'Quinn.'

'Hey, Terry.' There was a rasp to her voice, and he heard a long exhale before she said, 'What's up?'

'Listen, I got a strong line on Jennifer Marshall. But I'm gonna need a half a yard to buy the last piece of the puzzle.'

'I can get it.'

'Good. I think I might be able to make a grab tomorrow night.'

'We can do that.'

'We?'

'Well, one person generally can't do this right, Terry. I'll bring the van.'

'Okay, then. Okay.'

'Hold on a second.'

Quinn heard a rustling sound and waited for Tracy to get back on the line.

'Tell me where and when,' she said.

'You all right?'

'I'm in bed, Terry.'

'Oh.'

'I had to find paper and pen. Go ahead.'

'I don't know yet. What I mean is, I'll let you know.'

'You been out tonight?'

'Well, yeah.'

'You sound like you been drinking a little.'

'Just a little.'

'I bet you drink alone.'

'I don't like to,' said Quinn.

'Tell you what. We get this girl tomorrow, I'm gonna buy you a beer. You don't mind sitting next to a woman when you drink, do you?'

Quinn swallowed. 'No.'

'Good work, Quinn.'

Quinn sat there for a while thinking of the velvet sandpaper in Sue Tracy's voice, the sound of her long exhale, the way his stomach had kind of flipped when she'd said 'I'm in bed.' How 'Good work, Quinn' had sounded like 'Fuck me, Terry' to him. Well, he was just a man, as stupid as any other. He looked down, saw his hand resting on the crotch of his jeans, and had to grin. He was too tired to jerk off, so he went to bed.

Strange sat on the edge of the bed, Janine's strong thighs over his. She moved slowly up and down on his manhood, gyrating on the upstroke, that thing she did that made him feel twenty-one all over again. One of his hands grasped her ass and the other was flat on the sheets, and he pushed off, burying himself all the way inside her.

'You going for my backbone, sugar?'

'A man can try.'

She gave him her hips. 'Shit, yeah.'

'C'mon, baby.'

'I am on the way.'

She kissed him deep, her eyes wide and alive. She kept them open when they kissed. He liked that.

Strange licked and sucked at one of her dark nipples, and Janine laughed low. Quiet Storm was coming from the clock radio by the bed, playing Dorothy Moore. Strange had turned it up before undressing her, so that Lionel, in the next room over, could not hear them making love.

He shot off and kept himself in motion. She was almost soundless when she came, just a short gasp. Strange liked that, too.

Later, he stood in his briefs by the bedroom window, looking through the blinds down to the street. Greco had nosed his way through the door and was sleeping on a throw rug, his muzzle resting between his paws.

'Come to bed, Derek.'

He turned around and admired Janine, her form all woman beneath the blanket on the bed.

'I'm just wondering what's goin' on out there. All those kids, still walking around.'

'You're done working for today. Come to bed.'

He slid under the sheets and rested his thigh against hers.

'You better go to sleep,' said Janine. 'You know how you get cranky when you don't get enough.'

'Oh, I *got* enough.'

'Stop it.'

'Look, it's just, at the end of the day, all these things go racing through my mind.'

'Like?'

'Thinkin' on you, you want the truth. How I don't tell you enough what a good job you do. And what you mean to me.'

Janine ran her fingers through the short wiry hairs on Strange's chest. 'Thank you, Derek.'

'I mean it.'

'Go ahead.'

'What?'

'Usually, when you start going that way with me, it means you need to unload something off your mind. So what is it?'

'Ain't nothin' like that,' said Strange.

'Is it Terry?'

'Well, he's still a little rough around the edges. But he's all right.'

'Is it the job you're doing for George Hastings?'

'Uh-uh. I'm nearly done with that.'

'I'm almost done on my end with it, too,' said Janine. 'Got one more thing to check up on. You didn't find anything, did you?'

'No,' said Strange, and reached over to the nightstand and turned off the lamp.

He wasn't sure why he had lied to her. So Calhoun Tucker was a player, so what? But something about snitching on a guy about that to a woman didn't sit right with most men. It was a kind of betrayal, in an odd way. One betrayal too many in the day for Strange.

Quinn was disoriented from sleep when the phone rang by his bed. He reached over and picked up the receiver.

'Hello?'

'You called?' The voice was smooth and baritone. There was music playing in the background against the sound of a car's engine.

'Who is this?'

'Who's *this*? You called *me*. But you, uh, declined to leave your name.'

Quinn got up on one elbow. 'I'm looking for a girl.'

'You done called the right number then, slick. How'd you get it, by the way?'

'I'm looking for one girl in particular,' said Quinn. 'Girl named Jennifer, I think.'

'You think?'

'It's Jennifer.'

'Asked you how you got my number.'

'Why is that important?'

'Let's just say I like to know if my marketing dollars are well spent. You know, like, do I re-up with the Yellow Pages or do I go back heavy on those full-page ads in the *Washington Post*?'

The man on the other end of the line laughed then. It was a cut-you-in-the-alley kind of laugh, and the sound of it made Quinn's blood tick. His hand tightened on the receiver. He looked down at some CDs stacked carelessly on the floor. An old Steve Earle was atop the stack.

'A friend of mine, guy named Steve, recommended I call you. Said you could hook me up.'

'Oh, I can hook you up, all right. Your name is?'

'Earle.'

'Okay, Earle. But I'm a little curious; it's in my nature, if you don't mind. White boy like you, usually when I get a request from one, it's for some black pussy, understand what I'm sayin'? And Jennifer, it's the same girl we both thinkin' of, she's white all the way.'

'That's what I want. She's young, too, isn't she?'

'Oh, Jennifer's young, all right. They call her Schoolgirl, matter of fact. She'll be good to you, too. But I guess your boy Steve told you that.'

'He did.'

'Sure he did. Satisfied customer's the very best form of advertising. Steve, he mention specifics?'

'Just that he had a good time. That she'll do things.'

'Any goddamn thing you want. You can bring your friends and roll some videos, too. Have your own private record of the occasion. Fuck her mouth or her pussy. Ass-fuck her, you got a mind to. Course, you gonna pay for all that.'

'Look, I'm talkin' about a private party. You deliver her and you name the price. I got money.'

'You're gonna need it, Earle. 'Cause this is some fresh turn-out here. And I can't be givin' pussy this new away.'

Quinn kicked off his top sheet, swung his legs over the bed, and sat up. He reached for the pencil and pad he kept on the nightstand. Maybe he could make this happen without Stella. He didn't need her now that he had gotten through to Wilson.

'How do I hook it up?' said Quinn.

'Well, let's see. Where'd your boy Steve have his party?'

'He didn't say.'

'Oh, come on, Earle, you can tell me. See, I need to know, to satisfy that curiosity I was tellin' you about. Steve must have bragged on it. Man don't tell another man ass stories without goin' into the details.'

'It was out on New York Avenue,' said Quinn, feeling the sweat break upon his forehead. 'I think it was one of those motels they got out there on the way out of town.'

'You think?'

'It *was.*'

The man on the other end of the line laughed heartily. It ended with a chuckle, long and low.

'What's so funny?' said Quinn.

'Just that, you know, you done gone and fucked up right there. You talked too much, see? 'Cause I don't use those trick pads over on New York Avenue. Never have.'

'What difference does it make? I said I thought it was there—'

'You said it *was.* And I did like the way you said it, Earle. It *was.* So sure of yourself. So tough. So *much* like the rough and tough man you must be. Bet you got your little chest all puffed up, right about now. Got your fists balled up, too? So easy to be tough when you're speaking on the phone. Isn't it? *Earle.*'

His voice was singsong and mocking. Quinn unclenched his jaw and spoke through barely parted lips.

'My name's Terry Quinn.'

'Oh, I got your phone number now, so it would have been easy to get your name right quick. But thanks for providin' it for me; I'll remember it for sure. What're you, Vice, sumshit like that? You must be new, 'cause I got the patrol boys on my strip taken care of.'

'I'm not a cop.'

'Don't matter to me what you are, anyway. You don't mean nothin' more to me than some dog shit on my shoe. Look here, I better be goin'. I'd put your girl on the line, but she's suckin' a dick right now, makin' me some money.'

'Wilson—'

'So long, white boy. Maybe we'll meet someday.'

'We will,' said Quinn. But the line was already dead as the words came from his mouth.

So now Wilson had his name and number. It would be easy for him to get Quinn's address. In his mind, Quinn shrugged. When he was a cop, the threat that he'd be tracked down to his place of residence had been made many times. He'd lost count of those threats long ago.

Quinn turned off the nightstand lamp. He stood and went to the bedroom window. His hands were shaking at his sides. It wasn't fear.

Tomorrow night the girl would be his.

12

On Wednesday morning, Garfield Potter had Carlton Little and Charles White drop him at the Union Station parking garage, where he spotted a car he liked, a police-package, white-over-blue '89 Plymouth Grand Fury with a 318 engine and a four-barrel carb. Potter used a bar to break into the vehicle and a long-handled flat-head to pop out the ignition. He hot-wired the Plymouth and rolled down to the exit. Potter wore a skully and shades so that the booth camera could record very little of his face. As he didn't have a ticket, he paid the full-penalty parking fee and drove out of the garage.

Potter followed Little and White out to Prince George's County, pulling up behind them on a gravel shoulder running alongside a football field in Largo. He waited for his boys to wipe the prints out of the interior and off the exterior handles of the beige Caprice, as he had instructed them to do, and when they joined him inside the Fury he turned the car back toward D.C.

Potter and Little both had priors: possession, intent to distribute, and aggravated-assault beefs. Also, there had been one sodomy-rape charge on Potter, dropped when the victim would not testify. Eventually, they knew, some judge would have to give them time. Like many of his peers, Potter often bragged on the fact that violent death or a jail cell awaited him. But he didn't want to go down on something as mundane as grand theft. A charge like that was a bitch charge, and it bought you no respect inside the walls. So he was always careful to cover his tracks when he got rid of one of his stolen cars.

Old police cars, or those outfitted for police specifications, were the vehicle of choice for many young men in and around D.C. Potter heard you could buy them cheap off lots in Virginia, in places like Manassas and Nokesville, wherever that was. But he didn't like to cross over into Virginia for any reason, and anyway, lately he hadn't been buying shit. You could steal a car easily in the District, and if you rotated it out, say, once a week, you'd never get caught. Well, he hadn't been caught at it yet.

Potter looked at it like this: what you had to do was, you had to target a car owned by a young brother who lived in the city or near the PG County line. Some young brothers got their shit stole, they didn't even report it to the police, on account of they knew damn near nothing would come of it anyway, and there was also this unwritten thing about not talking with the MPD. Many of them didn't carry insurance either, so there wasn't no money reason to report it. Sure, the ones got their cars took kept their ears open and their eyes out for the thief, looking to get some street justice if they could. But so far, Potter, Little, and White had escaped that as well.

Potter floored the gas as he got on the entrance ramp to the Beltway.

'Shit moves,' said Potter.

'Better than that hooptie we done had, D,' said Little.

'Gonna buy us a Lex soon, though. I'm fixin' to own me a nice whip.'

'When?' said Little.

'Soon.'

Charles White sat in the backseat, letting the wind from the open window hit his face. He was listening to that song 'Bounce with Me,' done by that singer they called Lil' Bow Wow, who dressed like a gangster but wasn't nothin' much more than a kid. White was still up there from the hydro him and Carlton had smoked on the way out to Largo, and the song sounded good. He was into music; it was, like, his hobby. Sometimes he made tapes of himself over beats. Maybe someday he'd take some of the money they were making and go into a studio, lay somethin' down for real. But he figured that was for other people to do, like Bow Wow, had someone showin' him how to make it and all that. Someone to guide him, like.

In his true mind Charles White knew that he was stuck with what he had right here. The only family he had now, except for his grandmother, was the boys he'd come up with. Garfield and Carlton, before both of them turned cold and all the way hard, like they were now.

White's hand instinctively dropped to his side, but there was nothing there. He still thought of Trooper all the time. He missed him. He wished Trooper were sitting warm beside him on the backseat.

Potter looked in the rearview at White, breathing through his mouth, looking out the window with the wind beatin' on him, slumped in the backseat. Dumb-ass motherfucker, probably still stressin' over that stupid dog. Potter thought of White as a dog, too, in a way, a thing that just kind of followed him and Carlton around.

He was stuck with White. White still acted and thought like a kid sometimes. He hadn't changed much since the three of them had been tiny, growing up in the Waterfront Gardens, the Section Eight housing units down off M Street by the Southeast/Southwest line. Wasn't no 'waterfront' about it, though sometimes the seagulls did drop in from Buzzards Point and pick at the trash. Some government type actually did have the nerve to name that shit hole a Garden, too. One of those jokes you couldn't even laugh at. Not that Potter was crying about it or nothin' like that. If it wasn't for what he didn't have, and he never did have one good thing, he wouldn't have the ambition and drive he had today.

He could have used a father, he supposed, someone to throw a football to or sumshit like that. His mother didn't even have the strength to lift a ball, eighty-eight pounds of no-ass crackhead like she was, at the end.

He wasn't gonna cry about that either. Family and all that bullshit, it meant nothing to him, and it didn't get you anything when you counted the chips up at the end of the day. It was like them books his teachers was always tellin' him to read before they gave up on his ass, back about the fifth grade. He couldn't hardly read, and still he had a shoebox full of cash money in the closet at his place, clothes, cars, bitches, *everything*. So what was the point of books, or some piece of paper, said you went to school?

He had a good business going now. Him and Carlton, he guessed he had to call Charles a partner, too, they had some runners down on Georgia, below Harvard Street, and they sold the *shit* out of some dime bags of marijuana on that corner there. Marijuana, the good shit that was goin' around, the stuff grown hydroponic, was the way to go. In D.C., didn't matter whether you were in possession of a dime bag or ten pounds, it wasn't nothin' but a misdemeanor. You did go to court, most of the time it was no-papered, everyone in the life knew that. Black juries didn't want to send a young black man into the deadly prison system for some innocent charge like holding a little marijuana. Innocent, *shit*, Potter had to laugh at that. Young brothers killed one another over chronic just as dead as they did over crack and heroin. The people in charge would change the laws, make them tougher again when they figured all this out, but until then, hydro was the game.

So Potter had this business and he liked to keep it small. He didn't call him and his boys a 'crew' or a 'mob' or nothin' like that. You got into turf beefs and eyeball beefs that way; shit just got too complex. Potter was basically into having fun: stealing cars, taking off dumb motherfuckers who could get took, robbing crap games, shit like that. But he never fucked with those he knew to be hooked into crews, or their kin. Never that he knew, anyway. Only fuck with the weak, those who had no strength in numbers, that was his plan. He figured he hadn't made any big mistakes yet. He was still alive.

'Where we goin'?' said Little.

'Dime the rest of that key out and get it out to our troops,' said Potter. 'Maybe tonight we'll slide by Roosevelt, see if our boy Wilder is hangin' with his nephew on that football field.'

'You still on that?'

'Told you I wouldn't forget.'

They went back to their place, a row house they rented month-to-month on Warder Street in Park View, and dimed out the shit. They smoked a couple of Phillies while they worked. White went out for a bag of McDonald's, and when he returned there were a couple of young local girls up in the crib who'd dropped by. The new Too Short was up loud, and everyone was on the get-high and drinking gin and grapefruit. This pretty young thing, Brianna, was with Little, and they were laughing and then just gone, up in Carlton's room. Potter took the other one, couldn't have been more than thirteen, away with him next, kind of pulling on the sleeve of her Tweety Bird shirt. To White she didn't look like she wanted to go. A little while later White heard the bedsprings from back in Potter's room against the crying of that girl. White turned up the stereo so he didn't have to hear it, but he could still hear it deep in his head. So he went outside and sat on the stoop, where he rubbed at his temples and tried to remember if there had ever been a time in his life when he felt right.

Potter and the rest drove down to Harvard Street and found his main boy, kid named Juwan, sitting on a trash can. Juwan was one of those, like Gary Coleman, had a man's head on a boy's body. They took Juwan back to where the fence ran along the McMillan Reservoir. Juwan, sitting next to White in the backseat, passed a large Ziplock bag full of money, which he had taken from his knapsack, up to Little. Little took the money out, separated some for Juwan, and filled the Ziplock with dimed-out bags of marijuana. Juwan slipped the package back into his knapsack.

'Everything all right, little man?' said Potter.

'It's good, D. One thing, though. You know William, that boy got one leg shorter than the other? The po-lice took him in last night.

William be like, *thick* and shit. I done told him, Don't be carryin' when you steerin', you know what I'm sayin'? But he don't listen. I know he'll be out today, but—'

'Say what's on your mind.'

'Was gonna ask you, I got this cousin, just moved up from Southeast? He was lookin' to get put on, yo.'

'Put him on then, Jew. What I been tellin' you, man? Someone don't work out, go ahead and find someone else. Always gonna be kids out there wanna get in.'

They dropped Juwan back on Harvard and Georgia. Then Potter stopped at a market and bought a few forties of malt. They drove around some more, drinking the malt and getting smoked up. Little found a cassette tape, a Northeast Groovers PA mix that had been left in the glove box by the Plymouth's owner, and he slipped it in the deck.

'Shits ain't got no bass,' said White from the backseat.

Potter ignored White and turned up the volume. At a stoplight he stared down some young boy in a rice burner who he thought had been staring at him. The young boy looked away.

'Where we goin'?' said Little.

'Swing on up to Roosevelt,' said Potter.

'I don't want to be drivin' around all night lookin' for some ghost.'

'You got somethin' better to do?'

'Brianna,' said Little. 'I might just meet her again tonight, she can get out her mother's house. I tossed the *shit* out of that bitch today, boy.'

'She ain't look too satisfied to me.'

'Bull*shit*.'

'That's too much girl for you, man.'

'Shit, she was singin', 'Say my name, say my name' this afternoon. You saw her smilin' when she walked out the crib. Not like that girl you was fuckin', had tears on her face when she left.'

'I gave her the anaconda, she couldn't help but cry. Anyway, your girl Brianna wasn't smilin', she was *laughin'*.'

'At what?'

'At that itty-bitty thing you got between your legs.'

'Shit, I'm thick as a can of tuna fish down there, man.'

Potter side-glanced Little. '*Long* as one, too.'

They drove up to Roosevelt High and parked on Iowa. Potter walked down the driveway entrance to the lot, where several cars were parked, and went to the fence bordering the stadium. Kids in football uniforms were doing calisthenics on the field. Their call-and-response chant echoed up to the parking lot.

'*How y'all feel?*'

'*Fired up!*'

Potter didn't see Lorenze Wilder in the group of parents and relatives sitting in the stands. A bunch of men, looked like coaches, stood around on the field. One of them he recognized as the older dude with the gray in his natural, had been bold enough to study him and Little that time before. Potter spit on the ground and walked back to the car. He got behind the wheel of the Plymouth, his face gone hard.

They went back to their place. They got their heads up and drank some more and watched UPN and something on the WB. Little tried to sweet-talk Brianna out again, but her mother got on the telephone line and told him she was in for the night. Potter suggested they go out again, and Little agreed. White didn't want to, but he got up off the couch. Potter slipped his .357 into his waistband and put a Hilfiger shirt on, tails out, over his sleeveless T. He fitted his skully back on his head. White slipped on a bright orange Nautica pullover, his favorite, and followed Potter and Little out to the street.

They drove around, up and down Georgia. They checked on the troops. Potter drank another forty, and his face got more humorless and he drove from a lower position in the seat. It had been a long day of getting high and doing nothing, and it felt late to White. Anyway, it was full dark. Potter rolled the Plymouth into the Park Morton complex, driving real slow. Some kids were out, sitting like they always did on the entrance wall.

'Lorenze Wilder's sister live here,' said Potter.

Little said nothing. Like White, he was tired, and right about now would rather have been in front of the television, or in bed. He didn't like being out with Garfield when he'd been drinkin', had all that liquid courage inside him. Truth was, Little was kinda drunk, too.

Potter slowed the car. A lanky young man was walking across the narrow street, onto a plot of dirt that passed for a playground. He wore khaki pants, a pressed white T-shirt, and wheat-colored Timberland boots.

'Ask him he knows her,' said Potter.

'Yo,' said Little out the window. They were alongside the young man now. He was still walking, and the Plymouth was keeping pace.

'What?' said the young man, who looked at them briefly, for just the right amount of respect time, but kept his step.

'You know a woman name of Wilder lives here?' said Little. 'Got a little boy, kid plays football, sumshit like that. I got this friend owes her money, he asked me to swing by and tell her he'd be payin' it back to 'er next week.'

The young man looked at them again, scanned the front and backseat, his sight staying on the odd-looking young man in the bright orange pullover for what he feared might be a moment too long, then cut his eyes. 'I ain't know no one around here, no lie. I just moved up *in* here, like, last week.'

'Aiight then.'

'Aiight,' said the young man, moving off into the playground, walking with his shoulders squared, his head up, turning a corner and disappearing into the night.

'Maybe I ought to talk to that boy my own self,' said Potter, the lids of his eyes heavy, half shut.

'He said he didn't know, D,' said Little. 'Let's just let this shit rest for tonight.'

Potter kept the Plymouth cruising slow. He went around a kind of long bend that took him to the other side of the housing complex. They could see a group of people back in a stairwell lit pale yellow. Potter braked, steered the Plymouth up on the dirt, and cut the engine.

Potter said, 'C'mon.'

They got out of the car and followed him across the dirt to the stairwell entrance. There were three men crouched down there and a pink-eyed woman leaning against a cinder-block wall. In one hand the woman held both a cigarette and a bottle wrapped in a paper bag. Smoke hung in the yellow light.

Older cats, all of 'em, thought Potter. Didn't know nobody, didn't have nobody gave a fuck about 'em.

The dice-playing men looked up briefly as Potter approached, Little and White behind him. The oldest of the players, vandyked, wearing a black shirt with thin white stripes and a black Kangol cap, eyed Potter up and down, then rolled dice against the wall. The dice came up sixes. There was some talk about the boxcar roll, and money changed hands. Money was spread out on the concrete.

'Y'all want in,' said the roller, staring down the lane to the wall, shaking the dice in his hand, 'you're gonna have to wait.'

Potter didn't like that the man didn't look him in the eye when he spoke.

'That your woman?' said Potter, staring at the lady leaning on the wall. She took his stare, even as Potter smiled and licked his lips.

The dice man didn't answer. He made his roll.

'Asked you if that was your woman.'

'And I told you to wait,' said the man.

The other men laughed. One of them reached into his breast pocket and extracted a cigarette. None of them looked at Potter.

'Get up,' said Potter. 'Stand your tired ass up and face me.'

The dice man sighed some, then stood up. He grunted and rubbed at one knee as he did. He was old. But he was bigger than Potter expected, both in the shoulders and in height. He had a half foot on Potter if he had an inch. Now his eyes were twinkling.

'You got somethin' you want to say to me?'

Potter reached under his shirttail and drew the Colt. He held it at his hip, the muzzle on the midsection of the man. The man's eyes were calm; they didn't even flare.

'Give it up,' said Potter. 'All the cash.'

'Shit,' said the man, drawing it out slow, and he smiled.

'I'm gonna take your money,' said Potter. 'You want, I'll dead you to your woman, too.'

'Son?' said the man. 'I done had guns pointed at me, by real men, while I was layin' in rice paddies and mud, for two solid years. And here I am standin' before you. Do I look like I'm worried about that snub-nose you got in your hand?'

'This here?' Potter looked at the gun as if it had just showed up in his hand. 'Old-time, I wasn't gonna *shoot* you with it.'

Potter swung the barrel so quickly that it lost its shape in the light. He slashed it across the brow of the man, the blow knocking the cap off his head. The man's hand went to his face, blood seeping through his fingers immediately, and he stumbled back against the wall. Potter flipped the gun in the air and caught it on the half turn, so that he held it now by the barrel. He moved forward, ignoring the other men who had stood suddenly and backed away, and smashed the butt into the man's cheekbone. He hit him in the nose the same way, blood dotting the cinder blocks as the man's head whipped to the side. Potter laughed against the woman's screams. He reared back to beat the man again and felt someone grab his arm. Looking over his shoulder with wild eyes, he saw that it was Charles White who held him there.

'Man, *get* your got-damn hands off me, man!' yelled Potter.

'Let's just take the money,' said Little, moving into the light. 'You about to kill a motherfucker, boy.'

'Get the money, then,' said Potter. He smiled and spit on the man lying bloodied before him. 'You ain't standin' now, *are* you, Old-time?' Potter barked a laugh and raised his voice in elation. 'Can't nobody in this city fuck with Garfield Potter?'

Little and White gathered the cash up off the concrete. They backed up into the grassy area, turned, and walked quickly to the car. No one followed them or shouted for help.

Little counted the cash as they drove out of the complex. White looked in the rearview. A grin had broken, and was frozen, on Garfield Potter's face.

Lamar Williams said good night to his mother, a thirty-two-year-old woman with the face and body of a forty-year-old, who was leaning against the stove in their galley-sized kitchen, smoking a cigarette.

'Where you been at, Mar?'

'Practice with Mr Derek. I was watchin' wrestlin' with that kid Joe Wilder after that, over at his mother's.'

'I'm gonna need you in tomorrow night. I got plans.'

'Aiight.'

Lamar went down a hall and pushed open the door to his baby sister's room. She was lying atop her bed, stretched out in those pj's of hers, the ones had little roses printed on them. On her feet were those furry gold slippers she wouldn't take off, with Winnie the Pooh's head on the front. What was she now, almost four? Lamar covered her with a sheet.

He went back to his room, turned on his radio, sat on the edge of his bed, and listened to DJ Flexx talkin' to some young girl who'd called in with some shout-outs for her friends. Then Flexx played that new Wyclef Jean joint that Lamar liked, the one with Mary J., where they was talkin' about 'Someone please call 911.' That one was tight. It made him feel better, to hear that pretty song.

Lamar lay back on the bed. He could still feel his heart beating hard beneath his white T-shirt. He'd done right, not giving up anything to those boys who'd tried to sweat him from the open windows of that car, because whatever they wanted with Joe Wilder's mother, it was no good. But it was hard to keep doing right. Hard to have to walk a certain way, talk a certain way, keep up that shell all the time out here, when sometimes all you wanted to do was be young and have fun. Relax.

Lamar was tired. He rested the palm of his hand over his eyes and tried to make himself breathe slow.

13

Strange spent Wednesday morning clearing off his desk, his noontime testifying for a Fifth Streeter down in District Court, and his afternoon finishing his background check on Calhoun Tucker. He hit a couple of bars on U Street and then drove over to a club on 12th, near the FBI building, where George Hastings had said that Tucker had done some promotions.

All he spoke to that day told him that Tucker was an upstanding young businessman, tough when he had to be but fair and with a good reputation. At the 12th Street club, the bartender, a pretty, dark-skinned woman setting up her station, said that Tucker was 'a good guy,' adding that he did have 'a problem with the ladies, though.'

'What kind of problem?' said Strange.

'Being a man, you probably won't think of it as one.'

'Try me out.'

'Calhoun, he can't just be satisfied with one woman. He's a player, serial style. It's cool for a young man to be that way, but he's the type, he's gonna be a player his whole life, you understand what I'm sayin'? After a while you gotta check yourself with that, 'cause you are bound to hurt people in the end.'

'Did he hurt you?'

The bartender stopped slicing limes, pointing her short knife at Strange. 'It's my business if he did.'

Strange placed his card on the bar. 'You think of anything else you want to tell me about him, you let me know.'

Strange went back to his place, hit the heavy bag in his basement, showered, fed Greco, and got on the Internet, reading the comments on a stock chat room while he listened to the *Duck, You Sucker* soundtrack he had recently purchased as an import.

'See you later, good boy,' said Strange, patting Greco on the head before he headed out the door. 'Gotta get over to Roosevelt.'

They ran the team hard that night, as their game was coming up and the night-before practice would be light. The kids looked good. They weren't making many mistakes, and they had their wind. The Midgets were in numbers on one side of the field with Lydell Blue, Dennis Arrington, and Lamar Williams, and the Pee Wees occupied the other. Near dark, after the drills, Strange called the Pee Wees in and told them it was time to run some plays. Strange took the offense aside as Quinn gathered the defensive unit.

The offensive huddle broke and went to the line. Dante Morris took the snap from Prince on the second 'go' and handed off to Rico, who hit the five-hole off a Joe Wilder block, broke free from a one-handed tackle attempt, and was finally taken down twenty yards down the field.

Quinn took the kid who had missed the tackle aside. 'None of this one-handed-tackle stuff. You can't just put your arm out and say, Please, God, let him fall down. It doesn't work that way, you hear me?'

'Yes.'

'Hit him in the stomach. Wrap him up and lock your hands.'

The kid nodded. Quinn tapped him on the helmet with his palm, and the kid trotted back to the defensive huddle.

Joe Wilder slowed down as he passed Strange on the way to the offensive huddle. 'Forty-four Belly, Coach Derek?'

'Run it,' said Strange. 'And nice block there, Joe.'

Wilder ran the play into Dante Morris, who called it on one. It was a goal-line play, a simple flanker run direct through the four-hole. Wilder executed it perfectly and took the ball into the end zone. He did the dirty bird for his teammates and jogged back to Strange, a spring in his step.

'I be doin' that on FedEx Field someday, Coach Derek.'

'It's I *will* be doing that,' said Strange, who then smiled, thinking, I believe you will.

After practice, Strange talked with Blue awhile, then caught Quinn getting into his Chevelle.

'Where you off to so fast, Terry?'

'Got plans tonight.'

'A woman?'

'Yeah.'

'Thought you were gonna try and close that Jennifer Marshall thing tonight.'

'I am,' said Quinn. 'I'll let you know how it pans out.'

Prince, Lamar, and Joe Wilder were standing by Strange's Brougham. He put his football file into the trunk, let them in the car, and drove off the school grounds.

Strange turned up Prince's street, not far from the football field.

'There go my houth right there,' said Prince.

'I know it,' said Strange, stopping the car. 'Get in there straight away, boy, don't make no detours. Those boys on that corner over there, they try to crack on you, you ignore 'em, hear?'

Prince nodded and got out of the car. He went quickly up the steps to his place, where the light on the porch had been left on.

As they drove south on Georgia, Joe Wilder held two action figures in his hand. He was making collision sounds as he pushed their rubber heads together like warring rams.

'I thought those two was friends,' said Lamar, sitting beside Wilder.

'Uh-uh, man, Triple H be the Rock's *enemy*. H is married to the commissioner's daughter.' Joe Wilder looked up at Lamar. 'Will you come inside and watch it with me tonight?'

'Okay,' said Lamar. 'I'll watch it with you some.'

After Strange dropped them off, he popped a tape into the dash, a Stevie Wonder mix Janine had made him. Kids sat on the wall and dead-eyed him as he passed through the exit to the housing complex, Stevie singing 'Heaven Is 10 Zillion Light Years Away' from the deck. Strange couldn't help thinking how beautiful the song was. Thinking, too, how for those who'd been born in the wrong place through no fault of their own, how sad that it was true.

Sue Tracy picked up Terry Quinn at his apartment somewhere past ten o'clock that night. She stood in the doorway of his place while he shook himself into a waist-length black leather jacket over a white T-shirt. As he did this he blocked her way, his body language telling her to come no further. She watched him fumble his badge case into one jacket pocket and his cell into the other. Clearly he was anxious to slip out before she had a chance to get a good look at his crib. But Tracy had taken in enough to know that there was nothing much to see.

They walked out of the squat, three-story brick building, toward an old gray Econoline van parked on Sligo Avenue.

'Hey, Mark,' said Terry to a mixed-race teenage boy standing with a group of boys his age outside a beer-and-cigarette market on the corner.

'Wha'sup,' said the boy, not really looking at Quinn, muttering the greeting in a grudging, dutiful way.

Tracy stopped to light a cigarette. She dropped the spent match to the ground and exhaled smoke out the side of her mouth. 'Kid really likes you, Terry.'

'He does like me. It's just, you know, the code. He can't act like we're friends when he's hanging with his boys, you know what I'm sayin'? I have this gym set up in the basement of the building; I let some of these neighborhood guys work out with me, long as they show me and the equipment respect.'

They stood by the van, Tracy finishing her cigarette before getting in, Quinn letting her without comment.

'And you coach a football team, too.'

'I kinda help out, is all.'

'You're not so tough, Terry.'

'It's a way to kill time.'

'Sure.' Tracy ground out her cigarette. 'Where to first?'

'We'll pick up Stella. I got it all set up.'

The van dated back to the 1970s. It had front and rear bench seats and little else. The three-speed manual shift was a branch coming off the trunk of the steering wheel. A tape deck had been mounted where the AM radio had been, its faceplate loose, its wires exposed and swinging below the dash.

'I bet you only fly first class, too,' said Quinn.

'It was a donation,' said Tracy.

She wore a black nylon jacket over a black button-down blouse tucked into slate gray utilitarian slacks. She found a gray Scunci in her jacket pocket, put it in her mouth while she gathered her hair behind her, and formed a ponytail. The Scunci picked up the gray of the slacks. She pulled a pair of eyeglasses with black rectangular frames from the sun visor and slipped them on her face.

'Cool.'

'This van? Bet there's a bong around here somewhere, too, if you're interested.'

'I was talking about your glasses.'

'They'll keep us from getting killed. My night vision is for shit.'

They drove down into Northwest, cutting into Rock Creek Park at 16th and Sherrill and heading south. Tracy slipped a Mazzy Star compilation tape into the deck. Chicks and their chick music, thought Quinn, but this was guitar driven and pretty nice.

They didn't talk much on the ride into town. It wasn't uncomfortable. Quinn didn't feel like he did around most women, like he had to explain who he was, why he'd chosen the path he'd taken, the one that had put him on the way to becoming a cop. The singer's voice, breathy but unforced, was relaxing him, and arousing him, too. He looked over at Tracy, at the tendons in her neck, the elegant cut of her jaw as it neared her ear.

'What?' said Tracy.

'Nothing.'

'You're staring at me again, Terry.'

'Sorry,' said Quinn. 'I was just thinking.'

After a while they came up out of the park. Stella emerged from the shadows of a church at 23rd and P as they pulled the van along the curb.

'That her?'

'Yeah.'

'She looks fifteen.'

'Cobras live to be fifteen, too,' said Quinn.

'They do?'

'I'm making a point.'

'The back doors are open,' said Tracy. 'Tell her to get in there.'

Quinn rolled down his window as Stella reached the van. She wore black leather pants and a white poplin shirt, with a black bag shaped like a football slung over her shoulder. Her eyeglasses sat crooked on her face.

'You like?' said Stella, looking down at her pants. Her eyes were magnified comically behind the lenses of her glasses. 'I wore 'em for you, Officer Quinn. They're pleather, but that's okay. I get paid tonight, I'm gonna buy me a pair of leather ones on the for-real side.'

'You look nice,' said Quinn.

'What color should I get? The black or the brown?'

'The back door's open. Let's go.'

They drove east. Quinn introduced Stella to Sue Tracy. Stella was cool to her questions. She only became animated when responding to Quinn. Clearly she was eager for his attention. It was plain to Tracy that Stella had a crush on Quinn, or it was a daddy thing, but he was ignoring it. More likely, as with many men, the obvious had eluded him.

On 16th they saw some girls working the stroll, a stretch of sidewalk off the hotel strip south of Scott Circle.

'Around here?' said Tracy.

'Those aren't World's,' said Stella.

'Where, then?' said Quinn.

'Keep goin',' said Stella. 'He ain't into that visiting-businessmen trade. They talk too much, take too much time. Worldwide's girls walk between the circles. The Logan-and-Thomas action, y'know what I'm sayin'?'

Quinn knew. 'That's old-school turf. I remember that from when *I* was a teenager.'

Tracy shot him a look from across the seat.

'Strictly locals,' said Stella. 'Husbands whose wives won't blow 'em, birthday boys lookin' to get their cherry broke, barracks boys, like that. World's got some rooms nearby.'

'We're gonna try and take her in Wilson's trick-house?' said Quinn. 'Why?'

'Because she don't trust me,' said Stella. 'She won't meet me anywhere else.'

Tracy steered the van around Thomas Circle.

'North now,' said Stella, 'and make a right off Fourteenth at the next block.'

The landscape changed from ghost town–downtown to living urban night as soon as they drove onto the north side of the circle. Small storefronts, occupying the first floors of structures built originally as residential row houses, low-rised the strip. The commercial picture was changing, new theater venues, cafés, and bars cropping up with regularity. In fact, it had been 'changing' for many years. White gentrifiers tried to close down the family-run markets, utilizing obscure laws like the one forbidding beer and wine sales within a certain proximity to churches. The crusading gentrifiers cited the loiterers on the sidewalks, the kinds of unsavory clientele those types of businesses attracted. What they really wanted was for their underclass dark-skinned neighbors to go away. But they wouldn't go away. The former Section Eights were up the street, and so were families who had lived here for generations. It was their neighborhood. It was a small detail that the gentrifiers never tried to understand.

There weren't any hookers walking the 14th strip. But as they turned right and drove a block east, Quinn could see cars double-parked ahead wearing Maryland and Virginia plates, their flashers on, girls leaning into their driver's-side windows.

'Pull over,' said Stella.

Tracy curbed the van and cut the engine. Quinn studied the street.

A half block up, a couple of working girls, one black and one white, were lighting smokes, standing on the sidewalk outside a row house. One of them, the young white girl with big hair, wearing white mid-thigh fishnets and garters below a tight white skirt, walked up the steps of the row house and through the front door. A portly black man in an ill-fitting suit got out of his car, a late-model Buick, and went into the same house shortly thereafter.

'These all Wilson's?' said Quinn.

'Not all,' said Stella. 'You got a few independents out here, out-of-pocket hos. Long as they don't look him in the eye, disrespect him like that, then they gonna be all right. But those are World's trick-pads over there. All his. He rents out the top two floors, got, like, six rooms.'

'What about the car action?'

'That's okay for a quick suck. World gets money for the room, too, so he tells his ladies, Make sure you take 'em upstairs. Anyway, you don't want to be fuckin' a man in a car down here. Even the pocket cops, they see that, they got to take you in. This ain't the Bronx.'

'That where you come from, Stella?' said Tracy.

'I'm from nowhere, lady.'

'We waitin' on Jennifer?' said Quinn.

'You already saw her,' said Stella. 'She was that white girl with the white stockings, went inside.'

'It didn't look like her,' said Quinn.

'What, you think she'd still be wearing her yearbook clothes?' Stella laughed joylessly, an older woman's laugh that chilled Quinn. 'She ain't no teenager now. She ain't nothin' but a ho.'

'We could have grabbed her off the street.'

'We got to do this my way. I told you I'd come along, but I don't want nobody spottin' me, hear?'

'Keep talking.'

'I called Jennifer up. Soon after I met her, I boosted her Walkman and a few CDs she had. She never went anywhere without her sounds. I told her when I called her, I found her shit in some other girl's bag and I was lookin' to get it back to her.'

'Where?'

'Told her I'd meet her at eleven-thirty, up in three-C. That's the third-floor room nearest the back of the house. There's a fire escape there, goes down to the alley. The window leads out to the fire escape, one of those big windows, goes up and down—'

'A sash,' said Quinn.

'Whatever. World always tells the girls, leave that window open, hear, case you need to get out quick.'

Quinn checked his watch: close to eleven by his time.

'Think I'll drop in on her a little early,' said Quinn.

'I'm coming with you,' said Tracy.

'Who's gonna drive the van?' said Quinn, head-motioning over his shoulder. 'Her?'

Tracy looked out her window for a moment, then at Quinn. She reached back and pulled her leather briefcase from under the back bench. Her hand went into the briefcase and came out with a pair of Motorola FRS radios. She handed one to Quinn.

'Walkie-talkies?'

'That's right.'

'These come with a decoder ring, too?'

'Quit fuckin' around, Terry. You keep the power on, hear? There's a call alert; you'll hear it if I'm tryin' to get through to you.'

'All right.' Quinn turned the power on so that Tracy could see he had done it. He slipped the radio into his jacket.

'How long you gonna need in there?' said Tracy.

'Jennifer's where Stella says she is, I'd say ten minutes tops.'

'I'm gonna take the van back in the alley, but I'm gonna give you five minutes before I roll. I don't like alleys. I've seen too much shit go wrong in alleys, Terry—'

'So have I.'

'I don't want to get jammed up in there.'

'All right. I'll bring the girl down the fire escape. See you in ten, right?'

'Ten minutes.'

Quinn got out of the van and crossed the street. Go-go music came loudly from the open windows of one of the double-parked cars. The girl outside the row house, black girl with red lipstick and a rouged face, her ass cheeks showing beneath her skirt, looked him over and smiled as he approached.

'You datin' tonight, sugar?'

'I'm taken, baby. My girl's waitin' on me inside.'

Her eyes went dead immediately, and Quinn walked on. He took the row house steps and opened the front door, stepping into a narrow foyer. The door closed softly behind him. He looked up a flight of stairs to the second floor. The foyer smelled of cigarettes, marijuana, and disinfectant. He could hear voices above. Footsteps, too.

Quinn's blood was up. It was a high for him, to be back in the middle of it again. And to be in this place. It reminded him of his own first time with a prostitute, fifteen years earlier, in a house very much like this one, just a few blocks away from where he now stood.

He took the two-way radio out of his pocket and turned the power button off. He didn't need any gadgets. He didn't need any 'call alerts' or anything else to distract him while he was looking for the girl.

Quinn started up the stairs.

14

Worldwide Wilson cruised down 14th in his '92 400SE, midnight blue over palomino leather, the music down low. He had that Isley Brothers slo-jam compilation, *Beautiful Ballads*, on the stereo, Ronald singing all sweet, talkin' about, 'Make me say it again, girl,' coaxin' that man in the boat to show himself and drown.

Wilson had the seat back all the way. Still, even with that, his knees were high, straddling the wheel. He switched lanes, cutting the wheel quick to avoid hitting the dumb-ass in front of him who was making a sudden left without using the turn signal God gave him. As he swerved, the little tree deodorizer he had hung on the rearview swung back and forth.

He had recently had the steering wheel covered in fur, but the Arab he'd given the job to up at the detail shop, he'd fucked it all up. Put some cheap shit on there, so that the hairs were always coming off in his hands and flyin' around the car. Someone didn't know better, they'd think he owned a cat, some bullshit like that. Teach him to give his business to an Iraqi. And he should've known not to trust a man had a girl's name: Leslie.

Wilson's given name was Fred. Frederick, Freddie, he didn't like it any way you put it, what with the kids always callin' him Fred Flintstone and shit when he was a kid. Till he got the reputation, he would fuck them up good they said it again. Worldwide, that was more like it. He'd given himself that name after he returned from Germany, where he'd served in the army back in the late seventies. He'd put together his first little stable over there. Light-skinned girl with Asian eyes, and couple of blond bitches, too. German girls could lay a stamp on a black man, didn't even think twice about his color. Another thing he liked about being overseas.

Wilson punched numbers into the grid of the inverted phone he'd installed in the Mercedes. He liked the way the numbers lit the cabin up green at night. This was one pretty car, real classy, not a ride with too much flash, like those wanna-be pimps, just comin' up, were driving around. The fur steering wheel, that was the only thing he'd added. Oh, yeah, there was a working television and VCR in the backseat, and those stainless steel DNA exhaust pipes he'd recently put on. And the phone. And the Y2K custom wheels he had on this motherfucker. Those rims set the whole joint off right.

Wilson got through on the line and lifted the phone out of its cradle.

'What's goin' on, baby?'

'Slow.'

'I'm comin' in.'

Wilson turned off 14th. He went slowly down the block, checking out the action. Wasn't much. He passed a shitty old van and a couple other hoopties parked on the street, and went around a double-parked Chevy Lumina, where one of his women stood leaning in the driver's window. That particular girl, she talked too much, and when she did talk she had nothin' to say. One of those special-ed bitches, wore his shit out. Time he got that mouth of hers straightened around.

He pulled up in front of his row house, where Carola, another of his girls, his best producer but getting to be on the old side, stood. Wilson hit a button and let the window drop. Carola came over and leaned on the door.

'Where Jennifer at?'

'Schoolgirl's inside. Trickin' some old Al Roker–lookin' sucker.'

'What else?'

'I don't know. Some white boy just went in. I axed him for a date, but he said he already had a girl. Thing is, I didn't see him follow no one in.'

'He high?'

'Didn't look to be.'

'Vice?'

'He wasn't wearin' no sign if he is.'

'Okay. Why you standin' around, though?'

'Told you there wasn't nothin' goin' on.'

'Well, get out there and *make* somethin' go on. Get on back to the tracks and get a date.'

'I'm tired.'

'I'm tired, too. Tired of you talkin' about *bein*' tired and not earnin' shit. Now go on out there and market that pussy, girl.'

'My feet hurt, World.'

'C'mere.' Carola leaned forward to let Wilson stroke her cheek. 'You my bottom baby. You *know* this, right?'

'I know it, World.'

Wilson's eyes dimmed. 'Then don't *make* me get out this car and take a hand to your motherfuckin' ass.'

Carola stood straight and backed up a step. 'I'm goin'.'

'Good, baby.' Wilson smiled, showing a row of gold caps. 'I'll give you a foot massage later on, hear?'

But Carola was already off, walking down the block, Wilson thinking, Glad I got me that degree in pimpology. All you had to do was use a little psychiatry on these bitches, worked every time.

He cut the engine on the Mercedes and untangled his frame from the car. Big man like he was, it was a struggle to get out of these foreign rides. But his time in Berlin had given him a permanent love for German automobiles, and, though they were more roomy, he never had liked the way Cadillacs and Lincolns drove.

He stood beside his car, smoothed out the leather on his coat, and adjusted his hat. Before he closed the door of the Mercedes, he put one foot up on the rocker panel, then the other, and buffed the vamps of his alligator shoes with the palm of his hand. What was the point of spending five hundred dollars on a pair of gators if they didn't have a nice shine? He closed the door and stood straight.

Now he'd have to see what Carola was talkin' about. See what some white boy was doin' wandering around in his house without a woman he'd paid to fuck.

'Oh, shit,' said Stella, leaning forward, blinking hard behind her glasses. 'There go World.'

'Where?'

'That's his ride right there, the blue Mercedes. He's talkin' to Carola, up in the window there.'

Sue Tracy watched the girl step away from the tricked-out car and walk off down the block. Then she watched Worldwide Wilson get out of his car. He wore a full-length leather coat with tooled-out skin, and a hat with a matching tooled band. Wilson stood tall, a good six three, his shoulders filling out the soft cut of the coat. He had the walk of a big cat.

Tracy keyed the mic on the radio in her hand. There was no response.

Wilson walked up the row house steps. He pulled on the front door and moved fluidly through the space. The door closed behind him, and he disappeared into the house.

She tried the radio again and tossed it on the seat beside her.

'*Shit*, Terry.'

'What?' said Stella.

Tracy didn't answer. She ignitioned the van and slammed the tree up into first. She drove to the corner and cut a hard left.

Quinn's hand came off the shaky wooden banister as he stepped up onto the second-floor landing. The banister continued down a straight, narrow hall. The doors to the rooms, all closed and topped with frosted-glass transoms, were situated opposite the banister. Television cable ran from one room to the other in the hall, going transom to transom. Quinn heard no activity on the second floor. He took the hall to the next set of stairs.

Sounds from above grew louder as he ascended the stairs. It was the sound of furniture moving on a hard floor. Talk from a radio and the human bass of a man's voice and the unformed voice of a young girl.

Up on the landing, Quinn checked the sash window at the back of the house. It was open a crack, and he lifted it further and looked down through the mesh of the fire escape to the alley below. The alley was unlit, unblocked, and looked to be passable by car.

Quinn went to the first door, marked 3C in tacked-on letters broken off in spots. From behind the door came the talk radio and the man-girl sounds and the sound of bedsprings. The knob in his hand turned freely, and Quinn pushed on the door and walked inside.

A fat middle-aged black guy was on top of Jennifer Marshall on the bed. His fat ass and his fat sides jiggled as he pumped at her, and Quinn was on him just as he turned his head. He pulled him back by the shoulders and then pushed him roughly against the wall that abutted the bed. The man's head, bald on top and patched with black sides, made a hollow sound as it hit the wall.

Quinn speed-scanned the room: high ceilings and chipped plaster walls. A bed and a nightstand that held a lamp and a radio, with a bathroom coming off the room. Clothing lay in a pile beside the bed.

Jennifer had removed her skirt and panties only. She sat up against the headboard, her legs still spread. Her sex was pink and sparsely tufted with reddish brown hair. Quinn looked away.

'Get your clothes on,' said Quinn to the man, 'and get your ass out of here, *now*.'

The man, naked except for a pair of brown socks, didn't move. His face was still, and his swollen penis, sheathed in a condom, was frozen in place.

'I told you to get going.'

'What the fuck's goin' on?' said Jennifer.

Quinn picked up Jennifer's skirt and panties and tossed them before her on the bed. 'Put 'em on.' And to the man he said, 'Move.'

The man began to dress. Jennifer slipped on her panties and got off the bed, her skirt in her hands. She was thin of wrist, with skinny legs. Up close the heavy makeup could not conceal her age. She looked like a child who had gotten into her mother's things.

'Hurry up,' said Quinn.

'Who *are* you?' said Jennifer.

'I'm an investigator,' said Quinn. 'D.C.'

The door opened. Worldwide Wilson stepped into the room.

'An investigator, huh?' Wilson's gold-capped smile spread wide. 'You won't mind then, motherfucker, if I have a look at your badge.'

Sue Tracy pulled the van alongside the back of the building. Eyes glowed beneath a Dumpster, frozen in the fan of the headlights. As Tracy cut the engine and the headlights the alley went black. She let herself adjust to the sudden change of light. Lines of architecture began to take shape. A rat, then another, scampered across the alley in front of the van.

Residual light bled out from the curtained windows of a sleeper porch on the second floor and a window topping the fire escape on the third.

'That's it, right?'

Stella managed to get her head close to Tracy's window and look up. 'I guess it is.'

Tracy took a wad of cash from her briefcase and stuffed it into the pocket of her slacks. 'Wait here.'

'You're not gonna leave me, are you?'

'I'll be right back,' said Tracy.

'Don't leave me here in the dark,' said Stella.

'You jet, you don't get your money. Just remember that.'

Tracy stepped out of the van and carefully pushed on the driver's-side door. It closed with a soft click.

Wilson reached behind him, not turning his head, and closed the bedroom door. It barely made it to the frame. The man on the bed averted his eyes. He struggled from the sitting position to put on his pants. Some change slipped from the trouser pockets and dropped to the sheets. Quinn kept his posture straight and his eyes on Wilson's.

'I didn't do nothin', World,' said Jennifer.

Wilson took a few steps into the room, one hand in his leather, stopping several feet shy of Quinn. He looked down on Quinn and he looked him over and smiled.

'So what you *doin'* in here, man?'

Quinn didn't answer.

'You ain't datin',' said Wilson, his voice smooth and baritone.

Quinn said nothing.

'What'sa matter, white boy? Ain't you got no tongue?'

'I came for the girl,' said Quinn.

'You must be . . . ' Wilson snapped the fingers of his free hand. 'Terry Quinn. Am I right?'

Quinn nodded slowly.

The room was suddenly small. There was no window, and Quinn knew he'd never make it to the door. Wilson was a big man, but his fluid movement suggested he would be unencumbered by his size. The only way to bring him down, Quinn reasoned, was to hit him low and wrap him up. It was what he always told the kids. Quinn edged one foot forward and put some weight on that leg's knee.

'Now you gettin' ready to rush me, little man? That's what you fixin' to do?'

Wilson produced a switchblade knife from his coat pocket. Four inches of stainless blade flicked open, the pearl handle resting loosely in Wilson's hand.

'Picked this up over in Italy,' said Wilson. 'They make the prettiest sticks.'

The man on the bed clumsily drew on his shirt. Jennifer began to step into her skirt.

Wilson's eyes flared. 'You scared, *Terry*?'

Again, Quinn did not reply.

'Terry. That's a girl's name, ain't it?' Wilson laughed and stepped forward. 'Don't matter much to me, Terry. I need to, I cut a bitch up just as good as a man.'

The door was kicked open. Sue Tracy kicked it again on the backswing as she walked into the room. One arm was extended and holding a snub-nosed .38 Special. The other hand held her license case, flapped open.

'Fuck is that toy shit?' said Wilson.

'I'm an investigator,' said Tracy.

'Aw,' said Wilson, 'now y'all are gonna play like you police, huh?'

'Shut up,' said Tracy, the muzzle of the revolver pointed at Wilson's face. 'Drop that knife.'

Even as the words were coming from her mouth, Wilson was

tossing the knife to the floor. He was still smiling, though, his eyes lit with amusement, going from Tracy back to Quinn.

'Get outta here,' said Tracy to the fat man. She had a surge of adrenaline then, and she shouted, 'Get the fuck back to your wife and kids!'

The man picked what was left of his clothing up off the floor and quickly left the room.

Wilson chuckled. 'Damn, baby. You are like . . . you are like a *man*, you know it?' He head-motioned in the direction of Quinn. 'You got a lot more man to you than this itty-bitty motherfucker right here, I can tell you that.'

Tracy saw Quinn's face flush. 'Terry, get her out of here. I'm right behind you, hear?'

Quinn stood frozen for a moment, his eyes dry and hot.

'Take her!' said Tracy, still holding the gun on Wilson.

'Cavalry gonna hold the Indians back while the women and children leave the fort,' said Wilson.

Jennifer Marshall finished fastening her skirt. Quinn reached over and took her firmly by the elbow. She was shaking beneath his touch.

'I didn't do nothin', World.'

Wilson didn't even look at the girl. He was smiling at Quinn, who was moving Jennifer out of the room, going around Tracy, careful not to impede the sight line of her gun.

'Next time, *Theresa*,' said Wilson.

Tracy heard their footsteps out in the hall. She heard them going out the open window. The sound of their bodies knocking the window frame faded. She kept her gun arm straight.

'You got a name, too?' said Wilson.

Tracy waited. She could hear them on the fire escape and soon that sound faded, too. Then there was the man talking from the radio and Wilson's stare and smile.

Wilson studied her shape. 'Look here, I didn't mean nothin', callin' you a man like I did. Blind man can see you're all woman. I mean, you got some fine titties on you, baby. Can tell by the up-curve, even through that shirt. I bet they stand up real nice when you unfasten that brassiere. Do me a favor, turn around and let me get a look at that pretty ass.'

Tracy felt a drop of sweat slide down her forehead. It snaked off her brow and stung at her eyes.

'You got a nice pussy, too?'

Tracy snicked back the hammer on the .38.

'Go on, now,' Wilson said softly. 'I ain't gonna follow you or nothin' like that. I don't care to hurt a woman 'less she makes me. You ain't gonna make me, are you, darlin'?'

She backed out of the room. She backed down the hall and backed through the open window. She quickly looked down at the idling van in the alley as she got onto the fire escape, but she kept her eyes on the third floor and her gun pointed at the window all the way as she backed herself down the iron stairs.

15

Quinn drove out of the city, keeping to the speed limit and stopping for yellow lights. He had thanked Tracy when she got in the van, but they had barely spoken since. She knew that he was grateful for what she'd done. She also knew what kind of man Quinn was, and that he had been shamed.

Jennifer and Stella argued loudly, sitting beside each other on the back bench, for most of the way out of D.C. But as they crossed the line their voices grew quieter, and their conversation softened further still as Quinn took the ramp onto the Beltway. By the time Quinn was on 270 North, he looked in the rearview mirror and watched them embrace. For the first time since the row house snatch, Quinn loosened his grip on the wheel.

Tracy lit a cigarette and dropped the match out the window. 'You all right?'

'I'm fine.'

'Can I have my radio back?'

Quinn took it from his jacket and handed it over. 'This thing works for shit, y'know it?'

'Next time turn it on.' Tracy moved her hand to the tray and tapped ash off her cigarette. 'You don't have a problem with what happened back there, do you?'

'No problem,' lied Quinn. 'I'd be a class-A jerk if I did. I mean, you saved my ass.'

Tracy grinned. 'And the rest of you, too.'

'That was pretty smooth, you bustin' in like that. And you didn't even tell me you were carrying a gun.'

'My father gave it to me a long time ago. He bought it hot downtown. It's an old MPD sidearm, before they went to the Glocks.'

'It's, uh, illegal to have one of those in the District. You know it?'

'Really.'

'Yeah, you could get in a world of trouble, you get caught with it on your person. You could lose your license.'

'It's better than the alternative.'

'Just letting you know, is all.'

'I wouldn't walk into a situation like that without it.'

'Okay.'

'You tellin' me you don't own one?'

'I do own one. I'm just surprised that you do, that's all.'

'I wanted to kill him, Terry. I mean, I was close. It scared me a little, back there. Even more than he did, you know? You ever get a feeling like that?'

'All the time,' said Quinn.

In fact, Quinn was visualizing the room in the row house and Worldwide Wilson now.

'Anyway,' said Tracy, 'nice work. You found her quick. Even the hero stuff you pulled back there. Good, solid work.'

'Hero? Christ, what about you?'

Tracy smiled crookedly. 'What?'

Quinn looked her over. 'Bad-ass.'

Tracy pointed to the detention center across the highway that had become visible on their left. Quinn put the van into the right lane and took the next exit.

He parked in the lot of Seven Locks station. In the backseat, the two girls talked quietly. Stella was reaching into her football-sized handbag, pulling out a Walkman and then several CDs.

'I'm gonna be a while,' said Tracy. 'I don't have to, but I think I ought to wait for her mother and father to get here while the cops process the paperwork. I like to talk to the parents when I can.'

'No problem. You still want to grab a beer?'

'Sure.'

'Bars'll be closed by the time we're done here. Thought I'd go snag a six while you're inside.'

'Make it a twelve-pack.'

'I'll be out here waiting,' said Quinn.

Jennifer climbed out of the back of the van. Tracy tossed her pack of cigarettes back to Stella. Jennifer did not speak to Quinn as she passed by his window and went with Tracy up the sidewalk to the station. Tracy kept her hand on Jennifer's elbow all the way.

'Think we can find a beer store out here in Potomac?'

'*I* want one,' said Stella.

'Forget it,' said Quinn.

It took a while to locate a deli. When they returned to the lot Quinn cracked open a can of beer and took a long swig. Stella sat beside him and smoked one of Tracy's cigarettes. She had Quinn half turn the ignition key so that she could get some power to the van, and she pushed the Mazzy Star tape back into the deck.

'This is old,' she said, 'but it still sounds pretty cool.'

'Yeah, it's nice.'

'Bet it's your partner's tape.'

'That's right.' Quinn closed his eyes as he drank off some of his beer. It was cold and good.

'You're more like the Springsteen type.'

'Uh-huh.' He looked at the brick building lit by spots, remembering back to that time in high school when he'd spent a night out here in one of the cells. A D&D charge at a house party that had gone on way too long. He'd beaten up the host's father. Quinn wondered if the kid ever got over seeing his father on the ground, getting punched out by a seventeen-year-old boy. And all because the old man had looked at Quinn the wrong way and smiled.

'Hey, you listenin'?'

'Yeah, sure.'

'My father likes Springsteen. The old Springsteen, he says, which means, like, the stuff that's one hundred years old. Not that I'm comparing you to my father. You're younger than him, for one.' Stella dragged on her cigarette. 'My father was "weak and ineffectual." That's what the shrink my parents took me to said. This shrink, he wasn't supposed to say stuff like that to me, I know. But I was suckin' his little dick right there in his office, so he said all kinds of stuff.'

'I don't want to hear about it,' said Quinn.

'He said that I "gravitated toward strong men" 'cause my father was weak. What do you think of that?'

'No clue.'

'It's why I hooked up with World, I guess. Couldn't find a much stronger man than him. He turned me out quick, too.' Stella double-dragged on her smoke and pitched it out the window. 'But I couldn't produce for him. Nobody wanted to pay for this stuff, not that I blame them. I'm not much of a woman, *am* I, Terry? Do you think I am?'

'You're fine,' said Quinn.

'Yeah, I'm a beauty, all right. Anyway, that's how I got into the recruitment biz for World.'

'Stella—'

'I do like strong men, Terry. The shrink was right about that.'

She slid over on the seat so that she was close to him. Quinn could feel her warm breath on his face.

'That's not a good idea,' he said.

'Don't worry, green eyes, I'm not gonna hurt you. I was just lookin' for a little love. A hug, is all.' She moved back against the passenger-side door, her face colored by the vapor lights of the lot. Quinn could see that her eyes had teared up behind the lenses of her glasses.

'I'm sorry, Stella.'

'Ain't no big thing,' she said, a catch in her voice. She turned her face away from him and stared out the window.

They sat awhile longer, watching the uniformed cops moving in and out of the station. A minivan pulled into the lot. A man and a woman got out of it and hurried inside. Stella laughed joylessly, watching them.

'I love happy endings,' said Stella. The hard shell had returned to her face.

'You don't have to go back to working for Wilson. You know that, don't you?'

'Yeah, I know. Damn right, I am somebody, and all that.'

'I'm serious. And we both know it's not safe. One of these days he's gonna find out you been playin' him for the middle.'

'You didn't give me up to him back there, did you? You didn't say my name or nothin' like that.'

'No.'

'Course not. There wasn't nothin' in it for you.'

'That's not the only reason people do or don't do what they do,' said Quinn.

'Yeah, okay, whatever.' Stella lit another cigarette. 'Just so I get paid.'

A half hour later Tracy emerged from the station. Stella climbed into the back and Tracy took the shotgun seat.

'Everything go okay?' said Quinn.

'The parents have her,' said Tracy. 'They're taking her home. I can't tell you if it's going to stick.'

She drank a beer and Quinn drank another as they drove back into D.C. Quinn parked the van on 23rd, alongside the church.

Tracy gave Stella five hundred-dollar bills, along with her card.

'It was a pleasure doin' business with y'all,' said Stella. 'You want your smokes back?'

'Keep 'em,' said Tracy. 'I got another pack. And, Stella, you need to talk, anything like that—'

'I know, I know, I got your number right here.'

'Stay low for a few days,' said Quinn.

Stella leaned forward from the backseat and kissed Quinn behind the ear. Then she was out of the van's back door and walking across the church grounds. They watched her move through the inky shadows.

'Where do you suppose she's going?' said Quinn.

'Don't think about it.'

'I shouldn't even care, right? I mean, she's steering girls over to Wilson so he can turn them out.'

'Stella's a victim, too. Try to think of it like that. And remember, we got Jennifer off the street.'

'So how come I feel like we didn't accomplish shit?'

'You can't save them all in one night,' said Tracy. 'C'mon, let's go.'

Quinn looked back to the church grounds. Stella was gone, swallowed up by the night. Quinn put the van in gear, rolled to the corner, hooked a left, and headed uptown.

Sue Tracy invited herself into Quinn's apartment. He was relieved that she took the initiative but not surprised. He snapped on a lamp in the living room, gathering up newspapers and socks as he moved about the place, and told her to have a seat.

Quinn went into the kitchen to put the beer in the refrigerator, opened two, and brought them back out to the living room along with an ashtray. Tracy was on her cell, talking to her partner, telling her what had gone down. Karen, it went fine, and Karen this and Karen that. He heard Tracy say where she was, then listen to something her partner said. Tracy laughed, saying something Quinn couldn't make out, before she ended the call.

Tracy lit a smoke and tossed a match in the ashtray. 'Thanks. You don't mind if I smoke in here, do you?'

'Nah, it's fine.'

Quinn was by his modest CD collection, trying to figure out what to put on the carousel. It struck him, looking to find something that would be appropriate, that most of the music he owned was on the aggressive side. He hadn't really noticed it before. He settled on a Shane MacGowan solo record, the one with 'Haunted' on it, his duet with Sinéad. Good drinking music, and sexy, too, like a scar on the lip of a nice-looking girl.

Quinn had a seat on the couch next to Tracy. She had taken off her Skechers and tucked her feet under her thighs.

'To good work,' she said, and tapped her green can against his. They drank off some of their beer.

'What were you laughing about on the phone there. Me?'

'Well, yeah. Karen bet me I was gonna spend the night here. I took the bet.'

'And?'

'I told her I'd pay up the next time I saw her.'

Tracy stamped out her smoke and pulled the Scunci off her ponytail. She shook her head and let her hair fall naturally past her shoulders. Some strays fell across her face.

'Do I have anything to say about it?' said Quinn.

'Both times we've been together, you've been staring at me like you were from hunger. And Terry, I'm not as obvious as you are, but I've been looking at you the same way.'

'Christ, you got some balls on you.'

'It's not like I make a habit of this.' She unfolded her legs and swung them down to the hardwood floor. 'But, you know, when it's so obvious like it is right here, I mean, why dance around it?'

'You talked me into it.'

Tracy leaned into Quinn. He brushed hair away from her face and she kissed him on the mouth. Their tongues touched and he bit softly on her lower lip as she pulled away.

'Let's have another beer,' said Tracy. 'Relax a little, talk. Listen to some music. Okay?'

'You're in charge.'

'Stop it.'

'No, it's cool.' Quinn breathed out slow. 'Relax. That sounds nice.'

They drank their beers and Quinn went off for two more. Tracy was lighting a cigarette when he returned. He sat close to her on the couch. Quinn had downed three beers and was working on his fourth. His buzz was on, but he was still amped from the grab.

'Thought you were gonna relax.'

'I am.'

'You got your fist balled up there.'

'So I do.'

'Forget about what happened tonight with Wilson, Terry. He pushed my buttons, too. But he's history and we got the job done. That's the only thing that matters now, right?'

Quinn nodded. He was thinking about Wilson. Sitting here drinking a cold beer with a fine-looking woman he liked, ready to go to bed with her, and not able to stop thinking of the man who had punked him out.

'What makes you think I had Wilson on my mind?'

'I asked around about you, talked to a couple of guys Karen knew in the MPD.'

'Yeah? What'd they say?'

'Well, everyone's got a different opinion on what happened the night you shot that cop.'

'That black cop, you mean. Why didn't you just ask Derek? He did his own independent investigation into the whole deal.'

'That how you two hooked up?'

'Yeah.'

'The department said you were right on the shooting.'

'It's more complicated than that. You know what I'm sayin'; you were a cop yourself. But a whole lot of cops I come across, they're not too willing to forget about it. Some guys still think that shooting was a race thing. By extension, that I'm some kind of racist.'

'Well?'

'Sue, I'm not gonna sit here and tell you that I have no prejudice. For a white guy to say he sees a black man and doesn't make some kind of assumptions, it's bullshit, and it's a lie. And the same thing goes in reverse. Let's just say I'm no more a racist than any other man, okay? And let's leave it at that.'

'You know, even the ones who had that opinion of you, they also admitted that you were well-liked, and a good cop. You did have a reputation for violence, though. Not bully violence, exactly. More like, if anyone pushed you, you weren't willing to let it lie.'

Quinn drank deeply of his beer and stared at the can. 'You always background check the guys you're interested in?'

'I haven't been interested in anyone in a long time.' Tracy took a drag off her smoke and ashed the tray. 'Now you. Ask me anything you want.'

'Okay. First day I met you, I had the impression you had some daddy issues.'

'You're wrong,' said Tracy, shaking her head. 'Not like you mean. I loved my father and he loved me. I never felt I had to prove anything to him. He was always proud of me. I know 'cause he told me. He even told me the last time I saw him, in his bed at the hospice.'

'Was he a cop?'

'No. He did come from a family of them, but it wasn't something he wanted for himself. He was a career barman at the Mayflower Hotel, downtown.'

'They're all, like, Asian guys behind the bar down there.'

'That's now. Frank Tracy was all Irish. Irish Catholic. Just like you, Quinn.'

'And you.'

'Not quite. The Tracy part of me is. My mother was Scandinavian, where I got the name Susan and my blond hair.'

'You're a natural blonde?'

'Don't be rude.'

'I was just wondering.'

Tracy smiled. 'You'll find out soon enough.'

'You are something,' said Quinn.

They undressed each other back in his room, standing face to face before the bed. She helped him off with his T-shirt and then slipped out of her slacks, leaving on her black lace panties. They were cut high, and her thigh muscles were ripped up to the fabric. He unbuttoned her shirt and peeled it back off her strong shoulders. She wore a black brassiere that fastened in the front. He unfastened it and let it drop to the floor. He pinched one of her pink nipples and flicked his tongue around it.

'These are nice,' said Quinn.

'I've been told.'

He swallowed. 'I mean it, baby.'

'They hold my bra up,' said Tracy.

Quinn chuckled and kissed her lips. He got down to his knees and drew her panties down and kissed her sex. He blew on her pubis and kissed her there and split her with his tongue. Her fingers dug into his shoulder until it hurt. He sucked her flesh into his mouth and tasted her silk and she came standing there.

They moved to the bed and fucked on the edge of it, Quinn on top. His orgasm was like a punch in the heart. They talked for a while and took a shower and fucked again. Quinn lay beside Tracy and they looked at each other for a long time without speaking. He watched her eyelids slowly drop. In sleep she had a small smile.

Quinn got out of bed and walked to the window. It was late, nearly four. The street was still. A cop car from the station up the street blew down Sligo Avenue and was gone. He wondered if the guy was on a call, or if he was just driving fast, looking for the next piece of action. He wondered if he was that kind of cop, the kind Quinn had been.

It had happened fast with Tracy. He knew it would when he'd met her the first time, in the coffee shop. It had been simple, as simple as her uttering those few words. *Irish Catholic. Just like you, Quinn.* Nothing much needed to be said between them after that, as all was understood. There was her father, as much a part of her as the blood in her veins, and now him, equally familiar. He wondered, as he often did, if it wasn't more natural for people to stick with their own kind. Well, anyway, it was easier. Of this he was sure.

Tracy had been a cop, too, just like him. With her, he didn't have to pretend that he didn't care about the action, that he didn't crave it all the time. There wouldn't be any of that bullshit fronting, the mask he'd felt he had to wear when he was with other women. In that way, they were good for each other. She took him for who he was.

Quinn stood there looking out the window to the darkened street, picturing Wilson in that trick-house, seeing that gold-capped smile and hearing his smooth baritone and trying to forget. Trying to figure out where he was headed with this problem of his. Trying to figure out, himself, who he was. Who he was and where it would take him in the end.

16

On Saturday morning the team gathered at Roosevelt High School for a roster check. Strange and Blue wanted to be sure the kids were outfitted with the proper pads and mouthpieces, so that there would be no surprises before game time or injuries on the field of play. When they were done checking on those details, the kids got into the cars of the coaches and the usual group of parents and guardians and drove across town and over the river to the state of Virginia, where the Petworth Panthers' first game was to be played.

Their destination was a huge park and sports complex in Springfield that held tennis and basketball courts, picnic areas, and several soccer and football fields. A creek ran through the woods bordering the property. Complexes like this one were typical and numerous in the suburbs, especially farther out, where there was land and money. The kids from the Panthers had rarely seen playing fields as carefully tended as these, or sports parks situated in such lush surroundings.

'Dag, boy,' said Joe Wilder, his eyes wide, 'this joint is tight; check out those lights they got!'

'Look at thoth uniforms,' said Prince, pointing to a team warming up on a perfect green field, with big blue star decals on their helmets. 'They look just like the Cowboys!'

The kids were on a path between the road and the field, alongside a split-rail fence. Strange, Blue, Lionel Baker, Lamar Williams, Dennis Arrington, and Quinn were walking among them. Rico, the cocky running back, was telling the quarterback, Dante Morris, what he was going to do to the opposing team's line, and Morris was nodding, not really listening to Rico but keeping quietly to himself. Later, just before the first whistle, Morris would say a silent prayer.

There were several teams on and around the two main fields. Many had their own cheerleading squads and booster clubs. A game was ending on one of the fields. As the Panthers went through an open chain-link gate, they passed a group of boys in clean red-and-white uniforms, decked out in high-tech equipment, their gleaming helmets held at their sides.

'Y'all the Cardinals?' said Joe Wilder.

'Yeah,' said one of the boys, mousse in his studiously disheveled hair, looking down on Wilder and looking him over.

'We're playin' y'all,' said Wilder.

'In those uniforms?' said the kid, and the Cardinal next to him, pug nosed and with an expensive haircut like his friend, laughed.

'What, did you find those in the trash or somethin'?' said pug nose.

Wilder looked over at Dante Morris, who shook his head, Wilder taking it to mean, correctly, that Morris was telling him to keep his mouth shut. Rico took a step toward the two Cardinals, but Morris pulled on his sleeve and held him back.

Strange, who had heard the exchange and seen this kind of thing before, said, 'C'mon, boys, you follow me.'

The Cardinals were a team of white kids and the Panthers were all black. But it wasn't a white-black thing. It was a money–no money thing, a way for those who had it to show superiority over those who did not. Plain old insecurity, as old as time itself.

Blue checked in the team rosters to a guy in a Redskins cap whom he knew to be the point man for the league, then met Arrington, Lionel, and the Midgets for their pregame warm-ups. Strange and Quinn led the Pee Wees under the shade of a stand of oaks beside the main stadium and had them form a circle. Strange told Joe Wilder and Dante Morris, the designated captains, to lead the team in calisthenics. Lamar Williams stood by and made sure that they kept the circle tight.

'*How y'all feel?*'

'*Fired up!*'

'*How y'all feel?*'

'*Fired up!*'

'*Breakdown.*'

'*Whoo!*'

'*Breakdown.*'

'*Whoo!*'

Strange watched the Cardinals warming up down on the edge of the field. He watched their coach, a fat white man in Bike shorts, yelling out the calisthenics count to his team. Strange remembered this guy from a scrimmage late in the summer, a heart attack waiting to happen, and how he coached his kids to be intimidating and mean.

'You hear what went down back there?' said Quinn.

'I heard it,' said Strange.

'I hope we beat the shit out of these guys, Derek, I swear to God.'

There was only so much money in the program. The kids had to come up with fifty dollars to play for the squad, and some of them hadn't even been able to raise that. Dennis Arrington, who was flush from his job in the computer industry, had donated a couple of thousand dollars to the team. Strange, Blue, and Quinn had come up with a grand between them. It bought good pads and replacement helmets and mouthguards, but it didn't buy new jerseys and pants. The Panthers' green uniforms were faded, mismatched, and frayed. The number decals on their scarred helmets rarely matched the numbers on their jerseys.

'It's not the attitude we're trying to convey to the boys,' said Quinn, 'but I can't help feeling that way, even though I know it's wrong.'

'It ain't wrong,' said Strange. 'But we got what we got. Game time comes, it's not the uniforms gonna decide the contest. It's the heart in these kids gonna tell the tale.'

Strange called them in. They gathered around him and Quinn. Quinn talked about defense and making the big plays. Strange gave them instructions on the general offensive game plan and a few words of inspiration.

'Protect your brother,' said Strange when he was done, trying to meet eyes with most of the boys kneeling before him. 'Protect your brother.'

The boys formed a tight group and put their hands in the center. 'Petworth Panthers!' they shouted, and ran down to the field.

Both teams were rusty at the start of the opening quarter. Morris fumbled an errant Prince snap in the first set of downs but fell on the ball and recovered. They went three-and-out and punted. On first down the Cardinal halfback was taken down behind the line of scrimmage, and on second down he was stripped of the ball. A Panther named Noah picked up the ball off its bounce and ran ten yards before he was dropped. It was the gasoline on the fire the Panthers needed, a wake-up call that would carry them the rest of the game.

The offensive line began to make their blocks and open the holes. Rico hit those holes, and the chains began to move as the team marched down the field. The Cardinals' coach called a time-out and yelled at his defensive line. Strange could see the veins on the man's neck standing out from across the field.

'No heart,' said Strange.

'Their hearts are pumpin' Kool-Aid,' said Blue.

The line tightened its play and stopped a thirty-five-run call on the next play. Strange had Joe Wilder run in the next play to Morris, a triple-right. Morris lobbed a pass in the direction of the three receivers – halfback, end, and flanker – who had lined up on the right and gone out to the flats. Rico caught it and took it in, freed by a Joe Wilder block on the Cardinals' corner.

Strange stuck with the running game but took it to the outside. The Cardinals' left side was weak and seemed to be growing weaker the more the coach screamed at his players. At flanker, Wilder was taking out the defensive man assigned to him, pushing him inside, allowing Rico to turn the corner and just blow and go.

By halftime, the Cardinals were totally demoralized and the Panthers were firing on all cylinders. Barring an act of God, the game was theirs, Strange knew.

The second half went the same way. Strange played the bench and rested his first-stringers. The Cardinals managed a score against the Panthers' scrubs, causing an anemic eruption from the cheerleaders on the other side of the field. But the drive was just a spark, and even their coach, who threw his hat down in disgust when his team turned the ball over on their next possession, knew they were done. The Panthers moved the ball into Cardinal territory easily and were threatening again with a minute left to play.

Strange brought Joe Wilder out of the game and rested his hand on his shoulder. 'Next play, I want you to tell Dante to down the ball. Just let the clock run out, hear?'

'Let me take it in, Coach,' said Wilder. He was smiling at Strange, his eyes eager and bright. 'Forty-four Belly, that's my play.'

'We won, Joe. We don't need to be rubbin' it in their faces.'

'C'mon, Coach Derek. I ain't touched the ball all day. I know I can run it in!'

Strange squeezed Wilder's shoulder. 'I know you can, too, son. You got real fire in you, Joe. But we don't do like that out here. Those boys been beat good today. I don't like to put the boot to someone's face when they're down, and I don't want you doin' it either. That's not the kind of man I want you to be.'

'Okay, then,' said Wilder, the disappointment plain on his face.

'Go on, boy. Run the play in to Dante like I told you.'

The game ended the way Strange had instructed. At the whistle, the players gathered on the sideline. Wilder got a hug from Quinn and a slap on the helmet from Strange.

'Line up,' said Strange. 'Now, when you go to shake their hands, I don't want to hear a thing except 'Good game.' No trash-talking, you understand? You said all you needed to on the field. After what you did out there, don't shame yourselves now, hear?'

The Panthers met the Cardinals in the center of the field, touched hands as they went down the line. The Panthers said 'Good game' to each player they passed, and the Cardinals mumbled the same words in reply. Dante Morris stared into the eyes of the pug-nosed boy who had cracked on their uniforms, but Morris didn't say a word, and the boy quickly looked away. At the end of the line the Cardinals' coach shook Strange's hand and congratulated him through teeth nearly clenched.

'All right,' said Quinn, as the team returned and took a knee before him. 'I liked the way you guys played today. A lot of heart. Just remember, it's not always going to be this easy. We're going to be playing teams who have better athletes and are better coached. And you need to be ready. Ready in your minds, which means you keep your heads in the books during the day. And ready physically as well. That means we're going to continue to practice as hard as we ever have. We want the championship this year, right?

'Right!'

'I didn't hear you.'

'*Right!*'

'What time is practice Monday night?' said Strange.

'*Six o'clock on the dot, be there, don't miss it!*'

'I'm proud of you boys,' said Strange.

17

Later that afternoon, Quinn sat behind the counter of Silver Spring Books reading *The Pistoleer*, a novel by James Carlos Blake. His coworker, Lewis, was back in the military history room, straightening the shelves. A homeless intellectual whom everyone in the area called Moonman was sitting on the floor in the sci-fi room, reading a paperback edition of K. W. Jeter's *The Glass Hammer*. A customer browsed the mystery stacks nearby.

Quinn had put *Johnny Winter And* on the turntable, and the molten blues-metal classic was playing at a low volume throughout the store. Syreeta, the owner of the business, who was rarely on site, had instructed the employees to play the used vinyl in stock to advertise the merchandise. This disc, with its faded black-and-white cover portraits, had recently been inventoried as part of a large purchase, a carton of seventies albums.

Quinn cherished these quiet afternoons in the shop.

The mystery customer, a thin man in his early forties, brought a paperback to the register and placed it on the glass counter. It was Elmore Leonard's *Unknown Man No. 89*, one of the mass-market publications Avon had done with the cool cover art depicting a montage of the book's elements; this one displayed a snub-nosed .38, spilled-out shells, and an overturned shot glass.

'You ever read his westerns?' said Quinn. 'They're the best, in my opinion.'

'I go for the crime stuff set in Detroit. There's a lot of different Leonard camps and they've all got opinions.' The customer nodded to one of the speakers mounted up on the wall. 'Haven't heard this for a while.'

'It just came in. The vinyl's in good shape, if you want it.'

'I own it, but I haven't pulled it out of the shelf for a long time. That's Rick Derringer on second lead.'

'Who?'

'Yeah, you're too young. Him and Johnny, the two of them were just on fire on this session. One of those lightning-in-a-bottle things. Listen to 'Prodigal Son,' the cut leads off side two.'

'I will.' Quinn gave the man his change and a receipt. 'Thanks a lot. And take it easy, hear?'

'You, too.'

Quinn figured this guy had a wife, kids, a good job. You'd pass him on the street and think he was your average square. But one thing you learned working here was that just about everyone had something worthwhile to say if you took the time to listen. Everyone was more interesting when you got to know them a little than they initially appeared to be. That was the other thing he liked about working in a place like this. The conversations you got into and the people you met. Of course, he had met plenty of people on a daily basis in his former profession. But it almost always started from an adversarial place when you met them as a cop.

Quinn read some more of his novel. A little while later, Quinn watched Sue Tracy cross Bonifant Street on foot. She was wearing her post-punk utilitarian gear and had a day pack slung over her shoulder. Quinn's heart actually skipped, watching her walk. He was imagining her naked atop his sheets.

The small bell over the door rang as she walked in. Quinn let his feet drop off the counter, but he didn't get up out of his seat.

'Hey.'

'Hey.'

'New in town?'

'I missed you.'

'I've been missing you, too.'

'Got on the Metro and walked up from the station. Can you get away?'

'I can probably sneak out, sure.'

'It's a beautiful day.'

'I've got my car here. We can, I don't know, go for a ride.'

Tracy looked down at the book in Quinn's hand. 'What's that, a western?'

'Yeah, sort of.'

'What's with you and your partner? Strange went on about some scene from *The Magnificent Seven.*'

'That would be the one with Coburn shooting the rider instead of the horse.'

'Uh-huh.'

'He does go back to that one a lot.'

Lewis came forward from the back of the shop. His black hair was long, greasy, and tangled, and his thick glasses had surgical tape holding one stem to the frame. Yellow perspiration marks stained the armpits of his white shirt.

'Lewis, meet my friend, Sue Tracy.'

'My pleasure,' said Lewis. Tracy and Lewis shook hands.

'I'm gonna punch out for the day, Lewis. That okay by you?'

Lewis blinked hard behind the lenses of his glasses. 'Fine.'

Quinn gathered his things, marking the Leonard paperback off in the store's inventory notebook before he came around the counter.

'This Johnny Winter?' said Tracy.

'How'd you know that?'

'Older brothers. I had one played this till the grooves wore out on the vinyl.'

'That's Rick Derringer on second lead right here.'

'Who?'

'You're too young.'

They left the shop and walked up Bonifant.

'Lewis gonna be all right back there, all by himself?' said Tracy.

'He's the best employee Syreeta's got. A little lonely, though. Any suggestions?'

Tracy laced her fingers through Quinn's. 'I'm spoken for.'

'Maybe your partner, then.'

'He's not Karen's type.'

'What type is that?'

'The type who runs a comb through his hair every so often. The type who showers.'

'Picky,' said Quinn.

They stopped at his car, parked in the bank lot.

'Sweet,' said Tracy. Quinn had recently waxed the body, scrubbed the Cragar mags with Wheel-Brite and wet-blacked the rubber. The Chevelle's clean lines gleamed in the sun.

'You like, huh?'

Tracy nodded. 'You got the Flowmasters on there, huh?'

'I bought it like that off the lot.'

'What's under the hood, a three ninety-six?'

'Now you're making me nervous.'

'My older brothers.'

'C'mon, get in.'

She got into the passenger side. Quinn saw her admiring the shifter, a four-speed Hurst.

'You want to drive?'

'Could I?'

'I knew there was something else I liked about you. Aside from you being a natural blonde, I mean.'

'What can I say? I like fast cars.'

'Bad-ass,' said Quinn.

Tracy drove down into Rock Creek Park. They parked near a bridle trail on the west side of the creek and took the path up a rise and all the way to the old mill. On the walk back they sat on some boulders in the middle of the creek. Quinn took his shirt off, and Tracy removed her socks and shoes. She let her feet dangle in the cool water. They talked about their pasts and kissed in the sun.

Late in the afternoon they went back to Quinn's apartment and made love. They showered and re-dressed and had dinner at Vicino's, a small Italian restaurant Quinn liked up on Sligo Avenue. Quinn had the calimari over linguini, and Tracy had the seafood platter, and they washed it down with a carafe of the house red. They stopped for another bottle of red on the way back to Quinn's place and drank it while listening to music and making out on his couch. They fucked like teenagers in his room, and afterward they lay in bed, Tracy smoking and talking, Quinn listening with a natural smile on his face.

The day had been a good one. The kids had won their game, and in his mind Quinn could still see the look of pride on their faces as they had run off the field. Then Sue Tracy had surprised him and stopped by the shop.

Quinn looked at his hands and saw that they were totally relaxed on the sheets. He hadn't been thinking of the streets or if anyone had looked at him the wrong way or anything else but Sue, his girlfriend, lying beside him. He hadn't felt this comfortable with a woman for some time.

Strange dropped off Prince, Lamar, and Joe Wilder, then dropped Lionel at Janine's house uptown.

'You comin' for dinner tonight?' said Lionel, before getting out of the car.

'I haven't spoken to your mother about it,' said Strange.

'My mom wants you to come over, I know. Saw her marinating some kind of roast this morning before you picked me up.'

'Maybe I'll see you, then.'

'Whateva,' said Lionel, turning and going up the sidewalk toward his house.

Strange watched the boy and his loping walk.

Boy's still got that way of stepping. Had that walk since I been knowing him, back when he wasn't nothing much more than a kid. Thinks he's a man, but he's still a boy inside.

He grinned without thinking, watching him, and waited until Lionel got inside the house before driving away.

Strange picked up the Calhoun Tucker photos from the Safeway over on Piney Branch. Safeway was cheap and they did a good-enough job on the processing. It took a little longer when you used them, but he wasn't in any hurry on this particular job.

Back in his office, he inspected the photographs. The woman in the doorway, Tucker's somethin' on the side, was plain as day in the shot, letting him into her crib. Janine had gotten her name from the crisscross program, based on her street address. It was in the file he was building on Tucker, the one he was preparing for his friend George Hastings. Strange found the file and slipped the photographs inside it. He was just about done with the background check. He'd need to report on all this to George. Soon, thought Strange, I will do this soon. He wondered what was stopping him from getting George on the phone right now. Strange turned this over in his mind as he locked the file cabinet, then his office door.

Walking through the outer office, he noticed his reflection in the mirror nailed to the post, and stopped to study himself. Damn if his natural wasn't nearly all gray. The years just . . . they just *went.* Strange was bone tired and hungry. He thought about having a nice meal, maybe some Chinese. And a hot shower, too; that would do him right.

At dinner that night, Strange sat at the head of Janine's table, as he always did, in the one chair that had arms on it. It had been her father's chair. Lionel sat to his left and Janine to his right. Greco played with a rubber ball, his eyes moving to the dinner table occasionally but keeping control of himself, staying there on his belly, lying on the floor at Strange's feet.

Janine had *Talking Book* on the stereo, playing softly. She did love her Stevie, in particular the breakout stuff that he'd done for Motown in the early seventies.

'Where you off to tonight?' said Strange, eyeballing Lionel, clean in his Nautica pullover and pressed khakis.

'Takin' a girl to a movie.'

'What, you gonna walk her there?'

'Gonna pull her in a ricksha.'

'Don't be playin',' said Strange. 'I'm just asking you a question.'

'He's taking my car, Derek.'

'Yeah, okay. But listen, don't be firin' up any of that funk in your mother's car, hear?'

'You mean, like, *herb*?'

'You know what I mean. You get yourself a police record, how you gonna get to be that big-time lawyer you always talking about becoming?'

Lionel put his fork down on his plate. 'Look, how you gonna just *suppose* that I'm gonna be out there smokin' some hydro tonight? I mean, it's not like you're my father, Mr Derek. It's not like you're here all the time, like you know me all that well.'

'I know I'm not your father. Didn't say I was. It's just—'

'I wasn't even thinkin' about smokin' that stuff tonight, you want the truth. This girl I'm seein', she's special to me, understand, and I wouldn't do nothin', *anything*, that I thought would get her in any kind of trouble with the law. So, all due respect, you can't be comin' up in here, part-time, lookin' to guide me, when you don't even know me all that well, for real.'

Strange said nothing.

Lionel looked at his mother. 'Can I be excused, *Mom*? I need to pick up my girl.'

'Go ahead, Lye. My car keys are on my dresser.'

Lionel left the room and went up the hall stairs.

'I guess I messed that up pretty bad.'

'It is hard to know what to say,' said Janine. 'Most of the time, I'm just winging it myself.'

'I do feel like a father to that boy.'

'But you're not,' said Janine, her eyes falling away from his. 'So maybe you ought to go a little easier on him, all right?'

Janine got up out of her seat and picked up Lionel's plate off the table. She head-motioned to Greco, whose eyes were on her now and pleading. 'C'mon, boy. Let's see if you can't finish some of this roast.'

Greco's feet sought purchase on the hardwood floor as he scrabbled toward the kitchen, his nub of a tail twitching furiously. Strange got up and went to the foyer, meeting Lionel, who was bounding down the stairs.

'Hey, buddy,' said Strange.

'Hey.'

'You got money in your pocket?'

'I'm flush,' said Lionel.

'Look here—'

'You don't have to say nothin', Mr Derek.'

'Yeah, I do. Don't want to give you the impression that I'm just assuming you're always out there looking to get into trouble, doing somethin' wrong. Because I do think that you're a fine young man. I appreciate you helping out with the team like you do, and the way you help your mother around here, too.'

'I know you do.'

'I guess what I'm trying to tell you is, I'm proud of you. I give you advice you don't need, I guess, because I care about you, see? I'm looking to play some kind of role in your life, but I'm not quite sure what that is yet, understand?'

'Uh-huh.'

They stood there in the foyer looking at each other. Lionel put his hands in his pockets and took them out again and shuffled his feet.

'Anything else?' said Lionel. ''Cause I gotta bounce.'

'That's it, I guess.'

Strange shook Lionel's hand and then hugged him clumsily. Lionel left the house, looking over his shoulder at Strange one time before continuing on down the sidewalk. Strange watched him through the window and made sure he got safely into Janine's car.

'How'd that go?' said Janine, standing behind him with a cold bottle of beer in one hand and two glasses in the other.

'Uh, all right, I guess.'

'C'mon back out to the living room, then, and put your feet up.'

Strange followed her out of the foyer, through a hall. He watched her strong walk and the back of her head of hair. He could see she'd been to the beauty salon that day, and he hadn't even complimented her on it. He thought of how much he did love her, and the boy. And he thought of the stranger who had jacked his dick off on a massage table just a few hours earlier in the day.

'Goddamn you, Derek,' he said under his breath.

Janine looked over her shoulder. 'You all right?'

'I'm fine, baby,' said Strange.

He wished that it were so.

18

Garfield Potter, Carlton Little, and Charles White spent most of Monday driving around Petworth, Park View, and the northern tip of Shaw, checking on their troops, looking for girls to talk to, drinking some, and staying high. Early in the evening they were back in their row house, hanging out in the living room, where the smoke of a blunt Little had recently fired up hung heavy in the air.

Potter had been trying to get up with a girl all afternoon, but he hadn't been able to connect. He paced the room as Little and White sat on the couch playing Madden 2000 while an Outkast cut on PGC came loud from the box. White saw the shadow that had settled on Potter's face, the look he got when the girl thing hadn't gone his way. Truth was, most girls were afraid to be with Garfield Potter, something that had never crossed his mind.

Potter was working on his third forty of malt. He'd been drinking them down since early in the day.

'Y'all gonna play that kid shit all night?' said Potter.

'It's the new one they got,' said Little.

'I ain't give a good fuck about no cartoon football game,' said Potter. 'Let's go up to that field and see some real football.'

'That again?'

'I feel like smokin' someone,' said Potter. He rubbed his hands together as he walked back and forth in the room. 'Lorenze Wilder is gonna be got.'

'Ah, shit, D,' said Little. 'Let me and Coon just finish this one game.'

Potter went over to the PlayStation base unit and hit the power button. The game stopped and the screen went over to the cable broadcast. Potter stood in front of the couch and stared at his childhood friends. Little started to say something but thought better of it, looking into Potter's flat eyes.

'You want to go,' said Little, 'we'll go.'

Potter nodded. 'Bring your strap.'

Charles White didn't protest. He hoped they would not find this Lorenze Wilder up at the football field. He told himself that they would not. After all, they had gone back to the practice field a couple of times, and except for the first go-round when Wilder had been there, there hadn't been nothin' over there but a few parents, coaches, and some kids.

They met a few minutes later at the front door of the house, Potter wearing his skully. Both he and Little had dressed in dark, loose clothing. White had slipped on his favorite shirt, the bright orange Nautica pullover in that soft fleece, the one felt good against his skin.

'Take that shit off,' said Potter, looking at White's shirt. 'Like you wearin' a sign says, Look at me.'

'Why you buggin'?' said White.

''Cause I don't want no one to remember us later on,' said Potter, talking carefully as he would to a child. 'Could you be more stupid than you is?'

Lorenze Wilder stood by the stadium seats, leaning on the chain-link fence, watching the kids practicing while his hand dipped into a bag of french fries doused in ketchup. He shoved a handful of fries into his mouth and licked ketchup off his fingers. He hadn't thought to get some napkins from the Chinese chicken house he'd stopped into up on the strip. Cheap-ass slope who owned the shop, he was probably hiding the napkins in the back anyhow.

Wilder nodded to one of the parents of the kids who was seated nearby. Man barely gave him the time of day, just a kind of chill-over with his eyes. One of those bourgeois brothers, Wilder guessed, thought he was somethin' with his low-grade government job. Maybe he didn't like Wilder's T-shirt, had a big picture of a marijuana leaf on the front. Didn't like him wearing it in front of all these kids. Well, fuck him, too.

The coaches were working these boys tonight. That white-boy coach they had, he had set up three of those orange cones road crews used in the center of the field. The kids were running to the cones, and the white boy had the pigskin, and he was shouting 'Right' or 'Left,' and the kid would cut that way without looking over his shoulder and get the pass from that coach. The pass would always be there, on the money. Wilder had to admit, the white boy had an arm on him, but he should've thrown it much harder, taught those boys what it was like to feel the sting of a bullet-ball. That's what Wilder would do if he was the coach. He wouldn't mind getting out there himself, show them all how it was done.

The one named Strange was out there, talking to another coach, a brother with a gray mustache who looked even older than him. Wilder didn't care much for this Strange, who he could tell didn't want him hangin' around his little nephew, Joe. First time they'd met, Strange had given him one of those chill-looks, too.

Now the kids were being told to come in and take a knee. It had gotten near to dark, and Lorenze Wilder guessed the practice was coming to an end. Wilder had brought his car with him tonight. He wasn't gonna let Strange talk him out of spending time with his nephew. Joe was his own kin, after all. And Lorenze Wilder needed to speak to him about something important. He'd been looking to get up with the little man on it for a long time.

Charles White sat in the backseat of the Plymouth and watched Garfield Potter return from the fence bordering Roosevelt's stadium. In the passenger seat, Carlton Little ate a Quarter Pounder, his eyes closed as he chewed. He had made them stop at the McDonald's near Howard before doubling back up here to the high school. Little always got hungry behind the herb.

Potter crossed the lot slow, putting a down-dip to his walk, a kind of stretched-back grin spreading on his face. The things that made Potter smile were not the things that made other people smile, and White felt a tightening in his chest.

Potter leaned into Charles White's open window.

'You drivin', Coon. Get out and take the wheel. Roll over to Iowa and park on the street. We'll wait there for him to pull out.'

'Wilder's here?' said Little, looking up from his meal.

'Yeah,' said Potter. 'And we gonna dead this motherfucker tonight.'

Strange gave his usual closing talk to the Midgets and Pee Wees, and answered their questions patiently. Then he asked them for the starting time of the next practice, on Wednesday night.

'*Six o'clock on the dot, be there, don't miss it!*'

'See you then,' said Strange. 'Those of you on your bikes, get home now. If you're waitin' on a ride from one of the coaches or parents, you wait over there by the stands, or at the parking lot if you know the car.'

Strange looked over to the stands, saw the parents and guardians grouped together, waiting for their kids and for those who were not theirs but who depended on them for a lift home. He noticed Joe Wilder's no-account uncle standing apart from the rest, leaning on the fence, a brown bag of trash at his feet. He probably just dropped it there, thought Strange. Wouldn't think to move a few feet and throw it in a can.

Prince and Joe Wilder were walking together toward the stands.

'Prince! Joe! Y'all wait for me, hear?'

Joe Wilder turned his head, made a small wave back to Strange, and kept walking. Strange could see the boy's eyes blink under his helmet as he took out his mouthguard and fitted it in the helmet's cage. He was holding one of those wrestling figures of his tight in his hand.

If Lionel or Lamar were there, he'd tell them to go ahead and get up with the boys, make sure they waited up by his car. But Lamar was baby-sitting his little sister, and Lionel had stayed home to catch up on his schoolwork.

'Derek,' said Lydell Blue, coming up beside him and startling him with his voice. 'Can I talk to you a minute? Need some advice on what to do with my offensive line. I mean, they did nothin' on Saturday. You and Terry been handlin' yours pretty well.'

'I can't talk long,' said Strange.

'This won't take but a minute,' said Blue.

Some of the boys had stayed on the field and were throwing long passes, tackling one another, clowning around. Strange glanced over at Arrington and Quinn, who were gathering up the equipment on the far sideline.

'All right,' said Strange, 'but let's make it quick. I gotta get these boys back in their homes.'

Joe Wilder saw his uncle Lorenze standing by the fence as he neared the stands. Joe's mom was mad at his uncle or something, and Joe hadn't seen him around the apartment for quite some time.

'Little man,' said Lorenze.

'Hey, Uncle Lo,' said Joe with a smile.

'How you been doin'? You lookin' strong out there, Hoss.'

'I been doin' all right.'

'I got my car. C'mon, boy, I'll drive you home tonight.'

'Thanks, but I was gonna ride with Coach Derek.'

'You like ice cream, don't ya?'

'Yeah?'

'Well, c'mon, then. We'll grab a cone or a cup or somethin', and then I'll run you home.'

'*I* like ithe cream,' said Prince.

'Sorry, youngun,' said Lorenze. 'Only got enough to spring for me and my man here. Next time, okay?'

Joe Wilder looked back at Coach Strange, who was still on the field, talking with Coach Blue. His uncle seemed pretty nice. He wouldn't let anything happen to him or nothin' like that. And an ice cream sounded good.

'Tell Coach Derek I got a ride home with my uncle,' said Joe to Prince. 'All right?'

'I'll tell him,' said Prince.

Prince had a seat on the lowest aluminum bench in the stands and waited for Strange to finish what he was doing. Joe and his uncle climbed the concrete steps to the parking lot. The shadows of dusk faded as full dark fell upon the school grounds.

'There we go,' said Potter, looking through the windshield of the Plymouth from the passenger side. 'There goes Wilder right there.'

Lorenze Wilder was letting a uniformed boy into the passenger side of his car. As he went around to the driver's side, he looked around the parking lot, studying the cars.

Potter chuckled under his breath, then took a deep swig from a forty-ounce bottle of malt liquor. He slid the bottle back down between his legs.

'He got some kid with him,' said White. 'That's his nephew, right?'

'Whateva,' said Potter.

'Yo, turn that shit up, D,' said Little from the backseat. He was busy rolling a fat number, his hands deep in a Baggie of herb.

Potter turned up the volume on the radio.

'That's my boy DJ Flexx right there,' said Little. 'They moved him into Tigger's spot.'

'Put this shits in gear, Coon,' said Potter. 'They're pullin' out.'

'We gonna do this thing with that kid in the car?' said White.

'Just stay on Wilder. He probably gonna be droppin' that boy off at his mother's, sumshit like that.'

'We don't need to be messin' with no kids, Gar.'

'Go on, man,' said Potter, chinning in the direction of the royal blue Oldsmobile leaving the parking lot. 'Try not to lose him, neither.'

Lorenze Wilder's car was a 1984 Olds Regency, a V8 with blue velour interior, white vinyl roof, and wire wheel covers. The windows were tinted dark all the way around. It reminded Wilder of one of those Miami cars, the kind those big-time drug dealers had down there, or a limousine. You could see out, but no one could see inside, and for him it was the one feature of the car that had closed the deal. He had bought it off a lot in Northwest for eighteen hundred dollars and financed it at an interest rate of 24 percent. He had missed the last three payments and had recently changed his phone number again to duck the creditors who had begun to call.

Lorenze saw Joe running his hand along the fabric of the seat as they drove south on Georgia Avenue.

'You can get your own car like this someday, you work hard like your uncle.' In fact, Lorenze Wilder hadn't had a job in years.

'It's nice,' said Joe.

'That's like, *velvet* right there. Bet your father got a nice car, too.'

Joe Wilder shrugged and looked over at his uncle. 'I ain't never met my father, so I don't know what he drives.'

'For real?'

'Mama says that my father's just . . . She say he's *gone*.'

Of course, Lorenze knew all about the family history. It was this very thing Lorenze and his sister had argued about, that had set her shit off. She didn't want the boy to know about his father, that was her business. But here it was now, affecting him, Lorenze. Standing in *his* way. All he wanted was a little somethin', a way in. Lorenze tried not to think on it too hard, 'cause it only made him angry.

He glanced over at his nephew. Joe Wilder's helmet was next to him on the bench seat. He held an action figure in his hand, some guy in tights. Sunglasses had been painted on the man's rubber face.

Lorenze let his breath out slow. He hadn't been around kids too much himself. But as kids went, his nephew seemed all right. Lorenze made himself smile and tried to put a tone of interest in his voice.

'Who's that, Joe?'

'The Rock.'

'That's that Puerto Rican boy, right?'

'I don't know what he is, but he's bad. I got a whole rack of wrestlers like this at home.'

'Bet you ain't got no good ice cream at your mama's place.'

'Sometimes we do.'

'What kind of ice cream you like?'

'Chocolate and vanilla. Like, when they mix 'em up.'

'I think I know where this one place is.' They were south of Howard University now, and Lorenze turned the wheel and went east on Rhode Island Avenue. 'Let's see if it's open, okay?'

Had Wilder bothered to look in his rearview, he would have seen a white Plymouth following him from four or five car lengths back.

'He ain't droppin' that kid off,' said White.

'Just keep on doin' what you're doin',' said Potter.

Carlton Little passed the fat bone over the front seat to Potter.

Potter took it and hit it deep. He kept the smoke in his lungs for as long as he could stand it. He exhaled and killed the forty of malt and dropped the bottle at his feet. The music from the radio was loud in the car.

In the Edgewood Terrace area of Northeast, still on Rhode Island, Potter saw the blue Olds slow down up ahead. It turned into a parking lot where a white building stood, fronted with glass and screens.

'Keep drivin' by it,' said Potter.

As they passed the building, Potter saw that it was a take-out ice-cream joint, had a sign out front looked like a kid had drawn it. Next to it was a 7-Eleven with plywood over its windows and red condemnation notices stuck on the boards.

'Drive around the block, Coon.'

White made a left at the next intersection, and the next one after that. Potter reached into his waistband and drew the .357 Colt that he had there. He broke the cylinder and checked the load. He jerked his wrist to snap the cylinder shut, as he had seen it done in the movies, but it did not connect, and he used his free hand to finish the job. He tightened his fingers on the revolver's rubber grip.

'Get your shit ready, Dirty,' said Potter.

'I'm tryin' to,' said Little, with a nervous giggle. He had his 9mm automatic out from under the front seat. He had released the magazine and was now trying to slide it back in. Little had gotten this Glock 17, the current sidearm of the MPD, from a boy he knew who owed him money, a drug debt erased. But Little hadn't practiced with it much.

'Boy,' he said, 'I am *fucked up*.' The magazine found its home with a soft click.

White brought the car back out to Rhode Island, about fifty yards south of the ice-cream place.

'Park it here and let it run,' said Potter.

As they pulled along the curb, Potter watched Lorenze Wilder and his nephew up at the screen window of the joint, the place where you ordered and paid. Wasn't but one other car in the lot, a shitty Nissan. Well, it *was* September. The nights had cooled some.

'What're we gonna do?' said White.

'Wait,' said Potter.

The person worked in the ice-cream place, had a paper hat on his head, Potter could see it from back on the street, was taking his time. Potter looked around the block. He didn't see anyone outside the few residences that were situated around the commercial strip, but there could have been some people looking out at them from behind curtains and shit, you never knew. Later on, they might remember their car.

'Take it around the block again, Coon,' said Potter. 'I don't like us just sittin' here like this.'

Potter pulled the trans down into drive and rolled out into the street. As they neared the ice-cream shop, Potter saw Wilder and his nephew walk toward the Olds. Then he saw the kid hand Wilder his cone and head back toward the shop. The kid was going around the side, where they had hung some swinging signs over a couple of doors.

'Keep goin'!' shouted Potter, and then he barked a laugh. 'Oh, shit, that boy's goin' to the bathroom! Hit this motherfucker, man, go around the block quick. Just drive straight into that ice-cream lot when you get back onto Rhode Island, hear?'

White's foot depressed the gas. He fishtailed the car as he made the left turn, and the tires squealed as he made the next one.

'You ready, Dirty?' said Potter.

'I guess I am,' said Little, his voice cracking some on the reply. He bunched up the McDonald's trash by his side and flung it to the other side of the car. He thumbed off the Glock's safety and racked the slide.

'Motherfucker thinks he gonna rise up and take me for bad,' said Potter. 'He's gonna find out somethin' now.'

White made the next turn, and Rhode Island Avenue came up ahead. His hands were shaking. He gripped the wheel tightly to make the shaking stop.

Joe Wilder went around to the side of the building. He had to pee, and his uncle had told him they had a bathroom there. His uncle said to go now so he could enjoy his ice cream without squirming around in the car. But when Joe got to where the men's room was, he saw that someone had put one of those heavy chains and a big padlock through the handle of the door.

He could hold it for a while. And the thought of that ice cream, the soft chocolate-and-vanilla mix, made him forget he had to go. He went back to the car and got inside.

'That was quick,' said Lorenze, handing Joe his cone.

'It's all locked up,' said Joe. 'But it's all right.' He licked at the ice cream and caught some that had melted down on the cone.

'Good, huh?'

'Yeah, it's tight.' Joe smiled. His tongue showed a mixture of white and brown.

'Listen, Joe . . . you need to get up with your moms about your father and all that.'

'What about him?'

'Well, he ain't exactly gone, like *gone* gone, know what I'm sayin'?'

'Not really.'

'You really ought to meet your father, son. I mean, every boy should be in contact with his pops.'

Joe Wilder bit off the crest of the mound of ice cream sitting atop the cone.

'When you do meet him,' said Lorenze, 'what I want you to do for me is, I want you to tell him how nice I been to you. Like what we did right here tonight.'

'But my moms says he's gone.'

'Listen to me, boy,' said Lorenze. 'When you do talk to him, *wheneva* you do, I want you to tell him that Uncle Lo wants to be put on. Hear?'

Joe Wilder shrugged and smiled. 'Okay.'

Lorenze looked up at a tire sound and saw a white police-looking car pull very quickly into the lot. The car stopped in front of his Olds. Well, it wasn't no police. The car was too old, a fucked-up Plymouth, and anyway, it looked like a bunch of young boys just driving around. Dumb ones, too, if they thought he was gonna let them block his way when there were plenty of other spaces in the lot.

Both passenger-side doors opened on the car, and two of the young men jumped out, one coming around the hood and the other around the tail of the Plymouth. Lorenze's eyes widened as he recognized Garfield Potter at the same time that Potter and a boy with cornrows showed their guns and raised them, stepping with purpose toward the Olds.

'Hey,' said Joe Wilder, 'Uncle Lo.'

Lorenze Wilder heard popping sounds and saw fire spit from the muzzles of the guns. He dropped his ice cream and threw his body across the bench to try to cover his nephew just as the windshield spidered and then imploded. He felt the awful stings and was twisted and thrown back violently and thought of God and his sister and Please don't take the boy, God in that last long moment before his brain matter, blood, and life blew out across the interior of the car.

19

Friends, relatives, police, and print and broadcast media heavily attended Joe Wilder's showing at a funeral parlor near the old Posin's Deli on Georgia Avenue. At one point, traffic had been rerouted on the strip to accommodate the influx of cars. Except for a few acquaintances and a couple of black plainclothes homicide men assigned to the case, few came to pay their respects to Lorenze Wilder on the other side of town.

The boy and his uncle were buried the next day in Glenwood Cemetery in Northeast, not far from where they had been murdered.

Because of the numbing consistency of the murder rate, and because lower-class black life held little value in the media's eyes, the violent deaths of young black men and women in the District of Columbia had not been deemed particularly newsworthy for the past fifteen years. Murders of young blacks rarely made the lead-off in the TV news and were routinely buried inside the Metro section of the *Washington Post*, the details consisting of a paragraph or two at best, the victims often unidentified, the follow-up nil.

Suburban liberals plastered Free Tibet stickers on the bumpers of their cars, seemingly unconcerned that just a few short miles from the White House, American children were enslaved in nightmare neighborhoods, living amid gunfire and drugs and attending dilapidated public schools. The nation was outraged at high school shootings in white neighborhoods, but young black men and women were murdered without fanfare in the nation's capital every single day.

The shooting death of Joe Wilder, though, was different. Like a few high-profile cases over the years, it involved the death of an innocent child. For a few days after the homicide, the Wilder murder was the lead story on the local television news and made top-of-the-fold Metro as well. Even national politicians jumped into the fray, denouncing the culture of violence in the inner cities. As the witness at the ice-cream shop had mentioned the loud rap music coming from the open windows of the shooters' car, these same politicians had gone on to condemn those twin chestnuts, hip-hop and Hollywood. At no time did these bought-and-sold politicians mention the conditions that created that culture, or the handguns, as easily available as a carton of milk, that had killed the boy.

Strange was thinking of these things as he pulled his Brougham into Glenwood Cemetery, coming to a stop behind a long row of cars that stretched far back from Joe Wilder's grave site. Lydell Blue was beside him on the bench. Lamar Williams and Lionel Baker sat quietly in the back of the Cadillac.

Strange looked in his rearview. Dennis Arrington was pulling up behind him in his Infiniti. He had brought along Quinn and three of the boys from the team: Prince, Rico, and Dante Morris. Some of Joe's other teammates had attended the church service, a ceremony complete with tears-to-the-eyes gospel singing, in the Baptist church where Joe and his mother had attended services.

Strange looked out at the automobiles, and the people getting out of them and crossing the lawn. Joe Wilder's mother, Sandra Wilder, was stooped in the middle of a group of mourners who were helping her along to the grave site. She had just gotten out of an expensive German car. Lorenze's casket and Joe's, half the size of his uncle's, were up on platforms under a three-sided green tent beside two open graves.

Most of the cars parked along the curb and up on the grass had been waxed and detailed out of respect. There was a van in the mix that Strange knew to be a police van, its occupants taking photographs of the funeral's attendees. This was fairly routine in killings believed to be of the serial variety, as serial killers often showed up at the wakes and funerals of their victims.

Strange knew, and the police knew, that the killers would not show up here today. He was fairly certain what this had been about. This wasn't a serial killing. It was a gang killing, or turf beef, or eyeball beef, or a death collect on a drug debt. The target was Lorenze Wilder; his nephew Joe just happened to have been in the car. A simple, everyday thing.

Again, Strange studied the cars. Many of them were not just clean. Many of them were drug cars. High-priced imports tricked out in expensive customized options. The men getting out of them were very young and flashily dressed. Strange didn't even have to turn it over in his mind. It wasn't black-on-black racism. He had lived in the city his whole life. It was real.

'You thinking what I'm thinking?' said Blue.

'All kinds of young drug boys here,' said Strange. 'Question is, why?'

'No idea.'

'Joe wasn't even close to being in the life. I know his mother, and she's straight.'

'You see that car she got out of?'

Strange had seen it. It was a three-series BMW, late model, the middle of the line.

'I saw it.'

'She's got, what, a thirty-five-thousand-dollar car and she's living in government-assisted housing?'

'Could be a friend's car,' said Strange.

'Could be.'

'Something to think about. But this ain't the time or the place.'

They got out of the car. Lamar and Lionel joined Quinn, Arrington, and the boys from the team. They walked as a group to the grave site. Strange and Blue walked behind.

'You okay?' said Blue.

'Yeah,' said Strange. But to Blue's eyes his friend looked blown apart, both depleted and seething inside.

'I'm on midnights tonight,' said Blue. 'Was gonna take a car out. Was wonderin' if you wanted to do a ride-along.'

'I do,' said Strange.

'Just thought I'd see what's out there.'

'I'll be there.'

'Meet me at the station at around eleven-thirty. You're gonna need to sign some papers.'

'Right,' said Strange.

Dennis Arrington had asked the group to form a circle. He took the hand of Quinn, who was standing beside him, and the rest of the boys joined hands until the unbroken circle went back to Arrington. They all bowed their heads, and the young deacon led Quinn and the boys in a quiet prayer. Nearby, Strange and Blue also lowered their heads and prayed.

When Strange was done he looked over to the grave site and saw Joe's mother, Sandra, talking to a young man with closely cropped hair, immaculately dressed in a three-button suit. The young man looked over at Strange as Sandra Wilder talked. He kept his eyes on Strange and said something to the well-dressed young man beside him. His friend nodded. These two young men, Strange decided, were also in the life.

'Let's go, Derek,' said Blue. 'Looks like they're about ready to say the final words.'

Blue and Strange walked to the site. Fifteen minutes later, Joe Wilder, eight years old, was lowered into his grave.

Strange woke from a nap at about ten o'clock that night, showered and changed, fed Greco, and locked the house. He had called Janine before he left, telling her that he would be out most of the night and would probably not be back in the office until the following afternoon. He had not spent the night at Janine's place that week.

Strange drove north toward the Fourth District station house at Georgia, between Quackenbos and Peabody. Lydell Blue had already filled him in on the developments of the Wilder case. In the three days that had elapsed since the murders, much had been learned.

The ice-cream shop, called Ulmer's, carried two employees in the fall and winter seasons, a young Salvadoran named Diego Juarez and the owner, Ed Ulmer, African American and fifty-nine years old. On the night of the shooting, Juarez was on the clock. His car, a black Nissan Sentra, was the only one in the lot when Lorenze Wilder pulled in and parked his Olds. After serving Wilder and his nephew, Juarez noticed that the boy tried to use the bathroom around the side of the building but quickly returned to the Oldsmobile. Ulmer had padlocked the bathroom doors after several incidents of vandalism.

Shortly after the boy got into the Olds, joining the older man, a white Plymouth, stripped down like an old police vehicle, came into the parking lot at a high rate of speed. Driven by a young black man with 'a long nose, like a beak,' the Plymouth stopped in front of the Olds, blocking its forward path. Juarez stated that the 'rap music' coming from the open windows of the car was quite loud. Very quickly, two young black men got out of the car, one from the passenger seat and one from the backseat, drew handguns, and began firing into the windshield of the Olds.

Diego Juarez mentally recorded the sequence of letters and numbers on the D.C. license plate of the Plymouth before retreating into the back of the shop. At this point, he phoned the police and then locked himself in the employee bathroom until he heard the squad cars arrive, five minutes later. He had nothing to write with in the bathroom, and in his nervous excitement he had forgotten one of the license plate's two letters and most of its numerals. When he came out of the bathroom, he could recall none of the numerals. By then, of course, the shooters were gone.

One of the shooters, apparently, had vomited a mixture of alcohol and hamburger meat on the asphalt of the parking lot before he'd gotten back into the Plymouth.

Both victims had been shot several times. Lorenze Wilder had been shot in the back as well as the face and neck, indicating that he had initially tried to protect the boy. This was before the force of the bullets had spun him around. Joe Wilder had taken five bullets, one in the groin area, two in the stomach and chest, and two in the face and head. Both victims, lying in melted ice cream and blood, were dead when the police arrived. A rubber action figure, also covered in blood, was found near the boy's hand. A football helmet with a mouthguard wedged in its cage was found at his feet.

Ten 9mm casings were found in the lot consistent with those that would be ejected from an automatic weapon. Their ejection pattern suggested that they came from the gun of the shooter on the right, described by Juarez as the one with 'the braids in his hair.' There were no casings found from the gun of the second shooter. Either he had picked them up, highly unlikely, or they had remained in the chambers of his gun. If the latter was the case, the weapon he used was a revolver. Indeed, the slugs that had done the most damage to the bodies would later be identified as hollow-points fired from a .357.

Juarez described the second shooter as 'a tall and skinny black' with light skin and a skully. Juarez said that the shooter was smiling as he fired his weapon, and it was this smile that had persuaded him, Juarez, to retreat into the back of the shop. He had since worked extensively with police artists to come up with drawings that would closely resemble his brief recollection of the faces on the young men he had seen.

There were no other witnesses to the shooting, and none of the occupants of the nearby residences claimed to have seen a thing.

The white Plymouth was found the next morning on a rural stretch of road bordering a forest in Prince George's County. The car had been doused in gasoline and burned. The smoke rising above the trees had been seen by a resident of a community situated on the other side of the woods, which had prompted him to call the police. The first letter of the license plate matched the letter recalled by Juarez. This was the shooters' car. The arson job had been thorough, obliterating any evidence save for some clothing fibers; the automobile had been wiped clean of prints.

The Plymouth was registered to a Maurice Willis of the 4800 block of Kane Place in the Deanwood section of Northeast. Squad cars and homicide detectives were dispatched to his address, where Willis was taken in without resistance for questioning. The Plymouth belonged to Willis. It had been stolen from the Union Station parking lot while he was attending a movie at the AMC. He had not reported the theft, he explained candidly, because he had been driving the car without insurance. Based on his recollection of the movie he had seen and his certainty of its time, the detectives were able to pinpoint a two-hour window for the theft.

By the end of this next day, the surveillance tapes from the pay booth at the parking garage had produced a photographic record of the one who had stolen the Plymouth. The image was of a light-skinned young black man wearing a sheer black skullcap and shades. On top of these visual obstacles, the suspect had deliberately kept his face partially turned away from the camera while he paid the parking fee. The camera evidence wouldn't find them the shooter, but it would be useful in court.

Detectives continued to canvass the neighborhood where the shooting had occurred. They posted sketches of the suspects and kept the sketches on hand when interviewing potential wits. They interviewed friends and relatives of Lorenze and Joe Wilder extensively, focusing on the acquaintances of the uncle. Most important, the police department had issued a ten-thousand-dollar reward for any information leading to the arrest and conviction of the shooters. This was the most important element and effort of the investigation. In the end, Strange knew, it would be a snitch who would give them the identity of the killers.

They're doing a good job. A damn good job so far. They're doing everything they can.

Strange pulled into the parking lot behind the Fourth District station, found a spot, and cut the engine on his car.

Strange went around to the front of the station house, named in honor of Charles T. Gibson, the uniformed officer slain outside the Ibex Club a few years earlier. He went directly to the front desk in the unadorned, fluorescent-lit lobby. The police officer on desk duty, a woman he did not recognize, phoned Lieutenant Blue in his second-floor office while Strange signed two release forms for insurance purposes. These were required of all citizens requesting ride-alongs.

Blue appeared in uniform. He and Strange went back through the locker room and down a flight of stairs to the rear entrance. Blue told a sergeant, out in the lot catching a cigarette, that he was taking the Crown Victoria parked leftmost in a row of squad cars facing the building. He mentioned the car's number, displayed on its side and rear, to the sergeant as well.

Blue got behind the wheel of the Crown Vic, and Strange sat beside him. They drove out onto Georgia at just past midnight and headed south.

The Fourth District, known as 4-D, ran north-south from the District line down to Harvard Street, and was bordered by Rock Creek on the west and North Capitol Street on the east. It included neighborhoods of the wealthy and those of the extreme lower class. With a high rate of sexual assault, auto theft, and homicide, 4-D had become one of the most troubled districts in the city. Chief Ramsey had been considering an eighth police district to break up the Fourth, probably in the form of a substation near 11th and Harvard. It had gotten that bad.

The crime rate in the city, despite the propaganda issued to the media about 'New Day D.C.,' was rising once again. In the first six months of the new century, homicides were up 33 percent; rapes had increased by over 200 percent. In '97, detectives had been transferred and re-assigned citywide after an independent investigation had reported substandard performance. Anyone who knew anything about police work knew that results came from a network of informants and neighborhood contacts, and confidences, built up over time. The reassignment had destroyed that system. The result was that the current homicide closure rate was at an all-time low. Two out of three murders in the District of Columbia went unsolved – a closure rate of 31 percent.

The streets were fairly quiet. The temperature had dropped to sweater weather, and it was a work night, and kids had school the next day. But still, kids were out. They were out on the commercial strip and back on the corners of the residential streets, sitting on top of trash cans and mailboxes. A curfew law came and went in D.C., but even when it was in effect it was rarely enforced. No one was interested in locking up a minor who had stayed out too late. Police felt, rightly so, that it wasn't their job to raise other people's kids.

'Anything new since the funeral?' said Strange.

'Nothing on the forensic side,' said Blue. 'The detectives are doing some serious recanvassing of the neighborhood over there around Rhode Island. And they're heavily interrogating Lorenze Wilder's associates and friends.'

'He have any?'

'He had a few. The plainclothes guys at Lorenze's wake got some information until they got made. And they do have the sign-in book from the funeral home, has the names and addresses of those who bothered to use it.'

'Anything yet from those interrogations?'

'Lorenze was one of those fringe guys. Didn't work for the most part, least not in payroll jobs. Even his friends admit he was no-account. But none of 'em say he was a target. He wasn't mixed up in no big-time crews or anything like that. That's what they're telling our people, anyway.'

'I'd like to get a list of his friends,' said Strange.

'You know I can't do that, Derek.'

'All right.'

Blue had said it. He had to say it, Strange knew. And Strange let it lie.

They drove back into the neighborhoods between Georgia and 16th. Blue stopped to check on a drunken Hispanic man who was standing in the middle of Kenyon Street, his face covered in alcohol sweat. He said he had 'lost his house.' Blue talked to him carefully and helped him find it. At 15th and Columbia he slowed the patrol car and rolled down his window. A man sat on the stoop of a row house, watching a young boy dribble a basketball on the sidewalk.

'He's out kinda late, isn't he?' said Blue.

The man smiled. 'Aw, he's just hyped. You know kids.'

'I hear you,' said Blue, smiling back. 'But you need to get him inside.'

'Aiight then,' said the man.

Blue drove away. Strange noted how relaxed he was behind the wheel. Blue had always liked working midnights. He said that the danger in these hours was greater, but the respect between the citizens and cops actually increased between midnight and dawn. The squares had all gone home and were sleeping, leaving an uneasy alliance for those who remained.

Blue took a call on a domestic disturbance at 13th and Randolph. He asked the woman if she wanted the husband, whom she had accused of striking her, to spend the night in jail. She said she didn't want that, and this call, like most domestics the police answered, ended in peace.

'How's Terry doing?' said Blue, as he cruised east toward the Old Soldiers' Home.

'He's been quiet,' said Strange. 'Got a new girlfriend, I think, and he's been spending time with her. It's been good for him to be with a woman this week.'

'And you and Janine?'

'Fine.'

'Good woman. That son of hers is a fine young man, too.'

'I know it,' said Strange.

'Lionel gonna be at the game on Saturday?'

'I guess he is.' Strange hadn't thought much on the game.

'You know we got to play it.'

'Right.'

'Think we ought to have a short practice tomorrow night. Talk to the kids.'

'That's what we ought to do.'

'They need to pick themselves up, right about now,' said Blue. 'They're gonna see a lot of death in their young lives. I want them to remember Joe, but I don't want this to paralyze them. You agree?'

'Yes,' said Strange.

Blue looked over at his friend. They had hugged and patted each other's backs when they'd first seen each other after Joe Wilder's murder. The both of them felt extreme guilt, Blue for tying Strange up after practice, and Strange for letting Joe out of his sight. But they had been tight since childhood, and this was not something that needed to be apologized for or discussed. Blue was dealing with it in his own way, but he wasn't sure about how deeply it had burrowed into Strange.

'Listen, Derek—'

'I'm okay, Lydell. Just don't want to talk about it much right now, all right?'

Blue turned up Warder Street in Park View. They passed a group of row houses, all dark. Inside one of them, Garfield Potter, Carlton Little, and Charles White slept.

Blue drove around the Fourth. They bought coffee at the all-night Wings 'n' Things at Kennedy Street and Georgia, and drove around some more. They stopped to tell some kids to get off the streets, and answered a domestic. Blue answered another domestic on 2nd but was called suddenly to a disturbance a block away.

A fight had broken out in a bar on Kennedy at closing time, and it had spilled onto the street. Several squad cars were already on the scene. Officers were holding back the brawlers and trying to quiet some of the neighbors and passersby who had been incited by the police presence. The patrolmen carried batons. A guy shouted 'cracker motherfucker' and 'white motherfucker' repeatedly at the white policeman who had cuffed him. The policeman's partner, a black officer, was called a 'house nigger' by the same man. Blue got out of the car and crossed the street. Strange stepped out and leaned against the Crown Vic.

Down the street was the Three-Star Diner, Billy Georgelakos's place. Strange's father had worked there as a grill man for most of his career.

A riot gate covered the front of the diner. Nearby, concertina wire topped the fence surrounding the parking lot of a church.

Blue returned to the Crown Vic with sweat beading his forehead. Most of the bystanders on Kennedy had disappeared. Whatever this had been, it was over without major incident. It would go unreported to the majority of the city's citizens, safely asleep at home in their beds.

Strange asked Blue to make a pass through Park Morton, where Joe Wilder had lived, and Blue agreed. In the complex, few people were out. A boy sat on a swing in the playground of the dark courtyard, smoking a cigarette. Dice players and dope smokers moved about the stairwells of the apartments.

'We put flyers with the artist's renderings of the suspects in the mailboxes here,' said Blue. 'Gonna post them around the neighborhood as well.'

'That's good.'

'Most of the time we don't get much cooperation up in here. Drug dealers get chased by the police, they find a lot of open doors, places to hide, in this complex.'

'What I hear.'

'They even got community guns buried around here somewhere. We know all about it, but it's tough to fight.'

'You sayin' you think no one will come forward?'

'I'm hoping this case here is gonna be different. We're mistrusted here, maybe even hated. I got to believe, though, anyone with a heart is gonna want to help us find the people who would kill an innocent kid.'

On the drive out, Blue went by the brick pillars and wall that were the unofficial gateway to the housing complex. Two children, girls wearing cartoon-character jackets, sat atop the wall. The girls, no older than eleven or twelve, cold-eyed the occupants of the squad car as they passed.

'Where are the parents?' whispered Strange.

20

On Saturday morning, the Petworth Panthers defeated a Lamond-Riggs team on the field of LaSalle Elementary by a score of twenty to seven. Joe Wilder had not been mentioned by name in the pregame talk, but Dennis Arrington had led a prayer for their 'fallen brother.' The boys went to one knee and bowed their heads without the usual chatter and horseplay. From the first whistle, their play on the field was relentless. The parents and guardians in attendance stood unusually quiet on the sidelines during the game.

Afterward, as they were gathering up the equipment, Quinn put his hand on Strange's shoulder.

'Hey.'

'Hey, Terry.'

'You feel like gettin' a beer later this afternoon?'

'I gotta drop these kids off.'

'And I've got to work a few hours up at the store. Why don't you meet me up at Renzo's, say, four o'clock? You know where that is, right?'

'Used to be Tradesman's Tavern, up on Sligo Avenue, right?'

'I'll see you there.'

Lamar Williams, Prince, and Lionel Baker were waiting by Strange's Cadillac, parked on Nicholson. Lydell Blue's Park Avenue was curbed behind it. Strange told the boys to get in his Brougham as he saw Blue, holding a manila folder, approaching him from behind.

'Derek,' said Blue, holding out the folder. 'Thought you might want this Migdets roster back for your master file.'

Strange took it and opened his trunk. He started to slip the folder into his file box as Blue began to walk away. Strange saw some notation written in pencil on the Pee Wees folder. He pulled it and studied his own writing, the description of a car and a series of letters and numbers, on the outside of the folder. He thought back to the evening he had written the information down.

'Lydell!' he said.

Blue walked back to Strange, still standing by his open trunk. Strange took the papers out of the Pee Wee folder and handed the folder to Blue, pointing at the notation.

'Probably nothin',' said Strange, 'but you ought to run this plate here through the system.'

Blue eyed the folder. 'Why?'

'Not too far back, a week or so, I noticed some hard-looking boys up in the Roosevelt lot one night when we had practice. Thinking back on it, it was a night that Lorenze Wilder was down on the field, waitin' on Joe. I wrote down the plate number and car description out of habit. The car was a Caprice. I guessed on the year, but I do know it was close to the model year of the one I own. I put down it was beige, too.'

Strange flashed on the image of the boys. One of them wore his hair in close cornrows, like those on one of the shooters the ice-cream employee had described. But that meant nothing in itself, like noting he wore Timberlands or loose-fitting jeans; a whole lot of young boys around town kept their hair the same way.

'A beige Caprice. Why you got "beige-brown" on here, then?'

'Had one of those vinyl roofs, a shade darker than the body color.'

'Okay. I'll get it into the system right away.'

'Like I say, probably nothin'. But let me know it if turns up aces.'

'I will.'

Strange watched Blue go back to his car. He took the papers from the Pee Wee folder and decided to put them together with the Midget papers in the folder Blue had just given him. He opened the folder. Inside was a mimeographed list of Lorenze Wilder's friends and acquaintances, along with notations describing interview details, taken from the official investigation.

Strange turned his head. Blue had ignitioned his Buick and was pulling off the curb. Strange nodded in his direction, but Blue would not look his way. Strange put the papers together, slipped the folder into his file box, and closed the lid of his trunk.

Strange drove Lionel to his mother's house on Quintana. As Lionel was getting out of the car, he asked Strange if he was coming over for dinner that night. Strange replied that he didn't think so, but to tell his mother he'd 'get up with her later on.' Lionel looked back once at Strange as he went up the walk to his house. Strange drove away.

Prince was the next to be dropped. He had been quiet during the game and had not spoken at all on the ride. The boys who were always cracking on him were on their usual corner, across from his house. Prince asked Strange if he would mind walking along with him to his door. At the door, Strange patted Prince's shoulder.

'You played a good game today, son.'

'Thanks, Coach Derek.'

'See you at practice, hear? Now go on inside.'

Lamar Williams rode shotgun for the trip down to Park Morton. He stared out the window, listening to that old-school music Mr Derek liked to play, not really paying attention to the words or the melody. It was always that blue-sky stuff about love and picking yourself up, how the future was gonna be brighter, brother this and brother that. Lamar wondered if everyone had been more together back then, in the seventies or whenever it was. If those brothers weren't killin' each other every day, like they were now. If they were killin' on kids 'back in the day.' Anyway, that kind of music, it sure didn't speak to the world Lamar was living in right now.

'You thinkin' of Joe?' said Strange.

'Yeah.'

'It's okay. I was, too.'

Lamar shifted in his seat. 'That boy was just good. I never thought he'd die. You'd think he'd be the last one living in my complex who'd go out like that.'

'Just because he was a good boy? You know better than that. I've told you before, you always got to be aware of what's going on around you, living where you do.'

'I know. But I don't mean that, see? Word was, Joe was protected. Even the ones liked to step to everybody, they kept their hands off that boy. I mean, he was a tough little kid and all. But the word was out; everybody knew not to fuck with Joe.'

Strange started to correct Lamar from using the curse word, but he let it pass. 'Why you think that was?'

'No idea. Was like, people got the idea in their heads he was connected to someone you didn't want to cross. It was just one of those things got around, and you knew.'

'I saw some fellas at his funeral,' said Strange, 'had to be drug boys.'

'I saw 'em, too,' said Lamar.

'Any idea why they were paying their respects?'

'Uh-uh.'

'Was his mother involved with those people?'

'Not so I knew.'

'What about that car she came in?'

'Everybody drivin' a nice car these days, seems like. Don't make you in the game.'

'True. But you never saw her hangin' with people you thought were in the life?'

'No. There *was* these young boys, was lookin' for her one night. They rolled up on me when I was walkin' through the complex. Said they owed her money. I didn't tell 'em where she lived, though. They didn't look right.'

Strange looked over at Lamar. 'How *did* they look?'

'I don't recall, you want the truth. Don't mind tellin' you, Mr Derek, I was scared.'

'Did one of them have cornrows?'

'I don't remember. Look, I didn't even want to meet their eyes, much less study on 'em. I only remember this one boy in the backseat, 'cause he was, like, goofy lookin'. Had a nose on him like one of those anteaters and shit.'

'What about their car?'

'It was white,' said Lamar. 'Square, old. That's all that registered in my mind. That's all I know.'

'You did right not to meet their eyes, Lamar. You did good.'

'Yeah.' Lamar snorted cynically. 'It's all good. Good to be livin' in a place where you can't even be lookin' at anyone long for fear you're gonna get downed.'

Strange pulled into Park Morton and went slowly down its narrow road.

'You got be positive, Lamar. You got to focus on doing the things that will get you to a better place.'

Lamar looked Strange over. His lip twitched before he spoke. 'How I'm gonna do that, huh? I can't read all that good, and I'm barely gonna graduate high school. I got no kinda grades to get me into any kind of college. Only job I ever had was dustin' your office and taking out your trash.'

'There's plenty of things you can do. There's night school and there's trade school . . . whole lotta things you can do, hear?'

'Yessir,' said Lamar, his voice devoid of enthusiasm. He pointed to the road going alongside the playground in the courtyard. 'You can drop me right here.'

Strange stopped the car. 'Listen, you been good to me, Lamar. Conscientious and efficient, and I'm not gonna forget it. I'll help you in any way I can. I'm not going to give up on you, young man, you hear me?'

Lamar nodded. 'I'm just all messed up over Joe right now, I guess. I miss that boy.'

'I miss him, too,' said Strange.

He watched Lamar cross the courtyard, pushing on a rusted swing as he walked past the set. Strange thought about the description that Lamar had just given him: the white car, and the kid with the long nose. Juarez, the ice-cream-parlor employee, had described the Plymouth's driver as having a nose 'like a beak.'

Strange had the strong suspicion that this was not a coincidence. He knew he should phone Lydell Blue right now and give him the information he had just received. But he had already decided to keep Lamar's story to himself.

Strange was not proud of his decision, but he had to be honest with himself now. He was hoping to find the murderers of Joe Wilder before they were picked up by the police. He knew that if these little pieces were coming to him, a private cop, it would not be long before the police, fully mobilized, would have suspects in custody. He was wondering how much time he had before they took the killers in. Wondering, too, what he would do to them if he found them first.

Strange hit the heavy bag in his basement, showered and dressed, fed Greco, and locked down his row house. He drove uptown toward the District line. In his rearview he thought he saw a red car, vaguely familiar, staying with him but keeping back a full block at all times. The next time he checked on the car, up around Morris Miller's liquor store, it was gone, and Strange relaxed in his seat.

The events of the past week had elevated his sense of street paranoia. People living in certain sections of the city, Strange knew, felt the fear of walking under this kind of emotional sword every day. But he didn't like to succumb to it himself.

Strange parked on Sligo Avenue. As he was crossing the street, the beeper on his hip sounded, and he checked the numbered readout: Janine. He clipped the beeper back onto his belt.

Strange walked into Renzo's, an unbeautiful neighborhood beer garden in downtown Silver Spring. Renzo's housed a straight-line bar, stools along a mirrored wall, a pool table, and keno monitors. Bars like this one were common in Baltimore, Philly, and Pittsburgh, but rare around D.C. Quinn sat on a bar stool, reading a paperback and nursing a bottle of Bud in the low light. A heavy-set guy in a flannel shirt, a guy in camouflage pants, and several keno players, huffing cigarettes, sat with him along the stick. The bartender was a woman, nearly featureless in the low light, wearing a Nighthawks T-shirt and jeans. Smoke hung heavy in the air.

Strange got up on a stool next to Quinn. He ordered a Heineken from the tender.

'From a bottle,' said Strange. 'And I don't need a glass.'

'This is you,' said Quinn, producing a record album he had propped up at his feet.

Strange took it and studied the cover. He smiled at the photograph of Al Green decked out in a white suit, white turtleneck, and white stacks, sitting in a white cane chair against a white background. A green hanging plant and a green potted plant, along with the singer's rich chocolate skin, gave the cover its color. It looked like Al was wearing dark green socks, too, though some argued that the socks were black.

'*I'm Still in Love With You.*'

'You don't have to say it,' said Quinn. 'It's understood.'

'Al freaks called this "The White Album,"' said Strange, ignoring Quinn. 'Has "Simply Beautiful" on it, too.'

'You don't have it, do you? I thought it might be one of those you lost in that house flood you had.'

'I did lose the vinyl, you're right. I own the CD, but the CD's got no bottom.'

'Funny thing is, it came in with this carton of seventies rock, a lot of hard blues-metal and also weird stuff some pot smoker had to be listening to. I found Al Green filed alphabetically, after Gentle Giant and Gong.'

'Herb smokers used to listen to Al, too. People used to listen to all sorts of music then, wasn't no barriers set up like it is now. Young man like you, you missed it. Was a real good time.'

'I think you might have mentioned that to me before. Anyway, I'm glad you like it.'

'Thank you, buddy.'

'It's all right.'

Strange and Quinn tapped bottles. Strange then filled Quinn in on the ongoing investigation. He told him about the Caprice in the parking lot and the white car and its occupants that had rolled up on Lamar Williams. He told him about Lydell Blue's list.

'You get up with Joe's mother,' said Quinn, 'she might be able to narrow down the number of names for us.'

'I called Sandra a couple of times and left messages,' said Strange. 'She hasn't got back to me yet.'

They discussed the case further. Strange drank two beers to Quinn's one. Quinn watched Strange close his eyes as he took a deep pull from the bottle.

'Janine's been trying to get up with you,' said Quinn.

'Yeah?'

'She called me at the bookstore, said she's been beeping you. Something about finding the last piece of the puzzle on Calhoun Tucker.'

Strange drank off some of his beer. 'I'll have to see what that's about.'

'What's goin' on between you two?'

'Why, she say somethin' was?'

'Only that you've been avoiding her this week. Outside of work stuff, she hasn't been able to get through to you at all.'

'I'm not sure I'm right for her right now, you want the truth. Her *or* Lionel. When I get like this . . . Ah, forget it.' Strange signaled the bartender.

'You're not done with that one yet,' said Quinn, nodding to the bottle in front of Strange.

'I will be soon. But thanks for pointing it out.' Strange's elbow slipped off the bar. 'At least you're doin' all right with Sue. Seems like a good woman. Looks good, too.'

'Yeah, she's cool. I'm lucky I found her. But Derek, I'm talkin' about you.'

'Look, man, everything's been boiling up inside me, with Joe's death and all. I know I haven't been dealing with it right.'

'Nobody knows how to deal with it. When a kid dies like that, you look around you and the things you thought were in order, your beliefs, God, whatever . . . nothing makes sense. I've been fucked up about it myself. We all have.'

Strange didn't say anything for a while. And then he said, 'I should've let him run that play.'

'What?'

'Forty-four Belly. He wanted to run it in at the end of the game. Boy never did get to run that touchdown play, the whole time he played for us. He would've scored that day, too, 'cause he had the fire. Can you imagine how happy that would've made him, Terry?'

Strange's eyes had filled. A tear threatened to break loose. Quinn handed him a bar napkin. Strange used it to wipe his face.

Quinn noticed that the guy in the flannel shirt was staring at Strange.

'You want somethin'?' said Quinn.

'No,' said the guy, who quickly looked away.

'I didn't *think* you did,' said Quinn.

'Settle down, Terry. I'd be starin', too. Grown man, actin' like a baby.' Strange balled up the napkin and dropped it in an ashtray. 'Anyway. It's all water passed now, isn't it?'

'You did right,' said Quinn, 'telling Joe not to run up that score. You were teaching him the right thing.'

'I don't know about that. I don't know. I thought he had a whole lifetime of touchdown runs ahead of him. Out here, though, every day could be, like, a last chance. Not just for the kids. For you and me, too.'

'You can't think like that.'

'But I do. And it's selfish of me, man, I know. Plain selfish.'

'What is?'

Strange stared at his fingers peeling the label of the bottle of beer. 'These feelings I been having. About my own mortality, man. Selfish of me to be thinkin' on it, when a boy died before he even got started and I been fortunate enough to live as long as I have.'

'Men are always thinking about their mortality,' said Quinn. He sipped his beer and placed the bottle softly on the bar. 'Shit, man, death and sex, we think about it all the time. It's why we do all the stupid things we do.'

'You're right. Every time I start thinkin' on my age, or that I'm bound to die, I start thinking about getting some strange. Makes me want to run away from Janine and Lionel and any kind of responsibility. It's always been like that with me. Like having a different woman's gonna put off death, if only for a little while.'

'You need to be runnin' *to* those people, Derek. The ones who love you, man. Not to those girls down at those massage parlors—'

'Aw, here we go.'

'Just because they don't walk the street doesn't make 'em any different than streetwalkers. Those girls ain't nothin' but hookers, man.'

'For real?'

'I'm serious. Look, I've been with whores. So I'm not looking down on you for this. Just about every man I know has been with 'em, even if it was just a rite-of-passage thing. But what I've been seeing lately—'

'Your girl Sue got you converted, huh? Now you got religion and seen the light.'

'No, not me. But it's wrong.'

'Terry, these ladies I see, they got to make a living same as anyone else.'

'You think that's what they want to be doing with their lives?

Putting their hands on a man's dick they got no feelings for? Letting a stranger touch their privates? Shit, Derek, these Asian girls in those places, they've been brought over here and forced into that life to pay off some kind of a debt. It's like slavery.'

'Nah, man, don't even go there. White man starts talkin' about, *It's like slavery*, I do not want to hear it.'

'Ignore it if you want to,' said Quinn. 'But that's exactly what it's like.'

'I got to relieve myself, man,' said Strange. 'Where's the bathroom at in this place?'

Quinn drank the rest of his beer while Strange went to the men's room. When Strange returned, Quinn noticed that he had washed his face. Strange did not get back on his stool. He placed one hand on the bar for support.

'Well, I better get on out of here.'

'Yeah, I need to also. I'm seeing Sue tonight.'

Strange withdrew his wallet from his back pocket. Quinn put his hand on Strange's forearm.

'I got it.'

'Thanks, buddy.' Strange picked up his album and put it under his arm. 'And thanks again for this.'

'My pleasure.'

'Monday morning, I plan on getting started on that list Lydell slipped our way. You with me?'

'You know it. Derek—'

'What?'

'Call Janine.'

Strange nodded. He shook Quinn's hand and pushed away from the bar, unsteady on his feet. Quinn watched him go.

21

Strange stopped by Morris Miller's and bought a six. He opened one as he hit Alaska Avenue and drank it while driving south on 16th. Dusk had come. He didn't know where he was headed. He kept driving and found himself on Mount Pleasant Street. He parked and went into the Raven, a quiet old bar he liked, not too different from Renzo's, to get himself off the road. There, seated in a booth against the wall, he drank another beer.

When he came out he was half drunk, and the sky was dark. He said 'hola' to a Latino he passed on the sidewalk and the man just laughed. Strange's beeper sounded. He scanned the readout and looked for a pay phone. He had brought his cell with him, but he didn't know where it was. Maybe in the car. He didn't care to use it anyhow. He knew of a pay phone up near Sportsman's Liquors, run by the Vondas brothers. He liked those guys, liked to talk with them about sports. But their store would be closed this time of night.

Strange walked in that direction, found the phone, and dropped a quarter and a dime in the slot. He waited for an answer as men stood on the sidewalk around him talking and laughing and drinking from cans inside paper bags.

'Janine. Derek here.'

'Where are you?'

'Calling from the street. Somewhere down here . . . Mount Pleasant.'

'I been trying to get up with you.'

'All right, then, here I am. What've you got?'

'You sound drunk, Derek.'

'I had one or two. What've you got?'

'Calhoun Tucker. You know how I been trying to finish out checking on his employment record? I finally got the word on that job he had with Strong Services, down in Portsmouth? They were no longer operating, so I was having trouble pinpointing the nature of the business—'

'C'mon, Janine, get to it.'

There was a silence on the other end of the line. Strange knew he had been short with her. He knew she was losing patience with him, rightfully so. Still, he kept on.

'Janine, just tell me what you found.'

'Strong Services was an investigative agency. They specialized in rooting out employee theft. He worked undercover in clubs, trying to find employees who were stealing from the registers, like that. Which is how he moved on into the promotion business, I would guess. But my point is, at one time, Tucker was a private cop. He might have done other forms of investigation as well.'

'I get it. So now that completes his background check. Anything else?'

There was another block of silence. 'No, that's it.'

'Good work.'

'Am I going to see you tonight, Derek?'

'I don't think so, baby. It'd be better for both of us if I was alone tonight, I think. Tell Lionel . . . Janine?'

Somewhere in there Strange thought he'd heard a click. Now there was a dial tone. The line was dead.

Strange stood on the sidewalk, the sounds of cars braking and honking and Spanish voices around him. He hung the receiver back in its cradle. He walked back down toward the Raven and tried to remember where he had parked his car.

Strange parked in the alley behind the Chinese place on I Street and got out of his Caddy. The heroin addict who hustled the alley, a longtime junkie named Sam, stepped out of the shadows and approached Strange.

'All right, then,' said Sam.

'All right. Keep an eye on it. I'll get you on the way out.'

Sam nodded. Strange went in the back door, through the hall and the beaded curtains, and had a seat at a deuce. He ordered Singapore-style noodles and a Tsingtao from the mama-san who ran the place, and when she served his beer she pointed to a young woman who was standing back behind the register and said, 'You like?'

Strange said, 'Yes.'

He walked out into the alley. He had showered and he had come, but he was not refreshed or invigorated. He was drunk and confused, angry at himself and sad.

A cherry red Audi S4 was parked behind his Cadillac. A man stood beside the Audi, his arms folded, his eyes hard on Strange. Strange recognized him as Calhoun Tucker. He was taller, more handsome, and younger looking up close than he had appeared to be through Strange's binoculars and the lens of his AE-1.

'Where's Sam at?' said Strange.

'You mean the old man? He took a stroll. I doubled what you were payin' him to look after your car.'

'Money always cures loyalty.'

'Especially to someone got a jones. One thing I learned in the investigation business early on.'

Tucker unfolded his arms and walked slowly toward Strange. He stopped a few feet away.

Strange kept his posture and held his ground. 'How'd you get onto me?'

'You talked to a girl down in a club on Twelfth.'

'The bartender.'

'Right. You left her your card. She was mad at me the day she spoke to you. She ain't mad at me no more.'

The alley was quiet. A street lamp hummed nearby.

'You've been easy to tail, Strange. Especially easy to follow today. All that drinkin' you been doing.'

'What do you want?'

'You got a nice business. Nice woman, too. And that boy she's got, he seems clean-cut, doesn't look like no knuckle-head. Living up there on Quintana. You spend the night there once in a while, don't you?'

'You've been tailing me awhile.'

'Yeah. Let me ask you somethin': does your woman know you get your pleasure down here with these hos like you do?'

Strange narrowed his eyes. 'I asked you what you wanted.'

'All right, then, I'll get to it. Won't take up much of your time. Just wanted to tell you one thing.'

'Go ahead.'

Tucker looked around the alley. When he looked back at Strange, his eyes had softened.

'I love Alisha Hastings. I love her deep.'

'I don't blame you. She's a fine young lady. From a real good family, too. You got yourself a piece of gold right there. Somethin' you should've thought of when you were runnin' around on her.'

'I *think* of her all the time. And I plan to be good to her. To take care of her on the financial tip and be there for her emotionally, too. This is the woman who is gonna be the mother of my children, Strange.'

'You got a funny way of preparin' for it.'

'*Look* at yourself, man. Is it you who should be judging me?'

Strange said nothing.

'I'm a young man,' said Tucker. 'I am young and I have not taken that vow yet and until I do I am gonna *freak*. Because I am only gonna be this young and this free one time. But, you got to understand, that ceremony is gonna mean somethin' to me. I saw a bond between my mother and my father that couldn't be broken, and it set an example for me. For my brothers and sisters, too. I know what it means. But for now, I'm just out here having fun.'

'George Hastings is a friend of mine.'

'Then *be* a friend to him. I'm lookin' you in the eye and telling you, there is nobody out here who is going to love and respect his daughter, for life, like I know I am going to do.'

'I can only report your history and what I've seen.'

'You're not listening to me, Strange. Hear me and think about what I'm telling you. I *love* that girl. I love her fierce enough to make me do something I don't care to do. You want to take me down, fine. But you're gonna go right down with me.'

'You threatenin' me?'

'Just telling you how it's gonna be.'

Strange looked down at his feet. He rubbed his face and again met Tucker's eyes. 'Whatever I'm gonna do with regards to you, young man, I am going to do. You standing there talking bold, it's not gonna influence me either way.'

'Course not.' Tucker looked Strange over. 'You got principles.'

'You don't know me that well to be talking to me that way.'

'But I do know your kind.'

'Now wait a minute—'

'Let me put it another way, then. This is all about what kind of husband I'm gonna be to Alisha, right? Well, I can promise you this: I ain't gonna end up like you, Strange. Sneakin' around down here in your middle age, paying to have some girl you don't even know jack your dick. Out here tellin' on others when you got a fucked-up life your own self. So do whatever you think is right. I've said what I came to say. You want to listen, it's up to you.'

Tucker walked back to his car, got behind the wheel, and lit the ignition. Strange watched the Audi back out of the alley. Then it was just Strange, standing on the stones under the humming street lamp, alone with his shame.

Janine Baker came down the stairs and unlocked the front door of her house at a little past one in the morning. She had been lying awake in bed and had recognized the engine on Strange's Cadillac as he had cruised slowly down her block.

He was out there on the stoop, one step down from the doorway. She looked down on him, rumpled and glassy-eyed, as she stood in the frame.

'Come on in. It's cool out there.'

'I don't think I should,' said Strange. 'I just came by to apologize for being so short with you on the phone.'

Janine pulled the lapels of her robe together against the chill. Behind her, Strange could see Lionel coming down the staircase. He stopped a few steps up.

'Tell him to go back to bed,' said Strange softly. 'I don't want him seeing me like this.'

Janine looked over her shoulder and directed her son to return to his room. Strange waited for Lionel to go back up the stairs.

'Well?'

'I'm all turned around,' said Strange.

'And you're trying to say what?'

'I just don't feel . . . I don't feel like I'm right for you now. I know I'm not right for the boy.'

'You're looking to give up on us, is that it?'

'I don't know.'

'I haven't given up on *you.*'

'I know it.'

'Even while I knew how you been cheatin' on me these past couple years.'

Strange looked up at her. 'It's not what you think.'

'*Tell* me what it is, then. Don't you think I been knowin' about your, your *problem* for a while now? I might be forgiving, but I am human, and I still have my senses. Smelling sweet like lilacs or somethin' every time you come back from seeing her. Smelling like perfume, and you, a man who doesn't even wear aftershave.'

'Listen, baby—'

'Don't *baby* me. Derek, I can smell it on you *now.*'

Her voice was almost gentle. It cut him, Janine being so steady with him, so strong. He wanted her to raise her voice, let it out. But he could see she wasn't going to do that. It made him admire her even more.

Strange shifted his feet. 'I never loved another woman the whole time I been lovin' you.'

'That supposed to mean something to me? Should I feel better because you only been, what, cattin' around with hos?'

'No.'

'What about respectin' me? What about respecting yourself?'

Strange cut his eyes. 'When my mother was dying, that whole time . . . that was when I started. I couldn't face it, Janine. Not just her passing, but lookin' at my own death, too. Seeing that my turn was coming up, not too far behind.'

'And now Joe Wilder's been killed,' said Janine, completing his thought. 'Derek, don't go dishonoring that little boy's memory by connecting the one thing to the other. All these bad things out here ought to lead you to the ones who love you. In the face of all that, family and your faith in the Lord, it's what keeps you strong.'

'I guess I'm weak, then.'

'Yes, Derek, you are weak. Like so many men who are really just boys on the inside. Selfish, and so afraid to die.'

Strange spread his hands. 'I love you, Janine. Know this.'

Janine leaned forward and kissed him on the mouth. It was a soft kiss, not held long. As she pulled back, Strange knew that the feel of her lips on his would haunt him forever.

'I won't share you anymore,' said Janine. 'I am not going to share you with anyone else. So you need to think about your future. How you want to spend it, and who you want to spend it with.'

Strange nodded slowly. He turned and walked down the sidewalk to his car. Janine closed the door and locked it, and went into the hallway and leaned her back against the plaster wall. Here she was out of sight of Lionel and Strange. For a very short while, and quietly, she allowed herself to cry.

Terry Quinn sat naked in a cushioned armchair set by the window. His bedroom was dark, and outside the window the streets were dark and still. He stared out the window at nothing, his fist resting on his chin. He heard a rustling sound as Sue Tracy moved under the sheets and blanket. Her nude form was a lush outline as she brought herself to a sitting position in his bed.

'What's wrong, Terry? Can't you sleep?'

'I'm thinking about Derek,' said Quinn. 'I'm worried about my friend.'

22

The next morning, Strange willed himself out of bed and down to the kitchen, where he brewed a cup of coffee and slipped the sports page out of the Sunday *Post*. He drank the coffee black while reading Michael Wilbon's latest column on Iverson and a story on the upcoming 'Skins/Ravens contest, set for that afternoon. Strange then drove with Greco up to Military and Oregon, where he hung a left into Rock Creek Park. He and many others ran their dogs in a field there by a large parking lot.

Greco ran the high grass field with a young Doberman named Miata, a black-and-tan beauty whose primary markings were a brown muzzle, chest, and forelegs. Generally, Greco preferred the company of humans and chose his few canine playmates carefully. But he took to this one quickly, finding Miata to be an energetic and able-bodied friend. The dog's owner, Deen Kogan, was an attractive woman with whom Strange found it very easy to talk. In another life, he might have asked her out for a scotch, maybe a bite to eat. But she wasn't Janine.

Back on Buchanan, Strange showered and dressed in one of the two suits he owned. He emptied a full can of Alpo into Greco's dish and headed up to the New Bethel Church of Christ, on Georgia and Piney Branch. Driving north, he realized that he was being followed by a black Mercedes C-Class, a fine factory automobile cheapened in this case by the custom addition of a spoiler and over-elaborate rims. Up around Fort Stevens he circled the block, came back out on Georgia, and looked in his rearview: the Mercedes was still behind him. After his encounter with Calhoun Tucker, he could no longer blame his feeling of dread on paranoia. This was real.

Strange took a seat in a pew far back in the church, coming in at the tail end of the service. He could see Janine and Lionel in their usual place, a few rows up ahead. Strange prayed hard for them and for himself, and closed his eyes tightly when he prayed for Joe Wilder. He believed, he had to believe, that the spirit of that beautiful boy had gone on to a better place. He told himself that the corpse lying in the ground in that small box wasn't Joe, but was just a shell. He felt his emotions well up, more from anger than from sadness, as he prayed.

Outside the church Strange shook hands with the parishioners he knew, and with a few he was meeting for the first time. He felt a hand drop onto his shoulder and he turned. It was George Hastings, his daughter by his side.

'George,' said Strange. 'Alisha. Sweetheart, you look lovely today.'

'Thank you, Mr Derek.'

'Honey,' said Hastings, 'give me a moment alone with Derek here, will you?'

Alisha gave Strange a beautiful smile and found a friend to talk to nearby.

'Haven't heard from you in a while,' said Hastings.

'Been meaning to get up with you, George,' said Strange.

'You could stop by for the game. You got plans for the day?'

'No, I . . . All right. Maybe I'll drop by later on.'

Hastings shook Strange's hand and held the grip. 'My sympathies on that boy from your team.'

Strange nodded. He had no idea what he would say to his friend when they next met.

Strange caught up with Janine and Lionel as they walked to her car and asked them if they'd like to have breakfast with him at the diner. It was their Sunday morning ritual. But Janine said she had a busy afternoon planned and that she ought to get a jump on it. Lionel did not protest. Strange told him he'd pick him up for practice Monday night. Lionel only nodded, double-taking Strange with what Strange took to be a look of confusion before dropping into the passenger side of Janine's car. Strange hated himself then for what he knew he was: another man who was about to drift out of this boy's life. He wondered what Janine had told Lionel, and what he would tell Lionel himself if he had the chance.

On the way over to the Three-Star Diner, going east on Kennedy, Strange noticed the Mercedes, once again, in his rearview. The tricked-out car was only two lengths back. They're not even worried about being burned, thought Strange, and for one young moment he considered taking a sudden turn and punching the gas. He could lose them easily; he'd come up around here, and no one knew these streets and alleys like he did. But he let them follow him, all the way down to First, where he parked his Caddy in a space along the curb. The Mercedes pulled up behind him.

Strange locked his Brougham and walked toward the Mercedes,

memorizing the car's license plate and confirming the model as he approached. Strange reached the car as the driver's-side window slid down. Behind the wheel was a handsome, typically unfriendly looking young man with close-cropped hair. His suit and the knot of his tie were immaculate. Strange recognized him as one of the men who had attended Joe Wilder's funeral. He had been talking to Joe's mother, Sandra Wilder, by the grave.

In the passenger bucket was a man of the same age, same unsmiling expression, more flashily dressed. He sat low, with one arm leaning on the sill of his window, talking on his cell.

'What can I do for you fellas?' said Strange.

'A man needs to speak with you,' said the driver.

'Who?'

'Granville Oliver.'

Strange knew the name. The city knew Granville Oliver's name. But with Strange it was more; he had a history with Oliver's bloodline.

'And you are?'

'Phillip Wood.'

Wood's partner lowered the cell and looked across the buckets at Strange. 'Granville wants to see you *now*.'

Strange did not acknowledge this one or give him any kind of eye contact at all. He glanced over his shoulder through the plate glass fronting the diner. He could see Billy Georgelakos coming around the counter, his girth pushing against his stained apron, holding the pine baton that Strange knew had been hollowed out and filled with lead. Strange shook his head slightly at Billy, who stopped his forward path at once. Strange returned his gaze to the driver, Phillip Wood.

'Tell you what,' said Strange. 'I'm gonna go on in there and eat my breakfast. When I come out, y'all are still out here? We can talk.'

Strange gave them his back, left the idling Mercedes curbside, and walked into the Three-Star. The sound of gospel music, coming from the house radio, hit him like cool water as he entered the diner.

'Everything all right, Derek?' said Georgelakos, now behind the counter again.

'I think so.'

'The usual?'

'Thanks, friend,' said Strange.

Strange ate a feta-cheese-and-onion omelette sprinkled with Texas Pete hot sauce, and a half-smoke side, and washed it down with a couple of cups of coffee. Some after-church types were at the counter and some sat in the old red-cushioned booths. The diner was white tiles and white walls, kept clean by Billy and his longtime employee, Etta.

Billy Georgelakos, his bald head sided by patches of gray, ambled down the rubber mat that ran behind the counter and leaned his forearms on the Formica top.

'Where's Janine and the boy?'

'Busy,' said Strange, sopping up the juice left on the plate with a triangle of white toast.

'Uh,' grunted Georgelakos. His great eagle nose twitched. His glance moved through the window to the street, then back to Strange. 'What about it? They're waiting for you, right?'

'I *told* them to wait,' said Strange. He closed his eyes as he swallowed the last of his breakfast. 'Billy, you can't get a better egg and half-smoke combination in all of D.C. than you can right here.'

'The omelette was my father's recipe, you know that. But your father taught us all how to grill a half-smoke.'

'However it happened, it's beautiful music, that's for damn sure.'

'You sure you gonna be all right?'

'Pretty sure. Lemme see your pen.'

Georgelakos drew his Bic from where it rested atop his ear. Strange wrote something down on a clean napkin he pulled from a dispenser.

'In case I'm wrong,' said Strange, 'here's the license plate number of their car. It's a C two thirty, a two thousand model, in case it comes up.'

Georgelakos took the napkin, folded it, and slipped it under his apron. Strange left money on the counter and shook Georgelakos's hand.

On the way out, Strange stopped by the photograph of his father, Darius Strange, wearing his chef's hat and standing next to Billy's father, Mike Georgelakos, in the early 1960s. The photograph was framed and mounted by the front door. He stared at it for a few moments, as he always did, before reaching for the handle of the door.

'*Adio*, Derek,' said Georgelakos.

'*Yasou, Vasili*,' said Strange.

Out on the street, Strange stood before the open window of the Mercedes.

'Get in,' said Phillip Wood.

'Where we goin'?'

'You'll find out, chief,' said Wood's partner.

Strange looked at Wood only. 'Where?'

'Out Central Avenue. Largo area.'

'I'll follow you out,' said Strange, and when Wood didn't answer, Strange said, 'Young man, it's the only way I'll go.'

Wood's partner laughed, and Wood stared at Strange some more in that hard way that was not working on Strange at all.

'Follow us, then,' said Wood.

Strange went to his car.

Strange followed the Mercedes east to North Capitol, then south, then east again on H to Benning Road. Farther along they found Central Avenue and took it out of the city and into Maryland.

As he drove, Strange mentally recounted what he knew of Granville Oliver.

Oliver, now in his early thirties, had come up fatherless in the Stanton Terrace Dwellings of Anacostia, in Southeast D.C. His mother was welfare dependent and a shooter of heroin and cocaine. When he was eight years old, Granville had learned how to tie his mother off and inject her with coke, a needed jolt when her heroin nods took her down to dangerously low levels. He was taught this by one of her interchangeable male friends, hustlers and junkheads themselves, always hanging around the house. One of these men taught him how to go with his hands. Another taught him how to load and fire a gun. At the time, Granville was nine years old.

Granville had an older brother, two cousins, and one uncle who were in the game. Cocaine at first, and then crack when it hit town around the summer of '86. The brother was executed in a turf dispute involving drugs. The cousins were doing time in Ohio and Illinois prisons, dispersed there after the phase-out of Lorton. Granville's mother died when he was in his early teens, an overdose long overdue. It was the uncle, Bennett Oliver, who eventually took Granville under his wing.

Granville dropped out of Ballou High School in the tenth grade. By then he was living in a row house with friends in Congress Heights, south of Saint Elizabeth's. He had been a member of the notorious Kieron Black Gang in the Heights, but it was small change, a you-kill-one-of-us-and-we-kill-one-of-you thing, and he wanted out. So Granville went to his uncle, who took him on.

From the start it was apparent that Granville had a good head for numbers. After he had proven himself on the front lines – he was allegedly the triggerman in four murders by the time he was seventeen years old – he quickly moved into operations and helped grow the business. Through ruthless extermination of the competition, and

Granville's brains, the Oliver Mob soon became the largest crack and heroin distribution machine in the southeast quadrant of the city.

The center of the operation was a small rec center anchoring a rocky baseball field and rimless basketball court on the grounds of an elementary school in the Heights. There Bennett and Granville got to know the kids from the surrounding neighborhoods of Wilburn Mews, Washington Highlands, Walter E. Washington Estates, Valley Green, Barnaby Terrace, and Congress Park.

For many of the area's youths, the Olivers, especially the young and handsome Granville, were now the most respected men in Southeast. The police were the enemy, that was a given, and working men and women were squares. The Olivers had the clothes, the cars, and the women, and the stature of men who had returned from war. They gave money to the community, participated in fund-raisers at local churches, sponsored basketball squads that played police teams, and passed out Christmas presents in December to children in the Frederick Douglass and Stanton Terrace Dwellings. They were the heroes, and the folk heroes, of the area. Many kids growing up there didn't dream of becoming doctors or lawyers or even professional athletes. Their simple ambition was to join the Mob, to be 'put on.' Working out of the rec center, the elder Oliver had the opportunity to observe the talent and nurture it as well.

Granville and Bennett's hands no longer touched drugs. In the tradition of these businesses, the youngest shouldered the most risk and thereby earned the chance of graduating to the next level. The Olivers rarely killed using their own hands. When they did, they didn't hold the weapon until the moment of execution. The gun was carried by an underling; the squire, in effect, handed it to the knight at the knight's command.

So the Olivers were smart, and it seemed to the newspaper-reading public and to some of the police that they would never be stopped. There were possibilities: tax evasion was one, as were wires and bugs planted to record their conversations. The more likely scenario was that they would be ratted out by snitches: guys who needed to plead out or guys who had previously been raped in jail and would do anything to avoid being punked out again. The Olivers knew, like all drug kingpins knew, that they would go down eventually. And snitches would be the means by which they would fall.

In August of 1999, one week before he was scheduled to go on trial for racketeering after a wire recorded him discussing a major buy, Bennett Oliver was found murdered behind the wheel of his car, a new-style Jag with titanium wheels, idling a block from the rec center.

Two bullets had entered his brain, one had blown out an eye, and a fourth had bored a tunnel clean through his neck. The Jag was still idling when the police rolled up on the scene. There were no bullet holes in the palms of the hands, no defensive marks at all, indicating that Bennett knew and maybe even trusted his attacker and had been surprised by his own murder. The word on the street was that Bennett's nephew Granville, expecting his uncle to roll over and implicate him on the stand, had pulled the trigger or had ordered it pulled.

Granville Oliver had kept a relatively low profile since the murder of Bennett. Though he was still very much in the business, his name, and the name of his operation, had not appeared recently in the news. He had moved to a new home outside the city, in Largo, where he was said to be recording an album in a studio he had built in the basement of the house.

Strange steered his Cadillac off the main highway. He supposed that he was headed toward Granville Oliver's house now.

He parked behind the Mercedes in a circular drive in front of a large brick colonial. Another brand-new Mercedes, less adorned than the one Phillip Wood drove, was parked there, facing out.

The house was on a street with two similar houses, one of which appeared to be unoccupied. It wasn't a neighborhood, exactly, certainly not one of those gated communities favored by the new African American wealth of Prince George's County. Maybe Granville wanted the privacy. More likely, those kinds of people had moved behind the gates to get away from the Granville Olivers of the world. There were unofficial covenants protecting them; real estate agents working certain neighborhoods knew to discourage sales to his kind.

Wood's partner remained in the car. Strange followed Wood to the front door. He noticed an open garage, totally empty, attached to the side of the house. Beside the garage, a boy no older than twelve raked leaves.

They walked into a large foyer in which a split staircase led to the upper floor. Two hallways on either side of the staircases reached a state-of-the-art kitchen opening to a large area holding cushiony couches, a wide-screen television, and stereo equipment. They went through this area, past a dining room introduced by French doors, and into another sort of foyer that led to an open door. Wood was talking on his cell all the way. He made a gesture to Strange and stepped aside so that Strange could go, alone, through the doorway.

The room was a kind of library, with framed photographs on the walls and books shelved around a huge cherry-wood desk, and it smelled of expensive cologne. Granville Oliver sat behind the desk. He was a large man with light brown eyes, nearly golden, and handsome in an open-neck shirt under a dark suit. Strange recognized him by sight.

'Go ahead and close that door,' said Oliver.

Strange closed it and walked across the room.

Oliver stood, sized Strange up, leaned forward, and shook his hand. Strange had a seat in a comfortable chair that had been placed before the desk.

'This about Joe Wilder?' said Strange.

'That's right,' said Oliver. 'I want you to find the ones who killed my son.'

23

'You're Joe's father?'

'Yeah.'

'He never mentioned it.'

Granville Oliver spread his hands. 'He didn't know.'

The Motorola StarTAC on Oliver's desk chirped. Oliver picked up the cell, flipped it open, and put it to his ear. Strange listened to 'uh-huh' and 'yeah' over and over again. He was too wired to sit in the chair and digest what had been revealed. He got up out of the chair and walked around the room.

The wall cases were filled with books. Judging by the tears on the corners of the frayed jackets and the cracks in the spines of the paperbacks, the books had been read. Except for a few classic works of fiction by writers like Ellison, Himes, and Wright, most of Oliver's collection consisted of nonfiction. The subjects dealt with black nationalism, black separatism, and black empowerment. All were penned by black authors.

The photographs on the walls were of Oliver with local sports celebrities and politicians. One showed him with his arm slung over the shoulder of D.C.'s former mayor. There was a rumor, unsubstantiated, that Oliver had periodically supplied the mayor with both women and drugs. Another photo had Oliver standing on an outdoor court, presenting a trophy to a basketball team wearing black shirts with red print across the chests. The shirts read, 'Dare to Stay Off Drugs.'

The cell phone made a sound again as Oliver ended his call.

'You sponsor a team?' said Strange.

'Gotta give back to the community,' said Oliver, with no apparent irony.

Strange could only stare at him. Oliver nodded in the direction of his cell phone, which he had placed on a green blotter. 'I had to take that, but it's turned off now. We can talk.'

Strange sat back down in his chair.

'So what do you think?' said Oliver, waving his hand around the room, the gesture meant to include the entire house, his land, all his possessions. 'Not bad for a Southeast boy, right?'

'It is something.'

'Check this out.' Oliver shook a black-and-white photograph out of a manila envelope and slid it across the desk to Strange. It was a head shot of a scowling Oliver wearing a skully and chains, his arms crossed across his chest, a Glock in one hand and a .45 in the other.

Strange dropped the photograph back on the desk.

'That's my new promo shot,' said Oliver, 'for this record I just made. I brought this boy down from New York, used to run the mixin' board up there for some of the top acts. This boy put some beats behind me, made my flow tight. I got a studio right here in my basement, man. All new equipment, all of it the best. I mean, I got everything.'

'It does make an impression,' said Strange. 'But I hope you'll understand if I don't seem too impressed.'

'So now you gonna tell me, It's not what you have, it's how you got it, right?'

'Somethin' like that. All these pretty things you own around here? There's blood on 'em, Granville.'

Oliver's eyes flared, but his voice remained steady. 'That's right. I *took* it, Mr Strange. Wasn't no one gonna give me nothin', so I just went out and grabbed it. White man gonna try to keep a black man down from birth. But Bobo, he couldn't do it to this black man.'

'Okay, then. In your mind, you've done all right.'

Oliver blinked his eyes hard. 'I have. Despite the fact that I got born into that camp of genocide they used to call the ghetto. Poverty is violence, Mr Strange, you've heard that, right?'

'I have.'

'And it begets violence. Poor black kids see the same television commercials white boys and white girls see out in the suburbs. They're showed, all their young lives, all the things they should be striving to acquire. But how they gonna get these things, huh?'

Strange didn't reply.

Oliver leaned forward. 'Look, I got a good head for numbers, and I know how to manage people. I've always had that talent. Young boys wanted to follow me around the neighborhood when I wasn't no more than a kid. But do you think anyone in my school ever said to me, Take this book home and read it? Keep reading and get yourself into a college, you can run your own company someday? Maybe they knew, black man ain't never gonna run nothin' in this country 'less he takes it and runs with it his own self. Which is what I been doin' my whole adult life.

'So poor kids with nothin' are gonna want things. They start by gettin' into their own kind of enterprise, 'cause they figure out early there ain't no other way to get it. And these enterprises are competitive, like any business. Once you start gettin' these things, see, you're gonna make sure you keep what you got, 'cause you can't never go back and live the way you were livin' before. And now Bobo gonna act surprised when the neighborhoods he done herded us into start runnin' with blood.'

'You don't have to lecture me about being black in this country, Granville. I been around long enough to remember injustices you haven't even dreamed of.'

'So you agree.'

'For the most part, yes. But it doesn't explain the fact that a lot of kids who grew up in the same kinds of places you did, the same way you did, with no kind of guidance, got out. Got through school, went on and got good jobs, careers, are raising kids of their own now who are gonna have a better chance than they ever did. And they're doin' it straight. By hanging with it, by being there for their children. Despite all the roadblocks you talked about.'

'Didn't work out that way for me,' said Oliver with a shrug. 'But it sure did work out. So I hope you'll understand *me* if I'm not too ashamed.'

'That what you tell that young boy you got working for you, the one I saw outside?'

'Don't worry about that boy. That boy is gonna do just fine.'

Strange leaned back in his chair. 'Say why you called me out here.'

'I told you.'

'Okay. You claim Joe was yours.'

Oliver nodded. 'He was one of my beef babies, from back when the shit was wild. When I was out there getting into a lot of, just, *battles* and mad shit like that. Used to crib up with different girls I knew from around the way, just to go underground, keep myself safe until the drama cooled down. In those two or three years, I must have fathered three babies like that.'

And you think that makes you a man.

'But you were never there for Joe,' said Strange.

'His mother, Sandra, wanted it like that. She didn't want him to know about me. Didn't want him lookin' up to someone like me, Mr

Strange. It speaks to what you were just *lecturin'* me on just now. She wanted the boy to grow up with some kind of chance.'

God bless her, thought Strange.

'You gave her money?'

'She wouldn't take much. Didn't want me anywhere near the boy; no presents at birthday time, nothin' like that. She did take a whip I gave her, though. Told her I didn't want no son of mine ridin' around in that broken-down hooptie she was drivin'. A nice BMW. She couldn't turn that down.'

'I saw it,' said Strange. 'Why did you pick me?'

'Sandra says you all right. You been havin' that business down in Petworth for years, and you got a good reputation behind it. And she says you always were good to the little man.' Oliver smiled. 'Boy could play some football, couldn't he?'

'He had a heart,' said Strange, speaking softly. 'You missed out on the most beautiful thing that ever could've happened to your life, Granville. You missed.'

'Maybe. But now I want you to help me make it right.'

'Why? Okay, so you fathered Joe. But you never were any kind of father to him for real.'

'True. But some people know he was mine. Man in my position, he can't just let this kind of thing go. Everyone needs to know that the ones who took my kin will be got. You lose respect in this business I'm in, there ain't nothin' left.'

'The police are close,' said Strange. 'I'd say they're gonna find the shooters in a few days. They've got likenesses and they're putting them around the neighborhoods. This isn't your normal street beef where everybody keeps their mouths shut. The police aren't the enemy in a case like this. A child was murdered. Someone's gonna come forward soon and talk.'

'I want you to find them first.'

'And do what?'

'Gimme some names.'

'I've been working on it,' said Strange. 'I'm planning on talking to Lorenze Wilder's friends.'

'You got a list?'

'Somethin' like that.'

'Sandra will help you narrow it down.'

'I've tried to talk to her. She didn't seem to want to.'

'She'll talk to you now. I just got off the phone with her before you showed. She's waitin' on you to come by when we get done here.'

There was a knock on the door. Oliver raised his voice and said, 'Come in.'

Phillip Wood appeared as the door swung open but stood back behind the frame. 'You got an appointment in fifteen.'

'We'll be done by then,' said Oliver.

Wood nodded and pulled the door shut.

'There's an example of what I was talkin' about right there,' said Oliver to Strange. 'That boy, Phil Wood? Boy can't even read. But he's *drivin'* a Mercedes. He's *wearin'* twelve-hundred-dollar suits with designer tags. Young man is gainfully employed, Mr Strange, 'stead of lyin' around in his own pee, which is where he was headed if I hadn't put him on.'

'Where you think he's headed now?'

'True. We all know what waits for us. But we can't be thinkin' on tomorrow all that much, can we? The thing you got to do is enjoy the ride.'

'It's all good, right?'

'No, not all. Take Phil, for example. I'm gettin' near to the point, I got to be making a decision on his future. Phil Wood's taken a fall two times. The Feds know this, and they're lookin' to see him stumble, 'cause the third fall is gonna be long time. And Phil can't do no long time. He's weak that way. I know it, and he knows it, too.'

'You're afraid he's gonna roll over on you.'

'He will. Fond as I am of that young man, he will. Gonna be one of those "You too, Brutus" motherfuckers in the end. My very own Judas, gonna sell out Granville Oliver for his thirty pieces.'

'You comparing yourself to the Lord?'

'Matter of fact, the first example was out of *Julius Caesar*. I read a lot, case you haven't noticed. But, nah, it's just . . . You know what I'm sayin'. I got a decision to make. Just tellin' you, you know, this ain't all fun and games.'

Strange looked at his watch.

'Yeah, okay,' said Oliver. 'So, we got ourselves a deal, right?'

'No,' said Strange.

'What's that?'

'I don't think I'll be working for you.'

'You got a problem with my kind.'

'That's right.'

'Forget about me, then. Think about the boy.'

'I am.'

'Don't you want to see justice done?'

'I told you, the police will have this wrapped up quick.'

'We ain't talkin' about the same thing.'

'The cycle never ends, does it?'

'Oh, it'll *end*, you do what I ask you to do. That's my point. There ain't no death penalty in the District of Columbia, Mr Strange. You want to see those shooters go to prison, get warm meals, get to sleep real comfortable, maybe walk out in twenty, twenty-five? You think my son's ever gonna get to walk out his grave? Gimme some names, like I said. I'll make sure justice gets served.'

'You can't trade a bad life for a good.'

'What's that?'

'Something someone told me a long time ago.'

'I'm givin' you straight talk,' said Oliver, 'and you're over there talkin' proverbs and shit. Talkin' about *cycles*.'

Strange looked into Oliver's eyes. 'I knew your father.'

'Say it again.'

'They always say that D.C.'s a small town. Well, it's true. I knew your father, over thirty years ago.'

'You got one up on me, then, chief. 'Cause I never did get to meet the man. He died in sixty-eight, during the riots. Right around the time I was born.'

'He had light eyes, just like you.'

Oliver cocked his head. 'Y'all were tight?'

'He knew my brother,' said Strange. 'My brother passed about the same time as your father.'

'So?'

'Cycles,' said Strange, leaving it at that.

Strange got up out of his chair. Granville Oliver handed him a business card. It was for his record company, GO Entertainment. Under the logo, Oliver's cell number was printed.

'You call me,' said Oliver, 'you find anything out. And somethin' else: Sandra says you got a white boy, helps you coach that football team. Says he works with you, too. Well, I don't want him workin' on none of this, hear?'

Strange slipped the business card into his suit pocket.

'My sympathies on the death of your uncle,' said Strange.

'Yeah,' said Oliver. 'That was a real tragedy right there.'

Strange walked out of the house. He nodded to the boy raking leaves and received only a scowl. Phillip Wood and partner were leaning against their Mercedes in the circular drive. Strange passed them without a word, got into his Cadillac, and drove back into D.C.

24

The Park Morton complex looked different during the day. There were children using the playground equipment, and mothers, aunts, and grandmothers watching over them. A group of girls was doing double Dutch by the entrance, and the ones sitting on the brick wall nearby were actually smiling. Strange knew that Sundays were quiet time, even in the worst neighborhoods, and the fact that the sun was full in a clear blue sky, its rays highlighting the turning leaves, added to the illusion of peace. Also, most all the men around town, even the bad ones, were indoors watching the Redskins game.

Strange had been listening to it on the radio, the pregame and then the play-by-play, Sonny, Sam, and Frank on WJFK. The Ravens were in the house at FedEx, and the contest had just gotten under way.

Strange got the list Lydell Blue had given him out of his trunk and locked down the Brougham. He walked across the brown grass of the courtyard to the stairwell leading to Sandra Wilder's apartment. He noticed flyers with the likenesses of the shooters taped on the stairwell wall.

Strange knocked on the door of the Wilder residence. He waited patiently for a while and did not knock again. Then the door opened and Sandra Wilder stood in its frame. She gave Strange warm eyes.

'Sandra.'

'Derek.' She reached out and touched his arm. 'Come on in.'

They settled in a kind of living room the size of a den, at the end of a hall broken by an open entrance to a galley-style kitchen. The couch Strange sat on was marked with food stains and its piping was torn away from the fabric. A television sat on a stand past the rectangular table set before the couch; it was on and showing the game at a very low volume. On the wall behind the set were photographs torn from magazines and newspapers, taped crookedly, of Keyshawn Johnson and Randy Moss, along with a close-up of Deion wearing a do-rag. Tellingly, a poster of Darrell Green at the ready was the largest and most prominently displayed. It would be like Joe to honor the tireless workhorse above the flash. Strange could see him sitting on this couch, eating a snack or a microwaved dinner prepared by his mom, watching the game on a Sunday afternoon. He guessed that that was how the stains had gotten on the couch.

Strange drank a glass of instant iced tea, quietly watching the 'Skins move the ball upfield. Sandra sat beside him, leaning forward and making marks on the list Strange had given her, which she had placed on the table. Her lips moved as she read the names.

Though Sandra Wilder was in her mid-twenties, she appeared at first glance to be ten years older. She was heavy in the hips and waist, and her movements were labored. She had big brown eyes, freckles, a full mouth, and straight teeth. She was pretty when she smiled. Strange guessed she had given birth to Joe when she was about sixteen.

Today Sandra wore a pair of jeans with an untucked T-shirt showing a computer-generated photograph of a grinning Joe. The words 'We will not forget you' were printed beneath his image. Entrepreneurs offered T-shirts like this at the wakes and funerals of young people citywide, usually in the form of bulk sales to the grieving families. It had become a cottage industry in D.C.

'Here you go,' said Sandra, handing Strange the sheet of paper. 'Why are those Social Security numbers next to the names?'

'My friend hooked me up. I'll be using those numbers in my computer to get addresses, job histories, like that.'

'I circled the ones still come to mind.'

Strange studied the list. Sandra had highlighted three names: Walter Lee, Edward Diggs, and Sequan Hawkins.

'These your brother's closest friends?'

'The ones I recall. The ones who used to be around our house most when we were coming up.'

'Were they still tight with Lorenze?'

'I have no idea. I didn't have much contact with my brother these past few years. But you say these names came off the funeral home list, that book you sign when you pay your respects? So I figure, at least they're still around. Far as where they live or how to get in touch with 'em, I don't have a clue.'

'I can find them,' said Strange. 'You don't have to worry about that.'

'My mother would know. She had this address book, she used to keep all our friends' names in it, 'cause me and Lorenze, when we were young? We were, like, always slipping out, and she had to have a way of finding us. 'Specially Lorenze; that boy was buck wild, you couldn't keep him in the house at all.'

'Can I speak to your mother?'

'She's dead.'

Strange turned on the couch so that he was facing her. 'Where'd y'all come up, Sandra?'

'Manor Park, over there around North Dakota Avenue. South of Coolidge?'

'I know it,' said Strange, something catching his eye over Sandra's shoulder. On an end table abutting the couch sat a framed photograph of Joe in his uniform, his face shiny with sweat, a football cradled against his chest.

'Anything else?' said Sandra.

'You say you were out of contact with your brother. Why was that, you don't mind my askin'?'

'Lorenze was no-account. I loved him, but that's what he was. He wanted some of that bling-bling, but he couldn't even do that right, for real. He was always calling me, trying to get me to hook him up with Granville. Tellin' me he wanted Granville to put him on. But when Joe got born, I didn't want to have anything to do with Granville anymore. I didn't want Joe to know about him at all. Lorenze wouldn't leave it alone, so I broke things off with my own blood. You know I took a car from Granville, and I am not proud of that, but I swear to you, that's all I had to do with that man.'

'You don't need to apologize for anything.'

'But I do want you to know. I've been straight all the way. I been having the same job for years now and I'm never late on my bills . . . It's been hard, Derek, but I have been *straight*.'

'I know you have,' said Strange. 'Did Lorenze have enemies you knew of?'

'It's like I told the police. He didn't go lookin' for trouble. But it found him sure enough. It was his way. He just didn't take anything serious. Couldn't hold a job, and still, he always felt free to put out his hand. Never did take care of his debts. *Never* did. Laughed it off most of the time. He thought it was all a joke, but the ones he was laughin' at, they didn't see it that way. To them, Lorenze was tryin' to take them for bad.'

'You think that's why he was killed?'

'I expect.'

Strange folded the list and slipped it into the inside pocket of his suit coat. He took one of Sandra Wilder's hands. It felt clammy and limp in his.

'Listen,' said Strange. 'You did right by keeping your son away from Oliver, and away from your brother, too. And don't you ever think that you could have prevented what happened. Because you did right, and you did good. That boy was as special as they come, Sandra. And it's because of you.'

A smile broke upon her face. The smile was perfect, and her hair was beauty-shop done and in place, and her makeup was perfectly applied. Cosmetically, Sandra Wilder was completely intact. But Strange could see that her eyes were jittery and too bright, and her mouth twitched at the corners as he tried to hold the smile.

Strange put his arms around her and drew her toward him. She fell into his embrace without resistance, Strange catching the foulness of her breath. It was quiet in the room except for the faint voice of the announcer calling the game. After a while he felt Sandra's shoulders shaking beneath him and her hot tears where she had buried her face in his neck. He held her like that until she was cried out, and he left her there when he knew that there was nothing left.

The 'Skins/Ravens game was tied up three to three, a pair of field goals the only score, as Strange drove north. A pass interference call against Washington put the Ravens on the Redskins' one yard line with ten seconds to go in the half. From the radio, Sonny Jurgensen and Sam Huff discussed the most likely call for the next play. It would certainly be a run, Jamal Lewis up the middle. If he was stopped, there would still be time on the clock for a field goal to put the Ravens ahead before the end of the first half.

Strange pulled his Cadillac to the curb and let the motor run. He clockwised the volume dial.

'Come on,' said Strange. 'Hold 'em.'

Ravens quarterback Tony Banks did not hand the ball off to Lewis. He attempted a pass into the flat of the end zone to Shannon Sharpe, who was in the company of two burgundy jerseys. It was a bad play to call – if Banks were to throw it at all he should have thrown it away. Redskin linebacker Kevin Mitchell picked off the pass.

Strange's holler was one of disbelief. The roar of FedEx and the laughter of Sonny and Sam were in the car as Strange pulled down on the tree and continued uptown.

'Derek, come on in,' said George Hastings. 'You see that last play?'

'I been listenin' to it on the radio,' said Strange.

They walked through the hall of Hastings's brick tudor in Shepherd Park. Hastings wore a Redskins cap, but he was otherwise cleanly dressed in an expensive sweater and slacks. His house was just as clean.

'You believe that call Billick made?' said Hastings, looking over his shoulder as he led Strange into his den. 'You got Jamal Lewis, a tough young back, on the one yard line, and all you got to do is give it to him and let him run it up the gut, and you call a *pass*?'

'Tony Banks ain't exactly one of your top-tier NFL quarterbacks either.'

'Not yet, anyway.'

'Should have pitched it out of the end zone when he saw the coverage. That was his inexperience showing right there.'

Hastings pointed to one of two big loungers in the den. A large-screen Sony was set in a wall unit in the room; the second half was under way. 'Sit down, Derek. Can I get you something? I might have a cold beer myself.'

'Nothin' with alcohol in it for me, not today. A Co-Cola if you got it, George.'

Hastings returned with the drinks and had a seat. Both teams went scoreless in the third.

'Our defensive linemen got fire in their eyes today,' said Strange.

'Yeah, this is one of those classic defensive battles we got goin' right here,' said Hastings.

'They've stopped Stephen Davis, and we got hardly any receivers left except Albert Connell. Fryar's out.'

'Your boy Westbrook is gone for the season, too. *Again*.'

'And I thought it was gonna be his year, too,' said Strange sadly. 'Next year, maybe.'

At the start of the fourth quarter, Stephen Davis left the field with a pinched nerve in his shoulder. Skip Hicks replaced him for three downs at tailback and then Davis came back in. On second and seven, the teams lined up on the Baltimore thirty-three, with the Ravens showing blitz. Davis took the handoff from Brad Johnson and hit a hole provided by tackle Chris Samuels and fullback Larry Centers. Davis was off with only safety Rod Woodson between him and the goal line. Davis stiff-armed Woodson, dropped him to the turf, and sailed into the end zone.

Strange and Hastings were on their feet with instant high fives.

'Just like Riggo,' said Strange.

'Thought you said they were stoppin' Davis.'

'You can't stop that boy for long.'

George looked at his friend. 'Good to see you smiling, man.'

'Was I?' said Strange. 'Damn. Guess it's been a while since I have.'

They watched the rest of the game, knowing the contest was over with the Davis touchdown. The 'Skins had broken Baltimore's back with that one play. When the whistle sounded, Hastings hit the mute button on the remote and sat back in his lounger.

'All right, man,' said Hastings. 'Gimme the bad news.'

'Well, I don't think you can call it bad,' said Strange. 'Your future son-in-law is clean.'

'For real?'

'Don't look so disappointed.'

'What about all that Calhoun Enterprises jive?'

Strange spread his hands. 'Can't fault a man just 'cause he picks a bad name for his business. Far as his work ethic goes, and his reputation, the man is golden. He comes from a solid family who gave him a good example, by all accounts. I got no reason to think he won't be anything but a good provider for your daughter.'

'What else?'

'Huh?'

'I been knowin' you too long, Derek, and you know I can read your face. There's somethin' else, so why don't you say it?'

'Well, Calhoun Tucker likes the ladies.'

'Course he does. What, you think some *faggot*'s gonna be fallin' in love with my girl?'

'I don't mean that. I mean, he's got an eye for 'em.'

'Say what you're gettin' at, man.'

Strange looked down at his hands. He had been rubbing them together and he made himself stop.

'I don't know what I'm getting at exactly, George. I guess . . . I was wondering, not to get into your business, understand, but I was wondering how it was between you and Linda. The whole time you were married, I mean. Did you ever, you know, stumble? Did you ever find yourself steppin' out on her or anything like that?'

'Never,' said Hastings. 'You know me better than that, Derek.'

'But I remember how you were, back when the two of us were out there. When we were single and coming up, I mean. You had a lot of girlfriends, George. Wasn't like you ever just stuck to one.'

'Until I met Linda.'

'Right. But you and her were together for like, *two years* before you put the ring on her finger. How was it for you and other women in that time?'

'Well, naturally, you know, I continued to see other girls while I was dating Linda. I never did consider that to be any kind of sin. But once I made a pledge to her and the Lord in the church, though, that was it. I looked hard at plenty of women, but as far as lyin' down with someone other than my wife, after I was married? It was never an option for me again.'

'So you don't see nothin' wrong with cattin' around up to the wedding day.'

'Young man's only gonna be young once. You tellin' me Calhoun Tucker's a player?'

If he were to bring it up, now would be the time. But he had been leaning one way already, and this conversation with George had made up his mind. Strange shook his head.

'I guess I strayed off the topic some. To tell you the truth, I was askin' about it because . . . because I been having some problems with Janine. I been stumblin' like that with regards to her, George. Not just once or twice, understand, but as a matter of habit. It came to a head between us last night.'

'Sounds like you need to make some decisions. But you know, Derek, everybody's got to make those kinds of choices their own selves.'

'I hear you.'

'Anything else about Tucker?'

'Just this: I talked to some people who know him, here in D.C. They told me, to a one, how much he goes on about Alisha all the time, how deep he loves her. Sounds like he's sincere to me.'

'Who wouldn't love that girl?'

'True. But I thought you might like to know. Far as what kind of husband he's gonna be, only thing I can say is, neither one of us is gonna know that until time tells us. Right?'

'Yeah, you're right. I guess I been wantin' to find something wrong with that young man. It's like you told me back in your office: maybe the only thing wrong with him is that he's getting ready to take away my little girl.'

'Maybe. Wouldn't anybody blame you for feeling that way, though. The thing is, you just got to support her decision now and see what happens. Don't you agree?'

Hastings reached over and shook Strange's hand.

'Thank you, Derek.'

'I'll have a written report for you next week.'

'Send a bill along with it.'

'You know I will.'

Hastings removed his Redskins cap and rubbed the top of his head. 'Any progress on finding that boy's killers?'

'It won't be long,' said Strange. 'One way or another, they'll be got.'

*

Strange walked out the front door of the Hastings residence. Calhoun Tucker's Audi was parked behind Strange's Cadillac. Tucker, all Abercrombie & Fitch, leaned against the car. Alisha Hastings was with him, her eyes alight as she followed his every word, both of them beside the waxed Audi parked beneath the fiery colors of an oak. The tableau was like some advertisement for beauty and youth.

'Come here, Mr Derek,' said Alisha. 'I want you to meet someone.'

Strange crossed the lawn and went to the couple. He kept his eyes on Tucker's as Alisha introduced them to each other. They shook hands.

'I bet you and my daddy were in there watching the game,' said Alisha. 'I can't understand how you two could stay inside and watch television on a beautiful day like this.'

'It's always a beautiful day when the Redskins win,' said Strange.

'Y'all catching up on old times in there?' said Tucker.

'Just being a friend to my old buddy George.'

'Oh?'

'Been meaning to get by and congratulate him on the engagement of his lovely daughter here. Congratulations to the both of you as well.'

Tucker's eyes softened. 'Thank you, Mr Strange.'

'Make it Derek.'

They shook again. Strange tightened his grip on Tucker's hand.

'Good to meet you, young man.'

'You don't have to worry,' said Tucker, moving in close to Strange's face.

'See that I don't,' said Strange, his voice very low. He released Tucker's hand.

Strange kissed Alisha, hugged her and held her tightly. He kissed her again and walked toward his car.

'What was that about?' said Alisha. 'I couldn't hear what you two were saying, but it looked intense. You two don't know each other, do you?'

'No. It was nothing. Just, you know, pissin'-contest stuff between men.'

'Stop it.'

'I'm kiddin' you. He seems like a good guy. He coming to the wedding?'

'Yes. Why?'

'Looking forward to seeing him again is all.'

Tucker flexed his right hand to alleviate the pain. He watched

Strange drive away, orange and red leaves rising from the street in the Caddy's wake.

Strange stopped by the house to pick up Greco and a couple of CDs, then drove down to his place of business. In his office, he slipped *The Sons of Katie Elder* soundtrack into his CPU as he settled into his chair. The message light blinked beside his phone.

Lydell Blue had called to tell him that the beige Caprice had been found in an impound lot in Prince George's County. The Chevy was determined to have been a stolen vehicle, wiped down of prints. Clothing fibers, orange threads of a fleece material, found in the Chevy matched those found in the Plymouth driven by the shooters.

Strange was certain now that the boys he had seen in the Caprice idling in Roosevelt's parking lot were the killers of Lorenze and Joe Wilder. He had caught a look at the driver and especially the boy with the braids, and their faces loosely matched those of the artist's renderings posted around town.

He knew this. But he didn't phone Lydell Blue back to tell him what he knew.

Strange got into Westlaw and fed the names Walter Lee, Edward Diggs, and Sequan Hawkins, along with their Social Security numbers, into the program. It took a couple of hours to find what it would have taken Janine a half hour to find. Despite his rudimentary knowledge of the programs, Strange was still old world, and much better at his job when out on the street. He also tended to seek out distractions when he should have been working nonstop behind his desk. In those two hours he played with Greco, thought of Janine, and ate a PayDay bar she had left for him on his mouse pad. But finally he got the information he needed.

Using PeopleFinder and the reverse directory, he had secured the current addresses and phone numbers of the men. Also the names and addresses of their current neighbors. The Social Security numbers had given him their past and present employment data.

Strange phoned Quinn and got him on the third ring.

'Terry, it's Derek. You see the game?'

'I saw some of it.'

'Some of it. Your girlfriend over there, man?'

'Yes, Sue's here.'

'Been there all day, huh? Y'all even get a look at the sunshine today, man?'

'Derek, what's on your mind?'

'Wanted to make sure you were gonna be ready to go in the morning.'

'Told you I would be.'

'Meet me down at Buchanan at nine, then. We'll roll out together in my car.'

'Right.'

'And Terry?'

'What?'

'Bring your gun.'

25

Carlton Little swallowed the last of his Big Mac and used his sleeve to wipe secret sauce off his face, where it had gathered like glue on the side of his mouth. He had another Mac in the bag on the table in front of him and he wanted to kill it right now. The grease stain on the bottom of the bag, just lookin' at it made him hungry.

He was hungry all the time. Not hungry for real like he had been when he was a kid, but hungry just the same. Loved to eat anything you could take out of somebody's hand from a drive-through window. Taco Bell, Popeyes, and the king of it all, *Mac*Donald's. Little knew guys who had trouble with their movements, but not him. All the food he ate, the kind came in damp cartons and grease-stained bags? Damn if he didn't take three or four shits a day.

He supposed his love for food had somethin' to do with the fact that he didn't have any when he was a boy. His aunt, who he stayed with, she sold their food stamps most of the time to pay for her crack habit. She had food in there from time to time, but the men she was hangin' with, who were pipeheads, too, and always leaving a slug's trail around the house, ate it or stole it themselves. There was cereal sometimes, but the milk went fast, and he couldn't fuck with eatin' no dry cereal. Before he grew some, when he weighed, like, sixty pounds, Carlton used to hide the milk outside his bedroom window, on this ledge that was there, so it wouldn't get used up. In wintertime the milk froze and in summer it went sour, so you couldn't do it all the time. But it was a good trick that worked half the year. This teacher taught him how to do that after he collapsed one time at school 'cause he was so weak. Weak from not eating. Not that he was cryin' about it or nothin' like that. He had money now, and he wasn't weak anymore.

Man on the TV said that one third of the kids in D.C. lived below the poverty level, the same way he had. Well, fuck those kids. Nobody ever gave him nothin', and he made out all right. They'd have to figure a road out their own selves. If they *were* to ask him, he'd say that there was one thing he knew for sure about this life out here. You acted the punk, you were through. You wanted to make it, you had to be hard.

Little laid himself down on the couch.

Potter sat low in one of those reclining rocking chairs he loved. Potter had bought two of them at Marlo's, along with the couch Little lay on now, filled out the no-payment-till-whenever paperwork and had them delivered the next day. That was a year ago, and Potter had still not made a payment and never would. No Payments Till Forever, that's the way the sign read to him. Potter had given the African or whatever he was a different billing address than the delivery address, and the dude hadn't even noticed. Stupid-ass foreigners they hired out there, workin' those sucker jobs.

'You gonna eat that?' said Potter, one hand pointed lazily at the paper bag holding the last Mac.

'I was thinkin' on eatin' it right now,' said Little.

'I wouldn't even be feedin' that shits to a dog.'

'It's good.'

'You gonna throw it up out in the street, like you did the other day?'

'I ain't ashamed. Made me sick to see what happened to that kid.'

'Well, he shouldn't've been in that car.'

'Yeah, but those bullets you used done fucked him up for real.'

'Oh, it was just *mines* now.'

'It was those hollow points out of that three-five-seven you was holdin', did all that damage.'

'Couldn't handle lookin at it, huh?'

'Shit was just nasty is all.'

'Yeah, well, you keep eatin' that *Mac*Donald's, gonna make you worse than sick. Gonna kill you young.'

'I be dyin' young anyway.'

'True.'

They had been in the living room all day. Charles White had gotten into his Toyota at lunchtime and brought them back a big carton of Popeyes and biscuits for the Redskins game, and they had gotten high and eaten the chicken, and then they had watched the four o'clock game and told White they were hungry and to go out again. White had returned with a bag of McDonald's for Little and some Taco Supremes from the Bell for Potter, because Potter didn't eat McDonald's food.

Now the eight o'clock game was coming on ESPN, and the sound was off on the television because neither Potter nor Little could stand to hear Joe Theismann, the color man for the Sunday night games, speak. They put on music during the games, but the Wu-Tang Clan

CD they had been listening to had ended. For the first time that day, it was quiet in the room.

Potter and Little had been keeping a very low profile since the murders. They sent White out for all their food and beer. He was scared, they could tell it from his face and the way his voice kinda shook these past few days. But they knew him to be weak, knew that he would do as they asked.

Juwan, their main boy down in the open-air market, had been delivering the daily take to their place on Warder. Their dealer in Columbia Heights had agreed to drop off the product, as needed, at the house. They had burned the Plymouth and abandoned it, and dropped the guns off the rail of the 11th Street bridge into the Anacostia River. Far as evidence went, Potter reasoned, their asses were covered good.

Since the shooting, Potter had gone out twice. Once to buy a couple of straps from this boy he knew who arranged straw purchases out of that gun store, where you could pay junkies and their kind to buy weapons real easy, over in Forestville. The other time he went out was to buy a car, a piece of garbage sitting up on that lot on Blair Road in Takoma, across from a gas station and next to a caterer. Place where all the cars had $461 scrawled in soap on the windshields, all the same price, looked like a kid had written it. Potter bought something, he didn't even bother to look at it close, and paid cash. The salesman tellin' him how to get plates, get insurance, get it inspected, all that, Potter not even listening because he knew he wouldn't have the car long enough to worry about it anyway. Insurance, what the fuck was that? Shit.

So they were keeping low. Their pictures, drawings made to look like them, anyhow, were posted all around the neighborhood. Potter figured, who that could connect the pictures to their names was gonna rat them out? Wasn't anyone that stupid, even if the reward money was printed right there on the drawings, because that person had to know that if they did this, if they snitched on them, they would die. It was a good idea to stay indoors for a while, but Potter wasn't worried in a serious way, and if Little was worried he didn't act it. It was Charles White who was the loose end.

'Where Charles at?' said Potter.

'Up in his room,' said Little. 'Why?'

'You and me need to talk.'

'Well, talk.'

'Go put some music on the box. I don't want him to hear us.'

'He can't hear us. You know that boy's up in his bed with his headphones on, listening to his beats.'

'I expect.'

Potter fired a Bic up in front of the Phillie in his hand and gave the cigar some draw. He held the draw in and passed the blunt over to Little.

Little hit the hydro and exhaled slowly. He blew a ring of gray smoke into the room. 'So talk.'

Carlton Little knew what was about to come from Potter's mouth. He expected it, and didn't like it, but he would go along with it, because he knew Potter was right. Though Little fully expected to die on the street or in prison, it didn't mean he was in any hurry. He wasn't exactly afraid to die. He had convinced himself that he was not. But he did want to live as long as he could. His friend Charles White was fixin' to cut his life short, one way or another. Charles had to go.

'We got a problem with Charles,' said Potter. 'Boy gets picked up for somethin', he is gonna roll on us. Or maybe his conscience is gonna send him to the po-lice before that. You *know* this, right?'

'I do.' Little sat up on the couch and rubbed at his face. 'Shame, too. I mean, me and Coon, all of us, D, we go back.'

'I'll take care of it, Dirty.'

'Wish you would.'

'You know, Charles is like that dog of his,' said Potter. 'Good to hang around with, wags his tail when you be walkin' into a room and shit. But like that dog, he's a cur. And a cur needs to be put down.'

'When?' said Little.

'I was thinkin', later tonight, after we watch this game, get our heads up some? We take Charles out for a ride.'

Charles White had been lying in bed, listening to a Roc-a-Fella compilation through the headphones of his Aiwa, when the cups on the phones started to hurt him some. His ears got sore when he kept the phones on too long, and he had been having them on his head most of the day. He took the headphones off and moved onto his side, staring out the window at the night out behind the house. Wasn't nothin' but dark and an alley back there. He looked at it a little while, then got off the bed and walked out to the bathroom in the hall.

White could hear them playing the first Wu-Tang, the one that mattered, down in the living room. It was that last track the Clan had, 'Tearz,' before that spoken thing they did to close the set. This was the bomb, the kind of classic shit he wanted to record his own self when he got the chance. But of course, he knew deep down he would never get the chance.

White figured he better go downstairs and see what Dirty and Garfield was up to. See if they wanted him to run out for some burgers or malt or sumshit like that. But first he needed to get those dirt tracks off his face. He had been crying a little while ago, back in his room. Some of it had been over what they'd done to that kid, but most of it had been just cryin' for himself.

He bent over the bathroom sink, washed his face, toweled off the water, and checked himself in the mirror. He must have lost weight or something, what with the way he'd been stressin' since they'd killed that boy. His nose looked bigger than usual, his cheeks on either side of it nothin' but some flabby skin hanging on to bone. But you couldn't tell he'd been crying, now that he'd cleaned up. He looked all right.

White went along a hall, hearing their voices below and smelling the smoke of the cheeva they were hittin' drifting up the stairs. It was strange for things to be so quiet in this house. He heard Dirty say, 'So talk,' and then Garfield say, 'We got a problem with Charles.'

White's heart had kicked up and his fingers were shaking some as he went down the stairs halfway. There was a wall there that blocked a view from the living room, and carpet on the steps to muffle the sound of his descent.

He listened to their conversation. He heard his friend Carlton say 'When?' and Garfield, quick and cold in his reply, answered, 'Later tonight.' He said something else about watching the game and getting high, and then he said, 'We take Charles out for a ride.'

You ain't takin' me a *mother*fuckin' place, thought White as he backed himself slowly up the stairs.

Charles locked his bedroom door. They came up and asked why he'd locked himself in, he'd deal with it then.

He got into his Timbies and laced them tight. He found an old Adidas athletic bag, the size of a small duffel, in his closet. He stuffed it with underwear and a few pairs of jeans and some shirts, and one leather jacket, but he left most of the cold-weather stuff on the hangers because he had already decided that he was headed south. He had grabbed his toothbrush and shaving shit from the vanity over the sink on the way to his room, and he dropped it all in. There was still some room in the bag. He put his Aiwa in along with all the CDs, the newer joints, he could fit. He found some older stuff he still listened to,

Amerikkka's Most Wanted and *Doggystyle*, and jammed those in there, too.

White went to his bedroom mirror, where he had taped a photograph of his mother to the glass. In the original shot, some Jheri-curled sucker, all teeth and sweat, lookin' like he walked off the *Street Songs* cover, had his arm around White's mom. White had scissored the man off the picture so that now you could only see the hustler's hand. His mother was smiling in the photo, had a low-cut dress on, red, you could see her titties half hangin' out, but that was all right. At least she looked happy. Not like she looked when they'd cuffed her right at the apartment for robbery, the last of her offenses in a long line of them, and taken her off to that women's prison in West Virginia. Last time White had seen her, ten years back, before he went to live with his grandmother. Granmoms had been okay to him, but she wasn't his moms. He had no idea who his father was.

White carefully took the photograph down and slipped it into his wallet, along with eighteen hundred dollars in cash he found where he'd hidden it, under some T-shirts in the bottom of his dresser.

He opened the window by his bed and dropped the Adidas bag into the darkness. He heard it hit the alley and he closed the window tight.

White slipped himself into his bright orange Nautica pullover, swept the keys to his Toyota off his scarred dresser, and walked out of his room. He walked quickly, so he wouldn't have much time to think on what he was about to do. Wasn't like he could just drop himself out that bedroom window and ghost. He needed to talk to those two, act like everything was chilly. He needed to do this and be gone.

And now he was going down the stairs. And now he was down the stairs and into the living room, and he was twirling his car keys on his finger, wondering why he was doing that, tipping them off so soon that he was headed out the door.

'Where you off to, Coon?' said Little, lying on the couch. He said it casual, like he was still White's friend. White could see in Carlton's eyes that he was higher than a motherfucker, too.

'I'm hungry. *You* hungry, right?'

'I still got me a Mac.'

'I was gonna roll on up to the Wings n Things, man.' His voice shook some and he closed his eyes, then forced them open quick.

'Bring me some malt back,' said Potter.

'You got money?' said White.

He moved to the lounger where Potter sat.

Be hard, Charles. Give 'em somethin' bold to remember you by. Let 'em know you all there.

White opened his hand in front of Potter's face. Potter slapped the hand away. 'Man, *get* that shit out my face! Bring me some Olde English back, hear? Two forties of that shits.'

'And some wings,' said Little.

Potter and Little laughed, and White laughed, too.

'Aiight, then,' said White. He headed for the door.

'Coon,' said Potter, and White turned.

'Yeah?'

'What I tell you about wearin' that orange shirt out, man? You *want* people to be noticin' you? Is that it?'

'Cold out, D. Shit keeps me warm.'

'Damn, boy, you about the thickest motherfucker . . . Look, you ain't gonna be long, right?'

'Nah, I'll be back in like, an hour, sumshit like that.'

''Cause I thought we'd all roll out together for a while, later on.'

White nodded, went out the door, and closed it behind him. He walked down to the corner and when he was out of window-sight he ran around to the alley. He found his Adidas bag there and ran with it back to the street, where he walked to his Toyota parked along the curb. His heart was fluttering like a speed bag as he put his key to the driver's-side door.

White tossed the Adidas bag in the backseat, got into the front, and turned the ignition. He put the stick into first and heard the tires squealing as he pushed on the gas and let off the clutch. First time this old shit box had ever caught rubber. White didn't look in the rearview. As he neared Georgia Avenue he began to laugh.

White stopped at a market on Georgia, one of those fake 7-Elevens, places those Ethiopians named Seven-One or Seven-Twelve, for a big cup of coffee to go. A 4-D cop was parked in the lot, but that meant nothing in this neighborhood, 'less you were out here committing some obvious mayhem. Shoot, someone was smoking cheeva in a nearby car, you could smell it in the lot, and the cop was just sitting there behind the wheel, smellin' it too, most likely, sipping from a large cup. Why would that cop care to stress his self, make an arrest, when the courts would just kick that smoker right back out on the street?

White went into the store. He bought his coffee and a couple of Slim Jims, some potato chips, and a US road map, folded up wrong like someone had been using it without paying, which was in a slot next to the gun magazines they sold in that joint. White went back out to the lot, the map in one hand, the other stuff in a brown paper bag.

There was this boy standing near his Toyota, and when White came out the boy kind of backed away. He was wearing a white T-shirt and khakis, and White had the real feeling he knew this boy or he'd seen him before.

White wasn't a fighter and he wasn't brave, but when it looked like someone was fuckin' with your whip out here, ordinarily you had to say something. You couldn't let it pass, because then you were weak. Just a comment like, 'You got some business lurkin' around my shit?' or somethin' like that. But White didn't need no drama tonight, what with the police right there, and he let it pass.

As he pulled out of the lot and back onto Georgia, he noticed that boy, standing on the corner, staring at him and his car. But White wasn't gonna worry about it now. He was gone.

White got over to 14th Street and headed south. He took the 14th Street Bridge over the Potomac River and into Virginia, where he followed 395 to 95 South. Soon he was out of anything that looked like the city and seeing signs for places like Lorton, which of course he had heard of, and Dale City, which he had not. Down around Fredericksburg, just an hour into his journey, he saw a Confederate flag sticker on the back window of a pickup truck and knew he was already very far away, maybe a whole world away, from D.C.

The coffee had done its job. He was wired and bright with thoughts of the future. He was sorry that the little boy had been killed, but he was convinced that he couldn't have stopped it, and he knew for certain that he couldn't change what had happened now.

This was his plan: he had a cousin in Louisiana, a nephew of his mother's who had come up and stayed with his grandmother a couple of summers back. That summer, White and this boy, Damien Rollins, had got kind of tight. Damien worked in a big diner down there on the interstate, outside New Orleans, and told White that he would hook Charles up if he ever came down south. He said that the man who owned the diner paid cash, under the table. Charles had the idea that this would allow him to work there without incident, under an assumed name, in case anyone was still lookin' for him up in D.C.

White had an address on his cousin, and he had held on to it. About halfway down, he'd give him a call and tell him he was on his way. He had money in his pocket, so he'd also tell cuz that he'd be stayin' with him and help out with half the rent. He'd get that job at the diner and he'd hold it. He wouldn't get into any kind of bad shit down there and he'd stay away from those who looked wrong.

Maybe he'd make manager someday at that job.

26

Walter Lee worked for a big-box electronics retailer up by Westfield Shopping Center, the fancy new name for the mall that everyone in the area still called Wheaton Plaza, a few miles north of the Silver Spring business district. Lee wrote up answering machines, mini-tape recorders, cordless phones, and portable stereos at a computer station after the customers had basically picked the units out themselves. The human resources department gave him the title of sales counselor, but there were few professional salesmen left in the business, and Walter Lee was a clerk.

Strange and Quinn entered the store late in the morning. There was a sea of maroon shirts in the place and few customers at this hour. Most of the employees looked like African Americans, African immigrants, and Indians of some variety, with some Hispanics thrown into the mix to cater to the Spanish-speaking clientele. Strange found himself wondering if the manager of the store was white.

No one approached them or asked if they needed help. In fact, several of the sales counselors had scattered when the two of them had walked through the doors. Strange went up to a tall young African and asked him if he could point out Walter Lee. Strange already knew that Lee was on the schedule; he'd phoned the store on the ride out to Wheaton.

Walter Lee stood by the rack of boom boxes, fiddling with a radio dial, as Strange and Quinn approached. Lee looked up and saw a strong middle-aged man in a black leather jacket, a beeper and a Buck knife and a cell on his belt line, with a younger white dude, also in a leather, had a cocky walk, coming toward him. Lee saw two cops.

'How you doin' today?' said Strange.

'Good. What can I get for you gentlemen?'

Quinn got too close to Lee, crowding him, like he used to do when he wore the uniform. Strange did the same to Lee on his opposite side and flipped open the leather case he drew from his jacket. He let Lee look at the badge and license and closed the case before he had looked at them too long.

'Investigators, D.C.,' said Strange. 'This here's my partner, Terry Quinn.'

'What y'all want?'

''Bout a minute of your time,' said Strange. 'A few questions about Lorenze Wilder.'

'I already talked to the police.' Lee looked around the sales floor. He was in his early thirties and carried too much weight for his age. He wore a fade haircut that looked fine on Patrick Ewing but on Lee just looked tired. 'This ain't too cool, you know.'

'We won't be long,' said Strange. 'You were at the wake for Lorenze, right?'

'Sure.'

'Y'all were tight?'

'I already told the police—'

'Tell us,' said Strange.

'Tell us *again*,' said Quinn, his tone softer than his partner's.

Lee looked over Strange's shoulder, then breathed out slow. 'We hadn't been tight for, like, ten, fifteen. We ran together in high school, that was about it.'

'Coolidge?'

'Yeah. I came out in eighty-six. Lorenze, I don't think he finished up.'

'Lorenze have many enemies when you two were hangin' together back then?'

'Back then? I guess he did. He had this way about him, right? But if you're askin' me, Did he have enemies lately, or, Do I know who killed him? The answer is, I don't know.'

'Y'all didn't swing in the same circles,' said Strange.

'Like I said: not for a long time.'

'You use drugs, Walter?'

Lee's eyes, directly on Strange, narrowed, and he lowered his voice. 'This ain't right. You *know* this ain't right. Comin' up in here to a black man's workplace and tryin' to sweat him.'

'*If* you do drugs,' said Strange, plowing ahead, 'and if you cop from the same people, then maybe you know who Lorenze owed. 'Cause it could've been a drug debt got him doomed.'

'Look. I haven't been usin' any kind of drugs for a long time. Back in the eighties, yeah, I had a little problem with powder. Lotta people did. But I found my way out of it, see—'

'Let's get back to Lorenze.'

'No, you're gonna let me finish. I found my way *out* of it. This isn't the only job I have. I got a night job, too. I been holdin' two jobs down now for the last ten years, and all the time doin' it straight. Takin' care of my little girl, raising her right.'

'All right,' said Strange. 'You're so far away from all that, why'd you go to Lorenze's wake, then?'

'Because I'm a Christian. I went to say a prayer for my old friend. To pay my respects. Even you can understand that, right?'

'Did Lorenze still hang with some of the old crowd that you know?'

Lee relaxed his shoulders. It seemed he'd given up on reaching Strange's human side and now he just wanted this done. 'Most of them grew up and moved on. A couple of them passed.'

'Sequan Hawkins? Ed Diggs?'

'I haven't seen Sequan, so I don't know. Digger Dog? He's still around.'

'That's Diggs's street name?'

Lee nodded. 'I saw him at the funeral home. He's still livin' over there with his grandmother. He looks older, but the same, you know? He always was Lorenze's main boy.'

'Thanks for your time,' said Quinn.

'That it?' said Lee, his eyes still locked on Strange.

'That'll do it,' said Strange. 'We need you, I expect we can find you here.'

Strange and Quinn walked toward the entrance to the store. They passed a white guy in a maroon shirt, small, with a belly and patches of hair framing a bald top, trying to calm an angry customer. The manager, thought Strange.

Out in the lot, Quinn glanced over at Strange on the way to the car. 'You were kinda rough on him, weren't you?'

Strange stared straight ahead. 'We got no time to be nice.'

They drove out toward Potomac in Strange's white Caprice. Strange made a cell call to see if Sequan Hawkins was at his job. Then he phoned the office and got Janine. Quinn sipped coffee from a go-cup and listened to their short, businesslike conversation. Strange made another call, left a message on the machine at Lamar Williams's apartment, and left Lamar the number to his cell.

'What's going on?' said Quinn.

'Lamar's been trying to get up with me. Janine said he told her it was important.'

'Well?'

'He's got his classes right now. I'll get him later.'

'Any idea what he wants?'

'These boys rolled up on him a while back in Park Morton, lookin' for Joe's mother? Pretty sure it's the same hard cases I saw up at Roosevelt one night at practice. They were huntin' Lorenze, I'm certain of it now. Bet you they ain't nothin' but neighborhood boys, too. Maybe Lamar found out something more.'

'If they're stupid enough to stay in the neighborhood, it won't be long until someone turns them in.'

'You're right. If it doesn't happen today, it'll happen tomorrow, if you know what I mean. The police are gonna get those boys soon enough.'

'What if we find them first?'

'I haven't figured that out yet, Terry. To tell you the truth, right now I'm just goin' on blind rage.'

Strange kept the needle above eighty on the Beltway. Quinn didn't comment on the speed. He blew the steam off his coffee and took a long pull from the cup.

'You and Janine got some problems, huh?' said Quinn.

'Guess you heard that in my tone.'

'You two gonna make it?'

'Haven't figured that one out yet, either,' said Strange. 'Anyway, it's not up to me.'

Strange parked the Caprice in the lot of Montgomery Mall, near an upscale retailer that anchored the shopping center. In contrast to Westfield, the parking lot here was clean, and the multi-ethnic people walking from their luxury cars and SUVs to the mall might as well have had dollar signs stamped right on their foreheads.

Strange and Quinn went up to the second floor of the department store. The sound of piano met them as they reached the top of the stairs. A man in a tuxedo played the keys of a Steinway set near the escalators adjacent to a menswear section and a large layout of men's shoes. Middle-aged white men wearing pressed jeans and sweaters strolled the aisles. Strange wondered what they were doing here on a Monday, why they weren't at work. Living off the interest, he reckoned.

They walked along the display tables of shoes. Several well-dressed salesmen eyed them as they passed.

'You need any kicks?' said Strange.

'I got a wide foot,' said Quinn, 'and it's hard to fit. There's this salesman, though, at Mean Feets, down in Georgetown? Says he can fit me. Dude named Antoine.'

'Skinny cat, right? Always standin' outside in the doorway there, hittin' a cigarette.'

'That's him.'

'I know him. They call him Spiderman.'

'You know everyone in town?'

'Not yet,' said Strange. 'But it's a long life.'

To the side of the shoe department was a shoe-shine stand, where a kneeling man in suspenders was buffing the cap-toes of a suited white man sitting in a chair above him, up on a kind of elevated platform.

Strange and Quinn waited in an alcove-type area beside the stand. They could hear the white man talking to the shoe-shine man about the Redskins/Ravens game, praising only the black players. They could hear the white man ending his sentences with 'man' and they could hear him dropping his g's, talking in a way that he thought would endear him to the black man kneeling at his feet. Talking in a way he would never talk at work and in a way he would forbid his children from talking at the dinner table at home. Strange looked over at Quinn, and Quinn looked away.

Soon the white man left, and they went out to the stand, where the shoe shiner was straightening the tools of his trade.

'Sequan Hawkins?' said Strange, getting a short nod in return. 'I'm Derek Strange, and this is Terry Quinn, my partner. We phoned you a little while ago.'

Hawkins rubbed his hands clean with a rag that smelled of nail polish remover. He was a handsome, well-built man with a light sheen to his close-cropped hair and a careful hint of a mustache.

'Come on around here,' said Hawkins, indicating with his chin the alcove where they had stood.

They went back to the alcove and Strange said, 'This is about Lorenze Wilder, like I explained.'

'Let me see some identification, you don't mind,' said Hawkins.

Strange flipped open his leather case and produced his badge and license. Hawkins's mouth turned up on the right, a lopsided grin.

'You two are, like, cops.'

'Investigators, D.C.,' said Strange. 'We knew the young man who was murdered alongside Lorenze.'

'My sympathies,' said Hawkins, the grin disappearing at the mention of the boy. 'I got two of my own.'

'You went to the funeral home for Lorenze's wake,' said Quinn.

'That's right.'

'You were friends with him?'

'A long time ago.'

'What made y'all stop being friends?' said Strange.

'Geography,' said Hawkins. 'Ambition.'

'Geography?'

'I haven't lived anywhere near the old neighborhood for the past ten years.'

'Don't get back there much, huh?'

'Oh, I do. I drive over to the house I grew up in, like, once a month. Park outside of it at night sometimes and look through the windows. They got a new family in there now.'

'Why would you do that?'

'To look at the ghosts.'

Strange didn't feel the need to comment. He often went by his mother's house at night, parked on the street, and did the same thing. He didn't consider Hawkins's actions to be odd at all.

'You ever run into Lorenze Wilder on those trips?' said Quinn.

'Sure, I saw him now and again. He was still living in his mother's house; I guess it was paid for with life insurance after her death. He never did get a steady job I knew of. He was one of those . . . I don't like to speak ill of the dead. But it was plain Lorenze was never gonna make it.'

'How about Ed Diggs?' said Strange.

'I saw him around the way, too. He was living with his grandmother last time I ran into him. Ed was the same way.'

'Any other reason why you might have gone back?'

'What do you mean?'

'We're looking for someone who might have wanted to hunt down Lorenze,' said Strange. 'Maybe for a drug debt or somethin' like that.'

'I wouldn't know about that.'

'So, you'd go back to the neighborhood once a month for what, exactly?' said Quinn. 'Couldn't be to just park outside your house.'

'I went back to remember, Mr . . .'

'Quinn.'

'I'd see some of those guys still in the neighborhood, the ones who were already at that dead end, who weren't even lookin' to get through it anymore, and it just served to remind me.'

'Of what?'

'Of why I'm down on my knees here every day. See, I don't just work here. I *own* this concession. I got four of these around the Beltway and a couple downtown.'

'You must be doin' all right,' said Strange.

'Got a house on a couple acres out in Damascus, a wife I love, and a couple of beautiful kids. There's a Harley in my garage and a Porsche Boxster, too. It's not the Carrera, but I'm workin' on that. So yeah, I've done all right.'

'You read about the murders,' said Strange, 'and you knew Lorenze. Any ideas?'

'I think you're talkin' to the wrong man. You want to know if Lorenze died because of a street beef, you need to be talking to Ed. They were still as tight as any two men could be, way I understand it. But Ed's not the type to talk to the police, or even to someone got a toy badge, tryin' to *look* like they're police.'

'Okay,' said Strange.

'Couldn't resist,' said Hawkins. 'You need to be flashing that license quick, so no one can look at it too close.'

'Normally I do. Get back to Diggs.'

'All I'm saying is, if there's any information to be got, Ed's the one to talk to. But you're gonna have to be creative.' Hawkins looked them both over. 'Y'all got a couple of pairs of shoulders on you. Use 'em.'

'You say he still stays with his grandmother?'

'Far as I know.'

Strange shook Hawkins's hand. 'Thanks for your time.'

Crossing the lot to the Caprice, Quinn said, 'Just goes to show you, you can't judge a man by his appearance.'

'You tellin' *me* that?'

'Oh, so now you're gonna tell me you didn't look at that guy and think, Shoe-shine Boy.'

'Didn't see the word 'boy' flashin' through my head at any time, if that's what you mean.'

'You know what I'm sayin'. Man shines shoes for a living and he's got a Porsche in his garage.'

'It's not a Carrera, though.'

'He's workin' on that,' said Quinn.

Strange removed his keys from his pocket and tossed them to Quinn. 'You drive. I need to make some calls.'

'Right.'

Quinn hit the Beltway and headed back toward the city. Strange phoned Lamar, got no answer, and left another message. He found the number for Ed Diggs on his list and phoned the house. Quinn heard him talking to a woman on the other end of the line; he could tell it was an older woman from the patient tone of Strange's voice.

'Any luck?' said Quinn, as Strange hit 'end.'

'His grandmother says he's on his way out the door. I figure he's still home, still wearin' his pajamas, and now she's gonna tell him to get his shit together and get himself out the house.' Strange looked at the needle on the speedometer. 'You can get there quicker, we might still catch him in.'

'I'm already doin' seventy-five. Wouldn't want us to get pulled over. You might go showing that toy badge of yours to a real police officer, get us into a world of hurt.'

'Funny. C'mon, Terry, speed it up. Car's got a three-fifty square block under the hood, and you're drivin' it like a Geo and shit.'

'You want me to drive it like a race car, I will.'

'Pin it,' said Strange.

Lucille Carter lived on a number street off North Dakota Avenue in Manor Park, in a detached bungalow fronted by a series of small roller-coaster hills that stopped at a stone retaining wall before they reached the sidewalk. There were plenty of cars parked along the curb on this workday. This, along with the condition of the raked lawns and the updated paint on the modest houses, indicated to Strange that the residents were mainly retirees holding on to their properties and sheltering their extended families.

Strange and Quinn went up the concrete steps to the porch of Lucille Carter's house. Strange knocked on the front door, and it soon opened. Carter, short, bespectacled, narrow in the hips, and not yet completely gray, stood in the frame. She knew who they were. Her eyes were unsmiling and her body language told them that she wasn't about to let them in. As agreed, Quinn stepped back and let Strange take the lead.

'Derek Strange. This is my partner Terry Quinn.' Strange opened his badge case and closed it just as quickly. 'Like I explained to you on the phone, we're investigating the Lorenze Wilder homicide. We need to speak with your grandson Edward.'

'He already talked to the police.'

'I told you we needed to speak with him again.'

'And I told *you*, Mr Strange, that he was on his way out. As I am about to be, shortly.'

'Any idea where we can catch up with him?'

'He went out to his job—'

'He doesn't have a job, Miss Carter.'

'He went out to his job *search*. If you had let me finish—'

'All due respect, I don't have the time or the inclination to let you finish. You told Edward that we were on our way over here, and now he's gone. So let me make this easy for you and tell you how it's gonna be. Me and my partner here are gonna be back in an hour with a subpoena. Edward's not in, we'll come back the hour after that. Same thing the hour after that. We have to, we'll be here on the hour around the clock. Now, what do you suppose your good neighbors gonna think of that?'

'This is harassment.'

'Yes, ma'am.'

'Would you like me to call your supervisors?'

'I can't stop you.' Strange looked at his watch. 'We'll see you in about sixty minutes, then. Thank you for your time.'

They heard the door close behind them as they were walking down the steps.

'That was nice,' said Quinn. 'The Gray Panthers are gonna give you their humanitarian award for that one.'

'You want to find a man in this city, shake down his grandmother,' said Strange. 'Black man like Diggs always gonna respect the matriarch who treated him right. Plus, she's stronger than he is, and the last thing he's gonna want is to incur her wrath.'

'That cop knowledge?'

Strange shook his head. 'My mother always said it. "Kick the bush and the quail comes flyin' out." '

'So Diggs flies out of the bush. Then what? I mean, the cops have already talked to this guy.'

'They didn't know how close he was to Lorenze. And they didn't *talk* to him the way I'm gonna talk to him.'

'Okay, what now?'

'Let's get my car out of view so we can regroup.'

Strange pulled the Caprice around the corner and parked it a block south of the Carter residence and out of its sight lines. He phoned Lamar's apartment and this time he got him on the line. Strange made a writing sign in the air and snapped his fingers. Quinn handed him a pen. Strange wrote down a series of numbers, asked Lamar some questions, nodded as he listened to the answers, and said, 'Good work, son,' before ending the call.

'What?' said Quinn.

'Lamar saw one of those boys last night, one of the three who rolled up on him at Park Morton.' Strange was punching numbers into the grid of his cell as he talked. 'Said this boy was wearing the same bright shirt he had on when he saw him the first time.'

'Lotta bright shirts out here.'

'His face was hard to forget, had a nose like an anteater.'

'And?'

'Boy had a duffel bag in his backseat and a road map in his hand when Lamar saw him coming out the market, over there near the Black Hole. Looked to Lamar like he was runnin'.'

'What else?'

'Lamar got the license number off this boy's Toyota, too.' Strange gave him the hold-up sign with his hand as his call connected. 'Janine. Derek here. I need you to run a plate for me quick. You get an address on the owner of the car, I'm gonna need a phone number from the reverse directory, too.' Strange gave her the information and nodded as if Janine were in the room. 'I'll be waiting. Right.'

Strange hit 'end.' 'Janine will get it quick. She sends a Christmas card every year to this guy she's been knowin', over at the DMV? One of those little things she does, small gestures of kindness. Gets results.'

'She is good.'

'The best.' Strange pointed his chin up the block. 'You want the alley or the front of the house?'

'The alley.'

'Where's your gun at, case I need it?'

'Right here, under the seat.'

'Is it loaded?'

'Yeah.'

'You got your cell?'

'In my pocket.'

'Keep it live.' Strange kept the pen Quinn had given him and slipped a notepad into his jacket. 'The old lady will be going out, I expect. Either he's in there or she's gonna find him and tell him to get back to the house and take his medicine. But I don't trust him to do what she says. If you get sight of him, you call me.'

'What if you see him first?'

'I'll do the same.'

Strange positioned himself a half block east of the Carter home, his 10×50 binos around his neck.

Quinn walked down the alley, found the Carter bungalow, and quickly opened the link gate at the end of the weedy concrete path to the back porch of the house. Then he walked back and stood three houses away on the stones of the alley. A pit bull in a cage barked at him from a neighboring yard. No one came out to see what the barking was about, and no curtains moved from the back windows of the houses.

Quinn paced the alley for an hour. Then his phone chirped. He flipped it open.

'Yeah.'

'The old lady just left. She's drivin' off in her Ford right now.'

'Okay,' said Quinn.

Another thirty minutes passed. Then a sad sack of a man in oversize jeans and a T-shirt came out from the back of the Carter house. He stepped down off the peeling wood porch and reached into his jeans for a pack of cigarettes. He shook one out from a hole cut in the bottom of the pack and lit it with a match he tore from a book.

Quinn stepped back behind a tall lilac bush that still had leaves. He phoned Strange and kept his voice low.

'Derek, he's out in the yard. How do you want to play it?'

'Hard,' said Strange. 'Strong-arm him into the house and keep that back door unlocked. How much time you figure before he goes back inside?'

'However long it takes to smoke a cigarette.'

'Right,' said Strange.

Strange ran to the Caprice. He dropped his binoculars to the floor. He found Quinn's automatic, a black Colt .45 with a checkered grip and a five-inch barrel, underneath the seat. He released the magazine and checked the load: a full seven shots. It had been a long time since Strange had had the weight of a gun in his hand. He felt that he needed one today.

Edward Diggs took a last drag of his Kool, then a real last drag that burned his throat, and crushed the butt under his shoe. He picked up the butt and tossed it over the fence, into the yard of a neighbor who was also a smoker. Diggs's grandmother wouldn't let him smoke in the house, and she didn't like to see any evidence of it in her backyard. Mad as she had been this morning, he wasn't gonna do anything to get her back up more than it already was.

But fuck that shit if she thought he was gonna talk any more to the police. Let them deliver that subpoena. He had told them he didn't know shit about what had happened to Lorenze and that kid, and he didn't have to go on repeating it if he didn't want to. Far as telling them the truth, he had decided from the get-go to keep his mouth shut. Lorenze was his main boy, he loved him like a brother and all that, but all the talking in the world wasn't gonna bring Lorenze back. Diggs felt that the police wouldn't waste their time protecting a guy like him. All he wanted now was to live.

He turned and went back up the walkway, cracked and overgrown with clover and weeds. He thought he heard something behind him, but it couldn't be, it was just his own footsteps and that cur, wouldn't stop barking across the way.

His right hand was grabbed from behind and then bent at the wrist.

A bolt of electric pain shot up to his neck, and the shock of it nearly dropped him to his knees. But the man behind him held him up.

'Let's go, Ed.' A white man's voice, the one saying the words pushing him along the walkway to the back porch. 'Inside.'

'Fuck *is* this shit? You're hurtin' me!'

'Investigator, D.C. Move it.'

'I'm 'onna get your badge number, man.'

'Yeah, okay.'

'This is assault right here!'

'Not yet,' said Quinn. 'Open that door, let's go.'

Diggs did it and Quinn released him as they stepped inside. They were in a clean kitchen that held a small table and chairs. On the table was a coffee cup and the sports page of the *Washington Post.* A set of knives sat on the Formica counter, sheathed in a rubber stand. Diggs stood by the table, trying to give Quinn a hard glare. Quinn looked Diggs over carefully, thinking of the knives, deciding that Diggs would never make a play.

'Sit down,' said Quinn, pointing to one of the chairs. Diggs pulled one away from the table and sat in it. He mumbled to himself as he stared at the linoleum floor.

Quinn moved to the rear window and looked through it. Strange was coming through the open gate and moving quickly up the walkway. His shirttails were out over his jeans. Then Strange was opening the door and he was in the kitchen and closing the door behind him. He walked toward Ed Diggs. Diggs stood from his chair.

'Meet Ed Diggs,' said Quinn.

'Ed,' said Strange, and as Strange reached him he threw a deep right into Diggs's mouth and knocked him back over the chair. Diggs slid on the linoleum and stopped sliding when the back of his head hit the kitchen cabinet beneath the sink. Strange yanked him up by his T-shirt, kept his left hand bunched on the T, and hit him with a short, sharp right to the same spot. Diggs's neck snapped back and his eyes fluttered. His eyes came back, and he stared up at Strange as blood flowed over his lower lip and dripped onto his shirt. Strange released him and Diggs dropped to the floor. Diggs staggered back up to his feet.

'We tell you to stand?' Quinn righted the chair. '*Sit* your ass down.'

Strange pulled a chair over so it faced the one Diggs had been sitting on. He and Quinn listened to Diggs mumble and moan, and they waited for him to slouch across the room. Strange had split Diggs's lip wide, and blood came freely now from the cut.

Diggs sat down dead eyed, his shoulders slouched. Strange reached under his shirt and pulled the .45.

'Nah,' said Diggs in the voice of a boy. 'Uh-uh, man, nah, uh-*uh*.'

'Who killed Lorenze?' said Strange.

'I don't know who did that.' His diction was sloppy and wet.

'Somebody was huntin' him. Was it a drug debt?'

'I don't know.'

Strange racked the receiver on the Colt.

'Why you want to do that, brother? I *told* you I don't know.'

Strange got up out of his chair and with his free hand flat-palmed Diggs's chest. Diggs and the chair toppled back to the floor. Diggs grunted, and Strange crouched over him and forced the barrel of the .45 into his mouth.

'*You* know,' said Strange. He withdrew the barrel, touched it gently to the corner of Diggs's right eye, and then pressed it there with force.

'They'll kill me,' said Diggs.

'*Look* at me, Ed. *I'm* gonna kill you right now, I swear to God.'

'Derek,' said Quinn. It wasn't part of the act. Strange's eyes had long since veered from the script.

'*Look* at me, Ed.'

Diggs did look. His lip quivered and he closed his eyes. When he opened them again a tear sprung loose and ran fast down his cheek.

'Lorenze,' said Diggs, 'he owed money to this boy for some hydro he copped. I was there when Lorenze bought it. He was gonna pay this boy in his own time ... Wasn't nothin' but a hunrid dollars. Boy stepped to me at a dogfight back by Ogelthorpe; I could tell he was serious. I mean, that boy had nothin' in his eyes.'

'What'd this boy look like?'

'Tall and slim, light skinned, had this crazy smile.'

'He had partners, right?'

'The ones he came with to the fight. Boy with cornrows and show muscles. 'Nother kid, one with the dog, boy had this funny-lookin' nose and shit.'

'The main one, he say his name?'

'Garfield Potter.'

'You know where he stays at?'

'He said he was up on Warder Street, near Roosevelt.'

'What else you know?'

'Nothin' else.' Diggs blinked hard. 'You just doomed me, man. Don't you care nothin' about that?'

Strange slipped the Colt back under his shirt as he stood.

'Don't speak of this,' said Strange. 'Tell your grandmother you got jumped out on the street. Tell her you fell down and bounced a few times or anything you want. But don't tell her it was us came back. It's over for you, hear? You'll be fine.'

They left him lying on the kitchen floor and walked out the back door of the house and to the alley.

Strange handed Quinn his gun. Quinn slipped it into his waistband and side-glanced Strange.

'You got some anger management issues you need to work on, Derek. You know it?'

'My anger's been working pretty good for me today so far.'

'Thought you were gonna use the forty-five for a second back there.'

'Couldn't have used it if I wanted to. I emptied the magazine before I came to the house.'

'That gun felt too good in your hand, didn't it?'

'Scared me how good it felt,' said Strange. 'Your bullets are in the ashtray, back in the car.'

On the way to the Caprice, Strange answered his cell. He continued his conversation with Janine as he got under the wheel of the car. Quinn slipped the .45 back under the seat. As Strange listened to his call, writing in his notebook, Quinn's cell chirped. He answered, got out of the Chevy, and leaned against the rear quarter panel as he took the call.

Strange waited for Quinn to get back inside. He noticed that some of the color had drained from Quinn's face.

'Janine got me a name and address on that boy Lamar saw,' said Strange. 'Charles White. And guess what? His credit record shows his last address is up on Warder Street. I bet you he was the only one of the three qualified to sign for the utilities. She got me the phone number there, too.'

'Guess you got enough to call Lydell,' said Quinn, his eyes showing he was somewhere else. 'Time to send in the troops.'

'I'm not ready to do that yet,' said Strange, watching Quinn's stare go out the window. 'Terry, you all right?'

'I just got a call from the MPD. They got a girl down in the ER at Washington Hospital Center, she's all fucked up. Beaten close to death. It's an informant of mine, helped me on that snatch I did. She gave my name as the first contact. Girl named Stella.'

'You want to go there, then go. I can drop you at the hospital and pick this up my own self from here.'

'All right,' said Quinn. 'Let's go.'

Quinn phoned Sue Tracy as Strange turned off Georgia Avenue and headed east on Irving Street. Strange entered the complex of hospital buildings five minutes later and stopped the Caprice near the heliport adjacent to the ER entrance. Quinn opened his door and put one foot to the asphalt. He turned and shook Strange's hand.

'Don't do anything without me, Derek.'

'I won't,' said Strange.

Even as he said this, Strange was weighing a plan. It went against most everything he believed in. Still, he couldn't shake it from his mind.

27

Quinn went directly past the check-in desk, through the waiting area, and into the treatment facility. A security guard stopped him and walked him over to a plainclothes MPD cop who wore a black mustache. He held a go-cup of coffee in his thin, veined hand.

'You got a minute to talk?' said the cop.

'After I see the girl,' said Quinn. 'How is she?'

'According to the people here, she got beat up pretty bad. The man did it used his fists, but he didn't hold back. He punched right through her. Broke a few ribs, and she's bleeding inside. They're trying to stop that, and the doc thinks they will. Also, whoever this prince was, he carved up her face with a knife.'

'She gonna live?'

The cop shrugged. He sipped from a hole torn in the lid of the cup and looked Quinn over. 'You know, I recognized your name on the sheet, and then when you walked in, from the pictures they used to run in the papers. You're the same Terry Quinn used to be on the force, right?' The cop's eyes said curiosity rather than aggression.

'Yeah. Can I go?'

'Why'd she have you as contact number one?'

'I don't know why.'

'No fixed address, no mention of parents. And she wants to talk to you?'

'That's right.'

'Okay. She claims she got blindsided and never saw a thing. You got any idea who did this to her?'

'None.'

'Here's my card.'

Quinn took it and slipped it into his coat.

'Excuse me,' said Quinn.

Stella was on a gurney behind a portable curtain, at the end of a row of makeshift stalls. Her forehead and cheeks were nearly covered in surgical tape, damp and brownish red in spots. Her thin right arm, lying outside the blanket, was bruised black with large defensive marks and also in several places where a nurse had tried to find a vein for the IV. Tubes ran from somewhere under the sheets and into her nostrils. The fluid in the tubes was dirty, and brown particles ran through it as Stella inhaled, her breath labored and ragged.

Quinn found a hard chair and placed it beside the gurney, where he took a seat and held her hand. A nurse came by and told him that they were preparing to move Stella to the ICU and he couldn't stay much longer. Ten minutes later, Stella opened her eyes, bloodied in the corners and ringed in black. Her head remained in place as her eyes moved to his, and she squeezed his hand.

'Hey, Stella.'

'Green eyes.'

Her voice was barely audible, and Quinn bent forward and moved his ear close to her mouth. 'Say it again?'

'You came.'

'Course I did,' said Quinn. 'We're friends.'

Stella's lips began to move, but nothing came out. She tried again and said, 'Ice.'

A cup of ice chips sat beside Stella's eyeglasses on a stand next to the gurney. Quinn put the cup to her blistered lips and tilted it so that a few chips slid into her mouth. When he returned the cup to the table he saw a bag at the foot of the gurney containing Stella's clothing and shoes. A white plastic purse rested atop her possessions.

Quinn stroked her hand. 'Wilson do this to you, Stella?'

She nodded, her eyes straining as she looked up at Quinn. Quinn took her glasses off the stand and carefully fitted them on her face.

'Better?'

Stella nodded.

'You tell anyone else that he did this?'

Stella shook her head.

'I don't want you to tell anyone else, not yet. Do you understand?'

Stella nodded.

'*Why* did he do this, Stella? Did Jennifer Marshall tell him you'd set up the snatch?'

'She called him,' said Stella. 'She's out again . . . mad at her parents . . . and she called World.'

'All right,' said Quinn. 'That's enough.' The tubes running into her nose were dense now with brown particles, and her hand felt hot beneath his.

'Terry . . .'

'Don't talk. Sue Tracy, remember her? She's on her way down. I want you to talk to *her* when she comes. You need to tell her how to get in touch with your people. Your parents, I mean.'

'Home,' said Stella.

'Sue's gonna take care of that.'

The nurse returned and told Quinn he had to go. Quinn kissed Stella on her bandaged forehead, told her he'd be back to see her later, and walked out from behind the curtain. The cop was waiting for him by the swinging exit doors.

'She say anything?' said the cop.

'Not a word,' said Quinn, hitting a wall button and going through a space in the opening doors. He yanked his cell off his belt clip and dialed Strange as he walked. He had Strange's location by the time he left the building and hit fresh air.

Quinn looked ahead. Sue Tracy was coming down the sidewalk toward him, a cigarette in her hand. She hit the smoke and pitched the butt onto the street as they met.

'What happened?' said Tracy.

'Wilson got to her. He worked on her with his hands and a knife.'

'Why?'

'From what I can make out? Jennifer Marshall ran away from home again. She called Wilson and hipped him to Stella.' Quinn looked around, distracted, nervous as a cat. 'Listen, I gotta go.'

'Wait a minute.' Tracy grabbed his elbow. 'I think you need to take a deep breath here.'

'Go take a look at her yourself, Sue. See how peaceful it makes you feel.'

'All right, it's rough. We've both seen plenty.'

'Stay in neutral if that's what works for you.'

'You got a history, Terry. Don't make this an excuse to settle some score just because some lowlife looked at you wrong and called you a girl.'

'Right. Here's the part where you say, "We live in two different worlds. Yours is too violent. I don't want to live in your world anymore." Go ahead and say it, Sue, because I've heard it from women before.'

'Bullshit. I'm not giving up, and I'm not looking to walk away. Don't put me down just because I'm worried about you.'

Quinn pulled his arm free of her grasp. 'Like I said, I gotta bounce.'

'Where are you off to?'

'To hook up with Derek. We're working on something important and I can't leave him twisting out there.'

'You sure that's where you're going?'

'Look: Stella wants to go home. You need to find her parents. She'll cooperate.'

'I know what to do. You don't have to tell me, because I've been doing this for a long time. I hired you, remember?'

'There's a plainclothes in the ER; he'll be looking to talk to you. I didn't give him anything, understand?'

'You don't want me to talk to the police.'

'Not yet. You'll know when the time's right.'

'Why don't you want me to talk to them now?'

'Take care of Stella,' said Quinn.

He put his arms around Tracy and kissed her on her lips. He took in the clean smell of her hair. They broke their embrace, and Tracy stepped back and pointed her finger at Quinn.

'Keep your cell on, Terry. I want to know where you are.'

She watched him jog down the sidewalk toward a line of cabs idling near the main entrance of the hospital. She turned and walked into the ER.

Quinn got into the backseat of a purple Ford. The driver was talking on a cell phone and did not turn his head.

'Warder Street in Park View, off Georgia.'

The African looked at Quinn in his rearview but kept talking on his cell. He did not touch the transmission arm coming off the steering column.

Quinn flipped open his badge case, reached over the front seat, and held the case in front of the cabby's face.

'Haul ass,' said Quinn.

The cabby pulled down on the tree and fed the Ford gas.

'Lydell, it's Derek.'

'Derek, where you at?'

'Down near my office. Can you hear me?'

'Sure.'

Strange sat behind the wheel of his Caprice, parked along the curb on Warder Street, facing east. He was a half block down from the row house where Charles White and, he expected, Garfield Potter and the boy with the cornrows lived. Strange's binoculars hung around his neck.

'Lydell, I wanted to get up with you. I don't think me and Terry are gonna make it to practice tonight.'

'Why not?'

'We got a big surveillance thing we're working on. Can't break it; you know how that goes.'

'That's a lot of boys for me and Dennis to handle.'

'Call Lionel, and Lamar Williams; those two know the drills and the plays as good as we do. If you don't have their phone numbers, call Janine.'

'Yeah, okay. But what's up with this surveillance thing? Thought you'd be out talking to Lorenze Wilder's associates today.'

'We been doing that, too,' said Strange, looking at the empty row house porch. 'But nothin' yet.'

'Well, *we* might have something.'

'Yeah?'

'Woman called in, trying to get some of that reward money. Said she was out late one night, a few nights before the killings. Some male friends of hers was in a crap game got robbed by three young men, over there in Park Morton. One of the young men pulled a gun on one of her friends, man named Ray Boyer. Used it like a hammer and broke Boyer's nose. Woman says the one with the gun matched the description of the artist's drawing on the posters we put up in the neighborhood. And get this: she says the gun was a short-barreled revolver. You know that we've identified one of the murder weapons as a snub-nosed three fifty-seven.'

'Could've been a thirty-eight that boy pulled on that crap game. Could've been anything.'

'Could've been. But this is too much of a coincidence to leave alone.'

'I don't suppose the gunslinger left his name.'

'Matter of fact, this knucklehead did say his name. But she can't remember it. Admits she was too intoxicated and up on weed, and scared in the bargain. We're out looking for Ray Boyer right now. He didn't show up to his job today, so we're visiting the bars he likes to go to. Hoping that he'll remember this boy's name. Man's a Vietnam veteran, so I'm thinking he'll be able to identify the caliber of the gun as well.'

'Sounds promising.'

'Just a feeling, Derek, but it looks to me like we're gonna make an arrest on this today.'

'Keep me posted on it, you don't mind. You got my cell number, right?'

'I got it.'

'All right, then. Thanks, Lydell.'

Strange slipped his cell into its holster on his side. In his rearview, he saw Quinn walking up Warder, two cups of coffee in his hands.

Strange reached over and opened the passenger door. Quinn dropped onto the seat and handed Strange one of the cups.

'Thank you, buddy,' said Strange.

'I know you like to sip water on a surveillance.'

'Coffee makes me pee.'

'But you're gonna need the caffeine to make up for all the food we haven't eaten today.'

'I forgot all about it. Not like me to forget being hungry.'

Quinn chin-nodded up the street. 'Which one is it?'

'Third one down from the corner there. Only one has a porch got nothin' on it. There, see?'

'They show themselves yet?'

'No. But I expect, they got any brains at all, they're staying inside.'

'What about the one Lamar saw?'

'Charles White. His Toyota's not out here. Maybe Lamar's right about that boy leaving town.' Strange sipped his coffee. 'How's that girl, man?'

'Bad,' said Quinn.

Quinn described what he had seen, and how he had kept what he knew from the police. Strange told Quinn that he had spoken to Lydell Blue, and that he had kept everything from his friend as well. He told Quinn that the police seemed very close to finding the killers. He told Quinn what he had in mind.

'So you're just giving up on those boys,' said Quinn. 'No possible hope, ever, is that what you're sayin'?'

'For them? That's right.'

'You can call the MPD in now if you want to. End it right here.'

'You think that would end it?'

'There's no death penalty in the District, if that's what you mean. But they'd do long time. They'd get twenty-five, thirty years. Maybe on a good day they'd get life.'

'And what would that do? Give those boys a bed and three squares a day, when Joe Wilder's lying cold in the ground? Joe's gonna be dead forever, man—'

'Derek, I know.'

'Then you're gonna read in the paper how the police solved the murder. The big lie. Can't no murder ever be *solved.* Not unless the victim gonna get out of his grave and walk, breathe in the air. Hug his mother and play ball and grow up to be a man and lie down with a woman . . . live a life, Terry, the way God intended him to. So how you gonna *solve* it so Joe can do that?' Strange shook his head. 'I'm not lookin' to solve this one. I'm looking to *re*solve it.'

'You telling me, Derek? Or are you trying to convince yourself?'

'A little bit of both, I guess.'

'You do this,' said Quinn, 'you lose everything. You believe in God, Derek, I know you do. How you gonna reconcile this with your faith?'

'Haven't figured that one out yet. But I will.'

Quinn nodded slowly. 'Well, you're on your own.'

'You don't want any part of it, huh?'

'It's your decision,' said Quinn. 'Anyway, I've got something I've got to do tonight myself.'

Strange looked Quinn over carefully. 'You're goin' after that pimp.'

'I have to.'

'It's not just what he did to the girl, is it? That pimp tried to punk you out.'

'Like you said: it's a little bit of both.'

'Sure it is.' Strange smiled sadly. 'Shit's older than time, man. Garfield Potter killed Joe Wilder 'cause he thought Joe's uncle disrespected him on a hundred-dollar debt. Now I'm gonna do what I think I have to, my idea of making it right. And all of it started 'cause this boy Potter thought he got took for bad.'

Quinn finished his coffee and dropped the cup on the floor. 'I gotta go.'

'Go ahead, then. But don't forget your gun. It's under the seat there.'

'I won't need it.'

'Neither will I.'

'I better leave it. Can't be carrying it around town now, can I?'

'Plus, you wouldn't feel right, would you, to have any kind of drop on that pimp?'

'That's not it.'

'Okay. You need a ride?'

'I'll catch a Metrobus up Georgia. I can get off at Buchanan and pick up my car.'

'You gonna hang out at the bus stop, in this neighborhood? At night?'

'I'll be all right.'

Strange reached over and shook Quinn's hand. 'I'm gonna pray that you will be.'

'Keep your cell on,' said Quinn, 'and I'll do the same with mine. Let's talk later on, all right?'

Strange nodded. 'See you on the other side.'

Quinn got out of the car and shut the door. Strange eyed him in the rearview, walking down Warder in that cocky way of his, hands in his leather, shoulders squared, going by groups of young men moving about on the sidewalks and gathered on the corners.

Quinn went under a street lamp and passed through its light. Then he was indistinguishable from the others, just another shadow moving through the darkness that had fallen on the streets.

28

Strange made a call on his cell. He spoke to the man on the other end of the line for a long while. When their conversation was done, Strange said, 'See you then.' He hit 'end,' punched Janine's number into the grid, pressed 'talk,' and waited to connect. He got Janine on the third ring.

'Baker residence.'

'Derek here.'

'Where are you?'

'Workin' this Joe Wilder thing. Sittin' in my car.'

'*Where*?'

'Out here on the street.'

'You're not drinking coffee, are you?'

'I did.'

'You know how it runs through you.'

Strange found himself smiling at the sound of her voice. 'Just wanted to call and make sure Lionel got to practice.'

'Lydell came by and got him. Told me to tell you, if we spoke, that they found this guy, Ray something, and picked him up.'

'Ray Boyer. He say if Boyer gave him anything?'

'Not yet. Lydell said that Boyer wanted to lawyer up first. Something to do with making sure the paperwork's right so he gets the reward money.'

Strange knew now that he didn't have much time.

'Why don't you knock off for the day?' said Janine. 'Sounds like the police have this in hand.'

'I think I'll stay out some, see what happens.'

'Must be getting chilly in that car. And I know you're not lettin' the heat run. You, who's always telling Ron Lattimer that a running car kills a surveillance, what with the exhaust smoke coming out the pipes—'

'You know me too well.'

'That I do.'

'You asking me to come over and warm myself up?'

'Are you ready to do some serious talking?'

'Not yet,' said Strange. 'Soon. But I didn't just call about Lionel and practice.'

'Well?'

'Wanted to ask you something. My mother used to tell me, You can't trade a bad life for a good. Do you think that's right, Janine?'

'Do I think it's right? I don't know . . . Where *are* you, Derek? You don't sound right.'

'Never mind where I'm at.' Strange shifted his weight on the bench seat. 'I love you, Janine.'

'Us lovin' each other is not the issue, Derek.'

'Good bye, baby.'

Strange cut the call. He stared up the street at the row house. If he was going to do this, then he had to do it now. He found his notepad beside him, and on the top sheet, the phone number of the house. He punched the numbers into his cell. As he did, he went over in his head what he had planned. It was all risk, a long play. He couldn't waver or stumble now.

The phone rang on the other end. A silhouette moved behind the curtains of the row house window.

'Yeah.'

'Garfield Potter?'

'That's right.'

'Lorenze Wilder. Joe Wilder. Those names mean anything to you?'

'Who?'

'Lorenze Wilder. Joe Wilder.'

'How'd you get my number?'

'Not too hard, once you find out where a person lives. I been followin' you, Garfield.'

'Man, who the *fuck* is this?'

'Derek Strange.'

'That supposed to mean somethin' to me?'

'If you saw me, you'd remember. I was coachin' the football team that little boy played on. The boy you killed.'

'I ain't kill no boy.'

'I'm the one you and your partners were crackin' on, callin' me Fred Sanford and shit while I was walking to my car. Y'all were smokin' herb in a beige Caprice. You and a boy with cornrows, and another boy, had a long nose. Remember me now? 'Cause I sure do remember you.'

'So?'

Strange heard a crack in Potter's voice.

'I followed Lorenze and the boy the night you killed them. I was responsible for that boy, and I followed. Only, you weren't riding in a beige Caprice that night. It was a white Plymouth with a police package. Isn't that right, Garfield?'

'White Plymouth? That shit was on the news, any motherfucker own a television set gonna know that. You got somethin' serious you want to say, then say it, old-time.'

'Maybe *you* want to say something, Garfield. You kill a boy—'

'Told you I ain't killed no kid.'

'You kill a *boy*, Garfield, and you got to have somethin' to say.'

Save yourself. If you want to live, young man, then now's the time.

'What, some young nigger dies out here, I'm supposed to cry? I be dyin' young, too, most likely; ain't nobody gonna shed no tears for me.'

Strange spoke softly as he closed his eyes. 'I want to get paid.'

'What? I just told you—'

'I'm tellin' *you*, I was a witness to the murders. I saw the event with my own eyes.'

Strange listened to the hiss of dead air. Finally, Potter spoke. 'You so sure of what you saw, why ain't you gone to the police? Get your reward money and slither on back into that hole you came out of?'

'Because I can get more from you.'

'Why you think that?'

'Drug dealer like you, all that cash you got? Told you, I been followin' you, Potter.'

'How much more?'

'Double the ten they're offering. Make it twenty.' Strange squinted. 'Since you been insulting my intelligence, might as well go ahead and make it twenty-five.'

'Ain't even no murder gun no more. And I know you ain't gonna try and play me the fool and claim you got photographs or sumshit like that.'

'Not photographs. A videotape. I own an eight-millimeter camera with a three-sixty lens. I was parked a whole block back from that ice-cream shop on Rhode Island, but with that zoom the tape came out clear as day.'

'Tape can be doctored. Bullshit like that gets thrown out of court every day. Truth is, you can't prove a thing.'

'I can try,' said Strange.

More silence. 'Aiight, then. Maybe we should hook up and talk.'

'I don't want to talk about nothin'. Just bring the money. I'll give you the tape and we will be done.'

'Where?'

'I got a house I keep as a rental property; it's unoccupied right now. Figure you're not stupid enough to try somethin' in a residential neighborhood. I got some business I got to take care of first, so it's gonna take me about an hour, hour and a half to get out there.'

'Where is it?'

Strange gave Potter the directions. He repeated them slowly so that Potter could write them down.

'You still drivin' that black Cadillac that was parked outside Roosevelt?'

'You do remember me, then.'

'You still drivin' it?'

'Yeah.'

'I see any kind of police-lookin' vehicles outside that house, I am gone. I don't want to see nothin' but that Caddy, hear?'

'Bring the money, and come with your two partners. I want to keep my eye on all of you at once.'

'Ain't but two of us now,' said Potter.

'Hour and a half,' said Strange. 'I'll see you then.'

Strange ended the call, ignitioned the Chevy, and put it in gear. He drove quickly up to Buchanan, where he washed his face, changed his shirt, and fed Greco.

Back on the street, Strange walked toward his Brougham. Quinn had parked his car behind the Cadillac earlier that morning. The Chevelle was gone.

The guns Garfield Potter had bought were a six-shot .38 Special and a .380 Walther, the PPK double action with the seven-shot capacity. The revolver, a blue Armscor with a rubber grip, was for Potter. He stayed away from automatics, fearing they would jam.

Potter checked the load on the .38. He jerked his wrist and snapped the cylinder shut. He had been practicing this action in the mirror just this afternoon.

'You ready, Dirty?'

'Uh-huh,' said Little.

He was sitting on the couch, thinkin' on Brianna, how if she was here now how good it'd be to bust it out. He was flyin' like the eagle behind some hydro he'd just smoked, and his eyelids were heavy. He was happy. Hungry, too. He didn't really want to go out, but Garfield did. So there it was.

Little looked down at the automatic he held loosely in his hand. The grip was checkered plastic and had the Walther logo on it, the word written inside a kind of flag, like, looked like it was blowin' in a breeze. The safety was grooved, and there was this thing on the side, like a little sign, showed you when you had put one in the chamber, in case you forgot. Walther, they made a pretty gun.

'Dirty? You with me?'

'Yeah.'

'Come on, then,' said Potter, fitting his skully onto his head. He picked up two pairs of thin leather gloves off the table, one pair for him and one for Little. He knew Carlton would not think to bring a pair himself. 'Let's get this done.'

Little got up off the couch and looked in a mirror they had over a table by the stairs. His cornrows were lookin' raggedy and fucked. He wondered if maybe he ought to do those twisties in his hair, the short tips, like he'd seen the fellas around do. Little realized he had been staring at himself for a while and he chuckled. It sounded like a snort.

'Let's *go*, Dirty.'

'Yeah, aiight.'

Little got into his leather and holstered the Walther under his shirt. Potter put his leather on and dropped the .38 in its side pocket. He looked at Little and smiled.

'Damn, boy, you just smoke too *much* of that shit, don't you?'

'It's good to me, D. Wish you had a player in that hooptie you bought, though. We could listen to some beats on the way out the county.'

'We'll let Flexx roll on ninety-five point five. Anyway, I be havin' a Lex next time, with the Bose system in it, too.'

'You been talkin' about that nice whip for, like, forever, man. When you gonna get it?'

'Soon.'

Little and Potter laughed.

'Let's go,' said Potter. 'We need to take care of this tonight.'

'Maybe we'll peep Charles while we're out.'

'Coon's just hidin' somewhere, you know this.' Potter pulled his car keys from the pocket of his jeans. 'We do find him, we gonna down him, too.'

Little head-motioned to the TV set, a UPN show playing with the volume up. 'Should I turn it off?'

'Nah,' said Potter. 'We ain't gonna be gone all that long.'

They walked from the row house, the laugh track from the sitcom fading as they shut the door behind them.

*

Quinn did push-ups in his apartment while 'Jackson Cage' played loud from his speakers. He did five sets of fifty and stopped when he had broken a sweat and felt the burn in his pecs. When he came out of the shower he dropped a Steve Earle into his player and listened to 'The Unrepentant' as he dressed. His blood was up sufficiently now. He could feel his sweat again, cool beneath his flannel shirt.

Quinn slipped his cell into his jeans, put on his leather, and dropped a pair of cuffs into the side pocket. He locked the apartment down and walked out into the night air. A kid on the sidewalk nodded in his direction and Quinn said, 'Hey,' and kept walking without a pause in his step.

He got under the wheel of the Chevelle and fitted his key to the ignition. Quinn cooked it and headed downtown.

29

The man at the used-car lot on Blair Road had told Garfield Potter that there might be some white smoke at first, coming out the exhaust pipes of the '88 Ford Tempo he was about to sell him, but not to worry.

'It just needs a good highway run,' said the man, some kind of Arab, or a Paki, maybe; Potter couldn't tell one from the other. 'Blow the cobwebs out, and it's going be just like new.'

Potter knew the man was lying, but the price was right, and anyway, he was lookin' for something wouldn't attract much attention. An '88 Tempo? That was just about as no-attention-gettin' a motherfucker as you could get.

Looking in the rearview, going east on New York Avenue, he could see the white smoke trailing out behind the Ford. Carlton Little had made mention of it, as he always reminded Potter that what they were rolling in was a hoop, but he hadn't said much after that.

Little had turned the radio up loud. Flexx had a set going on PGC, the same list they played over and over every night, their most-requested jams. It had gone from Mystikal to R. Kelly to Erykah Badu since they'd left the house. Little had been kind of bobbing his head up and down, the same way no matter the beats, all the way. Potter didn't bother talkin' to him when he was chronicked out all the way, like he was now.

As he drove down the road, Potter saw a woman outside one of those welfare motels they had on New York. Woman had a boy by the hand and a cigarette hanging out her mouth, and she was leading the kid across the lot. Potter could see the boy's shirt, had one of those Pokémon characters on it, sumshit like that.

Potter had had a shirt with E.T. on the front of it when he was a kid. He was too young to have seen the movie in a theater, but his mother had bought the video for him from the Safeway on Alabama Avenue, and he had just about wore that tape out. He really loved that part where the boy kind of flew up in the sky on his bicycle against that big old moon. For a long time Potter had thought that if he had a special bike like that boy did, he could fly away, too. Until this man who was always hangin' around the apartment laughed at him one night when he talked about it, called him a dumb-ass little kid.

'You ain't flyin' *no* goddamn where,' said the man, Potter still remembering his words. 'You a project boy, and a project boy is all you will be.'

His mother should've said something to that man. Told him to shut his mouth, that her boy could do anything he wanted to do. That he could fly against the moon, even, if he had a mind to. But she hadn't said a thing. Maybe she knew the man was right.

Potter got the Tempo on the Beltway and forced the car up to sixty-five. The new Destiny's Child was on the radio. Little was bobbing his head, kind of staring out through the windshield, his mouth open, his eyes set.

Potter's mother, she had this smell about her, sweet, like strawberries, somethin' like that. It was these oils she used to wear. He remembered when she used to hold his hand like that woman was holdin' that kid's hand back in that lot. He could close his eyes and recall the way it felt. She had calluses on her palms from work, but her fingers were cushioned, like, sorta like that quilt blanket she'd cover him with at night. Her hand was always warm, like bein' under that blanket was warm, too. And sometimes when he couldn't sleep she'd sit by his bed, smoke a cigarette, and talk to him till he got drowsy. Once in a while, even now, he'd smell cigarette smoke somewhere, maybe it was the same brand she'd smoked, he didn't know, but it would remind him of her, sitting by his bed. When he was a kid and she was there for him, before she fell in love with that pipe. Forgetting she had a kid still needed her love, too.

But fuck it, you know. He wasn't no motherfuckin' kid no more.

'Dirty,' said Potter.

'Huh?'

'Read them directions to me, man, tell me where we at.'

Little squinted as he picked up the paper in his lap and tried to read Potter's handwriting, nearly illegible, in the dark of the car.

'Take the next exit,' he said. 'Take the one goes east.'

They took the exit and the road off of it, brightly lit at first and then dark where the county had ended the lamps. They went along woods and athletic complexes and communities with gates.

'You ever think of your moms, Dirty?'

'My mother?' said Little. '*I* don't know. I think of my aunt some, 'cause she owes me money.' He smiled as he heard the first few notes of a song coming from the radio. 'This is that new Toni Braxton joint right here, "Just be a Man"? I'd be a man to her, she let me.'

Potter didn't know why he bothered talking to Carlton. But he figured he'd keep hangin' with him anyhow. He didn't have Dirty, he didn't have no one at all.

'Where we at?' said Potter.

Little looked at the notepaper. 'Turn ought to be comin' up, past some church on the right-hand side.' Little pointed through the windshield. 'There go the church, right up there.'

A half mile past the church, Potter made a turn into an ungated, unmarked community of large houses with plenty of space in between them. Many of the houses were dark, but that didn't mean anything. It was a Monday night, and it had gotten late.

'Right turn up there,' said Little. 'Then a left.'

Potter made the first turn. Some light from a corner lamppost, made to look like one of those antique jobs, bled into the car and cast yellow on his face. Then his face was greenish from the light drifting off the dash.

'You know what to do,' said Potter, 'we get in there.'

Potter made the second turn.

Little pushed out his hips, withdrew his Walther from where he had fitted it, and racked the slide.

'Kill Old-time,' he said, refitting the gun under his shirt.

'Once we get the video,' said Potter, 'we'll down him quick. Put a couple in his head and get out.'

Little put on his gloves. He held the wheel steady as Potter did the same. They were on a cul-de-sac now that had only three houses set on oversize lots. The first house was dark inside, with only a lamp on over the front door. They passed the second house, completely dark, with two black Mercedes sedans parked in its circular driveway.

'There's the Caddy,' said Little, chinning toward the black Brougham parked in the circular drive in front of the last house on the street.

Potter parked the Ford along the curb and killed its engine.

They walked over grass and asphalt, then grass again, as they neared the steps of the brick colonial. The first-floor interior of the house was fully lit. An attached garage with a row of small rectangular windows across the top of its door was lit, too.

Potter and Little stood beneath a portico marking the center of the house. At Potter's gesture, Little rang the doorbell. Through leaded glass, Potter could see the refracted image of a man wearing black coming down a hall. The door opened. The football coach, the one who called himself Strange, stood in the frame.

'Come on in,' said Strange.

They stepped into a large foyer. Strange closed the door and stood before them.

Potter licked his lips. 'Somethin' you want to say to me?'

'Just wanted to have a look at you.'

'You had it. Let's get on about our business.'

'You got the money?'

'In my jacket, chief.'

'Let me see it.'

'When I see the tape.'

Strange breathed out slow. 'Okay, then. Let's go.'

'Hold up. Want to make sure you're not strapped.'

Strange spread his black leather jacket and held it open. Little stepped forward and frisked him like he'd seen it done on TV. He nodded to his partner, letting him know that Strange was unarmed.

'Follow me back,' said Strange. 'I've got a studio in the garage. The tape is back there.'

They walked down one of the halls framing the center staircase, leading to a kitchen and then a living area housing an entertainment center and big cushiony furniture.

'Thought you said this house was unoccupied,' said Potter.

'I rent it furnished,' said Strange over his shoulder.

And it's all high money, too, thought Potter. And then he thought, Somethin' about this setup ain't right.

'What you do to get this?' said Potter, elbowing Little, who was clumsily bumping along by his side, away.

'I own a detective agency,' said Strange. 'Ninth and Upshur.'

'Yeah,' said Potter, 'but what's your game? I mean, you can't be havin' all this with a square's job.'

'I find people,' said Strange.

They passed a door that was ajar and kept going, Strange stepping down into a kind of laundry room, then heading for another door and saying, 'It's right in here.'

'You can't be all *that* good at findin' people,' said Potter, 'to have all this.'

'I found *you*,' said Strange, and he opened the door.

Beyond the door was just darkness. Potter stared at the darkness, remembering the garage door and its little windows, remembering the light behind the windows as they'd walked toward the house.

'Dirty,' said Potter, and as he reached into his leather for his .38 he heard steps behind him and then felt the press of a gun's muzzle against the soft spot under his ear.

Little was pushed up against a wall, his face smashed into it by a man holding a gun to the back of his head. The man found Little's gun and took it.

Potter didn't move. He felt a hand in his jacket pocket and then the loss of weight there as his revolver was slid out.

'Inside,' said the voice behind him, and he was shoved forward.

Strange flicked on a light switch and moved aside as the four of them stepped down into the garage.

Potter saw a big man in a jogging suit with golden-colored eyes, standing with his hands folded in front of him. A young man in a dress suit stood beside him, an automatic in his hand. On the other side of the big man was a boy, no older than twelve, wearing an oversize shirt, tails out. Other than the people inside of it, the garage was empty. A plastic tarp had been spread on its concrete floor.

Potter recognized the big man as Granville Oliver. Everyone in town knew who he was.

Oliver looked over at Strange, still standing in the open doorway.

'All right, then,' said Oliver.

Strange was staring at the young boy in the oversize shirt. He hesitated for a moment. Then he stepped back and closed the door.

A row of fluorescent lights, set in a drop ceiling, made a soft buzzing sound overhead.

'You Granville Oliver, right?' said Potter.

Oliver stepped forward with the others. The two who had braced Potter and Little had joined the group. Potter and Little retreated and stopped when their backs touched the cinder-block wall of the garage. One of the men reached out and tore Potter's skully off his head. He threw it to the side.

'What is this?' said Potter, hoping his voice did not sound weak. But he knew that it did. Little's hand touched his for a moment, and it felt electric.

Oliver said nothing.

'Look, you and me ain't got no kinda beef,' said Potter. 'I been careful to stay out the way of people like you.'

The fluorescent lights buzzed steadily.

Potter spread his hands. 'Have I been steppin' on your turf down there off Georgia? I mean, you tryin' to build somethin' up there I don't know about? 'Cause we will pack up our shit and move on, that's what you want us to do.'

Oliver didn't reply.

Potter smiled. 'We can work for you, you want us to.' He felt his mouth twitching uncontrollably as he tried to keep the smile.

Oliver's eyes stayed on his. 'You want to *work* for me?'

'Sure,' said Potter. 'Can you put us on?'

'Gimme my gun,' said Oliver, and the young boy beside him reached under the tail of his shirt and withdrew an automatic. Oliver took the gun from the boy and jacked a round into the chamber. He raised the automatic and pointed it at Potter's face. Potter saw Oliver's finger slide inside the trigger guard of the gun.

Potter closed his eyes. He heard his friend beside him, sobbing, stuttering, begging. He heard Carlton drop to his knees. He wasn't gonna go out like Dirty. Like some bitch, pleadin' for his life.

Potter peed himself. It felt warm on his thighs. He heard the ones who was about to kill him laughing. He tried to open his eyes, but his eyes were frozen. He thought of his mother. He tried to think of what she looked like. He couldn't bring her up in his mind. He wondered, did it hurt to die.

Strange walked through the kitchen toward the stairway hall. He slowed his step and leaned up against an island holding an indoor grill.

Even from here, even with that door to the garage closed, he could hear one of those young men crying. Sounded like he was begging, too. The one with the cornrows, if he had to guess. Strange didn't even know that young man's name.

It wasn't that one, though, or Potter, who had given him pause. It was the young boy standing next to Oliver. The one he'd seen raking leaves the previous day, the one he'd never seen smile. Like he was already dead inside at eleven, twelve years old. Quinn would say that you should never give up on these kids, that it was never too late to try. Well, Strange wasn't sure about Potter and his kind. But he knew it wasn't too late for that boy who'd lost his smile.

Strange walked back the way he'd come. He opened the door leading to the garage without a knock. He stepped down onto the plastic tarp and entered the cold room. All heads turned his way.

Granville Oliver was holding an automatic to the face of Garfield Potter. Saliva threads hung from Potter's open mouth, and his jeans were dark with urine. The smell of his release was strong in the garage. The one with the cornrows was on his knees, tears veining his face. His eyes were red rimmed and blown out wide.

'You ain't got no business back in here,' said Oliver.

'Can't let you do this.'

Oliver kept his gun on Potter. 'You delivered our boys here. Now you're done.'

'I thought I was, too,' said Strange. 'Can I get a minute?'

'You *got* to be playin'.'

Strange shook his head. 'Look at me, man. Do I look like I'm playin' to you? Gimme one minute. Hear me out.'

Oliver stared hard at Strange, and Strange stared back.

'Please,' said Strange.

Oliver's shoulders loosened and he lowered the gun. He turned to the man in the suit, Phillip Wood, standing beside him.

'Hold these two right here,' said Oliver. To Strange he said, 'In my office.'

Strange said, 'Right.'

A phone chirped as Strange sat in the chair before Granville Oliver's desk. Oliver reached into his jacket for his cell.

'That's me,' said Strange, slipping his cell from its holster. 'Yeah.'

'Derek, it's Lydell. We got his statement.'

'Whose?'

'Ray Boyer, the craps player. Said the boy who broke his nose did it with a three fifty-seven snub-nose.'

'He remember the boy's name?'

'Garfield Potter. They're runnin' the name right now, should have a last-known on him any minute.'

'Potter's the one.'

'What?'

'I can give you his address,' said Strange, looking over Oliver's shoulder through the office window to the street, where Potter had parked. Potter's car was gone. 'But he ain't there just yet.'

'What're you talkin' about, man?'

'Here it is,' said Strange, and he gave Blue the Warder Street address. 'It's a row house, got nothin' on the porch. They ought to be there in about a half hour. Both Potter and his partner, the one with the cornrows. Potter's driving a Ford Tempo, blue, late eighties. The third boy, I can't tell you where he is. I believe he's gone.'

'How you know all this, Derek?'

'I'll explain it to you later.'

'Trust me. You will.'

'Get all your available units over there, Ly. Ain't that how they say it on those police shows?'

'Derek—'

'How'd practice go?'

'Say what?'

'Practice. The kids all right?'

'Uh, yeah. The boys all got home safe. Don't be trying to change the subject, man—'

'Good. That's good.'

'I'm gonna call you later, Derek.'

'I'll be waiting,' said Strange.

Strange hit 'end,' made a one-finger one-moment gesture to Oliver, and punched in Quinn's number. Quinn had turned his cell off. Strange left a message and stared at the dead phone for a moment before sliding it back in place.

'You done?' said Oliver.

'Yeah.'

'You know, what you did tonight ain't gonna change a thing in the end. Those two are gonna die. I'll make sure of that.'

'But not tonight. Not by my setup. Not in front of that little boy you got workin' for you.'

'Yeah, okay. We been all over that already.'

'I just want that boy to have some kind of chance.'

'So you said. But what would you have done if I had said no?'

'I was counting on reaching your human side. You proved to me that you have one. Thank you for hearin' me out.'

Oliver nodded. 'Boy's name is Robert Gray. You think I been ruinin' him, huh?'

'Let's just say that I don't see him hookin' up with your enterprise as an opportunity. You and me, we got a difference of opinion on that.'

'Strange, you ought to see what kind of conditions he was livin' in when I pulled him out, down there in Stanton Terrace. Wasn't nobody doin' a *god*damn thing for him then.'

Strange leaned back and scratched his temple. 'This Robert, he play football?'

'What's that?'

'Can he *play*?'

'Boy can jook. He can hit, too.' Oliver grinned, looking Strange over. 'You're somethin', man. What, you tryin' to save the whole world all at once?'

'Not the *whole* world, no.'

'You know, wasn't just my *human side* convinced me to let those boys walk out of here.'

'What was it, then?'

'I'm gonna need you someday, Strange. I had one of those, what do you call that, premonitions. Usually, when I get those kinds of feelings, I'm right.' Oliver pointed a finger at Strange. 'You owe me for what I did for you tonight.'

I owe you for more than that, thought Strange.

But he just said, 'I do.'

Strange drove back to the city in silence. Coming up Georgia Avenue, he tried to reach Quinn again on his cell but got a recording. He passed Buchanan Street and kept driving north, turning right on Quintana and parking the Cadillac in front of Janine's. She let him into her house and told him to have a seat on the living room couch. She joined him a few minutes later with a cold Heineken and a couple of glasses. The two of them talked into the night.

30

Quinn had been parked along the curb for half an hour when Worldwide Wilson's 400SE came rolling down the street. Quinn watched the Mercedes glide up in his rearview and he tucked his chin in and turned his head a little as it passed. The Mercedes double-parked, flashers on, as the driver's-side window came down. A woman Quinn recognized, the black whore who'd asked him for a date the night of the snatch, leaned into the frame. A minute or so went by, and Wilson stepped out of the car.

He wore his full-length rust-colored leather over a suit. He wore his matching brimmed hat and his alligator shoes. He walked toward his row house, and the black whore got under the wheel of his Mercedes and drove off to find a legal parking spot for her man's car. Worldwide Wilson moved like a big cat onto the sidewalk. He went up his steps and entered his house.

Quinn ignitioned the Chevelle and drove down the street, hooking a left at the next corner, and then another quick left into the alley. He parked the car in the alley along a brick wall. His headlights illuminated several sets of eyes beneath the Dumpsters. He cut the lights and in their dying moment saw rats moving low across the stones of the alley. He killed the engine and listened to the tick of it under the hood. He counted units and found the row house, lit by a single flood suspended from the roof. He saw a light go on in the sleeper porch on the second floor.

Quinn stepped out of the car and walked fast toward the fire escape. Dim bulbs lit the third-floor hall. He could see the third-floor window, but his long sight was gone, and he could not determine if the window was ajar.

He turned off his cell, got on the fire escape, and began his ascent. He could hear music from behind the wood walls of the sleeper porch as he climbed the iron mesh steps. The music grew louder, and he was grateful for that as he went low along the porch's curtained windows and kept going up. As he neared the third floor he could see the hall window clearly and he could see now that the window was open a crack.

He raised the sash and climbed into the hall. He could feel his sweat, and his blood pumping in his chest. The hall smelled of marijuana, tobacco, and Lysol. Behind one of the doors he heard thrusts and bedsprings, and the sounds of a man reaching his climax, and Quinn went on.

He moved down the hall, his hand sliding along the banister, and at the end of it he looked down the stairs to the second floor. The music, mostly bass, synthesizer, and scratchy guitar, was emanating from below. The music was loud and it echoed in the house. He started down the stairs. The music grew louder with each step he took.

Worldwide Wilson sat on a couch covered in purple velvet, swirling ice in a glass of straight vodka, listening to 'Cebu,' that bad instrumental jam ending side two of that old Commodores LP, *Movin' On*. Wilson had owned the vinyl, on the Motown label, for over twenty-five years. He still had all his wax, racked up here in this finished porch, where he liked to kick it when he wasn't at home. At his crib he listened to CDs, but here he kept his records and turntable, and Bang & Olufsen speakers, and his old tube amplifier, made by Marantz. Box had a lotta clean watts to it, the perfect vehicle for his vinyl. You just couldn't beat the bottom sound of those records.

Wilson tapped some ash off his cigarette. He drank down some of the vodka, now that it had chilled some, and let it cool-burn the back of his throat.

Wilson loved his potato vodka. He bought that brand in the frosty white bottle, with the drawing of the bare tree on it, up there at the store on the District line. He was different from all those other brothers, felt they had to drink Courvoisier and Hennessy just because everyone else did, because the white man told you to. Shit was just poison. There was a word for it, even: carcino-somethin'. Gave you cancer, is what the word meant. And the Man pushed that bad shit into the ghetto, through billboards and bus ads and ads in *Ebony* and *Jet*, the same way they pushed death through cigarettes. Well, Wilson did like his tobacco, but the point was, he wasn't buyin' into all that, 'cause he was his own man all the way. His brother, who read a lot, had explained this all to him once after they'd smoked some Hawaiian at his mother's house on Christmas Day. So he wasn't into no con-yak. But he did love his expensive vodka. He'd gotten a taste for it overseas.

This room was nice. He'd insulated the room and put radiator heat in it for the wintertime. He had it carpeted with a remnant, hung some Africa-style prints he'd picked up at a flea market on the wall, and bought those thick curtains for the windows. The curtains gave him privacy and made him feel as if he was in his own private club. He'd brought in the furniture and even had a chandelier, had a couple of bulbs missing but it looked good, up in this motherfucker. You could bring a young country-type bitch up here, straight off the bus, and impress her in this room. Girl got a look at all this, you could turn her out quick.

Wilson put his feet up on the table and dragged on his cigarette. He looked at the windows and thought he saw some kind of shadow pass out there beyond the curtains. He had another sip of vodka, moved his head some to the sounds coming from the stereo, and finished his cigarette.

Wilson got off the couch, went to the windows, and spread the curtains. He looked out, down the fire escape, and then up to the third floor. Wasn't nothin' out there he could see. But he thought he'd go out to the hall for a minute, have a look out there. Never did hurt to double-check.

Quinn had reached the bottom of the stairs and was standing on the landing when the door to the sleeper porch swung open at the end of the hall. Worldwide Wilson stood there, a drink in his hand, wearing a light green suit over a forest green shirt and tie. A look of perplexity creased his face. Then a smile of recognition broke upon it. His chuckle was long and low.

'Damn if it ain't Theresa Bickle,' said Wilson. 'You come to knock me for another woman? That why you came back? 'Cause I am fresh out of young white girls, *Theresa*.'

Quinn moved quickly down the hall.

'Guess you ran into your friend Stella. Shame what that bitch made me do to her, huh?'

Quinn broke into a run.

'Now what?' said Wilson. 'You gonna rush me now, little man?'

Quinn's stride reached a sprint, and he put his head down as Wilson dropped the glass and tried to reach into his jacket pocket. Quinn hit him low, wrapping his arms around Wilson and locking his fingers behind his back, and both of them went through the open door and into the room.

Quinn ran Wilson through the room and slammed him against the window. The window shattered behind the curtains, and shards of glass fell as Quinn whipped Wilson around, still holding on. Wilson was laughing. Quinn ran him into a stand holding a turntable, and as they toppled over the stand, Quinn's hands separating, there was the rip of needle over vinyl and the music that was pounding in their heads suddenly came to an end.

Quinn and Wilson stood up, six feet apart. Quinn saw blood on his hands. The glass from the window had opened up one of them or both of them. He didn't know which.

'You fucked up my box,' said Wilson, incredulous.

'Let's go,' said Quinn with a hand gesture, seeing the slice along his thumb now, seeing that it was bleeding freely and that the slice was deep.

Wilson stepped in. Quinn put his weight on his back foot, tucked his elbows into his gut, and covered his face with his fists. He took Wilson's first blows like that, and the punches moved him back and the pain of them surprised him. He took one in the side and grunted, losing his wind, and Wilson laughed and hit him in the same spot again. Quinn dropped his guard. Wilson hit him in the jaw, and the blow knocked Quinn off his feet. He rolled and came up standing. He moved his jaw, and the pain was a needle through his head. Wilson smiled, and his gold tooth caught the glow off the chandelier.

Quinn charged in. Wilson jabbed at his face as he advanced, but Quinn swatted it off and threw a right. The right glanced off Wilson's cheek, and as Wilson moved a hand up to fend off another blow, Quinn put one in his gut and buried it there. Wilson jacked forward, then squared himself straight. They traded body blows. Quinn threw a vicious uppercut in the space between Wilson's hands and connected square to Wilson's chin. Wilson's eyes rolled up, and Quinn hit him there again. Wilson staggered back. He shook the cobwebs out and kicked the table violently away from the couch. He wasn't smiling anymore.

There was a large space, cleared now, in the middle of the room. They circled the space and met in its center.

Wilson stepped on Quinn's foot and punched through his guard. Quinn's neck snapped back as he took the short right. He tasted the blood flowing over his upper lip, and Wilson threw the same jab. Quinn blocked it with his palm, quickly wrapped his arms around Wilson, and locked his hands behind him once again. Wilson ran him straight into a wall. Quinn felt a picture frame splinter behind his back. He reared back and butted his forehead into Wilson's nose. Wilson's blood mingled with his, and Quinn heard an animal sound that was his own and he butted Wilson again. Tears welled in Wilson's eyes, and Quinn released him. They both stepped back and tried to breathe.

Below his nose, blood covered Wilson's face. His blood was brown on his green suit. Quinn's shirt was slick with blood.

'Enough,' said Wilson, reaching into his suit pocket. His hand emerged with a pearl-handled knife, and its blade flicked opened as Wilson walked toward Quinn. The scream of a woman now pierced the room.

Wilson's arm whipped forward. The blade winked in the light, and Quinn tried to move out of its arc, but as he felt the impact, like a punch, he knew that he had failed. Fresh blood warmed his face.

Wilson turned the handle in his hand so that the blade revolved and he tried to make a backswing, but Quinn caught his forearm and held it. Wilson's legs were spread wide, and Quinn kicked him in the balls, aiming for three feet behind them and following through. Wilson coughed. Quinn felt the tension go out of Wilson's forearm, twisted the arm behind him, and kicked Wilson's right leg out from under him at the shin. Wilson went down on one knee, and Quinn got his wrist and bent it forward until Wilson released the knife. The knife dropped to the carpet. Quinn put everything he had into it and kicked Wilson in the face. There was a wet cracking sound. Wilson's body jerked up, and blood arced up with it. Wilson fell on his side and then onto his back, where he remained. His face was featureless and ruined.

Quinn picked up the knife. He folded the blade into its handle and pocketed it. He dragged Wilson to the radiator and cuffed him to one of its tubes.

A woman was screaming obscenities at Quinn. She was standing in the doorway, ass-out in a short skirt and fishnets, but not attempting to enter the room.

Quinn reached into his jeans for his cell. He sat on the purple couch, squinting at the keyboard of the cell, and with a shaky hand punched in 911. He asked for squad cars and an ambulance and gave the dispatcher his general address. He ended the call and tried to think of Strange's number. He tried to think of Sue's. He couldn't bring either of their numbers to mind.

He breathed slowly. He knew that he was still bleeding because he could feel it going down his neck. He could feel the wetness of it on his upper chest and behind his collar. He wanted to bring his heart rate down to slow the flow of blood. The air was full on his wounds now, and the pain had ratcheted. He stared at the ripped curtains and the broken glass, and after a while he heard sirens and an odd sound coming from his lips.

Wilson said something from across the room. It was hard to hear him because the woman was still alternately sobbing and berating Quinn.

'What?' said Quinn.

'Somethin' funny?' said Wilson.

'Why?'

'You *laughin'*.'

'Was I?' said Quinn.

It didn't surprise him. It didn't scare him or make him feel any way at all. Quinn let his head drop back to the couch. He closed his eyes.

31

On the stoops of the row houses of Buchanan Street, the jack-o'-lanterns of Halloween had begun to wilt. Time and the weather had mutated the faces carved into the pumpkins, and hungry squirrels had mutilated their features. Gloves and scarves had come out of the closets, and lawn mowers had been drained of gas and put away in basements and sheds. Colors had exploded brilliantly upon leaves, then the leaves had dried and gone toward brown. One holiday was done and another was approaching. Thanksgiving was just a week away.

Strange drove his Cadillac up his block, waving to an old woman named Katherine who was out in a heavy sweater, slowly raking her small square of yard. Katherine had been an elementary school teacher in D.C. for her entire career, put two sons and a daughter through college, and had recently lost a grandson to the streets. Strange had been knowing that woman for almost thirty years.

Strange hooked a right on Georgia Avenue. He looked in his shoebox of tapes and slipped an old Stylistics mix into the deck. Bell and Creed's 'People Make the World Go Round' began with a wintry prologue, Russell Thompkins Jr's incomparable vocal filling the car. As Strange drove south on Georgia he softly sang along. At a stoplight near Iowa, he noticed a flyer with the likenesses of Garfield Potter, Carlton Little, and Charles White still stapled to a telephone pole. By now, most of those flyers had been torn down.

Potter and Little had been arrested at their house on Warder Street without incident. They had been arraigned and were now incarcerated in the D.C. Jail, awaiting trial. The trial would not come for another six months. The whereabouts of the missing suspect, Charles White, would continue to be a source of speculation for the local media from time to time. A year and a half later, White's identity would surface in connection with another murder charge outside of New Orleans. White would eventually be shanked to death, a triangle of Plexiglas to the neck, in the showers of Angola prison. The story would only warrant a paragraph in the *Washington Post*, as would the violent fates of Potter and Little. As for Joe Wilder, the memorial T-shirts bearing his face had been discarded or used for rags by then. For most metropolitan-area residents, Wilder's name had been forgotten. 'Another statistic.' That's what hardened Washingtonians called kids like him. One name in thousands on a list.

Strange parked on 9th and locked the Brougham down. He walked by the barber shop, where the cutter named Rodel stood in the doorway, pulling on a Newport.

'How's it goin', big man?'

'It's all good.'

'Looks like you could use a touch-up.'

'I'll be by.'

He went down the sidewalk and looked up at the logo on the sign hung over his place: Strange Investigations. There were a few dirt streaks on the light box, going across the magnifying glass. He'd have to get Lamar on that today.

Strange was buzzed into his storefront business. Janine was on her computer, her eyes locked on the screen. Ron Lattimer sat behind his desk, a porkpie hat angled cockily on his head. The color of the hat picked up the brown horizontals of his hand-painted tie. Strange stopped by his desk and listened to Lattimer's musical selection for the day, a familiar-sounding horn against a slamming rhythm section.

'Boss.'

'Ron. This here is Miles, right?'

Lattimer looked up and nodded. '*Doo-Bop*.'

'See, I'm not all that out of touch.' Strange looked at the paperwork on Lattimer's desk. 'You finishin' up on that Thirty-five Hundred Crew thing?'

'I'll be delivering the whole package to the attorneys next week. Major receivables on this one, boss.'

'Nice work.'

'By the way, Sears phoned in. They said your suit's been altered and you can pick it up any time.'

'Funny.'

'Serious business. The cleaner down the street called, said your suit and shirts are done.'

'Thank you. I got a wedding to go to this weekend. You remember George Hastings, don't you? His little girl's.'

'The dress I'm wearing is down there, too, Derek,' said Janine, not taking her eyes off the screen. 'Could you pick it up for me?'

'Sure.'

'You don't mind my saying so,' said Lattimer, 'you goin' to a wedding, you *ought* to do something about your natural.'

'Yeah,' said Strange, patting his head. 'I do need to get correct.'

Strange passed Quinn's desk, littered with old papers and gum wrappers, and stopped at Janine's.

'Any messages?'

'No. You've got an appointment down at the jail, though.'

'I'm on my way. Just stopped in to check up on y'all.'

'We're doing fine.'

'You comin' to the game this afternoon? It's a playoff game, y'know. Second round.'

Janine's eyes broke from her screen, and she leaned back in her seat. 'I'll be there if you want me to.'

'I do.'

'I was thinking I'd bring Lionel.'

'Perfect.'

Janine reached into her desk drawer and removed a PayDay bar. She handed it to Strange.

'In case you're too busy for lunch today.'

Strange looked at the wrapper and the little red heart Janine had drawn above the logo. He glanced over at Ron, busy with his work, and back to Janine. He lowered his voice and said, 'Thank you, baby.'

Janine's eyes smiled. Strange went back to his office and closed the door.

Lamar Williams was behind Strange's desk, reaching for the wastebasket as Strange walked in. Strange came around and took a seat as Lamar stepped aside. Lamar stood behind the chair, looking over Strange's shoulder as he logged on to his computer.

'You getting into that People Finder thing?' said Lamar.

'Was just gonna check my e-mails before I go off to an appointment. Why, you want to know how to use the program?'

'I already know a little. Janine and Ron been showin' me some.'

'You want to know more, I'll sit with you sometime. You and me'll get deep into it, you want.'

'I wouldn't mind.'

Strange swiveled his chair so that he faced Lamar. 'You know, Lamar, Ron's not gonna be here forever. I know this. I mean, good people don't stay on in a small business like this one, and a fair boss wouldn't expect them to. I'm gonna need some young man to replace him someday.'

'Ron's a pro.'

'Yeah, but when he first came here, he was green.'

'He had a college degree, though,' said Lamar. 'I'm strugglin' to get my high school paper.'

'You'll get it,' said Strange. 'And we get you goin' in night school, you'll get the other, too. But I'm not gonna lie to you; it's gonna take a lot of hard work. Years of it, you understand what I'm tellin' you?'

'Yes.'

'Anyway, I'm here for you, you want to talk about it some more.'

'Thank you.'

'Ain't no thing. You coming to the game?'

'I'll be there.'

Lamar walked toward the door, the wastebasket in his hand.

'Lamar.'

'Yeah,' he said, turning.

'The sign out front.'

'I know. I was fixin' to get the ladder soon as I emptied this here.'

'All right, then.'

'Aiight.'

Strange watched him go. He picked up the PayDay bar he had placed on his desk. He stared at it for a while, and then he shut down his computer and walked out of his office. He stopped in front of Janine's desk.

'I was wondering,' said Strange, 'if Lionel couldn't just take your car home after the game. I thought, if you wanted to, you and me could go for a little ride.'

'That would be good,' said Janine.

'I'll see you up at the field,' said Strange.

Strange drove down to the D.C. Jail at 1901 D Street in Southeast. He parked on the street and read over the notes he had taken from the news stories he had researched on the Net.

Granville Oliver had recently been arrested and charged in one of the most highly publicized local criminal cases in recent history. He had fallen when Phillip Wood, his top lieutenant, was arrested for murder on an anonymous tip. The murder gun had been found, and Wood was charged accordingly. He had pleaded out and agreed to testify against Oliver on related charges. It was exactly what Oliver had predicted Wood would do when he and Strange had first met.

Oliver had been hit with several federal charges, including the running of a large-scale drug operation and racketeering-related murder. At a recent press conference, broadcast on all the local stations, the attorney general and the U.S. attorney had jointly announced that they would aggressively seek the death penalty in the case. Though the citizens of D.C. had gone to the voting booths and overwhelmingly opposed capital punishment, the Feds were looking to make an example of Granville Oliver and send him to the federal death chamber in Indiana.

Strange closed his notebook and walked to the facility.

He checked in and spent a long half hour in the waiting room. He was then led to the interview room, subdivided by Plexiglas partitions into several semiprivate spaces. There were two other meetings being conducted in the room between lawyers and their clients. Strange had a seat at a legal table across from Granville Oliver.

Oliver wore the standard-issue orange jumpsuit of the jail. His hands were cuffed and his feet were manacled. Behind a window, a guard sat in a darkened booth, watching the room.

Oliver nodded at Strange. 'Thanks for comin' in.'

'No problem. Can we talk here?'

''Bout the only place we can talk.'

'They treating you all right?'

'All right?' Oliver snorted. 'They let me out of my cell one hour for every forty-eight. I'm down in Special Management, what they call the Hole. Place they put the high-profile offenders. You're gonna like this, Strange: guess who else they got down there with me.'

'Who?'

'Garfield Potter and Carlton Little. Oh, I don't see 'em or nothin' like that. They're in deep lockup, just like me. But we're down there together, just the same.'

'You've got more to worry about right now than them.'

'True.' Oliver leaned forward. 'Reason I'm telling you is, I got contacts all over. Last couple of years I made friends with some El Ryukens. You know about them, right? They claim to be descended from the Moors. Now, I don't know about all that. What I do know is, these are about the baddest motherfuckers walkin' the face of this earth. They fear nothing and take shit from no man. They got people everywhere, and like I say, me and them are friends. Wherever Potter and Little go, whatever prison they get sent to? They will be got.'

'You don't need to tell me about it, Granville.'

'Just thought you'd like to know.'

Strange shifted his position in his chair. 'Say why you called me here.'

'I want to hire you, Strange.'

'To do what?'

'To work with my lawyers. I got two of the best black attorneys in this city.'

'Ives and Colby. I read the papers.'

'They're going to need a private detective to help build my case against the government's. It's routine, but this case is anything but.'

'I know how it works. I do this sort of thing regularly.'

'I'm sure you do. But this here ain't the usual kind of drama. It's life and death. And I'll only have a black man working on my case. You do good work, so there it is. What those lawyers are gonna need is some conflicting testimony to the testimony the government is gonna get out of Phillip Wood.'

'In a general sense, what's he saying?'

'I'll tell you specifically. He's gonna get up on the stand and say that I ordered the hit on my uncle. That I gave Phil the order directly, and he carried it out.'

'Did you?'

Oliver shrugged. 'What difference does it make?'

'None, I guess.'

Oliver turned his head and stared at one of the room's blank white walls as if it were a window to the outside world. 'They got Phil next door, you know that? In the Correctional Treatment Facility. He's in one of those low-number cells, like CB-four, CB-five, sumshit like that. The special cells they got reserved for the snitches. Phil got punked out the first stretch he did. Got ass-raped like a motherfucker, and he can't do no more prison. That's what all this is about. Course, he could be got the way Potter and Little gonna be got. But that would take some time, and time is something I do not have.'

'Told you I don't need to know about that.'

'Fine. But will you help me?'

Strange didn't answer.

'You wouldn't want to sit back and watch someone kill me, would you, Strange?'

'No.'

'Course not. But they got me on these RICO charges, and that's what they aim to do. You remember that photo I showed you, that promo shot I did for my new record, with me holding the guns? The prosecution's gonna use that in court against me. You know why? Do you know why they picked *me* to execute, the only death penalty case in the District in years, instead of all the other killers they got in D.C.? Well, that picture says it all. They got a picture of a strong, proud, I-don't-give-a-good-fuck-about-nothin' black man holding a gun. America's worst nightmare, Strange. They can *sell* my execution to the public, and ain't nobody gonna lose a wink of sleep over it. 'Cause it's just a nigger who's been out here killin' other niggers. To America, it is no loss.'

Strange said nothing. He held Oliver's stare.

'And now,' said Oliver, 'the attorney general wants to help me right into that chamber where they're gonna give me that lethal injection. She and the government gonna *help* me now. Wasn't no government lookin' to help me when I was a project kid. Wasn't no government lookin' to help *me* when I walked through my fucked-up neighborhood on the way to my fucked-up schools. Where were they then? Now they're gonna come into my life and *help me.* Little bit late for that, don't you think?'

'You had it rough,' said Strange, 'like a whole lot of kids. I'm not gonna deny you that. But you made your own bed, too.'

'I did. Can't say I'm ashamed of it, either.' Oliver closed his eyes slowly, then opened them again. 'Will you work for me?'

'Have your lawyers call my office,' said Strange.

Strange signaled the guard. He left Oliver sitting at the table in chains.

'*How y'all feel?*'

'*Fired up!*'

'*How y'all feel?*'

'*Fired up!*'

'*Breakdown.*'

'*Whoo!*'

'*Breakdown.*'

'*Whoo!*'

'*Breakdown.*'

'*Whoo!*'

The Petworth Panthers had formed a circle beside the Roosevelt field. Prince and Dante Morris were in the center of the circle, leading the Pee Wees in calisthenics. Strange and Blue and Dennis Arrington stood together in conference nearby, going over the roster and positions. Lamar and Lionel tossed a football to each other on the sky blue track.

In the stands, Janine sat with the usual small but vocal group of parents and guardians. Among them were the parents and guardians rooting for the opposing team, the Anacostia Royals.

Arrington noticed a white man and white woman walking slowly across the field, the woman's arm through the man's, where two refs stood conferring at the fifty-yard line. Arrington nudged Strange, who looked across the field and smiled.

'Terry,' said Strange, shaking Quinn's hand as he arrived. 'Sue.'

'Hey, Derek,' said Sue Tracy, pulling an errant strand of blond away from her face.

'Runnin' a little late, aren't you?' said Strange.

'Had a meeting with my attorney,' said Quinn. His cheek was bandaged. His jaw line was streaked yellow, the bruise there nearly faded away.

'They're not gonna drop the charge?' said Strange.

'Assault with intent,' said Quinn, nodding. 'They got to charge me with something, right?'

'Well,' said Strange, a light in his eyes, 'wasn't like Wilson came to your apartment and kicked *your* ass.'

'Right,' said Quinn. 'But with Stella's testimony, he's gonna do some time.'

'Soon as they take those straws out his nose and rewire his jaw.'

'It'll keep him off the stroll for a while, anyway. As for me, my lawyer says, I get sentenced at all, it'll be suspended.'

'The authorities don't want no one mistaking you for a hero.'

'I'm no hero,' said Quinn. 'I got a temper on me, is all.'

'You think so?' said Strange. He nodded to Quinn's cheek. 'Still need that bandage, huh?'

'All these scars, I look like Frankenstein.' Quinn grinned, looking ten years older than Strange had ever seen him look before. 'I don't want to scare the kids.'

'Bring it in!' said Blue, and the teams ended their six-inches drill and jogged over to their coaches, where they took a knee.

'Glad you could make it,' said Arrington, looking Quinn over as they met the boys.

'I'm like you,' said Quinn. 'I wouldn't miss it.'

'Just doing God's work,' said Arrington, and he shook Quinn's hand.

Quinn and Blue went over positions and told the boys what they expected of them. Arrington led them in a prayer, and Strange stepped in to give them a short talk as Dante, Prince, and Rico, the designated captains, went out to the center of the field.

'Protect your brother,' said Strange. 'Protect your brother.'

The game began, and from the start the contest was fierce. Many times when one of the black teams from D.C. played a primarily white suburban team, the contest was over before the first whistle. White boys taught by their parents, indirectly or directly, to fear black boys sometimes gave up and lay down the moment they saw black players running onto the field. That fear of the unknown was the seed of racism itself.

But this was not the case here. Today there were two teams from the inner city, a Northwest-Southeast thing, kids battling not for trophies but for neighborhood pride. You could see it in the charging style of play, in the hard eyes of the defenders, the way it took three kids to bring one kid down. And you could hear it in the ramlike clash of the pads, echoing in the bowl of Roosevelt's field. By halftime, Strange knew that the game would be decided not by one big play, but by one fatal mistake. With the score tied in the fourth quarter, with the Petworth Panthers controlling the ball and threatening on their own twenty, that was exactly how it went down.

On one, Prince snapped the ball to Dante Morris, who handed off to Rico, a simple Thirty-two play, a halfback run to the two-hole. The Petworth linemen made their blocks and cleared an opening. But Rico positioned his hands wrong for the handoff and bobbled the ball as he tried to hit the hole. He ran past the ball, leaving it in the air, and the fumble was recovered by Anacostia. The play broke the Panthers' spirit. It took only six running plays for Anacostia to score a touchdown and win the game.

At the whistle, the boys formed a line at center field and congratulated their opponents. To their counterparts, the coaches did the same.

'Take a knee!' said Lydell Blue.

The boys formed a tight group, the parents and guardians, along with Lamar, Lionel, Janine, and Sue Tracy, standing nearby. Blue looked at Arrington, and at Quinn, visibly upset. Quinn chinned in the direction of Strange. Strange stepped up to address the boys.

He looked down into their faces. Turf was embedded in their cages, and some of their helmets were streaked with blue, the color of Anacostia's helmets. Dante was staring at the ground, Prince on one knee beside him. Rico was crying freely, looking away.

'All right,' said Strange. 'We lost. We lost this one game. But we didn't lose, not really. You don't have to be ashamed about anything, understand? Not a thing. Look at me, Rico. Son, *look* at me.'

Rico's eyes met Strange's.

'You can hold your head up, young man. You made an error, and you think it cost us the game. But if it wasn't for your running out there, the courage and the skill you showed, we wouldn't have even been *in* this game. That goes for all a y'all.'

Strange looked down at the boys, trying to look at each and every one of them, holding his gaze on them individually, before moving on.

'We had a tough season. In more ways than one, it was so tough. You lost one of your fellow warriors, a true brother. And still you went on. What I'm trying to tell you is, every so often, every day, you are going to lose. Nobody is going to give you anything out here, and you will be knocked down. But you got to stand back up again and keep moving forward. That's what life is. Picking yourself up and living to fight, and win, another day. And you have done that. You've shown me what kind of strong character you have, time and time again.'

Strange looked over at Lionel. 'You know, I never did have a son of my own. But I know what it is to love one like he was mine.'

Strange's eyes caught Janine's as he returned his attention to the team kneeling before him.

'You *are* like my own.'

Rico ran the back of his hand over his face. Dante held his chin up, and Prince managed a smile.

'I am so proud of you boys,' said Strange.

Strange left Prince, Lamar, and Janine sitting in his Cadillac, said good-bye to Blue and Arrington, and walked toward Quinn, who was beside Sue Tracy, leaning on his Chevelle. Leaves blew across Roosevelt's parking lot, pushed by a cool late-afternoon wind that had come in out of the north.

Strange greeted Tracy and kissed her on the cheek. 'Sorry I didn't get to talk to you much today.'

'You had your hands full,' said Tracy.

'So,' said Strange. 'You gonna throw us any more work?'

'I had the impression,' said Tracy, 'you didn't want to get involved with this prostitution thing.'

Strange looked at Quinn, back at Tracy. 'Yeah, well, I had some personal issues I had to take care of with regards to that subject. I believe I've got it worked out.'

'There's always work,' said Tracy. 'We did get Stella back to her home in Pittsburgh. We'll see how long that lasts.'

'What about the one you snatched away from Wilson?' said Strange.

'Jennifer Marshall. She left home again, and she's missing. So far, she hasn't turned up.'

'Gotta make you wonder sometimes, why you keep trying,' said Strange.

'Like you told the kids,' said Tracy. 'Live to fight another day.'

'We're getting a beer, Derek,' said Quinn. 'You and Janine want to join us?'

'Thank you,' said Strange. 'But I need to get up with her alone on something, you don't mind.'

'Some other time.'

Strange shook Quinn's hand. 'It was a good season, Terry. Thanks for all your help.'

'We did the best we could.'

'I'll call you tomorrow. Looks like I'm picking up a big case, and I might need your help. You gonna be at the bookstore?'

'I'll be there,' said Quinn.

They watched Strange cross the lot and climb into his Brougham.

'I told Karen, the first time we met him,' said Tracy, 'that he was gonna work out fine.'

Quinn put his arms around Tracy, drew her in, and kissed her on the mouth. He held the kiss, then pulled back and touched her cheek.

'What was that for?' said Tracy.

'For being here,' said Quinn. 'For sticking around.'

After dropping Prince and Lamar, Strange stopped by Buchanan, going into his house to pick up Greco while Janine waited in the car. They drove up to Missouri Avenue, turned left, and continued on to Military Road. Strange parked in a small lot on the eastern edge of Rock Creek Park.

Strange leashed Greco and the three of them walked onto the Valley Trail, up a rise along the creek. Strange held Janine's arm and told her about his meeting with Granville Oliver while Greco ran the woods through bars of light. They returned to the car as the weak November sun dropped behind the trees. Greco got onto his red pillow in the backseat and fell asleep.

Strange kept the power on in the car so they could listen to music. He played some seventies soul, and kept it low.

'You going to take the Oliver case?' said Janine.

'I am,' said Strange.

'He represents most everything you're against.'

'I know he does. But I owe him.'

'For what he did with Potter and them?'

'Not just that. The way I see it, most all the problems we got out here, it's got to do with a few simple things. There's straight-up racism, ain't no gettin' around it, it goes back hundreds of years. And the straight line connected to that is poverty. Whatever you want to say about that, these are elements that have been out of our hands. But the last thing, taking responsibility for your own, this is something we have the power to do something about. I see it every day and I'm convinced. Kids living with these disadvantages already, they need parents, *two* parents, to guide them. Granville Oliver was a kid once, too.'

Strange stared through the windshield at the darkening landscape. 'What I'm saying is, Oliver, he came out of the gate three steps behind. His mother was a junkie. He never did know his father. And I had something to do with that, Janine.'

'What are you talking about?'

'I knew the man,' said Strange. 'I killed his father, thirty-two years ago.'

Strange told Janine about his life in the 1960s. He told her about his mother and father, and brother. He recounted his year as a uniformed cop on the streets of D.C., and the fires of April 1968. When he was done, gray had settled on the park.

Strange pushed a cassette tape into the deck. The first quiet notes of Al Green's 'Simply Beautiful' came forward.

'Terry gave me this record,' said Strange. 'This here has got to be the prettiest song Al ever recorded.'

'It's nice,' said Janine, slipping her hand into Strange's.

'So anyway, that's my story.'

'That's why you brought me here?'

'Well, there's this, too.' Strange pulled a small green jewelry box from his leather and handed it to Janine. 'Go on, take a look at it. It's for you.'

Janine opened the box. A thin gold ring sat inside, a diamond in its center. At Strange's gesture, she removed the ring and tried it on.

'It was my mother's,' said Strange. 'Gonna be a little big for you, but we can fix that.'

'You planning to ask me something, Derek?'

Strange turned to face her. 'Please marry me, Janine. Lionel needs a father. And I need you.'

Janine squeezed his hand, answering with her eyes. They kissed.

Strange kept her hand in his. They sat there quietly in the Cadillac, listening to the song. Strange thought of Janine and of her heart. He thought of Joe Wilder, who had fallen, and of all the kids who were still standing. Outside the windows of the car, the last leaves of autumn drifted down in the dusk.

Deep fall had come to the city. It was Strange's favorite time of year in D.C.

Soul Circus

To Michael, with gratitude

May

1

The chains binding Granville Oliver's wrists scraped the scarred surface of the table before him. Manacles also bound his ankles. Oliver's shoulders and chest filled out the orange jumpsuit he had worn for half a year. His eyes, almost golden when Strange had first met him, were now the color of creamed-up coffee, dull in the artificial light of the interview room of the D.C. Jail.

'Looks like you're keeping your physical self together,' said Strange, seated on the other side of the table.

'Push-ups,' said Oliver. 'I try to do a few hundred every day.'

'You still down in the Hole?'

'You mean Special Management. I don't know what's so special about it; ain't nothin' but a box. They let me out of it one hour for every forty-eight.'

Strange and Oliver were surrounded by Plexiglas dividers in a space partitioned by cubicles. Nearby, public defenders and CJA attorneys conferred with their clients. The dividers served to mute, somewhat, the various conversations, leaving a low, steady mutter in the room. A thick-necked armed guard sat watching the activity from a chair behind a window in a darkened booth.

'It won't be long,' said Strange. 'They finished with the jury selection.'

'Ives told me. They finally found a dozen D.C. residents weren't opposed to the death penalty, how'd they put it, *on principle.* Which means they found some white people gonna have no problem to sit up there and judge me.'

'Four whites,' said Strange.

'How you think they gonna find me, Strange? Guilty?'

Strange looked down and tapped his pen on the open folder lying on the table. He didn't care to take the conversation any further in that direction. He wasn't here to discuss what was or was not going to happen relative to the trial, and he was, by definition of his role as an investigator, uninterested in Oliver's guilt or innocence. It was true that he had a personal connection to this case, but from the start he had been determined to treat this as just another job.

'The prosecution's going to put Phillip Wood up there first,' said Strange.

'Told you when I met you the very first time he was gonna be my Judas. Phil can't do no more maximum time. Last time he was inside, they took away his manhood. I mean they ass-raped him good. I knew that boy would flip.' Oliver tried to smile. 'Far as geography goes, though, we still close. They got him over there in the Snitch Hive, Strange. Me and Phil, we're like neighbors.'

Wood had been Granville's top lieutenant. He had pled out in exchange for testimony against Oliver. Wood would get life, as he had admitted to being the triggerman in other murders; death had been taken off the table. He was housed in the Correctional Treatment Facility, a privately run unit holding informants and government witnesses in the backyard of the D.C. Jail.

'I've been gathering background for the cross,' said Strange. 'I was looking for you to lead me to one of Phillip's old girlfriends.'

'Phil knew a lot of girls. The way he used to flash . . . even a bitch can get some pussy; ain't no trick to that. Phil used to drive this Turbo Z I had bought for him around to the high schools, 'specially over in Maryland, in PG? Drive by with that Kenwood sound system he had in there, playin' it loud. The girls used to run up to the car. They didn't even know who he was, and it didn't matter. It was obvious he had money, and what he did to get it. Girls just want to be up in there with the stars. It's *like* that, Strange.'

'I'm looking for one girl in particular. She swore out a brutality complaint against Wood.'

'The prosecution gave you that?'

'They don't have to give you charges, only convictions. I found it in his jacket down at the court. This particular charge, it was no-papered. Never went to trial.'

'What's the girl's name?'

'Devra Stokes. Should be about twenty-two by now. She worked at the Paramount Beauty Salon on Good Hope Road.'

Oliver grunted. 'Sounds right. Phil did like to chill in those beauty parlors. Said that's where the girls were, so he wanted to be there, too. But I don't know her. We went through a lot of young girls. We were kickin' it with 'em, for the most part. But we were using them for other shit, too.'

'What else would he have used a girl like Devra Stokes for?'

'Well, if she was old enough, and she didn't have no priors, we'd take her into Maryland or Virginia to buy a gun for us. Virginia, if we needed it quick. We paid for it, but she'd sign the forty-four seventy-three. What they call the yellow form.'

'You mean for a straw purchase.'

'A straw gun, yeah. Course, not all the time. You could rent a gun or get it from people we knew to get it from in the neighborhood. It's easy for a youngun to get a gun in the city. Easier than it is to buy a car. Shoot, you got to register a car.'

Strange repeated the name: 'Devra Stokes.'

'Like I say, I don't recall. But look, she was workin' in a salon, chance is, she still doin' the same thing, maybe somewhere else, but in the area. Those girls move around, but not too far.'

'Right.'

'Phil's gonna say I killed my uncle, ain't that right?'

'I don't know what he's going to say, Granville.'

Oliver and Strange stared at each other across the desk.

'You standin' tall, big man?' said Oliver.

Oliver was questioning Strange's loyalty. Strange answered by holding Oliver's gaze.

'I ain't no dreamer,' said Oliver. 'One way or the other, it's over for me. The business is done. Most of the boys I came up with, they're dead or doin' long time. One of the young ones I brought along got his own thing now, but he's cut things off with me. Word I get is, he still got himself lined up with Phil. Shoot, I hear they got two operations fighting over what I built as we sit here today.'

'What's your point?'

'I feel like I'm already gone. They want to erase me, Strange. Make it so I don't exist no more. The same way they keep poor young black boys and girls out of the public's eyes today, the same way they did me when I was a kid. Warehousin' me and those like me down in the Section Eights. Now the government wants to bring me out and make an example out of me for a hot minute, then make me disappear again. And I'm a good candidate, too, ain't I? A strong young nigger with an attitude. They want to strap me to that table in Indiana and give me that needle and show people, that's what happens when you don't stay down where we done put you. That's what happens when you rise up. They want to do this to me bad. So bad that they'd fuck with someone who was trying to help me to stop it, hear?'

You left out the part about all the young black men you killed or had killed, thought Strange. And the part about you poisoning your own community with drugs, and ruining the lives of all the young people you recruited and the lives of their families. But there were some truths in what Granville Oliver was saying, too. Strange, following a personal policy, did not comment either way.

'So I was just wondering,' said Oliver. 'When they try to shake you down – and they will – are you gonna stand tall?'

'Don't insult me,' said Strange. 'And don't ever let me get the idea that you're threatening me. 'Cause I will walk. And you do not want me to do that.'

Strange kept his voice even and his shoulders straight. He hoped his anger, and his fear, did not show on his face. Strange knew that even from in here, Oliver could have most anyone killed out on the street.

Oliver smiled, his face turning from hard to handsome. Like many who had attained his position, he was intelligent, despite his limited education, and could be a charming young man at will. When he relaxed his features, he favored his deceased father, a man Strange had known in the 1960s. Oliver had never known his father at all.

'I was just askin' a question, big man. I don't have many friends left, and I want to make sure that the ones I *do* have stay friends. We square, right?'

'We're square.'

'Good. But, look here, don't come up in here empty-handed next time. I could use some smokes or somethin'.'

'You know I can't be bringin' any contraband in here. They bar me from these meetings, it's gonna be a setback for what we're trying to accomplish.'

'I hear you. How about some porno mags, though?'

'I'll see you next time.'

Strange stood.

'One more thing,' said Oliver.

'What is it?' said Strange.

'I was wonderin' how Robert Gray was doin'?'

'He's staying with his aunt.'

'She ain't right.'

'I know it. But it's the best I could do. I got him all pumped up about playing football for us this year. We're gonna start him in the camp this summer, comin' up.'

'That's my little man right there. You're gonna see, that boy can jook. Check up on him, will you?'

'I get the time, I'll go by there today.'

'Thank you.'

'Stay strong, Granville.'

Strange signaled the fat man in the booth and walked from the room.

Out in the air, on the 1900 block of D Street in Southeast, Derek Strange walked to his car. He dropped under the wheel of his work vehicle, a white-over-black '89 Caprice with a 350 square block under the hood, and rolled down the window. He had a while to kill before meeting Quinn back at the office, and he didn't want to face the ringing phone and the message slips spread out on his desk. He decided he would sit in his car and enjoy the quiet and the promise of a new day.

Strange poured a cup of coffee from the thermos he kept in his car. Coffee was okay for times like this, but he kept water in the thermos when he was doing a surveillance, because coffee went through him too quick. He only sipped the water when he knew he'd be in the car for a long stretch, and on those occasions he kept a cup in the car with a plastic lid on it, in which he could urinate as needed.

Strange tasted the coffee. Janine had brewed it for him that morning before he left the house. The woman could cook, and she could make some coffee, too.

Strange picked up the newspaper beside him on the bench, which he had snatched off the lawn outside Janine's house earlier that morning on his way to the car. He pulled the Metro section free and scanned the front page. The *Washington Post* was running yet another story today in a series documenting the ongoing progress of the Granville Oliver trial.

Oliver had allegedly been involved in a dozen murders, including the murder of his own uncle, while running the Oliver Mob, a large-scale, longtime drug business operating in the Southeast quadrant of the city. The Feds were seeking death for Oliver under the RICO act, despite the fact that the District's residents had overwhelmingly rejected the death penalty in a local referendum. The combination of racketeering and certain violent crimes allowed the government to exercise this option. The last execution in D.C. had been carried out in 1957.

The jury selection process had taken several months, as it had been difficult to find twelve local residents unopposed to capital punishment. During this time, Oliver's attorneys, from the firm of Ives and Colby, had employed Strange to gather evidence, data, and counter-testimony for the defense.

Strange skipped the article, jumping inside Metro to page 3. His eyes went to a daily crime column unofficially known by longtime

Washingtonians as 'the Roundup,' or the 'Violent Negro Deaths.' The first small headline read, 'Teen Dies of Gunshot Wounds,' and beneath it were two sentences: 'An 18-year-old man found with multiple gunshot wounds in Southeast Washington died early yesterday at Prince George's County Hospital Center, police said. The unidentified man was found just after midnight in the courtyard area behind the Stoneridge apartments in the 300 block of Anacostia Road, and was pronounced dead at 1:03 a.m.'

Two sentences, thought Strange. That's all a certain kind of kid in this town's gonna get to sum up his life. There would be more deaths, most likely retribution kills, related to this one. Later, the murder gun might turn up somewhere down the food chain. Later, the crime might get 'solved,' pinned on the shooter by a snitch in a plea-out. Whatever happened, this would be the last the general public would hear about this young man, a passing mention to be filed away in a newspaper morgue, one brief paragraph without even a name attached to prove that he had existed. Another unidentified YBM, dead on the other side of the Anacostia River.

River, hell, thought Strange. The way it separates this city for real, might as well go ahead and call it a canyon.

Strange dropped the newspaper back on the bench seat. He turned the key in the ignition and pushed a Spinners tape into his deck. He pulled out of his spot and drove west. Just a few sips of coffee, and already he had to pee. Anyway, he couldn't sit here all day. It was time to go to work.

2

Two house wrens, a brownish male and female, were building a nest on the sill outside Strange's office window. Strange could hear them talking to each other as they worked.

When Strange was a child, his mother, Alethea, had held him up to their kitchen window on mornings just like this one to show him the daily progress of the nest the birds made there each year. 'They're working to make a house for their children. The same way your father goes to work each day to make this a home for you and your brother.' His mother had been gone two years now, but Derek Strange could recall her words, and he could hear the music in her voice. She still spoke to Strange in his dreams.

Late-spring light shot through the glass, the heat of it warming the back of Strange's neck and hands as he sat at his desk. The wedge-shaped speaker beside his phone buzzed. Janine's voice, transmitted from the office reception area up front, came from the box.

'Derek, Terry just came in.'

'I'll be right out.'

Strange glanced down beside his chair, where Greco, his tan boxer, lay. Greco looked up without moving his head as Strange rubbed his skull. Greco's nub of a tail twitched and he closed his eyes.

'I won't be gone long. Janine'll take care of you, boy.'

In the reception area, Strange nodded at Terry Quinn, sitting at his desk, a work station he rarely used. While Quinn tore open a pack of sugarless gum, Strange stopped by Janine's desk.

She wore some kind of pants-and-shirt hookup, flowing and bright. Her lipstick matched the half-moons of red slashing through the outfit. It would be like her to pay attention to that kind of detail. Strange stared at her now. She always looked good. *Always.* But you couldn't get the full weight of it if you saw her seated behind her desk. Janine was the kind of tall, strong woman, you needed to see her walking to get the full appreciation, to feel that stirring up in your thighs. Like one of those proud horses they marched around at the track. He knew it wasn't proper to talk about a woman, especially a woman you loved, like she was some kind of fine animal. But that's what came to mind when he looked at her. He guessed it was still okay, until the thought police came and raided his head, to imagine her like that in his mind.

'You okay?' said Janine, looking up at him with those big browns of hers. 'You look drunk.'

'Thinking of you,' said Strange.

Strange heard Lamar, seated at Ron Lattimer's old desk, snicker behind him. For this he turned and stared benignly at the young man.

'I ain't say nothin',' said Lamar. 'Just over here, minding my own.'

Strange had been grooming Lamar Williams to be an investigator as soon as he got his diploma from Roosevelt High and took up some technical courses, computer training or something like it, at night. In the meantime, Strange had Lamar doing what he'd been doing the past couple of years: cleaning the office, running errands, and keeping himself away from the street-side boys over in the Section 8s, the nearby Park Morton complex where Lamar lived with his mom and little sister.

Strange looked back at Janine, then down to the blotter-style calendar on her desk. 'What's my two o'clock about?'

'Man says he's looking for a love.'

'Him and Bobby Womack,' said Strange.

'His *lost* love.'

'Okay. We know him?'

'Says he's been seeing our sign these last few years, since he's been "frequenting an establishment" over on Georgia Avenue.'

'Must be talkin' about that titty bar across the street. Our claim to the neighborhood.'

'Georgetown's got Dunbarton Oaks,' said Janine with a shrug. 'We've got the Foxy Playground.'

Strange leaned over the desk and kissed Janine fully on the lips. Their mouths fit together right. He held the kiss, then stood straight.

'Dag, y'all actin' like you're twenty years old,' said Lamar.

Strange straightened the new name plaque on the desk. For many years it had read 'Janine Baker.' Now it read 'Janine Strange.'

'I didn't have it so good when I was twenty,' said Strange, talking to Lamar, still looking at Janine. 'And anyway, where's it say that a man's not allowed to kiss his wife?'

Janine reached into her desk drawer and pulled free a PayDay bar. 'In case you miss lunch,' she said, handing it to Strange.

'Thank you, baby.'

Terry Quinn stood, a manila folder under his arm. He had the sun-sensitive skin of an Irishman, with a square jaw and deep laugh ridges framing his mouth. A scar ran down one cheek where he had been cut by a pimp's pearl-handled knife. He kept his hair short and it was free of gray. The burst of lines that had formed around his green eyes was the sole indication of his thirty-three years. He was medium height, but the width of his shoulders and the heft of his chest made him appear shorter.

'Can I get some of that Extra, Terry?' said Lamar.

Quinn tossed a stick of gum to Lamar as he stepped out from behind his desk.

'You ready?' said Strange.

'Thought you two were gonna renew your vows or something,' said Quinn.

Strange head-motioned to the front door. 'We'll take my short.'

Janine watched them leave the office. Strange filled out that shirt she'd bought him, mostly cotton but with a touch of rayon in it for the stretch, with his broad shoulders and back. Her man, almost fifty-four, had twenty years on Terry, and still he looked fine.

Coming out of the storefront, they passed under the sign hanging above the door. The magnifying-glass logo covered and blew up half the script: 'Strange Investigations' against a yellow back. At night the light-box was the beacon on this part of the strip, 9th between Kansas and Upshur, a sidearm-throw off Georgia. It was this sign, Janine's kidding aside, that was the landmark in Petworth and down into Park View. Strange had opened this business after his stint with the MPD, and he had kept it open now for over twenty-five years. He could just as well have made his living out of his row house on Buchanan Street, especially now that he was staying full-time with Janine and her son, Lionel, in their house on Quintana. But he knew what his visibility meant out here; the young people in the neighborhood had come to expect his presence on this street.

Strange and Quinn passed Hawk's barbershop, where a cutter named Rodel stood outside, dragging on a Newport.

'When you gonna get that mess straightened up, Derek?' said Rodel.

'Tell Bennett I'll be in later on today,' said Strange, not breaking his stride.

'They got the new *Penthouse* in,' said Quinn.

'You didn't soil it or nothin', did you?'

'You can still make out a picture or two.'

Strange patted his close-cut, lightly salted natural. 'Another reason to get myself correct.'

They passed the butcher place that sold lunches, and Marshall's funeral parlor, where the white Caprice was parked along the curb behind a black limo-style Lincoln. Strange turned the ignition, and they rolled toward Southeast.

3

Ulysses Foreman was just about down to seeds, so when little Mario Durham got him on his cell, looking to rent a gun, he told Durham to meet him on Martin Luther King Jr Avenue, up a ways from the Big Chair. Foreman set the meeting out for a while, which would give him time to wake up his girl, Ashley Swann, and show her who her daddy was before he left up the house.

An hour and a half later, Foreman looked across the leather bench at a skinny man with a wide, misshapen nose and big rat teeth, leaning against the Caddy's passenger-side door. On Durham's feet were last year's Jordans; the *J* on the left one, Foreman noticed, was missing. Durham wore a Redskins jersey and a matching knit cap, his arms coming out the jersey like willow branches. The back of the jersey had the name 'Sanders' printed across it. It would be just like Durham, thought Foreman, to look up to a pretty-boy hustler, all flash and no heart, like Deion.

'You brought me somethin'?' said Foreman.

Durham, having hiked up the volume on the Cadillac's system, didn't hear. He was moving his head to that single, 'Danger,' had been in heavy rotation since the wintertime. Foreman reached over and turned the music down.

'Hey,' said Durham.

'We got business.'

'That joint is tight, though.'

'Mystikal? He ain't doin' nothin' J. B. didn't do twenty years back.'

'It's still a good jam.'

'Uh-huh. And PGC done played that shit to death.' Foreman upped his chin in the direction of Mario. 'C'mon, Twigs, show me what you got.'

Mario Durham hated the nickname that had followed him for years. It brought to mind Twiggy, that itty-bitty model who was popular from back before he was born. It was a bitch name, he knew. There wasn't but a few men he allowed to call him that. Okay, there was more than a few. But Ulysses Foreman, built like a nose tackle, he sure was one of those men. Durham reached down into his jeans, deep inside his boxers, and pulled free a rolled plastic sandwich bag containing a thick line of chronic. He handed it across the bench to Foreman.

Foreman's pearl red 1997 El Dorado Touring Coupe was parked on MLK between W and V in Southeast. Its Northstar engine was quiet, and no smoke was visible from the pipes. Foreman didn't like to tax the battery, so he was letting the motor run. He sat low on the bench, his stacked shoulders and knotted biceps filling out the ribbed white cotton T-shirt he'd bought out that catalogue he liked, International Male.

Across the street, a twenty-foot-tall mahogany chair sat in the grassy section off the lot of the Anacostia Medical/Dental Center, formerly the sight of the Curtis Brothers Furniture Company. The Big Chair was the landmark in Far Southeast.

'This gonna get me up?' said Foreman, inspecting the contents of the bag.

'You know me,' said Durham. 'You know how I do.'

Foreman nodded, glancing in the rearview. A Sixth District cruiser approached, coming slowly from the direction of St Elizabeth's, the laughing house atop the hill. Foreman never worried. If he didn't know the beat police in this part of town, then he could name-check some of their older fellow officers, many of whom he had come up with back in the late eighties, when he had worn the uniform himself in 6D. Being a former cop, still knowing existing cops, it was usually worth a free pass. Leastways it stopped them from searching the car. The cruiser went by and was soon gone from sight.

Foreman reached under the seat and produced a Taurus 85, a five-shot .38 Special with a black rubber boot-shaped grip and a ported barrel. He handed it to Durham butt out, keeping it below the window line. Durham admired it in the morning sunlight streaming in from the east.

'It's blue.'

'For real. Pretty, right?'

'Damn sure is.'

Durham turned it in the light, the barrel now pointed at Foreman. Foreman reached out and with the back of his hand moved the barrel so that it pointed down at the floor of the car.

'It's loaded?' said Durham.

'You got to treat every gun like it's live, boy.'

'I hear you. But is it?'

'Yeah, you're ready.'

Durham nodded. 'When you want it back?'

Forman weighed the plastic bag in his hand. 'I say you rented about five days of strap right here.'

'That's a hundred worth of hydro in that bag. I coulda *bought* a brand-new three eighty for, like, ninety dollars.'

'You talkin' about a Davis? Go ahead and buy one, then. But give me back my *real* gun before you do.'

'That's all right.'

'There you go then, little man. You want to ride in style, you got to pay.' Foreman pushed his hips forward to slip the bag into the pocket of his jeans. 'What you need the gun for, anyway?'

'Need to make an impression on someone, is all it is. Why?'

'I can't be fuckin' with no murder gun, hear? You plan to blow someone up behind this shit, I got to know. 'Cause I can't use no gun got a body attached to it. We straight?'

Durham nodded quickly. 'Sure. Do me a favor, though. Don't be tellin' my brother about you rentin' me this gun.'

'Why not?'

'He might say somethin' to our mother. I don't want her stressin' over me.'

'I can understand that. We don't need to be worryin' your all's moms.'

Foreman had already decided that he would tell Dewayne Durham that he had rented a gun to his half brother, Mario. Dewayne might not like that, but it would be better if he knew up front. Foreman figured, what harm would it do? This miniature man right here wouldn't have the courage to use the gun anyway. Foreman would have it back in five days, and he had some free hydro to smoke in the bargain. Didn't seem to be any kind of problem to it that he could see.

They shook hands. Durham ended the ritual with a weak finger snap.

'Let me get on back to Mer-land where I belong,' said Foreman.

'I got an appointment I got to get to my own self.'

'You need me to drop you somewheres close?' Foreman had no intention of driving Mario Durham anywhere, but he felt it made good sense to be polite, go through the usual motions and ask. Foreman's business relationship with Dewayne Durham was on the rise.

'Nah, I'm just down there around the corner.'

'Awright, then,' said Foreman.

'Aiight.'

Durham dropped the pistol into the large pocket of his oversize jeans and stepped out of the car. He walked down the hill and cut left. Foreman watched him, wearin' a boy's-size Redskins jersey, a slip of nothing in his Hilfigers, hanging like some sad shit on his narrow ass. 'I'm just down there around the corner' – that was some bullshit right there. Twigs didn't own no car, or if he did it wasn't nothin' but a bomb. Most likely he was headed for the Metro station to catch a train to that appointment he had. Must be a real important date, too. Foreman had to admit, though, Mario Durham always did have some good chronic to smoke. Dewayne, a dealer over in Congress Heights, advanced him however much he wanted.

Durham walked toward the Metro station in Barry Farms, passing hard-eyed boys on the sidewalk, thinking how different it felt when you had a gun in your pocket. Different on the physical tip, like he'd grown taller and put on fifty pounds of muscle. Lookin' in those young boys' narrowed eyes, thinking, Yeah, go ahead, fuck with me; I got somethin' right here gonna make your eyes go wide. Having that .38 just touching his leg through the fabric of his Tommys, it made him feel like he had four more inches of dick on him, too.

He'd catch a Green Line train and take it over the river to the Petworth stop. The man's office, he'd seen the sign out front with the magnifying glass on it all those times he'd been to that titty bar they had across the street from it, on Georgia. His office, it wasn't far from the station stop.

Durham wondered, could the man in that office find Olivia? Because his kid brother wasn't gonna wait much longer without taking some kind of action his own self. Sign out front claimed they did investigations.

Strange Investigations.

That's what it said.

4

'There it is right there,' said Quinn, pointing to the in-dash cassette deck in Strange's Chevy.

'He said "hug her." ' Strange sang the words: ' "Makes you want to love her, you just got to hug her, yeah." '

' "You just got to *fuck* her," ' said Quinn. 'That's what the man's sayin'. Rewind it and listen to it again.'

They were on eastbound H Street in Northeast, where the sidewalks were live with pedestrian traffic, folks hanging out, and deliverymen moving goods from their curbed trucks to the shops. They passed a Murray's Steaks, several nail salons and hair galleries, and a place called Father and Son Beer and Wine. Strange turned right on 8th and drove toward Southeast. He rewound the tape and the two of them listened again to the line in question.

'There it is, man,' said Strange. 'He said "hug her." '

'He said "fuck her," Dad.'

'See, you're focusing on the wrong thing, Terry. What you ought to be doing, on a beautiful day like this, is groovin' to the song. This here is the Spinners' debut on Atlantic. Some people call this the most beautiful Philly soul album ever recorded.'

'Yeah, I know. Produced by Taco Bell.'

'*Thom* Bell.'

'What about those guys Procter and Gamble you're always goin' on about?'

'Gamble and Huff. Point is, this is pretty nice, isn't it? Shoot, Terry, you had to have—'

'Been there; I know.'

'That's right. You take all those slow-jam groups from that period, the Chi-Lites, the Stylistics, Harold Melvin, the ballad stuff that EWF was doin', and what you got is the most beautiful period of pop music in history. It's like America got their own . . . they finally got their own opera, man.'

Quinn turned up the volume on the deck. He chuckled, listening to the words. 'Derek, is that what you mean by opera, right there?'

'What?'

' "Makes a lame man walk . . . makes blind men talk about seein' again." '

'Look, the song's called "One of a Kind (Love Affair)." Ain't you never had the kind of love that could rock your world like that?'

'When I was bustin' a nut, maybe.'

'That's what I can't understand about you young folks, Generation XYZ, or whatever you're calling yourselves this week. Y'all ain't got no romance in you, man.'

'I had plenty in me last night.'

'Oh, yeah?' Strange looked across the bench. 'How's Sue doin', anyway?'

'She's fine.'

'Yeah, and she's *fine*, too.'

On M Street, Strange cut east. They took the 11th Street Bridge over the river and into Anacostia, bringing them straight onto Martin Luther King Jr Avenue.

The welcoming strip in this historic part of town was clean and carefully tended. Merchants swept the sidewalks outside their businesses, and the cars along the curb were late model and waxed. Commercial thinned out to residential as the Chevy began to climb the hill in the direction of St. E's. Strange and Quinn drove by the Big Chair without remark. Farther up, on the left, Strange mentally noted the nice lines on a pretty red El Dorado parked along the curb. He loved the beauty of big American cars.

' "I Could Never Repay Your Love," ' said Strange, upping the volume on the deck.

'Thank you, Derek,' said Quinn.

Strange ignored him, settling low on the bench. He smiled as the vocals kicked in. 'Just listen to this, man. Philippe Wynne really testifies on this one here.'

Strange found Devra Stokes on their third stop. He had first gone to the Paramount Beauty Salon on Good Hope Road, where no one claimed to remember the girl. Strange checked his files, located in the trunk of his car: Janine had located Devra's mother, Mattie Stokes, using the People Finder program on her computer. Strange found her, a tired-looking woman in her late thirties, at her place in the Ashford Manor apartments, down by the Walter E. Washington Estates off Southern Avenue. She informed Strange that her daughter was working in another beauty parlor on Good Hope Road, a block east of the Paramount.

Quinn stayed in the car while Strange entered the salon. He went directly to an oldish woman, small as a child, whom he figured to be the owner or the manager. He told the hard-faced woman that he was looking for Devra Stokes and was pointed to a young lady braiding another woman's hair. A little boy, no older than four, sat at the foot of the chair, playing with action figures and making flying noises as he moved the figures through the air. When the older woman told Devra that a man was here to see her, she glanced at him with nothing telling in her eyes and returned to her task at hand. Strange had a seat by the shop-front window and flipped through a copy of *Essence* magazine. The miniature woman he had spoken to was looking him over as if he had just come calling on her granddaughter with flowers, chocolates, and a packet of Trojan Magnums. He tried to ignore her and studied the photos of the models in the magazine.

Ten minutes later Devra Stokes walked over to Strange and sat down beside him. Time and her environment had not yet bested her. She had almond-shaped, dark brown eyes and a wide, sensuous mouth.

'You lookin' to talk to me?'

'Derek Strange.' He flashed her his license. 'Investigator, D.C.'

'This about Phillip and them?'

'Yes.'

'Knew y'all would be along.'

'Will you speak with me?'

'I can't today. I got appointments.'

'But you will?' Devra looked away. Strange gently touched her arm to bring her back. 'You filed a brutality complaint against Wood.'

'That was a while back.'

'When the time came to take the stand, you changed your mind.'

Devra shrugged and looked in the direction of the little boy, still playing beside the chair. Strange was certain that Phillip Wood had paid her to stay away from court. It was possible, also, that Wood had fathered her child. Wood would be put away forever, and with him any money he could provide to Stokes and her son. Strange was counting on her awareness that she'd been permanently dogged out. He hoped it burned her deep.

'I just need some background information,' said Strange. 'Chances are you won't have to testify.'

'Like I say, I can't talk now.'

'Can I get up with you here?'

'Where else I'm gonna be?' said Devra, looking down at her shoes.

'What time you get off today?'

'About five, unless my clients run over.'

'Your little boy likes ice cream, right?'

'He likes it.'

'How about I see you around five? We'll find him some, and we'll talk.'

Devra's eyes caught light and her mouth turned up at the sides. She was downright pretty when she smiled. 'I like ice cream, too.'

Course you do, thought Strange. You're not much more than a kid yourself.

At the Metro station Strange idled the Caprice while Quinn passed out flyers to Anacostians rushing to catch their Green Line trains. The flyers were headed with the words 'Missing and Endangered' and showed a picture of a fourteen-year-old girl that Sue Tracy, Quinn's girlfriend, had been hired to find. Tracy and her partner, Karen Bagley, had a Maryland-based business that primarily took runaway and missing-teen cases. Bagley and Tracy Investigative Services also received grant money for helping prostitutes endangered by their pimps and violent johns. Quinn had first met Tracy when he agreed to take on a case of hers that had moved into D.C.

Strange watched a cocky and squared-up Quinn through the windshield, the only white face in a sea of black ones. Quinn was drawing fish eyes from some of the young men and a few double takes from the older members of the crowd. Strange knew that Quinn was unfazed by the attention. In fact, he liked the challenge of it, up to a point. He was, after all, a former patrol cop. As long as he was given the space he gave others, every thing would be cool.

But it often didn't happen that way. And when Quinn was shown disrespect, the kind that went down with a subtle eye sweep from a black to a white, it got under his skin, and baffled him a little bit, too.

Something was said by a couple of young males to Quinn as he began to walk back to the car. Quinn stopped and got up in the taller of the two's face. Strange watched Quinn's jaw tense, the set of his eyes, the vein wormed on his forehead, the way he seemed to grow taller as the blood crept into his face. Strange didn't even think to get out of his car. It was over without incident, as he knew it would be. Soon Quinn was dropping onto the bench beside him.

'You all right?'

'Guy *told* me to give him a dollar after he called me a white boy.

Like that was gonna convince me to pull out my wallet. God, I love this town.'

'It was the *boy* part got your back up, huh?'

'That was most of it, I guess.'

'Think how it felt for grown men to be called boy every day for, I don't know, a couple hundred years before you were born.'

'Yeah, okay. So now it's my turn to get fucked with. We all gotta have ourselves a turn. For some shit that happened, like you say, before I was even born.'

'You don't even want to go there, Terry. Trust me.'

'Right.' Quinn breathed out slowly. 'Look, thanks for stopping here. I told Sue I'd pass some of those out.'

'Who's she looking for, anyway?'

'Girl named Linda Welles. Fourteen years old, ninety-nine pounds. She ran off from her home in Burrville last year, over near Woodson High, in Far Northeast? Couple of months later, her older brother recognizes her when he's with his boys, watching one of those videos they pass around.'

'She was the star, huh?'

'Yeah. It was supposed to be a house party, freak-dancing and all that, but then a couple of guys start going at it with her back in one of the bedrooms, right on the tape. Not that she wasn't complicit, from the looks of it.'

'Fourteen years old, complicit got nothin' to do with it.'

'Exactly. The brother recognized the exterior shot of the street where they had the party. It was on Naylor Road, up around the late twenties, here in Anacostia. That was a while back. The girl's just vanished, man – nothing since.'

'So, what, you gonna go deep undercover down here to find her?'

'Just passing out flyers.'

''Cause you're gonna have a little trouble blending in.'

'But I feel the love,' said Quinn. 'That counts for something, doesn't it?'

They drove back to W Street, passing the Fredrick Douglass Home, then cut up 16th toward Minnesota Avenue, where they could catch Benning Road to the other side of the river and back into the center of town. They passed solid old homes and rambling bungalows sitting among tall trees on straight, clean streets, sharing space with apartments and housing complexes, some maintained but many deteriorating, all surrounded by black wrought-iron fences. Many of the apartment buildings, three-story brick affairs with the aesthetic appeal of bunkers, showed plywood in their windows. Hard young men, the malignant result of years of festering, unchecked poverty and fatherless homes, sat on their front steps. Strange had always admired the deep green of Anacostia and the views of the city from its hilly landscapes. It was the most beautiful section of town and also the ugliest, often at the same time.

'You can't find one white face down here anymore,' said Quinn, looking at a man driving a FedEx truck as it passed.

'There's one,' said Strange, pointing to the sidewalk fronting one of the many liquor stores serving the neighborhood. A cockeyed woman with a head of uncombed blond hair and stretch pants pulled up to her sagging bustline stood there drinking from a brown paper bag. 'Looks like they forgot to do their head count this morning up at St E's.'

Strange was hoping to bring some humor to the subject. But he knew Terry would not give it up now that he'd been stepped to.

'Bet you there's some down here, they'd tell you that's one too many white people on these streets,' said Quinn.

'Here we go.'

'You remember that loud-mouth guy they had in this ward, ran for the city council, Shazam or whatever his name was? The guy who wanted everyone to boycott the Korean grocery stores?'

'Sure, I remember.'

'And?'

'And, nothin',' said Strange.

'So you agreed with that guy.'

'Look. People down here got a right to be angry about a lot of things. They talk it out among themselves, in the barbershop and at the dinner table, and when they do they talk it out for real, the pros and the cons. But one thing they don't do is, they don't go shittin' on that guy you're talking about, or our former mayor, or Farrakhan, or Sharpton, or anyone else like that to people like you.'

'People like me, huh?'

'Yeah. Black folks don't put down their own so they can feed white people what they want to hear.'

'This guy ran his whole election on fear and hate, Derek.'

'But he didn't win the election, did he?'

'Your point is what?'

'In the end, in their own quiet way, the majority of the people always prove that they know the difference between right and wrong. What I'm saying is, there's more good people out here than there are bad. Once you get hip to that, that anger you're carrying around with you, it's gonna go away.'

'You think I'm angry?'

'Look at the world more positive, man.' Strange reached for the tape deck, looking for some music and some peace. 'Trust me, man, it'll help you get through your day.'

5

'I see you're a 'Skins fan,' said Mario Durham, nodding at the plaster figure with the spring-mounted head on Strange's desk.

'I see you are, too,' said Strange, his eyes passing over the Sanders jersey Durham wore as he sat slumped in the client chair.

'I do like Deion. Boy can play.'

'He couldn't play for me. Biggest mistake the 'Skins ever made, gettin' rid of a heart-and-soul player like Brian Mitchell for a showboat like Deion. Mitchell used to get that whole team up, man. That's what happens when a new owner comes in, doesn't understand the game.'

'Whateva. You a longtime fan, though, I can see. This right here must go back to Charley Taylor and shit.' Durham reached out and flicked the head of the plaster figure. Greco, lying belly down on the floor, raised his head and growled.

'Watch it,' said Strange. 'My stepson painted that, and it's special. Money can't replace it.'

'That dog all right? Animals and me don't get along.'

'You interrupted his beauty sleep,' said Strange.

Durham shifted in his chair. 'So anyway, like I was sayin', I'm lookin' for this girl.'

'Olivia Elliot,' said Quinn, seated beside the desk.

'Right. I was knowin' her for, like, two months, and I thought we was gettin' along pretty good.'

'Where'd you two meet?' said Strange.

'I was tryin' to hook up with this other girl, see, worked at this nail and braid salon in Southeast. I went in there lookin' to date this girl, and I see Olivia, got some woman's hand in her lap, paintin' it. Y'all know how that is, when you get a look at a certain kind of woman and you say, uh-huh, *yeah*, that right there is gonna be *mine*.'

'You had a lot of girlfriends, Mario?'

'I ain't gonna lie to you; I been a player my whole life,' said

Durham. He smiled then, showing Quinn and Strange two long, protruding front teeth surrounded by space. 'But this was different right here.'

'And then she left,' said Quinn.

'She just *up* and left, and I ain't heard from her since.'

'You two have an argument, something like that?' said Strange.

'We was cool,' said Durham, 'far as I know.'

'Where was she staying when she disappeared?'

'She had this apartment, stayed with her son, young boy. They stayed in this place they rented off Good Hope.'

'Her son's name?'

'Mark.'

'Same last name? Elliot?'

'Uh-huh.'

'And he's in school?'

'Elementary, down in that area they was stayin' in, I guess, but I don't know the name.'

'You try her mother, any other family?' said Strange.

'She never spoke of any kin,' said Durham. 'Look, fellas, I'm worried about the girl.'

'Why hire private cops?' said Quinn.

'What my partner means is,' said Strange, 'you suspect some kind of foul play, what you need to do is, you need to report it to the police.'

'Black girl goes missin' in Southeast, police ain't gonna do shit. But it ain't like that, anyway. Olivia was the kind of girl, it was a cloudy day or somethin', it would bust on her groove. She'd be, like, cryin' her eyes out over somethin' simple like the weather. I'm worried in the sense that she's sad, or got the depression, sumshit like that. I just want to know where she is. And if we do have some kind of problem between us, then maybe we can work it out.'

'All right, then,' said Strange. 'Give Terry here the details on what you just told us. Addresses, phone numbers, all that.'

Strange went out to the reception area while Quinn took the information. He phoned Raymond Ives, Granville Oliver's attorney, and left a message on his machine informing him that he was making progress on the gathering of countertestimony against Phillip Wood. When Strange returned to his office, Mario Durham was standing out of his chair. He wasn't but five and a half feet tall, and he couldn't have weighed more than a hundred twenty-five pounds.

'We all set, then,' said Durham.

'Just give my office manager out there your deposit on your way out,' said Strange, 'and we'll get going on this right away.'

'Fifty, right?'

'A hundred, just like Janine told you when you spoke to her on the phone.'

'Damn, y'all about to bankrupt a man.'

'It's a hundred. But this shouldn't take too long. Our rate is thirty-five an hour, and if it comes out to be under the hundred, then you're gonna get what we didn't earn back.'

'Put a rush on it, hear? I can't even afford the hundred, seein' as I'm in between jobs right now. I'm just anxious to see my girl.'

Durham began to walk from the room. Greco got up and followed him, sniffing at the back of his Tommys as he walked. Greco growled some, and Durham quickened his step. Greco stopped walking as Durham passed through the doorway. Quinn shut the office door.

'Animal doesn't like you,' said Strange, 'must be a reason.'

'We don't usually ask for one-hundred-dollar deposits, Derek.'

'I made an exception for him.'

'It's because he's black, right?'

'It's because he's a no-account knucklehead. That hundred's the only money we're ever gonna see out of him. He's got no job, wouldn't even give Janine a fixed address. Said if we needed to get him we could look up a friend of his called Donut in Valley Green.'

'Donut, huh? You can bank that.'

'And his only phone number is a cell.'

'You think there's something funny about his story?'

'Course there is. Somethin' funny about half the stories we hear in this place. Maybe she owes him money, or he's just tryin' to find out if she's shackin' up with someone else.'

'You don't think a woman would leave a prize like him for another man, do you? That'd be like, I don't know, driving across town for a Big Mac when you got filet mignon cooking on the grill in your backyard.'

'Was it just me, or was that man butt-ugly?'

'Playa hater,' said Quinn.

'Almost feel like pressing his money back in his hand, giving him the phone number to a good dentist.'

'Last time I saw two teeth like that, they were attached to somethin' had a paddle for a tail and was chewin' on a piece of wood.'

'Well, a hundred dollars is a hundred dollars. If any of that information he gave us is accurate, I'll find that girl this afternoon.'

'Quit bragging.'

'No brag,' said Strange, 'just fact.'

'*Guns of Will Sonnet*,' said Quinn. 'Walter Brennan.'

'Damn, boy, you surprise me sometimes.'

'You need me,' said Quinn, 'I'm puttin' in a few hours at the bookstore today.'

Strange said, 'I'll call you there.'

6

Strange went back down to Anacostia and had a late lunch at Mama Cole's. Its sign claimed they served 'the best soul food in town,' and if that wasn't enough, the cursive quote on the awning out front added, 'Martin Luther King would have eaten here.' Strange didn't know about all that, but the food was better than all right. He ordered a fish sandwich with plenty of hot sauce, and when he had his first bite he closed his eyes. That pricey white-tablecloth buppie joint on the suit-side of town, claimed it was South authentic, didn't have anything this good coming out of its kitchen.

'How you doin', Derek?' said a man at a deuce as Strange was making his way toward the door.

'I'm makin' it,' said Strange, shaking his hand. The man was an assistant coach for the football squad that played their home games at Turkey Thicket, but Strange could not remember his name.

'You gonna be ready this year, big man?'

'Oh, we got a few surprises for you, now.'

'All right, then.'

'All right.'

They shook hands. Quinn would say something now, if he were here, about Strange running into someone he knew in every part of the District. It was true, but Strange never found it surprising. He'd lived here, and only here, for over fifty years. For its permanent residents, D.C. was in many ways still a small town.

Strange got into his Caprice. He was full and happy. He pushed in a mix tape and found 'City, Country, City,' the War instrumental that he always returned to when he was under the wheel on a fine spring day. He drove to the nail salon where Mario Durham had first met Olivia Elliot and entered the shop.

The owner of the place, a youngish woman who looked like she had a ropy bird's nest set atop her head, hadn't seen or heard from Olivia in a long while. She didn't ask why Strange was looking for Elliot, and he didn't bother to invent a ruse. She had marked him as a bill collector, most likely, an assumption he did not confirm or deny. If Elliot had left her job on bad terms, then this would work in his favor.

'You have no idea where she's working now?' said Strange.

'I don't believe she could hold a job for long,' said the owner.

'Girl was keepin' bad company, too,' said another woman, unprompted, from across the shop.

'She didn't know Jesus,' said the owner. 'So how could she know herself?'

Strange drove toward the complex where Olivia Elliot had lived. He passed Ketchum Elementary and wondered if Olivia's son, Mark, was a student at this school. But it wasn't like this was the only grade school in the area; Strange had noticed another one, and another still, just in the small distance he'd covered since leaving the shop. There was no shortage of babies being made in this part of town.

He parked in the lot of the Woodland Mews, a grouping of several tan brick units surrounded by the ubiquitous black iron fence. The grounds were on the clean side and the parking lot, half filled on this workday, was mostly free of trash. Strange wrote down the name of the complex's management company, posted with a phone number under an 'Apartment Available' notice hung on the fence. He called this in to Janine and asked her to check with the company to see if Elliot had left a forwarding address. If she had put a security deposit down, he reasoned, she would be looking for them to send it to her.

Strange crossed the lot, going by two young men standing beside a tricked-out Honda. An old Rare Essence track came from the open windows of the car. The young men's conversation halted as he passed. Strange wore his cell on a holster, along with a Leatherman Tool-in-One looped through his belt. He wore his Buck knife as well when he felt he had the need to show it, but had left it in the office today. He carried a spiral notepad with a pen fitted into the rings.

Strange walked as he had taught Lamar and the kids on his football team to walk when they were out on the street. Chin up, shoulders square, at a steady clip but not too fast. The effect was confidence and, in his case, authority. Among those who were acquainted with the traits and mannerisms that are common to police, Strange would always be made as a cop, even though he had not worn the uniform for thirty-some-odd years. The young men resumed their conversation as Strange made his way into the stairwell of a nearby unit.

The stairwell's interior walls were the usual dull cinder block. The words 'Mews Crew' were spray painted on the wall, artlessly, along with several nicknames. 'Black,' that most popular of D.C. street names, was among them. Strange had become acquainted with most of the gang names down here in the course of his long investigation related to Granville Oliver, but he had not heard this one mentioned. He figured that the wall tag was just the work of hopeful kids.

Strange knocked on the apartment door where Olivia Elliot had lived. No one answered, but there was music behind the door, and Strange knocked again. A girl opened the door to its chain length and peered out. He could smell marijuana through the opening, and the girl's eyes told him she was high. Strange caught a glimpse of an older boy, shirtless above the waist, backing into the hallway of the apartment.

'I'm looking for Olivia Elliot,' said Strange.

'I ain't know her,' said the girl.

'Is your mother at home?'

'At work.'

'How long have you been living here?'

'We only been stayin' up in here, like, a month.'

'What—'

'Bye.'

She closed the door. Strange was accustomed to having doors closed in his face, and he wasn't about to knock again just to get the same response. Anyway, he had the feeling that this was a dead lead. The management company was the way to go. But he figured he'd upturn all the stones he could while he was here.

Strange knocked on another door, then tried a third. He walked back down the stairs to the open air. A man in the parking lot, smoking a cigarette beside a Dumpster, stared him down. Strange looked him over and walked on. With his cell holstered to his belt and his pen and pad, Strange was obviously some sort of official, cop, or inspector. He didn't feel the need to explain himself or acknowledge the smoker in any way. Besides, Strange had sized up the man and decided that if it came down to it, he could kick his ass. Didn't matter how old you got, there was always some kind of satisfaction for a man in knowing that.

He walked around the unit to the back, where the apartments' balconies faced a small playground holding rusted and broken equipment. Strange studied the balconies. He noticed a boy's bicycle in the 20-to-23-inch range chained to a rail on the third floor. That size bike would belong to a child who was somewhere between seven and twelve years old. He counted the apartments and where they were in relation to the stairwell, and he returned to the front of the building and took the steps to the door he thought he was looking for. He knocked on the door and soon it opened.

A dark-skinned, unkempt woman whose facial features had begun to collapse stood in the frame. Hung on a chain around her mottled neck was a large wooden crucifix that lay on a threadbare housedress. The furniture in the room behind her followed the lead of the dress. A piece of rug art, a brown-and-white pony standing in a field of black, was tacked to the wall over a shredded sofa.

'Yes?'

'Yes, ma'am.' Strange softened his eyes. 'I'm trying to get up with Mark Elliot, little boy lives here, down on the floor below you. Trouble I'm having, the phone number I had on his mother, when I dial it I get a recording, says it's been disconnected.'

'Well, that's because they moved out.'

'I was afraid it might be that.'

The woman looked him over and crossed her arms beneath her sagging breasts. 'And you are?'

'Excuse me. My name is Will, uh, *William* Sonnett. I've got a football team I coach every fall over in Turkey Thicket, run it through the, uh, church group. We do this camp in the summertime, kind of ease the kids into their conditioning, if you know what I mean. I was hoping to recruit Mark into the Pee Wee division. I heard from some of the neighborhood boys that he could play.'

The woman's features untightened and she let her arms fall at her sides. 'Mark would have liked to have played, if he still lived here. He's a good little athlete. He played with my grandson all the time when he was living here.'

'That so.'

'Yes, they rode their bikes together day and night.'

Damn, thought Strange, I am good. His blood ticked the way it always did when he was getting close. He'd like to see Terry's face when he told him that, just as he had predicted, he had found the woman in one afternoon.

'You don't know how I can get in touch with Mark or his mother, do you?'

'No, I'm sorry. They left without a word.'

'And she hasn't called you or nothin' like that.'

'No. *She* hasn't.'

'What's that?'

'Well, Mark has called. He calls my grandson 'bout once a week or so. I think he must be lonely, wherever they're stayin' at.'

'So your grandson, he must call him back.'

'I don't allow Daniel to call out on our phone.'

'Oh.'

'But I think Mark called here a couple of days ago. Maybe I still have the number on the caller ID.'

Strange smiled. 'I sure would appreciate it if you'd check.'

In the small kitchen the woman handed Strange a cordless phone. He pressed the directory button and thumb-wheeled through the record of calls printed out, one by one, on a lit yellow screen. There were thirty old calls listed in the directory.

'I never think to erase them,' said the woman.

'Neither do I,' said Strange.

Strange found a number with the name Olivia B. Elliot printed above it. He copied the number onto his pad.

'Thank you,' said Strange.

The woman, ugly by anyone's standards but with a peculiar bright-eyed energy to her, looked up at Strange with admiration. 'You're doing the Lord's work helping these kids like you do, Mr Sonnett. Praise God!'

'Yes, ma'am,' said Strange, unable to meet her eyes. 'I better be on my way.'

In the car Strange phoned Janine.

'Derek, I didn't have any luck with the management company. Apparently she moved out without giving them any notice and she left no forwarding address.'

'That's okay. I got a phone number on her. You ready?'

Strange gave her the number. Over the years, Janine had cultivated contacts all over town. But her contact at the phone company was the most valuable. Strange sent Christmas cards out to all the people he did business with. A few of these cards contained gift certificates. At Christmastime, Strange sent Janine's contact at the phone company a Tower Records certificate along with a crisp one-hundred-dollar bill.

'I'm going to meet Devra Stokes,' said Strange. 'Call me on my cell when you get an address.'

Strange's cell rang as he parked in the lot of the strip center on Good Hope Road. Janine was on the line with Olivia Elliot's address. Strange wrote it down, thanked her, and cut the connection. Then he phoned Quinn.

'Terry, can you get out for a while?'

'I think Lewis can handle the shop.'

'Yeah, what else is a cat like Lewis gonna be doin' with his time? All right, write this down. Just need you to verify that she's at the address.'

Quinn took down the information. 'That's up around Lincoln Heights. Northeast, right?'

'Yeah, it's on the north side of East Capitol.'

'Took you, what, two hours to find her?'

'Some of it was lunch. And most of the rest was drive time.'

'You are one macho motherfucker.'

'And I drink the bad dude's brew.'

'Gonna make beaver boy happy.'

'He's gonna get some change back, too.'

'Why can't you take care of this yourself?'

'I got some more work down here in Anacostia. The character wit I called on today, on the Oliver thing.'

'I'll take care of it,' said Quinn.

Strange hit 'end' on his cell.

He looked through the window of the hair salon. Devra Stokes's little boy was holding on to her pants leg as she gathered up her things. Even his timing was on today. Sometimes, Strange thought, every thing just goes right.

7

Dewayne Durham checked himself in a full-length mirror hung crookedly on a nail pushed into a bullet hole in a plaster wall. He wore a new pair of jeans his mother had pressed for him and a Nautica shirt with a black-and-beige Hawaiian print. He wore a pair of black Jordans, the Penny style, on his feet, which picked up the black of the shirt real nice. He looked good and he looked strong. A little on the thin side, but that was his fun-house reflection in the cheap mirror, which one of his boys musta bought from Target or someplace like that. He'd have to talk to that boy. Wasn't no such thing as a bargain; you had to spend money to get nice things.

Trick mirror or no, he'd have to watch his weight, make sure he didn't go in the direction of one of those sad-sack motherfuckers, had no ass and got no respect. Like his half brother, Mario, had to be the saddest, most okeydoke-lookin' motherfucker in Ward 8. Mario'd be dead by now, picked off just for sport, if it wasn't known that he was kin to Dewayne.

'Your brother's out by your car,' said Bernard Walker, a.k.a. Zulu, Dewayne's next in command.

'Aiight, then,' said Dewayne, patting his hair, shaved nearly down to the scalp, one last time in the mirror before walking from the room. There was a mattress in the room, the mirror, and nothing else. Walker followed him down a narrow hall.

The house, a duplex on Atlantic Avenue in Washington Highlands, near 6th, was unfurnished except for some folding chairs and a couple of card tables where Dewayne's boys bagged up and bottled up their shit. Plywood filled the window frames. The house had radiators but no gas, and the electricity and water had been shut off long ago. The 600 Crew, Dewayne's outfit, used the house during the day to conduct their business, and also used it as a place to cut up, roll dice, play cards, and hang.

They passed an open door to the bathroom, where excrement,

urine, and paper clogged the toilet and filled half the tub. Dewayne's crew peed in the bathtub and sometimes they shit in it, and on occasion they hid their airtight, weighted bundles of marijuana and cocaine underneath the mess. Dewayne had figured that no police would stick his hand down in there, and he was right; the last time they'd been raided, the uniform had stood there for only a couple of seconds, hardly looking into the bathtub, gagging while he was shaking his head, and then walked out. Later, Dewayne would let some young boy with ambition fish out the product. The stench in the house didn't bother him or any of the fellas. Got so now they didn't even notice it.

Four boys were bagging up some chronic at a table in what used to be the dining room as Dewayne and Walker came down the stairs. Dewayne's New York connect had made a delivery the night before.

Walker had to bow his head at the foot of the stairway, since the ceiling there was kind of low. He had gotten the name Zulu partly because of his skin color, which was close to black, but mainly because of his height and build. He was six and a half feet tall and could throw a scare into Charles Oakley on a dark street. Walker was a feared enforcer down here in Anacostia. He was an unhesitant triggerman, but it was known that he could also go with his hands. It was said by Dewayne's rivals that Zulu Walker was the long hair on Samson's head. You cut it, and Dewayne Durham wouldn't be shit.

'Y'all gonna have it ready to go for the shift tonight?' said Dewayne.

'We good,' said a medium-skinned, handsome boy named Jerome Long, a.k.a. Nutjob, seated at the table. He made eye contact with his boy Allante Jones, a.k.a Lil' J, who was beside him. The two, equally tall, had come up together in Stanton Terrace. Both were fatherless. With one mother on a slow junk-ride down and another in and out of jail, they had been raised by Long's grandmother until she could no longer handle them. To this day they were rarely seen apart.

An electronic scale sat on the table along with boxes of zip lock bags of various sizes purchased at Price Club. Pounds of marijuana rested at the feet of the boys in grocery store paper bags. A beat box, running on batteries and playing an old Northeast Groovers go-go PA tape, sat beside the table on the floor. Another boy stood by the window frame at the front of the dining room, looking through a quarter-size hole punched out of the plywood, checking the street for police.

'My troops,' said Dewayne, giving them the verbal pat on the back he felt they needed but meaning it in his heart, too. Dewayne was only twenty-three and hadn't gone past the tenth grade, but he felt he knew more about business instinctively than those who went to those kind of schools had ivy growing up the walls. One thing he did know: a man, however big he believed himself to be, wasn't nothin' without his employees.

'We'll roll on back in a little while,' said Dewayne.

Jerome Long watched them go down a hall and through the kitchen. When he heard the back door open and shut he head-motioned to Allante Jones and the two of them got up from the table. They went back to the kitchen and looked out the window over the kitchen sink, the only window in the house that had not been boarded up.

'Check them out,' said Long, looking past Dewayne and Walker, on the concrete walk now, to the Yuma Mob members sitting on the back steps of a house on the other side of the alley.

'All bold and shit,' said Jones.

'I'm tired of sittin' at that table.'

'So am I.'

'You ready to make some noise, Lil' J?'

'Drama City.' Jones elaborately shook Long's hand. ''Bout time someone in this town remembered our names, too.'

Long forced a smile. He felt he had to talk this way sometimes, so his friend and the others would believe that he was hard. But he wasn't hard for real. He didn't want to kill no one, and he didn't want to die.

Going out the back door, Dewayne and Walker went down a concrete walk split with weeds cutting a small yard of dirt. Past the alley, where Mario stood leaning against Dewayne's Benz, Dewayne could see the fenced backyards of the street that ran parallel to Atlantic. About three houses down, on the back steps of another duplex, a group of boys sat drinking out of bags in the late-afternoon sun, listening to their own box, passing around a fat one and getting high. These were members of the Yuma Mob, headed up by Horace McKinley, who had risen under Granville Oliver, Phillip Wood, and them. Crazy boys, 'cause they were trying to make a rep, the worst kind. Especially those two cousins, the Coateses, who had come up from the South. Dewayne briefly locked eyes with one of them, because this was what he was expected to do, then kept walking toward his car.

Dewayne didn't sweat behind the competition. He expected them to be there. Shoot, you didn't go openin' no *Mac*Donald's, then get surprised when a Burger King moved in across the street. There was business enough for everyone down here, just so everyone knew their place and kept to it. That is, if you stayed on your strip. Once in a while, at night, if anyone was still down here, his boys would fire off a shot in the Yuma Mob's direction to let them know they were still around, and they'd fire one back. Turf etiquette: we're down and there's peace if we stay behind our imaginary lines. Even the square motherfuckers lived on these blocks, had payroll jobs and kids and shit, got used to the sound of occasional gunfire. Long as those boys didn't come into your house and start shittin' on your bed, then every thing would be cool.

'Little brother,' said Mario, stepping off the car.

Dewayne shook Mario's hand, hanging off a wrist you could circle with your thumb and pinkie, then pulled his older brother in for the standard half-hug. To say Mario was thin was to say that Kobe had a little bit of game. Mario was famine-in-Africa kind of thin. You saw a photo of him, you'd start sending money to that company on TV, claimed they could feed kids for eighty-nine cents a day.

'Zulu,' said Mario, 'how you been?'

Walker allowed him a nod. 'Twigs.'

It hurt Mario to hear Walker call him that name, but he managed to hold a friendly smile.

'What's up, son?' said Dewayne.

'Wanted to get up with you, D. Let you know I'm gettin' close to finding the girl.'

'Yeah?'

'Uh-huh. Hired me one of those private investigators to do it.'

'Okay. And what you gonna do then?'

'I'm gonna make it right.'

'You find her, you let me know where she at, *I'll* make it right.'

'Nah, man, this here is me.'

''Cause you can't be lettin' no bitch do you like she did, and I don't care how good that pussy was. She took me off, too, and I can't *have* none of that.'

'Said I'm gonna square it.'

'Don't tell me. *Show* me that you will.'

'We're kin,' said Mario. 'I won't let you down.'

Kin. Who would know it? thought Dewayne. Boy looked like a water rat ain't had nothin' to eat for, like, forever. They shared the same mother; that was true. Mario's father, a nothing by all accounts, had died in a street beef when Mario wasn't nothin' but a kid. He must have been one ugly man. Dewayne had never known his father. His mother, Arnice Durham, had claimed that he was handsome. He was doing a stretch, last Dewayne had heard, in some joint in Pennsylvania. Didn't mean shit to Dewayne anymore, if it did mean something to him to begin with. Whateva. Anyway, he had promised his mother he'd look after Mario, and there wasn't anything Dewayne wouldn't do for his moms.

Dewayne looked down at Mario. He reached into his pocket and pulled out a roll of bills. He handed a couple of twenties to Mario.

'Here you go,' said Dewayne. 'Go out and buy you some new stuff, don't look like last year. Shit's hangin' off you, boy. And Deion ain't even with the squad no more.'

Mario held up the bills. 'I'm gonna get this back to you, too, soon as I get myself situated with a job.'

Mario slid the bills into his pants pocket, alongside the Taurus, thinking, now I got some of the hundred back I gave to that Strange in Petworth, and it's right here next to my gun. It feels good.

'Okay, then. You need a ride somewhere?'

'Nah, man, I got my short right up there at the end of the alley.'

'I don't see no car.'

'It's down the street some.'

'Holler at you later,' said Dewayne.

Mario turned and walked away. Dewayne watched him hitch up his Tommys as he went down the alley.

'That boy ain't got no whip,' said Walker.

'I know it,' said Dewayne. 'I don't know who's more stupid, a man can't afford no car or a man who'd rather walk than admit it.'

Some kids on bikes had been circling them in the alley, not lingering but keeping within Dewayne's sight. They all knew who Dewayne Durham was. They were hoping to catch his eye in some way, get noticed. They were hoping, someday, to get in with him if they could.

'Hey, D,' said one of them, riding by, 'when you gonna put me on?'

Dewayne didn't answer. The one who had asked was bold on the outside but was hiding his insecurities and his fears. Dewayne had noticed how this one always backed down when someone called him on his words. The kid standing on the pegs of the back of the bike, that was a kid to look out for. He didn't speak too much, but when he did the other kids listened. And they stepped out of his way when he was walkin' toward them, too. He wasn't but eleven or twelve, but in a couple of years Dewayne would start him out as a lookout by the elementary school, across from the woods of Oxon Run, where he moved product at night. Give him the opportunity to rise up above all this.

'Yo, little man,' said Dewayne to the kid riding the pegs. 'Move that shit out the head of the alley so we can roll on out of here.'

The kid nodded and gave directions to the one steering the bike. They rode to the T of the side street and moved some old tires and trash cans placed there to discourage the police from entering the alley. Then they rode back and continued to circle the car. Dewayne held out a five-dollar bill to the kid on the pegs as he made a pass. The kid refused the tip with a short shake of his head. Another thing Dewayne liked about this one: he was looking toward the future. He was smart.

'Better go see Ulysses,' said Dewayne, head-motioning Walker toward his car. 'Told him we'd be out.'

Dewayne got under the wheel of the Benz, and Walker got in beside him. They drove slowly down the alley, the kids on the bikes following their path. Walker got PGC up on the radio. Soon he grew tired of the commercials and scanned down to KYS. They listened to the song, that Erick Sermon joint that sampled Marvin Gaye. Marvin was a D.C. boy originally, and anything had his voice in it was all right. Least they hadn't played this cut out, the way they liked to do.

'You think Mario's gonna fuck up?' said Walker after a while.

'Maybe he won't this time.'

Dewayne kept his eyes on the road and tried not to show that sick feeling he'd been having inside his stomach these days. Running a business was easy. Dealing with family, that was hard.

Horace McKinley stood in the back window of the house on Yuma and watched Dewayne Durham's Benz roll out the alley. McKinley, large like Biggie, looked even heftier today in his warm-up suit. He wore a large crucifix on a platinum chain that hung outside his shirt. He wore the latest And Ones on his feet. A four-finger ring, spelling YUMA in small diamonds set in gold, was fitted on his right hand.

McKinley's body filled the window's frame. Kids around the way called him Candyman when he was coming up, not from that horror movie but from that big fat actor whose heart went and blew up in his chest. McKinley was fat then, and he was still fat, but no one called him Candyman anymore.

He had been watching Dewayne Durham talking to that sad-ass, no-job-havin', retard-lookin' brother of his across the alley. If Horace had a brother like that he wouldn't claim him. But Dewayne was soft that way. That soft spot was gonna get him dead someday, he didn't look out.

Truth was, Dewayne didn't seem to have the fire no more to keep up what he'd got. McKinley'd seen the way Dewayne had cut his eyes away when one of the cousins, out on the back steps, had stared him down. It was cool not to look for trouble, but sometimes you had to give a little attitude just to wake up the troops. Bottom line was, these boys were in this shit to begin with for the drama, like the way boys used to be all eager and shit to go off to war. That's what most folks didn't understand. But Horace McKinley did. Once in a while you had to feed your boys some conflict, just to give them something to do.

A cell phone rang behind him. He heard his man Michael Montgomery, a.k.a. Monkey Mike, talk into the phone. Then Mike was beside him by the window, hitting the 'end' button on the cell.

'That was Inez over at your hair shop,' said Montgomery.

'He came back?'

Montgomery nodded. 'She say he looks like some kind of police. Drivin' a police-lookin' car, anyway. He's been sittin' in the parking lot waitin' on Devra. Look like she's fixin' to meet up with him, sumshit like that.'

Horace looked over at Montgomery, his arms longer than shit, his hands hanging down around his knees. How he got the name Monkey, Horace suspected. But he never had asked Montgomery to confirm it. Didn't serve no purpose, other than to rile his ass up. Monkey was loyal, but when he was fierce he was fiercer than a motherfucker, like someone went and crossed the wires and shit inside his head. At the same time, there was something soft behind his eyes, too. McKinley had never been able to figure that part of him out.

'Better keep an eye on her,' said McKinley.

'I'll get a couple fellas from out back.'

'Get the cousins,' said McKinley, and Montgomery went to the back steps, where James and Jeremy Coates were with the others, getting high.

McKinley mopped the sweat off his forehead as he watched through the window. Montgomery was out there now, telling the Coateses to get up and come with him. The two of them, had the same last name 'cause their fathers were brothers, stood like they were on springs. That's what McKinley liked, how ready those two always were. Course, they *were* a couple of stone 'Bamas, only having lived up here for the last two years. And they drove a 'Bama car, one of those Nissans, the 240SX, trying to be a Z but wasn't even close. But you didn't want your boys driving whips as nice as yours, anyway. They needed to see what you had and want it bad enough to work for it their own selves. Want it bad enough, up to a point.

Horace McKinley understood a lot of things about running a business. He had learned them, mostly, from Granville Oliver, and he had learned some from Phillip Wood. Granville Oliver wasn't comin' out, and maybe Phil wasn't either, but if they put Oliver down with a needle, that left Phil alive.

So he'd put his chips in with Phil. Stayed in contact with him, got him cash and cigarettes, and passed him messages through the guards at the Correctional Treatment Facility, the ones who took money to look the other way. And he kept an eye out here for those who could undermine Phillip Wood with regard to his upcoming testimony.

McKinley believed in staying on the winning side. Like every leader who had come to terms with the long-range prospects of being in the life, he knew this was going to end for him in one of two ways. Either he'd be got by one of his rivals or he'd go to prison. He might be doing time his own self someday, and if he was, he might be lookin' to Phil Wood for protection.

He had told all of this to Mike Montgomery when Mike had asked why they were going through all this trouble. Mike couldn't really see why they were looking after Wood when it was damn near certain that he would be in forever. The way McKinley explained it, Mike almost seemed to believe it. Almost. Anyway, Mike followed orders. He always had.

There *was* a good reason for McKinley's protection of Phil Wood, and it did have to do with McKinley's well-being. But he'd been told not to give Montgomery, or anybody else, the full, true story. Just like he'd been *told* to track Phil Wood's enemies while the Oliver trial was in effect. And you couldn't fight the ones who was doin' the tellin'. McKinley never did have much school, but he was smart enough to know that. Smart enough to do as he was told.

One thing he did know, and that was that Granville Oliver was as good as dead. So, regardless of his motivation, there wasn't no upside to gettin' behind Oliver. That was the other part about being a good businessman: you had to know who to stand with when things started to come apart.

8

Ashley Swann stood on the back deck of the house she shared with Ulysses Foreman, dragging on a Viceroy, tapping the ash into a coffee mug set on a wooden rail. In her other plump, pink hand was a glass of chardonnay. She wore a pair of silk pajama shorts, salmon colored with a matching top, and leopard-print slides on her feet. Her hair had a streak of black running through the part, but the remainder was blond with an orangish tint. There was a little bit of green in it, too, but that was from the chlorine in the Dream Dip, what they called the indoor pool at this cheap motel she and Ulee had stayed at in Atlantic City. Thank God the green was finally starting to fade.

Having a smoke with her white wine on the back deck was one of Ashley's true pleasures. She preferred to smoke outside rather than in the house, especially on nice days like this one, where she could listen to the birds and look into the woods that bordered their backyard. It reminded her of the tree line on the edge of her father's soybean farm down in Port Tobacco, where she had been raised.

Hard to believe that they were within a mile of Anacostia, just over the District line in Maryland, off Wheeler Road. Once you crossed that line there was even a country store, telling you, abruptly, that you'd left the city behind. Right past a Citgo gas station, not too far from the country store, was their place.

Ulysses had been smart, like he had been smart about so many things, when he'd bought this house right here, set back like it was in a stand of trees. Close to his business but protected. Made you feel like you were far away from the drama. You could even hear crickets chirping on summer nights, though those sounds were sometimes mixed with the occasional crack of gunshots riding up from Southeast, if the wind was right.

Even when she'd first got to know him, when he'd been a patrol cop and she'd been a dispatcher in 6D, Ulysses had talked about having a house in the country. All right, so this wasn't exactly the country. But he'd had ambition, unlike most men she'd known, including her husband, who was happy working on small motors and such. For Ulysses, the ambition was more than just talk. Since she'd met him, he had always got close to what he'd set his sights on. She loved that about him, that and his size. A woman could feel secure with a big, driven man like Ulysses Foreman.

He was coming through the rambler now, toward the back deck. She could hear his footsteps, large as he was, and now she was thinking, You should've changed up out of these pajamas, girl; he's gonna say something first thing.

'Damn, Ashley,' said Foreman, coming out into the open air. 'You ain't dressed yet?'

'Thought I'd ease into my day.'

'Well, you better ease your fine ass inside and get into some street clothes. I got a business meeting out here any minute.'

Ashley made a half turn, blowing out an exhale of smoke and smiling, giving him a look at her ass cheeks hanging out the bottom of those shorts.

'Don't you like the way I look in these, Ulee?'

Foreman took her in and felt his mouth go dry. Her hindparts were bigger than most, but that was the way he liked them. And with those dimples and wrinkles and shit, it looked like someone had thrown oatmeal onto the back of her thighs. She had some veins on her, too, like blue lightning bolts, back there. But you didn't see all that when you closed your eyes. Same thing went for her belly, and the shotgun-pellet-lookin' marks on her face, and her little upturned nose, didn't even look large enough to let the air in, to tell the truth. That switch on the bedside lamp was what he liked to call the Great Equalizer. You could excuse a lot with a woman who could buck like Ashley.

Lord, she had a set of big, full lips, too. Woman could suck a man's dick without touching her teeth to it, the way a dog gives love to a porterhouse bone. Okay, she wasn't fine by any stretch, nothin' you'd want to march around in front of your best boys. But there were things she did he'd never go looking for anywhere else. Black women loved you like that for a night; a white woman, though, once you gave her some of that good thing? They'd love you the Heatwave way: forever and a day.

'I do like those jammies on you, baby, you know I do.' Foreman pointed his chin toward the back door. 'But hurry up on in there, now, and get dressed.'

Ashley stubbed out her Viceroy in the cup. She had another sip of wine and hustled herself inside. Foreman found himself grinning. It was hard to get mad at her, and he was still up, anyway, having burned some of that hydro Mario had traded him. That smoke was nice.

Foreman checked his watch. Dewayne Durham would be showing up any minute.

He didn't care to do business here, what with the risk. But he made an exception for those who headed up the various factions in Southeast, especially the leaders of the largest ones. What with Granville Oliver gone, there were plenty of players vying for the action now. Dewayne Durham, from the 600 Crew, and Horace McKinley, holding the Yuma Mob together, had to be the top two. They expected to be treated right, to have their meets down in his basement, sitting in comfortable chairs, having a sip of something, instead of in some car parked out on the street. Having them over the house was worth the risk. Business was good.

Oliver had been his first hookup. He'd started taking payoff money from Oliver when he, Foreman, had been a cop. It was about then that Foreman had seen a way to make big money for real. His years as a police officer had given him insights into the criminal mind, and he'd learned the mechanics of illegal gun sales, straw buys and the like, the same way. Oliver had been his first customer, and his best up until the time the Feds busted him on those RICO charges.

But even with Oliver and his boys put away, there would always be a market down here. This new breed of hard boys comin' up, they all wanted shiny new guns, the same way they wanted nice whips. And the turnover was high, on account of you couldn't hold on to any one crime-gun too long. Long as there was poverty, long as there wasn't no good education, long as there wasn't no real opportunity, long as kids down here had no fathers and were looking to belong to something, then there was gonna be gangs and a need for guns. This textbook he'd had called it supply-and-demand economics. Foreman had learned about that during the one semester of courses he'd taken at the community college over in Prince George's County.

So he'd quit the force, citing the burnout effect of the job. Six months later, Ashley Swann, who he'd been doing since he met her, resigned from the MPD as well. She left her white-boy husband, a lawn mower repairman, no joke, and moved into this house with him. Ashley hadn't worked a day since.

She didn't need to work. She didn't need to get out of those pajamas or put her wineglass down, she didn't want to. Foreman was making good money moving guns around, and he worked about twenty hours a week as a security guard on top of that, just so he could show something to the IRS come tax time.

Course, he wasn't the only dealer in this part of the city. But he was the quality man. He didn't sell Davis or Lorcin or Hi-Point or Raven, none of those cheap-ass guns project kids bought on their first go-round. He carried fine American, Austrian, and German pieces, pistols, mostly, and occasionally special-order stuff the young ones had seen in the gun mags and the movies, AKs and Calico autoloaders, carbines, and the like. He customized some of the guns himself. You could still buy a Hyundai down here, you wanted to, but he was the Benz dealer in this part of town. His goods were marked way up, but he had no problem moving them. Shit, the high price tag was a badge of honor for these kids, like bragging that you had spent a couple thousand on a Rolex watch or a clean grand on a set of rims.

Foreman had a couple of boys working for him. These boys rounded up young girls, just old enough and with no priors, to do the straw buys in the gun store over in Forestville on the Maryland side, and in Virginia, in these shops they had way down Route 1. They used junkies and indigents, too, long as they had no record. You had to be careful with the junkies, though. The 4473 had a question, asked if you used drugs, and if you got caught lying on a federal form after the trace, that was a felony. Filing off the serial number, that was another amateur play right there, something Foreman would never do. Another felony, good for an automatic five. It was the way police squeezed testimony out of suspects and got them to flip. As far as solving cases went, shaking down suspects to give up other suspects worked better than ballistics and forensics every time.

Another of Foreman's boys was a student at Howard who had been raised in Georgia. He made the 95 South run in his trap-car once a month to his hometown, where family and friends made purchases in the area on his behalf. This boy was putting himself through college with what Foreman was paying him. It was true that D.C. had a handgun ban, but its good neighbor states, especially those to the south, did not. So there wasn't no thing to getting a gun in the District. Simple as buying a carton of milk. And you didn't even need big money to do it. You could rent a gun or trade drugs to get one, or the community could chip in to buy one. What they called a neighborhood gun. In many of the Section 8s there was a pistol buried somewhere, could be got to quick, in a shoe box. Most everyone knew where that shoe box was.

It was an easy business to be in and manage. Situation wasn't getting any better for these kids, so there would always be a need, and the money continued to flow in. So why was Foreman feeling those burning pains in his chest? Had to be the start of an ulcer, or what he imagined an ulcer to be. It was because he had been a cop, and in that time he had learned something about criminals, and being a criminal himself now, this is what he knew: his time was gonna come. No one in this game, be he gun dealer or gang leader or dope salesman, lasted forever. It could be the police or someone younger, stronger, or crazier than you, but the fact remained that someone was going to take you down.

It was kinda like playing the stock market. You had to know when to sell, not let greed make you stay in too long. He knew he had to get out, and get his woman out the clean way, too. The question was, how?

Foreman heard some heavy bass as a car pulled off the road, came down his long asphalt entrance, and slowed, arriving at the circular drive that fronted the house. That would be Dewayne Durham. Prob'ly had that big-ass sucker they called Zulu with him, too.

Foreman slipped back into the house and went down the stairs off the kitchen. He hoped Ashley had got herself dressed by now. She could show Durham in, and his personal giant, too.

Foreman had spread out several pistols on the felt of his pool table down in the recreation room of the rambler. He had bought a ring once for Ashley, and this was the way the jeweler had presented it to him, on a square of red felt. When Foreman had chosen his pool table at that wholesale store he went to, he had gone for the red, remembering how he had been sold on the ring. This was the way he presented all his goods.

Five guns were set in a row, turned at a forty-five-degree angle to the line of the table. Above them were boxes of ammunition, 'bricks,' the contents of which fit the guns. A Heckler & Koch 9mm automatic was at the head of the row. A Sig Sauer .45 was next, followed by a stainless steel Colt of the same caliber, then a Glock 17. The Glock was the MPD sidearm and, Foreman knew, was always a sure sale. The young ones wanted what the police carried, nothing less. At the end of the row was a Calico M-110 auto pistol, a multiround, 22-caliber chatter gun. It was generally ineffective and hard to conceal but had recently gained popularity on the street due to its round capacity and exotic look.

'That's pretty right there,' said Dewayne Durham. He was pointing to the Colt .45 set between the Sig and the drab plastic Glock. Foreman had placed the gun there strategically, knowing it would stand out.

'You like it, huh?'

'What kinda grips you got on there?'

'That's rosewood,' said Foreman. 'The checkered style. Ordered them from Altamont and put 'em on my own self. Looks good against the stainless, right?'

Durham picked up the gun, felt its weight in his hand. He racked the slide and dry-fired at the wall. He placed the gun back on the table.

'Pretty,' repeated Durham, Foreman knowing right then that he had made a sale. 'That's like that gun you got, right?'

'Same gun,' said Foreman. 'Only I got the ivory grips on mine.'

'You had it long?'

'Just came in. Got bought at a store down in Virginia and changed hands once since. Never even been fired.'

'How you know?'

'Smell it.'

'Okay, then. I'm gonna take that Glock, too, if it's clean.'

'You could eat off it, dawg.'

'Aiight, then.'

'What about that?' said Bernard Walker. Foreman had been watching the tall man's eyes and knew he was talking about the Calico.

'Brand-new,' said Foreman.

'Where the bullets come from?'

'Right up top there, why it's long like it is. They call it a helical feed.'

'What you need that for, Zulu?' said Durham. 'Shit ain't even, like, practical.'

'I guess I don't need it,' said Walker. 'I was just askin' after it, is all.'

Durham said to Walker, 'I'm buyin' you the Glock.' To Foreman he said, 'How much for the two?'

Foreman closed his eyes like he was counting it up. He had already decided on a price.

'Sixteen for the both of them is what I'd normally charge. With those grips and all, price got up.'

'Sixteen hundred for two guns?' Durham made a face like he had bitten into a lemon. 'Damn, boy, you gonna make me pay list price, too. What, you see me pull up in my new whip and the price went up? Or I got the word *sucker* stamped on my forehead and nobody done told me.'

'I said it's what I'd *normally* charge. I'm gonna make it fifteen for you. And I'll throw in the bricks.'

Durham looked down at his Pennys. He had made up his mind, but he was going to let Foreman wait. They both knew it was part of the process.

Durham looked up. 'You got anything to drink up in this piece?'

Foreman smiled. 'I'll throw that in, too.'

Foreman got them a couple of beers from the short refrigerator he kept running behind his bar and opened one for himself. He brought them frosted pilsner glasses he stored in the fridge for his guests. They sat in leather chairs grouped around a leather couch studded with nail heads, a glass-topped table in the center of the arrangement. Italian leather on the couch, Durham guessed, soft as it was. Foreman did have nice things. Why wouldn't he, with the prices he charged?

The room was paneled in knotty pine. Foreman had always wanted a room like this, a room that he imagined a secure man would own, and now he had it. To him, the wood had the smell of success. There was the pool table and a deep-pile carpet, wall-to-wall, and a wide-screen Sony with a flat picture tube, the best model they made, with a DVD player racked beneath the set. His stereo, with the biggest speakers they had in the store, was first-class. He had a gas-burning fireplace in here, too, and the bar with the imitation marble top. He was all hooked up. He'd rather sit down here and catch a game than go out to the new football stadium or the MCI Center, matter of fact. He'd rather sit down here and chill than do just about anything else.

Durham took a taste of beer. He had a look around the room. Looked like some old man, wore his pants up high, owned it. Foreman was playing some old-school stuff on the stereo, Luther Vandross from when Luther could sing, had some weight behind his voice. Music from the eighties, that fit this place, too.

'Saw your woman,' said Durham, after enjoying a long sip of beer. 'She looked good.'

'Thank you, man,' said Foreman.

It made Durham kinda sick just to think about her. Why it was, he wondered, that black men who went for white women always went for the most fugly ones. When a white boy had a black woman she always seemed to be fine. You could bet money on that shit damn near every time.

Foreman's woman, she had come to the door in some JCPenney's-lookin' outfit, no makeup on her face and wine breath coming out her big mouth. Looked like she just dragged her elephant ass out of bed; must have remembered that it was feeding time, sumshit like that. Talkin' about, 'How you two be doin'?' A big-ass, ugly-ass white girl trying to talk black, her idea of it, anyway, from ten years ago.

'Yeah,' said Durham, 'she looked good.'

'She's gettin' her rest,' said Foreman.

Foreman took a Cuban out of a wooden box on the glass table

before him, clipped it with a silver tool set beside the box, and lit the cigar. He got a nice draw going and sat back.

'Saw your brother, Mario, today,' said Foreman casually, as if it had just come into his mind.

'So did I,' said Durham. 'Just a little while ago.'

'This was in the morning,' said Foreman. 'I had a little transaction with him.'

'Yeah?'

'No big thing. Rented him a gun. Traded him five days' worth for a little bit of hydro he was holding.'

Walker glanced over at Durham. No one said anything for a while, as Foreman had expected. But he wanted his business with Twigs to be up front, on the outside chance that some kind of problem came up later on.

Durham's eyes went a little dark. 'Now why you want to do that? I'd get you some smoke, you needed it.'

'Well, for some reason, Mario's always got the best chronic.' Foreman chuckled. 'The older I get, seems I need the potent shit to get me high.'

'What, mine don't get you up?'

'The truth? It hasn't lately. When Mario lays some on me, I trip behind it.'

'Cause what I give to Mario, I give to him out of my private stash, thought Durham. And you know this.

Durham exhaled slowly, trying to ignore the ache in his stomach. 'What he needs a gun for, anyway?'

'Said he was lookin' to make an impression on someone. I didn't get the feeling he was gonna use it.'

'He ain't say nothin' to me.'

'Boy's harmless, though, right?'

Durham cut his eyes away from Foreman. 'He ain't gonna do nothin', most likely.' He did believe this in his heart.

'What I thought, too. Now look, he didn't want me to tell you. Didn't want to worry you or y'all's moms. But I just thought it might be better if you knew.'

'Okay, then.'

'We all right, dawg?'

Durham nodded. 'Yeah, we're good.'

'We better be gone,' said Walker, placing his empty pilsner on the table.

'Gotta see the troops get out for the night,' said Durham.

'I'll get you a bag for your guns,' said Foreman.

Durham pulled a roll of cash from out of his jeans. 'Fourteen, right?'

'Fifteen,' said Foreman, standing from his chair.

'Why you want to do me like that?' said Durham, but Foreman was ignoring him, already walking toward a side room where he kept his supplies.

Foreman stood on the stoop of his house, watching the Benz go down the drive. He was under a pink awning that Ashley loved but he hated. It was a little thing, though, one of them concessions you make to a woman, so he told her that he liked the awning, too.

He had played it right, telling Dewayne about Mario and the gun. Now there wouldn't be no misunderstanding later on. If Dewayne didn't like it, well, next time he'd give him some of that good smoke he kept in the family. Everything was negotiation in this business, nothing but a game.

'It go okay?' said Ashley, coming up behind him with a fresh glass of wine in her hand.

'Went good.' Foreman put his arm around her waist, looked her over, then kissed her neck. 'Those boys were noticing you.'

'You jealous?'

'I don't think you're goin' anywhere.'

'You got that right, boyfriend.'

'I better keep an eye on you, though. Fine as you look, someone might try to steal you out from under me.'

'That's where they'd have to steal me from, too.'

Foreman kissed Ashley on the mouth. She bit his lower lip, and they both laughed as he pulled away.

9

'You ever been back in there?' said Strange, looking through the windshield to the brick wall bordering St. Elizabeth's.

'Once,' said Devra Stokes. 'This girl and me jumped the wall when we was like, twelve.'

'I interviewed a witness there, a couple of years back.'

'Hinckley?'

'Naw, not Hinckley.'

'I was just playin' with you.'

'I know it.'

They sat in the Caprice, across from the institution, eating soft ice cream from cups that they had purchased at the drive-through of McDonald's. Juwan, Devra's son, sat in the backseat, licking the drippings off a cone.

'It was this dude, though,' said Strange, 'had pleaded insanity on a manslaughter charge, we thought he might have some information on another case. He seemed plenty sane to me. Anyway, we sat on a bench they have on the grounds, faces west, gives you a nice look at the whole city. This is the high ground up here. Those people they got in there, they got the best view of D.C.'

'I wouldn't mind getting taken care of like they take care of those folks in there. You ever think like that?'

'It's crossed my mind, in the same way that it would be easy to be old. Walk around wearing the same raggedy sweater every day, don't even have to shave or mind your hair. But I don't want to be an old man. And I wouldn't want to be locked up anywhere, would you?'

'Sometimes I think, you know, not to have all this pressure all the time . . . not to have to think about how I'm gonna make it for me and Juwan, just for a while, I mean. That would be nice.'

'I know it's got to be rough, raising him as a single parent,' said Strange.

'I got bills,' said Devra.

'Phil Wood's not taking care of you and your little boy?'

'Juwan's not his. Juwan's father—'

'Mama!'

Devra turned her head. The boy's ice cream had dripped and some of it had found its way onto the vinyl seat. Devra used the napkin in her hand to clean the boy's face, then wipe the seat.

'Mama,' said Juwan, 'I spilt the ice cream.'

'Yes, baby,' said Devra, 'I know.'

'Don't worry about that,' said Strange. 'You see that red cushion back there? My dog sleeps on that, and he has his run of the car. So I ain't gonna worry about no ice cream. This here is my work vehicle, anyway.'

'I'm sorry.'

'Ain't no thing,' said Strange. 'Look here, what about Juwan's father, then?'

Devra shrugged. 'He's in Ohio now. They had him incarcerated out at Lorton, but they moved him a few months ago. Once a week, me and Juwan used to take the Metrobus, the one they ran special from the city, out there to see him. But now, with him so far and all, I don't think Juwan's even going to remember who his father is.'

Strange nodded at the familiar story. A young man fathered a child, then went off to do his jail time, his 'rite of passage.' Lorton, the local prison in northern Virginia, was slowly being closed down, its inhabitants moved to institutions much farther away. Lorton's proximity to the District had allowed prisoners and their families to remain in constant contact, but that last tie between many fathers and their children was ending now, too. Juwan's future, like the futures of many of the children who had been born into these circumstances, did not look promising.

'Can't Phil help you out with some money?'

'Phil's got no reason to give me money. He had a whole rack of girls. I was just one.'

'But he paid you to stay away from court on that brutality rap.'

'That was a one-time thing.'

'I'm gonna need you to talk about it with me, you don't mind.'

'Talk about what?'

'Well, the fact that he was beatin' up on you, for one. Plus, the time you filed the original charges was about the same time some of the murders went down that they got Granville up on. Including the murder of his own uncle. So I need to know, did Phil ever discuss any of those murders with you? Or did you hear anything else about those murders from anyone close to Phil or Granville around that time?'

'I got no reason to hurt Phil.'

'It's not about hurtin' Phil. The prosecution's gonna put him up on the stand to testify against Granville. What the defense does, they want to give a complete picture of the prosecution's witness to the jury. If Wood was the kind of man who would take his hand to a woman, that's something the jury ought to know. Throws a shadow, maybe, over the stuff he's saying about Granville.'

'How's that gonna change anything? Ain't nobody denying that they were in the life.'

'True. But that's how it works. Their side claims something and our side tries to refute it. Or make it more complicated than it really is.'

'Sounds like bullshit to me.'

'It is. But I'm still gonna need your help.'

'I don't know.' Devra looked out her open window, away from Strange. 'I don't want to get back into all that. I moved away from it, hear? I got my little boy . . .'

Strange turned his body so that he faced her. 'Look here. They're gonna try and put Granville to death. Some folks feel that only God gets to decide that. And a lot of folks in this city, they don't see how killing another young black man is gonna solve any of the problems we got out here.'

'Granville did his share of killin', I expect.'

'Maybe so, Devra. But this is about something more than just him.' Strange touched her hand. 'It's important. I need you to talk to me, young lady, tell me what you know.'

'I gotta think on it,' she said.

'Give me your phone number and the address where you're stayin' at, you don't mind.'

Stokes did this, and Strange wrote the information down. He withdrew his wallet and opened it.

'Let me give you my business card,' said Strange. 'Got a bunch of different numbers on it; you can reach me anytime.'

Strange turned the ignition and drove the Caprice off the McDonald's property. An E-series Benz and a beige 240SX followed him out of the parking lot and down the hill of Martin Luther King.

Strange dropped Devra Stokes by her old Taurus in the lot of the salon on Good Hope Road. He waited for her to strap Juwan into a car seat and get herself situated and drive away. He noticed the older woman who owned the shop staring at him through the plate glass window. And he noticed the two cars that had been following him since back at the McDonald's idling behind him, about a hundred yards and several rows of spaces back.

Strange drove out onto Good Hope. In his rearview he studied the vehicles, a black late-model Benz, tricked out with aftermarket wheels, and a beige Nissan bomb, the model of which he could not remember but which he recognized as the poor man's Z.

Strange went down Good Hope and cut left onto 22nd Place without hitting his turn signal. The Benz fell in behind the Nissan and they stayed on his tail. He took another left on T Place and did not signal; the other cars did the same. T Place became T Street after a bit, and he took that to Minnesota Avenue. They were still there, about five car lengths back. Okay, so now he knew they were following him. But why?

Down near Naylor Road, Strange slowed down, moved into the middle lane, and came to a stop at a red light. Cars were parked along the curb to his right. The Benz stopped behind him and the Nissan pulled up to his left. He moved his car up into the crosswalk, as there were no cars there to block his exit. If he needed to make a move he could do so now. The Nissan did the same and pulled up even with his driver's-side door.

Could be this was a trap. If that was the case, the rider on the Nissan's passenger side would be the shooter. But Strange wasn't ready to look over at them yet.

In the rearview, Strange could read the front tag on the Benz and he committed it to memory. He said it aloud so that he would get used to the sound of the sequence, and he said it aloud again. He saw a fat young man in the driver's seat, a ring across the fingers that were gripping the wheel. Another young man, with no expression on his face at all, sat beside him.

He heard a whistle and looked to his left. Two young men with similar features, thick noses and bulgy eyes, were looking straight at him. A bunch of little tree deodorizers hung from their mirror, and music played loudly in their car. The bass of it rattled their windows. The one in the passenger seat grinned at him, raised his empty hand, and made a quick slashing gesture across his own throat.

Strange was startled by the loud beep of a car horn. He looked in his rearview and saw the fat man in the Benz making the gun sign with one hand. He pointed the flesh gun in the direction of Strange. And then Strange realized that the fat man was pointing his finger over the roof of Strange's car, at the traffic light in the intersection. Strange looked ahead at a green light; the fat man was telling him that the light had changed and it was time to move on through.

Strange gave the Caprice gas. He heard the fading laughter of the two on his left under the throb of their music as he went down the road. The Benz and the Nissan pulled out of the intersection as well but turned right on Naylor Road and vanished from his sight.

It might have been paranoia, a middle-aged man thinking negative things about a group of young black Anacostians who had the look of being in the life. Strange was angry at himself, and a little ashamed, for the assumptions he had made. But he had also been living in this very real world for a long time. He wrote down the plate number that he had memorized in the spiral notebook he kept by his side.

Strange had first met Robert Gray, not yet a teenager, at Granville Oliver's opulent house in Prince George's County the previous fall. Oliver had pulled Gray out of a bad situation in the Stanton Terrace dwellings and had been grooming him for a role in the business he was still running at the time. When Oliver had been arrested and incarcerated, Strange had promised Granville, and had made a promise to himself, that he would look after the boy and try to put him on the right path.

But it hadn't been an easy task. There was the geography problem, in that Strange lived in Northwest and Gray's people were down in Southeast, so he couldn't see the boy all that much. And Strange wasn't about to take him under his own roof, especially now that he was dealing with having a new family of his own; Janine and his stepson, Lionel, were his first priority, and he was determined to do everything he could to make that work. So Strange had seen that Gray was put up with his aunt, the sister to his mother, who was doing a stretch for grand theft and assault, her third fall. Through Granville Oliver's lawyer, Raymond Ives, Strange had arranged for a monthly payment to be made to the aunt, Tosha Smith, as one would pay foster parents for their services. The money was Granville Oliver's.

Tosha Smith lived in a unit of squat redbrick apartment buildings on Stanton Road. Strange parked on the street and walked up a short hill, across a yard of weed and dirt, past a swing set where young children and their mothers had congregated. One girl, wearing a shirt displaying the Tweety Bird cartoon character and holding a baby against her hip, looked no older than fifteen. Strange navigated around two young men sitting on the concrete steps of Smith's unit and ascended more stairs to her apartment door.

Tosha Smith, fright-time thin with a blue bandanna covering her hair, opened at his knock. Her initial expression was adversarial, but in a practiced, unemotional way, as if this were her usual greeting for every unexpected visitor who came to her door.

'Tosha,' said Strange.

'Mister Strange.' Her face softened, but not by much. Strange had visited her many times, but the look of relaxation that came with familiarity did not seem to be in her repertoire.

A grown man, on the thin side, with bald patches in his hair, sat on the couch playing a video game, staring at the television screen against the wall as a cigarette burned in an ashtray before him. He did not look away from his game or acknowledge Strange in any way.

Even in the doorway, Strange could take in the unpleasant odor of the apartment, not unclean, exactly, but closed up, airless, with the smell that always reminded him of an unminded refrigerator. And every time he had come by it was dark here, the curtains drawn over shuttered blinds. So it was today.

'You wanna come in?' said Tosha.

'Robert in there with you?'

'He's out playin' with his friends.' Tosha noticed something cross Strange's face and she grinned lopsidedly, showing him grayish teeth. 'Don't worry, I always know where he's at. We don't allow him to go more than a block or two away from here.'

'We?'

Tosha jerked her head over her shoulder. 'I got Randolph stayin' here with me now. Boy needs a man around, don't you think?'

'If it's right.'

'You don't have to worry about that. Randolph keeps him in line, tells Robert to mind his mouth when he gets the way young boys get. Randolph'll go ahead and smack the black out him, his tongue gets too bright.'

Strange could hear a baby crying from back in the apartment. He shifted his feet. 'You say Robert's in the vicinity?'

'You'll find him out there somewheres close, ridin' his bike. Tell him to get in here before dark comes, hear?'

Why don't you drag your junkie ass on out here and tell him yourself? thought Strange. But he only nodded and went back down the stairs.

'I'll be lookin' for my money this month,' said Tosha to his back.

Strange kept going, finding relief in the crisp spring air as he made his way outside. The sun had begun to drop behind the neighboring buildings, and shadows had spread upon the apartment grounds.

Strange circled the block in his car, then widened his search to the adjacent streets. He spotted Robert Gray standing around with a group of boys, most of them older, on the corner of another apartment complex. The boys, some wearing wife-beaters with the band of their boxer shorts showing high above the belt line of their jeans, studied Strange as he got out of his curbed Chevy. Gray said something to one of the boys, got on his bike, and rode it over to Strange, now leaning against the front quarter panel of his car out in the street.

'How you doin', Robert?'

Gray's eyes went past Strange to somewhere down the street. 'I'm all right.'

'Look at me when I talk to you, son.'

Gray fixed his gaze on Strange. He had intelligent eyes, and he was polite enough. But Strange could not recall ever seeing him smile.

'How's school going?'

Gray shrugged. 'We nearly out. Ain't all that much left to do.'

'Your aunt and them treating you okay?'

'I get along with 'em.'

'The boyfriend, too? He's not eatin' up your share of the food, is he?'

'Him and my aunt don't eat all that much, you want the truth.' Gray cocked an eyebrow. He was a handsome boy, one of those who already had the features of a man. 'You see Granville?'

'Saw him today. He was asking after you.'

'They gonna kill him?'

'I don't know. Whatever happens, it doesn't look like he's ever gonna come out of jail. It's important you know this. All that bling-bling you and your friends always talking about and lookin' up to, the whips and the platinum and the Cristal, you get in the life, it always goes away. Forever, you understand?'

Gray half nodded and quickly looked off to the group of boys standing on the corner. Strange felt impotent then. To Gray he wasn't much more than a fool, and an old man in the bargain. This much he knew.

'Look here,' said Strange. 'You still up for my football camp?'

'Yeah, I'll play.'

'I hear you *can* play.'

'You *know* I can.'

'We're gonna start the camp in August. Now, all the boys who play for me, they need to show me their last report card from the school year. So I want you to finish up strong.'

'I'll do all right. But how I'm gonna get over there to where y'all practice?'

'I'll work that out,' said Strange, realizing that he hadn't figured it out yet. But he would. 'All right then, why don't you get on home before it gets dark.'

'I will, in a little while.'

'Take care of yourself, young man.'

Gray wheeled off on his bike and joined his friends. Strange got back in his car.

Strange phoned Quinn from his cell as he drove across Anacostia. Quinn told him that he was outside the address given on Olivia Elliot, and he was getting ready to confirm. He asked Strange for the son's name. Strange gave it to him and told Quinn that if he needed him he could reach him at Janine's house, which he had not yet gotten used to calling home.

Strange was looking forward to holding his woman and talking to his stepson, sitting at the dinner table, just being with the ones he loved. Seeing the things he saw out here every day, he figured he deserved a couple of hours of that kind of peace.

He turned the radio on and moved the dial to PGC. The Super Funk Regulator was on the air, talking to a woman who had called in from her car.

'Where you at right now?' asked the DJ.

'I'm on Benning Road, headed home from work.'

'Who you goin' to see?'

'My son Darius,' said the woman giggling, obviously hyped to be on the radio and live. 'He's ten years old.'

'You have a good one,' said the DJ. 'Thanks for rollin' with a brother.'

'Thanks for lettin' a sister roll.'

Strange smiled. He did love D.C.

10

It was Terry Quinn's habit to keep a paperback western on the car seat beside him when he was on a job, since there were often long stretches during surveillance when he found himself with little to do. Today he had brought along *They Came to Cordura*, an out-of-print novel by Glendon Swarthout, from the used-book store where he worked in downtown Silver Spring. Sitting in his vintage hopped-up Chevelle, looking at the group of boys playing outside the building where Olivia Elliot had apparently settled, he didn't think he'd have that extra reading time to kill.

He was on a street numbered in the high fifties, in the neighborhood of Lincoln Heights, a residential mix of single-family homes and apartments at the forty-five-degree angle of border close to the Maryland line. This portion of the city, on the east side of the Anacostia River, was called Far Northeast, just as Anacostia was known as Far Southeast by many who lived in that part of town.

Nearby was the W. Bruce Evans Middle School. Administrators there had recently sent a group of 'problem students' to the D.C. Jail to be strip-searched in front of prisoners, one of whom had masturbated in plain sight as he watched the kids disrobe. Some District school official had apparently decided to reenact an unauthorized version of Scared Straight. Quinn wondered how that 'strategy' would have settled with the parents of problem kids out in well-off Montgomery County or in D.C.'s mostly white, mostly rich Ward 3. But this controversy would fade, as this was a part of the city rarely seen by commuters and generally ignored by the press, out of sight and easily forgotten.

Lincoln Heights was not all that far from Anacostia, a couple of bus rides away. If Olivia Elliot was trying to put some distance between herself and Mario Durham, she had made only a half-hearted effort. But Quinn wasn't surprised. Washingtonians were parochial like that;

even those who were running from something didn't like to run too far.

He grabbed a blank envelope from the glove box and neatly wrote 'Olivia Elliot' across its face. He folded a sheet of blank notebook paper, slipped it inside the envelope, and sealed it. Then he got out of his car, locked it down, and crossed the street.

There were plenty of kids, girls as well as boys, out of doors, though the sun had dropped and dusk had arrived. School was nearly done for the year, and if there was any parental supervision to begin with, it was even more lax this time of year. As Quinn went down the sidewalk toward the kids he saw rows of buzzers in the foyers of the attached homes, indicating that these houses had been subdivided into apartments. An alley split the block halfway, leading to a larger alley that ran behind the row of houses. Not unusual, as nearly every residential street in town had an alley running behind it, another layout quirk unique to D.C.

Quinn stopped close to the address Strange had given him, where four boys had built a ramp from a piece of wood propped up on some bricks in the street. A kid on a silver Huffy with pegs coming out of the rear axle circled the group.

'Hey,' said Quinn. 'Any of you guys know where I can find Mark Elliot?'

A couple of the boys snickered and looked Quinn's way, but none of them replied. The kid on the bike pulled a wheelie and breezed by.

'He might be new in the neighborhood,' added Quinn.

They continued to ignore him, so he walked on. He saw some girls on the next corner, one of them sitting atop a mailbox, and he decided to see if he would fare better with them.

He heard, 'Hey, you guys!' in a straight, white voice, and then, 'He might be new in the neighborhood!' in the same kind of voice, and then he heard the boys' laughter behind him. Quinn felt his blood rise immediately; it was hard for him to handle any kind of disrespect. He wondered, as he always did, if he would have been cracked on down here, like these kids were cracking on him now, if he were black.

'Mister,' said a voice behind him, and he turned. It was the kid on the bike, who had followed him down the street.

'Yeah.'

'You lookin' for Mark?'

Quinn stopped walking. 'Are you Mark?'

The kid pulled up alongside him and stopped the bike. He was young, lean, with an inquisitive face. 'Your face is all pink. You all right?'

'I'm fine.'

'You *mad*, huh?'

'No, I'm all right.'

'Shoot, they're only messin' with you because you're white.'

'Y'all think there's something wrong with that?'

'I don't know. It's just, we don't see too many white dudes around here, is all it is. And when we do see 'em, they act like they scared.'

'I'm not scared,' said Quinn. 'Do I look scared to you?'

'Yeah, okay. But why you lookin' to get up with me?'

'You're Mark Elliot, then.'

'Yeah, I'm Mark.'

'I was looking for your mother.' Quinn held up the envelope. 'I gotta give her this.'

'You a police?'

'No.'

'A bill collector, right? 'Cause, listen, she left out of here a while ago and I don't know where she's at.'

'She's gonna be back soon?'

'I prob'ly won't see her. I'm gonna be watchin' the Lakers game tonight over at my uncle's. He's fixin' to pick me up right about now.'

'Listen, Mark. I'm not looking to hurt her; I'm trying to give her something. She entered a contest. A raffle, you know what that is?'

'Like they do at church.'

Quinn nodded. 'She won a prize.'

'What kind of prize?'

'I'm not allowed to say what it is to anyone but her. And I need to put this in her hand.'

'She's out gettin' a pack of cigarettes.'

'Thought you didn't know where she was.'

'Just give it here,' said Mark, reaching out his hand. 'I'll make sure she gets it.'

'I can't. It's against the rules. I'll drop it by later.' Quinn eye-motioned toward a redbrick structure, two houses back. 'I know where you live. You're up on the third floor, right?'

'We in two-B,' said Mark, and his features dropped then. He knew he had made a mistake. He kicked ineffectually at some gravel in the street. 'Dag,' he said under his breath.

'I'll come back,' said Quinn. 'Thanks, Mark.'

Quinn began to walk quickly back toward his car. The kid followed on his bike.

'What's your name?' said Mark, cruising alongside Quinn.

'Can't tell you that,' said Quinn, who kept up his pace. 'It's against the rules.'

'I told you mines.'

Quinn didn't answer. He went by the group of boys in the street, who appeared not to notice him at all this time, and he put his key to the driver's lock of his car.

'Is it fast?' said Mark, who had stopped his bike and was standing behind Quinn.

'Yeah, it's fast,' said Quinn, opening the door.

'You live out in Maryland, huh?'

Quinn figured the boy had made his plates. Quinn kept his mouth shut and started to get into his car.

'You don't want to talk to me no more, huh?'

Quinn turned and faced the boy. 'Look, you're a good kid. I'd like to talk to you some more and all that, but I gotta go.'

'If I'm good, then why'd you want to go and do me like you did?'

'Like how?'

'You tricked me, mister.'

'Listen, I gotta get goin'.'

Quinn settled in the driver's seat and closed the door. He looked once more at the kid, who was staring at him with disappointment, something worse than anger or hate.

Quinn cranked the engine and rolled down the block. He found East Capitol and took it west.

Just before Benning Road, Quinn pulled over beside St. Luke's Church and let the Chevelle idle. He found Mario Durham's cell number in his notebook and punched the number into the grid of his own cell. Mario Durham answered on the third ring.

'Mario,' said Quinn. 'It's Terry Quinn, Strange's partner. I got an address for you.'

'Damn, boy, that was fast.'

'I know it,' said Quinn, his jaw tight. 'Write this down.'

Minutes later, driving across Benning Bridge over the Anacostia River, he noticed that his fingers were white and bloodless on the wheel.

Quinn knew, as every seasoned investigator knew, that to find a parent you always went first to the kid. Relatives and neighbors rarely gave up another adult to an investigator or anyone who looked like a cop. But kids did, often without thought. Kids were more trusting, and you used that trust. If you were in this game, and it was a game of sorts, this was one of the first things you learned.

So Quinn was doing his job. But he couldn't get Mark Elliot's face, his look of disappointment, out of his head. Quinn should have been up with the buzz of success. Instead he was ashamed.

Mario Durham noticed that the letter *J* had fallen off the word *Jordan*, printed real big across one of his sneakers, while he was riding the bus down Minnesota Avenue. He had those red, black, and white ones from last year he had bought off this dude said he didn't want the old style in his closet anymore. They had looked good to Durham, but now he realized maybe he had got beat for twenty-five dollars. If he was here now, his brother, Dewayne, would say, That's what you get for buying used shoes. But he had smelled the insides before he bought them, and they were clean, like they still sitting on the shelf at Foot Locker. They had looked all right to him.

Durham took off the shoe still had a *J* on it and worked at the letter with his fingernail until it started to peel at the edge. He tore it off. Good. Now both of his shoes looked alike.

He was still holding this shoe when he heard a girl laughing, and he looked around to see these two girls, sharing one of the seats a couple of rows up. They were staring at him, holding that shoe. A guy who wasn't with them, sitting nearby, was looking around to see what they were laughing at, and now he was looking back at Mario and he was kinda smiling, too.

People had been laughing at Mario Durham all his life. Wasn't anything special about this bus ride right here.

Soon those people went on about their business. He found that this was usually so, that folks would leave him alone after they got over the first thing they saw about him that made them crack on him and laugh: that he was skinny, or funny lookin', or that he was tearing a letter off his shoe. And that was worse than being laughed at sometimes – just being ignored. Feeling that he wasn't even important enough to notice, that's what really cut him deep.

Dewayne said that when someone stepped to you, then you had to step back. But what was he gonna do, even strapped like he was right now? Kill a Metrobus full of people for smilin' at him? But it did make him mad. You came into this life trusting people to be good, and it seemed like they always did you dirt in the end.

Like Olivia. She said she loved him and to prove it she was giving him that good thing, too. So when she asked him, could he ask his brother to front a pound of hydro so that they could sell it, make a little money together, and have some stash to smoke for their own selves, he had to say yes. She was the first woman who had shown some interest in him in a long while.

Dewayne gave him the LB after a lecture about being responsible and shit, and this being his chance to show his kid brother that he could do right. And then Olivia had disappeared with the chronic, just took her son and booked right out of Southeast, and shamed him to his brother. Mario Durham had stood for just about everything, but he couldn't stand for that. Now she was going to have to give the hydro back to him, or the money she'd made from it if she'd gone and sold it already. Because Dewayne had only been half right saying it was his 'chance.' Really, it was his last chance, and he couldn't let it slip by. He needed to show Dewayne that he could stand tall, that Dewayne could trust him, not just as a brother but also as a man. Maybe Dewayne would even put him on. Finding Olivia, getting back the pound she'd took, that's how he could redeem himself in his brother's eyes. For what she'd done, one way or another, the bitch was gonna pay.

Mario Durham reached up and pulled the signal cord, as his stop was coming up ahead. He needed to transfer over to the Benning Road line and take that bus east. He wasn't far now from where Olivia was at.

Durham walked the aisle toward the door, hitching up his Tommys as he passed the two girls. He heard one of them laugh, and he heard the dude nearby say something about Secret Squirrel, then, 'You lookin' good, Deion' from one of the girls, then more laughs. He bit down on his lip and took the steps down off the bus, passing through the accordion doors that opened to the street.

Olivia Elliot fired up a joint and sat back on the sofa. She took a good hit off it and held the smoke in, letting it lie in her lungs while she squinted at the TV set, had a rerun going of *Martin.* She thought she'd seen this one before, but she figured on watchin' it anyway. Truth was, wasn't one of these shows all that different from the others. Martin Lawrence was funny, too; he had come up over in Landover or something, which made his show more interesting to watch, 'cause she knew this girl who knew this other girl who claimed she knew his family. It was like Olivia felt she knew him herself.

The sound was low on the set. She had the stereo going, Missy Elliot gettin' her freak on, the remix joint that the Super Funk Regulator played on PGC.

Olivia had another hit of the hydro and then she had to put it down. She'd learned not to take too much of this, to back up off it quick, because it was potent. Must have come from Dewayne Durham's private stash. She had the feeling when she'd met his funny-lookin' older brother, Mario, that he'd be good for something. This shit right here was what it was.

It was like God had sent Mario down to her, and then the pound of herb with him. She hadn't intended to take it straight off, not exactly, but it came to her, big surprise, when she was high up on it one night, not long after Mario had brought the pound over to her apartment. She had been way up and got to thinking, Why do I need Mario to make some money off this? Why don't I keep it my own self, go somewheres away from here and sell it off? Mario, he wasn't gonna be no problem. And, okay, Dewayne, he was a drug dealer for real, and he had a gang and a rep and all the bad shit that went along with it. But everyone knew those boys didn't leave too far from their neighborhoods, not even to settle a beef, and especially not over some girl and her kid.

So she decided to take the chronic and go away. Not too far, 'cause you didn't have to go that far, but at least into Northeast. And then she'd seen that notice in the newspaper talking about a short-term sublease, fully furnished, and she was gone. Gathered up her clothes, and Mark's clothes, and his bike, and not much else. The furniture she had, she was paying for it on time, and she had stopped making payments on it anyhow. The car she'd bought, a used Toyota Tercel, she was doing that the same way. She moved herself and Mark out of that place in Woodland Mews in a couple of hours, and she'd been living here since.

For the first time since she'd left high school, in the tenth grade, she had some money in her dresser drawer. She'd sold off half of the chronic in one-hundred-dollar bags, just to friends and to people she'd met in the apartments around hers and to people they knew. And now she was flush. She didn't have a job or nothin' like that, but she intended to start looking for one soon. The important thing was, no one had found her or come looking for her, far as she knew, up till now. Mark had mentioned that some white dude had been by that day, and he was all embarrassed and stuff for telling the white dude where they lived, but she told Mark not to worry over it too much. The white dude was probably some bill collector, like from the furniture company or somethin' like that.

It touched her, the way Mark was always trying to please her and protect her. The flip side of that was, the only thing she worried about in her own life was Mark. She did love her boy and she wanted him safe. But he seemed to be adjusting to this new neighborhood. He looked happy most of the time and he made friends easy. She'd never lived in Northeast, but this was east-of-the-river Northeast, not too different from the Southeast side where she'd come up, and it seemed cool.

Mark was smiling when she'd kissed him good-bye. She'd just seen him off a few minutes ago. Her brother, William, had picked him up, was gonna take him over to his place to watch the playoffs, the Lakers against the Sixers, and spend the night. William was going to keep Mark for a couple of days, the way he always did.

Olivia missed him when he was gone, even for a night, but it was good for Mark to be around a man, and William was a strong role model and as straight as they came. He'd always disapproved of her lifestyle, telling her constantly to get herself together, but mostly she'd let it roll off her like everything else, 'specially since she knew deep down that her brother was right. And these nights that William took Mark, it allowed her to kick back, burn some smoke without having to hide it, listen to music by herself, and laugh at whatever was playin' on the TV.

Maybe she could fix this place up some, get an extension on the lease, settle here. Put curtains up or somethin', 'cause the way they had this place painted, it was dark and kinda gray. Get an exterminator out here for the roaches that showed up all over the kitchen when you turned the lights on back there. Some new sheets for Mark's bed. She had the money. It was hid good, too, right in between her mattress and box spring. Along with the rest of the herb.

The buzzer rang from over by the phone. It was that buzzer from downstairs, said that someone was wantin' to get in. She wasn't expecting anyone, so she stayed where she was. Probably someone was down there hittin' all the buzzers, just lookin' to get inside.

She shook a Newport out of her pack and lit it. The menthol, it tasted good after you smoked some get-high. Olivia smiled, looking at the face Martin was making on the TV show. The music sounded good, too, coming from the stereo. She looked at the joint resting in the ashtray and considered picking it back up. But she was already trippin' behind this shit, so she let it lay there where it was.

11

Sue Tracy had met Quinn over at his apartment on Sligo Avenue, in a boxy brick structure near a small convenience market in Silver Spring. When they spent the night together they did it at his place. More often these days, Sue, who had a one-bedroom off Rockville Pike, seemed to prefer to stay on his side of town.

Silver Spring had beer gardens and restaurants within walking distance of Quinn's, and live music if you wanted it, and you could leave the house and go to any of those places wearing whatever you had on without thinking twice. The city was starting to take on the concrete sterility of white-bread Bethesda, and it was getting the same upscale chains, and the fake Mexican cantinas, and the grocery store where people could be 'seen' eating overpriced sushi in the window booths and overpaying for vegetables in the checkout lines. But Silver Spring hadn't lost its personality or its mix of working immigrants and blue-collar eccentrics yet. You could still rest your can of Bud on the engine block of your car while you fiddled around under the hood on a sunny day and not get a reproachful look. You could say that you liked women, not just as people but also in bed, and not feel as if you were wearing a swastika band around your arm. If that ever changed, Quinn swore he'd be gone.

Earlier in the evening they'd had dinner at Sue's favorite place, Vicino, on Quinn's street. Then they caught a set of Bill Kirchin's band up at the Blue Iguana on Georgia Avenue. Quinn had suggested it, as the drummer, a guy named Jack who lived in the neighborhood, cooked. They bought a six on the way back to Quinn's place. They could have walked everywhere, but they took Quinn's '69 Chevelle, a 396 with Cregars and Flowmaster pipes. Sue was used to driving her work vehicle, a gray Econoline van, so it was a treat for her to get behind the wheel of something that had some muscle. She especially liked to move the Hurst shifter through its gears.

They were a little high on red wine and beer when they got to his spartan apartment. Sue opened a couple of cold ones while Quinn searched his CDs for something she would like. He was into Springsteen, Steve Earle, and the like, his collection running toward big guitars, male singers, and male concerns. Sue had come up in the fabled eighties D.C. punk movement. Occasionally their tastes converged.

'What do you want to hear?' said Quinn. 'Dismember Your Man?'

'It's the Dismemberment Plan,' said Tracy. 'And you don't own any, so shut up. Why don't you put on the new Dave Matthews?'

'Cute. You know I don't get that guy. Music for old people who look like young people. It's not rock, it's not jazz. What the fuck *is* it?'

'I'm kidding.'

'How about some Neil?'

'Neil's good.'

Quinn dropped *Everybody Knows This Is Nowhere* into the carousel and let it play. 'Cinnamon Girl' came forward as he joined Tracy on the couch. She wore a sky-blue button-down stretch shirt out over slate gray pants. Her blond shag-cut hair fell to her shoulders. The shirt was open three buttons down and showed the curves of her breasts, full and riding high. Quinn thinking, This is a sweet night right here.

They drank off some of their beer. Sue removed her Skechers, put her feet up on the table set before the couch, and smoked a cigarette while Quinn told her about his day.

'Anything on Linda Welles?' said Tracy.

Quinn shrugged. 'I passed out flyers down at the Metro station in Anacostia.'

'I appreciate it.'

'Her brother, he called the police, right?'

'Sure, but the police don't get all that mobilized for a missing girl in the city.'

It usually was reported to Youth and Preventive Services and pretty much sat. Most were runaway and not criminal cases. The girls stayed local and moved quadrant to quadrant. So families went to people like Sue for help finding them.

'She could be shacked up with some older boy, has drug money, a nice car,' said Quinn.

'That's right, she could be,' said Tracy, crushing her cigarette in the ashtray. 'But we still need to find her.'

'I will.'

'My hero.'

Quinn put his beer bottle down on the table and slipped his hand under the tail of Tracy's shirt and around her waist. 'I'm larger than life.'

'Don't be so boastful.'

Quinn kissed her. He unbuttoned her shirt and kissed the tops of her breasts, then pulled one cup of her bra down to kiss her darkish nipple. It hardened at the lick of his tongue, and he felt her stretch like a cat beneath him. Quinn tried to undo her bra but fumbled it.

'You got oven mitts on or something?'

'I need a manual for this thing.'

'It's a back-loader, Terry.'

'Oh.'

Tracy's chest was flushed pink and her hair was a beautiful mess. She sat up, undid her bra, and pulled it free. Quinn drew her shirt back off her shoulders.

'Gulp,' said Quinn.

'You look surprised.'

'I always am,' said Quinn. 'And thankful, too.'

They undressed quickly, 'Cowgirl in the Sand' filling the room. Quinn laughed as her panties flew past his head. They embraced and were down on the pillows and then knocking the pillows off the couch. They were all over each other and she moved him roughly to her center. She was wet there, and Quinn smiled.

'Damn, girl, where's the fire?'

'You don't know?'

'What I mean is, why the rush?'

'Quit fucking around.'

Soon he was all the way in her, her back arched to take it, her mouth cool on his, her damp muscled-up thighs flanking his sides. Quinn thinking, This is something God dreamed up, has to be. Something this good, it can't be an accident.

Strange picked up Greco at the office and drove the dog up to the row house on Buchanan Street. Strange had lived here for many years before marrying Janine. He was perfectly content and comfortable at Janine's place and as certain as any man could be that their marriage was going to last. But he still spent time at his old house. The house was paid for, so there weren't any issues with money, and he had not considered selling it.

He told Janine that he needed this place to keep his duplicate case files and to work away from his primary office. But there were other reasons for his reluctance to give up the Buchanan residence. It had been his first and only real-estate purchase, and the pride of home ownership was, for him, still strong. And of course he needed to know that there was always some other place he could go to, *run to*, some would say, when the space between him and Janine and Lionel got too close. He had lived with women briefly, but in those cases there'd always been an exit door. He'd been a bachelor his whole life and he had married in his fifties. This new life, this whole new thing, was going to take some getting used to.

Strange went down to his basement and did three sets of ab crunches, lying on a mat. He then did a dumbbell workout and put in fifteen minutes on the heavy bag with a pair of twelve-ounce gloves, more than enough to break a good sweat. Then he showered, fed Greco, and went on up to the second floor to his office.

He tore the shrink-wrap off a couple of soundtrack CDs he had purchased through the Internet that had just come to this address in the mail today. A Morricone import called *Spaghetti Western*, which held six tracks from the film *A Gun for Ringo*, among others, had arrived in the shipment. He slipped the CD into the CPU of his computer and sat down behind his desk. The music came through the Yamaha speakers on his desktop, and he nodded his head. This was exactly what he had hoped it would be. He had been looking for this particular soundtrack for some time.

Strange filed that day's Xeroxed records on the Granville Oliver case into the cabinets that supported the rectangle of kitchen-counter laminate that served as his desktop. He did some bills, killed more time listening to his CD, and then went looking for Greco, who was lying by the front door and ready to go. Strange grabbed some cruising music, locked the house down, and walked with Greco to his free-time vehicle, a black-over-black '91 Cadillac Brougham with a chromed-up grille.

He popped some Blue Magic into the dash deck and drove north on Georgia Avenue. The school year had not quite ended, and night had fallen, but there were plenty of kids out, hanging on corners and walking the streets. In fact, he had seen his young employee, Lamar, heading on foot toward the Capitol City Pavilion, a go-go venue the young ones called the Black Hole, on a recent evening. Strange wondered, as he always did, what these kids were doing out so late, and he wondered about the adults who were responsible for them, why they had let them out of their sight.

Janine's house was a clapboard colonial, pale lavender, set on a short, quiet, leafy street called Quintana, around the corner from the Fourth District police station in Manor Park. Lionel's car, a Chevy beater he had recently purchased, was out front, and Janine's late-model Buick was in the drive. Strange used his key to open the front door. He entered the house with Greco beside him, his nub of a tail twitching back and forth.

'It is me,' said Strange, his voice raised, not yet used to letting himself into Janine's house.

'That you, Derek?' said Janine from back in the kitchen.

'Nah, it's Billy Dee,' said Strange.

'Gettin' to look like him, too,' said Lionel, tall and filled out, coming down the center-hall stairs and patting his head, which barely had any hair on it at all.

'I know,' said Strange. 'Didn't have a chance to get that taken care of today. Gonna get to it tomorrow.'

'You know that album you got, has those guys with the big ratty Afros hanging out by the subway platform, talkin' about, 'do it till you're satisfied'?'

'B.T. Express.'

'Yeah, them. You're lookin' like the whole B.T. Express put together.'

'Said I was gonna take care of it.'

Lionel reached his hand out as he hit the foot of the stairs. Strange took it, then brought him in for the forearm-to-chest hug.

'How you doin,' boy?'

'I'm good,' said Lionel. 'You gonna watch the game with me tonight?'

'You know it. What's your mom got on the stove?'

'I think she made a roast or somethin'.'

'Was wonderin' what it was,' said Strange, 'smelled so good.'

'Smells like home,' said Lionel with a shrug.

Couldn't put my finger on it, thought Strange. But, yeah, there it is.

They ate in the dining room after Strange said grace, and the food was delicious. Lionel was graduating from Coolidge High, and the ceremony was coming up soon. He had been accepted to Maryland University in College Park and would start there in the fall. He had been down on the fact that he would not be able to afford to live on campus, but Strange had bought the old Chevy for him, his first car, and that had somewhat offset his disappointment.

'How's that car running?' said Strange.

'Good,' said Lionel. 'I took it up to the detail place and had them brighten up the wheels.'

'You check the oil?'

'Uh, yeah.'

''Cause you got to do that,' said Strange. 'You need to change that oil every three or four months, at the outside.'

'Okay.'

'You want that car to last you, hear?'

'I said okay.'

'You don't change the oil, it's like gettin' on with a woman without giving her a kiss.'

'Derek,' said Janine.

'It might feel real good when you're doing it, but you want her to be there for you the next time you get the urge.'

'Derek.'

'What I mean is, a woman ain't gonna be stayin' around too long if you don't treat her right. Car's the same way.'

Lionel shifted in his seat. 'You mean, like, changing the oil on the car is kinda like giving a woman flowers, right?'

'Exactly,' said Strange, relieved that Lionel had gotten him out of the woods.

Lionel cocked his head. 'You supposed to do that every time you hit it, or every three or four months?'

'Lionel!'

'Sorry, Mom. It's just, *Derek* is getting deep with me here, and I wanted to make sure I understood.'

Janine flashed her eyes at Strange.

'Dinner's delicious, baby,' said Strange.

'Glad you're enjoying it,' said Janine.

The three of them watched the game in the living room. Strange and Janine were for the Lakers, and Lionel was for the Sixers. It was a generational thing, like Frazier–Ali had been thirty years back.

On the television screen, Robert Horry was sinking foul shots like there was nothing on the line, though this was the championship series and the game was close, with less than a minute to play.

'Man is ice,' said Strange. 'Experience beats youth, every time.'

'Girl at school told me today I look like Rick Fox,' said Lionel.

'Must've been a blind girl,' said Strange.

'Funny.'

'I'm playing with you. But what's up with his hair?'

'The girls be geekin' behind it.'

'You ever grow your hair like that, you and me are gonna have to have a talk.'

'You think all dudes are funny, don't look a certain way.'

'He could afford a comb, at least, all that money he's got.'

'You're just old-time.'

'You think that's what it is?'

'I got news for you. Women love that dude, Pop.'

Strange grinned. Lionel had been calling him 'pop' more and more these days. He couldn't even put into words the way it made him feel. Proud and happy, and scared, too, all at once.

'All I'm saying is,' said Strange, 'you don't need to be gettin' any fancy hairstyles for the girls to like you. And anyway, you look good the way you are.'

Later, Strange and Janine sat on the couch splitting a bottle of beer. Lionel had gone out to see a girl he liked, who called the house several times a night. He had assured his mother that he wouldn't be late.

'That was pretty smooth tonight,' said Janine. 'Comparing women to cars.'

'Yeah, I know. You got to remember, though, I came to this game late. You had sixteen years of practice with that boy before I even came through the door.'

'You're doing fine.'

'I'm trying.'

'Oh, Derek, I almost forgot. Some man called today asking if he could talk to you about the Oliver case.'

'Was it one of the lawyers?'

'No, this was a white guy, and anyway, I recognize those lawyers' voices by now. But this guy hung up before I could get a number.'

'Caller ID?'

'It said "No Data" on the screen.'

'He'll call back,' said Strange. He turned and kissed Janine on the side of her mouth. 'Listen, we got some time before Lionel gets home . . .'

'I don't feel like going up just yet,' said Janine. 'I'm happy sitting right here for a while, you don't mind.'

'I'm happy, too,' said Strange.

And he was. He couldn't think of anyplace he'd rather be. Strange didn't know for the life of him why he was fighting all this. These were the people he loved, and this was home.

Sue Tracy lit a cigarette and got up naked off the couch. Quinn watched her move to the stereo to change the music and felt himself swallow. To have a woman, a woman who *looked* like a woman, all hips and breasts and just-fucked hair, parading around his crib without a stitch like it was the most natural thing in the world to do, this was what he had dreamed of since he was a boy, when he'd found those magazines behind the toolshed in his backyard. Quinn was so stoked now he wanted to phone his friends. But then he thought, Shit, my friend is right here in front of me. He had never figured on this part back when he was twelve years old. The stroke mags never taught you that.

'What?' said Tracy.

'What?'

'You're staring at me and you've got a silly smile on your face.'

'You look nice.'

'Yeah, so do you. You want another beer?'

'Okay.'

He heard her washing herself in the bathroom, and soon she returned with two more beers and a towel for Quinn. She sat on the couch and stretched her legs out, her toes noodling with the hair on Quinn's thighs.

'Good night,' said Tracy.

'Really good,' said Quinn.

They tapped bottles and kissed.

'You were late getting here,' said Tracy.

'I was finishing up something for Derek, over in Northeast. Confirming an address on a woman for a client of ours. It was a bullshit job, but I took care of it.'

'Why was it bullshit?'

'I don't know,' said Quinn, the self-disgust plain in his voice.

'Why?'

Quinn looked away. 'I had to lie to this kid, the son of the woman, to confirm the address. I tricked him, see? The look he gave me afterwards . . . I bet you money he's been told all his life to distrust white people, that in the end white folks are always gonna fuck you over if you're black. And you know how I feel, that it's wrong to plant that kind of seed in any kid's head, no matter what color you're talking about, because it never gets unlearned. So it just got to me, to see that look he gave me, like every thing he'd been taught had come true. And you know he's never gonna forget.'

'Who's looking for his mother?'

'A loser. That was the other thing that bugged me. That we just found this woman for this client, knowing this client's type, without giving it any kind of thought. 'Cause whoever this client is, he's no good, just a bad one to put anywhere near that boy's life. But Derek and me, we treat it like a game sometimes, who's got the bigger set of balls, like that, without thinking about the consequences. I don't know; I'm just pissed off at myself, that's all.'

'You're angry.'

'As usual, right? Derek tells me I gotta relax.'

Tracy looked down at Quinn's equipment, lying flaccid between his legs. 'You look pretty relaxed to me.'

'I'm just resting. You want me to rally, I will.'

She touched his cheek. 'Look, Terry. It's just a job. You agreed to do something for money and you did it. Don't make it more complicated than it is.'

'It's wrong when there's kids involved.'

'You're probably worried about nothing.'

'I'm right about this,' said Quinn. 'What we did today, it was fucked.'

12

The street was quiet and inked with shadows as Mario Durham moved down the sidewalk, his head low. He shifted his eyes from side to side. On the surrounding blocks there had been some kids hanging out, but on this street there were none. No cars running, either. No kind of drug strip, nothin' like that. Dogs barked in the alleys, and muted television and music sounds came from behind the walls of the apartments and row houses he passed. The nights were still cool, and the windows of the residences were shut or just opened a crack. Durham thinking, That's good.

He went by Olivia's hooptie, that old Toyota Tercel of hers, parked along the curb, then took a few steps up and went down a walkway to the address given him by that white-boy detective. He found the front door locked and was not surprised. There were a couple of rows of buttons outside the door, and he flattened out both of his palms and pushed on all the buttons at once. He had seen this done on TV shows. It always seemed to work on those shows, and it worked now. A click was audible as the lock was released, and he opened the door and went through it and then up a set of wooden stairs.

The second floor was unlit and held two apartments, one that faced the front of the house and one that faced the back. Two-B, Durham decided, would be the one to face the back. Durham went to that door. He could hear both television and stereo noise coming from inside the crib. Had to be Olivia in there, 'cause she liked to get high, watch TV and play her music at the same time. The door was heavy and wooden and had a peephole in its center. Durham knocked on it and stood back. He reached forward and knocked again.

The television sound faded down. He heard footsteps approaching from behind the door. He looked at the peephole and watched as it went dark.

'Open up, Olivia,' said Durham, and when he got nothing he repeated his instructions the same way.

'Go away, Mario,' was the reply.

They went back and forth for a while, but eventually she did open the door. Durham had known she would, after she'd thought it out. What else was she going to do?

Olivia Elliot turned down the television volume and went to see who was at the door. When she looked through the hole and saw Mario, she didn't jump. She wasn't scared, and her heart didn't race inside her chest or nothin' like that. Some people got paranoid when they burned smoke, but it had always evened her out, made her see things more clear.

She let him stand out there and call her name a couple of times, though, while she figured out what her next move ought to be.

'Go away, Mario,' she said.

'I ain't goin' *no* goddamn where,' said Durham.

'You gonna need some of that Grecian stuff, then, 'cause you gonna go gray, standin' out there, thinkin' you're comin' inside.'

'Then I'll go gray. And I'll *go* get my brother, too.'

She leaned against the door. This was what she didn't want to hear, but at least Dewayne Durham wasn't out there on the landing with a couple of his boys now. She'd need to handle this with Mario alone, work it out and end it tonight.

Leaning against the door, she put the tip of her finger in her mouth while she let it all bounce around in her mind. Her mother had told her to take her finger out her mouth all the time when she was a kid, that it would buck her teeth. But the habit had never left her.

'Olivia! C'mon, girl.'

Finally she opened up the door. And when he stepped in, his fists all balled up at his sides like he was gonna get physical with her, she nearly laughed. Lookin' like Lil' Romeo or sumshit, wearin' a Redskins jersey and a matching cap, like a kid would. Shoot, Lil' Romeo had more heft on him than this little slip of nothin' right here.

'Damn, Olivia, how you gonna let a man stand in the hall all night long?'

She motioned him inside, shutting the door behind him as he entered, one hand in his pocket, bobbing his head in that way he did, like it was mounted on a spring.

'So you found me.'

'Didn't you think I would?'

'You want a drink or somethin'?'

'Nah, baby. I ain't here to drink.'

Durham had forgotten how fine she was. She wasn't tall, but she was put together right. And she liked to look clean, even just hanging inside her place. She had on a summer dress and some shoes, sandals with heels and no backs, on her feet. On her chest where the dress separated were a few black hairs. Girl had some hairs on her chest and around her nipples, too. But that was the only fault Durham had found in her. Other than that, she was all right.

Olivia walked over to a grouping of furniture and Durham followed. Music, that 'Fiesta' joint by R Kelly and Jay Z, was up real loud, and Durham could smell blunt smoke mixed with her cigarette smoke in the room. The blunt smell was sweet, the good stuff, had to be his brother's. Well, maybe she still had some of it left.

'Where your son at?' He moved toward her and she held her place. She was up against the arm of the couch.

'He's stayin' with my brother for a couple of days.'

'It's good he's not here. 'Cause you and me need to have a very serious conversation.'

'Ain't no big drama to it, Mario.'

'Oh, yeah? Guess it wasn't no thing to you. Including the thing we had together, right?'

'I was fixin' to call you and straighten it all out.'

'When?'

'Look here, Mario, you gonna let me talk?'

He was nodding his head quickly and his eyes flared. It was comical to her, high as she was, watchin' him act all overdramatic, like he was in one of those old silent movies. She bit down on her lip, but she guessed that her eyes showed that she was amused.

'Somethin' funny?'

'Nah, it's just . . . Look, I shouldn't have left up on you like I did. I'm sorry for that. But it wasn't workin' between us, you know this. You *know* this, Mario.'

He was still nodding his head, trying to act hard, but Olivia noticed that the flame had gone out of him. She had wounded him now.

'Mark,' said Olivia, 'he's funny about having men around our house, and you got to understand, I put my son above everything else. I knew you wouldn't understand. I didn't know how to talk to you about it, so I just booked and came over here.'

'What about the hydro?'

'I didn't steal it, that's what you mean.'

'Explain what you *did*, then.'

'I gave it to this dude I knew, said he could sell it for a good price, only take a little off the top. He was a friend of a good friend, so I knew he wouldn't do me dirt. And he didn't. The herb got sold.'

'And you were gonna do what with the money?'

'Give half to you, the way we talked about.'

'Uh-huh. So you got the money now?'

'It's coming,' said Olivia, folding her arms across her chest.

He knew it was a lie. She could see it in his eyes, the way they'd got hot again. 'Cause on top of what she'd done to him, stole from him and shamed him to his brother, now she was telling these stories to him, too.

'So the money's comin',' he said.

'Yeah.'

'When?'

'Soon.'

'*Bull*shit.'

And now what? she thought. More of these one-word sentences, prob'ly, and then he'd just flare his eyes some more and turn around and leave. Get his brother, but not tonight, which would give her time to book, gather up Mark and her personal shit and move on to something else. Wasn't gonna be no fun, but then she'd known what she was getting into from the start. The important thing was, nothing was gonna happen tonight. You got down to it, what was this little man right here gonna do on his own, for real?

She looked down at his shoes and laughed. She didn't mean to, but the chronic, it had fucked with her head. And this really was one sorry motherfucker right here. Couldn't even afford no Jordans, had pair of 'ordans' on his feet. And then he looked down and knew right away what she was laughing at. And he got this funny look on. Not *acting* mad anymore but mad for real.

He slapped her square across the face.

It stung her and surprised her. It surprised *him*. For a moment, Durham looked at his hand, the one that had slapped her. He had never hit a woman before. He had never hit a man. But when she had laughed, it was like it was all those people on the bus and everyone else who'd ever cracked on him was standing there before him, laughing. *All* of them, not just her. Well, he damn sure did have her attention now.

No one had ever looked at him before the way she was looking at him this minute. She was showing fear, and something else: respect.

She touched at the spot that had already reddened. Then, slowly, she stood straight and cocked up her chin. That look of fear, it had passed as quickly as it had come.

'That's all you got?' said Olivia.

'I'll give you more, you want it.'

'You dare take a hand to me?'

'Bitch, I will close my hand next time, you don't mind your mouth.'

She chuckled and looked him over. 'Oh, shit. Now Steve Urkel gonna act all rough and tough, huh?'

'Olivia, I'm warning you, you are fuckin' with the wrong man.'

'Man?' She looked him over and moved in a step so that her face was close to his. 'I don't see no man. You see a man in this room, point him out.'

'I'm about to—'

'You about to *what?* Slap me again?' Her eyes caught fire. 'Mother*fuck* you, punk.'

Spittle flew from her mouth as she spoke those words, and she raised her hand to strike him. Durham grabbed her wrist. She drew her free hand back and he grabbed that wrist, too. He pushed her away, releasing his hold on her, and she backpedaled and hit the couch. She charged him then.

He stepped in as she neared him. Her arms were spread and she was open in her middle, and he punched her in the stomach with all he had. He was trying to stop her, but he realized as his fist sank into her doughy flesh that he had caught her good. He felt a power then that he had never known before.

Olivia hinged forward at the waist. Her sour breath hit him as it was expelled. Her eyes bulged in pain and surprise. And as she jacked forward he drove his fist up into her jaw, putting everything into it. The uppercut lifted her off her feet. The noise it made was like a branch snapping off a tree.

Olivia staggered and found her feet. She lowered her head and put her hands on her knees. She retched and spit out blood. She spit out a tooth. A thread of mucus ran from her nose and hung in the air.

'Oh, sweet God,' she said.

The revolver from the pocket of his Tommys appeared in his hand. He gripped it by its barrel.

She looked up at him, at the gun, and her eyes went wide, humble and afraid. He liked the way it made him feel. He was strong, handsome, and tall, everything he had never been before. He wished Dewayne were here to see him now.

'Nah,' said Olivia, standing out of her crouch, unsteady on her feet. A glaze came to her eyes and she spread her hands. She wanted to plead to him but couldn't get the words. She was thinking of her son.

The gun in his hand was electric, and he swung it like a hammer. The butt of it connected to her face. She turned her face and a sprinkle of blood jumped in the same direction, and while she tried to keep her feet he whipped her there again, harder this time. Her body spun. She tumbled over the couch. Her legs dangled off the arm of it and one of her sandals dropped to the floor.

Olivia wasn't making any kind of noise now. The music was still playing, and so was the television. But it seemed real quiet in the room.

Durham walked around to the front of the couch and looked down at her. Her face was all fucked up. The socket was caved in around one of her eyes, where he guessed the gun had connected. It was a mess, but through the blood and bone he could see that the eye had popped out some and was layin' down low. It seemed the way the eye was pointed that she was lookin' off to the side. The eye was an inch or so lower than where it should have been, and it was exposed nearly all the way around. Nerves and muscles and shit was the only thing still holdin' it on her face. Her jaw had turned color and was set off to the side kinda funny, and it had already swelled up, too. Her hands were bent at the wrists in the center of her chest, like she had arthritis or sumshit like that. If she was breathing, he couldn't tell.

I guess I killed her, thought Durham. I just murdered the fuck out of that bitch.

He dropped the gun back in his pocket.

He walked around the apartment for a little while. How long, he didn't know. He searched her room and took her keys off her nightstand. He searched the room where her son slept. He looked under the boy's bed and through his drawers. The usual kid shit was thrown around the room: CD cases and game cases and wires and controllers coming from the PlayStation he had hooked up to a small TV. Ticket stubs from a Wizards game. He had a Rock poster and a magazine picture of Iverson taped up on his wall, too. But no chronic and no money. He went to the kitchen and then the bathroom and searched through the cabinets and all but found not one thing. In the bathroom mirror he saw his face and noticed the dirt tracks on it. His forehead had sweat bullets across it and his eyes were bright.

He sat down on the toilet seat and wrung his hands.

He couldn't just leave her here, that much he knew. Take her somewhere else, dump her body, let her go missing for a while until he figured out what to do. When they did find her it would look like she got herself killed at random. She'd said her boy would be with his uncle for a couple days, and that would give him some time.

He took the shower curtain down off its rings. Out in the living room he spread the curtain on the floor and picked Olivia up off the couch. She hadn't gone cold yet and she wasn't stiff like he'd thought she'd be. Blood trailed on the wood floor as he carried her and dropped her roughly on the curtain's edge. He rolled her up in it and looked at the mess she had left behind.

He couldn't take her down the front stairs. He went to the back door that led to a rickety old porch overlooking the alley. It was quiet back there, except for the dogs. A light from down the way showed that below the porch was a narrow yard of dirt. He knew what he'd do, but he wasn't ready yet.

He found some Comet or something like it in the kitchen, wet some paper towels, and shook some of the cleanser on the couch where most of the blood was. He rubbed at it and it got soapy and also turned the brown couch to beige. Must've had some bleach in it or somethin', and anyway, didn't look like the blood was coming out. He got up what she'd spit out and all and used more cleanser on the floor, and that came out all right. But the couch was going to be a problem. He couldn't bring the color back to it, that was a fact. He had fucked that up good. But he rubbed at it some more as if he could. Then he flushed all the paper towels down the toilet, one by one so they wouldn't clog it, and waited to make sure they had disappeared.

He started to talk to himself as he worked. 'You all right, Mario,' and 'You okay, boss,' like that. He noticed he was sweating right through his jersey. His hands were slick with sweat.

Durham found a rag under the sink and went around the apartment wiping off his fingerprints at the places he could remember he'd touched. He must have touched damn near every where, he knew. Still, he did the best he could. He put the rag in his pocket, then went back out to the living room. The shower curtain was red where Olivia had bled out. He bent down over what had been Olivia and picked her up, lifting mostly with his legs. He had no bulk on him and little muscle, so it was hard. He felt his back strain as he carried her out to the porch. He looked around but not too carefully, as he knew now that the rest of it would run on luck.

He dropped Olivia off the back porch. She came out of the curtain halfway down. When she hit, the sound was dull, like she wasn't nothin' but a bag of trash. He thought he heard her moan for a second, but he knew that it had to be in his mind. There wasn't no sounds out there, not really. The dogs that had been barking all night were still barking, and that was all.

After turning off the television and stereo, and the lights, Mario Durham got Olivia's Tercel and drove it back into the alley with its lights off. He rolled her back up in the curtain, noticing that one of her arms was bent funny and most likely had got broke from the fall. He had to fold her some to get her body in the trunk of the car. She still hadn't gone stiff.

Durham drove into Southeast. He knew a place he could dump her there.

It surprised him, how calm he was. He was sorry he had killed Olivia and all, but he couldn't take it back now, and anyway, he had done this thing for Dewayne. What else was he gonna do, go back to his brother with empty hands, tell him that Olivia had given his chronic to someone else and it was just gone? Dewayne had always taught him that when someone stepped to you, you had to step back. And when Mario had promised to square it, Dewayne had said, 'Don't tell me, *show* me,' and this is what Mario had done. Now, finally, Mario would be a man in his kid brother's eyes.

He turned the radio on and kept the volume soft.

The thing he had to look out for now was the police. He didn't want to go to no prison for this. That was the only thing that scared him right there. Fuck all that rite-of-passage bullshit he heard the young ones talkin' about. He knew he wouldn't last in no kind of lockup.

He'd get rid of Olivia and lay up with his best boy Donut for a while. Let his mother and Dewayne know where he'd be at, but only them. Dewayne would front him cash, he needed it. The underground time, it wouldn't be all that long. The police didn't waste too much clock on murder cases down here. And once those cases got cold, they stayed cold; this much he knew.

He stopped the car on Valley Avenue, near 13th Street in Valley Green, along the Oxon Run park. Donut lived only a few blocks away; Durham could walk to his place from here.

Oxon Run was a long, deep stretch of woods controlled by the Park Service, cut by one of those concrete drainage channels down the middle. The Park Service had signs posted warning trespassers to stay out, trying to discourage the dealers and their runners from using the woods as an avenue of escape. Kids weren't even supposed to play back in there. Durham knew they did, he saw kids back up in there all the time, but he hoped those signs would work to keep some of them out.

It was late and the street was quiet. Durham waited a few minutes to get his nerve. Then he got out of the car and opened up the trunk. He had parked close to the woods. It wouldn't be easy to carry her, but it wasn't all that far.

It was tricky getting her out, trickier still to close the trunk lid with her in his arms. But he did it, and he walked like a man cradling a bundle of wood across the unmowed field and into the woods. He could smell his own sweat by the time he hit the trees.

He went deep in. He was talking to himself again, saying that every thing was all right, because he was afraid of animals and especially snakes. Was a moon out, and he managed to make a kind of path by that light and ignore the thin branches that were swiping at his face, and he went on. He dropped Olivia on the ground when he couldn't walk no more.

Durham had hoped to dig a shallow grave with his hands, but he broke a fingernail on the hard earth as soon as he tried. He decided to cover her up with leaves and stuff instead. That would work just as good.

He unrolled her from the shower curtain, 'cause the curtain was light in color and in daylight maybe it could be seen by some kid just walking by. He did this, and she tumbled out. He heard more air come out her and figured that was natural, like how they said people still breathed sometimes in those funeral homes and shit, even though they was dead. And then he heard her moan some and knew that she had not died after all.

He stood over her and tried to make her out in the little light that came down through the trees. She wasn't moving. But her good eye was open, and it was fixed straight up on him.

He couldn't stand to hit her again with a rock or nothin' like that, so he brought out the pistol and shot her three times in her chest. It was louder than a motherfucker, and the bullets made her body jump some from where it lay. Smoke kind of moved slow through the moonlight and its smell was strong. Well, he thought, she is dead now.

He didn't bother with covering her up. The gunshots had unnerved him, and anyway, she seemed protected enough back here. He dropped the gun in his Tommys and gathered up the shower curtain and folded it as he walked in the direction he'd come. He stumbled here and there and heard his own voice saying something about God and Please, and he felt the sweat drip down his back.

He went back to the street and stuffed the curtain down an open sewer near the car. He wiped the car down good, the steering wheel and every thing, with the rag he'd kept in his pocket. Then he locked the car and threw the keys down the same sewer slot. Far as he could tell, wasn't no one had been around to see a thing.

He got his bearings, trying to figure where Donut lived from here. Wasn't all that far, just a few blocks south and then east. He started walking that way, keeping his head down low.

13

That same night, on the other side of Oxon Run, near an elementary school in Congress Heights, Dewayne Durham sat in his Benz, parked on Mississippi Avenue, surveying his troops. Next to him sat Bernard Walker. Walker had the new Glock 17, purchased from Ulysses Foreman, resting in his lap. His head was moving to that Ja Rule he liked, 'I Cry,' as he finger-buffed the barrel of the gun.

'We did some business tonight, Zu,' said Durham. 'Made a whole rack of money out here.'

'Weather's good,' said Walker. 'People want to get their heads up when it's nice out.'

'Thinkin' of adding some bodies to the army.'

'We could use it.'

'That kid, the one ridin' the pegs on that bike this afternoon, back by Atlantic? The one I tried to tip some money to?'

Walker nodded. 'Quiet boy, gets respect.'

'Him. He got a father you know of?'

'Ain't even got much of a mother, what I've seen. He's out all hours of the night.'

'We'll put him on the crew. That'll be his new family right there. I'm gonna start him as a lookout down here, soon as school lets out.'

'That ain't gonna be but another week or so.'

'We'll start him then.'

Durham looked up at the school from their position on the street. Boys stood around the flagpole, holding the portioned-out mini-Baggies of marijuana and some similarly portioned, foiled-up units of cocaine. The dope went hand-to-hand from the runners to the sellers, who stood on the midway and corner of the strip. Lookouts rolled up and down the street and on surrounding streets on their bikes. They carried cells with them to phone and warn the workers positioned around the school in the case of any oncoming heat.

The elementary school sat on a rise, and behind it were a couple of boxy apartment buildings and some duplexes going up the block, all backed by a series of alleys. Across the street was a field leading to the woods of Oxon Run.

Dewayne Durham had chosen this spot because of the many avenues of escape. The police from 6D rolled by regularly, and once in a while they stopped, using their mikes and speakers or sometimes just yelling from the open windows of their cruisers for the boys to get on home. On rare occasions they got out of their cars in force and gave half-assed chase, but they never followed the troops into the woods. Every so often the police would roll in with a major shakedown and make a few arrests, but it did nothing to slow down the business. Marijuana possession, up to half a pound, was a misdemeanor in the District, so if the kids did draw an arrest, priors or not, they generally did no time. They were also out on the street in a very short period; in D.C. a bond was as easy to come by as a gun.

Dewayne's choice of location had to do with the convenience of the school grounds as well. You could hide drugs in several spots, especially around the flagpole, where holes had been dug out and re-covered with turf for just that purpose. Or you could just drop the goods in the grass if you had to, things got too deep.

So this was a good spot. Horace McKinley and the Yuma Mob had one almost like it on the southern side of the park.

Up by the flagpole, Durham could see Jerome 'Nutjob' Long and Allante 'Lil' J' Jones standing around, giving occasional orders to the troops.

'I need to drop by my mom's,' said Durham. 'Maybe we'll see my brother somewhere if we drive around, too.'

'Where he's stayin' at now?'

'I don't know. He shows up at my mother's from time to time, but he ain't been there lately. Probl'y with that friend of his, calls himself Donut, down around Valley Green.'

'The one be sellin' dummies?'

'That's the one.'

'You worried?'

'I don't like that fool havin' a gun.'

'You wanna book out now?'

'Sure. Nut and J can take care of things. We'll swing by again later on. Give Nutjob the gun.'

'You sure?'

'He needs to get used to holdin' it. And get the money from 'em while you're there.'

'Right.'

Walker slid the Glock under his waistband as he got out of the car. He crossed the street and went up the rise to the flagpole, chin-signaling one of the sellers, who held the money, as he passed. The seller followed Walker up the hill.

Walker had a look around the street before passing the gun over to Jerome Long.

'Here you go, Nut. Take care of things.'

Long glanced down at the gun as he weighed it in his hand. 'It's live?'

'Yeah, you all set.'

Long took the automatic and slipped it under his shirt and behind the belt line of his khakis. He wore the flannel shirt tails out. Though it was already too warm this time of year to have flannel on his back, he favored the material for three seasons because he liked the way it looked on him. It went nice with his khakis and his Timbs.

'I'll hold it down, chief,' said Long.

The seller handed Walker a thick wad of cash and jogged back down the hill.

'We'll roll on back in here in a while,' said Walker, stashing the money in his jeans. He turned and went down to the idling Benz.

Long and Jones watched the Benz pull off and move down the street.

'That gun looked new,' said Jones.

'They went to see Foreman this afternoon,' said Long. 'So I guess it is.'

'Why Zulu show you all that love just now?'

'What you mean?'

'Why he give that gun to you and not me?'

'Gave it to the first one of us he came up on, I guess. Anyway, we *both* in charge, you know that.'

'Can I hold it?'

'Nah, uh-uh.'

'Why not?'

'Dewayne and Zulu wanted you to hold the gun, they would've put it in your hand.'

'Damn, boy, why you do me that way?' Jones looked over at his friend. 'Feels good to have it, though, right?'

'Yeah,' said Long. 'I dare a motherfucker to start some shit out here tonight.'

James and Jeremy Coates had been drinking and smoking hydro since the afternoon, and now James was getting stupid behind it, daring other drivers at stoplights with his eyes, flashing that kill-grin he had, shit like that. Jeremy had seen him get like this too many times before, but he knew better than to comment on it, and anyway, Jeremy's head was all cooked, too.

James called himself J-1 and Jeremy called himself J-2. They had argued briefly over who would get the number one designation at the time they had come up with the names. James had won the argument, since he was the older of the two.

They had been driving around for an hour or so, looking for girls, rolling up in the usual spots, the Tradewinds and other places in PG, but as yet had found no luck.

The cousins had not done well with D.C. women. They were not attractive in any way, though they did not know this or would not admit it, and they had not yet found their sense of city style. So if they had women at all, they usually had to buy them with money or drugs. Sometimes, if the girl was game, and sometimes even if she was not, they would share a girl or scare one enough to give herself up.

Often they couldn't even tempt a girl into the car with cash or cocaine. This had been one of those nights. James and Jeremy looked an awful lot alike: both were small and wiry, with bulbous noses and thyroid-mad eyes, and when they were high and sweaty like they were now, it scared girls some to look at them. Scary or no, the Coateses didn't like to be turned down. James especially, when he wanted some of that stuff and couldn't get it, he got mean.

They were driving through Washington Highlands on Atlantic, going over the drainage ditch of Oxon Run. Jeremy was under the wheel of their beige-over-tan '91 240SX, shifting into third on the five-speed as he pushed the car up the hill. It was a four-cylinder rag, but they hadn't known that or even asked about it when they'd bought the car. It had a spoiler on the back of it, and it looked kinda like a Z, so they had figured the ride was fast.

'Boulay bookoo chay abec moms, ses-wa,' sang James as he turned the radio up high.

'Turn that bullshit down,' said Jeremy. He reached for the volume dial and heard a horn sound as the 240 swerved into the oncoming lane. He brought the car back to the right of the line.

'That's French, yang,' said James. 'Talkin' about the Moo-long Rooge. They be sayin', Do you want to fuck with my moms? or sumshit like that.'

'I don't give a fuck what they be singin' about. Sounds like they're screamin' more than singin', you ask me.'

'Which one of them bitches from the video you like the best?'

Jeremy Coates screwed his face up into a grimace as he thought it over. 'Not the white bitch, I can tell you that. No-ass bitch, looks like a chicken with those legs comin' out her like they do. I guess Maya, I had to choose.'

'I like Pink. Pink has got some ass on her, yang.' James smiled. 'I bet it's pink inside, too.'

'Shit, even a mule is pink inside.'

'You ought to know. Remember that time I came up on you on the farm, back in Georgia?'

'*Shut* the fuck up. I was just cleanin' that mule off.'

'I ain't see no brush.'

'I was washin' it.'

'Yeah, looked like you was waxin' it, too.'

'Aw, *fuck* you, man.'

James laughed. He punched his cousin on the shoulder and got no response. Jeremy turned right on Mississippi. As he did, the batch of little tree deodorizers hanging from the rearview swung back and forth.

'We goin' to see the Six Hundred boys?' said James.

'Thought we'd drive by and see what's what.'

'I saw that Jerome Long outside a club last night with a girl. Girl was laughin', lookin' at him like she was lookin' up at Taye Diggs or sumshit like that.'

James had a beef with Nutjob Long, who had looked at him the wrong way and smiled one night at a club. Long was known to be good with the women. James Coates hated Long for that, too.

James pulled a gun up from under the seat. It was a 9mm Hi-Point compact with a plastic stock and alloy frame, holding eight rounds in its magazine. The gun was a starter nine, popular with young men because of its low price. James had traded a hundred and twenty dollars' worth of marijuana to get it. He fondled the gun as he held it in his lap.

Jeremy looked down at the gun, then back at the road. 'Damn, boy, you ought to be ashamed to be holdin' some cheap shit like that.'

'It shoots.'

'And a Geo gets you from place to place, too. You don't see me drivin' one, do you?'

'I'm gonna get me one of those Rugers next.'

'Sure you are.'

James looked through the windshield at the elementary school, coming up on their left. 'Slow this piece down, yang. I want them to see us while we pass.'

They cruised slowly by the school. They ignored the kids who were selling on the street and the lookouts riding their bikes, and they stared hard up the hill toward the two young men standing by the flagpole. James made sure the young men could see his smile.

'That's Long,' said James. 'That's his boy Lil' J up there beside him, too.'

'So?'

'So keep on going a few blocks, then turn this motherfucker around and bring it back. Drive past 'em a little faster this time.'

'Tell me what you doin' before you do it, hear?'

'We're in their house, right?'

'Yeah, we in it.'

'We're just gonna announce ourselves, then.'

Jeremy gave the Nissan gas. James pulled back the receiver on the Hi-Point and laughed. They were having fun.

'That's them,' said Jerome Long as the Nissan went down the block. 'That's those cousins from the Yuma.'

'They be tryin' to mock us,' said Allante Jones.

'They can try.'

'You see all those little trees they got swingin' from their mirror?'

'And that spoiler, too.'

'Like it's gonna make that hooptie go faster. Next thing they gonna do is paint some flames on the sides.'

''Bamas,' said Long.

The taillights on the Nissan flared as the car slowed down.

Jones squinted. 'Looks like they're stopping.'

'They ain't stoppin',' said Long. 'They turnin' around.'

The Nissan had U-turned and was now accelerating back in the direction of the school. Long could hear the driver, the one named Jeremy, called himself J-2, going through the gears. And then he saw James Coates, ugly like his cousin but crazier by an inch, leaning out the window of the passenger side, smiling at them, laughing, as they came up on the school. And then he saw the gun in his hand, and saw a puff of smoke come from it just about the time he heard the pops. Long froze; he couldn't make his hand go to the Glock and he couldn't move his feet. He felt his friend Lil' J tackle him to the ground.

As he went down it looked all jittery, like one of those videos where the camera can't sit still. Long saw the troops diving for cover, a lookout on his bike pedaling like it was the devil behind him, and he heard more shots and it was as if he could feel them going by. There was a metallic sound as a round sparked off the flagpole, and Long put his head down and covered his ears. When he uncovered them, there was just the laughter of James Coates and the music they were listenin' to. Under all that was the sound of their four-banger struggling up the street as they sped away.

The troops were slow getting up.

Jones released his hold on Long and rolled off of him, standing to his feet. Long brushed the dirt off his clothes as he stood. He locked hands with Jones and pulled him in for the forearm-to-forearm hug.

'My boy,' said Long, his voice sounding high to his own ears.

'You know I got your back.'

'Better tell everyone to pull it off the street for a while. All those shots, you know someone's bound to call up the police.'

'I'll do it. We could use a break our own selves, too.'

It shamed Long that his hands were shaking. It shamed him that he had frozen up the way he had. He buried his hands in the pockets of his jeans. He was embarrassed now, standing next to his friend, as he'd just been bragging about daring a motherfucker to come by here and start something tonight. And here he was, trembling like a kid. He hadn't even been able to pull his gun.

'They surprised us,' said Jones, as if he could read Long's mind. 'You didn't even have no time to think on it.'

'I knew they was stupid,' said Long. 'But I didn't know they'd be so bold.'

'They need to be got,' said Jones.

'They will be.'

'You know where they stay at?'

'I know this girl who does,' said Long. 'And I'm gonna remember that car.'

Arnice Durham lived in a nice town house her son Dewayne had bought for her in the Walter E. Washington Estates near the Maryland line. She had given birth to Mario when she was sixteen, and Dewayne came, by another man, when she was twenty-six. Arnice was now creeping up on fifty but didn't feel it. Her friends told her she carried her age good.

She had always took care of her body. Though many of her men smoked and used drugs and alcohol, she did not. She was also a regular at church. It was true that she had been poor and looked ghetto most of her life, but that changed when Dewayne started earning the money that he had been bringing in the past two years or so. With Dewayne's cash she bought furniture for her new house, and clothes and jewelry, and she made two trips a week to the hair salon and had her nails done while she was there. Money kept you young. Anyone who said different ain't never had none.

She let Dewayne and his friend Bernard into the house. Dewayne kissed her on the cheek, and she said hello to Bernard and asked if he was wanting on something to drink. She had told Dewayne that his friends were always welcome here.

They went past the slipcovered furniture and wide-screen TV of the living room into the dining room, where a scale was set in the corner along with a cash counting machine. Durham used his mother's place for work – bagging up, scaling out, packaging, and counting – at night, mostly, when it wasn't smart to burn the candles in that house on Atlantic. She knew to let his troops in whenever they came by, long as they went and called ahead first. And she knew not to talk to the police about anything, anytime.

Arnice Durham never questioned her son about his business, and she didn't question her own involvement in it, either. Wasn't any opportunity where Dewayne had come up, and the people in those schools where he went had barely taught him how to read. He was out here now, making his way the best he could, and he was doing fine.

She did worry about Dewayne's safety, though, and she prayed for him regular, not just on Sundays, but every night before she went to bed. She prayed for her first son, Mario, too, but for different reasons. The Lord would watch over both of her sons, because at bottom they were good. This was something she believed deep in her heart. Sometimes, also, she said prayers of thanks for the life Dewayne had given her. She knew she was blessed.

Dewayne was seated at the dining-room table, running money through the cash counter. When he was done he read the number on the display and handed Bernard some bills. He stood and backed away from the table.

'You hear from Mario, Mama?'

'No,' said Arnice. 'He's all right, isn't he?'

'Oh, yeah, I saw him today; he looked fine. Just checkin' is all; thought he might have rolled on by.'

'He might be stayin' up with that boy Donut.'

'All right then. Let me get on back to my place.'

Dewayne smiled at his mother. She had deep brown, loving eyes. She wore a new dress and she had a necklace on, spelled 'Arnice' out in diamonds, all of the letters hanging on a platinum chain.

'You driving me to church this Sunday, Dewayne?'

'I'll pick you up like always.'

He kissed her good-bye and left the apartment with Walker.

Dewayne tossed Walker the keys to the Benz as they walked across the lot.

'Drive me home, Zu. You can check on everything when you come back into the city, hear?'

Walker said, 'Right.'

Walker drove into Maryland on Branch Avenue, headed toward Hillcrest Heights. Durham kept an apartment there, near the Marlowe Heights shopping center. The building he lived in looked kinda plain, but inside his crib Durham had it all: stereo and flat-screen TV, DVD, everything. It was real nice.

The rule was, you kept your business in the city, in the neighborhoods you came up in, but you lived outside of town. You needed to get out of the city to breathe, but you couldn't get no love in Maryland or Virginia on the business side. There wasn't no good way to get a bond, and you got charged with somethin' there, you'd do long time. Plus, there was the PG County police, who had a rep for being ready on the beat-down and quick on the trigger. The only thing those states were good for, on the business tip, was to buy a gun. So you lived in the suburbs and you did your dirt in town.

Durham's cell rang and he answered it. Walker made out that Dewayne was talking to Jerome Long, and when Dewayne was done, Walker asked him what was up. Durham told Walker about the drive-by over at the school, and who had done it.

'What you want to do about that?' asked Walker.

'Nothing now.' Durham slid down low in his seat. 'I don't want to think on it tonight.'

He tried not to, and closed his eyes.

Strange got up out of bed without waking Janine and went to the window that fronted the street. He knew he had dozed some and he could not remember hearing Lionel come in the house. There was his old Chevy, though, parked along the curb. Strange felt his hands relax. He reached down and patted Greco, who was standing by his side.

Lionel had detailed the car out, like he said, and it looked nice. The chrome wheels shined under the street lamp, and the tires had been sprayed with that fluid, made them look wet. Strange wondered when the last time was that Lionel had checked the oil.

Well, anyway, the boy was in the house.

Strange thought about Robert Gray, if anyone listened for his footsteps coming through the front door, or if that junkhead aunt of his or her hustler-looking boyfriend looked into Robert's bedroom at night to see if he was covered up. And then he got to thinking about

Granville Oliver, and if anyone had ever thought to show that kind of concern for Oliver when he was a kid.

It was hard to imagine that a killer and kingpin like Oliver had once been a boy. Strange couldn't picture that hard man in manacles as one in his mind. But everyone started out as an innocent child. It's just that the poor ones didn't come out of the gate the same way as those who had money, a set of loving parents, and everything that went along with them. It was like those kids were crippled, in a way, before they even got to run the race.

Strange ran his hand through his beard and rubbed at his cheek.

'Derek,' said Janine's groggy voice behind him.

'I know,' he said. 'Come to bed.'

'Lionel get in?'

'Yes, he's here.'

'You're done working for today,' said Janine. 'Whatever you're thinking about, stop.'

He got back into bed. Because Janine was right. He wasn't going to do anybody any good just standing by that window, and there wasn't anything more he could do tonight. His day was done.

14

The Granville Oliver trial was being held in Courtroom 19 at the U.S. Courthouse on Constitution Avenue and 3rd Street, in Northwest. Strange passed by the nicotine addicts standing outside the building in the morning sun. The air was still, and the smoke from their cigarettes hung in the light. It would be a hot spring day, a reminder that the dreaded Washington summer was not far behind.

Strange passed through a security station and caught an elevator up to the fourth floor. All of the courtrooms were active, with attorneys, clients, and the clients' relatives and friends standing out in the hall. Outside of one room, a mother was raising her voice to her sloppily dressed, slouching son, and Strange heard a clap as she slap-boxed his ear. Most of the activity was down around 19, where a portable metal detector had been set up. Strange went through it, was thanked by a man in a blue uniform, and entered the courtroom.

The spectator section in the back of the room was half filled, with the first two rows of seats left unoccupied by rule. There were several young ladies, pretty, made up, and nicely dressed, seated on the pewlike benches. A couple of tough young men wearing suits, whom Strange pegged as being in the life, were among them, along with a woman who had the age on her to be a mother or an aunt. A young journalist, a small white male wearing black-rimmed eyeglasses and punkish clothes, sat alone.

FBI agents and other types of cops were scattered about the room. They were there to ensure that there would be no spectator intimidation directed at witnesses in the courtroom. Their hairstyles went from crew cut to flattop, and many of them wore facial hair, mustaches for the veterans and goatees and Vandykes for the young. Some had just made the height requirement, and Strange noted mentally that the shortest ones had bulked themselves up to the monkey-maximum. All of them filled out their suits. A few gave Strange the fish eye as he found a seat. They knew who he was.

In the body of the courtroom there were two tables for the defense and the prosecution. The defense team, from Ives and Colby, was all black, per the request of Oliver, though many of the firm's white attorneys had been working the case from behind the scenes. Raymond Ives had already made eye contact with Strange, as it was Ives's habit to watch the spectators as they entered.

Granville Oliver sat at the defense table wearing an expensive blue suit. He wore nonprescription eyeglasses, a nice touch suggested by Ives, to give him a look of thoughtfulness and intelligence. Underneath the suit he wore a stun belt, by decree of the court.

The jurors had entered the courtroom and were seated. The selection process had taken months, and its progress was heavily monitored in the local news. Nearly two hundred District residents had been excused because they had admitted on a questionnaire that they were unlikely or unable to render a death sentence. Prosecutors had been allowed to continue the process until they were satisfied that they had a 'death-qualified' jury. So the jurors who were ultimately selected were hardly an accurate representation of the D.C. community, or its sentiments.

In the jury box were four whites. Two of them were bookish and rumpled and the other two wore unfashionable sport jackets with long, wide lapels. The remaining jurors were black and mostly elderly or nearing retirement age. From the looks of them, they appeared to be upstanding citizens, on the conservative side, lifelong workingmen and -women. Not the type to sympathize, particularly, with an angry young man of any color who in the past had publicly flashed his ill-gotten, blood-smeared gains.

The U.S. attorney for the prosecution began his opening remarks, telling the jury what the case was 'about.' As he spoke of greed and power and the notion of 'street respect,' a series of photographs of Granville Oliver were presented on several television monitors placed about the courtroom. These were stills from a rap video Oliver had produced to promote his recording career and recently founded company, GO Records. The origin of the stills was not mentioned. When the prosecutor was done with his speech, he showed the video in its entirety for the jury.

The images would be familiar to anyone under the age of thirty: Oliver in a hot tub with thong-clad women, Oliver behind the wheel of a tricked-out Benz, Oliver in platinum jewelry and expensive threads, Oliver holding twin .45s crossed against his chest. The usual bling-bling, set to slow-motion female rump shaking, drum machine electronica, Fred Wesley-style samples, and a monotone rap coming from the unsmiling, threatening face of Granville Oliver. Any kid knew that the images contained props that were rented for the shoot. Perhaps these images would be less familiar, though, in this context, especially to the older members of the jury.

Strange had come down to speak to Ives because he felt he needed to brief him today. And he also thought he'd sit and hear the opening statement for the defense, describing Oliver's early life in the Section 8 projects. Ives would detail his fatherless upbringing, his crack-dealer role models, his subpar education, and how, as a youngster, he had learned to shoot up his mother with cocaine to bring her up off her heroin nod.

It was all propaganda, from both sides, when you got down to it. But something about the prosecution's presentation that morning had stretched the boundaries of dignity and fairness, and it had angered Strange. He stood, made the telephone-call sign to Ives with two fingers spread from cheek to ear, and left the courtroom.

An FBI agent followed him out the door. Strange didn't look at him or acknowledge him in any way. He kept walking and he kept his eyes straight ahead. He was used to this kind of subtle intimidation.

Down on the first floor, he ran into Elaine Clay, one of the public defenders known as the Fifth Streeters, who had been in the game for many years. Strange had bought countless LPs from Elaine's husband, Marcus Clay, when he'd owned his record stores in Dupont Circle and on U Street before the turnaround in Shaw.

Elaine stopped him and put a hand on his arm. He stood eye to eye with her and relaxed, realizing he had been scowling.

'Derek, how's it going?'

'It's good. You're lookin' healthy, Elaine.'

'I'm doing my best.'

She was doing better than that. Elaine Clay was around his age, tall, lean, with strong legs and a finely boned face. She had most definitely kept herself up. Elaine had always commanded respect from all sides of the street, a trial lawyer with a rep for intelligence and a commitment to her clients.

'Marcus okay?'

'Consulting still, for small businesses opening in the city. Complaining about his middle spreading out and the new Redskins stadium. Wondering why he still watches the Wizards. But he's fine.'

'Y'all have a son, right?'

'Marcus Jr. He's college bound.'

'Congratulations. I got a stepson starting next fall my own self.'

'Heard you finally pulled the trigger and settled down.'

'Yeah, you know. It was time. Glad I did, too.'

She looked him over. 'You all right?'

'Just a little perturbed, is all. I been working the Granville Oliver thing for Ives and Colby, and I was just up at his trial. Some bullshit went down in there that, I don't know, got to me.'

'You got to roll with it,' said Elaine.

'I'm trying to.'

'So that means you been prowlin' around Southeast?'

'That's where the history is,' said Strange.

'You need any kind of insight to what's going on down there, give my office a call. I've got an investigator I use, he's been on the Corey Graves Mob thing for me down there for a long time.'

'Corey Graves? I was down in Leavenworth a couple of weeks ago, interviewing an enforcer for Graves, used to be with Granville. Boy named Kevin Willis.'

'I know Willis. You get anything out of him?'

'He talked plenty. But I got nothin' I could use.'

'Call me if you want to speak to my guy.'

'He got a name?'

'Nick Stefanos.'

'I've heard of him.'

'He knows the players, and he does good work.'

'That's what I heard.'

'Feel better, hear?'

'Give love to your family, Elaine.'

'You, too.'

Strange watched her backside move in her skirt without guilt as she walked away. He had to. Didn't matter if she was a friend or that he was married and in love. He was just a man.

Outside the courthouse, Strange phoned Quinn at the bookstore as he walked to his Chevy. When he was done making arrangements, he placed the cell back in its holster, hooked onto his side.

Strange's temper had cooled somewhat talking to Elaine Clay. But it hadn't disappeared. By showing that video, the prosecution was presenting Granville Oliver as a scowling young black man with riches, cars, and women, every thing the squares on that jury feared. The Feds wanted the death penalty, and clearly they were going to get it in any way they could. Their strategy, essentially, was to sell Granville Oliver to the jury as a nigger. No matter what Oliver had done, and he had done plenty, Strange knew in his heart that this was wrong.

In Anacostia, Ulysses Foreman's El Dorado idled on MLK Jr Avenue, a half block up from the Big Chair. Foreman wheeled the thermostat down on the climate control and let the air conditioner ride. It was a hot morning for spring.

Mario Durham sat in the passenger seat beside him, fidgeting, using his hands to punctuate his speech when he talked. Foreman noticed that Durham still wore that same tired-ass outfit he'd had on the day before. And those shoes, too, one of them had the *J* missing off the Jordan, read 'ordan.' Forman studied them and saw that Durham had done them both now the same way. And then he saw the blood smudge across the white of the left one.

Had to be Mario Durham's own blood, 'cause he couldn't have drawn no blood from anyone else. Somebody must have given the little motherfucker a beat-down, and he went and bled all over his own shoes. Foreman didn't ask about it, though. Far as he cared, Durham could just go ahead and bleed hisself to death.

'Wanted to turn this in,' said Durham, patting the pocket of his Tommys, where it looked like he held the gun.

'What you said on the phone.'

'You don't mind, do you?'

'Why would I mind?' Foreman chin-nodded at a brand-new Lexus rolling up the hill of the avenue in their direction. 'You see that pretty Lex right there?'

'Sure.'

'I been seein' that Lex all over Southeast these last few weeks. And every time I do see it – same car, same plates – a different motherfucker is under the wheel, drivin' it.'

'So?'

'It's a hack. Someone done bought that car just to rent it out. For drugs, money, a gun, whatever. This rental business is the business of the future in D.C. Shit, white people been doin' it to us with furniture and televisions and shit forever. We're just now gettin' behind it our own selves.'

'What's your point?'

'Why would I mind if you give me back my merchandise early? I'll just go ahead and turn it over to someone else, 'cause I got the market locked up. The question is, though, why would you give it up so early? You had five days on it, man.'

'I was done with it. Thought I'd get some kind of credit on the time I *didn't* use, sumshit like that.'

'Yeah, well, you were wrong about that. You want to turn that gun in early, that's your business, but we don't do no store credits up in here. Anyway, I done smoked up all that herb you gave me for it.'

'Damn, boy.'

Foreman's eyes went to Durham's pocket. 'Let me have a look at the gun.'

Durham passed it low, under the sight line of the windows, to Foreman. Foreman looked in the rearview and glanced though the windshield, then turned his attention to the Taurus. He broke the cylinder and saw that it had been emptied. He smelled the muzzle and knew that the gun had been fired.

'You shot some off, huh?'

'A few.'

'To make that impression you were talkin' about?'

'Nah, I didn't need it for that, turns out. I just shot off the gun in the air a few times, late last night, like it was New Year's or the Fourth of July. I was high and I wanted my money's worth, is all it was.'

'Okay, then.' Foreman slipped the Taurus under the seat. 'Pleasure doin' business with you, Twigs.'

Foreman watched with amusement as Durham's eyes flared and his bird chest filled with air.

'I don't like that name,' said Durham, his voice rising some. 'I don't want you callin' me that anymore.'

'You don't want me to, I won't.' Foreman looked him over. 'You need a ride somewhere?'

'Nah, man, my short's just down the street.'

'Where you stayin' now?'

'I'm up with a friend, why?'

'Just like to know where you're at, case we need to hook up.' Foreman smiled. 'Man returns his strap after one day on a five-day rent, he might just become my best customer.'

'Yeah, well, you need me, you can reach me on my cell.'

'Take care of yourself, dawg.'

'You, too.'

Foreman watched Durham walk down the hill, going in the direction of his 'short.' The only cars he'd be headin' toward was the ones parked outside the Metro stop. 'Cause that's where he was going, any fool knew that.

Still, raggedy as Mario Durham did look, there was something different about him today. Stepping up and saying that he didn't want to be called by that bitch name no more, for one. And his walk was different, too. He wasn't puttin' on that he was bad; he *felt* bad for real. Like he'd just got the best slice of pussy he'd ever had in his life, or he'd stepped to someone and come out on top.

Foreman was curious, but only because he liked to have all the street information he could. Knowing where the little man was staying, that was a bone he could give his brother, Dewayne, and get some points for it, if it came up. It was real useful to be holdin' those kinds of cards, if you could. Mario had said something about laying up with a friend. Had to be that boy they called Donut.

Donut was a 'dummy' dealer down by where he lived in Valley Green. He sold fake crack, wasn't nothin' but baking soda dried out, to the drive-though trade from Maryland. Those kids got fucked over, then were too afraid to come back into town for some get-back. Still, Donut was gonna get his shit capped someday for what he was doin'. Foreman had seen him and Mario together a few times, walking the streets.

Foreman's cell rang. He unholstered it and hit 'talk.'

'What's goin' on, boyfriend?'

'Ashley, you up?' Her gravelly voice told him she still hadn't wiped the sleep out of her eyes.

'Got woke up by a call. It was that dude, Dewayne Durham?'

'Talk about it.'

'Says he needs something from you, if you got it.'

'Boy's on a buying spree.'

'He says he don't want nothin' fancy. And no cutdowns or nothin' like that. Says he doesn't want to pay too much, 'cause it's not for him. It's for this kid he's got, they call him Nutjob.'

'Jerome Long,' said Foreman, knowing him as a comer in the 600 Crew. He hung tight with his partner, a boy named Allante Jones, a.k.a. Lil' J.

'Dewayne says he wants somethin' today.'

Foreman thought it over. He had the Calico, the Heckler & Koch .9, and the Sig Sauer, and that was about it. He was low on product now. The H&K and the Sig would retail for more than Dewayne wanted to spend. That left the Taurus under the seat. Dewayne didn't have to know that this was the gun Foreman had rented to his dumb-ass brother. Wasn't like it had a body hangin' on it or nothin' like that. The gun had been fired, but it wasn't hot. Foreman would just need a little time to clean it up.

'Call Dewayne, baby. Tell him to have his boy meet me at the house in an hour or so. And get yourself dressed, hear?'

'Why don't you come back here and undress me first?'

Foreman felt himself getting hard under his knit slacks. He did like it when she talked to him that way.

'Tell Dewayne to make it an hour and a half.'

'I'll be waitin' on you.'

'Want me to pick up some KY or somethin' on the way?'

'We won't need no jelly. I'll get it all tuned up for you; you don't have to worry none about that. Hurry home, Ulee.'

'Baby, I'm already there.'

Foreman figured an hour and a half was plenty. He could knock Ashley's boots into the next time zone and have the gun like new by the time Nutjob and his shadow came by.

Foreman pulled down on the tree, swung his Caddy around, and headed for the Maryland line.

15

Bright and sunny days did nothing to change the atmosphere of the house on Atlantic Street. The plywood in the window frames kept out most of the light. The air was stale with the smoke of cigarettes and blunts, and there was a sour smell coming from the necks of the overturned beer and malt liquor bottles scattered about the rooms.

Dewayne Durham and Bernard Walker sat at a card table with Jerome Long and Allante Jones. The four of them had been discussing the shooting by the school and what needed to be done next.

'Those cousins just came up on us, Dewayne,' said Long. 'James Coates was poppin' off rounds and smilin' while he was doing it. Wasn't like we provoked 'em or nothin' like that.'

'That's how it was,' said Jones.

'The cousins,' said Long, his lip curling, 'they sittin' on the back steps of the house on Yuma, across the alleyway, right now.'

Long and Jones had been watching them from the kitchen window moments ago. They were over there, getting high with others from the Yuma, on the porch steps. James would look over toward the house on Atlantic now and again, and do that smile of his. Long hated that the Coates cousins were so bold, knew that in part he was hating on himself for his cowardice the night before. It was eating at him hard inside.

'Why you ain't fire back last night?' said Walker. 'I *gave* you my gun. You just want to look like a gunslinger or you want to be one?'

'I ain't had no time, Zu,' said Long. 'They came up on us so quick. I was about to reach for it when Lil' J tackled me to the ground.'

'That's how it was,' repeated Jones.

'We could make it happen right now,' said Long, 'you want us to.'

'I ain't lookin' for no full-scale war in broad daylight,' said Durham. 'This here is between you two and the cousins. You representin' Six Hundred, don't get me wrong. But it's up to y'all to make it right.'

Dewayne Durham stared across the table at the two young men. He knew them better, maybe, than they knew themselves. Allante Jones was loyal to his bosses and his friend, fearless, and on the dumb side. Jerome Long was handsome, a player, and, considering his lack of education, smart. What he was missing was courage. He had always avoided going with his hands and he had never killed. This here was a test and an opportunity, to see if these boys were ready to go to the next level, and to reduce the numbers of the Yuma Mob by two, thereby weakening them and Horace McKinley. So it would also be good for business.

'You tell us what to do, D,' said Long, 'and it's done.'

'You need to roll up on those cousins out on the street,' said Durham.

'We gonna need a gun,' said Long. 'I gave the Glock back up to Zulu.'

'Are you gonna use it?' said Durham.

'I'm ready to put work in,' said Long. He was assuring Durham that he was willing to make his first kill.

Durham phoned Ulysses Foreman from his cell. He got Foreman's woman, the big white girl, on the line. He told her what he needed and what he wanted to pay for it, and they all sat around and talked some more about the business and cars and girls. A short while later, Ashley Swann phoned him back with instructions. He thanked her and cut the call.

'Give him about an hour and a half,' said Durham, 'then tip on over to his house.'

'I won't let you down,' said Long.

'It's all over to y'all,' said Durham. 'I'm gonna be out today, so I'm countin' on you two to get it done.'

'Where you gonna be at?'

'I'm taking my son to King's Dominion.'

'Thought we was goin' to Six Flags,' said Walker.

'Whateva,' said Durham, who saw his son, Laron, a beef baby he had fathered four years ago, once or twice a year. 'Point is, I might not be back in town till late.'

'We're gonna take care of it,' said Long, Jones nodding his head in agreement.

'Go on about your business,' said Durham, officially ordering the hit. He flipped some cash off his bankroll for the gun purchase and handed it to Long. He and Walker watched them walk from the room and listened for the door to shut at the front of the house.

'Think he can do it?' said Walker.

'I don't know. What do *you* think?'

'Boy's a studio gangster, you want my opinion.'

'One way or the other,' said Durham, 'we gonna find out now.'

Terry Quinn was seated behind the glass case of the used-book-and-record store where he worked, reading a Loren Estleman western called *Billy Gashade*, when Strange phoned him from his cell. He was headed down into Southeast and was looking for company, wondering if Quinn would like to ride along. Strange said that they could hook up at his house. Quinn said he would ask Lewis if he could cover for him, and Strange said, 'Ask him how to get the dirt stains out of my drawers while you're at it. I bet he's an expert at that.' Quinn told Strange he'd meet him at his row house on Buchanan and hung up the phone.

Lewis was back in the sci-fi room, rearranging stock. His thick glasses were down low on his nose, and surgical tape held them together at the bridge. His hair was unwashed and his skin was pale. He wore a white shirt with yellow rings under the arms. Strange called it his trademark, the Lewis Signature, the look that made all the 'womenfolk' fall into Lewis's arms.

'That record came in you were looking for,' said Lewis.

It was *Round 2*, by the Stylistics. Quinn had ordered it from his contact at Roadhouse Oldies, the revered vinyl house specializing in seventies funk and soul, over on Thayer Avenue.

'Don't sell it,' said Quinn. 'I got it for Derek but he doesn't know about it. He's got a birthday coming up.'

Lewis nodded. 'I'll put it in the back.'

'I'm going out for the day,' said Quinn. 'All right?'

Lewis had recently bought half the shop from the original owner, Syreeta Janes, and he was more than happy to cut Quinn's hours whenever possible.

'Go ahead,' he said.

Out on Bonifant Street, Quinn went up toward the Ethiopian coffee shop beside one of his neighborhood bars, the Quarry House, to grab a go-cup for his drive down Georgia. He walked by a group of young men who were headed into the gun store, a popular spot for sportsmen and home-protection enthusiasts. It was also a hot destination for those D.C. residents who wanted to touch the guns they had seen in magazines and heard about in conversation. Though it was illegal for them to purchase guns in this shop, they could buy or trade for these same models later on the black market or rent them very easily on the street. The store was conveniently located just a half mile over the District line in downtown Silver Spring.

*

Sitting at his desk in his house, listening to a new CD, Strange stared at the tremendous amount of paper spread before him. He had been on the Oliver case for some time, and it had been easy to forget, busy as he'd been, just how much work he had done.

He had started with the original indictment and set up dossiers on all the codefendants and the government witnesses who were scheduled to testify against Oliver. He had studied the discovery, which was everything the government had seized on the case: autopsy files, bullet trajectories, and coroner's reports among the data. He'd read the 302, the form the FBI used to describe the debriefing of its cooperating witnesses. The names of those witnesses had been blacked out; it was Strange's job to identify them through careful reconstruction. He'd used the PACER database to turn up previous charges on the witnesses. By law, these charges did not have to be mentioned in the reports provided by the government prosecutors.

All of this was office work, the first phase of the process. The second phase was done out on the street.

Here Strange took his research and went out to the civilian population, looking for character witnesses and witnesses for the defense: those who had direct knowledge of the actual 'events' referred to in the indictment. In court jackets he looked for assault cases, complainants in domestic disputes, and codefendants who might have a beef against his client. He was looking for any kind of background that could be used during cross-examination. Most of the people he spoke to would never make it to the stand.

Strange looked at it all as a stage play with a large cast of characters. In the beginning, he had written Oliver's name on a large sheet of paper and connected lines, like tentacles, from it to the names of those who had known him or had been affected by his alleged deeds. These included the current drug dealers who had stepped into Oliver's abandoned territory. All of this was an awful lot of work, but by doing it, he found that the various relationships and their possible ramifications sometimes became more graphic, and evident, to him.

Many of the leads he'd gotten were false leads, and though he suspected them to be from the get-go, he still went after anything he could. He had even traveled down to Leavenworth, on the nickel of Ives, to interview a former member of Oliver's gang, Kevin Willis, who had later gone to work for the Corey Graves Mob in another part of Far Southeast. Willis had talked on tape about everything he knew: who was 'hot' on the street and who would or would not most likely flip. He had talked freely about charges still pending against him. Strange had the tapes in his office off Georgia and duplicates here in his house. But, as with many of the interviews he'd done, the tapes had given him nothing.

But Strange had a feeling about Devra Stokes. He sensed that Stokes, one of Phillip Wood's former girlfriends, had more to tell him. He had phoned the hair and nail salon and been told she was working today. He had gotten Janine to start the process to obtain a Federal Order of Subpoena, in the event that he would need her to testify.

Greco's sharp bark came from the foyer down on the first floor. When Strange went out to the landing and saw Greco's nose at the bottom of the door, his tail twitching, he knew that this was Quinn.

Quinn, a folder under his arm, came up to the office and waited as Strange gathered up the papers he needed for the day.

'What the hell is this?' said Quinn, chuckling, holding up a CD he had picked up off the desk. '*My Rifle, My Pony and Me?*'

Strange looked down at his shoes. 'Meant to put that away before you came by. Knew you'd give me some shit about it if you saw it.'

'It's a song from *Rio Bravo*, right?'

Strange nodded. 'Dean Martin and Ricky Nelson sing it in that scene in the jail.'

'*What* scene in the jail? Christ, half the movie's set in the jail.'

'I know it. But look, they got another twenty-five tracks just like that one on there, too. Title tunes with vocals from old westerns.'

'Okay. You haven't actually seen all these, have you?'

'Most of 'em, you want the truth. But I got a twenty-year jump on you.'

'Seen *The Hanging Tree* lately?' said Quinn, reading off the CD.

'No, but I saw a damn good one the other night on TNT. I forgot the name of it already, but I been meaning to tell you about it. Italian, by that same guy did *A Bullet for the General*.'

'I liked that one.'

'Anyhow, in this movie, they're gettin' ready for the big gunfight at the end. The hero gets off his horse and faces a whole bunch of gunmen standing in this big circle of stones, like an arena they got set up.'

'That's been done before.'

'Well, they do that Roman Coliseum thing for the climax of these spaghetti westerns all the time. They're Italians, remember?'

'I'm hip.'

'So they're all starin' at each other for a while, like they do. Squintin' their eyes and shiftin' them around. Then this hero says to these four bad-asses, before he draws his gun, "What are the rules to this game? I like to know the rules before I play." And the main bad-ass, got a scar on his face, he smiles real slow and says, "It's simple. Last man standing wins." '

Quinn grinned. 'I guess that put a battery up your ass, didn't it?'

'I did like that line, man.'

'You need to get out more, Derek.'

'I'm out plenty.' Strange stood, slipping the papers he needed into a manila folder. He undid his belt, looped it through the sheath of his Buck knife, moved the sheath so that it rested firmly beside his cell holster on his hip, and refastened the belt buckle. 'You ready?'

Quinn nodded at the knife. '*You* are.'

'Comes in handy sometimes.'

'You had a gun, you wouldn't need to carry a knife.'

'I'm through with guns,' said Strange. 'Let's go.'

Down the stairs, Strange put a bowl of water out by the door and dropped a rawhide bone to the floor at Greco's feet.

'He gonna be all right here all day?' said Quinn.

'Too hot to have him in the car,' said Strange. 'He'll be fine.'

Driving down Georgia in the Caprice Classic, Strange had the Stylistics' debut playing in the cassette deck; 'Betcha By Golly, Wow' was up, symphonic and filling the car. Strange was softly singing along, closing his eyes occasionally as he tried to hit the high notes on the vocals.

'Careful, man,' said Quinn. 'You keep shutting your eyes when you're gettin' all soulful like that, you're gonna get us killed.'

'I don't need my eyes. I'm driving by memory.'

'And you're gonna bust a stitch in your jeans, the way you're trying to reach those notes.'

'Tell me this isn't beautiful, though.'

'It's dramatic, I'll say that much for it. Kinda like, I don't know, an *opera* or something.'

'Exactly. What I was trying to tell you yesterday.'

'The singer's really got a nice voice, too.' Quinn's eyes smiled from behind his aviators. 'What's her name?'

'Quit playin'. That's a dude, Terry! Russell Thompkins Jr.'

'Produced by Albert Belle, right?'

'Funny,' said Strange.

'You got all of this group's albums?'

'I'm missin' *Round Two*. You asked me the same question last week.'

'I did?' said Quinn.

They got down into Anacostia. They drove the green hills as the sun came bright and flashed off the leaves on the trees. Generations of locals were out on their porches, talking on the sidewalk, and working in their yards.

'Just another neighborhood,' said Strange.

'On a day like this one, it does look pretty nice.'

'I was just thinking, looking at these people who live here . . . The world we run in, all we tend to see is the bad. But that's just a real small part of what's going on down here.'

'Maybe it is a small part of it. But a mamba snake is small, and so is a black widow spider. Doesn't make those things any less deadly.'

'Terry, when you say Far Southeast, or Anacostia, it's like a code or something to the rest of Washington. Might as well just add the words "Turn your car around," or just "Stay away." '

'Okay, it's a lot nicer here than people think it is. It's an honest-to-God neighborhood. But the reality is, you're more likely to get yourself capped down here than you are in Ward Three.'

'True. But there's also the fact that Anacostia's damn near all black. That might have a little somethin' to do with the fear factor, right?'

'Absolutely.'

'Yeah,' said Strange, 'absolutely. And it's bullshit, too. But you can almost understand it, the images we get fed all the time from the papers and the television news. Listen, I had this friend, name of James, who lived down here. Still does, far as I know. He was a cameraman, worked for one of the network affiliates. So this network was doing a story down here, one of those segments on "the ghetto," and they found out that my buddy James lived in this part of the city. So the producer in charge got hold of him and said, "Take your video camera and go get some tape of black people down in Anacostia." '

'He said it like that?'

'Exactly like that. This was about fifteen, twenty years back, when you could still say those kinds of stupid-ass things and not worry about gettin' sued. So James does his thing and takes the footage back to the studio. They run it for the producer and it's not exactly what he had in mind. It's images of people leaving their houses to go to work, cutting their grass, dropping their kids off at school, like that. And the producer gets all pissed off and says to James, "I thought I told you to get some footage of black people in Anacostia." And James says, "That's what I got." And the man says, "What I meant was, I wanted shots of people standing outside of liquor stores, dealing drugs, stuff like that." And James said, "Oh, you wanted a *specific kind* of black person. You should have said so, man." '

'What happened to your friend?'

'I don't think he got any work out of that producer again. But he's doin' all right. And he says it was worth it, just to make that point.'

Strange pulled into the parking lot of the strip shopping center on Good Hope Road. He fit the Caprice in a space near the hair and nail salon and had a look around the lot. Strange didn't see Devra Stokes's car, though the woman he had talked to on the phone had said she would be working today.

Quinn picked up his folder off the seat beside him. 'I brought some flyers for Linda Welles, that girl went missing.'

'That's all your doin' on that is passing out flyers?'

Quinn hesitated for a moment before answering Strange. He had spent some time on a rough stretch of Naylor Road, knocking on doors, talking to people on the street. And he had tried to speak to a group of hard young men who seemed to gather daily on the steps of a dilapidated apartment structure that had been visible in the Welles video. But the young men had given him blank kill-you stares and implicit threats, and he hadn't hung with them long, despite the fact that he felt they had to know something about the girl. In the end, he had walked away from them with nothing but shame.

'I've interviewed her family,' said Quinn. 'I've talked to her friends and I went down to the neighborhood that shows up on the video. I got nothin', Derek, so I'm down to doing this.'

'Sue's gonna keep you hard on the case, huh?'

'It's not just Sue. I'm trying to do something positive for a change. That Mario Durham thing left a bad taste in my mouth, you want the truth.'

'Mine, too, I can't lie about it. But I'm running a business, and I got employees like you to support, not to mention a new family. It was quick money and I took it.'

'It stunk, just the same.'

'We can talk about that over a beer later on, you feel like it.'

'All right. In the meantime, maybe I'll go over to that grocery store and pass some of these out while you talk to Stokes.'

Strange reached for the handle on the door. 'I'll meet you back at the car.'

16

'That was Inez, over at the shop,' said Horace McKinley, flipping his cell closed. 'That police, or whoever he is, came by to see Devra.'

'Same one we tailed yesterday?'

'He's drivin' the same car. He showed Inez some kind of badge, told her he was an investigator for D.C., some bullshit like that.'

'He leave his name?'

'Said it was Strange.' McKinley, in fact, had known Strange's name for some time now.

'The girl ain't there, though, right?' said Michael Montgomery.

'Nah, Inez sent her home for a couple of hours when that man called, said he was rollin' on down.'

'Guess he shouldn't have called ahead.'

'Yeah, we one step ahead of the motherfucker, for now. He gets her to testify against Phil Wood, we got us a serious problem we got to fix. I'm talkin' about the girl.'

Montgomery nodded without conviction. He wasn't into the way McKinley roughed up the women. Gettin' violent on women didn't sit well with him; he'd seen a whole lot of men – if you could call them men – beat on his mother through the years when he was a kid. One of them finally beat his mother half to death. Years later, that man had got his brains blown out across an alley by a gun in Montgomery's hand. Montgomery's mother and his younger brother were staying with some relatives now in a suburb of Richmond. He hadn't seen his mom or the little man for some time.

They stood in the house on Yuma, McKinley's great girth filling out the fabric of his warm-up suit. 'Monkey Mike' Montgomery's arms hung loosely at his sides, his hands reaching his knees.

'What you want to do, for now?' said Montgomery.

'Grab the Coates cousins off the back stoop,' said McKinley. 'Tell them to get over to the apartment where Devra Stokes stays at. Strange told Inez he knew where she stayed, so that's where he's off to next. Tell 'em to make sure this Strange knows they're around.'

'They took a few shots at the Six Hundred boys last night. You knew about it, right?'

McKinley nodded. He had heard them bragging on it out back, and he was down with what they had done. Once in a while you had to let the rivals know you were out here and still alive. Except for Dewayne and Zulu Walker, the 600 Crew was light. The one they had shot at, called himself Nutjob, like the name would mean somethin' just by saying it, he wasn't nothin' but a punk.

'I musta knew somethin' when I took those cousins on.' McKinley smiled, showing the three silver 'fronts' on his upper teeth. 'Those boys are ready.'

'You want them to talk to Stokes, too?'

'Nah,' said McKinley. 'Those two are like a couple of horses, man. I don't want to be ridin' them too hard. You and me, we'll visit the bitch when she gets back to work. In the meantime, let's roll over to that barbecue place on Benning Road and get us some lunch.'

Montgomery left the house to give the Coateses their orders for the day. McKinley walked toward the front door, where he'd be far enough away from the others. He dialed a number, got a receptionist, gave her a name that was a code, and was transferred to the man he had asked to speak to.

'Strange is still on it,' said McKinley. 'But you don't have to worry about nothin', hear?'

McKinley ended his call and mopped some sweat off his forehead with a bandanna he kept in his pocket. All this weight he was carrying, it was starting to get to him. He'd been meaning to lose some, 'cause lately he'd been feeling tired and slow all the time.

McKinley could think about that later, though. Right now, all he could get his head around was lunch.

An elderly man wearing a straw boater sat on a folding chair in the shade outside the hair and nail salon, smoking a cigarette. Strange passed by him, nodded by way of a greeting, and received a slow nod in return.

Strange entered the salon and saw that Devra Stokes was not in, or at least was not in the front of the shop. He went over to the older woman who had been giving him the cold looks the day before, and who seemed to be in charge. Strange guessed her height at four-foot-ten or four-eleven, straddling the line between short and dwarf. Her face was unforgiving, without laugh lines or any other evidence that she knew how to smile.

'Devra in?' said Strange.

'She is not.'

Strange flipped open his badge case and showed it to her for a hot second. His private detective's license read 'Metropolitan Police Department' across the top. It was the one thing that most people remembered, especially if it was shown and put away in a very short period of time.

'Investigator, D.C.'

This was his standard introduction. Officially, the description was correct, intended to give the impression that he was with the police. Anyway, it wasn't a lie.

'That supposed to mean somethin' to me?'

'My name is Strange. I spoke to you on the phone a little while earlier. You said Devra would be in today.'

'I sent her home early.'

'But you knew I was comin' by.'

'So?'

'You're interfering with an investigation.'

'So?'

Strange stepped in close to the woman. He had more than a foot of height on her, and he looked down with intimidation into her stone-cold face. She didn't back up. Her expression didn't change.

'Yesterday,' said Strange, 'when I came by here, I got followed on my way out. You know anything about that?'

'Why would I? And if I did know, why would I care? And why would I care to tell you?'

'You got a name?'

'I got one. But I got no reason to give it to you.'

'I know where Devra lives,' said Strange, realizing it was childish the moment the words left his mouth. 'I'll just go over there now.'

'You mean you ain't gone yet?'

Strange left the shop, muttering something about a tough-ass bitch under his breath.

He heard the old man in the chair chuckle as he headed toward the parking lot. Strange stopped walking, stared at the old man for a second, then relaxed as he saw the friendly amusement in the old man's eyes.

'Little old girl stonewalled you, right?'

'That's a fact,' said Strange.

'You a bill collector? 'Cause if you are, you ain't gonna get nary a penny out of Inez Brown.'

'I can see that. She the owner of that shop?'

The old man dragged the last life out of his cigarette and dropped it to the concrete. He ground the butt out with the sole of his black leather shoe as he shook his head.

'Drug dealer owns that shop,' said the old man.

'You know his name?'

The old man continued to shake his head, smoke clouding around his weathered face. 'Big boy, wears jewelry. Got this ring that covers his whole hand. Has silver teeth, too. It ain't unusual for his kind to put money into these places. Those young boys like to hang out where the young ladies do.'

Strange nodded slowly. 'Can't blame them for that.'

'No. You can blame 'em for a lot, but not for that.'

'You have a good one,' said Strange.

'Gonna be hot today,' said the old man. 'Hot.'

Back in the Caprice, Strange eyeballed Quinn, who was outside the grocery store, his face close to the face of a young man, both of their mouths working furiously. Even from the distance, Strange could see that vein bulging on the left side of Quinn's forehead, the one that emerged when he got hot.

Strange found what he was looking for in the small spiral notebook by his side. He phoned Janine and asked her to run the plate numbers from the Mercedes that had tailed him the day before. He had her look into any priors on an Inez Brown, and he gave her the address of the salon and its name so that she could check on who it was, exactly, who held its lease.

'Anything else?' said Janine.

'I got some shirts hangin' back in my office, need some cleaning.'

'Thanks for the opportunity to serve you. You want those shirts pressed, too?'

'Not too much starch, baby.'

'When you need 'em by?'

'Yesterday.'

'Consider it done. Now, maybe you got something else you want to say to me.'

'You mean about how much I appreciate all your good work?'

'Thought you were just gonna imply it.'

'You don't give me a chance, all that sarcasm.'

'Okay, go ahead.'

'I do appreciate you. Matter of fact, you're the backbone of my everything. And I've been thinkin' about you, you know, the other way, too. Haven't been able to get you out of my mind all day.'

'For real?'

'I wouldn't lie.'

'You'll be home for dinner, right?'

'I'll call you. Me and Terry were gonna stop and have a couple beers.'

'Let me know.'

'I will.'

'I love you, too, Derek.'

Strange picked up Quinn outside the grocery store. They drove out of the lot.

'Everything all right back there?' said Strange.

'Yeah. Guy was wondering how he could join the Terry Quinn fan club. I was, like, giving him the membership requirements. How about you?'

'Well, Tattoo's sister wasn't no help. But I did find out a thing or two.'

'Must have been that quality detective work you're always going on about.'

'Not really. Old man I never even met just went and volunteered all sorts of shit.'

'Good day at Black Rock,' said Quinn.

'It happens once in a while,' said Strange. 'I didn't even have to ask.'

Devra Stokes lived off Good Hope Road in an apartment complex where 'Drug-Free Zone' signs were posted on a black wrought-iron fence. Strange pulled into the lot and cut the engine.

'You coming?' said Strange.

'I'm not really into the Free Granville Oliver movement,' said Quinn. 'So I think I'll hang, you don't mind.'

'I'll leave the keys,' said Strange, 'case you want to listen to some of my music.'

'You got that one about lame men walkin'?'

'It's in the glove box. Help yourself.'

Quinn watched Strange cross the lot and disappear into a dark stairwell.

Juwan Stokes sat on the floor of Devra Stokes's apartment, playing with some action figures, while Strange and Stokes sat at the dining-room table. The apartment, filled with old furniture and new electronics, was in disarray and smelled of marijuana resin and nicotine. Devra apologized, explaining that her roommate, a young woman who worked in another salon, had recently brought an inconsiderate, no-account man into the place against Devra's wishes. This man was unemployed, liked to burn smoke and drink at all hours, and was responsible for the mess.

'Not too good for the boy, I expect,' said Strange.

'We're looking to get out.' As she said it, she looked out the apartment's large window.

'I can help you, short-term.'

'How you gonna do that?'

'Defense has witness relocation capabilities, same as the prosecution.'

'Like Witness Protection?'

'Not really. You don't change your name, and you don't have anybody looking after you. Basically, they have funds set aside that can get you into a place, an apartment like this one, in another part of town.'

'The Section Eights, right?'

'Sometimes.'

'I'm not movin' Juwan into no Section Eights.'

'Maybe we can do better than that. We can try.' Strange leaned forward. 'Look, I think you know things that would help out our case. You were with Phil Wood back when the murder of Granville's uncle went down. Phil must have talked to you about it then.'

'He talked about a lot of things,' said Devra. 'But listen, Phil and Granville and their kind, all of 'em been into some serious shit. None of them's innocent. This is the Lord, now, giving them their due. I don't want to get in the way of that. I don't want to be involved.'

'I can subpoena you, Devra.'

'Nah, hold up.' Devra Stokes raised one hand and her lovely eyes lost their light. 'I don't like to be threatened. That's something you're gonna find out, you get to know me better. When Phil started taking a hand to me, that's when we broke up. But it wasn't the physical thing so much as it was what was coming from his mouth. "Bitch, I will do this" and "Bitch, I will do that." I was like, Do it, then, motherfucker, but don't be threatenin' me. That's when I filed charges against him. I just got tired of all those threats.'

'But you dropped the charges.'

'He paid me to. And I had no reason to hurt him that bad. It was over for us anyway by then.' Devra looked down at her son. 'That life is behind me, forever and for real. I got no reason to go back there. None.'

'Mama,' said Juwan, 'look!' He was flying an action figure, some hillbilly wrestler, through the air.

'I see, baby,' said Devra.

'This isn't personal,' said Strange. 'But you need to understand: I am going to do my job.'

'Ain't personal with me, either. But I'm not lookin' to get involved, and I've told you why. Now, I need to get back to work.'

'Thought Inez gave you the day off.'

'Not the whole day. She told me that it was slow and to take a couple of hours of break and then come back.'

'I see,' said Strange. 'Inez doesn't own that place, does she?'

'No.'

'Do you know who does?'

Devra nodded, cutting her eyes away from Strange's. 'Horace McKinley.'

'McKinley. Wears one of those four-finger rings, got silver on his teeth?'

'Yeah.'

'He's a drug dealer, right?'

'That ain't no secret. Plenty of these salons down here got drug money behind them. Same way with the massage parlors all over this city, too.' Devra stood, picked up Juwan, and held him in her arms. 'Look, I gotta clean him up and get back to work.'

'There's plenty you haven't been telling me, isn't there?'

'Seems like you're doing all right without my help.'

'Go ahead and take care of your son,' said Strange. 'I'll walk you out.'

Strange went over to the large window that gave to a view of the lot. A beige Nissan with a spoiler mounted on its rear was driving very slowly behind the Caprice, where Quinn waited in the passenger seat. The bass booming from the vehicle vibrated the apartment window. Strange studied the Nissan, sun gleaming off its roof, as it passed. He knew that car.

17

It took Devra a while to get herself and the boy ready. Strange waited for her to do whatever a woman felt she had to do and saw Devra and Juwan to her Taurus. As he walked back to his Caprice, he noticed that the car seemed to be in the general area where he had left it, but there was something off about how it was parked. Strange guessed it was the way it was slanted in its space; he didn't remember putting it in that way.

Quinn was impassive, leaning against the passenger door as Strange got behind the wheel.

'You see that Nissan,' said Strange, 'was cruising slow behind you, little while back?'

'Saw it and heard it,' said Quinn. 'They passed by twice. I could see them smiling at me in my side mirror. My pale arm was leaning on the window frame the second time they went by. They must not have liked the look of it or something. That's when they split.'

'You make the car?'

'Early nineties, Nissan Two Forty SX. The four-banger, if I had to guess.'

'You could hear the engine over the music?'

'The valves were working overtime.'

'Okay. How those boys look to you? Wrong?'

'All the way. But that could just be me, profiling again.'

'Once a cop,' said Strange.

'Tell me you know 'em,' said Quinn.

'I do. Those two rolled up on me at a light yesterday. Both of them had those bugged-out eyes.'

'Like Rodney Dangerfield and Marty Feldman got together and made a couple of babies.'

'They could be brothers. One of 'em made the slash sign across his throat. Another car, a Benz, was trying to hem me in from behind.'

'Sounds like it was planned.'

'A classic trap,' said Strange. 'And you know that gangs hunt in packs. Anyway, I thought I was imagining this shit at the time, but I don't think so anymore. They're trying to warn me off of talking to Stokes.'

'You want me to, I can show you where they went.'

'You followed them, didn't you?'

The lines around Quinn's eyes deepened, star-bursting out from behind his aviators. 'I figured, loud as they were listening to that music of theirs, they wouldn't make me, that is if I played it right. And if they did make me, so what? I stayed behind other vehicles, five or six car lengths back, the whole way. Just like you taught me, Dad.'

'Thought there was something different about my car from where I'd left it.'

'I parked it one space over.'

'Knew it was something.'

'Was wondering if you were gonna catch it. They stopped at another apartment complex, not far from here.'

'Nice work,' said Strange, pulling his seat belt across his chest. 'Let's run by the parking lot of those apartments.'

'I need to eat something,' said Quinn. 'And I could use a beer.'

'I could, too,' said Strange.

Mario Durham took a shower at Donut's apartment, then dressed again in the clothes he'd been wearing the past two days. He had some fresh clothes over at his mother's house, but he didn't want to go there just yet. The Sanders jersey and his Tommys, they were a little ripe but not awful. He had put his nose to them and they didn't smell all that bad.

Mario needed to talk to Dewayne when the time was right, kind of ease him into the events of the night before, then wait for Dewayne's instructions. But not yet; he'd just hang back for today. He was looking forward to seeing that shine in Dewayne's eyes, though. He was thinking Dewayne was gonna be proud to have a big brother who finally went and stepped up.

Mario Durham's whole outlook had changed since he'd killed Olivia. He had taken a life, done what he'd only heard others talk about. Sure, Mario was scared of getting caught, but he was high on the fact that he now belonged in the same club as his brother and Zulu and all the others who bragged about killing around the way. The gun in his hand had changed everything he'd been before. It had made him a man. He was happy to be rid of that gun, but it would be good to get another. He'd do that in time, too.

Mario hadn't told Donut why he needed to lay up with him for a few days, and Donut hadn't asked. But he was itchin' to tell somebody, and he needed some advice. Donut, who got that name 'cause he loved those sugar-coated Hostess ones so much when he was a kid, was his boy from way back.

Donut was on the couch, holding a controller, playing NBA Street. Over the television was a rack, plywood on brackets, holding Donut's blaxploitation and exploitation video collection. He favored Fred Williamson's and Jim Brown's body of work, and also the low-budget, high-grossing B films from the seventies: *Macon County Line, Jackson County Jail, Billy Jack*, and the like. He had his pet actors from that period, too. He liked Carol Speed and Thalmus Rasulala, and especially Felton Perry, played in the second Dirty Harry movie and the first one in that series about the redneck sheriff. There was a time when Donut had fantasized about being an actor his own self, but every mirror he looked into told him different, and eventually reality had beaten down those dreams.

The remains of a fatty sat in an ashtray on the table before him, as did a can of beer. Donut was small like Mario and close to ugly, and he hadn't ever held any kind of payroll job. But he did all right. He sold marijuana to his network of friends and dummies to the suckers drivin' by out on the street.

Donut's window air conditioner rattled in the room.

'You feel better?' said Donut.

'Shower did me right,' said Durham.

'I'm goin' out in a little bit, need to pick up some shit.'

'I'll just rest here, you don't mind. Kinda hot to be walkin' around.'

Donut looked over at his skinny friend, standing by the couch looking at him like a dog waitin' on a treat, one hand in his pocket, jingling change. Long as Donut had known him, that was the way Mario stood: slouched, his hand in his pocket, needy eyed, always wanting something.

'What's up?' said Donut.

'Need to talk to you, Dough.'

Donut's eyes went to the couch, then back to Durham. 'Then sit your ass down and talk.'

Durham sat down beside Donut as Donut put some fire back to the joint. They passed the marijuana back and forth.

Slowly, building it up with drama, Durham told Donut what he'd done. As he related the murder of Olivia Elliot, he began to embellish the story, making her an all-out bitch, making himself stronger, more heroic, and more justified than he had been. His head had gotten up quick from the chronic, and the tale sounded good to his ears.

'Damn, boy,' said Donut, 'you did it for real.'

'She took me off, and my brother, too. What was I supposed to do, let it ride?'

'They gonna find that girl. You know this, right?'

'I put her deep in the woods. But yeah, eventually they will. After that, shit, I get by a few days without no one pickin' me up, maybe I'll be all right. Seems like the whole police force is out there lookin' for that white girl was fuckin' that congressman, so maybe they'll just forget. Cases get cold quick down here anyway; you know that. If the police *are* lookin' for me, well, everyone knows who my brother is. Ain't nobody gonna point me out. But maybe they won't come lookin' for me. I done fixed all the evidence, I think.'

'What about that gun?'

'It was a hack. I rented it from that dealer does business with Dewayne. Ulysses Foreman, lives over in PG? I already gave it back.'

'You tell him it was a murder gun?'

'Sure,' said Mario, still embellishing, still bragging. 'I mean, he took one look at me, he knew what I'd done. You can't hide something like that.'

'What you gonna do now, then, just wait?'

'I guess.'

Donut nodded his head, his eyes pink from the chronic. Durham could tell that Donut was just trying to think things out.

'You can lay up here for a little while, I guess. But not forever, hear? You my boy, but I can't be no accessory to no homicide. With my priors, I'm looking at long time.'

'I won't stay long. The thing of it is, I could use some money to stake me, so I can move on out of Southeast for a while.'

'I'm light right now.'

'Oh, I wasn't askin' for you to give me no cash. I got some in my pocket, my brother gave me. What I was thinkin', I could double it, maybe triple it, with your help. I'll give you what I got for some dummies I can sell out there on the strip. I can make a quick rack of money like that. The quicker I do, the quicker I'm gone.'

'Yeah, but you need to be careful behind that shit.'

'You don't have to worry about me, Dough,' said Durham, shaking his friend's hand. 'I'm harder than you think I am. I'll be all right.'

Donut looked down at Durham's feet. 'You get some money, first thing you need to do is buy you some new sneaks.'

'I do need to get myself into the new style.'

'Looks like some of that bitch's blood got on 'em, too.'

'I guess it did.' Durham looked stupidly at the PlayStation 2 controllers lying on the floor. 'You wanna play some Street before you tip out?'

'I will, if you're ready to lose.'

'I'm done with losin',' said Durham. 'Do I look like I could lose to you?'

Horace McKinley snapped the lid down on his cell as he crossed the parking lot with Mike Montgomery, walking toward the hair shop. He was moving slow, and his stomach hurt some. He had eaten too much barbecue at lunch, but it had tasted too good for him to stop.

'That was James,' said McKinley. 'Him and Jeremy circled around that Strange's car a couple of times, then went back to their place.'

'They make an impression?'

'Some white boy was in the car. But they say they got their point across. I told them to stay where they're at for a while. Sun ain't down yet, and James sounds like he's all fucked up on somethin' already.'

'He usually is.'

'Yeah, but those two earned it. They done enough for today.' McKinley tipped his large head in the direction of Devra Stokes's Taurus. 'She's in there. There go her car.'

They went into the shop. Devra was painting the nails of a woman her age, a goosenecked lamp throwing light on the table between them. Juwan sat at Devra's feet, his plastic wrestlers in his lap and on the linoleum floor. Inez Brown was seated behind a desk, reading a magazine. She stood and smoothed out her skirt as McKinley lumbered through the door.

Devra and the young woman had been talking, but they stopped at the sight of the fat man and his long-armed companion. The new Eve was coming from the store stereo, and it had become the only sound in the room.

McKinley took a half-smoked cigar and a silver lighter from the pocket of his warm-up suit and flamed the cigar's end. When he was satisfied with the draw he replaced the lighter in his pocket. He looked at the cigar lovingly as he exhaled, then gazed at the young customer as if he were noticing her for the first time.

'Sorry to interrupt your session, baby,' said McKinley, 'but you're gonna have to leave for a while, come back later on. Me and my employee need to discuss some business up in here.'

'She ain't even done with my nails,' said the young woman.

McKinley lodged the cigar in the side of his mouth, reached for his wallet, withdrew a ten, and dropped it on the table. 'Go on, get yourself some MacDonald's, sumshit like that.'

'I ain't hungry.'

'You look hungry to me.'

Her eyes went up and down his rotund body. 'How would *you* know what hungry looks like?'

McKinley leaned down and put his face close to hers. 'Go on, now,' he said. 'Before I lose my composure.'

She looked away from him and stood quickly. She gathered her possessions and left the shop.

'All right, girl,' McKinley said to Devra, smiling pleasantly, showing her his fronts. 'Let's have a talk in the back.'

'I need to look after my son,' said Devra.

'Mike'll look after the boy,' said McKinley. 'He's good with kids.' To Inez Brown he said, 'Lock that front door.'

Devra got up from her chair and Juwan stood up with her. She danced her fingers through his short, tight hair. 'Mama's just going in the other room. I'll be out in a while. Stay out here and play.'

The boy sat back down but kept his eyes on his mother as she walked through a doorway behind the register desk. He watched the fat man with all the jewelry follow her. He watched his mother's boss, that little lady who wasn't never nice to him, put her key to the lock of the front door.

'What you got there, little man?' said Montgomery, who had crouched down beside the boy, his forearms resting on his thighs. 'Who's that, the Rock?'

'That's Afro Thunder!' said Juwan, pointing to one of the action figures. He didn't mind talking to this man. His eyes told Juwan that this man was all right.

'My mistake,' said Montgomery, gently tapping the boy's shoulder. 'Tell me the names of the other ones you got, too.'

The back room, cluttered with supplies and lit with a forty-watt naked bulb, was little more than a narrow hall leading to a dirty bathroom. A door near the bathroom had a small window, barred on both sides, that gave to a view of an alley.

'Stand over there,' said McKinley, pointing to the door. Devra went to the door, crossed her arms, and leaned her back against the bars.

McKinley drew hard on his cigar and walked toward her. Smoke swirled off of him as he approached. It settled in the dim glow of the naked bulb. He stood three feet from her and smiled.

'You lookin' fine, baby.'

'Thank you.'

'You makin' some money here, right?'

'I'm doin' okay.'

'That's good,' said McKinley. 'Good to remember why you doin' okay, too.'

'I do,' said Devra.

'I know you do. I know you remember when you lost your other job, how that felt. I know you remember that it was Phil Wood who asked me to put you on. How it was him who was lookin' out for you.'

'I remember.'

'Sure you do. So my question is, why you want to go and do him dirt now?'

Devra's palms had begun to get sticky. She dropped her hands to her sides.

'You been talkin' to the police, haven't you?' said McKinley. 'That man they call Strange.'

'He's not police,' said Devra. 'He's private. Gathering evidence for Granville's defense. They be trying to talk to everyone knew Phil and Granville.'

'They tryin'. Except for some dry snitches they got inside, though, they ain't had too much success. What we got some concern about is you.'

'You don't need to worry.'

'Strange took you out somewhere yesterday, ain't that right?'

'He bought some ice cream for my boy and me, is all.'

'What about over at your apartment, a little while back? He buy you some ice cream there, too?'

'We talked,' said Devra, hating the sound of the catch in her voice. 'But I didn't talk to him about the case. He asked me to, but I didn't. Everything he knows he already knew, or he found out his own self. We just talked. Wasn't anything more than that.'

McKinley nodded slowly. He dragged on his cigar. The smoke reached her and it was foul. He looked at the cigar and then put it behind his back. Smoke coiled up over his broad, round shoulders.

'I'm sorry, baby. This bothering you?'

'It's all right.'

'You know,' said McKinley, 'I'm glad we're straight on this. Seems like you got your priorities together, I mean, with your little boy and all. Seems like a good kid.'

'He is.'

'I know you want to be a good mother. Seein' as how you had some problems with your own mother and all that. See, Phil told me about her. Granville and him knew her some around the way, when you wasn't but a slip of nothin'. She goes by the name of Mattie, right?'

'She don't have those problems anymore,' said Devra. 'She's good now.'

'But she did have some problems while you was growin' up. Phil says she was one of those rock stars, from back when they had that, what do they call it, *epidemic* here in the city.'

'She's good now,' repeated Devra.

'But she wasn't back then. Heard she was a real chicken-picker. Would give up her face for ten dollars.'

Devra said nothing.

'Was she pretty like you?' said McKinley. 'Probably not when she was geekin' behind that shit. They lose their ass at that point. But I wonder, at one time, if she was as fine as you. If she had the ass on her that you got on you now.'

McKinley stepped in and put his free hand, thick as a mitt, on Devra's hip. Then, suddenly, he moved it to the crotch of her slacks. He rubbed her clumsily through the fabric. She pushed herself against the door and felt the bars of the windows press into her back. She wanted to cry out. She wanted to look away, but she kept her eyes on his.

'You are fine,' said McKinley, his voice soft and raspy.

'Don't,' said Devra.

He pressed harder at her objection, and she said, 'Uh.'

'That hurt you? I didn't mean to.' McKinley inspected her body. 'Let's see what else we got here.'

His hand slid up and over her shirt and went to her right breast. He kneaded it and found her nipple. His forefinger made small circles there. Her nipple grew hard. He pinched it between his thumb and forefinger and it grew harder still.

'There you go,' said McKinley, smiling silver. 'Your body is betrayin' you now.'

He pinched her nipple harder and heard her breath catch. Devra's eyes filled with tears and one broke free and rolled down her cheek. He tightened his fingers more, pinching her there until she closed her eyes completely. He got very close to her face.

'I know you'll stand tall,' said McKinley. 'You gonna do this for your son. Make sure he has the kind of childhood you never had. Boy needs his mother, right?'

Devra's lip trembled. She couldn't bring herself to speak. She nodded instead.

McKinley released her and stepped back. He brought the cigar around and put it to his mouth. He drew on it and backed up toward the doorway. At the open frame he stopped and looked at her.

'We understand each other, right?'

Devra said, 'Yes.'

But in her mind she said, You have made a mistake.

18

That afternoon, a boy was cutting through the woods of Oxon Run and came upon a body lying on its back in a small clearing beside an oak. The body was bloated and ripe from the heat. If not for the smell and the sound of the flies, the boy might have missed it.

He picked up a stick. He approached the body cautiously and touched the stick to its side. It was a woman. She was dead, and he was frightened, but he had the curiosity of a boy, and even as he trembled he knew that this would be a story to tell his friends later on.

Flies buzzed all around him, some scattering momentarily as he bent down to inspect the body. There were three bullet holes he could count, two in her stomach and another in one of her breasts. The blood around the holes was close to black and looked thick, like syrup. The thing that made him run was her face: the bottom part of her jaw was set off from the top part, and her lips were drawn back over her teeth so it looked like she had died trying to smile. Also, one of her eyes had come out some and was lying on her fat purple cheek. In the empty socket, maggots clustered and writhed where the flies had laid their eggs.

The boy, who was named Barry Waters, bolted from the woods, saying things like 'Go, boy' and 'Go now' under his breath as he ran. He realized that the woman was beyond the need of help, but he went directly to Greater Southeast Community Hospital, which he knew to be close by. He tried to tell the woman behind the desk of the ER what had happened, and as he did she tried to calm him down. Barry Waters would be a celebrity of sorts in his neighborhood for the next few days. For years he would dream about the maggots, and in those nightmares he would see that anguished thing that looked something like a smile.

Sixth District police officers and homicide detectives were dispatched to the scene. For the next couple of hours a forensics team and photographers worked over the body before it was moved by ambulance to the D.C. morgue. Neighborhood people watched as 'the white shirts' – lieutenants and the like – arrived in their unmarked vehicles. Obvious gang-related killings and hits on young men did not usually draw this kind of official attention; murders of women and children brought out both suit and uniform heat.

It wasn't long before the investigation became focused on a Toyota Tercel, one of two cars parked on the street closest to the entrance to the woods. Blood was visibly smudged on its driver's door handle. In a nearby sewer police found a shower curtain stained with blood along with the keys to the car.

The Tercel was dusted for prints. The car had been wiped down but not thoroughly. Its glove box yielded a registration in the name of Olivia Elliot, with an Anacostia address. Prints on the car would be matched to the prints of the corpse, and a photo ID of Elliot, in the system, would be matched to her body as well. When this was done, a homicide detective would notify family and next of kin. The notification would also serve as the initial investigation into the case.

This would fall to homicide cop Nathan Grady, formerly of the Fourth District. His territory now, in the aftermath of the recent duty realignment, was citywide. Grady, like most of the men and women who shared his kind of shield, hated this part of the job. It would be a while, but not too long, before the final identification was made, but his gut told him that the woman found in the woods was the owner of that Tercel. Once he knew for sure, he'd go tell the husband, or the kid, or whomever, that their loved one was forever gone.

Ulysses Foreman had scored Ashley Swann a real nice gun for Christmas, a piece she had been wanting for a long time. The revolver had come from that retail gun store down in Virginia, his most frequent source. As was his usual practice, he had paid a commission to a clean Virginia resident to make the buy.

Ashley sat on the edge of their bed in her pajamas, having changed back into them after Long and Jones, Dewayne Durham's boys, had come, bought that pretty blue Taurus .38, and gone. She had taken her gun out of the drawer of her nightstand, which is where she kept it all the time. Ulysses had instructed her that this would be its most useful spot; he kept his, the 9mm Colt, the one with the custom bonded ivory grips, in his own nightstand on his side of the bed.

She was giving the gun a good inspection. She liked the weight of it in her hand.

It was the Smith & Wesson 60LS, the LadySmith, a .357 stainless-steel revolver with a speed-loader cutout and smooth rosewood grips, specially contoured to fit a woman's hand. The grips were smooth and carried the S&W monogram; Ashley oiled them often, and she used her Hoppes kit to clean the chambers and barrel at least twice a month. It was a beautiful gun. She had her eye on a similar model, the 9mm auto, manufactured in frosted stainless with matching gray grips.

'Ulee?'

'Huh.' He was lying on his back on the bed, his head propped up on pillows, his eyes on their flat-screen Sony.

'You know that LadySmith nine, the pretty one I seen in the magazine, all gray?'

'Yeah.'

'I want one.'

'Yeah, okay.'

Foreman was watching ESPN Classic. Ashley didn't know how men could stand to look at some old basketball game, had been played years before, when they knew how it was gonna end. But she did like to see him lying there, one arm behind his head, his bicep rounded, that rug of tight, curly hair covering the upper part of his chest.

'I'm thinkin' on goin' to see my daddy down in Port Tobacco,' said Ashley.

'Go ahead.'

On the tube was game 6 of the Bulls-Jazz finals from '98, played in Salt Lake. He watched Karl Malone take a dish from Stockton – white boy had to do something about those tight drawers, but he could orchestrate the shit out of some ball – and go underneath for a one-handed reverse dunk.

'The Mailman,' said Foreman with admiration.

'Ulee?'

Foreman thought about how Malone was wastin' hisself out there in Morman land. Handsome man like him, going home to his dull-ass family after the games, listenin' to country music and shit, when he could be playing in a real city like New York, spending his dollars in clubs, gettin' fresh pussy every night. To Foreman it seemed like Malone wasn't having any fun. Playing with Stockton and his short shorts, and that other white boy, wiped his face like there was somethin' runnin' down it every time he got to the foul line. Lack of fun was probably the reason why Malone had never won the ring.

'Ulee, come with me.'

'Huh?'

'To Port Tobacco!'

'Maybe I'll meet you down there,' said Foreman. 'I got business to attend to.'

The truth was, he was a city boy and wasn't cut out for no farm. Also, her father, had one of those lantern-holdin' negroes set on his lawn, made Jesse Helms look like Jesse Jackson. Pop wanted to bite right through his tongue every time Foreman came to visit. There was this other thing, too, bothered him some. Black men down there, deep in southern Maryland, some of them acted like they was back in 1963. Yessirin' and all that, walkin' down those country roads in the summertime, scratchin' at the top of their heads.

Ashley put the gun back on the nightstand. She picked up the glass that was sitting there and had a sip of chardonnay.

'I'm thinkin' of heading down there tomorrow.'

'Tomorrow? Baby, I need to stay home. I got some serious demand for low-end product right now, and I am light.'

'What about that boy goes to Howard? I thought he was coming up from Georgia.'

'He is. He's bringing a load up Ninety-five in that trap car of his. But he's not due up in here for a few more days.'

'What you gonna do, then?'

'I got that kid stays in Virginia, keeps a bunch of girls down there, over in Alexandria? I don't know where he gets these girls, but he gets 'em. Anyway, the girls he finds, they got no priors.'

'They old enough?'

'Course they are; I wouldn't waste my time they weren't of age. He's gonna come by tomorrow so I can give him the cash to make the buy.'

'I wish you could come with me.'

'So do I, baby, but work is work. Maybe I'll have him see if they got one of those LadySmith nines in stock while he's down there.'

'For real?'

'Why not?'

Foreman heard her place the glass of wine back on the nightstand. He heard the rustle of cloth and her gutter-girl giggle. When he looked over at her she had peeled her pajama top off her shoulders and was crawling toward him across the bed. The bedsprings were crying on account of her weight. Her titties hung low, and those silver-dollar nipples of hers were grazing the sheets.

Foreman didn't have to watch the rest of the game. He'd seen it. And anyway, four minutes to go, Jordan on the court with that look in his eye, any fool would know how it was going to end.

Ashley lowered herself upon him, her greenish-blond hair tickling his face, and kissed him deep. Her nipples felt hot on his chest. Her tongue was hot, too. Lord, could she kiss. He closed his eyes so he didn't have to look at her. She wasn't good-lookin' or nothin' close to it, but he did love her. And the woman could buck like a horse.

'Uh,' she said. 'Uh-huh.'

The way she was on him now, making those sounds she liked to make? His dick was so hard a cat couldn't scratch it. He'd had her earlier that day, but that was hours ago. She kept playin' like this, he was just gonna have to go ahead and toss the shit out of her again.

'Gimme some of that,' said Jerome Long.

'You sure?' said Allante Jones. He had just put fire to a joint, double rolled in EZ Widers.

'Gimme it. I need that shit to calm my nerves.'

'Shaky, huh?'

'A little.'

'You'll be all right, after. You'll feel good then.'

They were in their car, purchased for them by Dewayne, a plush 2000 Maxima with seventeen-inch tires and custom alloys, with a V6 under the hood. Jones sat behind the wheel, and Long was beside him. The Taurus .38 was under Long's seat.

The Maxima sat on the street, facing the lot of the apartments where the Coates cousins lived. This girl Long knew from the clubs, who mentioned once that she'd been with one of the cousins before, had told him where they stayed.

Their hooptie, the old 240SX with the spoiler, was parked in the lot. It was dark out now, and they'd been waiting on the street for an hour or so. But so far the cousins had not come out.

Long got the joint from Jones and hit it. He took the herb into his lungs, watching a man in a wheelchair roll down the sidewalk toward their car. The man was dressed in black and wore a black skully on his head. Not far behind him were two young girls, smiling, elbowing each other, having fun.

'Boy musta caught one in the spine,' said Jones.

Long closed his eyes. When he opened them the man in the wheelchair was gone. The young girls were alongside the car, laughing as they walked by. Long hit the chronic again, wondering what those girls had to laugh at, and passed it back over to his friend. Sometimes Long didn't know how anyone could laugh, the way they lived.

'You know that Muslim dude,' said Long, 'always be sellin' *Final Call* newspapers and shit down by the Metro?'

'Young dude wears the dark suit?'

'They all young. This one's light-skinned, got a real faint mustache.'

'I seen that dude, yeah.'

'He was talkin' to me the other day, tryin' to tell me about the life I was livin'. How I wasn't doin' nothin' but playin' into the white man's plan of a black holocaust.'

'You mean like how they done to them Jews.'

'Except he was sayin' that we're doin' this to ourselves. Killin' each other like we do.'

'Whateva.'

Long took the joint but didn't hit it. 'Man said it was like we were in some kind of circus down here.'

'He did, huh?'

'And we in the ring, performing like the white man expects us to. One big ring of souls, killin' each other while Mr Charlie claps. You think it's like that?'

'I don't know if it is or if it isn't. But take a look around you, boy. What else we gonna do? 'Cause there *ain't* nothin' else.' Jones shook his head. 'Nothin'.'

Long was high. He stared through the windshield. He saw nothing and no way out. Though the night air was warm, he felt a chill run through him. The cold feeling went all the way down to his feet.

'Don't you ever get scared?' said Long.

'Not really,' said Jones. He looked away from Long then. He did get scared sometimes. But he couldn't tell his friend that he did.

The cousins emerged from a stairwell in the apartment complex, crossed the parking lot, and walked toward the Nissan.

Jones chucked up his chin. 'There they go, Nut.'

'I see 'em.'

Jones turned the ignition. 'Time to go to work.'

19

Strange and Quinn had some barbecue at a place Strange liked, around 18th and U, then went over to Stan's, near McPhearson Square, for drinks. The crowd was unpretentious, mixed race and class. The house signature was a full glass of liquor with a mixer side. The music was always tight. This was Strange's idea of a bar.

The tables in the main area were full, so Strange and Quinn found stools at the stick.

Strange drank Johnnie Walker Red with a soda back. Quinn had a Heineken. *Here, My Dear* was on the house stereo, and the bartender was letting it roll from front to back.

'Marvin's masterpiece,' said Strange.

'He was local, right?'

Strange nodded. 'He came back to sing at Cardozo once, after he got huge. But they say he wasn't really into being back in D.C. All those memories with his old man, I guess. Course, he had all sorts of demons, not just family stuff. I remember back in the seventies, cats were walkin' around sayin', Is Marvin gay?'

'It bothered you, didn't it?'

'Yeah, sure. I'm not gonna lie. And I'm not sayin' he was or he wasn't, 'cause I don't know. But I couldn't understand the concept then and I still can't get all the way comfortable with it today. You get old enough, you're gonna see young people doin' shit you can't get behind, either. Y'all's generation is all right with a man being with a man. I'm not exactly against it, but don't expect me to embrace it, either. In my time, it's not the kind of thing we were taught to accept.'

'All of these hatreds get taught,' said Quinn.

'Sure they do,' said Strange. 'We get schooled by the people around us, and it stays inside us deep.'

'Yesterday, when I tricked that kid into giving me his mother's apartment number?'

'Olivia Elliot's boy.'

'Him. You should have seen the way he was looking at me, Derek. Like he should've known from the get-go that the white guy was gonna fuck him.'

'That's like blaming the meter maid's color for the ticket she wrote. You were just doing your job.'

'The job stinks sometimes.'

'You took those kinds of looks regular when you were a cop. Like you were part of the occupying army or something. On my side, when I wore the uniform, I caught that house-nigger rap all the time. Again, it's part of the job.'

Quinn finished his beer and asked Strange if he wanted another drink. Strange put his hand over the top of his glass. Quinn signaled the bartender and was served another Heineken.

'So anything we do,' said Quinn, 'it comes under the heading of just another job.'

'If you accept it going in, yes.'

'Like Granville Oliver?' said Quinn. 'That just a job to you, too?'

Only Janine knew the truth: that Strange had been responsible for the death of Granville Oliver's father, back in 1968. That Oliver had spared the lives of two killers at Strange's request, in exchange for Strange's help, less than a year ago.

Strange looked into his drink. 'It's more complicated than that.'

'You were making a living before you took Oliver's case. You didn't have to take it.'

'I know you think it's wrong.'

'Damn right I do. Piece of shit killed or had killed, what, a dozen people. He infected his community and he ruined the lives of all the young men he took on, and their families.'

'Most likely he did.'

'Then why shouldn't he die?'

'It's not him I'm working for. For me, it comes down to one thing: I don't believe any government should be putting its own citizens to death. Here in D.C. we voted against it, and the government's just gonna say, We don't give a good goddamn *what* you want, we're gonna execute this man anyway. And that's not right.'

'Maybe it will make some kid who's thinking about getting into the life think twice.'

'That's the argument. But in most civilized countries where they don't have the death penalty, they've got virtually no murders. 'Cause they've got the guns off the street, they've got little real poverty, and they got citizens who get involved in raising their own kids. The same people who are pro-death penalty are the ones want to protect the rights of gun manufacturers to export death into the inner cities. Hell, we got an attorney general sold on capital punishment and at the same time he's in the pocket of the NRA.'

'Well, yeah, but he doesn't think people should dance, either.'

'I'm serious, Terry, shit doesn't even make any sense. Look, an active death row doesn't deter crime; ain't nobody ever proved that. It's all about some politicians lookin' to be tough so they can get reelected the next time around. And that makes it bullshit to me. I'd do this for anyone who was facing that sentence.'

'What about McVeigh?'

'You know what they do in prison to people who kill kids? McVeigh got off easy, man; that boy just went to sleep. They should've put him in with the general population for as long as he could live. Trust me, wouldn't have been long. But they did him to get the ball rolling on this wave of executions we got coming. Wasn't nobody gonna object, for real, to McVeigh's death. A week later, they put that cat Garza down, and nobody even blinked an eye. Now that the ice got broke, next thing, a line of black and brown men gonna go into that chamber in Terre Haute, and bet it, it'll barely make the news.'

'Here we go.'

'Look here, Terry. Out of the twenty men they got on federal death row right now, sixteen are black or Hispanic.'

'Could be they did the crimes.'

'And it could be they got substandard representation. Could be they found a death-qualified jury that's more likely to find guilt than the other kind. *Could* be the prosecutors used those Willie Horton images to convince the jury that what they had was another nigger needed to be permanently took off the street. And I'm not even gonna talk about where these men came from, the opportunities and guidance they *didn't* have when they were coming up. You gonna sit there and tell me that this isn't about class or race?'

'It's about Granville Oliver, to me. Everything you're saying, it makes some sense. But it all comes down to the simple question: did Oliver do what they say he did?'

'That's off the point.'

'It is the *whole* point, way I look at it. If he did those things, then I wouldn't want to do anything to help him get off. I'm looking to stay on the right side from now on. You keep on the Oliver thing, you want to. But it's not for me.'

Strange and Quinn noticed that their faces had become close and their voices had risen. They both moved back and sat straight. Strange looked down the bar and nodded to a man he knew, a Stan's regular.

'What's goin' on, Junie?'

'I'm makin' it, Strange.'

Strange sipped at his scotch while Quinn had a pull off his beer and set the bottle on the bar.

'I'm gonna use the head,' said Quinn.

'That vein of yours is standin' out on your face.'

'So what?'

'Don't get up in anyone's shit, is all I'm sayin'.'

'Yeah, okay.'

Quinn walked toward the men's room. At a large table near the hall, a man wearing sunglasses sat with a group of six. As Quinn neared him, the man's white cane, which had been leaning against his chair, fell to the floor. Quinn picked it up and replaced it.

'Thank you,' said the man.

'No problem,' said Quinn.

Junie moved down a stool so he could get closer to Strange. When they ran into each other, the two of them generally talked about local sports, who was coming out of what high school and where they were headed, and the 'Skins.

'That friend of yours is wound up a little tight, isn't he?' said Junie.

'He's okay.' Strange smiled over Junie's shoulder at a nice-looking woman who was smiling at him. It was a habit he would never break.

'You two were arguing about something?'

'My boy just gets passionate about shit sometimes. So do I, I guess.'

Junie took a sip of his drink. 'What you think about Jeff George and the new coach? He gonna listen to Schott?'

'George don't need a coach,' said Strange. 'You ask me, man needs a shrink.'

Quinn came back and finished his beer. As they settled up their tab, Quinn's cell vibrated in the pocket of his jeans. He answered the phone and the lines in his face smoothed out. Strange figured it was Sue on the line.

'What's up?' said Strange when Quinn was done.

'Sue's all stoked. She's over at the Black Cat at some show.'

'On Fourteenth?'

'Yeah. Says she was up front, center stage for this guy Steve Wynn. She's fired up and wants to see me.'

'We better get going, then. All that piss and vinegar you got in you, you don't want to waste it on me.'

They put down twenty on fifteen and crossed the room. Quinn nudged Strange and directed his attention to the man in the black sunglasses.

'What the fuck is he starin' at?' said Quinn with a scowl.

'He ain't starin' at nothin', Terry. The man is blind.'

'I'm just fuckin' with you, man.'

Out in the night they moved toward the Caprice. Strange held out his keys.

'You feel like driving?'

'Why, you got drunk on one scotch?'

'Nah, just tired.'

'I better not,' said Quinn. 'I can't see for shit at night.'

'You got driving glasses, don't you?'

'I didn't bring 'em. And I probably wouldn't wear them if I had.'

'Afraid someone might mistake you for your boy Lewis?'

'Something like that.'

They stopped at the car.

'We all right?' said Strange.

Quinn shook Strange's hand. 'You know it, Derek.'

'Always interesting with you around, buddy.'

'Yeah,' said Quinn. 'You, too.'

20

'Turn this joint up right here, yang.'

'Missy?'

'It's got Jay-Z and Ludacris on it, too.'

'I ain't like that song.'

'Why not?'

'She be talkin' about not wantin' no one-minute man. Cuttin' on some dude 'cause he busts a nut in her too quick.'

'So?' said James.

'That's what I'm sayin',' said Jeremy. 'She's complainin' when she ought to be thankin' him. What the fuck's up with that?'

The Coates cousins were rolling down the road in their Nissan to one of those Chang markets where they knew they sold the cheapest White Owls. James wanted to smoke a fat one while they watched that new Bokeem Woodbine movie, called *BlackMale*, they'd bought off the street. All they had was rolling papers around the crib; James said that papers weren't good enough when you wanted a long-player smoke. Plus they could pick up more beer at the market while they were there.

They'd been goin' hard at the hydro and alcohol since the afternoon. They didn't have other relatives or girlfriends in the area, and neither of them had made any friends. There wasn't anything to do but hang together and get their heads up when they weren't working. They were high now, and knew that they could get higher still.

Well behind the Nissan, under the cover of other vehicles, Long and Jones cruised in the Maxima. They had been listening to 95.5 on the radio for a while, because they had one of those blocks of music goin' without commercials. They were letting it play.

'How you want to do it?' said Long.

'It's on you, Nut. You got to call it.'

'Wc could trap 'em at a light.'

'I don't like it,' said Jones. 'Too many witnesses like that.'

'Yeah, you right.' Long's thumb rubbed the barrel of the five-shot Taurus revolver in his lap. He had been rubbing at it, the sweat from his thumb oil-streaking the gun, for the past couple of miles. 'Ain't no good place to do it, right?'

'You want me to, I'll pull the trigger.'

Long wanted nothing more. But he said, 'It's my time.'

'Let's just see where they goin',' said Jones.

Long reached over to the radio and hiked up the volume.

'You like that song?' said Jones.

'Missy? It's somethin' to listen to.'

Jones shook his head. 'I don't know what that bitch is complainin' about, though. Do you?'

Jeremy Coates pulled over in front of a small neighborhood market in Congress Heights.

'You got your gun on you?' said Jeremy.

'Right here,' said James, indicating that the 9mm Hi-Point was wedged behind the belt line of his trousers, under his shirt.

'Leave it,' said Jeremy.

'I don't go nowhere without this shits,' said James. 'You want a gun, you need to buy one your own self.'

'Whateva. Go on, then.'

'Want to listen to the rest of this song.'

'They playin' the remix, man, this shit's gonna go on forever!'

'All right, I'm goin'.'

'Get me some rinds while you're in there, too.'

'Get your own got-damn rinds, boy.'

'Get me some.'

'Gimme some money then, yang.'

'What they doin'?' said Long.

'Talkin', I guess,' said Jones. 'Decidin' what to buy. *I* don't know.'

'Pull back,' said Long. 'They gonna see us, we sit here too long.'

They were on the cross street, looking at the Nissan idling, smoke coming from its pipe. Jones backed the Maxima up so that they were out of the Coateses' sight. He kept the engine going and turned the radio off.

'Now they can't see us,' said Jones, 'but we can't see them.'

'I can hear their car,' said Long, a shake in his voice. 'They still there.'

It was true. They could hear the motor knocking on the cousins' car, and the same music they'd been listening to coming from its open windows.

'Go on, then,' said Jones. 'You gonna do it, do it now, cause now's the time.'

'I will.'

'Just walk right up to that car and fire inside it. Head shots if you can. You got five in that motherfucker, right?'

Five's all I need, thought Long, intending to say it, wanting to be loose and cool, but unable to because his mouth was so dry. It was like those dreams he had sometimes, when he'd be tryin' to speak and couldn't get his lips unglued.

'Go ahead, Nut,' said Jones, his voice gentle. 'I'll pick you up there.'

'Lil' J,' said Long.

'You don't have to say nothin'. You know I got your back.'

Long got out of the car and closed his door without force. His legs were weak as he crossed the street. He held the blue revolver tight against his leg and he made it to the side of the market, where he flattened his back against its brick wall. He looked back at his friend for a moment, then pushed away from the wall. He turned the corner and stepped off the sidewalk. He walked toward the Nissan idling along the curb.

In the market, James Coates unrolled some cash as the woman behind the counter bagged up his shit.

'Put them rinds on top,' said James.

She was some kind of slope. He didn't know which kind and he didn't care. All of them who had these stores looked the same to him. This one had a kid, had one of those big-ass heads with a flat face. He was sitting near the entrance to the back room, playing with some toy cars and shit.

The woman placed a six-pack of beer in the bag, along with a pack of White Owls and a large plastic bag of pork rinds up top. She took his money, gave him his change, smiled, and thanked him.

James Coates said nothing. He took the bag off the counter and cradled it under his left arm. He heard gunshots from outside and turned his head.

Long approached the Nissan. The music was coming loud. Still the same song, Long thinking, How long can this motherfucker play? He could see the head of one of the cousins, bobbing as he sat low in his seat. He could see the cluster of little tree deodorizers hanging from the rearview. He could see no one on the passenger side. The other one must be in that store, thought Long. But he didn't look at the store. He needed to keep moving. His pace was steady, and his adrenaline was pushing him toward the car.

The cousin behind the wheel turned his head some as Long came up on him. His expression was like nothing as Long shot the gun directly into his face. The cousin's blood came back at Long in a spray, and Long fired again and one more time as the cousin pitched over to the side. The cousin's face was all over the interior of the car, and Long dropped the Taurus to the asphalt and puked up what he'd had for lunch.

He felt something like the stab of a knife between his shoulder blades and he heard a gunshot at the same time and knew he'd been shot hisself. He fell onto his back and kind of turned his head to the side and saw the other cousin walking toward him. The other cousin had a bag of groceries or sumshit in one hand and a gun in the other, and he was smiling and tears were going down his face.

Long tried to get to his feet, but he couldn't move at all. He could feel the puke chunks on his lips and it felt warm on his behind where he'd shit hisself.

The cousin was standing over him now. His eyes were mad-bulged as he pointed the gun at Long's face.

'Aaah,' said Long.

Long saw the cousin's gun hand shake. He saw the cousin's finger pull back on the trigger. He tried to scream but never got it out.

James Coates fired three rapid shots – face, neck, chest – into the jumping body of Jerome Long. He heard the cry of tires on asphalt and turned.

A Maxima was fishtailing around the corner. He could hear the engine roar as the driver pinned the gas. The car was coming right at him.

Coates fired into the windshield. He stayed where he was and he kept firing and he felt himself lifted off the street and a shower of beer and pork rinds around him. The world spun crazily, and he heard himself gurgle and felt nothing but confusion. His back had been broken and so had his neck. His eyes saw nothing forever.

The Maxima sideswiped two parked cars down the block and came to a stop near the next corner when it crashed into a telephone pole. Behind the wheel, Allante Jones sat low, his jaw slack, his eyes fixed. Had he been able to see, he would have seen a spidered windshield and upon it his own blood. A bullet had entered his forehead, tumbled through his brain, and ended his life.

Outside the market, the street was quiet, except for a Missy Elliot song coming from the open windows of a Nissan 240SX.

Inside the market, a woman named Sung locked the front door, extinguished the lights, and sat down on the floor with her little boy. His name was Tommy. She held him tightly and told him not to cry.

21

While Quinn went into a market on Georgia for a six, Strange idled the Chevy along the curb and made a couple of calls on his cell. He talked to Janine, found out what she had learned from his requests earlier in the day, and told her he'd be home after picking up Greco at the row house on Buchanan. Then he found attorney Elaine Clay's card in his wallet and punched in the number to her pager. He talked about the private investigator she used and learned how to reach him.

'He straight?' said Strange.

'He's got his ghosts, if that's what you mean,' said Elaine. 'He's trying to beat drinking, and I think it's a long fight. But on the work side of things, there's no one more straight.'

'*Ste*fanos,' said Strange, reading aloud what he'd written.

'Ste*fa*nos,' said Elaine, putting the accent on the correct syllable. 'These Greeks get touchy about their names.'

'I heard *that*,' said Strange, knowing then where he would try to meet this Stefanos face-to-face. 'Thanks, Elaine. Say hello to Marcus for me, hear?'

Ten minutes later, Strange and Quinn stood beside Quinn's Chevelle on Buchanan Street.

'Can you get out tomorrow?' said Strange.

'Every day, you want me to. Lewis is cutting me back.'

'Phil Wood's taking the stand tomorrow, so my time is getting short. I could use the company and the help.'

'And you can help me on the Welles runaway thing.'

'Right. I'm gonna try and get us a meeting with this PI, knows all the players down in Southeast.'

'Okay. Call me in the morning.'

'Bring your eyeglasses, man. Maybe I'll let you drive some.'

Quinn nodded toward the row house, where they could both hear Greco alternately barking and crying from behind Strange's door. 'You better see to your dog.'

Strange watched Quinn's car turn left onto Georgia as he walked up the steps to his house. Nearing the door, he noticed that a section of its window had been shattered and the jamb was splintered. The door was closed, but Strange knew he'd been burgled. The door opened without a key.

Stepping into the foyer, he found Greco lying on his belly, rubbing his eyes with his front paws. His tail was twitching at the sound and smell of Strange's entrance, but he was crying.

'All right, boy,' said Strange softly, 'let me get a look at you.'

Strange lifted the paws away from Greco's face. His eyes were pink and nearly red at the rims. The intruders had used something, pepper spray most likely, to immobilize him.

Strange went to his second-floor bathroom and got some Murine eyedrops out of the medicine cabinet. As he passed the doorway to his office, he noticed that the room had been completely tossed. It was the only room he had seen so far that had been misarranged. He did not stop but went directly down the stairs to Greco.

Strange put drops in Greco's eyes and then got spring water from the refrigerator and flushed his eyes further, splashing the water from a juice glass. Greco stood after a while and shook himself, then touched his nose to Strange's calf. Strange patted the top of his head.

'You're like that one-eyed fat man, boy,' said Strange. 'You got what they call true grit.'

Strange was angry that anyone would do this to a good animal. But he was thankful that the dog was alive.

Strange went up to his office. The Granville Oliver files, including paper and audio tapes, were gone. Other files were missing as well. Some of the cases on his western CDs were broken into pieces. Everything atop his desk, except for his telephone and message machine, had been swept onto the floor.

He had duplicate files and tapes in his daytime offices. He guessed that the storefront on Buchanan had been inspected and found to be wired for security. It wasn't as if they couldn't beat his simple alarm system if that was what they wanted to do. But the home break-in was deliberate in that it carried a deeper meaning.

The message light blinked 2 on his machine. Strange hit the receive bar.

Devra Stokes had called. She said she wanted to talk.

The next message was from a white man: 'You interviewed a Kevin Willis in Leavenworth. In your conversation, Mr Willis talked about a pending capital case. Obstruction of justice in a capital case is the highest form of obstruction and carries the most severe penalty. Eight to ten years, medium security. The loss of your license forever. How much are you willing to lose?'

The message ended there. Strange listened to the message again and transcribed it exactly. He saved the message and checked the directory on the readout of the phone. The call following Devra's said 'No Data.' Strange phoned Raymond Ives at home and got the attorney on the line. He read the message to Ives.

'You save it?'

'Yeah.'

'You'll never be able to trace that call.'

'I know it.'

'Call the police, report the burglary, and have them come to the house. Get a record of the event.'

'What else?'

'Nothing.'

'What?'

'Nothing.'

Strange listened to Ives breathe. He was telling him that he would talk no further about the subject, not on this line. So Ives suspected that Strange's phone was bugged.

'I'll speak with you later,' said Strange.

'Right,' said Ives.

Strange phoned the police. He was told that some officers would be dispatched to his place in the next half hour.

He phoned Janine on his cell. If the home phones were tapped, then surely his cell calls were being monitored as well. He didn't care. If the government was after him, FBI or whoever, there wasn't all that much he could do. He wasn't going to spend his time making pay-phone calls and worrying about conversations indoors. He was getting angrier by the moment. All that talk about loss of license and eight-to-ten. He didn't take to threats. This was bullshit, was what it was. They had misjudged him, thinking he would cave to their office-toss and phone messages. And they shouldn't have fucked with his dog.

He got Janine and gave her the facts without conjecture. She asked him if he was sitting down.

'I just watched the news, Derek. Someone found the body of Olivia Elliot in Oxon Run late this afternoon.'

'Lord,' said Strange.

'You better call Lydell,' said Janine.

'I will,' said Strange, rubbing at his face. His anxiety shifted from thoughts of himself and the government to his role in this girl's death.

And then there was Quinn and Mark Elliot, Olivia's son. The hardest part would be telling Quinn.

'Derek, you there?'

'Yes. I'll be home in a couple of hours. I'm waitin' on the police.'

'I'll save you dinner.'

'You got anything special for Greco? Some bones, maybe?'

'I'll find something.'

'I love you, baby.'

'See you soon.'

Strange phoned his friend Lydell Blue, a lieutenant in the Fourth District, at home. He told Blue that he was calling about Olivia Elliot, the woman whose murder had made the TV news. He gave Blue Mario Durham's name and cell phone number, and told him what Durham had paid him to do.

'That's your man right there, I expect.'

'No address?'

'What I gave you is what I have.'

'You better come in tomorrow morning. I'll find out who's got the case in Homicide and have him meet us at the Gibson building. Say nine o'clock?'

'I'll be there. I'll bring Quinn, too.'

'All right then, Derek. Thanks for the call.'

Blue hung up on his end. Strange heard the police knocking on the door on the first floor and went down to let the two uniformed cops in. He spent some time with them, then left them to do their job. He went to the living room, sat on his mother's old couch, and stared at the cell phone he still held in his hand. There wasn't any way to put it off any longer. He phoned Quinn.

Dewayne Durham had gotten the cell message on the way back from Six Flags amusement park informing him of the deaths of Jerome Long and Allante Jones. One of his young men at the elementary school had made the call. Word of the quadruple homicide had spread quickly on the street.

Durham and Bernard Walker dropped off Durham's son, Laron, at his mother's place in Landover. Durham hugged Laron without feeling and sent him into his apartment holding balloons and candy. Durham watched him, thinking, That boy has grown some, not realizing or caring that it had been six months since he had seen him last.

There were still a couple of balloons in the backseat of the Benz as Durham and Walker drove back into the city. Walker tried to look around them in the rearview as he changed lanes.

'Boy who called me said Nutjob shot first,' said Durham.

'I guess Jerome did have that fire in him after all,' said Walker. 'He ain't had enough to save his life.'

'We lost two to get two of theirs. Makes us even, right?'

'That's not the way it works; you know that. Some young boy now in Yuma is gonna see this as a way to prove he can put work in. All's this is gonna do is make the killin' start.'

'We'll be ready, then.'

'We gonna have to be.' Durham shifted in his seat. 'Go on over to Mississippi Avenue. Let's see what's up, get the rest of the story from the troops.'

When they got to the elementary school in Congress Heights, there were few of their people around. Durham could see a kid up by the flagpole, standing back in the shadows, and another boy, a lookout no older than twelve, up there on a bike. The kid rode his bike down the rise to the Benz, which Walker had put beside the curb. He wheeled around to the passenger side of the car as Durham's window glided down.

'Wha'sup, youngun?'

The boy's face was streaked with sweat, and excitement lit his eyes. A cell phone in a holster lay against his hip. 'It was me called you up.'

'I'll remember it, too.'

'Five-O already came by twice, askin' after you. Same car both times.'

They heard the whoop of a siren blast then, as if on cue, as an MPD cruiser came down Mississippi.

'Here they come again,' said Walker.

'Book, little man,' said Durham, and the kid took off on his bike. He went up the cross street, past the elementary school, and disappeared into an alley.

'What you want me to do?' said Walker.

'Kill the engine. You don't got your gun with you, do you?'

'You told me not to bring it, 'cause of your son.'

'We all right, then.' Durham moved to the left so that he could see the Crown Vic cruiser in the rearview, idling behind them with its headlights on, radioing in for backup. He could read the car number, but he suspected that this was more than a routine stop.

The Maryland-inflected, deep female voice on the cruiser's loudspeaker told them to put their hands outside the open windows of the car. They did this, then were approached by two officers. One of them had drawn his sidearm, a Glock 17, and was holding it out and pointed at the driver's window with his elbow locked.

'Why they're not waitin' on more cars?' said Walker.

Durham said, 'They want to talk to me first.'

The officers separated them outside the car. Walker was led to the side of the cruiser by a tall officer with a thick black mustache. Durham was frisked against the Benz by an eight-year veteran of the force, a wide-bottomed woman with short bottle-blond hair. Her name was Diane Beard.

Beard pushed on Durham's head until it was bowed and got close to his ear. 'We're taking you in for questioning soon as the backup gets here.'

'For what?'

'The shooting tonight.'

'I don't know nothin',' said Durham, his standard response to any police question.

'Course you don't,' said Beard.

'Why you here?' said Durham, lowering his voice.

'Jerome Long and Allante Jones are dead. The Coates cousins, too.'

'Tell me somethin' I don't know.'

'Your brother, Mario, is hot.'

'What?'

'A woman named Olivia Elliot was found murdered in Oxon Run this afternoon. Mario's the number one suspect. It just came out over the radio.'

Durham said, 'God*damn*.'

His first thought: Couldn't be. He didn't believe Mario had murder in him. But then, it fit together. Dewayne had told Mario to find the woman for some get-back. He had only meant be a man. He didn't mean for the fool to kill the bitch.

Durham's second thought: Mario would be hidin' out with that boy Donut. And the police would be talking to their moms straightaway. But she wouldn't give Mario up. No one would. They knew who his brother was, after all.

More squad cruisers converged on the scene. Officer Beard yanked up on Durham's arms, which she held behind his back, and pulled him away from the hood of the Benz.

'Little rough, ain't you?'

'Gotta make it look good,' said Beard, a small degree of pleasure in her voice.

'I ain't payin' you to make it look that good,' said Durham.

Beard pushed him along. Pocket-cops, thought Durham. They hate everyone. Most of all, they hate themselves.

22

'The police gonna want to talk to us,' said Mike Montgomery.

'I ain't hidin',' said Horace McKinley.

And I ain't worried, neither. The police can't touch me.

'Too bad about the cousins, though.'

'Find that boy we see down by the liquor store. The one makes them T-shirts?'

'I know his sister.'

'Find him. Get some T-shirts made up for the cousins. "RIP, We Will Not Forget," sumshit like that. You know what to do.'

'They ain't had no family or friends.'

'It ain't for them. We need to show the street, the Yuma honors their own.'

'I'll get it done.'

They sat in the abandoned house at a card table, beer and malt bottles strewn about the scarred hardwood floor and the stairs leading to the second floor. The lights were on in the house. McKinley smoked a cigar.

'Gonna be a war for a while,' said McKinley, admiring the Cuban in his hand. 'We gonna need some guns.'

'We'll go see Ulysses, then.'

'Six Hundred gonna want to have some go. You know this.'

'They ain't but across the alley.'

'Then that alley's gonna be one of those DMZs you hear about.'

'Right,' said Montgomery. He didn't know what McKinley was talking about. He didn't know if McKinley knew.

'Phil Wood's takin' the stand tomorrow,' said McKinley.

'You told me.'

Montgomery reached into his pocket. He had walked out of the hair salon with one of those little wrestling figures by mistake. He'd been using the figure to play one of those hide-and-go-seek games with that boy Juwan. It had been fun hangin' out with him. Relaxing. He was tired of this life he was leading, and that boy had reminded him, in a pure kinda way, that not everyone out here was involved in this drama that always ended in death. That boy had been friendly, and not because he was afraid of Mike or knew who McKinley was or nothin' like that. That boy was nice.

'Phil's gonna be up there for a couple of days.' McKinley drew on his cigar and exhaled a cloud of smoke that further fogged the room. 'So we need to watch the Stokes bitch for a little while longer.'

'Okay.'

'I think she got the message today, but you never know. Girl had some fire in her eyes, I'll give her that. She don't respond to the way I put it to her, next thing is, we gonna have to squeeze her little boy.'

Montgomery fingered the plastic wrestler in his pocket.

'Mike?' said McKinley.

'What.'

'You heard me, right?'

'I heard you,' said Montgomery.

But I ain't gonna do nothin' to hurt that kid.

Strange drove uptown in his Cadillac, Greco beside him on his red cushion, War's 'Lotus Blossom' coming from the box. War was one of those groups Strange always went back to when he wanted to think and breathe. They were known as a jam band, but it was their ballads that really cooled him out.

Kids were out on Georgia's sidewalks, like they always were. There wasn't any curfew anymore, like there had been for a while in D.C. The curfew hadn't worked because the responsibility for the children had been put in the wrong hands. It never should have been up to the police to raise other people's kids.

Strange thought of Mark Elliot, now an orphan. And he thought of Robert Gray, living with that junkie aunt of his and her equally damaging boyfriend.

Strange drove by a church set back on Georgia. He saw a banner outside of it, read, 'Member: One Kid, One Congregation.' He knew of the program and had once met the man who ran it. He made a mental note to give that man a call.

Lionel was out on Quintana, standing under a street lamp, the hood up on his car, as Strange parked the Brougham. Lionel had a rag in his hand and he was using it to wipe oil off a dip stick.

Strange got out of the Caddy. He waited for Greco to jump out before he closed the door. Greco stayed with him every step of the way as Strange came up on Lionel.

'Hey,' said Strange.

'Pop. Rough night, huh?'

'I'm still standin'.'

'Mom kept some food on.'

Strange brought Lionel to him and held him close.

'Don't stay out here too long, hear?'

Lionel nodded, somewhat embarrassed by the affection, somewhat confused. Strange let him go and walked toward the house, Greco's nose bumping at his calf. Janine was waiting for him behind the screen door. Strange wondered where he had found the luck to have all this, when others had none at all.

Durham and Walker were taken to the Sixth District substation on Pennsylvania Avenue, Southeast, and interviewed separately by homicide detectives working the shootings outside the market. Predictably, both said that they knew nothing about the event. Detective Nathan Grady entered the interview room where Dewayne sat and asked him about the whereabouts of his brother, Mario. Dewayne gave him nothing except for the address of his mother, which he knew they could easily find or already had. There was nothing to hold them on, so Dewayne and Walker were told they could leave. Their car was waiting for them out on Pennsylvania.

Back in the Benz, Dewayne called his mother. She was crying and said that the police had already been to her town house. She told Dewayne that she didn't know where Mario could be. Their mother was smart enough not to mention Mario's friend Donut while talking on the cell.

Dewayne Durham told his mother not to worry. He'd stop by later and bring along some sweets that he knew she liked, truffles he could get in a late-night market by her place.

'Drive over to Valley Green, Zu,' Durham said to Walker. 'Make sure we don't get followed.'

Down in Valley Green, near the hospital, they cruised a cluster of streets: Blackney Lane, Varney Street, and Cole Boulevard among them. Durham was looking for Donut's car, a silver blue Accord, as he didn't know exactly where Donut lived. But then they saw Mario, wearing that stupid-ass Redskins getup, standing on a street corner up ahead. Mario stood with one hand in his pocket, slouched, just looking around. Looked like he was waiting for something, he didn't know what. Just like he'd been doin' his whole sorry life.

'Fool,' said Dewayne under his breath. 'Pull over, Bernard.'

Dewayne got out of the car and crossed the street to the corner where Mario stood. Mario kind of puffed out his chest then, like he was one of his brother's kind. But he saw Dewayne's eyes and deflated himself quick.

'What you doin' out here, huh?' said Dewayne.

'Nothin',' said Mario.

He had some fake crack in his pocket, a whole rack of dummies, but he hadn't sold a dime's worth yet. He didn't think his brother wanted to hear about it now.

'Don't you know you wanted on a homicide?'

'They found her, huh?'

Dewayne took a deep breath and let it out slow. 'Who you stayin' with? Donut?'

'Uh-huh.'

'Where he live at, man?'

Mario told him.

'You got your cell on you?' said Dewayne. At Mario's nod, Dewayne said, 'Give it to me.'

Mario handed Dewayne his cell. Dewayne dropped it on the concrete and stomped on it savagely, breaking it into pieces. He kicked the various shreds into the worn grass and street.

'They can find you like that, trace your ass right through your phone when you be usin' it. Don't you know *nothin'*?'

Mario looked up into Dewayne's eyes. 'Don't be mad at me, D.' Dewayne didn't respond.

Mario said, 'You *told* me the bitch needed to be got.'

'Stupid motherfucker,' said Dewayne. His hand flew up and he slapped Mario's face.

The blow caught them both by surprise. Mario rubbed his cheek and slowly turned his head back to face Dewayne. Mario's eyes had welled up with tears and his bottom lip shook.

'Why'd you do me like that?' said Mario, a tremor in his voice. 'You my kid brother, man.'

Dewayne brought him into his arms. Mario was right. He had punked his brother, shamed him in front of Walker, who had surely seen it from his spot in the Benz. And that was wrong.

'Come on,' said Dewayne, leading Mario across the street, one arm around his shoulders. 'We got to put you underground.'

'Where I'm goin'?'

'To stay with this girl I know who owes me.'

'That gonna be all right with her?'

'It'll be all right if I tell her it will. C'mon.'

From behind the wheel, Bernard Walker watched as Dewayne led his retard, no-ass, no-job-havin' brother toward the car. As they neared, Walker noticed the blood-stained shoes on Mario's feet. Yesterday he had had one 'ordan,' and today he had him a whole pair. Walker thinking, That's progress, to *him.*

Terry Quinn and Sue Tracy were fucking like animals in Quinn's bed when Strange called. Quinn reached over and swept the phone off the nightstand without missing a stroke. Fifteen minutes later Strange called again. Quinn had put the receiver back in its cradle, and Sue was in the bathroom washing herself when the phone rang. Quinn sat up naked on the bed and answered the call.

'What's goin' on?' said Tracy, coming out of the bathroom, seeing Quinn's pale, drawn face.

'It was Derek,' said Quinn, nodding toward the phone. He repeated, briefly, the details Strange had given him. She asked some questions, but he waved her off and got up from the bed. He dressed in jeans and a white T-shirt, and got into his leather.

Quinn stood dumbly in the center of the room and stared at his bureau. His Colt was in there. He took a step toward his dresser and stopped. What would he do with his gun now? The gun was his crutch, he knew. Violence was his answer, had always been his answer, to every conflict, threatened or imagined, he'd ever had. But there wasn't even a target now. Not unless you counted that pathetic little man in the Deion jersey. No, it was Quinn who had gotten that boy's mother killed.

He walked from the bedroom. Tracy heard him pacing the living room and then a crash. It was the sound of a toppled chair. He came back in, and the vein was up on his face.

'I'm going out.'

'Where?'

'For a walk.'

'I'll come.'

Quinn's eyes cut away from Tracy's. 'No.'

He walked up Sligo Avenue, past houses and apartments and the Montgomery County Police station, the 7-Eleven and the bus station on Fenton, and then along the car repair garages and auto parts stores lining the strip. The closed-mouth kiss of gentrification and the replacement of mom-and-pops by national chains had not yet reached this far south in Silver Spring. Quinn generally stayed in this part of town.

He turned left on Selim, crossed the street at the My-Le, the Vietnamese restaurant there, and went over the pedestrian bridge spanning Georgia Avenue that led to the commuter train station and the B&O and Metro tracks. He stood on the platform and looked down Georgia, his nearsighted eyes seeing only the blur of headlights, street lamps, and streaks of neon. He turned toward the tracks, hearing the low rumble of a freight train approaching from the south. It reached him eventually. When it did, he reached his hand out so that he almost touched the train and could feel its wind. He closed his eyes.

Now he was away from his world. Enemies and allies were easily distinguished by hats of black and white. Honor and redemption were real, not conceptual. Justice was uncomplicated by the gray of politics and money, and, if need be, achieved at the point of a gun.

Quinn knew he was out of step. He knew that his outlook was dangerous, essentially that of a boy. And that it would catch up to him in the end.

He opened his eyes. The train still rumbled by. Up on Selim, his Chevelle was idling outside My-Le. He crossed back over the bridge and went to the open passenger window. He leaned into the frame. Sue Tracy was behind the wheel, her right hand moving the Hurst shifter through its gears.

'Thanks for checkin' up on me, Mom.'

'Look, I don't know what you dream about up here, cowboy, but it doesn't get anything solved.'

'In my mind it does.'

'Okay. But it sounds to me like you've got some work to do tomorrow. I just wanted to make sure you got some sleep tonight.'

'What you wanted was to drive my sled.'

'There was that.'

'I'll be home in a little while.'

'C'mon, Terry,' said Tracy, reaching across the bucket and opening the door. 'Get in.'

23

Strange and Quinn sat at a table on the second floor of the Brian T. Gibson Building, the Fourth District station, in the office of Lieutenant Lydell Blue. Homicide detective Nathan Grady sat with them. Four Styrofoam cups holding coffee were on the table, along with a file. There were no windows in the office, no rays of sun, no bird sounds, no indication at all that it was a beautiful morning late in spring. It could have been any time of day. The fluorescent lights in the drop ceiling above gave them all a sickly pallor.

'So where we at?' said Strange.

'You first,' said Grady.

'I gave Lydell everything I had.'

'Tell *me*,' said Grady.

Strange repeated the story of Mario Durham's visit to his office. He left out no detail of their meeting, except for one. He relayed the particulars of the subsequent investigation, including the conversations with his interviewees and those of Quinn. Quinn interjected to give further recollections as needed.

'Some man matching your description,' said Blue, 'talked to a neighbor of Olivia's at her old address. He used some ruse about being a football coach, called himself Will Sonnet. Like that old TV show with Walter Brennan. You know, "No brag, just fact." '

'She came forward, huh?' said Strange.

'Soon as she saw on the TV news that they found the Elliot woman,' said Blue.

'Nice to know we got some good citizens out there.'

'I figured that was you.'

'And you told the son that his mother had won a raffle,' said Grady, addressing Quinn.

'Yes,' said Quinn.

'Tricky.'

Quinn ignored the editorial remark. 'How'd he connect me?'

'The boy got a partial on your plates.' Grady stared at Quinn for a moment, then looked down at a small lined pad, where he tapped his pen. When he looked back up at Quinn he said, 'You were a patrol cop here in Four D, weren't you?'

'That's right.'

Next thing you'll tell me I look familiar, but you already know who I am. I'm the cop that shot that other cop two years ago. Never mind that I was cleared. All of you will never forget. And now I'm private, a joke, tricking kids so that I can get their mothers killed. The opposite of what a cop does. Why don't you just say it so we can move on?

'We had no reason to think we were going to cause that woman any harm,' said Strange.

'True,' said Grady.

'Mario Durham looked less than harmless.'

'I appreciate your cooperation on this. I really do.'

'Anything we can do to help.'

Strange knew Grady by reputation and by sight, a tall man with gray-blond hair and ice blue eyes, looked like an older version of that Scandi actor, played in the later *Walking Tall* movies, Bo something. Blue said that Grady was all right. Odd, but all right. He was known to keep crime-scene photos of victims mounted on the walls of his apartment, where he lived alone. Cops who'd been by his place described them: there was one of a young man lying on his back on a Capitol Hill street, his hands still tented in prayer from before he had been shot. Another showed a woman who had hung her cat from the basement pipe, then hung herself beside it. That one was framed above the mantel. Outsiders would say that Grady was disturbed to keep such photos on display. Cops knew that this was Grady's way of dealing with his job.

'Y'all are positive it was Mario Durham who killed her, right?' said Strange.

'As positive as you can be. He left prints all over the apartment and her car. His prints were on her car keys, the shower curtain he wrapped her in, everything.'

'Any idea on motive?' said Strange.

Grady shrugged. 'They found cash between her mattress and box spring. There was marijuana in there, too, looked like it might have been a little more quantity than for personal use. Mario's got a connection to a dealer—'

'What connection?' said Quinn.

'I'm gonna get to that,' said Grady. 'So maybe this had something to do with a drug debt unpaid. Or it was one of those crimes of passion. The way you described him, Mario must have been a real player.'

'How's the son doing?' said Quinn.

'He's staying with his uncle, William Elliot. It's where he was when she was killed, and why she wasn't reported missing right away. The way I understand it, the arrangement's going to be permanent. The uncle's about as straight as they come. A government employee, married, secure. Doesn't tolerate knuckleheads or any kind of foolishness. Loved his sister but hated her lifestyle, all that.'

'Sounds like a really fun guy,' said Strange.

'Let's be honest,' said Grady. 'The boy's never gonna get over the death of his mother. But from my point of view, he's going to have a more secure environment now than he had before.' Grady's eyes went from Strange's to Quinn's. 'I'm not tryin' to make you two feel good about yourselves, either. Just giving you my opinion.'

Strange nodded. 'You get anything from Durham's cell number yet?'

'Nothing yet,' said Grady. 'If he uses it, we'll get a trace. If he's smart, he's destroyed the phone by now, or dumped it somewhere to throw us off.'

'He's not smart,' said Quinn.

'Shouldn't be too hard to find him, either,' said Strange.

'You'd think it'd be easy, even if he did move from place to place. And you know he's not going far. Anacostia's a small town. Talk to his mother, find out who he hangs with, all that. But there's this connection he's got, the one I was mentioning before.'

'Go ahead,' said Strange.

'Mario's younger brother is a guy named Dewayne Durham. Leads a gang called the Six Hundred Crew. Marijuana sales, primarily, with cocaine in the mix. Dewayne's got priors, was a suspect in several murders in his younger days, the typical profile. He's the big Magilla in his corner of the world.'

'So nobody's gonna flip on his brother,' said Quinn.

'Exactly,' said Grady.

'You bring Dewayne in?' said Strange.

'Yeah,' said Grady. 'He gave us jack shit.'

A brief silence fell.

'The gun he used is in the river right now, I expect,' said Strange.

'No,' said Grady. 'Here's where it gets interesting. You guys hear about that quadruple homicide in Southeast last night?'

'I read about it in the Metro section this morning,' said Strange. 'They withheld the names of the victims.'

Grady leaned forward and issued a joyless show of yellowed teeth, meant to be a smile. 'One of the guns used in the shooting was the same gun Mario used to shoot Olivia Elliot.'

'What the fuck?' said Quinn.

'How'd you get that so quick?' said Strange.

'There was an alert officer on the crime scene, remembered the caliber of the murder gun in the Elliot case. They sent one of the slugs and a casing out and ran them through the IBIS program, you know, with the ATF?'

'IBIS?' said Quinn.

'Inter Ballistics ID System,' said Grady. 'You been away.'

'Not too long.'

'The slug from the shooting matched the slugs taken out of Olivia Elliot. A Taurus thirty-eight. It wasn't just the same model of gun. The markings made it as the same exact piece.'

'Keep talking,' said Strange.

'Two of the victims of the shooting were known employees of Dewayne Durham. Jerome Long and Allante Jones. Allante. Christ, someone named their kid after a Cadillac, you believe it? And not even one of the good Caddies.'

'And?'

'One of them used the Taurus before he died.'

'Who'd he use it on?' said Quinn.

'Jeremy Coates. He and his cousin James worked for a rival dealer, this fat cat named Horace McKinley.'

McKinley. Strange's blood ticked through his veins. James and Jeremy Coates owned the beige Nissan that had been tailing him the past two days; Janine had gotten him the information from her MVA contact after Quinn had taken their plate numbers off the 240.

'Funny,' said Grady. 'Right?'

'If all else fails,' said Strange, 'I guess you can follow the gun.'

'Oh, we're already on that. We did a trace, the ATF again, God love 'em. The serial number was still on there, which tells us the gun came from a pro middleman. It was purchased in a gun store down in Virginia, way down off Route 1, called Commonwealth Guns. It'll be a straw buy, we're pretty sure. Probably went to an intermediary dealer who works the District. Anyway, we're looking into it.'

'So the gun sale was legit,' said Quinn.

'Most likely. Purchased at an FFL – that's federal fire arms licensee to you, Quinn. Since you been away so long.'

'And that makes it legal?'

'Legal, not moral. But so what? Legal's enough. Hard to stop straw buys, anyway, even if you wanted to. Sixty percent of the crime guns recovered in D.C. come from legitimate stores in Maryland and Virginia. In Virginia you can buy a gun, do an instant background check, and walk out of the store, that day, with the gun in your hand. Nice, huh?'

'If you're buying a gun for protection or sport, then it makes sense,' said Quinn. 'So I guess it depends on how you look at it.'

'Maybe you ought to ask Olivia Elliot's son,' said Grady. 'How he looks at it, I mean.'

'Anything else?' said Lydell Blue, cutting the tension that had come to the room.

'Yeah,' said Grady. 'Anything else you two can tell *me*?'

'I've given you everything, I think,' said Strange.

But he hadn't mentioned Donut, Mario's friend. He and Quinn had agreed: they were saving that bit of information for themselves.

'You think of anything else, let me know,' said Grady, pushing two business cards across the table. 'I've got to get down to the substation in Six D. They just brought Dewayne in for another go-round. I wanna see his face when we tell him about the gun.'

'If I run into Mario,' said Strange, sliding his own card in front of Grady, 'I'll mention you're looking for him.'

'Oh, I'll probably run into him first.'

The two men smiled cordially and shook hands as they stood.

'Where you off to?' said Blue.

'Running down to check on the Granville Oliver trial,' said Strange.

'Another solid citizen,' said Grady. Strange didn't respond.

'I talk to you a minute?' said Blue.

Strange nodded as Quinn and Grady left the room.

'Anything more on that break-in last night?' said Blue.

'I don't expect I'll be hearing anything,' said Strange. 'It was a professional burglary. I'm not gonna let it interfere with what I'm doin'.'

Blue stroked his thick gray mustache. 'You mean you're not going to take the warning.'

'I've pretty much decided I'm just gonna keep doing my job.'

'You can't fight the government, if that's who it is.'

'True,' said Strange. 'But I don't know what else to do.'

Strange and Blue, friends for thirty-some-odd years, shook hands.

Quinn was waiting for Strange out in the hall. They took the stairwell down to the first floor.

'Interesting meeting,' said Quinn.

'I'm thinking about it,' said Strange.

Strange's Caprice was beside Quinn's Chevelle in the lot behind the station. Strange motioned for Quinn to come with him.

'Where we headed?' said Quinn.

'Gotta get myself lookin' right first. Then the office, then downtown.'

'We're gonna need two cars today. You and me got different things planned.'

'We'll pick yours up later. We're swinging back up here for our lunch appointment anyway.'

They settled onto the front bench of the Caprice.

'That Grady guy,' said Quinn, 'he's the one keeps death photos, like art or something, hanging in his crib.'

Strange turned the ignition. 'Yeah, that's him.'

'Man looks like that actor played in *Walking Tall.* Not Joe Don Baker. Parts two and three, I mean. The ones that sucked.'

'Bo something or other,' said Strange.

'Derek?'

'Funny.'

'It's Svenson, dude.'

'That's it. *Damn.*' Strange pulled out of the lot. 'Was killing me, looking at Grady across that table. I just could not remember that cat's name.'

Strange had his hair cut and his beard trimmed at Hawk's, then walked to the office, where he met Quinn, who had been making some calls and gathering equipment and files. Greco greeted Strange as he entered the storefront, settling back onto his red cushion after receiving a rub on the head. Lamar Williams was up on a ladder, changing a fluorescent bulb, and Janine was seated behind her desk, tapping the keyboard of her computer.

'Good morning,' said Janine. 'You look nice.'

'My neck itches,' said Strange, picking up his messages off Janine's desk. 'I'll be right back out.'

In his office, Strange looped his belt through the sheath of his Buck knife and retrieved a sand-filled sap from his top desk drawer. He slipped the sap into the back pocket of his jeans and pulled his shirttail out to cover it. He made a phone call, then grabbed some files and other items, and went back out to the front of the shop.

'Here you go,' said Janine, handing him a PayDay bar, his favorite snack. 'In case you miss a meal.'

'Thank you, baby,' said Strange. 'Stick to your desk if you can today. I'm gonna need to keep in contact with you, hear?'

Strange looked up to Lamar, on the top step of the ladder.

'What's goin' on, boss?' said Lamar.

'What's goin' on with *you*?'

'Keepin' this place clean. Taking care of my mother and my baby sister. Studying for my final tests. Same old same old.'

'Were you studying for your tests when I saw you walkin' down Georgia toward the Black Hole the other night?'

'Dag, Mr Strange, you got eyes every where? I was just checking out some go-go they had up in there, wanted to see if I could run into this girl I wanted to get to know. I'm allowed to have some fun, ain't I?'

'Long as you take care of that other stuff you claim you're doing, too.'

'I am.'

'You keep it up, then.'

Quinn got up from his chair, a file in one hand and a fresh pack of sugarless gum in the other.

'Can I get one of them Extras, Terry?' said Lamar.

Quinn handed Lamar a stick of gum. 'You ready, Derek?'

Strange nodded. 'Let's go.'

Out on the street, walking to Strange's car, Quinn said, 'You're a little rough on him, aren't you?'

'He thinks I am now,' said Strange. 'When he's older and he understands what I was trying to do, he'll think of me different.'

'The kid's trying, Derek.'

'I know he is,' said Strange. 'Lamar's good.'

On the way downtown they stopped at the offices of One Kid, One Congregation, below Massachusetts Avenue, where Strange had made a short introductory appointment with Father John Winston, the nonprofit's director. Winston was a former police officer, now a minister, out of a large metropolitan area in the Midwest, who had brought his program to D.C. Strange talked with Winston briefly in the office and knew right away that he liked the man and what he was trying to do. Both were ex-cops, so there was that connection as well.

Back in the Caprice, Strange drove down toward 3rd and Constitution.

'What was that about?' said Quinn.

'Robert Gray,' said Strange.

'That boy you inherited from Granville Oliver.'

'He's in a bad place right now. I'm gonna try and get him into this program, where a church kind of adopts a kid. It's a citywide thing, and I've heard it works. Might be just what Robert needs. This guy Winston, he's started a similar program for addicts here, too.'

'Sounds good.'

'If I can swing it, we'll get him into a family up near us, so we can have him on the football team, too.'

Quinn looked at his friend across the bench. 'Derek Strange, always looking to save the world.'

'A kid or two, maybe,' said Strange. 'That would be enough for me.'

24

Strange and Quinn entered courtroom 19, where the Oliver trial was in progress, after a thorough security check. The heads of a few spectators and several law enforcement types turned as they walked in and took their seats. Strange and Quinn did not return their stares.

Judge Potterfield, rotund and jowly, had asked attorneys from both sides to approach the bench for a consultation. Phillip Wood, sharply dressed and freshly shaved, was on the stand. Granville Oliver sat placidly, his stun belt beneath his blue suit, staring at Wood through nonprescription glasses.

The prosecution's questions for Wood resumed. His testimony had been rehearsed and came off that way. It could have been recorded as a primer for the life, D.C.-style, complete with name checks of familiar clubs, go-go bands, motels, skating rinks, favorite models of automobile, brands of champagne, Calico autos and AK-47s. Wood was asked about Bennett Oliver, and if Granville had ever discussed killing his uncle or having him killed.

'Granville told me he suspected his uncle Bennett was gettin' ready to flip to the Feds,' said Wood. 'They had his uncle talkin' about a buy on a wiretap and they were gonna send him up. Granville thought his uncle was gonna cut a deal.'

'What were Granville's thoughts about that?' said the prosecutor.

'Objection,' said Ives. 'Mr Wood's interpretation of the defendant's thoughts calls for speculation.'

'I'll rephrase, your honor. Did Granville Oliver ever *say* that he would in any way try to stop his uncle from talking to federal agents?'

'He said it was time for Bennett to be got.'

'To be got?' said the prosecutor.

'To be killed. Next thing I heard, Bennett Oliver was dead.'

'I see.' The prosecutor paused for effect and softened his tone. 'Do you love Granville Oliver, Mr Wood?'

'Yes,' said Phillip Wood, looking straight at Oliver. 'That's my main boy right there. I love Granville like my own blood.'

Oliver's expression remained flat and unreadable.

Judge Potterfield called a short break in the proceedings. Strange caught the eye of Raymond Ives, Oliver's primary defense attorney, and head-motioned him to follow.

Strange and Quinn met Ives, immaculate and trim in a William Fox pinstripe, outside the courthouse. They stood on the sidewalk of Constitution where the bus and car sounds would serve to mute their conversation. A man who looked like a federal cop watched them, standing near the building's front steps among the cigarette smokers, not smoking himself.

'Maybe we should discuss this alone,' said Ives.

'I don't have a problem with him being here,' said Strange, speaking of Quinn.

'Okay,' said Ives. 'I went over the message left at your house. You say the voice was the voice of a white man.'

'Same one, probably, who called my office on Ninth and spoke to my wife. This is no gang member leaving me death threats. Those boys in Southeast want to fuck with me, they'd do it direct. This here's not their style.'

'The voice spoke of your conversation with Kevin Willis down at Leavenworth.'

'I got nothing from Willis on the Oliver case.'

'Right. I reviewed the transcripts of your tapes.'

'And?'

'At several points Willis talks about people in protective who are hot or who are about to flip. He's referencing potential witnesses who have nothing to do with the Oliver trial. These are cases that are still pending, Derek.'

'Make your point.'

'They have grounds for an obstruction charge.'

'You should have warned me about that.'

'I did warn you.'

'I don't remember you sayin' anything.'

'I went over it with you before you left town; it's in my notes of our meeting. Now, understand, if the government wants to go after your license or prosecute you further, they're within their rights to try.'

'The Feds had Willis set me up.'

'Maybe. That would be damned hard to prove.'

'You want me off the case?'

'If you dropped out now, I'd understand. But I need you more than ever. What I'm telling you is, you've got to be aware of the possible situation you have here. Let's assume we're talking about the FBI. They can bug your office, your house, your bedroom, even your car.'

'I know all that.'

'They can monitor your phone conversations, including your cell. At the very least you ought to be communicating with your people through pay phones.'

'Whatever,' said Strange.

'You don't seem too concerned.'

'I'm staying on this.'

'Okay. Good. When the time comes to resolve your problem, I'll represent you, gratis.'

'I was counting on that.'

'In the meantime,' said Ives, 'you heard the testimony in there. I need something from the Stokes girl, if there is anything, right away. Something to refute Phil Wood's testimony that Granville hit his own uncle or had him hit.'

'I'm working on it,' said Strange.

He asked Ives about what they could do for the girl and her son. Ives described the arrangements that could be made. When he was done he said, 'I don't need to tell you to watch your back.'

Strange and Ives shook hands. Quinn and Strange walked toward the Caprice.

'Hope you're hungry,' said Strange.

'It depends.'

'The Three-Star Diner.'

'That Greek place where your father worked,' said Quinn.

'We're meetin' a Greek,' said Strange. 'So it makes sense.'

They sat in a booth, its seats covered in red vinyl, along the window of the Three-Star on Kennedy Street. Quinn had a cheeseburger with mustard and fried onions only, and a side of fries. Strange ate eggs over easy, grilled half smokes, and hash browns, his usual meal.

Sitting across from them was Nick Stefanos. He had the half smokes and hash browns like Strange, but took his eggs scrambled with feta cheese. Both of them had scattered Texas Pete hot sauce liberally atop the dish.

'I remember this place,' said Stefanos. 'My grandfather knew old man Georgelakos. They went to the same church, St. Sophia. And they were in the same business.'

'Your grandfather had a lunch counter?'

'Nick's.'

'Fourteenth and S, in Shaw. I can picture the sign out front.'

'Right. He used to run up here from time to time. ' "I'll be right back; *Kirio* Georgelakos needs a few tomatoes, I'm gonna run some up to him." Like that.'

'That's his son,' said Strange, pointing behind the counter to Billy Georgelakos, wide of girth and broad of chest, nearly bald, working with a Bic pen wedged behind his ear. 'My father worked here, too. He was the grill man in this place.'

'Small town,' said Stefanos, smiling pleasantly at Strange.

Stefanos wore a black summer sweater over a white T-shirt, simple 505 jeans, and black oilskin shoes. He kept his hair short and distressed. His face was flecked with scars, white crescents and tiny white lines on olive skin. He wasn't handsome or ugly; his looks would have been unremarkable except for his eyes, which some would have called intense. His height and build were medium, and he kept his stomach reasonably flat for his age. Strange put him in his early forties. He looked as if he had lived a life. Strange could almost see this one as a younger, reckless man. He sensed that Stefanos had been about good times in his youth, and wondered if drugs were his thing today, and if not, what had replaced them. Maybe it was the adrenaline jolt from the job, or something else. Elaine Clay had said that he had his problems with drink.

'Elaine told me you had a wire on the gang situation in Southeast.'

'I've been working RICO cases and the Corey Graves thing for a long time. You just naturally pick up a ton of information, and misinformation, when you're canvassing those streets.'

'Like any cop,' said Quinn.

'Exactly,' said Stefanos, looking Quinn over.

'I interviewed Kevin Willis down in Leavenworth recently,' said Strange. 'Willis was an enforcer with Granville Oliver before he went over to Corey Graves.'

'Be careful with Willis. Kid talks so much, you lose track of what he's sayin'. He's charming, but he's got those long teeth, if you know what I mean.'

'I got bit, too.' Strange told Stefanos about being burgled, and the phone call, and its relation to the Willis tapes.

'So he talked about hot wits in pending cases,' said Stefanos. 'That's where the obstruction could come in.'

'I know it. *Now.*'

'You fucked up.'

'Thanks for all your support,' said Strange, a dry tone entering his voice. But he liked Stefanos's candor.

Billy Georgelakos's longtime waitress, Ella, came to the table with a pot of coffee and refilled their cups with a shaking hand. Stefanos thanked her as she poured, tapping unconsciously on the hardpack of Marlboro reds set on the table beside his plate.

'Tell me what you know about Horace McKinley,' said Strange.

'Yuma Mob,' said Stefanos. 'You remember that Cary Grant movie *Mr Lucky*?'

'Was there a horse in it?' said Quinn.

'If they were gonna remake that movie,' said Stefanos, 'they'd put Horace McKinley in the title role. He's got that rep. Been hard-busted a few times, but nothing seems to stick.'

'Why's that?' said Strange.

'Could be he has good attorneys; could be no one can get any wits to post. Could be he's connected in other ways, too.'

'As in, some kind of law with juice has the finger on him.'

'I can't say.' Stefanos pointed his fork at Strange. 'You don't know too much, huh?'

'I know some. My wife, Janine, she works for me. She dug up plenty of good information since yesterday. But I'm trying to piece all the players together down there. You know I'm working the Granville Oliver trial.'

'For Ray Ives.'

'Uh-huh. So keep in mind that everything I'm looking for, it's got to go back to Granville.'

'Most things do in that part of the world. Granville was the king for a good while down there, and he went deep into the community. Take McKinley. He got put on and brought up by Granville when Horace wasn't much more than a fat kid.'

'That would mean McKinley knew Phil Wood, too.'

'Phillip Wood,' said Stefanos. 'As in the cat who's flipping on Granville as we speak.'

'The same.'

Stefanos closed his eyes as he took in a forkful of half smoke and chewed. '*Damn*, that's good.'

'My father's signature,' said Strange. 'Keep talking about McKinley.'

'What I hear, Horace is standing tall with Phil Wood. He figures that Granville is gonna get the needle or life without parole, so there's no upside with him. McKinley runs Yuma, but his loyalty's with Phil. Like I say, this is only what I hear.'

'That would explain his intimidation,' said Strange.

'It could explain it,' said Stefanos. 'You'd have to go deeper than you been going to find out for sure.'

'How do you know all this?' said Quinn.

'I keep my ears open all the time. Stand by the pay phones and talk into a dead receiver, shop in those neighborhood markets for nothing. Ride the Green Line once in a while and listen. Young men down there talk about the day-to-day rumors of gang business every day, the way other young men talk about sports.'

'That's your secret? Take the Green Line train and keep your ears open?'

'My main secret? My snitches. I can ride the Metro all I want, but without informants I wouldn't have shit. I hand out a lot of twenty-dollar bills, Terry.'

Stefanos returned his attention to his plate.

'What about Dewayne Durham?' said Quinn.

They waited for Stefanos to swallow another mouthful of food. He started to speak, then raised one finger to hold them off and finished his meal. He pushed the plate away from him and centered his coffee cup where the plate had been.

'What was the question?'

'Dewayne Durham.'

'Yeah, Dewayne. Runs the Six Hundred Crew. Same kind of business, marijuana sales mostly. The two gangs work different strips. I hear they even work out of abandoned houses, one on Yuma and one on Atlantic, and stare at each other across the same alley. Once in a while they cross paths and shots get fired.'

'Like last night,' said Strange.

'I heard. Four dead – over nothing, most likely. A hard look, or someone walked down the wrong street, whatever. Just another war story to tell around the campfire. Like boys coming home from battle, wearing the medals and the uniforms, getting the eyes from the ladies. That little window of glory. Something to show that they were here. That's all this is, you know? It doesn't have a goddamn thing to do with drugs.'

'In my time,' said Strange, 'they would have met somewhere and gone with their hands to see who could take who.'

'Guns make the man now,' said Stefanos.

'Nothing wrong with guns,' said Quinn. 'It's the ones using them make the difference.'

'You don't have to tell me,' said Stefanos. 'I'm a man. I like the way a gun feels in my hand and I like the way it feels when I squeeze the trigger. I've used guns when I had to. But we're not talking about hunting or target practice, and this isn't the open country. It's an East Coast city with plenty of poverty. Guns don't belong here.'

'That's why they're illegal in D.C., I guess.'

'You'd never know it, with all the pieces on the street. All these fat-shit congressmen, blaming culture and rap music for the murder rate while they got their hands out to the gun manufacturers and their lobbyists. Don't you think that's wrong?'

'I guess we've got a difference of opinion.'

Strange cleared his throat. 'Let's get back to Dewayne Durham. Dewayne's got an older brother. Little guy, looks like a beaver, goes by Mario?'

'I don't know him,' said Stefanos.

'We're kinda lookin' for him on something else,' said Strange. 'No one's gonna help us out, on account of who his brother is, and I figure by now Dewayne has put him underground.'

'The cops'll get him.'

'We want to get to him first. It's crazy, I know. But it'll make us feel better if we do.'

'Go out and find some rumors, then,' said Stefanos. 'You guys ever used to congregate at a liquor store or a beer market when you were younger, to find out where the action was for the night?'

'Country Boy in Layhill,' said Quinn.

'For me it was Morris Miller's,' said Stefanos. 'In Anacostia it's Mart Liquors, at Malcolm X and Martin Luther King. Or any bank of pay phones. The gas stations are good for that. Bring plenty of cash, and don't forget the diplomacy. And humility, too.'

'Fuck humility,' said Quinn.

'Suit yourself. Me, I want to be around at the end of the race.' Stefanos looked from one man to the other. 'You guys are busy.'

'The gun in that shooting last night,' said Strange, 'it matches a gun used by Mario Durham in another killing.'

'Like I say, I don't know him.' Stefanos shrugged. 'My advice would be to follow the gun.'

'I've been thinking the same way.'

Stefanos picked up his pack of 'Boros, then put it back down. He looked at Quinn, back at Strange, and back at Quinn once more, squinting his eyes. 'You're the cop who shot that other cop a couple of years ago, aren't you?'

'I got cleared,' said Quinn, his own eyes narrowing. 'You're pretty direct, aren't you?'

'People say I am. To a fault sometimes.'

Quinn leaned back in his seat. 'It's better that way, I guess.'

'You look like you could use a smoke,' said Strange to Stefanos.

'I've got to get going anyway.'

'I'll walk you out.'

Stefanos slid out of the booth and shook Quinn's hand. 'Nice meeting you, man.'

'You, too.'

Stefanos stopped and looked at the photograph mounted on the wall by the front door. In it, a tall black man stood by the grill beside a short Greek, both of them in aprons. Stefanos saw the resemblance of the Greek to his larger son behind the counter; in the tall man he saw Derek Strange.

'That's him,' said Strange. 'That's my father right there.'

'*Yasou*, Derek,' said Billy Georgelakos from across the store.

'*Yasou, Vasili*,' said Strange, pointing to the booth where Quinn still sat. 'Give the check to my son over there, hear?'

'You speak Greek?' said Stefanos.

'A few key phrases. I know what you folks call a black man – the nice word, I mean. I know how to call someone a jerk off, and I know the word for, uh, pussy.'

'Prove it.'

'*Mavros, malaka*, and *moonee*.'

'The three M's. You're just about fluent.'

'It'll come in handy, I happen to get over to Athens for the Olympics.'

Out on Kennedy, Stefanos put fire to a smoke. He took the first drag in and held it deep. Strange stood beside him, watching.

'Tastes good, huh?'

'After a spicy meal like that? Damn right.' Stefanos gave Strange the once-over and smiled. 'Strange Investigations. I drive by your place all the time.'

'You know my sign?'

'Magnifying glass over half the letters. How'd you ever come up with that?'

'That logo with the guy smoking the pipe, wearing that hat's got two bills on it? It was taken.'

'Maybe I'll stop by sometime.'

'If the light in the sign's turned on, I'm in. You're welcome anytime.'

'How about your partner? Think he wants me around?'

'I think he liked you, to tell you the truth. Terry's carrying some baggage with him, is what it is.'

'Aren't we all.' Stefanos dragged on his cigarette, looked at it, and hit it again.

'Just so you know, you and me got some similar opinions about guns. I figure, we sat down in a bar together, we might have a lot to talk about.'

'I'm trying to stay out of bars. But I wouldn't mind hooking up with you sometime.'

'You know, I'm working this death penalty case for a reason.'

'Another thing we agree on. It's why I'm on the Corey Graves thing. The federal prosecutors were looking to make it a capital case and they just got the go-ahead from the attorney general.'

'I heard.'

'There's been too much death in this city already, Derek. I've had enough of it.'

'I have, too.'

'The neighborhoods you guys work, your partner's gotta be careful, with that personality of his. He shows some smarts and less emotion, he's gonna live longer.'

'I tell him all the time.'

'I remember what that guy went through, with the newspapers and television and all, after he shot that other cop. He's got some shit flying around in his head; it's understandable. For what it's worth, I liked him, too.'

'Don't forget to stop by. Ninth and Upshur.'

'I'll be around.'

'Thanks for your help, Nick.'

Stefanos shook Strange's outstretched hand and said, 'Right.'

Strange watched him walk toward a Mopar muscle car, a white-over-red Dodge with aftermarket Magnum 500 wheels. He listened to the cook of the Detroit engine and went back into the diner. Quinn was dropping money on the table, a toothpick rolling in his mouth.

'You ready?' said Quinn. 'I need to pick up my car.'

Strange nodded. 'Let's go to work.'

25

Bernard Walker waited in the idling Benz as Dewayne Durham walked out of the Sixth District substation on Pennsylvania Avenue in Southeast. He could see that screwed-up look on Dewayne's face, which meant confusion. Trouble, something to do with his family. Often it was his mother, always needin' something. Money, jewelry, clothes, a ride to church. But today it was that brother of his, who'd fucked up big with that girl. When the police had called him into the station that morning – 'You wanna come in, Dewayne, or should we send a car to pick you up?' – they said it had to do with Mario. Somethin' about an 'interesting' new development they had in the case.

'Everything all right?' said Walker, so tall in the driver's seat that his hair was touching the headliner of the car.

'Mario,' said Durham, as if that were explanation enough. He reached to the radio and turned down the sound.

'Well?'

'The gun he used to kill that bitch? It was the same gun Jerome used on that Coates cousin.'

'Same model?'

'Same exact *gun*.'

'Foreman's woman said that gun was clean.'

'I know it. Foreman told her it was. He took a gun had a body on it, a murder gun attached to my own brother, and sold it to Long. Why you think he'd want to put me in that kind of situation?'

'Maybe he didn't know.'

'Could be he didn't. Or maybe someone wanted to see me get jammed up.'

'You think Foreman would set you up like that? Why?'

'That's what I need to find out.'

'We better go talk to your brother,' said Walker.

'Nah, uh-uh. I don't trust what he'll tell me, scared as he is. And I don't trust myself to be around him right now. I'm tellin' you, Zu, I'm about to kill a motherfucker today. I see him and he starts to lie, I might just go ahead and dead my own brother. I don't want to do that to my moms.'

'We could talk to his fool friend, see if Mario said anything about it to him.'

'Yeah,' said Durham. 'Let's do that.'

Donut's apartment was dirty and it smelled like resin and cigarettes. A window air conditioner ran low and kept the smell in the two-bedroom unit. Donut sat on the couch, wires and controllers around him from the PlayStation 2 connected to his TV. Normally these things were on the living-room table in front of the couch, along with his ashtray and other smoking paraphernalia, his cell, and his CD and game cases. But Bernard Walker had kicked the table over on its side as soon as Donut had let him in, and now Donut's shit was scattered about the room.

'I don't know nothin',' said Donut. His hands were between his thighs, and he was scissoring his knees together compulsively while staring straight ahead.

Walker bent his long torso forward so that he could speak softly to the ugly man on the couch. 'We ain't asked you nothin' yet.'

'Go ahead and ask me whateva. I got no call to lie.'

'Just wanted to come by and thank you for looking after my brother like you did,' said Dewayne Durham, standing beside Walker, his voice friendly and calm.

'This how y'all thank me?' said Donut, his hands spread toward the mess on the living-room floor.

'I got a couple of questions for you, is all,' said Durham. 'Answer straight, and we'll be gone.'

'I'm listenin'.'

'That gun my brother had, the one he used on that girl. He tell you where he got it from?'

'That Foreman dude,' said Donut.

'Good. You doin' all right. Keep answering fast like that and don't think too hard before you do. Now, Mario say anything about his conversation with Foreman? When he returned the gun to him, I mean.'

'Like what?'

'Like, did Foreman know that Mario had used that gun on the girl?'

Donut nodded quickly. 'He said Foreman knew it was a murder gun. He knew.'

Durham looked over at Walker, who nodded one time. They stood there for a while, saying nothing. Donut guessed they were deciding what to do with him. He knew a lot of shit. He prayed they wouldn't kill him for what he knew. And now he had put the finger on Foreman, too, that big horse, used to be a cop. But he could worry about Foreman later. First thing was, he needed to get out of this situation right here.

'Donut?' said Durham.

'Huh?'

'Listen close.'

'I am.'

'You know where Mario's at?'

Donut knew. He knew the address of that girl he was stayin' with and he knew the phone number, too. It was written down on a pad of paper, lying somewhere on the floor with everything else. Mario had called him that morning, talkin' about the girl and how her ass looked in her jeans, and also about the trouble he was in. But Donut wasn't about to tell Dewayne Durham all that.

'No,' said Donut. 'I ain't talked to him since he left out of here.'

'That's good for you,' said Walker. 'You need to keep it that way.'

'You know I will.'

'And you do see him again,' said Durham, 'you don't want to be getting him involved in that dummy bullshit you peddlin' out on the street.'

'I wouldn't do that.'

'Aiight, then,' said Durham. 'You got my cell number, case you remember anything else?'

'Mario wrote it down. I know where it is.'

'Let's go, Zu.'

Walker stepped on Donut's case for NBA Street and broke it on the way out the door.

In the Benz, Dewayne Durham used his cell to phone Ulysses Foreman. Walker listened to Durham question Foreman about the gun. Durham's voice was cool and controlled. He never raised it once, not even at the end, when he said to Foreman, 'We ain't settled this yet.'

'What'd he say?'

'Said he knew the gun had been fired, but Mario told him he was just testin' it, like it was the Fourth of July, sumshit like that.'

'So he says he didn't know.'

Durham nodded. 'That's what he says.'

*

Donut looked through the slots of his venetian blinds, waiting for the Benz to leave his parking lot. When he was sure they were gone, Donut phoned his friend.

'Mario.'

'Dough?'

'Your brother was here, askin' about some shit. That gun you used? Maybe it got used in another murder or somethin' after you turned it in.'

'I ain't know nothin' about that.'

'I ain't say you did.'

'Why was he buggin', then?'

'I don't know. He was just *agitated* and shit.'

Donut listened to dead air. He could almost see Mario, his mouth open, staring into space, walking around the room with the cordless in his hand, the other hand in his pocket, jingling change.

'What else is goin' on?' said Mario.

'What else? Mario, you wanted for *murder*.'

'I know it.'

'Look here, Mario, those rocks I gave you? Throw that shit away, man. The vials, too, every thing. Your brother don't want you fuckin' with no dummies.'

'Yeah, okay. Dewayne didn't rough you or nothin', did he?'

'Nah,' said Donut. 'That Bigfoot-lookin' motherfucker of his, though, he broke my game case. Just, like, *stepped* on it.'

'Madden?'

'NBA Street.'

'That shits was already broke.'

'That ain't the point.' Donut rubbed his finger along his jawline. 'So how's that girl Dewayne put you in with?'

'She's at work.'

'How *is* she, though? Is she fine?'

'Yeah,' said Mario. 'I already told you, she got a nice round onion on her, man.'

'I just like thinkin' about it.'

'Donut?'

'What?'

'Don't give me up. You know I can't do no time.'

Donut said, 'You're my boy.'

Strange sat behind the wheel of his Caprice in the parking lot of the St Elizabeth's McDonalds, the Aiwa minirecorder in his hand barely making a sound as the tape whirred, recording the conversation in the car. Devra Stokes was beside him on the bench. Her son, Juwan, sat in the back, diligently working on a cup of soft chocolate ice cream, humming to himself from time to time. It was hot inside the car; Strange had kept the windows rolled up most of the way in an effort to reduce the ambient noise.

'And he said this where?' said Strange.

'This one time?' said Devra.

'This time you distinctly remember.'

'Me and Phil were in his car, the Turbo Z. The one Granville had bought him? We were out in the lot of Crystal Skate. Back around then, that used to be where the mob liked to hang. I liked to roller-skate then, and so did Phil. Phil was good.'

'Do you have a date on this?'

'Not exactly. It was, like, a few days before Bennett Oliver got murdered in his Jag.'

'Why do you remember that so clearly?'

''Cause when it happened, I thought of Phil right away.'

'Why?'

'This night at the skating park, Phil had drunk some wine and had a little smoke. We was in his Z that night, just talkin'. Phil said to me that Bennett had been caught on a wiretap. He said that Granville believed his uncle was gonna flip on him to the Feds, one of those plea-outs they do.'

'And?'

'Phil said that Bennett needed to be got.'

'To be murdered, right?'

Devra nodded.

'Answer for the tape, please, Devra.'

'Yes, to be murdered.'

'Did Phil say he was going to do it himself?'

'Yes. Phil said he was the one that would put the work in.'

'Clarify, please.'

'Phillip Wood told me that he was gonna kill Bennett Oliver.'

'Why him? Why not Granville?'

'Phil said it would be good for him to do it. Good for his career, I mean. It would remove another person above him, make him closer to Granville. In Granville's eyes, it would make him his main boy.'

'Were there other instances where Phil talked about this plan?'

'I guess. But I don't remember, like, specific. The night at Crystal Skate, it sticks in my mind.'

'And what happened next?'

Devra shrugged. 'Bennett got shot.'

'Did Phil Wood say he'd done it?'

'No. After, he never said nothin' about it again. And I didn't ask. I just thought, you know, since he'd told me he was gonna do it, that he'd been the one. I figured it was better I didn't know for sure. I'd seen what happened to some other people, knew too much.'

Strange shut off the recorder. 'Thank you, Devra. That's good. That's exactly what we need.'

'Will I testify?'

'Yes, I think you will. My wife will have the subpoena today. It's not that we're against you; it's only to make it official.'

'And then what?'

'I talked to Ray Ives. They're going to get you and Juwan into an apartment, probably over in Northwest. Not the Section Eights. A step or two up.'

'What, I get a new name or somethin'?'

'No, it's not like that. You keep your name and you're not under any kind of guard. Witnesses are relocated in this city all the time. Long as you're in another quadrant and you go about your life quietly, usually it's fine.'

'Usually.'

'Right.'

'You know, living here in Southeast, you hear all about what happens to people who are hot. That Corey Graves thing?'

'I'm familiar with it,' said Strange.

'They got him charged with a whole lot of stuff besides the drug business he was runnin'. Witness intimidation. Hiding witnesses. Not to mention all the beef murders he did.'

'I'm not gonna lie to you. I know it's risky, and so do you. Question is, why are you being so courageous?'

Devra looked out the window. ''Cause that motherfucker threatened me. He threatened my son, Mr Strange. He talked mad shit about my mother, too. And he did things to me he shouldn't have done.'

'Horace McKinley.'

'That's right.'

'*What* did he do?'

Devra turned her head so that she faced him. 'He put his hand on my privates and rubbed it there. He pinched one of my nipples until it hurt so bad I wanted to cry out. But I didn't cry out. I kept it in. That fat man with his cigar breath, up in my face. I could have killed him then, I had a way. I had so much hate in me.'

'Where does he stay at?' said Strange. He heard a catch in his voice and swallowed, checking his anger.

'I don't know. He hangs with his boys over on Yuma, the six hundred block, in a house, looks like a crack house with all that plywood in the windows, during the day.'

Strange touched Devra's forearm. 'I'm sorry you had to go through that. I admire you, the way you stood strong.'

'I'm ashamed for what I did when I was younger. Who I hung with, too. But that will never be me again. Just to do nothing, try to put it behind me, it's not enough. I figure, sometimes you got to *do* something. Isn't that right?'

'You're a brave young woman.'

'Not really. Maybe I'm just foolish, like I always been.'

'I don't think so.'

'Anyway, what should I do now? Just go back to work?'

'Yes, for right now. How long you on for?'

'Till closing time. She stays open till ten o'clock.'

'You don't want anyone to think anything's wrong. I'll call you later at your place and tell you about the next step and the arrangements we've made.'

'Mom,' said Juwan, 'this ite cream's good.'

'I know it, baby,' said Devra, looking over the seat and smiling at her son.

'You're keeping him with you?' said Strange.

'Yes.'

'What did you tell Inez today when you left?'

'That I was taking a break.'

'She wouldn't follow you?'

'She was the only one in the shop. She wouldn't leave it for nothin'; that shop is everything to her.'

'That's a bad little woman right there. My wife works for me, and she did some checking on Inez Brown. Assault priors, check kiting, everything.'

'I'm not surprised.' Devra's eyes took all of him in. It was an unexpectedly uncomfortable moment, and Strange shifted in his seat. 'So you're gonna look after me yourself?'

'Me and my partner. A guy named Terry Quinn.'

'Where's he at?'

'Here in Southeast. We're workin' on a couple of things today.'

'You ever lose a witness?' said Devra.

'I've made mistakes,' said Strange, thinking of Olivia Elliot. 'But I'm not gonna lose you.'

*

From her car on the street, a forest green Hyundai, Inez Brown watched the parking lot of McDonald's. She had put the Hyundai along the curb just right, so she could see the white Caprice, its tail facing her. She could see Strange and the girl, and the top of the boy's head in the backseat. But she figured, the way she was behind him, way back on the street, he'd be awfully lucky to notice her car, if Strange even knew what kind of car she drove.

Devra had said she was goin' out for lunch and some ice cream for the boy. That's where she'd fucked up. 'Cause Inez knew the little kid, ran that mouth of his all day long, liked that Golden Arches ice cream best.

Inez sat on a couple of cushions so she could see over the wheel. She had good eyes. She could see the two of them, the fake cop and the girl, lippin' in the front seat of his car. That's all the fat man had asked her to do: find out if these two were still talking, even after she'd been warned. Stupid little bitch, with her young ass, too.

Inez checked her watch. She'd done her job and now she needed to get back. She didn't like to be away from her business, not even for a few minutes. No telling the customers she'd lost, doing this thing right here. She'd head back to the salon now. Phone Horace when she got there, tell him what he wanted to know.

26

Quinn put time in out front of Mart Liquors, talking to some of the men and women who were entering and leaving the shop. He spoke to the regulars who hung outside the place as well. Quinn asked them about Mario Durham and a guy named Donut. He showed them the flyer of the missing teenager, Linda Welles. Some answered politely and some were bordering on hostile, and a few didn't bother to respond to his questions at all. He got nothing from any of them. They had made him straight off as some kind of cop.

He tried the Metro station. He tried the phone banks at the gas stations and accompanying convenience marts. He received the same nonresponse.

Quinn drove the neighborhoods next. He had no plan. He cruised Stanton Road, passing liquor stores and squat redbrick structures surrounded by black iron fences. He went down Southern Avenue, then got on Naylor Road. On Naylor were more liquor stores, Laundromats, and other service-oriented businesses. Around 30th Street, on a long hill, were the Naylor Gardens apartments, a complex as well tended and green as a college campus. Farther along, up past Naylor Plaza, the apartments abruptly went from clean and pampered to ghetto grim. And farther still were a couple of stand-alone units like those Quinn had visited several times before.

He slowed his Chevelle and idled it on the street. This was the complex that Linda Welles's brothers had recognized in the sex video. The party had been held in one of these units. It was where she had last been seen.

Quinn looked up a rise of dirt and weeds to a three-story bunker of brick. On the stoop sat several young men wearing wife-beaters and low-hung jeans revealing the elastic bands of their boxers, skullies and napkin bandannas. They were passing around a bottle in a brown bag. They looked down at the street, where Quinn's engine rumbled. One of them, a heavyset young man with blown-out hair, looked directly at Quinn and smiled.

Quinn pulled off from the curb. He had tried to interview that group earlier, remembered the smiler and his hair. He had had the sense then that they knew something about the fate of Linda Welles, but he hadn't pushed it. He hadn't done his job. He remembered feeling weak and punked as he'd driven away from them the last time. And he felt that way now.

Quinn drove over to the area of Valley Green. He pulled the Chevelle up along some street-side kids on their bikes. He asked about Mario Durham and 'a dude named Donut.' He got some shrugs and smart remarks, and watched impotently as the kids rode away, doing wheelies, laughing, cutting on one another and the white man in the old car.

He parked at a small market and went inside. He questioned the woman behind the counter and got a shrug. He bought a pack of sugarless gum and thanked her for her time. Then he walked next door, into a Chinese carryout, where a thin man with fat freckles across the bridge of his wide nose stood in a small lobby in front of a Plexiglas wall with a lazy Susan in it. A Chinese woman stood behind the Plexiglas; her smile was welcoming, but her eyes were not. She looked friendly and frightened, both at once. Quinn got the woman's attention and talked into a slotted opening above the lazy Susan.

'I'm looking for a guy named Mario Durham,' said Quinn.

'I don't know.'

'How about a man they call Donut?'

'You want food?'

Quinn looked down at the linoleum floor and shook his head.

'*I* know Donut,' said the man with the freckles. 'Boy owes me ten dollas.'

Quinn turned. 'You know where he lives?'

'The building he lives in ain't but two blocks from here. I don't know the apartment number where he stays at, though.'

'The building's good enough. He owes you ten?'

'Boy took me for a Hamilton, like, a year ago. He thinks I forgot. But I'm gonna get it someday.'

'You'll get that ten sooner than someday,' said Quinn, 'you give me the address.'

'Make it twenty,' said the man, 'and I'll give it to you now.'

Homicide Detective Nathan Grady got a break soon after meeting with

Strange and Quinn. A young man named Richard Swales, picked up on an intent-to-distribute beef, had offered his help, in exchange for some 'consideration,' in locating Mario Durham. He told the arresting officer that he knew from talk on the street that Durham was wanted in a murder. From the substation, where they were keeping Swales in a holding cell, Grady was called and told of the lead. Grady said he'd be right in.

In the interview room, Swales admitted that he did not know Mario Durham personally or his whereabouts. But there was a guy folks called Donut, Durham's 'main boy,' who most likely could point the police in the right direction. Grady learned that Donut's real name was Terrence Dodson. He asked Swales where he could find Dodson. Swales said that he didn't know, but he knew the 'general area he stayed at.'

'Can I get some love?' said Swales.

Grady said that if the information he'd given him was correct, and if it led to an arrest, yes, it could help Swales's case.

That's all Grady had been looking for. Someone less afraid of Dewayne Durham than he was of prison. A two-time loser about to strike out. It was how most cases were solved.

It took a hot minute to find Terrence Dodson's address in Valley Green and get a record of his priors. Grady took his unmarked and, accompanied by a cruiser and a couple of uniformed officers, went to the address. One of the uniforms stayed out on the street with the cars. The other uniform went with Grady into the building, where they found Dodson's apartment door. Grady knocked, the uniform behind him, and the door soon opened. As it did, Grady flashed his badge.

'Terrence Dodson?' said Grady, looking down on the small, ugly man who stood in the door frame, one eye twitching, trying to manage a smile.

'That's my given name. Ain't nobody ever call me that, though.'

Grady slipped his badge case back into his jacket. 'Donut, then, right?'

'That's right.'

'You know a Mario Durham?'

'Why?' said Donut, chuckling weakly. 'He done somethin'? What, that fool spit on the sidewalk, sumshit like that?'

'Mind if I come in?'

'You got a warrant?' Donut barked out a laugh. 'I'm just playing with you, officer, *I* got nothin' to hide.'

Donut stepped aside to let the white man pass. Big motherfucker, too. Looked like that man played in the sequels to that movie with Felton Perry, about the redneck sheriff with the bat. The ones that weren't no good.

Horace McKinley sat in a vinyl nail-studded chair meant to look like leather in what used to be the living room of the house on Yuma. He talked on his cell as Mike Montgomery paced the room.

McKinley flipped the StarTAC closed. His forehead was beaded with sweat. There was sweat under his arms and it ran down his sides.

It had been a busy morning. He had learned from his own boys that Mario Durham was wanted in a murder. He had spoken to Ulysses Foreman, who had taken a call from Dewayne Durham, angry that the gun used by Mario had also been Jerome Long's murder gun in the Coates killings. Foreman had called McKinley to give his condolences on the cousins, and also to assure him that he hadn't known, of course, that one of his guns would be used against the Yuma Mob. McKinley saw an opportunity for an alliance with Foreman, and maybe to gain a favor or something free. He told Foreman that this was simply the cost of doing business for both of them and that no offense had been taken. And now that little old girl, ran his salon, had phoned with some disturbing news.

'That was Inez,' said McKinley. 'The Stokes girl's been talking to that Strange again.'

'What're we gonna do?'

McKinley breathed in deeply and heard a wheeze in his chest. He was carrying too much weight. Now would be a good time to give up on those Cubans, too.

'Ice her down for a while, I guess.'

'Kill her?'

'No, I don't want to kill the bitch 'less I have to. I was thinkin' we'd hide her until she comes around. I figure, we separate her from her little boy for a few hours, she'll change her mind about talking anymore.'

'We could use some help.'

'The troops been depleted, Mike. I got everyone on the street and I told them I needed a big cash night. It's just you and me.'

'You want me to stay with the kid?'

'You'd do better with him than I will. Me, I'm better with the girls.' McKinley smiled at Montgomery, who was frowning. His long hands were jammed deep in the pockets of his jeans. 'You gonna hold that boy tight? I don't want you gettin' soft on me now. This is business here; that's all it is. We got to protect our own and what we got.'

Montgomery nodded. McKinley was only a couple of years his senior, but he was the closest thing to a father he'd ever had.

'I'm behind you, Hoss. You know this.'

'No doubt. You my right hand, Mike.'

'We gonna do this now?'

'No. We can get over to the salon later, take care of the girl. She ain't goin' nowhere else today.'

'What we gonna do now, then?'

'Let's roll over to Foreman's first and buy us another gun. I spoke to him, and he's still got this Sig I had my eye on for a while. He's expecting another piece later on today, too, case we need it. He's got a boy he uses, gonna make a run.'

Montgomery pulled the keys to the Benz from his pocket and twirled them on his finger. 'I'm ready.'

'We gonna have us our little war, I guess.'

'Might not happen too soon. Durham's got his head turned around, lookin' after that fool brother of his.'

'That might be the time to hit him,' said McKinley, rising laboriously from the chair. 'While he's weak.'

Ulysses Foreman stood on the back deck of his house, smoking a cigar. Ashley was back in their room, packing for her trip down to her daddy's in southern Maryland. She had the stereo on in there, Chaka Khan singin' about 'I'm every woman,' Ashley singing along. She loved Chaka. So did Ulysses, back when she was with Rufus. That was a fine motherfucker right there.

Foreman held one arm out and flexed as he drew on his cigar. He needed to get over to the gym, looked like he was starting to atrophy. Man had to pay attention to his body, especially in times like these.

It had been a morning. A call from Dewayne Durham about that brother of his and that goddamn gun. That was his own fault, renting the Taurus to Twigs. Once a fuck-up, et cetera. Foreman should have known. Apparently Mario had claimed that he knew about the gun being hot, too. Foreman had told Dewayne that this wasn't so, but he wasn't sure it had registered all the way. Now he'd have to do something for Dewayne just to keep his fire down. A gift, *that* would work; he could lay a gun on him, nothing too expensive, but no cheap-ass Lorcin, either, nothin' like that. The kid from Alexandria was making a run for him today; he'd have him pick something up.

Then he'd talked to Horace McKinley, who had acted all unconcerned that he had sold that gun to Durham's boy Jerome Long, who'd gone and used it on the cousins. The fat man *acting* unconcerned, but always strategizing. Foreman wondered what he'd want in the end.

Foreman moved his head around some, back and forth, trying to get the ache out his neck. Shit was just building *up*.

'I'm ready,' said Ashley, behind him.

He hadn't heard her, with all that thinking he'd been doing. But he could smell that body spray she liked, raspberry, from that 'collection' of Nubian Goddess fragrances she bought at the CVS.

Foreman turned. She had on some shorts-and-top thing, looked like pajamas to him. When he'd said so she'd laughed and told him that it was a daytime outfit she'd bought at Penney's. She was carrying a glass of chardonnay in one hand, had one of her Viceroys in the other.

'You done packing?'

'Said I was ready, sugar. I was wondering, should I take my gun?'

'Leave it,' said Foreman. 'You won't need it down on that farm, anyway. And the way you drive with that lead foot of yours, you might get pulled over. No reason to risk that.'

Ashley moved forward, held her cigarette away so that the smoke didn't crawl up into his eyes. He could smell the wine and nicotine on her breath as she kissed him deep. The woman could hoover a man's tongue. He had hit it that morning, just a couple of hours ago, but he felt himself growing hard again. He reached down and stroked the back of her thighs, felt the ridges and pocks there. He liked every thing about her, even those marks.

'I love you, Ulee.'

'I know you do.'

'Couldn't you just say it back?'

'I show you every day, don't I?'

'Wish you could come with me.'

'So do I, but I got business to attend to. Keep your cell on, hear?'

'I will.'

'You always *say* you will, but then I get that voice says, Leave a message.'

'I'll keep it on.'

'I'll call you later.'

From the front steps, he watched her pull away in that Cougar of hers, feeling strange as she turned onto Wheeler Road, like maybe he should have gone with her this time, just gotten the fuck away. But this house, the woods, the seclusion, it had all been bought with sweat and hard work; none of it came easy. You needed to remember how much you loved your lifestyle when it came time to protect it. That's why, despite the funny rumbling in his gut, he was hanging back here today.

A car soon came down the drive, that boy was gonna make the buy and some girl he knew. A little while from now, Foreman figured, McKinley and that sidekick of his, one with the long arms they called Monkey, they were gonna be rollin' in here, too.

Detective Nathan Grady stood over Donut, who sat on the couch. Donut had invited Grady to have a seat with him, but Grady had said that he preferred to stand. Always look down on the person you were interviewing, and crowd them when you could.

Donut's legs were scissoring back and forth, and sweat had formed on his upper lip, betraying his friendly, accommodating smile.

'So you don't know about the whereabouts of your friend Mario.'

'Nah, uh-uh.'

'And you weren't aware that he was wanted on a murder?'

'No, I wasn't aware of that situation right there.'

'Seems like everybody in Anacostia's heard about it but you.'

'Now that you tell me, though, I feel real bad about that girl got herself dead.'

'You haven't heard from your friend in the past few days, have you?'

'Been a long while. I was just wonderin' today where he been at.'

'I suppose we could go into your phone records. Ask around with your neighbors, too. Maybe they've seen him coming in and out of here.'

'You should. I'd like to know my own self where he is.'

Grady rocked back on the heels of his Rocksports. He looked back at the uniformed officer standing by the door, then lifted his head and made a show of sniffing the air. Donut watched him, thinking, Here it comes.

'That marijuana I smell, *Dough*-nut?'

'I don't smell nothin'.'

'You got some priors, so it made me think, you know, you might still be dealing.'

'That was the old me. I been rehabilitated. And I go to church now, too.'

'So you wouldn't mind if I looked around?'

Donut shrugged. This motherfucker did find something, it wouldn't be but an ounce or so. What they call personal-use stuff. He'd be on the street in an hour, and the charge would get thrown out, anyway, come court date. He knew it, and so did this bobo with a shield. As for the stuff he had that looked like crack, shit, that wasn't nothin' but baking soda cooked hard. Make them all look stupid when they got it back to the lab.

'You know what an accessory-to-homicide conviction would do to you, with your history?'

'I got an idea. But, see, I don't know where Mario is.'

'We're gonna talk again. You're holding out on me, it's not gonna go your way come sentencing time.'

'You find Mario,' said Donut, 'let me know. He borrowed a shirt from me and didn't return it. A Sean John – wasn't cheap, either.'

'Anything else?' said Grady, his jaw tight.

'Boy owes me five dollas, too.'

Quinn drove down the block, saw the unmarked with the GT plates and the 6D cruiser outside Donut's building, and kept his foot on the gas. He turned the corner and idled the Chevelle against the curb. He phoned Strange on his cell.

'Derek.'

'Terry, what's going on?'

'I found the building where Mario's friend Donut lives. But I think Grady or some other cop might have found him first. They got cars outside the place now.'

'We can visit him later on.'

'Where are you?'

'I'm tailing Horace McKinley as we speak. I waited for him near his place on Yuma after I finished up with Devra Stokes. I followed him and his boy when they drove out in their Benz.'

'And?'

'They're headed out of the city, going onto Wheeler Road right now. Passing a Citgo station . . .'

'Stay several car lengths back and try not to get made.'

'Funny,' said Strange.

'Want me to meet you?'

'I'll call you in a few minutes. There they go, they're turning.'

'Into where?'

Quinn waited. He could almost see Derek's face, intense, as he watched the car up ahead.

'Looks to me,' said Strange, 'like they're driving right into the woods.'

27

Strange parked his Caprice beside the Citgo station, near the rest rooms and out of sight. He grabbed his 10 x 50 binoculars from the trunk, locked the car down, jogged around a fenced-in area holding a propane tank, and ran into the woods. He went diagonally in the direction that McKinley and his sidekick had gone, hoping that they were headed for a house set back not too far off Wheeler Road. He crashed through the forest like a hooved animal, unconcerned with the noise he made, and saw brighter light about a quarter mile in. He slowed his pace, approaching the light, which he knew to be a clearing, with care.

Strange took position behind the trunk of a large oak. A brick rambler, looked like it had some kind of deck on the back of it, stood in the clearing at the end of a circular drive. Parked in the drive were a late-model red El Dorado, McKinley's black Benz, and a green Avalon with aftermarket alloy wheels.

Strange looked into his binos. McKinley and his sidekick, young dude with some long-ass arms, were getting out of the Benz. McKinley, big as he was, and with a strained look on his face, tired from all that weight, was getting out more slowly than the other young man.

There were three people standing at the top of the rambler's steps, on a small concrete porch under a pink awning. The color of the awning told Strange that a woman lived in the house. Two of the three people, a handsome young man and an attractive woman, were in their early twenties. The third was a bulked-up man heading toward the finish line of his thirties. The older man, smoking a cigar, wore a ribbed shirt highlighting his show muscles. He descended the steps to greet McKinley. With that barracuda smile of his, the bulked-up man looked like some kind of salesman.

Strange lowered his binoculars. Was this McKinley's drug connect? Probably not. Most of the major quantities sold down here came from out of town. But this here looked like more than a backyard barbecue. The muscleman was selling something.

Strange stepped back about twenty yards and phoned Quinn. He told him to park beside the Citgo station, and where he could find him, approximately, in the woods.

Horace McKinley shook the hand of Ulysses Foreman, taking the pliers-like strength of his grip, Foreman always eager to show off what he had.

'Damn, big man, you ain't lost nothin'.'

'You the big man, dawg,' said Foreman, nodding at Mike Montgomery but not bothering to shake his hand.

McKinley wondered where that white rhino of Foreman's was. She was usually here to greet them, too, trying to talk like a black girl, coming off like some strand-walking ho, showin' off her big pockmarked ass cheeks.

'Where your woman at?' said McKinley.

Foreman dragged on his cigar. 'She went off to see her daddy down in southern Maryland.'

'I'll catch her next time, then. You got somethin' for me?'

'C'mon in.'

McKinley and Montgomery went up the steps to where the young man and woman stood. It was crowded up there, and the woman backed up as McKinley introduced himself, extending his hand to her, ignoring the man.

'Couple of associates of mine,' said Foreman from behind them, not bothering to state their names.

'Horace McKinley. Pleased to meet you, baby.' Horace turned to the young man, then made a gesture to the Avalon with the Virginia plates parked in the drive.

'That you?'

'Yeah,' said the young man, smiling with pride.

'Why don't you get you a real car? Avalon ain't nothin' but a Camry with some trim on it, and a Camry ain't nothin' but shit.'

The young man didn't know how to react. He had been disrespected in front of the girl, but he wasn't going to step to this Horace McKinley. Probably a dealer, 'cause that's who Foreman did business with. Looking at him, wasn't no *probably* about it; with all that ice, the four-finger ring and the necklace, he was a drug dealer for sure. Wouldn't do any good to his health to show the fat man any kind of defiance.

'I got my eye on a Benz I like,' said the young man, but McKinley had already moved his attention back to Foreman, standing at the bottom of the steps.

'Where we goin'?' said McKinley.

'Down to the rec room,' said Foreman.

'Nah,' said McKinley. 'Nice day like this? Why don't you get me one of them good cigars you smokin', and a cold beer or two, and meet us out on the back deck. We can do our business out there.'

'Fine. Go on through the house and I'll see y'all out there.'

McKinley and Montgomery went into the house. Foreman came up to the porch, reached into his jeans, and extracted a roll of bills. He peeled some money off and handed it to the young man.

'Let me give this to you now,' said Foreman, 'lighten up this wad I got.'

'What you want me to get?' said the young man, taking the money and slipping it into his khakis.

'I got to think on it,' said Foreman. 'Come down to the basement while I take care of him. You and your girl can kick back and shoot some pool, or just watch some TV, while I'm working things out with the fat man.'

The young man grinned sheepishly. 'Can I get one of them *ci*gars, too?'

'That didn't take long,' said Strange.

'I followed your scent,' said Quinn. 'Fill me in.'

'Nothin' for a while now.' Strange looked at the house. 'Dude with muscles, between your age and mine, lives there. He met McKinley and his boy out front. That's their Benz, the one followed me the other day. The Toyota with the chrome on it belongs to a young man, has a nice-looking girl with him.'

'And?'

'Muscled-up dude gave the young man some cash and they all went into the house. I moved around some and saw McKinley on the back deck. Came back here to meet you so you wouldn't get lost. You remember the path you took?'

'I dropped some bread crumbs on the ground on my way in, just in case.' Quinn reached for Strange's binoculars, took them, and looked at the house through the glasses. 'You get what you needed from Stokes?'

'Yeah. Right after I talked to her I went to the post office and mailed the tape to Ives. Then I drove over to Yuma, the six hundred block, and watched this shit-hole-lookin' house where McKinley hangs.'

'Stokes gonna be okay?'

'Long as we keep an eye on McKinley.' Strange gave Quinn the details of McKinley's assault on Devra Stokes.

'Guy's a real gentleman.'

'Man does that to a woman is a coward. I'd like to get him alone and see how he holds up.'

'Maybe you'll get your chance.'

Strange looked Quinn over. 'Nice work finding that boy Donut.'

'Like your boy Stefanos said, just hang out and listen.' He handed the binoculars back to Strange. 'What do you think's up with all this?'

'They got me all curious now,' said Strange. 'Let me get closer and take the plate numbers off that Caddy and the Avalon. You got a pen on you, something to write on?'

'Yeah.'

'I'll read the numbers out to you, unless you want to read 'em off to me.'

'Your eyes are better than mine.'

'I know that, man. Just didn't want you feeling like my lackey, is all.'

When Strange had gotten the numbers off the plates closer in, they moved back to their spot in the woods.

'Now let's move around to that place I found before,' said Strange. 'Get a better look at that deck.'

While the young man shot some pool, smoked a cigar, and tried to impress his girl, Foreman put some red felt over one of those trays he used to rest his food on while he watched TV. Then he laid the rest of his inventory, the Sig Sauer .45, the Heckler & Koch .9, and the Calico M-110, atop the tray. He placed bricks of corresponding ammunition above the guns, a couple of beers with pilsner glasses on the side, and two cigars laid out just so. Presentation was everything in this business. It was his trademark, setting him apart from the other arms dealers in town.

'Don't be drinkin' none of my beer while I'm gone,' said Foreman to the young man. 'I want you together when you go down to that store.'

'I don't drink no beer nohow,' said the young man, winking at the girl. 'My drink is Cris.'

Foreman could have guessed. These young studio gangsters were all the same. 'I won't be too long, hear?'

Foreman carried the tray up the stairs and out through the sliding doors to the back deck. McKinley had made himself comfortable on one of the deck chairs, came with two others and a lounger, recently purchased at one of those outdoor-furniture stores. Looked like

McKinley was testing the weight limit on it, the way the cushion was riding low. Montgomery stood with his back against the wooden rail.

'Here we go,' said Foreman, placing the tray on a circular glass table Ashley had insisted they buy with the set.

McKinley managed to get himself out of the chair. Foreman handed him a cigar and lit it for him, holding the flame so that McKinley could get a good draw. He offered a cigar to Montgomery, who declined. Foreman almost double taked checking out Montgomery's arms. Boy was a knuckle-draggin' motherfucker. Wasn't no mystery why they called him Monkey Mike.

'Let's see what you got,' said McKinley.

Foreman lifted the Heckler & Koch off the tray and handed it butt out to McKinley.

'H and K nine,' said Foreman. 'Ten-shot magazine, stainless, got a roughed-up stock so it don't slip out your hand. German engineering.'

'Like my car.'

'High quality. You know how they do.'

'How much?'

'Seven fifty.'

McKinley returned the gun to Foreman. 'Let me see that other one right there.'

Foreman picked up the Sig Sauer. He turned it so it caught the sunlight. He admired it before handing it over, stroking the checkered black grip, making a show of its beauty. He knew Mc Kinley liked the gun and had deliberately waited before giving it to him.

'That's the deluxe Sig right there,' said Foreman. 'Forty-five with the eight-shot magazine. Double action, slide stays open after the last shot so you know to reload. Trigger guard's squared off, like them combat guns. I got it tricked out with all the options. Nickel slide, and those Siglite sights for the nighttime.'

'Nice,' said McKinley. 'What you want for it?'

'Nine hundred, for you.'

'For me? Shit.'

'I could sell you a Davis for a lot cheaper, I guess. I figured, you driving a Mercedes, you don't want to be carrying the kind of gun be in the glove box of a Neon.'

'True. But that don't mean I'm gonna take my money and burn it in the street.'

'Nine hundred is damn near close to my cost. And I'm gonna throw in another brick of bullets for you, like I always do.'

'What about another magazine?'

'I got one. But you're gonna have to purchase that.'

'Just the bullets, then, man.'

McKinley sighted down the barrel, then inspected the piece. The truth was, he knew as little about guns as he knew about cars. But he always ordered the most expensive item on the menu. Man had to show off the rewards of his hard work, otherwise none of it meant shit.

McKinley placed the gun back on the tray. He poured some beer into a pilsner glass and had a long swig. 'That young boy downstairs, he makin' a buy for you today?'

'Yeah, he's leaving soon.'

'I'm lookin' for somethin' on the low-end side. A revolver, maybe, for one of my troops.'

Foreman had planned to lay a cheap piece on Durham, to simmer him down over the mix-up with Mario. Now he'd have to think of something else.

'I can do that,' said Foreman.

'Might have some trouble coming up; want to make sure all my people are ready.'

Foreman nodded. He didn't want to talk about Dewayne Durham if that's where this was going. He had always stayed at a distance during these wars, and he was determined to remain neutral in this latest conflict.

'Might need you to deliver it to me, later on,' said McKinley.

'Prefer to do it right here,' said Foreman in a friendly way. 'You can always send one of your boys, you don't want to come back out yourself.'

'You don't want to get involved, huh?'

Foreman shrugged. He looked over at Montgomery, who was kind of staring off, not paying much attention to the two of them.

'You ain't afraid of Dewayne Durham, are you?' said Mc Kinley.

'I sell to everyone,' said Foreman. 'I told you that the first time I met you. The thing is, I wouldn't want anyone thinking I was taking sides. Someone like Durham might see me over at your place on Yuma, get the wrong idea. And why wouldn't he see me? He ain't but across the alley. Wouldn't be good for my business.'

'He's gonna go down,' said McKinley. 'When he does, I'm gonna remember who stood next to me. That might be good for your business.'

As you'll go down, too. You all do. And you ain't all that special, either, thinkin' you're the only one's gonna keep me in business. There's never a shortage of young men down here to take your place.

'I'll keep it in mind.'

'Or maybe I should tip on back here,' said McKinley, 'seein' as how I missed your woman. I do like to look at her.'

Foreman felt his face grow warm at the implied threat. He knew of McKinley's violent reputation with women.

'You're always welcome,' said Foreman, forcing a smile. 'I'll call you later, soon as my boy comes back with that piece.'

'Here's your money,' said McKinley. He rested the beer glass on the tray and peeled off nine hundred-dollar bills from a roll. He holstered the Sig in the waistband of his warm-up pants and dropped the matching top out over the band. Montgomery picked up a box of bullets without asking if he should.

'I'll meet you out front with that brick,' said Foreman.

'Nice doin' business with you.'

Foreman shook McKinley's sweaty hand. 'You too, dawg.'

McKinley head-motioned Montgomery. 'Let's go, Mike.'

Strange and Quinn walked through the woods to their original vantage point, where they could see the front of the house. Soon they watched McKinley and his sidekick emerge from the door, pass under the pink awning, and stand by the Benz in the circular drive.

'They're leaving,' said Quinn, keeping his voice low.

'Fat boy got his new gun,' said Strange, 'so I guess they're done. Least we know now what's going on in that house. I'll be giving Blue the plate numbers off muscleman's Caddy. If I'm guessing right, that's his ride. I'm sure the MPD and the PG County boys, not to mention the ATF, will be happy to get a local arms dealer off the street.'

'Why are they hanging around?'

'Maybe that salesman's gonna give them a good-bye kiss. I wonder what that young man and his girlfriend are doing for this guy.'

Quinn watched as the man in the muscle shirt walked out of the house. 'What now?'

'McKinley and his boy know my car. I got away with tailin' him a little while ago, but I was lucky. I'm gonna need you to follow McKinley, you don't mind. Shame you got that car says, Look at me, but you play it smart and don't get too close to him, you'll be all right. When you're satisfied he's not going after the Stokes girl, get over to the nail salon where she works and sit tight in the lot. I'll meet you there later on.'

'What are you gonna do about the girl then? You can't watch her all night.'

'I was thinkin' I'd take her home, to Janine's, I mean, for a couple of days. Until me and Ives can get her someplace else.'

'Look, I got some business to take care of,' said Quinn, thinking of Linda Welles and the boys at the apartment house on Naylor Road. His reluctance to talk to them earlier had been eating at him since.

'Still looking for Sue's runaway?'

Quinn nodded. 'I want to check out a lead.'

'Fine. I know you don't want to get involved in the Granville case. But this here is something else; you'll be doing one of those good things you been wanting to do. Just make sure Devra's all right.'

'What're you gonna do?'

'Follow that young couple, they move out of here. Like I said, I'm curious.'

'Leave your cell on,' said Quinn.

Strange shook Quinn's hand. Quinn turned and booked through the trees.

28

Looking at the needle on his gas gauge, Strange began to worry that he was going to run out of fuel. He'd been driving for a half hour now, following the Avalon, and as yet the young man behind the wheel had shown no signs of nearing a destination.

The Avalon was on Route 1 in Virginia, heading south. Strange had tailed him and the woman on the Beltway, over the Wilson Bridge, and onto 1, at that point called Richmond Highway.

To Strange, Virginia's Route 1 looked the same as Maryland's stretch of Route 1 from Laurel to Baltimore, a blacktop badland now dominated by chain and family-style restaurants and big-box retailers but still littered with trick-pad motels, last-stand truck stops, and drinker's bars. Confederate flag stickers appeared on some cars the farther south he drove, 'Tradition, Not Hatred' written below the stars and bars. Strange realized just how far off his turf he had come.

The road had stoplights but was straight and heavily trafficked, the easiest kind of tail job. Being made wasn't the problem, though. The problem was keeping up, as the boy was a lane changer with a lead foot.

Strange listened to *Let's Stay Together*, front to back, on the trip. The one had Green looking like a high school kid on the cover, 'How Can You Mend a Broken Heart' a highlight of the set. Ordinarily he'd enjoy a drive like this, the window down, the Reverend Al at his peak on the box. But he was worrying about the gas gauge, and the Stokes girl, and Quinn. And wondering if the boy in the Avalon was ever going to slow down.

Down below the Marine Corps base in Quantico, on a stretch of deep forest-lined highway absent of any commercial enterprise, he saw the Toyota's right turn signal flash. The car pulled off on the shoulder and then went into a graveled lot cut out of the woods. Strange stayed behind a Chevy pickup and kept his foot on the gas, glancing over at the Avalon as he kept his speed. The boy was parking in front of what looked like an old house, standing alone well back off the road. A sign, going the width of the house's porch, said 'Commonwealth Guns.'

Strange drove for another mile or so, found a cut in the median strip intended for official use only, and made an illegal turn. He drove north and made the same kind of turn a mile past the store. He drove into the graveled lot and parked beside the Avalon. These were the only two cars in the lot, and anyway, there wasn't any place to hide his car. If the young man hadn't made him yet, he'd be all right.

Strange walked about fifty yards up a path to the house. He stepped onto the front porch, where a Harley Softail was chained and padlocked to a post. He entered the shop.

It had the feel of a sportsman's store at first glance. The displays showed rods, bows, and knives, in addition to rifles and shot guns. Signs supporting gun ownership and gun owners' rights were hung on all the walls. Accessories, holsters, and cleaning kits crowded the aisles. The aisles led to the destination point, a glass case in the back of the store.

Strange went directly to the case. The young man and his companion were there, looking down at the handguns housed under the glass. A little white man stood behind the case. He greeted Strange and told him he'd be with him as soon as he finished with these folks. Strange told him to take his time. The young man glanced over, perhaps only registering Strange's size, gender, and race, and returned his attention to the guns.

Strange stayed to the right side of the case and examined its contents. The guns seemed to be arranged by type and caliber, with brands kept together and graduated by price. Davis and Lorcin went to Taurus, S&W, and Colt; Hi-Point went to Beretta, Glock, Browning, Ruger, Sig Sauer, and Desert Eagle. Derringers moved into revolvers and then on to automatics. The highly priced, coveted Dan Wesson revolvers, long-barreled .357s and .44 Mags, were set off from the rest.

The young man was holding a Taurus revolver, hefting it in his hand.

'It's meant to be heavy,' said the little man. 'Thirty-four ounces, most of it's in the barrel. Soft rubber grip. Good stopping power. Similar to what the police used to use before they went over to autos. Your basic thirty-eight special. This here is one of my most popular models. Perfect for protection. All those home invasions you hear about – in the city, I mean. I can't keep these in stock.'

Strange knew the police pitch was intended to sell the young man. The rest was just bullshit. The little man wore an automatic holstered on his waist. It looked large on his narrow hips. Strange figured that big motorcycle outside was his, too. Big gun, big bike, little man. Wasn't anything surprising about that.

'How much?' said the young man.

'Two ninety-five for the blue finish. The stainless will run you another fifty.'

'I'll take the blue.'

'It's for you?'

'Nah, it's for her.'

The young woman smiled. She was pretty and looked innocent enough. Strange wondered if she knew, exactly, what she was doing. If she thought this was just a favor for her boyfriend, or if she imagined herself to be a player in some kind of adventure.

'You're a Virginia resident, right, sweetheart? Over twenty-one?'

'Yeah,' said the girl.

'You'll need to fill out a form, and then I have to call it in. Instant check. I can have you out of here in ten minutes. The government hasn't screwed that part up yet, not in the commonwealth, anyway.'

The little man got the form, and while the young woman was filling it out, he approached Strange.

'Can I answer any questions for you quick?'

'I'm lookin' for some home protection myself. But right now I'm just scouting around.'

'I'll be finished up here soon and we can talk.'

Strange resumed his browsing. The little man was right. Didn't take but ten minutes after the girl had filled out the form, and the transaction was nearly done. The part left was the money. The young man removed some large bills from his wallet and handed them to the girl, who paid the merchant and got a receipt. Then they walked out of the shop with a handgun and a box of ammunition.

Obviously the gun was for the young man. He had paid for it with his own money in plain sight. But the form had been filled out by the girl, who was of age and had no prior convictions. That was all that was required for the two of them to make the straw purchase. The merchant had done nothing illegal and technically had obeyed every law. Another handgun would now be circulated in D.C. It would end up being used, most likely, in some kind of violent crime.

'Now,' said the little man, coming back to Strange. 'What can I do for you?'

'Nothing,' said Strange, looking into the man's eyes.

Strange left the shop.

Quinn tailed McKinley to the house on Yuma and kept driving as the

Benz came to a stop. There wasn't a turnoff nearby, and he had gotten too close to their car. The only option was to keep moving, just plow straight on ahead.

Passing by the Benz, Quinn did not look their way. But he felt the eyes of McKinley and his sidekick on him as he went by. It wasn't a surprise to Quinn that he'd been made. Strange had been riding him to get a work vehicle less conspicuous than his Chevelle for some time now. And he was white. Unless he was some kind of cop, or buying drugs, there was no good reason for him to be in this part of town. Still, he was angry at himself for not paying full attention to the street layout as he'd neared their house.

Quinn looked in his rearview as he prepared to make a left at the next corner. McKinley was getting out of the passenger side of the vehicle, staring at the Chevelle.

Quinn punched the gas, going up 9th. He headed for the salon off Good Hope Road.

The strip center was quiet as Quinn entered the lot. He parked his car two rows away from the salon, facing it. From this space he could look through its plate glass storefront. Even with his poor long vision, he could make out the tiny owner, talking on the phone. The Stokes girl was there, looked like she was working on a customer. He could see her son, walking around and then dropping to the floor, in there, too. All of them were secure in the shop. It didn't look to Quinn that the girl or her boy was in any kind of danger.

Those couple of hours of weekday activity, people getting off work and grabbing groceries and fundamentals on their way home, had come and gone. Until now, Quinn had not even noticed that the day had passed. The rumble in his stomach told him that he had not eaten anything since the meeting at the diner. The sun was dropping fast, lengthening the shadows in the parking lot as it fell.

The customer came out of the shop, examining her nails in the last light of day before dusk. She walked out into the lot and got into an old green Jag. Quinn sat for a little while longer, then phoned Strange.

'Derek here.'

'Where you at?'

'Someplace on Richmond Highway, near the city. I'll tell you where I been when I see you. I'm gonna catch the Beltway and come around now. Where are *you*?'

'Baby-sitting Stokes, like you told me to. McKinley's at his place on Yuma.'

'*Three-Ten to Yuma.*'

'Was wondering when you were gonna make that connection.'

'I'll be there in about a half hour.'

'I'm gonna roll over to Naylor, check on that Welles lead.'

'Your call. You think the girl's okay, go ahead.'

'Looks like business as usual in there. She looks fine.'

'I'll meet you back there, then,' said Strange. 'In the lot.'

'There he goes,' said McKinley, talking into his cell, watching through the windshield of the Benz as the Chevelle backed out of its space and drove from the parking lot.

'That Strange's boy?' said Montgomery, his cell to his ear, sitting behind the wheel of his late-model Z in the lot near the Benz.

'His partner.'

'How you know?'

'The Coates cousins said some white boy was in Strange's car while he went to talk to Stokes at her apartment.'

And I been told.

'Oh, yeah.'

'Boy's stupid, too. Trying to be all undercover and shit, driving a loud-ass car. Anyway, we better hurry up. Man's prob'ly just going to take a pee.'

'We gonna go in the back?'

'Like we said. Let me get off here and call Inez. You follow me then, behind the store.'

In the salon, Devra sat at her work station, watching as Inez Brown went to the phone. She spoke to the caller briefly, then ended the call. Inez went around the counter, taking her keys with her, and locked the front door.

Devra looked out into the parking lot. It had begun to get dark.

'Come here, Juwan,' said Devra. The boy got up from where he was playing, his action figures scattered around him, and walked to her. She brought him into her arms.

'What's wrong, Mama?' said Juwan. He could see something funny in his mother's eyes.

'Nothin'. You just stay here *with* me, now.'

Inez Brown went into the back room, then quickly returned to the front of the shop, coming over to where Devra sat in a chair, holding the boy.

'Why you lockin' the door?' said Devra. 'It ain't closin' time.'

'It is for you,' said Brown, showing a little row of white teeth. It was the first time Devra could remember seeing her smile. The smile scared her some.

'Why you doin' this?'

'You don't *know*? Girl, you fucked up. Runnin' that pretty-ass mouth of yours.'

'I never did you no wrong.'

'I just don't like you, is what it is. Did I mention that you were fired, too?' Brown laughed from somewhere shadowed and deep. As she laughed, Horace McKinley walked in from the back room.

'Let's go,' said McKinley. 'Out the back.'

'Where?' said Devra, her voice catching as she stood, keeping her hand on her son's shoulder.

'You're coming with me,' said McKinley. 'The boy's gonna stay with Mike.'

'No.'

'No *nothin*'. I got no time to argue with you. You didn't listen, and now we got to do somethin' else. We're just gonna put you somewhere, let you think about the things you did that I told you *not* to do. See how quick you get to missing your little boy.'

Devra backed up a step. McKinley reached over and grabbed her arm. She flinched as his fingers dug into her flesh. He pulled her toward him and she let him, grabbing her purse off the table as she went past. Her knees were weak, but she moved and brought the boy along. They stopped to pick up a few of the wrestling figures and kept on. It felt like she was floating as they made their way to the back room. The back door was open, and they stood in the frame. McKinley's Benz was in the alley and a black Z was idling behind it. The one named Mike, who had kind eyes and played nice with her son, was standing beside the driver's door.

'I don't want to hear no screamin' or nothin' like it,' said McKinley. 'Say good-bye quick.'

Devra got down on her haunches so that she was close to her son. He was crying, but trying not to.

'Baby,' said Devra, 'I want you to go with that man. The one you were playing with before?'

'I want to go with *you*.'

'You know where home is, right?' said Devra. She whispered the street name and apartment number in his ear, and the name of Mrs Roberts, who lived on their floor.

'I know.'

'We gonna be there together, real soon. I'll catch up with you, hear? It's gonna be all right.'

She kissed him roughly and smelled his scalp. She turned him then and pushed on his back until he took a few steps. She watched him walk toward the black car. Mike opened the passenger door for him, and he got inside the Z.

Devra moved toward the Benz. Nearing the car, she caught the eyes of Mike Montgomery and held his gaze. Looking at Montgomery deep, she wasn't so afraid for her son anymore. But she wondered if she'd ever hold him again.

The girl had come home from work, taken a shower, and then was just gone. She'd left without telling him where she was going. Said something about some sodas in the refrigerator and a key in a bowl by the front door, that was it. He heard the door close, and that was how he'd known she'd left out the place. He hadn't said nothin' out of line to her or nothin' like that. Girl just wasn't *social*, is what it was.

Mario was bored. He hadn't talked to no one since Donut had called him that last time, and his brother hadn't called all day. He had turned on the TV, but there wasn't anything on worth watching. Bitch didn't even have the cable. Who the fuck didn't have cable these days? Even the no-job-havin' motherfuckers he knew paid for the service. If she had it, at least he could sit and watch some of those joints they ran on *106 & Park*, that video show they had on BET.

He decided to go out on the street and try his luck, sell a couple of vials of that fake crack.

He was off his turf. Somewhere in Northeast – he hadn't bothered to take notice of the particulars when Dewayne drove him to the woman's place. Truth was, he didn't know *where* he was. No idea. But that was cool. An opportunity, since no one around here knew who he was. He could sell some of these dummies and then disappear. Move on, soon as the heat died down. All he had to worry about was the police.

He gathered up his shit and went out the door. Going down the stairwell of the apartment house, he could smell himself, and it wasn't pretty. It was the clothes he'd been wearing these past few days, that's what it was. He could put some deodorant on; he'd seen some in that girl's medicine cabinet. Or take a shower, like he'd done at Donut's, if he had the time.

He went down to the corner. It had gotten dark out. Not full dark yet, but near to it. There was some kids out playin', but nobody else. A market was on the corner, but wasn't anybody hanging outside of it. And on the corner was a street lamp that hadn't been broken. That would be a good place to stand, under that light.

He went there and assumed the position. One hand in his pocket, kind of staring out into the street. Like he was waiting for a ride but in no hurry to get it. He'd seen enough of these boys to know how they did it.

Some cars passed. A white car turned the corner, and Mario stepped back into the shadows. It was a Crown Victoria with big side mirrors, but it wasn't the police. Just some kids who liked to drive the same kind of car the Five-O drove. Stupid-ass kids.

A gray Toyota hooptie slowed down nearing the corner and came to stop in the middle of the street. Two hard-looking young men were in the front seat. The driver had marks on his face, looked like he'd been cut.

'You sellin'?' said the driver in a dry, raspy voice.

'I might be,' said Mario.

'Come closer, man. I can't hear shit with you standing there.'

Mario walked out to the car and leaned his elbows on the frame of the open window. He could smell that the driver and his friend had been drinking beer, and they were wearing fucked-up clothes. These two couldn't be undercover or nothin' like that. No one could make themselves look that ghetto 'less they *were* ghetto for real.

'I got some rock.'

'Talk about it.'

'What you want, a dime?'

'Do I look like a dime-smokin' motherfucker to you? Gimme a fifty, man.'

Mario looked around and reached into his pocket. He brought out some vials Donut had given him and found one that he had filled with what looked like fifty dollars' worth of rock. He put it in the hand of the driver while the one in the passenger seat checked the mirrors for any signs of law.

The driver scowled. 'Fuck is this shit?'

Mario's heart beat hard in his chest. 'What's wrong with it?'

'This looks like a hundred dollars' worth, not fifty. Fuck you tryin' to pull?'

'I'm new on this strip,' said Mario. 'Just tryin' to be generous so I can get some of that repeat business.'

The driver studied Mario's face. 'This shit better be right.'

'It is,' said Mario, nodding his head quickly.

The driver paid Mario with a ten and two twenties. The bills were damp.

'Pray you ain't fuckin' with me, *Deion*,' said the driver. His friend was laughing as the Toyota pulled away.

Yeah, okay, thought Mario. I'll fuck with you anytime I want.

'Cause I am gone up out of this piece, soon as things cool down. And you ain't never gonna see my face again.

'Bitch,' he said under his breath.

He puffed out his chest, feeling bold right about then. But soon he began to lose his nerve and he walked back toward the woman's apartment, his head down low. He could come out later, he wanted to, and sell a little bit more. In the meantime, he'd go and kick back on that girl's couch. See if there was anything worth watching on the box. Maybe take a shower, he had time.

29

Quinn pulled over on Naylor behind a new red Solara, tricked out with gold-accented alloys. He let the car idle as he looked up to the three-story, bunkerlike structure that sat atop a rise of dirt and weeds. The pipes on his Chevelle were sputtering and loud, and the young men on the front stoop all turned their heads at the sound. Quinn cut the engine and let himself relax, but not to the point of inaction. He knew if he deliberated too long, if he was sensible, he'd just pull away.

Do your job.

He grabbed the manila folder on the seat beside him and got out of the car. He locked it down and walked up the steps to the apartment unit.

There were chuckles and comments as he neared. All of them were staring at him now. He sensed that they hadn't moved since the afternoon. A halogen light that hung from the building cast a yellow glow on the stoop. The light bled to nothing as the hill graded down. Quinn stopped walking ten, fifteen feet away from the group.

A couple of them were drinking from brown paper bags. The air smelled of marijuana, but none was going around; a faint fog of smoke hung in the light. The young men's eyes, pink and hooded, told him they were up.

'Terry Quinn.' He flashed his license, which looked like a badge. 'Investigator, D.C.'

A couple of the young men looked at each other, smiling. He heard someone mimic him, 'Terry Quinn. Investigator, D.C.,' in the voice of a game-show announcer, and there was low laughter then, and movement as several of them adjusted their positions. One of them, wearing a napkin bandanna and smoking a cigarette, leaned forward, his forearms on his thighs. He was bone skinny, no older than thirteen, with the flat eyes of a cat.

'I remember you,' said a heavyset young man with a blown-out

Afro, his shirttails out over his jeans. Quinn remembered him, too. He was the smiling one from earlier that afternoon.

'I was looking for a girl named Linda Welles,' said Quinn. 'I'm still looking. Last time she was seen was in this neighborhood. Her family's worried about her. She's fourteen years old.'

He removed a flyer from the folder and held it out to the heavyset young man. The young man looked at it, and his eyes flared, but just as quickly lost their light. Quinn knew with certainty then that this one could help him find the girl.

'Take it,' said Quinn, still holding out the flyer. But the young man left his hands at rest. He hadn't moved at all since Quinn had come up on the group.

It was quiet now. They were all staring at Quinn, and even the drinkers were holding their bags still between their knees.

'You know where the girl is, don't you?' said Quinn.

The young man said nothing.

'You don't tell me now, I'm gonna come back.'

'Why you gonna come back?' said the young man. 'You here *now*.'

'I'm gonna come back,' said someone in that same announcer's voice, and another voice said, 'With the cavalry and shit.' Quinn heard chuckling and an 'Oh, shit.'

The heavy young man pulled back the tail of his shirt and let it drop back against his waist. The butt of an automatic, stainless with black grips, rose out of his waistband and lay across the elastic of his boxer shorts. Quinn couldn't seem to move. His face was hot. He was frozen there.

'You know why I remember you?' said the young man. 'Wasn't because of no girl.'

'What was it, then?' said Quinn.

'I remember you 'cause you were so little, and so white. Mini-Me, comin' up here, acting so tough. 'Cause you knew that we wouldn't hurt no white boy down here, bring all sorts of uniforms to our neighborhood. And you were right, the first time around. I don't want to do no time over some miniature motherfucker like you, don't mean shit to me *no* way. But you keep on standing around here, I might just go ahead and take my chances.'

Quinn could feel his free hand shaking and he balled it up to make it stop. He stood straight and kept his eyes locked on the heavy young man's.

'You want somethin' else?'

'I'm comin' back,' said Quinn.

'Yeah, okay. But for now? Walk while you still can.'

Quinn turned and headed back toward his car. He heard someone say, 'Mini-Me,' and a burst of laughter, and the slapping of skin. It was like he was a kid again, cutting through the woods at night. His humiliation was chasing him like something horrible, a screaming, maggot-covered corpse with an upraised knife. He was ashamed, and still he wanted to run.

Quinn dropped into the bucket of his car. It would be different if he still had the street power of a cop. But he knew he'd never have that kind of power again. He turned the ignition key and drove away from the curb.

Quinn wished he'd brought his gun.

The salon was dark inside when Strange arrived. On the glass door was a hand-painted sign that gave the store hours. That Inez Brown had gone and closed the store up two hours early, but Devra had said she'd be working till closing time.

Strange paced the sidewalk while he phoned Devra from his cell. She wasn't in, or wasn't answering. He left a message on her machine.

Strange looked around. Where was that old man, the one who'd given him the information yesterday, when he needed him? The real question was, where the fuck was Quinn?

Even as he was thinking it, he watched the Chevelle pull into the lot, easing into a space beside the Caprice. Strange dropped off the sidewalk to the asphalt and walked to the driver's side of the car. He put his palm on the roof as he leaned in the open window.

'Where's Devra?'

'She's not in there?' said Quinn. He looked through the windshield at the darkened shop.

'God*damnit*, Terry, I told you to keep an eye on her.'

'You said it was my call,' said Quinn, his face pale and taut. 'Looks like I shit the bed.'

Strange studied Quinn's troubled eyes and doughy complexion. 'What's wrong with you, man?'

'I found some guys who know where the Welles girl is, but I got nothin' out of them. Matter of fact, I let myself get punked out.'

'Shit, that's all this is?' Strange shook his head. 'Terry, I let people out here disrespect me every *day*. It's part of how we do our job. Let them have their little victory and get what you can.'

'It was worse than disrespect.'

'Besides, you come down here gettin' violent on people, how long you think you'd be able to work these neighborhoods? You'd be a marked man, and it doesn't even matter if the people you fucked with got put away. They have friends and relatives, and those people never forget. I started shakin' down people like I was wearin' a uniform again, I'd be out of business. Get it through your head, man, you're not a cop.'

'This was something else,' said Quinn. He stared straight ahead, unable to look at his friend. 'It never would have happened, I had my gun.'

'Nah, see, you don't even want to be considering that. You had your gun, you'd a killed someone and got yourself some lockdown, or got your *own* self killed. Either way, you'd be fucked.' Strange put his hand on Quinn's shoulder. 'Look, man, I don't have time for all this now. I got to find that girl and her kid. Time to visit McKinley. You with me?'

'Let's go,' said Quinn.

'I'll follow you,' said Strange.

Bernard Walker lit the candles on the first floor of the house on Atlantic and put a couple on the steps going up to the second floor. He came back into the living room, where Dewayne Durham sat at a card table ending a call. Durham flipped the cell phone closed and placed it on the table.

The house was oddly quiet. Dewayne had sent out all his people to work the school on Mississippi. He had told Walker that he didn't want him playing that beat box tonight like he liked to do, and Walker had complied. So it was just the two of them and the silence now.

Dewayne nodded at the cell. 'I just called my brother at the girl's place. He ain't there.'

'Maybe he's taking a shower,' said Walker.

'He better be. What he better *not* be is out. I told him to sit tight.'

Durham rubbed his face and stood, walking into the hall that led to the galley kitchen and the door at the rear of the house. Walker followed. They stood beside each other and looked across the darkened alley at McKinley's house on Yuma. All of McKinley's people, it looked like they were out working, too.

McKinley had the lights on all over the first floor. Though the front of the house had wood in its windows, there wasn't any plywood on the back windows, only curtains, and most of those had been torn down. They could see McKinley walking around in there slowly, gesturing to someone who was half his size.

'There go the Candyman right there,' said Walker. 'Looks like . . . Shit, he's got a woman with him.'

'Ain't like him to be *any* goddamn where without that boy Monkey,' said Durham. 'Much less with a woman.'

'He don't know how to treat a woman *no* way,' said Walker.

Durham squinted. 'Zu? Why is it we're in here lightin' candles and shit, worried about the police, when fat boy is over there with all the lights burning bright?'

'He's bold, I guess.'

'Right,' said Durham. 'He is bold. Just ain't right, how bold he is.'

Walker felt his stomach rumble. 'I'm hungry. Thirsty, too. You want to go out for a while, pick up somethin'?'

'Need to rest, think some,' said Durham. 'I'm gonna go upstairs and lay out on that mattress for a while.'

'Aiight, then.'

'Swing by Mississippi, get the money from the troops while you're there.'

'Anything else?'

'Bring me back a couple of sodas,' said Durham, 'and a Slim Jim.'

'Damn, boy, I am hungrier than a motherfucker.' McKinley punched in numbers on his cell, got the pizza joint on the line, was put on hold. 'Girl, you want anything?'

'No.'

'We gonna be here awhile.'

'I don't want no pizza.'

'Suit yourself.' The sucker who worked at the pizza place got back on, and McKinley ordered two pies with meat and a rack of super-sized sodas. He didn't think he could eat two pizzas by hisself, but they had a special on, saved you money when you bought two. And you never could have too much soda round the house.

McKinley gave the sucker his address.

Devra was sitting on the hardwood floor of the living room, her back against the chipped plaster wall. Her purse was beside her; McKinley had checked it out and found nothing but her keys that she could hurt him with, and he had reasoned that she would never try. McKinley shut his phone down and put it in a holster he kept clipped to his side. He walked to Devra and stood over her. He noticed she had coiled up some as he approached.

McKinley's warm-up top was zipped down and open, showing the wife-beater he wore underneath. He'd let his chains hang out. His new gun, the Sig .45, was under the waistband of his pants, the grip slanted and tight on his belly. The girls liked ice and automatics, this he knew.

Devra met his eyes, then took in the rest of him. He was sweating, and his fat belly was spilling out over his drawers, looked like dough was gonna swallow up that gun of his.

'You could sit in a chair,' said McKinley.

'I'm fine.'

'You don't have to make it too hard on yourself, girl. Ain't like I got you chained up or nothin' like that. You free to walk around. We just gonna sit tight together for a while till you come to your senses.'

'I want my son.'

'You'll get him, too. Tell me you're not gonna talk to that man no more, and I'll put y'all back together. Tell me for real, though, 'cause I won't take no more lies. I'll keep you here for a couple of days, till they're done crossing your old boyfriend Phil, and you can go free.'

'All's we was doin' was havin' some ice cream.'

'That again? Shit. Fine as you are, I don't believe you even eat ice cream.' McKinley smiled again, showing her his teeth. The girls liked that, too. 'Look here, I'm sorry for touchin' you rough yesterday. That don't mean we can't be friends *today*.'

'Mother*fuck*er,' said Devra, feeling her eyes get teary and trying to hold it in. 'Why can't you just . . . just leave me alone.'

'Damn, girl, you don't have to get all upset.' McKinley rolled his shoulders. 'Just sit your ass there, then. Don't say nothin', you can't say nothin' nice.'

McKinley walked away, wondering why the women did him like that. The only girls he'd had lately he'd had to pay for. Didn't make any difference to him. Pussy was pussy. One way or another, it cost you money.

A half hour later, the pizza delivery boy arrived. McKinley undid the chain, flipped the dead bolt, and opened up the door. Boy was wearin' some stupid-ass-striped shirt, looked like a barber pole. He put the pizzas and the sodas inside the door while McKinley counted out some money. He gave him two quarters on top of the bill. Boy didn't even say thank you or nothin'. He had been staring kind of wide-eyed into the house the whole time he was standing out there on the stoop. Prob'ly looking at the girl, like any girl could go for him. Looked like a scared animal or something. Sucker with a minimum-wage job, out here armed with nothin' but pizza, risking his neck at night with everything going on. Maybe he was seeing his future, why his eyes were wide. Boy was right to be scared.

McKinley closed the door and picked up the boxes that had been laid at his feet.

'Sure you don't want none of this? It's better when it's hot.'

The girl didn't answer, hugging herself against the wall.

McKinley said, 'Suit your *own* damn self.'

*

Strange and Quinn were in the Caprice on Yuma, a half block down from the McKinley house, parked behind Quinn's Chevelle. They watched the pizza boy deliver a load to the house and they watched him go back to his car, a rusted-out Hyundai.

As he pulled away, Strange ignitioned the Caprice and followed the delivery boy down to 9th. The Hyundai cut right on Wahler and headed toward Wheeler Road. At the stop sign at Wheeler, as the delivery boy slowed down, Strange goosed the gas and pulled up alongside the Hyundai on its left side. Strange honked his horn to get the driver's attention. Quinn was already leaning out, his license case flipped open, holding it face out so the driver could see.

'Investigators,' said Quinn, 'D.C.'

'What I do?' said the driver.

Strange's Caprice looked like a police vehicle, down to the heavy chrome side mirrors. He slanted it in front of the Hyundai, as a cop would do, and kept it running. He and Quinn got out and went to the Hyundai. Quinn took the passenger side and Strange stood before the open driver's-side window. Strange flashed his license.

'That house you just delivered to,' said Strange. 'Tell me who you saw.'

'Some fat dude paid me.'

'Anyone else?'

'Girl was sittin' in there on the floor, too.'

'Describe her, please.'

The delivery boy did, his hands tight on the wheel.

'The fat man, he have a bunch of locks on that front door?'

'Heard him turn somethin' and slide a chain, is all.'

'You don't need to be talkin' to anyone about this, hear?'

'I won't.' The delivery boy looked up at Strange. 'You lookin' at that fat boy for somethin'?'

'Nothing to concern yourself with.'

'I ain't concerned. I hope you get him if he's wrong, though.' The driver wiped his face. 'Wearin' all that ice, and all he could see to give me was fifty cents.'

'You have a good one,' said Strange. 'And thank you for your time.'

After getting out to move some debris blocking the entrance, Strange and Quinn cruised slowly down the alley between Atlantic and Yuma. Strange had killed his headlights and was navigating by his parking lights. There didn't seem to be anyone out, not even kids. On the Atlantic side of the alley he saw houses, some bright, some dark, one lit dimly by the flicker of flames, all partitioned by chain-link fences in various states of disrepair.

'There it is,' said Quinn, looking at the back of a house on the Yuma side. 'I counted back from the corner. That's the one, with the lights. I don't see anyone, though.'

'Pizza boy said it was just McKinley and the girl, what he could make out. McKinley's down on his big-ass haunches now, wolfin' that pizza, I expect.'

'Be a good time to hit him.'

'I guess we better do that, then, before we change our minds.'

Strange turned onto the street at the head of the alley and parked behind Quinn's Chevelle. Strange went over what they had already discussed.

'It's not much of a plan,' said Quinn.

'Ain't no plan at all,' said Strange. 'I'm countin' on that girl having the stones I think she does. I figure that McKinley's partner has the boy, and she's gonna be focusing on getting back with him. I know how much she loves her son.'

'What if it goes wrong?'

'One of us goes down, the other one's got to get the girl out quick. Take her to her apartment and figure it out then.'

'You know he's got a gun.' Quinn looked at Strange's hip, where his knife was sheathed. 'You gonna take him on with that?'

'I got somethin' else for him, I get close enough. You remember his gun, too, Terry. Don't stay back there too long and get your ass shot.'

'I'll do my best.'

'You got your cell?'

'In my pocket.'

Strange looked at Quinn's bright, jacked-up eyes. 'Look, man, you don't have to do this. You don't owe anybody anything.'

'When you side with a man, you stay with him,' said Quinn. 'And if you can't do that, you're like some animal. You're finished.'

'Oh, shit,' said Strange with a low chuckle. 'You are something.'

They shook hands. Quinn got out of the car and closed the door behind him. He bolted across the sidewalk, up a rise, and moved into the shadows between two duplexes farther down the block.

Strange got a coil of rope out of his trunk and patted his back pocket. He walked up toward the house.

30

Horace McKinley was in the living room, eating a slice of pizza topped with hamburger and pepperoni, when he heard someone banging on the back door. His heart skipped as he swallowed what was in his mouth. Couldn't be Mike; he always came in through the front. He dropped the slice into the open cardboard box at his feet. Neighborhood kids, most likely, pullin' pranks and shit, like they liked to do.

'Don't you move now,' said McKinley, standing out of his chair, talking to Devra, who was still against the wall, hugging her knees. 'I'll be right back.'

McKinley pulled the automatic from his waistband and racked the slide.

Devra watched him walk into what would be the dining room in a normal house. He went through an arched cutout there, barely fitting through it, and back into a hall. The hall led to the galley kitchen and the back door, she knew. When he got into the hall she heard him curse and then start to run, his heavy steps vibrating the wall at her back. And then she heard him opening the back door and yelling something out, his voice fading now 'cause he was outside.

Devra looked at the front door. Only thing stopping her was a deadbolt latch and a chain. Thinking, If I am going to see my baby again, now is the time to try.

Quinn stood on the back porch, knocking on the window and its frame, talking to himself, saying, 'Come on, fat man, come and get it,' and then smiling right into the man's sweaty face as he turned sideways to get himself through an opening and appeared in the hall. Quinn heard his muffled curse as he raised the gun in his meatball hand. Quinn held his position and his smile, knowing he was firing up the fat man, watching him run straight toward him through the kitchen to the door.

Quinn turned and leaped off the porch. His feet scrabbled for purchase on the dirt as he made it to the chain-link fence that surrounded the patch of backyard. He put his hand on the rail of the fence and was over it clean as he heard the back door swing open. The fat man was yelling at him now, and Quinn ducked his head. He zigzagged combat style down the alley and heard the first shot, thinking, I am not hit, and he heard himself humming as the second shot sounded and a whistle of air passed his ears. And now he just hit it, dug deep for speed and ran straight. He came to the end of the alley where it dropped onto the street, cut left, and slowed to a jog. His short bark of laughter was all relief, a burst of pressure release with the knowledge that he had cheated death.

He looked back toward the alley, wondering if he had given Derek enough time.

It was that white boy, Strange's partner. Had to be.

McKinley slipped the Sig back inside his drawers. He rolled his shoulders and looked around. A light came on in one of the houses, and a dog, that rott two doors down, was barking fierce. Wasn't but two shots. No one in this neighborhood was going to call the police 'cause of that. And if they did, wasn't no police gonna bother to respond.

McKinley walked across the dirt, stepped up to the porch, and entered the house. He closed the door behind him, mumbling as he locked it. He heard himself wheezing and felt the sweat dripping down his back as he walked through the kitchen into the hall. He went by the arched cutout, not wanting to squeeze through it again, and straight into the living room, where Devra Stokes was standing, one hand kind of playing with the fingers of the other.

'I tell you to get up?' said McKinley, standing before her.

'Heard gunshots, is all.'

'Girl, *sit* your ass back down.'

He looked over the girl's shoulder and saw the chain hanging free on the front door. He said, 'What the *fuck*?' just as he felt the presence of someone behind him and turned.

What he saw in that last second was a man with size, and McKinley reached for his gun. He had his hand on the grip when something whipped up toward him fast, a blur of flat black. When the flat black thing hit him under the chin, the pain was cold electric and the room spun crazy. His feet weren't holding him up, and he was floating, could almost see himself, like a balloon in one of those parades. The spinning room was the last thing he saw as his world shut down.

*

When McKinley opened his eyes and his vision cleared, there were a couple of men in the room with the girl, all of them standing over him, talking about him like he wasn't there. It was Strange and the white boy, the one he'd chased down the alley. McKinley burped and smelled the garlic and meat on his own breath.

'Look who woke up,' said Quinn.

'Told you he was all right,' said Strange.

McKinley was propped up against the plaster wall. His hands were together behind his back, and he moved to separate them. They were tied. He went to move his feet, and they were tied, too. McKinley turned his head to the side and spit out some blood. He rolled his tongue in his mouth. His teeth ached and one of the side ones he chewed with was loose. It was just kind of sitting in there, connected by threads. He could move it all around with his tongue.

Strange had fucked him up. That thing in his hand, looked like a sap, it must have been what he'd hit him with. He was slipping it into his back pocket now. And there was his own new Sig sticking out the waistband of the man's pants. This man has no idea what I can do to him, thought McKinley. None. But the thinking made him tired, and he closed his eyes.

'He's going out again,' said Quinn.

'He's just resting,' said Strange.

'What now?'

'We make a trade.'

Strange took McKinley's cell phone off his belt holster, getting down in front of him. He grabbed McKinley by the chin in the spot where he had laid the sap up into him. It opened McKinley's eyes.

'That doesn't smart too much, does it?' said Strange.

'Motherfucker,' said McKinley sloppily.

'Mind your language,' said Strange. 'What's your boy's cell number?'

'His name is Mike,' said Devra, her arms crossed with her purse clutched tight, looking down hard at McKinley.

McKinley gave Strange the number and Strange had him repeat it, knowing it hurt McKinley to talk. He punched the number into the cell.

'He gets on the line,' said Strange, holding the phone to McKinley's ear, 'I want you to tell him to bring the boy here. Tell him the condition you're in, and how important it is that he not even dream about doin' anybody any violence. Because you will be the first one to suffer. Do you understand?'

McKinley nodded. He listened to the phone and said, 'Mike ain't pickin' up.'

'Leave a message when it tells you to. We'll try again.'

They did, with the same response. And tried again, ten minutes later. McKinley left his third message, and Strange stood.

'Get her out of here,' said Strange to Quinn. 'Take her back to her apartment. I'll be in contact with you by phone. We'll meet up in a little while.'

'What are you gonna do?'

'Talk to our friend here alone,' said Strange. 'We got a few things to discuss in private.'

Devra Stokes spit on McKinley on her way out. Neither Strange nor Quinn moved to stop her.

After Quinn and Devra left, Strange shut down most of the lights in the house and returned to the living room. On the floor was a lamp with no shade, holding a naked bulb, and he picked it up and carried it over to McKinley. He placed it beside him and left it on. The bulb threw off heat, and its glow highlighted the bullets of sweat on McKinley's forehead and the tracks of it moving down his face.

Strange got back down on his haunches and pulled up McKinley's wife-beater, exposing his chest and belly.

'What you doin'?'

Strange drew his Buck knife from its sheath. He held it upside down and pressed the heavy wood-and-bronze hilt against the blackened area of McKinley's jawline. McKinley recoiled as if shocked.

'That hurts, I expect,' said Strange. He moved to press the spot again but did not make the contact. 'What's your partner Mike's full name?'

'Montgomery.'

'And where's he stay at?'

McKinley gave him the address. Strange asked him to repeat it so he could remember, and McKinley complied.

Strange rested one knee on McKinley's thigh and put his weight there. He touched the edge of the blade to the area below the nipple of McKinley's right breast.

'You got titties like a woman,' said Strange. 'You know that?'

'Man, what the fuck you *doin'*?' said McKinley in a desperate way.

Strange moved the knife so that the blade now rested with its edge above the purple aureole of McKinley's nipple.

'You put your hands on that girl, right about where I'm touchin' this blade. *Didn't* you, boy?'

'I didn't mean to hurt her. I didn't cut her, man.'

'You like the way this feels, *Horace*?'

'Don't.'

'You tellin' me?'

'God*damn*, don't be cuttin' on me with that knife.'

'You gonna leave the girl alone, right?'

McKinley nodded.

'The boy, too.'

'Both of 'em, man.'

''Cause I don't want you gettin' near her at all. Her or her son, you understand?'

'I hear you, Strange. We good, right?'

Blood splashed onto Strange's hand as he sliced into McKinley's flesh, sweeping the knife savagely across his breast.

McKinley bucked and screamed. The tendons stood out on his neck as he writhed from the pain. The scream became a sob that McKinley could not stop. Strange found it odd to hear a big man cry so free.

'Now we're good,' said Strange, wiping the Buck off on McKinley's shirt and sheathing it. 'You just sit there and try to relax.'

Strange moved the lamp as close as it would get to McKinley. The heat from the bulb, he guessed, was now hot on his face. Strange then dragged a chair over and set it before the fat man. He had a seat.

McKinley had stopped sobbing. His breathing had subsided to a steady wheeze. The dirty flap of nipple, nearly severed and dangling off McKinley's chest, had begun to turn from purple to black. The blood had stopped flowing from the cut Strange had made.

'What now?' said McKinley, elbowing the lamp away from him as best he could. 'Ain't you done enough?'

Strange drew the Sig from his waistband. He pointed it at McKinley's face and moved his finger inside the trigger guard. McKinley's lip trembled as he closed his eyes.

Strange lowered the gun. He turned it and released its magazine, letting it slide out into his palm. He checked to make sure a round had not been chambered.

'Just wanted you to experience what you put that girl through,' said Strange. 'That kind of helplessness.'

'*Fuck* you, man.'

'I'll just keep this.' Strange stood, the magazine in his hand. 'You can have the rest.'

He dropped the body of the .45 onto McKinley's lap. McKinley was cut, bleeding, and beaten. Worst of all, a piece of his manhood was forever gone. McKinley was past being frightened now. One eye twitched, and a thread of pink spittle dripped from his mouth.

'What makes me so different?' he said.

'What's that?'

'You out here trying to save Granville Oliver, and at the same time lookin' to harm me? Shit, him and me, we're damn near the same man. He ain't no better or different than me. I *worked* for him when I was a kid.'

'I know it,' said Strange. He had been thinking the same thing himself, trying to separate it out in his mind.

'So why?'

'Cops, private cops, whatever, they got this saying, when one of y'all kills another one like you: it's the cost of doing business. What it means is, you got your world you made, and we're in it, too. And no one outside that world is gonna shed tears when you go. But it's an unspoken rule that you don't turn that violent shit on people you got no cause to fuck with.' Strange slipped the magazine into a pocket of his jeans. 'You shouldn't have done what you did to that girl.'

'What, you don't think Granville's ever done the same?'

'I don't know for sure,' said Strange. 'But he's never done it to anyone I knew.'

McKinley looked down at the body of the Sig lying in his lap, then back up at Strange. 'Why didn't you kill me? I'd a killed you.'

'I'm not you,' said Strange. 'And anyway, ain't enough left of you to kill. You're through.'

'You don't know nothin', Strange,' said McKinley, grimacing horribly, showing his bloody teeth. 'You the one's through. One phone call from me is all it's gonna take. You and everyone you know, all a y'all gonna be under the eye. You gonna lose everything, Strange. Your license, your business, your family. Everything.' McKinley tried to smile. '*You* the one's through.'

The fat man's threats rippled through him. Strange stared at him but said nothing more. He redrew his knife, bent down, and cut the bindings on McKinley's feet. Then he severed the ropes that held his wrists. McKinley brought his arms around and dropped his hands at his sides.

Strange walked from the house.

McKinley found his cell on the floor. He grunted and got himself up on his feet. He went around the house turning lights on as he dialed Mike Montgomery's number. But he only got the message service again. He hit 'end' and dialed the number for Ulysses Foreman.

'Yeah.'

'McKinley here.'

'What's goin' on, dawg?'

'I need you out here to my place on Yuma. Bring that extra magazine for the Sig with you, man. I lost the one you sold me. I'm alone right now; I'm not even strapped.'

'I can get it to you tomorrow. Or you can send someone out here—'

'I wanted it tomorrow I would have *called* you tomorrow. Now, you gonna damage our business relationship over this?'

'You got no call to take a tone with me.'

'Just bring it, hear? Or maybe your woman would like to bring it out herself.'

McKinley listened to dry air. Foreman's voice, when it returned, was strangely calm.

'Ain't no need for you to bring my woman into this, big man.'

'You gonna bring it?'

'Yeah, I'll come out.'

'And stop by the CVS store for some gauze, and that surgical tape stuff, too. I'll get you for it later.'

'You have an accident?' Foreman's tone was almost pleasant.

'Never mind what I had,' said McKinley. 'I expect to see you soon.'

McKinley cleaned his chest up over the sink. The cut started to bleed again, and he pressed a rag to it to make it stop. While he held it there, he tried Mike Montgomery again.

'Goddamn you, Monkey,' said McKinley when he got the recording. 'Where the fuck you at?'

Ulysses Foreman got his leather shoulder holsters from out of the closet and put them on. He found his 9mm Colt with the bonded ivory grips, checked the load, and slipped it into the left holster. From the nightstand he withdrew Ashley's .357 LadySmith revolver holding jacketed rounds. He holstered the LadySmith on the right. He stood in front of the bedroom's full-length mirror and cross-drew both guns. He holstered the weapons and repeated the action. The revolver was a little light.

Foreman got into a leather jacket. It was warm for any kind of coat, but necessary to wear one in order to conceal the guns. In the basement he found the Sig's extra magazine and put it into a pocket of his leather. He clipped his cell to his side, got a few cigars out of the humidor, and a cold beer out of the refrigerator, and went outside to the back deck. He lit a cigar, drank off some of his beer, and looked up into the sky. It was a clear night, with most of a moon out and a whole burst of stars.

Foreman phoned Ashley Swann on her cell. She answered on the third ring.

'I've been waiting for you to call,' she said.

'Told you I would,' said Foreman. 'Wanted to get up with you, 'cause I got to go out and do some business for a while.'

'Everything all right?'

'Fine,' he said, closing his eyes. 'Tell me where you're at.'

'I'm out beside the soybean field. My daddy hasn't cut the grass yet. It's tickling my toes, long as it is. It's wet from the dew.'

Foreman tried to imagine her then. In his mind she had on that pair of salmon-colored pajamas and she was barefoot, holding a glass of chardonnay in one hand, holding a Viceroy with the other. Smiling 'cause she was speaking to her man. Standing under the same moon and stars he was standing under right now. Not beautiful like a model or nothin' like it, but his. And he was smiling now, too.

'I love you, baby,' said Foreman.

She chuckled. 'That wasn't so hard now, was it?'

'No,' said Foreman. 'Wasn't hard at all.'

'Can you come down here? Daddy would like to see you.'

'I will,' said Foreman. But even to his own ears his voice sounded unsure.

'Tell me you love me again, Ulee.'

He told her so, and ended the call. He stood there for as long as he felt he could, thinking of all he had and what he'd do to keep it. Smoking, drinking, and admiring the sky.

When Strange had cleared out of the immediate neighborhood, he pulled the Caprice over to the curb and phoned Quinn.

'Terry, it's Derek. You at Devra's place?'

'I am.'

'I got Montgomery's address. I don't know how we're gonna handle this—'

'Derek, it's all right.'

'What is?'

'Mike Montgomery's right here, in Devra's apartment. So's the boy. Everything's all right.'

Strange felt his grip loosen on the wheel. 'I'll be right over. Don't let Montgomery go nowhere, hear?'

'Figured you'd want to talk to him,' said Quinn. 'We're waitin' on you now.'

31

Quinn met Strange at the door and let him into the apartment. Quinn was smiling and so was Devra, the boy at her side. He was holding on to the tail of her shirt and did not let go of it when she moved to embrace Strange.

'Thank you,' she said. 'You okay?'

'I'm real good now,' said Strange. 'We alone here?'

'My roommate hasn't been home for a couple of days. She's been layin' up with her boyfriend ever since I told her I don't want that man burning smoke in front of my son.'

'Montgomery's in the kitchen,' said Quinn. 'Devra hooked him up with a soda.'

'What happened?' said Strange.

'Montgomery said he took Juwan to his place, but the boy couldn't stop crying. Montgomery figured, he brought the boy back here, he could pick up some of his toys, might make him feel better.'

'He could have bought the boy some toys at a store,' said Strange.

'True,' said Quinn.

'How'd they get in?'

'Lady across the hall, a Mrs Roberts, has a key. Devra reminded Juwan of that before they got split up.'

'Smart boy,' said Strange, and Juwan smiled.

'I've been getting our things together,' said Devra.

'Good,' said Strange. 'I'm gonna call my wife, have her get a bed ready in our guest room and a sleeping bag for the boy. You can stay with us for a few days until Ray Ives figures out a better arrangement. You'll like Janine, and she'll like having a woman around for a change. I got my stepson, Lionel, he's kid-friendly, too. And a dog. You into dogs, Juwan?'

'Will he bite me?'

'Nah, old Greco's a boxer. Boxers love kids.'

'I'll just finish packing up,' said Devra.

Quinn and Strange watched her walk down a hall, Juwan holding her shirttail tight.

'Let's go talk to Montgomery.'

'Don't be too hard on him,' said Quinn. 'He doesn't want to admit it, all that bullshit about picking up some toys here. He was bringing the kid back. He did a good thing.'

'I know,' said Strange. 'I want to thank him, is all.'

Quinn looked at the dried drops of blood on Strange's shirt and the blood still on his hand.

'You cut yourself?'

'Not *my* self, no.'

'You come down here, get all *violent* on people, Derek, it's gonna be bad for business.'

'Come on, man, let's go.'

Mike Montgomery was in the kitchen sitting at a small table, leaning back, his long hand around a can of Coke. Strange said, 'Mike,' and extended his hand, but Montgomery did not move to take it, and Strange had a seat. Quinn leaned against the counter.

'I just wanted to tell you,' said Strange, 'you did a real good thing tonight.'

Montgomery nodded but did not meet Strange's eyes.

'You like kids, don't you, Mike?'

Montgomery shrugged.

'How about football, you into that?'

Montgomery swigged from the Coke can and set it back down on the table.

'I got a football team for young men, just getting close to their teens. I could use a guy like you to help me out.'

'Shit,' said Montgomery, shaking his head, smiling but without joy. 'I don't think so, man.'

'Okay, you're tough,' said Strange. 'But you don't have to be so tough all the time.'

'What else I'm gonna be?' said Montgomery, now looking at Strange. He wore his scowl, but it was a mask. His eyes told Strange that he could be, *was*, someone else.

'You can be whatever,' said Strange. 'It's not too late.'

Again, Montgomery said nothing. Strange slipped a business card from his wallet and dropped it on the table between them. Montgomery made no move to pick it up.

'You hurt him?' said Montgomery, his eyes moving to the blood across Strange's shirt.

'Took him down a few notches, is all.' Strange leaned forward. 'Tell me something: who's protecting McKinley?'

Montgomery shifted his weight in his seat. 'I don't know what you're talkin' about. And if I did know I wouldn't say. I already betrayed him once tonight. Don't be askin' me to do it again.'

'You're better than you think you are,' said Strange.

Montgomery looked away. 'Tell the little man I said good-bye, hear?'

He got up from the table and left the kitchen. Soon after, Strange and Quinn heard the front door open and close.

'You tried,' said Quinn.

Out in the parking lot, Mike Montgomery got into his Z, a car McKinley had paid for in cash and given him as a gift. He hit the ignition and drove over to Suitland Road, taking that out of D.C. and into Maryland. The cell phone on the seat beside him began to ring. He had programmed it to go to messages after six rings, but three was enough for his ears, and he reached over and turned the power off. McKinley had been trying to get him all night, and that ringing sound was like someone screamin' in his head. Horace was his father and older brother, all in one. But he shouldn't have hurt that girl like he did. And he shouldn't have fucked with no kid.

Montgomery had no job and no way to get one. He could hardly read. Would be hard to punch a clock, have some boss in his face all the time after sitting high where he'd been these past couple of years. Trying to be straight, knowing he'd killed. But he'd have to figure all that out. For now, he had around fifteen hundred cash he'd saved and a full tank of gas. A gym bag, holding a change of clothes and his toothbrush, was in the trunk.

Montgomery followed Suitland Road over to Branch Avenue, which was Route 5. He knew that 5 connected with 301 when you took it south. And 301 went all the way to Richmond, you stayed on it long enough.

His mother was down there, and his baby brother, too. He was looking forward to throwing a football around with the boy. The little man loved football, and Montgomery did, too.

Mike hadn't seen them for quite some time.

In the salon parking lot, Quinn and Strange carried Devra's bags to her car. Strange had phoned Janine, and after some discussion and debate, the plans had been made. Strange gave Devra the directions to the house on Quintana and strapped the boy into his car seat while Devra said good-bye to Quinn.

'Aren't you gonna follow me?' said Devra to Strange.

'I'll be along in a little while. Me and Terry got some more business to take care of tonight.'

She kissed him on the cheek and got into her car. They watched her drive away.

'So what did you do to McKinley?' said Quinn.

'You been dyin' to know, haven't you?'

'You had that look in your eye.'

'I just cut him some. Nothin' a good brassiere won't hide.'

'What was that shit in there about who he was working for?'

'I'll tell you later. Still rolling it around in my mind.' Strange shifted his shoulders. 'Can you handle a little more work?'

'I'm hungry.'

'I'm about to chew on my arm, too.'

'Donut doesn't live too far from here.'

'I'll follow you,' said Strange. 'We find Mario, maybe we can end this day right.'

32

When Mario Durham woke up on the couch, the television was still showing something he didn't want to watch, and he was still alone. Quiet as it was, he guessed the girl Dewayne had put him up with hadn't come home. He wouldn't be surprised if she spent the night somewhere else. She wasn't the friendly type, or maybe she was afraid of him, or afraid of what she'd do if she got around him too long. Dewayne prob'ly told her not to think about gettin' busy with him, that he had too many women problems as it was. On the other hand, she could be one of them Xena bitches, didn't like men.

Compared to most, Olivia had been a good woman, except for that one mistake she'd made. Shame she'd done him dirt, made him have to do her like he did. Anyway, he couldn't change nothin' about that now.

Durham washed his face and rolled on some of the girl's deodorant from out of the medicine cabinet. He went to the kitchen and looked around for something to eat, but he couldn't find nothin' he liked. Then he thought of that market on the corner. He could get a soda and some chips down there, couple of those Slim Jims that his brother liked to eat and that he liked, too. And then he thought, While I'm down there, might as well do a little more business, put some cash money in my pocket. It had gone pretty smooth the last time.

He gathered up the rest of the dummies, and some cash to make change, and dropped the vials in a pocket of his Tommys. He fitted his knit Redskins cap on his head, adjusting it in the mirror so it was cocked just right, and left the apartment.

Mario walked down the darkened street to the corner where the market was still open and the streetlight stood. It was quiet out now. He didn't wear a wristwatch and hadn't thought to check the time. But he knew it must be late.

He stood on the corner, one hand in his pocket, his posture slouched.

A car came and went, and it was nothing. Then another came, five minutes later, and slowed down. The driver rolled his window down and Mario went there and they caught a rap. It was even easier this time, knowing when to listen and what to say. He was busy selling the driver a couple of dimes, so he didn't notice the old gray Toyota as it passed.

Mario did his business and the car drove away. He pocketed two twenties for a double dime and walked back to the corner and stood under the light. He put one hand in his pocket and jiggled the vials he had left. He looked furtively around the street.

Mario heard light footsteps behind him. Before he could turn, he felt something hard and metallic pressed against the base of his skull.

'*Deion*,' said a dry, raspy voice.

He didn't hear the shot or anything else. The bullet blew his brains and some of his face out onto the street.

33

'So you got no idea where your boy is,' said Strange.

'None,' said Donut, sitting on the couch, his knees scissoring back and forth. 'I told the other cop all this already. How many of y'all they gonna send over before someone believes what I got to say?'

Quinn was standing by the shelf holding Donut's video collection. He picked *The Black Six* out of the row and had a look at its box. 'Hey, Derek, you know Carl Eller starred in a movie?'

'*Black Six*,' said Strange. 'Mean Joe Greene, Mercury Morris. Gene Washington was in it, too.'

'Like a *Magnificent Seven* with black guys, huh?'

'Except they didn't need seven. Eller counted as two.'

'Don't mess with that,' said Donut. 'Please.'

Quinn returned the tape to its space. He was just killing time while Strange worked the ugly little man. It had taken them a while to find his apartment. This time of night, Donut's neighbors had been reluctant to answer the knocks on their doors. But an old man on the first floor had given them Donut's unit number.

'Donut,' said Strange. 'You don't mind I call you by your nickname, do you?'

'Ain't nobody call me anything else.'

'We'll leave right now, you tell us where Mario is.'

'Believe me, if I knew, I would.'

Strange stared down at him, all sweat and nerves. 'Maybe you could put us up with his brother.'

'That wouldn't be such a good idea.'

'We got time. We could sit around here, see if the phone rings. Mario calls you, we'd all know you been lying to us. That's obstruction in a homicide. I'm guessing, and it's just a guess, mind you, that you might have some priors.'

'Shit, y'all just enjoy fuckin' with a man, don't you?'

'Dewayne's number?'

'I got it somewhere in this mess,' said Donut. 'But don't tell him where you got it from, hear?'

After they'd left, Donut watched from his window as the salt-and-pepper team walked across the parking lot.

Donut smiled, pleased with himself. All these police trying to get him to talk, and not one of them had. He could hardly wait for Mario to call him, so he could tell his boy that he hadn't gave him up.

Strange and Quinn walked toward their cars.

'Surprised he even let us in,' said Strange.

'You impersonating a police officer had something to do with it.'

'I only told him I was with the police. As in, I'm *behind* them one hundred percent.'

'Okay. You gonna call Dewayne?'

'I don't know what I'll say to him. But I can't think of anything else to do.'

Strange's cell rang. He unclipped it from his belt. The caller ID read 'Unknown.'

'Derek Strange here.'

'It's Nathan Grady. Where you at?'

'Southeast.'

'Mario Durham's been shot to death. I'm at the crime scene right now. Thought you and your partner would want to know.'

'Damn.'

'He went cleaner than the Elliot girl. You can come over if you want to have a look at him. I'm gonna be here awhile.'

'Give me the directions,' said Strange.

Strange told Quinn the news, then followed him into Far Northeast.

Dewayne Durham was sleeping on the mattress in the second-floor bedroom when his cell rang and woke him. He had not heard or even been subconsciously aware of the two shots McKinley had fired out in the alley. Durham had been in a very deep sleep, and he had been dreaming. As he reached for the phone, he tried to bring back pieces of his dream. Something about his mother, but he couldn't recall what it was.

That homicide detective, Grady, was on the phone. He was calling to tell Dewayne that his brother, Mario, had been shot dead over in Northeast. One bullet to the head, close range. 'What kind of gun?' said Dewayne. Grady found the question odd but told him that it had most likely been a .45, as a spent shell casing had been found near Mario's body. Dewayne asked him how they knew it was Mario, and

Grady described his Redskins getup, telling him that the clothing description coming over the radio was what had sent him to the scene.

Dewayne shook his head. Fool never even thought to change his shit.

Grady told Dewayne that he'd called him first as a courtesy. That he would call his mother next if he wanted him to. Dewayne said he'd prefer to go to her place, give her the news in person. Then he could come to the scene and identify the body if that was what the detective wanted him to do. Grady said fine, and not to rush, since the ME crew and photographers would be there for some time. He gave Dewayne the address and cut the line without saying good-bye.

Dewayne Durham sat on the edge of the mattress and rubbed at his face. If he was gonna cry, then now would be the time. Get it done up here, alone, then go down and tell Zulu what was going on. But he couldn't even will himself to cry.

He'd shed tears with his mother later on, he supposed. Seeing her cry, that would be what would set him off. But for now all he could think of was the get-back. Wondering who hated him enough, and who was bold enough, to do something like this to a member of his family. Because that person had to know that he'd signed his own death certificate tonight.

Dewayne picked up the stainless Colt .45 with the rosewood checkered grips that lay on the floor and got up off the mattress. He slipped the gun under his waistband and slanted it so that the butt was within easy reach of his right hand. Then he went down the stairs.

Bernard Walker sat at the card table in the soft glow of the candlelight. There were a couple of Slim Jims and an open bag of chips lying on the table, along with Walker's Glock. Walker was listening to some go-go, the new 911 PA tape he'd bought off a street vendor, on his box, but the volume was way down low.

'I kept it soft,' said Walker, looking up at Durham, 'so you could sleep.'

'I'm up now,' said Durham. 'And I got some news.'

Ulysses Foreman handed Horace McKinley a full magazine. McKinley slapped the clip into the butt of his Sig.

'There we go,' said McKinley, smiling. His gums were spider webbed red, and some of the blood had seeped into the spaces between his teeth. 'Don't feel so naked now.'

'Brought you that first-aid shit you asked for,' said Foreman, eyeing the big man's saddlebag chest. There was a damp burgundy stain on his wife-beater, where his right tit was.

'Gimme it,' said McKinley. He holstered the Sig in his warm-up pants and reached for the white plastic bag that held the gauze and tape. 'What I owe you for that?'

'Nothin',' said Foreman.

'You can take your jacket off, you want to.'

'I'll just leave it on.'

'Got your shit on underneath, right?'

'You *know* I do.'

'Have a seat,' said McKinley. 'I'll be right back.'

Foreman watched McKinley go into a hall toward the kitchen. It was shorter to go through the dining room, but McKinley would have trouble squeezing through the space. Fat mother fucker must have stock in McDonald's, Burger King, and KFC all at the same time, thought Foreman. He couldn't understand how a man could let his body go like that.

In the kitchen, McKinley washed himself over the sink. He had water and electric, unlike those Little Orphan Annie motherfuckers across the alley. As he thought of them, he glanced through the back-door window and saw the house on Atlantic, lit by candlelight. Looked like Dewayne Durham and Bernard Walker were having one of those romantic dinners and shit. Now would be a good time to interrupt him.

McKinley made a pad from the gauze and tape. He grunted, holding his flap of nipple flat as he stuck the gauze on his chest. He was still bleeding some. He'd have to go to the clinic tomorrow, maybe get some stitches put on there to hold it tight. But that was tomorrow. He needed to find Mike, warn him to move the boy someplace safe. And he had some business with Foreman, too.

He phoned Monkey Mike but got a dead line.

He went back out to the living room where Foreman sat. He had a seat himself and smiled at the man with the show muscles who, after all those years out of uniform, still looked like a cop. Being a cop was like having those grass stains he used to get on the knees of his jeans when he was a kid. You could never get those out.

'I feel better now,' said McKinley.

'You want a cigar?'

'Never turn down one of your Cubans.'

McKinley slid two out of the inside pocket of his leather, handed one to McKinley, lit his own, lit McKinley's. They sat there in the living room in the light of the bare-bulb lamp, smoking, getting their draws.

'Nice,' said McKinley. 'Look here, I didn't mean to give you the wrong impression on the phone a while back. I was just *agitated* at the time.'

'Ain't no thing,' said Foreman, looking at the spot, still leaking, on McKinley's chest. 'What happened?'

'Someone took advantage of the fact that I was alone here, unarmed, and made the mistake of tryin' to step to me. I'm gonna take care of that situation my own self.'

'Where's your boy at?'

'Mike? I'd like to know myself.' McKinley chin-nodded in the direction of Foreman's leather. 'What you holdin', man?'

'My Colt.'

'That's a pretty gun, too, got those ivory handles. What else?'

Foreman reached into his jacket and slid the revolver from one of the shoulder holsters. He handed it butt out to McKinley, who weighed it in his hand. He turned the gun, admiring the contrast of the polished rosewood grips against the stainless steel.

'LadySmith Three fifty-seven,' said Foreman.

'It's light.'

'Yeah, but you could put your fist through the hole it makes. 'Specially on the exit. It's light 'cause it's made for the hand of a woman. That's Ashley's gun right there.'

McKinley handed the gun back to Foreman, who holstered it.

'How is your woman?' said McKinley.

'She's good.'

'Bet that pussy's good, too. I ain't never had a white girl I ain't paid to have. It's all pink anyway, right?' McKinley laughed, reached over and clapped Foreman on the arm, watching his narrowed eyes. 'Oh, shit, c'mon, big man, we just talkin' man-to-man here. I mean you no disrespect.'

Foreman sat back and dragged on his cigar. 'Say why you brought me out here, for real.'

'Okay, then. This situation we got, you sellin' to my competition, I come to the conclusion it ain't workin' for me. Two of my boys just got deaded by one of your guns; you *know* this.'

'And they lost two of theirs the same way. I'm sorry those boys had to die, but it ain't none of my concern. I didn't pull those triggers, any more than the dealer plunges the needle into a junkie's arm.'

'Like I said, it ain't workin' for *me*. You tryin' to stay neutral, all right, you've made yourself clear. But Durham's done, man, finished. All's that's left is for someone to come along and throw some dirt on him. I'm gonna take over his territory soon, you can bet on that like the sunrise.'

'That ain't none of my business, Horace.'

'I'm gonna be *all* your business, man. 'Cause eventually it's just gonna be me and my troops down here, understand?'

'So?'

'What we gotta do now is make that happen tonight. Cement our relationship so we can move forward, man.'

Foreman tapped ash off his cigar. 'No.'

'What you mean, *no*?'

'I mean I won't do it. You askin' me to cross a line that I won't cross.'

'It's gonna be good for your future, man.'

Foreman kept his tone friendly. 'Thanks for thinkin' of me, but I'm already doin' all right.'

'I'm not talkin' about you doing better. I'm talkin' about you makin' the right decision here so you can keep what you got.'

Foreman stared through the roiling smoke at McKinley. He nodded slowly, his dark eyes shining wet in the light.

'You should have got straight to the point from the get-go. I understand you now, Horace.'

'Good. It's just a short walk from here to there.'

'Who we talkin' about, exactly? And how many?'

'Dewayne. Zulu, I expect.'

'You got some kind of plan?'

'Simple. We walk on over there, cross that DMZ, and knock on their door. Tell 'em we want to give them, what do you call that, one of them olive branches. Tell 'em we want to talk. There's been too much killin' lately, can't we all get along, some bullshit like that. They let us in the house, we take 'em down. Like I said, simple. We outnumber their guns, and we got surprise on our side. Shouldn't be a problem.'

'When?' said Foreman.

McKinley said, 'They're over there right now.'

Foreman stood out of his chair, dropped his cigar to the scarred hardwood floor, and crushed it under his shoe. He released the safeties on both of his guns, reholstered the revolver, racked the slide on his Colt .9, reholstered it, and straightened out his leather.

'We gonna talk all night,' said Foreman, 'or we gonna do this thing?'

'Damn, big man,' said McKinley, 'you make a decision, you don't fuck around.'

'You the one made the decision, Hoss. I'm just a man with a couple of guns.'

*

Mario Durham lay on his back. The bullet had taken out the bridge of his nose and one of his eyes. His hat was still fitted to his head, which rested on the street in a river of blood.

'He looks real casual, doesn't he?' said Nathan Grady. 'Like he just laid down in the street to take a nap. I like the way he's got his hand in his pocket, too, don't you? Except for his face, you wouldn't even know he was dead.'

Strange and Quinn were inside the yellow crime tape, standing beside Grady. Kids and adults from the neighborhood were behind the tape, some talking to uniformed officers, some laughing, some just staring at something that would give them bad dreams later that night. The photographers and forensics team were still working over the body and had not yet covered Mario up.

'Why is he like that?' said Quinn.

'My guess is the bullet severed his cerebral cortex,' said Grady. 'When that happens it freezes the victim at the moment of death. I've seen it before. Mario was probably standing on the corner, his hand in his pocket, when he took the bullet. He died instantly, I'd say.'

'Standing on the corner doing what?' said Strange.

'Well, one of the locals said they saw little Mario there earlier in the evening, looked like he was selling something, or trying to. When we get into his pockets we'll find out.'

'He got killed over drugs?'

'Could be. Looks like an amateur killing. A pro wouldn't put a forty-five to a man's head. I mean, a twenty-two would have been sufficient, right? One thing's for sure: he didn't get killed for his sneakers. You see 'em?' Grady laughed. 'My man here is sportin' a pair of 'ordans.' Or maybe I'm missing something and that's the rage these days.'

Strange and Quinn did not comment.

'Anyway, he's dead. Justice in Drama City, right? Thought you guys would want to see him. For closure and all that.'

'You call his kin?' said Strange.

'His brother, the drug dealer. He's coming down in a while to ID the body. I'm gonna let him tell their mother.'

'Thanks for calling us,' said Strange.

'Yeah, sure. Take care.'

Grady motioned to the photographer, indicating that he should take another picture of the corpse. Strange guessed that the photograph of a bloody Mario Durham, 'sleeping' in the street with his hand slipped into his pocket, would soon be hanging on Grady's wall.

Strange and Quinn ducked the crime tape and walked to their cars.

'Get in for a minute, Terry,' said Strange, nodding at his Caprice. 'I want to talk to you before we go home.'

Dewayne Durham looked out the back window at the alley and the house on Yuma. The house was all lit up inside, and McKinley was standing in the kitchen with a man, big like him but muscular, not fat.

'Foreman,' said Durham. He raised his voice. 'Bernard, better get in here.'

Soon Durham felt Walker behind him, looking over his shoulder.

'That's Foreman, right?'

'Yeah.'

'What the fuck's goin' on?'

'I don't know. But they're leavin' the house.'

'Maybe they're just goin' to their car.'

'You see either one of their cars out in that alley?'

Durham heard Walker pull back the receiver of his Glock and ease a round into the chamber of the gun.

'They're comin' over here,' said Walker.

Durham watched them cross the alley. His fingers grazed the grip of his gun. 'He ain't hidin' nothin', either.'

'I can smoke 'em both, they get close enough.'

'Before you do that,' said Durham, 'let's see what they got on their minds.'

34

The overheads of cruisers flashed the crime scene and threw colored light upon the faces of Strange and Quinn. A meat wagon had arrived for Mario Durham, and its driver was leaning against the van, smoking a cigarette. The neighborhood crowd had begun to break up and many were walking the sidewalks back to their homes. Some kids had set up a board-and-cinder-block ramp in the street and they were taking turns jumping it with their bikes.

'Same old circus,' said Strange, looking through the windshield from behind the wheel of the Caprice. He was holding his cell phone, flipping its cover open and closed.

'You feel robbed?'

'A little. In my heart I know I shouldn't, but there it is.'

'*I* do,' said Quinn. 'Everything we did today, all the running around and all the sweat, and I feel like we didn't accomplish jack shit. Like we were one step behind everyone else.'

'Well, we're not the law. They do have a little bit of an advantage on us. Anyway, we got the girl and her kid to a safe place. That was something.'

'Not enough for me. I'd feel a whole lot better if I'd accomplished something.'

'There's always tomorrow.'

'I was thinkin' you'd come with me over to Naylor before we head back to Northwest. Talk to those boys about Linda Welles.'

'Tonight?'

'Damn right.'

'Nah, man, my day is done. I'm gonna go home and have a late dinner with Janine, see my stepson, make sure Devra and the boy got settled in all right. Pet my dog. You need to go home, too.'

'Yeah, okay.'

'Look at me, Terry. Promise me that's what you're gonna do.'

'I'm going home,' said Quinn.

'Good man,' said Strange.

Quinn listened to the click of the cover, then looked at the cell in Strange's hand. 'You gonna use that or just wear out the parts?'

'I been debating on making a call.'

'To who?'

'Dewayne Durham. I got his number from Donut, remember?'

'And what would you tell him?'

'It would be an anonymous call. I'd tip him that his brother got done by Horace McKinley or one of his people. I was thinkin', a call like that, it might speed along McKinley's demise.'

'Why would you do that?'

'McKinley threatened me, Terry. Threatened my family. Talked about me losing my license, my business, everything.'

'Wouldn't be the first time you been threatened. You said it earlier, you let yourself get disrespected like that every day.'

'This was a different kind of threat. Boys like that don't concern themselves with licenses and businesses. They want to take you out, they take you *out*. Got me to thinkin', it was the same kind of threat I got on my answering machine the night my office got burgled.'

'He's working for the same people broke into your place.'

Strange nodded. 'Would explain for real why he was so interested in hiding this witness. And he got all emotional back there, implied that he was protected. Which is why he goes about his business down here and doesn't take the long fall.'

'Protected by who? The FBI?'

'Whoever. The government. Mr Big. I don't know for sure, and I never will know, most likely. You get the general idea.'

'But you're not gonna make that call, are you, Derek?'

'No. I'm not in the business of killing young men, no matter who it is. Anyway, McKinley's gonna die or be locked up soon enough, I expect, without my help. They can't keep him out of jail forever.'

'And then you'll be out here defending him.'

'Could be. But not defending *him*. Defending his *rights*. And yeah, there's a difference. McKinley himself called me on that one earlier tonight. And I've been trying to work it out.'

'So have you?'

'Not entirely. It's an ongoin' process, I guess.'

'What are you going to do about the ones watching you?'

'Nothin'. Just keep doing my job. I already decided I'm not gonna let them fade me.'

Strange made a call to Lieutenant Lydell Blue. He told him about the house in the woods off Wheeler Road, gave him the license plate numbers off the red El Dorado and the Avalon, relayed what he'd seen and some of his suspicions, and reported on the death of Mario Durham. Blue thanked him, said that they'd get the local branch of the ATF involved, and commented that Strange and Quinn had had a full day. It prompted Strange to remind Blue about a full day they had both had together, thirty years earlier, involving two Howard girls, a bag of reefer, and a couple bottles of wine. Strange laughed with his friend and ended the call.

'Well, let me get on my way,' said Strange. 'I'm about ready to go to sleep right here.'

'I'm gone, too,' said Quinn, touching the handle of the door.

'Terry,' said Strange, holding his arm. 'Thanks for your help today, man. You know I couldn't have done any of this without you.'

'No problem.'

'Go *home*,' said Strange, staring into Quinn's eyes.

Quinn pulled his arm free. 'I will.'

'Always interesting with you around, man.'

Quinn smiled. 'You, too.'

Strange watched him walk across the strobing landscape to his car. Head up, strutting, with that cocky way of his. He wanted to scream out Terry's name then, call him back, tell him something, though he didn't know what or why. But soon Quinn was in his Chevelle, cooking the big engine, and driving up the block.

Strange started the Caprice and slid an old O'Jays, *Back Stabbers*, into the deck. That nice ballad of theirs, 'Who Am I,' with Eddie Levert singing tender and tough like only he could, filled the car, and Strange felt himself unwind. He put the car in gear and headed for home.

'You crossed that line,' said Dewayne Durham. 'Might give me the impression you want to do me some harm.'

'I wanted to talk to you, is all,' said Horace McKinley. 'Didn't think it would work too good, us shoutin' at each other across the alley.'

'Ain't nobody here but me and Zulu.'

'My troops are all out workin', too. What with all this talk I hear about us goin' to war, thought it'd be a good time to sort some shit out.'

'What about you?' said Durham, looking at Foreman. 'You always talkin' about stayin' neutral. Why you out here, Ulysses? Why you standin' next to *him*?'

'Horace called me,' said Foreman. 'Asked me if I'd mediate this discussion. Said y'all would need someone in the middle, someone who wasn't gonna take no sides. It's in my interest that the two of you work this out. So here I am.'

Durham and Walker stood on the back steps of the house on Atlantic, looking down at McKinley and Foreman, who stood in the weedy patch of yard. On McKinley's ribbed wife-beater, high on his cowlike chest, was a wet purple stain. The butt of his gun rose from the waistband of his warm-up suit. He wasn't trying to hide that he was strapped, and neither were Durham or Walker. Durham guessed that Foreman was wearing his iron, too. They all knew. But to mention it would be akin to admitting fear. And this was something none of them would ever do.

'We gonna stand out here all night?' said Foreman.

'C'mon in,' said Durham.

Durham and Walker gave them their backs and walked through the door, electing to lead rather than step aside to let the others pass. They were followed by McKinley and Foreman into a dark kitchen lit by a single votive candle and then a hall, where they found their way by touch against the plaster walls. Then they were all in a living room furnished with a card table and a couple of folding chairs. Candles had been set and lit on the floor, on the card table, and on the stairway. Drums and bass played softly from a beat box on the floor.

Durham and Walker stopped walking and turned. McKinley and Foreman also stopped and faced them, the card table between them. They stood with their legs spread and their feet planted. The big men filled the room. Candlelight danced in their faces and the flames from the candles threw huge shadows up on the walls.

'Go ahead and talk,' said Durham.

McKinley spread his hands, keeping them in the area of his gun. 'We just need to slow down some, think before we let our pride go and start some kind of drama we can't take back.'

'Keep talking.'

'Want you to know, straight away, that I didn't tell the Coates cousins to fire down on your boys at the school that night.'

'They did it anyway.'

'Those 'Bamas was just wild like that,' said McKinley, searching out the corner of his eye for movement from Foreman. But Foreman was just standing with his shoulders squared, looking straight ahead.

'New gun?' said Durham, nodding at the grip of the automatic, tight against the folds of McKinley's belly.

'Sig forty-five,' said McKinley.

Durham felt heat come to his face. 'My brother, Mario, was shot dead tonight.'

McKinley nodded solemnly, thinking that it had happened about thirty years too late. Someone should have shot the motherfucker when he'd popped out his mama's pussy, much good as he'd been to anybody his whole sorry-ass life.

'Too bad he died,' said McKinley.

'You wouldn't know nothin' *about* it, then.'

'I guess the po-lice caught up with him. Heard he had some trouble with a girl.'

'Nah,' said Durham, his lip trembling. 'Wasn't the police.'

'Who it was, then?'

'Oh, I don't know. Prob'ly just some fat motherfucker with a forty-five.'

The four of them stood there, staring at one another, saying nothing, watching the light shift in the room.

'Well, Zulu,' said Durham, 'I guess we done talked too much.'

Foreman reached and cross-drew his guns just as Durham and Walker went for theirs. They never touched their guns. They dropped their hands to their sides, knowing they had been bested, looking at their own deaths down the barrels of the .357 and the .9. McKinley pulled his Sig and held it on the men.

'You did talk too much,' said Foreman, snicking back the hammer of the revolver, disgust on his face. '*Too* got-damn much. For a minute there I thought you were gonna try and talk us to death. You had the draw on us, too. Motherfuckin' kids out here playin' gangster. Shit.'

McKinley laughed shortly. 'Do it, big man.'

'Yeah,' said Foreman. 'Okay.'

Foreman turned the LadySmith on McKinley and squeezed off two quick rounds. McKinley's blood blew back at him and Foreman kept firing, moving the gun from McKinley's belly to his chest, plaster exploding off the wall as the bullets exited his back. McKinley grunted, reached out for something, and lost his feet. As he fell, Foreman shot him in the groin and chest. Then the hammer fell on an empty chamber with an audible click.

Foreman still had the Colt trained on Durham and Walker. He holstered the revolver expertly, without looking for the leather, and faced them. Smoke was heavy in the candlelight. Foreman's ears rung from the boom of the Magnum. He did not squint, looking at them, and he kept his voice even and direct.

'Hope you learned a lesson here tonight,' said Foreman. 'I was a cop. Still am in my mind. You punk-ass motherfuckers out here, think you can threaten a police officer. You are wrong. Tellin' me what's good for my business. I don't give a good fuck about him, or you, 'cause there's always gonna be someone to come along and take y'all's place. You who think you're so special. Y'all ain't shit. Think about that the next time you get the idea you're gonna rise up.'

Durham said nothing. He had raised his hands in defense and they were shaking. He wanted to lower them, but he couldn't move them in any direction at all.

'I hear sirens,' said Walker.

'Police gonna have to respond to this one,' said Foreman. 'That gun does make some noise. Anyway, it's your problem, not mine. I know you won't mention I was here.'

'We'll take care of it,' said Walker.

Foreman stood over McKinley and fired two shots from the Colt into his corpse. The force of the rounds lifted him up from the hardwood floor. Then the body settled in the mix of plaster and blood.

'That's for talkin' shit about my woman,' said Foreman, holstering the Colt.

He walked off, disappearing into the darkness of the hall. Durham lowered his hands, hearing the back door open and shut.

'D,' said Walker, 'I'm gonna need some help to drag Hoss out there to the alley.'

But Durham did not answer. He was staring at his shaking hands.

35

Strange parked the Caprice on Quintana, killed the engine, and looked at the house he shared with his wife and stepson. Janine and Lionel were standing on the front lawn with Devra Stokes, in the light of a spot lamp Strange had hung above the door himself. Strange smiled, seeing the puff Lionel put in his chest as he talked to the girl. Juwan was playing with Greco, throwing him that red spiked rubber ball the tan boxer loved, then chasing him around the yard. Greco allowed the boy to catch up, letting him put his hand in his mouth, trying but failing to get the ball free.

Strange got out of the car. Greco's nub of a tail twitched furiously as he heard the familiar slam of the Caprice's door, but he stayed with the boy. Strange crossed the sidewalk and met the group in the light of the yard.

'What's goin' on, family?' said Strange. He hugged Lionel, then Janine. He kissed her and kept his arm around her shoulder after breaking their embrace.

'We're just getting acquainted,' said Janine, smiling at Devra.

'Everyone's nice,' said Devra.

'Yeah, they're all right,' said Strange.

'Where you been, Pop? Keeping the streets safe for democracy?'

'While the city sleeps,' said Strange.

'Hungry?' said Janine.

'You know I am.'

'I saved you some meat loaf.'

'Knew there was a reason my car turned down this street on its own.'

'You could have stopped at any old restaurant,' said Janine.

'It wouldn't be home,' said Strange. He kissed her again, and this time did not break away. 'Ain't nothin' better than this.'

Quinn went home to a quiet, empty apartment. He hadn't heard from

Sue Tracy all day and hadn't expected to. She and her partner, Karen, were close to finding a girl they'd been looking for for the past month or so. They'd planned to snatch her off the street that night.

The message light on his machine was blinking and Quinn hit the bar. It was Sue, asking him to call her on her cell.

He took off his shirt, washed his neck and face over the bathroom sink, and washed under his arms. He changed into a clean white T-shirt, went to the kitchen, found a Salisbury steak dinner in the freezer, and put it in his microwave oven. He set the power and time and touched the start button, then moved out to the living room and phoned Sue.

'Sue Tracy.'

'Terry Quinn.'

'Stop it.'

'Where are you?'

'Out at Seven Locks with Karen. We got our girl. We're processing the paperwork with the police, and her mother is on the way.'

'Can you come over?'

'It's gonna be a couple of hours.'

Quinn looked at his watch. 'Christ, it's late.'

'Too late?'

'No, no. I want to see you.'

'Good. Did you have a productive day?'

'A lot happened,' said Quinn. 'I don't know about productive.'

'What about Linda Welles? Anything?'

'Yeah, plenty,' said Quinn, too quickly. 'I'll give it to you when you get here.'

'You might be sleeping.'

'Wake me up.'

'I'm going to, believe me. Listen, Terry, they're calling us in. Love you.'

'I love *you*,' said Quinn.

The line went dead. Quinn stared at the phone.

I'll give it to you when you get here.

He had a couple of hours to kill before Sue would be by. Enough time to go down there, get it, and have it for her when she arrived.

It wasn't about finding Linda Welles. It was about doing something, and in the process, getting back a piece of his pride. He knew this, but he pushed the knowledge to the back of his mind.

Quinn went to the kitchen. He had a few bites of the Salisbury steak and some of the accompanying potatoes and mixed vegetables. Just enough to make his hunger headache fade but not enough to make him heavy and slow. He threw the rest of the dinner in the trash. He drank a large glass of water and walked to his bedroom.

Quinn retrieved his Colt, a black .45 with checkered grips, a five-inch barrel, and a seven-shot load, from his chest of drawers. He released the magazine, examined it, and slapped it back into the butt. He racked the slide. Quinn had bought the piece, a model O, after a conversation in a local bar.

It never would have happened, I had my gun.

Quinn holstered the Colt behind the waistband of his jeans and put on his black leather jacket.

Okay, so he'd been punked. He could fix that now.

He thought of Strange. He hadn't lied to him. He'd gone home like he'd promised.

Quinn grabbed some tapes, a pen, and the Linda Welles file on his way out the door. He walked out into the night air, letting the mist cool his face. He ignitioned the Caprice and put *Copperhead Road* into the deck and turned it up. As he was going south on Georgia, the traffic lights flashed yellow. Quinn's long sight was gone and the lights were a blur. He downshifted coming out of the tunnel under the pedestrian bridge leading to the railroad tracks. A freight train neared the station as he passed. Going up the hill, Quinn punched the gas.

In Far Southeast, Quinn stopped the Chevelle on Southern Avenue near Naylor Road. He withdrew his Colt and flicked its safety off, then refitted it under his jacket. He turned off Southern and drove up Naylor. He passed the well-tended Naylor Gardens complex, the buildings deteriorating in appearance as he moved on. Up past Naylor Plaza he saw the group of young men sitting on the front steps of their unit at the top of a rise of weeds and dirt. He swung the Chevelle around in the street and parked behind a red Toyota Solara with gold-accented alloy wheels and gold trim.

Do your job.

Quinn was out of the car quickly, walking up the hill. The young men had heard his pipes and were watching his approach. He walked through the mist and the hang of smoke in the halogen light. His blood jumped as he walked, watching the faces of the heavyset young man with the blown-out Afro and the skinny kid with the napkin bandanna and the others who had been there earlier in the day. He reached behind him. His hand went up under his jacket. Finding the grip of the gun, he was not afraid. He pulled the Colt, going directly to the heavyset young man. He grabbed the young man's shirt and bunched it in his left fist, touching the barrel of the Colt under his chin.

'Put your hands flat beside you,' said Quinn. 'Your friends don't want to fuck with me. Believe it.'

The young man did it. No one made a comment or laughed. No one moved.

'I ain't strapped,' said the young man.

'I don't *care*,' said Quinn. 'Linda Welles.'

'Who?'

'The girl on the flyer I showed you. You know where she is, who she's with. Gimme a name.'

The barrel of the gun dented the young man's skin as Quinn pressed it to his jaw.

'She stayin' with this boy Jimmy Davis, up on Buena Vista Terrace. Up there off Twenty-eighth.'

'Where on Buena Vista?'

'He's in this place, got a red door.'

'Say it again.'

The young man repeated the name and address. Quinn released his shirt and stepped back. He held the gun loosely at his side. He looked around at the faces of the boys on the steps. They stared at him with nothing in their eyes. One of the young men raised a brown paper bag and tipped its bottle to his lips.

Quinn backed up a few steps. He holstered the gun. He turned and walked down the rise to his Chevelle. He got under the wheel, started the car, and pulled off the curb.

At the next corner, Quinn stopped and wrote down the name and location the young man had given him on the back of one of the flyers. He ejected the Steve Earle tape and slipped *Darkness on the Edge of Town* into the deck. 'Adam Raised a Cain' came forward, and he turned it up. Quinn rolled down his window and began to laugh. It was easy. Fire with fire. All it took was a gun.

He drove down Naylor and onto 25th, and looked around at the unfamiliar sights. He didn't know this stretch of road, and anyway, his night vision was for shit. Street lamps and headlights were haloed and blurry. He wasn't lost. He'd come out on Alabama somewhere and from there he could hit MLK. He wasn't in a hurry. He was enjoying his Springsteen, his victory, the night.

He pulled up behind a car at a stoplight. Cars were parked along the curb at his right. In his rearview he saw a red import, tricked out in gold. He looked to his left. A white car with tinted windows rolled up had pulled alongside him. He couldn't see the occupants of the car. He heard Strange's voice in his head: *A classic trap. Gangs hunt in packs.*

Quinn's eyes went back to his rearview. The driver of the red car was heavy and wore his hair in a blown-out natural.

Quinn reached behind him and fumbled under his jacket. He found purchase on the grip of the Colt and began to draw it out. As he did this, he looked out the open window, feeling the presence of someone there.

He saw a skinny boy with a napkin bandanna on his head and a stainless automatic in his hand. The boy's finger went inside the trigger guard just as Quinn freed his gun and cleared it from his waist, seeing the stainless piece swing up, knowing he was far too late.

Quinn thinking, *He ain't nothin' but a kid*, as the world flashed white.

August

36

Granville Oliver's biceps pushed against the fabric of his orange jumpsuit. His manacles and chains scraped the table before him as he lowered his hands.

'Thanks for coming by,' said Oliver.

'Ain't no thing,' said Strange.

'Sentencing's today.'

'Ives told me.'

'Whichever way it goes, I figure we won't be seeing each other again. So I thought we should, you know, say good-bye, eye to eye.'

Strange nodded. The room was quiet except for the muffled voices of attorneys and their clients seated in other cubicles behind Plexiglas dividers. A guard with heavy-lidded eyes sat in a darkened booth, watching the room.

'You did everything you could,' said Oliver.

'I tried.'

'Yeah, you and that white boy was working with you, y'all did a good job.'

Strange leaned forward. 'Say his name.'

'Quinn.'

'That's right.'

'You two did all right, bringing that girl in like you did. For a while, seemed like her testimony was really gonna help my case. Sayin' that Phil was talkin' to her about plannin' to kill my uncle and all that. Course, when they crossed her, the prosecutors tried to make her look like a common ho, what with her havin' that boy out of wedlock, and the lifestyle she was into when she was kickin' it with Phil. But she kept her composure up there. She was good.'

'She was.'

'Where's she at now?'

Devra Stokes was living in Northwest, working in a salon, going to Strayer and taking secretarial classes around her hours in the shop. She and Juwan were renting an apartment, found by Ives, in a fringe but not deadly neighborhood. She and the boy were doing fine. But there was no reason for Strange to give Oliver, or anyone else connected with the trial, her whereabouts.

'I don't know,' said Strange.

'Anyway, I guess it's all over now. Relieved to have it behind me, you want the truth.'

After the defense had rested its case and closing arguments had been presented, jury deliberation lasted less than two weeks, an unusually short time for a case with this kind of life-and-death ramification. Once the verdict was read, a kind of minihearing had commenced in which Raymond Ives and his team argued mitigating circumstances in hopes of avoiding the death penalty. That phase, too, had concluded, leaving only Judge Potterfield's sentencing to complete the trial.

'Too bad it didn't work out for you,' said Strange.

'Aw, shit, I knew how it was gonna end from day one. That jury they handpicked, they decided what they were gonna do the first time they got a look at me. I mean, you get down to it, they didn't even need to go through the trouble of havin' that trial.'

'Maybe you're right.'

'Ain't no maybe about it. It wasn't no kind of shock to me when they found me guilty. Question now is, will I live or die?'

Strange sat impassively, looking into Granville Oliver's golden eyes.

'You know, it's funny,' said Granville. 'There was that day, when the Stokes girl was testifyin', that I actually thought that there was a chance I might walk. She had planted that, what do you call it, *seed of doubt* up in that whole courtroom. And I remember thinkin', Wouldn't that be some shit, if it was what she was sayin' that was gonna get me off?'

'Why would that be funny?' said Strange.

'Phil Wood told that girl he was gonna kill my uncle Bennett? Shoot, Phil was just talkin', pumpin' his own self up for the benefit of that pretty young ass. Phil had killed before to get his stripes, but he wouldn't never pull the trigger on my own kin, not unless I ordered him to do it. And I never did.'

'What are you telling me?'

'*I* killed my uncle, Strange. Walked right up to the open window of his new Jag and shot that snitch motherfucker to death. Man was about to flip on me, and it was down to that. Him or me, and I wasn't gonna do no long time, not for blood or anyone else.' Oliver looked Strange over. 'You surprised?'

'Not really. In my heart, I guess I knew all along.'

'Didn't make no difference to you, huh?'

'No. I suppose it didn't.'

'You knew I was who they said I was and still you kept on it. Why?'

Because I took your father out, thirty-some years ago. Because it was me who put you behind the eight ball, like all these other kids out here, got no fathers to teach them, by example, right from wrong. How to be tough without being violent, how to walk with your head up and your shoulders square, how to love one woman and be there for your children and make it work. Because it was me who put you on the road that took you where you are today.

'I was just doing my job,' said Strange.

'Well, you stood tall,' said Oliver.

'I did my best.'

'And I appreciate it. Wanted you to know.'

Their hands met in the middle of the table. Strange broke Oliver's grip and stood.

'How's the little man doin'?' said Oliver, looking up, managing a smile.

'Robert's fine. He's with that family affiliated with the church. I'm going to see him at practice this evening.'

'Boy can play, can't he?'

'Yes, he can,' said Strange.

'Holler at you later, hear?'

'I'll pray for you, Granville.'

And for myself, thought Strange, as he turned and walked from the D.C. Jail, leaving Granville Oliver in chains.

Strange had no live cases on the week's schedule. He was restless and had time to kill before evening practice, so he went about filling up his day. He visited a technical school in Northwest that Lamar Williams had mentioned to him as a place that offered computer training on a noncollegiate level. Strange had promised Lamar that he would contribute half to the cost of classes if he thought the school was okay. He picked up a brochure and got their rates from one of the admission staff, and had a look at the facilities. Then he called Janine on his cell. He asked her if she'd like to meet him at the old Crisfield's, up on Georgia, for a late lunch.

After raw oysters, soft-shell crab sandwiches, and a couple of beers at the U-shaped bar, Strange and Janine went back to the house on Quintana and made slow love in their bedroom as Greco slept at the foot of the bed. The house was quiet, with only the sounds of their coupling and the low hum of the window air conditioners running on the first and second floors. Lionel was in College Park, having started his freshman orientation.

Strange and Janine held each other for a while, kissing but saying little, after both of them had come. She looked up into his eyes and wiped some sweat off his brow.

'You're troubled.'

'Even with all this,' said Strange. 'I mean, with all I have, with you and Lionel. It's crazy, I know.'

'You can't hide it. Especially not in our bed.'

'I just feel like doin' something. Making some kind of a difference. 'Cause damn if it don't seem like I been chasing my tail these past months.' Strange put his weight on one elbow. 'You know, the night Terry got shot—'

'Derek.'

'The night he got *shot*, Janine, he told me that all he wanted was to feel like he accomplished something.'

'Derek, don't.'

'That's what I want to feel now, too.'

'Maybe you haven't felt that way lately. But you will.'

'I never should have let him go home alone like he did. I should have brought him back here that night to hang with all of us.'

'But that's not what happened.'

'I know it.'

'Lie down,' said Janine. 'Hold me and let's go to sleep. Can't remember the last time we had an afternoon to ourselves like this, just to do nothing but rest.'

'Okay,' said Strange. 'I need to rest. That sounds good.'

But when he awoke, late in the afternoon, his feelings had not changed.

Strange drove down to 9th and Upshur. He had not yet read the paper, so he picked up that day's *Post* at Hawk's barbershop and told one of the cutters he would return it.

Going into his shop, he went through the reception area and into his office, where he had a seat behind his desk. The vinyl version of *Round* 2, the Stylistics' follow-up to their debut, was leaning up against the wall, facing out, directly behind his chair. Lewis, from the used-book store in downtown Silver Spring, had mailed it to Strange, and Strange had not yet taken it home. Like the gum wrappers still in the top drawer of Quinn's desk, it was something he had not wanted to deal with just yet.

Strange went right to the Metro section. Between the roundup columns, 'In Brief' and 'Crime,' there had been five gun-related murders reported over the past weekend. Many of the victims had gone unnamed and all were in their late teens or early twenties. One had occurred in east-of-the-park Northwest and the others had occurred in Far Southeast. At the city's annual Georgia Avenue Day celebration, a teenager had been shot by random gunfire, sending some families fleeing in panic and causing others to dive on their children, shielding them from further harm.

Strange went to the A section. Deep inside, a congressman from the Carolinas dismissed the need for further handgun laws and vowed to continue his fight to hold Hollywood and the record industry accountable for the sexual content and violent nature of their product. This same congressman had threatened to cut off federal funds to the District of Columbia, earmarked for education, if D.C. did not agree to change its Metro signs from 'National Airport' to '*Reagan* National Airport.'

Strange turned his head and looked at the Stylistics album, a birthday gift from Quinn, propped up against the wall.

Do something.

'I will,' said Strange, though there was no one but him in the room. His voice was clear and emphatic, and it sounded good to his ears.

Strange turned on the light-box of his storefront, returned the newspaper to Hawk's, and drove north to his row house on Buchanan. From his basement he retrieved a couple of red two-gallon containers of gasoline, one of which was full, and carried them out to the trunk of his Caprice. He went to the Amoco station next, filled up his tank and filled the empty container with gas. He placed it next to the other in the trunk and used his heavy toolbox to wedge them tight against the well. Then he drove down Georgia to Iowa Avenue along Roosevelt High and parked in the lot between Lydell Blue's Buick and Dennis Arrington's import.

The boys were down in the Roosevelt 'bowl,' doing their warm-ups in the center of the field. The quarterback, Dante Morris, and Prince, another veteran player, were in the middle of the circle, leading the team in their chant. Strange could hear them as he took the aluminum-over-concrete steps of the stadium to the break in the fence.

'How y'all feel?'
'Fired up!'
'How y'all feel?'
'Fired up!'

'Breakdown.'

'Whoo!'

'Breakdown.'

'Whoo!'

Strange shook hands with Blue and then with Arrington, a computer specialist and deacon who was a longtime member of the coaching staff. The boys were warming up together but would soon break into their Pee Wee and Midget teams, determined by weight, for the remainder of the practice.

'You're a little late,' said Blue.

'Had to get some gas,' said Strange.

'We got a scrimmage set up for this weekend.'

'Kingman,' said Arrington.

'They're always tough,' said Strange.

'I like the way that boy Robert Gray is playing,' said Blue. 'Boy runs with authority. He's not much of leader, but he can break it.'

'He's just getting to know the other kids,' said Strange. 'And he's naturally on the quiet side. Plus he's smart; he already learned the plays in just a week's time. Be a change from Rico, anyway, the way that boy runs his mouth.'

Rico was the team's halfback, a talented but cocky kid who had a complaint ready for every command.

'Gray'll keep Rico on his toes,' said Blue. 'Make him appreciate that position he's got, and work harder to keep it.'

'I was thinkin' the same thing,' said Strange. 'And who knows? Maybe Robert'll earn that position himself.'

'You gonna take the Pee Wee team alone, Derek?' said Blue, his eyes moving to Arrington's. ''Cause me and Dennis here got our hands full with the Midgets.'

Strange nodded. 'I'll handle it.'

'You could use some help.'

'I know it,' said Strange, and ended the conversation at that.

After practice, the coaches had the boys take a knee and told them what they had seen them do right and wrong in the past two hours. The boys' jerseys were dark with sweat and their faces were beaded with it. When Strange and Blue were done talking, Arrington asked them what time they should show up for the next practice.

'Six o'clock,' said a few of the boys.

'What *time?*' said Arrington.

'*Six o'clock, on the dot, be there, don't miss it!*' they shouted in unison.

'Put it in,' said Strange.

They all managed to touch hands in the center of the circle.

'*Petworth Panthers!*'

'All right,' said Strange. 'Those of you got your bikes, get on home straightaway. If you got people waitin' for you, we'll see you get in the cars up in the lot. For you others, Coach Lydell and Coach Dennis and myself will drive you home. I don't want to see none a y'all walking through these streets at night. Prince, Dante, and Robert, you come with me.'

Strange crossed the field in the gathering darkness, Robert Gray beside him, his helmet swinging by his side.

'You looked good out there,' said Strange.

Gray nodded but kept his face neutral and looked straight ahead.

'It's okay to smile,' said Strange.

Gray tried. It didn't come naturally for him, and he looked away.

'It's a start,' said Strange. 'Gonna take some work, is all it is.'

Strange dropped Dante Morris, Prince, and Gray at their places of residence. Pulling off the curb from his last stop, Strange got WOL, the all-talk station on 1450 AM, up on the dial. The local headline news had just begun. From the female reporter, Strange learned that Judge Potterfield had sentenced Granville Oliver to death.

Driving south on Georgia, Strange saw a boy standing in front of his shop on 9th. He swung the Caprice around, parked in front of the funeral home, and walked toward the boy. He wasn't any older than seven. His dark skin held a yellow glow from the light-box overhead. The boy took a step back as Strange approached.

'It's okay,' said Strange. 'That's my place you're standing in front of, son. I was just coming by to turn off the light.'

The boy looked up at the lighted sign. 'That your business?'

'That's me. Strange Investigations. I own it. Been in this location over twenty-five years.'

'Dag.'

'What you doin' out here this time of night all by yourself?'

'My mother went to that market across the street. Said she couldn't hold my hand crossing Georgia with those market bags in her hand, so I should wait here till she comes back.'

'What's your name, young man?'

The boy smiled. 'They call me Peanut Butter and Jelly, 'cause that's what I like to eat.'

'Okay.'

'Mister?'

'What?'

'Will you wait with me till my mother comes back? It's kinda scary out here in the dark.'

Strange said that he would.

After the mother had come, and after Strange had given her a polite but direct talk about leaving her boy out on the street at night, Strange put his key to the front door of his shop. He had a slight hunger and knew that he could find a PayDay bar in Janine's desk. As he began to fit the key in the lock, he heard the rumble of a high-horse, big American engine, and he turned his head.

A white Coronet 500 with Magnum wheels was rolling down the short block. It pulled over directly in front of the shop and the driver cut its engine. Strange recognized the car. When the driver got out, Strange could see that, indeed, it was that Greek detective who worked for Elaine Clay. As he crossed the sidewalk, Strange could see in the Greek's waxed eyes that he was up on something. And as he grew nearer, he smelled the alcohol on his breath.

'Nick Stefanos.' He reached out his hand and Strange took it.

'I remember. What you doin' in my neighborhood, man?'

'I was driv ing around,' said Stefanos. 'You said that if the light-box was on I should stop by.'

'I was just fixin' to turn it off,' said Strange.

'Too late,' said Stefanos with a stupid grin. 'I'm here.'

37

Strange and Stefanos walked to the Dodge, parked under a street lamp. Stefanos leaned against its rear quarter panel and folded his arms.

'I heard the news about Oliver on the radio,' he said. 'I guess it's why I thought of you and took a shot at stopping by.'

'They'll give him the needle now, up in Indiana.'

'Not just yet. There's plenty of appeal time left. Anyway, you did what you could.'

'That's what everyone tells me,' said Strange. 'So you were just driving around, huh?'

'Yeah, my girlfriend, woman named Alicia, she's out with friends. I got itchy hanging around my crib.'

'Smells like you made a few pit stops on your way here,' said Strange. 'Thought you were staying away from drinking.'

'I said I was tryin' to stay out of bars. It's not the same thing.'

'You fall off that wagon much?'

Stefanos shrugged. They stood there for a while without speaking. Stefanos lit a Marlboro and tossed the match onto the street.

'You sure did stir up the bees down in Southeast,' said Stefanos.

'I guess I did.'

'After Horace McKinley was found in that alley, it started the ball rolling, didn't it? The ATF got involved and put together a case against that gun dealer, lived over the line in Maryland.'

'Ulysses Foreman. But it wasn't McKinley's death that triggered all the activity. It was Durham's boy Bernard Walker gettin' arrested for an unrelated murder a month later. The Feds flipped him on Durham and got him to detail the Foreman operation – what he knew about it, anyway. Apparently it was Foreman who blew up McKinley's shit. They even indicted Foreman's girlfriend as a coconspirator in the gun trafficking charge. Getting defendants to flip beats good police work every time.'

'I guess I ought to thank you for the job.'

'What job?'

'The Dewayne Durham thing, the whole Six Hundred Crew operation, it's gonna be a RICO trial now. Elaine Clay was the PD assigned to the case. I'm doing the investigative work for the defense.'

'Congratulations,' said Strange.

'It's work,' said Stefanos. He reached into the open window of his car, pulled free a pint bottle from under the front seat. 'What ever happened with that little problem you had with the authorities?'

'Nothing. No more burglaries, no more threats. Never heard another word after McKinley got chilled.'

'No reason to go after you anymore. They got their verdict.'

'I guess.'

Strange watched him unscrew the top and tip the bottle to his lips. He watched the bubbles rise in the whiskey as Stefanos closed his eyes. The Greek wiped his mouth with the back of his hand when he was done.

'Here you go,' said Stefanos, offering Strange the bottle. 'Shake hands with my old granddad.'

'Crazy motherfucker,' said Strange, waving the bottle off.

'Suit yourself,' said Stefanos. He dragged deeply on his cigarette and blew smoke at his feet.

Strange looked him over. 'Feel like going for a ride?'

Stefanos said, 'What'd you have in mind?'

Strange told him.

'Guess you caught me in the right frame of mind,' said Stefanos.

'You want to take a pee, wash your face or somethin', before we go? It's a long drive.'

'No. But let's pick up a six-pack. I need something cold to go with this bourbon. We can take my ride, you want to.'

'I'll drive,' said Strange. 'You're half blind.'

They drove out of the city via New York Avenue, took the tunnel to 395, and were soon into Virginia and on Route 1. They spoke very little. Strange listened to his tapes, and Stefanos drank and smoked. He seemed to enjoy the wind in his face.

The road became more barren as they drove south.

Forty minutes later, they passed the Marine Corps base at Quantico and continued on.

'Won't be long now,' said Strange.

'What's the plan?'

'No plan. Get in quick, burn the motherfucker down, try to get out without getting nailed.'

'Viva la revolution,' said Stefanos.

'I need you as a lookout.'

'But I'm half blind.'

'Funny.'

'I got the matches. Don't I get to play?'

'Yeah, okay.'

'We gonna wear gloves or something?'

'And ski masks, too. Shit, we get caught, we're gonna get caught on the site. I ain't gonna worry about fingerprints or nothin' else but haulin' ass out of there. Let's just do this thing, all right?'

Deep forest lined both sides of the highway. Strange took his foot off the gas pedal and let a car pass on his left. Soon he slowed the Caprice down and swerved off onto the berm, then he made a right onto a gravel drive where Stefanos had seen a cut in the trees. What looked like a house stood alone back off the road. A sign reading 'Commonwealth Guns' was strung along a porch holding barred windows. A light in a glass globe mounted beside the door illuminated the porch.

Strange killed the headlights as he drove the car onto the grass and parked alongside the house. The motorcycle was not on the porch.

'Let's go,' he said.

They got out and went to the trunk. Strange opened it and took out the two cans of gas. A car approached on the highway and he closed the trunk lid, extinguishing its light.

'There's gonna be cars from time to time goin' by,' said Strange. 'Just keep working fast.'

'You got a rag in there?'

'Yeah.'

'Give it to me. I'll find a stick to tie it around while you do your thing. After I take care of that porch light. Leave some gas for the torch.'

'Okay, man. Let's go.'

Stefanos waited for the rag, wrapped it around one hand, then went up to the porch and unscrewed the hot lightbulb inside its shield. Then he moved to the treeline in the nearly total darkness and hand-searched the ground until he found a small branch. He wrapped the rag around the top of the branch and tied it tightly so that it would not slip off.

Strange doused the porch with gasoline and continued around the house, flinging the liquid against its walls. When he was done with one can he went back for the other and continued his circular path. Cars sped by on the highway, but none stopped.

Strange met Stefanos at the trunk of the car.

'We all set?' said Stefanos.

'Yeah. It's an all-wood house, should go up good.'

'Here,' said Stefanos, holding out the branch. Strange poured gasoline onto the rag, careful not to get any near the car.

'That's good. Drive the car up to the road. I'll be right with you, hear?'

Stefanos smiled. 'Set 'em off, Jefferson: one, two, three, four.'

'You are something. Gimme your matches.'

'Here you go, Dad.'

Strange felt the book pressed into his hand.

Stefanos took the car up to the road, let it idle on the berm. He looked south and in the rearview took in the northern view. There were no cars coming in either direction. He flipped the headlights on and then off.

Strange lit the rag atop the branch. The light from it was startling and he swung the branch and released it, pinwheeling it onto the porch of the gun store. The porch caught fire immediately and then the rest of the house seemed to explode into a ring of flame. Strange stepped back, feeling the heat of the fire, watching it engulf the house. He heard the sound of his own car's horn but stayed where he was. He admired the power of the fire and the color dancing against the trees. He heard his horn again and he turned and jogged to his car. Stefanos was in the passenger seat, sweat shotgunned on his forehead. Strange got under the wheel and pulled down on the tree. He fishtailed off the berm, pinning the accelerator as he hit the asphalt.

Stefanos unscrewed the top from his pint bottle and had a drink. He handed it to Strange, who tipped it to his lips. The two of them laughed.

Strange handed the bottle back. 'Thanks, buddy.'

'You feel better now?'

'Yeah, I feel good.' He thought of the cleansing warmth of the fire and the beauty of the flames.

'It's a long jolt, we get popped for this. We ruined a man's livelihood. He was running a legal business there.'

'He has insurance, I expect,' said Strange. 'The way I look at it, we just saved a bunch of lives.'

Stefanos lit a cigarette. He looked at the white divider lines on the highway, rushing under the car. 'I'm sorry about your friend.'

'They found that girl he was looking for,' said Strange, smiling some, thinking of Quinn. 'He had written down her location on the back of a flyer. It was sitting there right next to him on the seat.'

Stefanos looked across the bench at Strange. 'Not many of us left out here.'

'No.'

'I guess I'm in it for life.'

'I guess I am, too.'

'Seems like a long game, doesn't it?'

'Long but simple,' said Strange. 'Only got one rule.'

'Just one?' said Stefanos.

Strange nodded. 'Last man standing wins.'

Acknowledgments

Thanks to Joe Aronstamn, Russell Ewart, Father George Clements, ATF Special Agent John D'Angelo, ATF Special Agent Harold Scott Jr, ATF Division Director Jeffrey Roehm, Sloan Harris, and Alicia Gordon, for their assistance and guidance in the writing of this book. As always, much love to Emily, Nick, Pete, and Rosa, for their patience and support.